The Treasure of Silver Lake

Unabridged Translation of the
Original Karl May Manuscript Published under the Title

Der Schatz im Silbersee

A Travel Narrative
by
Karl May

Translated by
Herbert Windolf

Original German text by Karl May [1842 – 1912]
First published 1890-1891
in 'Der Gute Kamerad', in serial format

English translation by Herbert Windolf

ISBN: 0-9766400-4-X

This book is printed on acid free paper.

Nemsi Books - rev. 04/30/2005

Acknowledgements

Without Dr. Albert William (Bill) Bork, a friend and native of Prescott, AZ, historian and font of knowledge -- who corralled me into translating Karl May's "The Oil Prince" which he dearly desired to see in print -- this subsequent translation of "The Treasure of Silver Lake" would never have come to be.

My thanks go to Frank Starrost who, following my translation and publication of Karl May's "The Oil Prince" by Washington State University Press, contacted me by e-mail from Kiel, Germany, and directed me to the Karl May Gesellschaft e.V. website: http://www.karl-may-gesellschaft.de of which he is a co-editor.

Here I found the writings of Karlheinz Everts, another May aficionado, who had laboriously posted on the Internet May's entire story, called in German "Der Schatz im Silbersee", which I used as a source for this translation. With the permission of both men, I downloaded the classic text of "The Treasure of Silver Lake" as published in a German magazine in 1890/91, and went to work.

While my translation has remained faithful to the original, May's plot development required some adjustments to maintain consistency as the translation proceeded.

Don Levenson, my Prescott friend and editor, and at times also my collaborator, was invaluable in properly "Americanizing" my work to make plot development more consistent and logical and to give, for instance, one of the novel's characters, an English lord, the right British manner of expression, something which was, of course, impossible for May to do in German.

Grant D. Brown, another good friend, assisted in the identification and correct translation of several botanical issues. Felipe A. Morales kept the Spanish expressions in good order.

For six months, my wife, Ute, bore with me through the often intense involvement as I hunched for long hours over my computer.

My thanks also go to George Jackson for a final thorough proof reading of the manuscript.

Without all these supporters, the English language version of "The Treasure of Silver Lake" would not have come to life; at least it would have turned out differently. Thanks again to you all!

If any errors or inconsistencies in the story remain, they are my responsibility alone.

Herb Windolf

Karl May – translated by Herbert Windolf

Foreword

Towards the end of the 19th century, there arose a uniquely European genre of stories about the American West, a frontier by then tamed from the general lawlessness that had prevailed in earlier decades. Influenced by James Fenimore Cooper's novels dating from the first half of that century, Buffalo Bill Cody's shows and other accounts, British, Scandinavian and German writers developed their own characters and plots in which they portrayed an American Wild West which was then already both legend and history.

The stories of the most prolific writer, the German Karl May, (pronounced "my") have been translated into many other languages. Sales of his books in Europe are exceeded only by those of the Bible. Generations of Germans grew up reading May, the titan of popular German writings, much more than literary greats like Goethe, Schiller, Hölderlin, Heine, Nietzsche and others.

While May's plots and character development are generally not deep, he never failed to create exciting stories, catching the enthusiasm of readers young and old even as long as a century later, among them such luminaries as Albert Einstein.

May's tales of adventure take place in locales all over the world, but are played out mostly in the Middle East and the American West. Although he was able to travel only after he had written many of his novels, May relied very much on others' travel accounts and on researched background material. Where detail required it, he amended geographical and historical fact from his imagination. Interestingly, a Karl May Atlas has been developed, displaying fact and fiction of the locales depicted in his many works.

For readers not yet familiar with this much-admired story teller, May was born in Ernstthal, Germany, a small village in Saxony, as a poor weaver's son on February 25, 1842. Becoming blind in his first year due to severe malnutrition, the boy's sight was restored at age five after his mother had consulted two prominent physicians. As a young adult he went through a period of severe emotional stress and had several run-ins with the law resulting in a series of imprisonments.

May's first stories set in the American West were written in the late 1870s. They subsequently appeared in serial form in family and youth publications. Finally, between 1892 and 1894 his novels were first published in book form.

Never during his lifetime did May have the opportunity to visit the Wild West of which he wrote so prolifically, having made it only as far as Niagara Falls on a brief trip with his second wife, Klara, in 1906. Previous journeys had taken him to Ceylon and Sumatra, as well as Turkey and Egypt.

The recurring protagonist in May's Middle Eastern novels is Kara ben Nemsi. In those of the American West, the frontiersman, Old Shatterhand. In both characters, May projected himself personally. Both are highly ethical personalities, interesting when contrasted with May's earlier brushes with the law. One at times gets the impression that his intense involvement with these two characters, together with the story material itself, led May to identify somewhat with each of them to the extent that his imagined world may have at times encroached on reality.

In 1895, May was able to purchase a personal residence in Radebeul, near Dresden, which he named "Villa Shatterhand."

In "The Treasure of Silver Lake", Hobble-Frank expresses his much-wished ambition to build a villa on the bank of the Elbe River in Saxony. In "The Oil Prince", he has fulfilled his dream: The "Villa Bärenfett" (which translates as "Villa Bear Fat"). A western-style blockhouse by that name still stands in May's home town, Radebeul, at the Elbe River. There too is the Karl May Museum, said to hold one of the leading -- if not the best -- collection of Indian artifacts in the world. The museum displays some 850 Native American pieces.

May died on March 12, 1912, at the age of seventy. His widow, Klara, continued to add to her late husband's artifact collection during a trip in 1930 to New Mexico and Arizona. Before returning to her native Germany, she was received by then-President Herbert Hoover.

Here now is a brief reference to May's data and background material from which the Silver Lake tale sprang:

The town of Lewisburg on the Arkansas River -- the paddle-wheeler's stopover in the first chapter of "The Treasure of Silver Lake", -- is nowadays not readily found on a map, since it lost its importance as a commercial river port by the development of Morrilton and Interstate 40 just north of it.

What May called "tramps" in German I have named "rovers" in the translation, so as not to confuse the reader by this misnomer. The term "rover" has two meanings: The one commonly known is "wanderer or roamer". The second, applicable here is "pirate, robber, plunderer", derived from the archaic term "to reave". The rover background, however, May took from the historical fact of the roving bandits who terrified Kansas and neighboring states following the Civil War. Quantrell and his raiders who devastated Lawrence, Kansas, and killed more than a hundred men are among the most vivid examples.

And when May refers to the "treasure" having been buried by an ancient people who had been pushed out by invaders from the north, it's interesting to note that some of today's scientific scholars place the origin of the Aztecs in the American West.

The events portrayed in "The Treasure of Silver Lake" precede those recounted in my translation of May's "The Oil Prince" by a few years. In fact, they are even mentioned in this later novel. Some of the characters you meet in this book such as Old Shatterhand, Winnetou, Aunt Droll and Hobble-Frank also appear in "The Oil Prince"; many others, particularly Old Firehand, are newcomers.

May you enjoy all the excitement and suspense in "The Treasure of Silver Lake."

Herbert Windolf, Prescott AZ., June 20, 2004

Karl May – translated by Herbert Windolf

Contents:

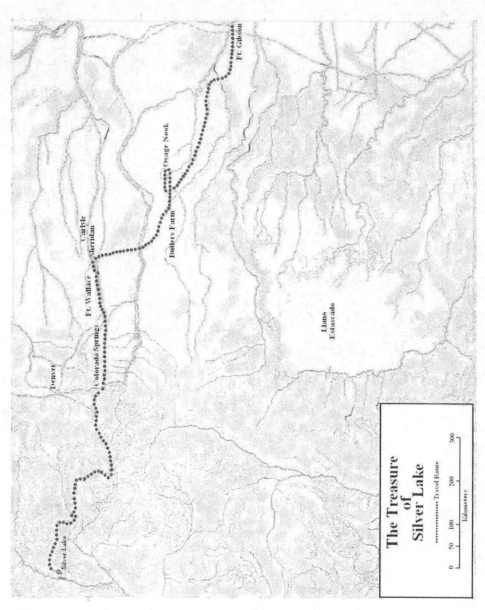

Map of the Silver Lake Travel Route supplied by Herbert Windolf

The Treasure of Silver Lake

Karl May – translated by Herbert Windolf

1. The Black Panther

It was about noon on a very hot June day when the "Dogfish", one of the largest passenger and cargo steamers on the Arkansas, whipped the waters of the river with its mighty paddle wheels. It had left Little Rock earlier this morning and was soon to arrive in Lewisburg and would tie up there if additional passengers or cargo was to be had.

The oppressive heat had driven the better-off travelers to their cabins. Most of the deck passengers lay behind barrels, crates and other luggage pieces affording them a bit of shade. Underneath a spread tarp, the captain had set up a bar table for these passengers. On it stood an assortment of glasses and bottles, whose burning contents were certainly not intended for discriminating palates. Behind the bar sat a barkeep with eyes closed, tired from the heat, his head nodding. If his lids opened at times, a quiet curse or other strong word crossed his lips. His annoyance was addressed to a group of about twenty men sitting in a circle on the floor in front of the table, passing a dice box from hand to hand. They played for a round of drinks that the loser had to buy for every participant at the end of a game. Because of that, the barkeep was denied his nap he so dearly desired.

For sure, these men had not met up here on the steamer, for they called each other by their first names and seemed to know exactly their respective relationships, made obvious by occasional remarks. Excluded from this general intimacy, however, was one among them, addressed as "colonel", to whom rather a certain respect was extended.

This man was tall and lean, had a sharp-featured, clean-shaven face with a bristly goatee. Fiery-red too was his close-cropped hair, as one could see, since he had slipped his old, battered felt hat far back on his neck. His dress consisted of heavy, nail-studded leather shoes, Nanking leggings and a short jacket of the same material. He did not wear a vest; instead he wore a wrinkled dirty shirt whose broad collar, not held together by a bandanna, stood wide open, showing his bare, suntanned chest. Around his hips he had tied a red-fringed piece of cloth from which showed the handles of a knife and two pistols. Behind him lay a rather new rifle and a linen knapsack with two straps for carrying it on his back.

The other men were dressed in a likewise careless and dirty manner, however were very well armed. There was not a single one among them to whom trust could have been extended on first sight. They played their game of dice with great passion, all the while conversing in such coarse language that a halfway decent person would surely not have remained standing with them for even a minute. In any case, they already had had many a drink, for their faces were not just heated from the sun, but rather the spirit of the brandy.

The captain had left the bridge to go to the quarterdeck to give some necessary instructions to the wheelman. This completed, the latter asked, "What

1

do you think of those fellows sitting up front there over dice, captain? I think they are the kind of people one doesn't quite like to see on board."

"I think so too," nodded the captain. "They identified themselves as farm laborers, harvesters, on their way out west to work on the land, but I wouldn't want to be the man they apply to for work."

"Well, sir, I myself feel they are right and true rovers. Let's hope they will keep the peace while on board."

"I wouldn't advise them to bother us more than usual. We have enough hands on board to throw them all into the old, blessed Arkansas. By the way, get ready for landing; in ten minutes Lewisburg will be in sight."

The captain returned to the bridge to issue the necessary orders for docking. Soon one could see the buildings of the town to which the ship responded with a drawn-out scream of its steam whistle. From the dock a signal was given that freight and passengers were to be picked up by the steamer. Travelers from below decks came up to enjoy the brief interruption of the otherwise boring trip.

Not that an entertaining spectacle was offered here. At the time, this place was, by far, not yet of today's importance. At the dock. only a few idle people hung around, and there were but several crates and packages to be loaded. There were only three new passengers boarding. When paying for their passage, they were hardly treated as gentlemen by the officer in charge.

One of them, a white, was of a tall, extremely husky build. He also sported a full dark beard, so that only the eyes, the nose, and the upper part of the cheeks were visible. On his head an old beaver cap was nearly furless from years of wear. To define its original form was impossible; it may have had already all kinds of shapes. The man's dress consisted of pants and a jacket of sturdy, gray linen. His broad leather belt held two revolvers, a knife, and several small implements indispensable to a frontiersman. In addition, he carried a double-barreled rifle to whose butt a long ax had been tied for easier carrying of the two.

Having paid the fare, he threw an inquiring glance across the deck. The well-dressed cabin passengers were apparently of no interest to him. But his eyes were drawn to some of the others, who had risen from their game to survey the boarding travelers. He saw the colonel and immediately averted his eyes, as if he had not even noticed him. At the same time, though, he growled under his breath, while pulling up the slipped legs of his high waders to his mighty thighs, "Behold! If that's not Red Brinkley, I'm going to be smoked and eaten with the skin! The purpose for which he has gathered such a troupe can surely not be a good one. I hope he doesn't remember me."

The one talked about had noticed him too. Addressing his companions in a low voice he asked, "Look at the black-bearded fellow! Does any one of you know him?"

None did.

"Well, I must have once come across him and that in a situation not pleasant to me. There's that faint memory."

"Then he would likely remember you too," remarked one. "He looked us over, but didn't even seem to notice you."

"Hmm! Maybe I'll remember. Even better, I'll ask him for his name. Once I hear it, I'll know where I'm at. Faces I do forget, but not names. Let's have a drink with him!"

"Provided he joins us!"

"Refusing would be a scandalous insult, as you all know. In this country, whenever a man declines the offer of a drink, one has the right to respond with the knife or the pistol, and if he puts down the offender, no questions are asked."

"But he doesn't look like he can be forced to partake in something he doesn't like."

"Pshaw! You bet?"

"Yes, bet, bet!" it came from everybody. "The loser pays three rounds."

"Okay by me," declared the colonel.

"Me too," said the other. "But there must be an opportunity for revenge. Three bets and three drinks."

"Who with?"

"Well, first with the black-bearded one you claim to know without knowing who he is. Then with one of the gentlemen still standing there, gaping at the shore. Let's take the tall fellow, looking like a giant among dwarfs. And then with the Indian, who boarded with his son. Or are you afraid of him?"

General laughter was the response to this question, to which the colonel answered contemptuously, "Me -- afraid of this red mug? Pshaw! Then rather of the giant you want to set me up with. By the devil, how strong this man must be! But particularly such giants tend to have the least guts. He's dressed so nicely that he most likely is more at home in salons than knowing how to deal with people of our kind. Okay, I hold to the bet. A round of three glasses for each of the three. And now to work!"

He had shouted the last three sentences so loudly that he must have been heard by all the passengers. Every American and every frontiersman knows the significance of the word 'drink', particularly when it is exclaimed so loudly and threateningly, as was the case here. Therefore all eyes now faced the colonel. One could see that he as well as his companions were already half drunk, but no one left, for everyone expected an interesting scene to develop and wanted to find out who the three were, and to whom the drinks were to be offered.

The colonel had his glass filled, took it in his hand, approached the black-bearded man, who was still searching for a comfortable place for himself, and said, "Good day, sir! I want to offer you a drink. Of course I think you a gentleman, for I drink only with truly noble people and hope you will empty this glass to my health!"

3

The full beard of the one addressed broadened and contracted again, the sign of a merry smile having crossed his face.

"Well," he answered, "I'm not averse to do you this pleasure, but I would like to know first who's doing me this honor."

"Right-o, sir! One must know who one drinks with. My name's Brinkley, Colonel Brinkley, if it pleases you. And yours?"

"My name is Grosser, Thomas Grosser, if you don't mind. Then to your health, colonel!"

He emptied the glass, while the others followed suit, and returned it to the colonel, who felt like the victor. Looking the other over from head to toe in an almost insulting way, he asked, "It seems to me this is a German name. That makes you a damned Dutchman, eh?"

"Not at all, but a German, sir," responded Grosser in a friendly voice, without getting riled by the other's rudeness. "You must deliver your 'damned Dutchman' to a different address. It doesn't catch on with me. Thanks for the drink then and good day!"

Turning sharply on his heel and quickly walking away, he mumbled to himself, "Then it is truly this Brinkley! And 'colonel' he calls himself now! The chap can't be planning anything good. Who knows how long we'll share the deck. I'll keep my eyes peeled."

Although Brinkley had won the first part of the bet, he didn't look so victorious any more. His expression had changed, showing that he was annoyed. He had hoped that Grosser would refuse and threats would have been needed to force him to drink. But the German had been the smarter one, had drunk first, and then shown openly that he was too clever to have given cause for a quarrel. This irritated the colonel. He then approached his second intended victim, the Indian, after he had had the glass filled again.

Two Indians had come aboard with Grosser, an older one with a youngster, the latter maybe fifteen years old. The unmistakable similarity of their facial features made it clear they were father and son. They were dressed and armed alike, so that the son appeared to be the exact, younger mirror image of the father.

They were clothed in fringed leggings and yellow-dyed moccasins. No hunting shirt or jacket could be seen, since their bodies were covered from the shoulders down in colorful Zuni blankets, which often sell for more than sixty dollars apiece. Their black hair was combed back simply and from there fell down their backs, giving them a somewhat feminine look. Their full, round faces gave the impression of extreme good-naturedness, increased by their having colored their cheeks with cinnabar vermillion red. The rifles both held seemed to be worth less than half a dollar each. On the whole the two looked entirely harmless, then too rather odd, so that they had caused laughter among the drinkers. They had stepped aside as if afraid of other people, and were now

4

leaning against a long, sturdy crate that was as high and broad as a man. They did not appear to pay attention to anything, even when the colonel approached, their eyes not rising until he stood hard in front addressing them, "Hot weather today! Or is it not, you red fellows? A drink will feel good. Here, take it, oldster, and pour it down your gullet!"

The Indian did not move a limb and answered in broken English, "Not drink."

"What, you don't want to?" the owner of the red goatee roared. "It's a drink, understand, a drink! To refuse it is a bloody insult to a veritable gentleman like me, one that needs to be repaid with the knife. But before that, I need to know who you are. What's your name?"

"Nintropan-hauey," the thus-questioned responded quietly and modestly.

"What tribe do you belong to?"

"Tonkawa."

"To the tame reds then, afraid of every cat, understand, every cat, even the littlest kitten. I'll make no bones with you. Well then, are you going to drink?"

"I not drink firewater."

He said this, despite the threat the colonel had issued, just as quietly as before. But then the latter reached out and resoundingly boxed the Tonkawa's ear.

"There's your reward, you red coward!" he shouted. "I don't want to revenge myself any other way since a rascal like you stands so much lower than I."

Barely had the slap been given, when the hand of the Indian boy slipped beneath the Zuni blanket, seeking a weapon, yet at the same time he looked up at his father's face to see what he would now do and say.

The visage of the red man had totally changed, so that one almost would not have recognized it any more. His stature seemed to have grown, his eyes had lit up, and his features had come alive with energy. Just as quickly, though, his eyelashes dropped again, his body slumped, and his face resumed the previously displayed humble expression.

"Now what do you say?" the colonel asked sneeringly.

"Nintropan-hauey thanks."

"Did my boxing your ear please you so much that you thank me for it? Here, have another one!"

Once more he reached out but since the Indian had quick as lightning lowered his head, his hand hit the crate against which the Indians were leaning, resounding loudly. From its inside sounded a short, sharp snarl and spit, quickly rising to a wild, ghastly scream, followed by such a thunder-like roar that one could imagine the ship was trembling from these horrible sounds.

The colonel had jumped back several steps, dropped his glass and shouted in a frightened but vehement voice, "Heavens! What is that? What kind of beasty

5

is in this crate? Is that permissible? One can die from fright or at the least catch epilepsy!"

The scare had not only affected him but also the other passengers. The other men on deck, like the colonel, had also cried out loudly. Only four of them had not batted an eyelash, namely the blackbeard, who now sat way up front at the bow, the giant gentleman that the colonel had wanted to invite for the third drink and the two Indians. Like everyone else, those four had neither known of the wild animal being on board, but possessed such strong, long-practiced self-control that it was not difficult for them to hide their surprise.

The roar had also been heard below decks in the cabins. Screaming loudly, several ladies had come running up to inquire what danger was threatening them.

"It's nothing, ladies and gentlemen," answered a very well-dressed gentleman, who had earlier come out of his cabin, "It's only a little panther, nothing else! A most cute Felis panthera, only a black one, just a little black one, gentlemen!"

"What? A black panther!" yowled a little, bespectacled man, who obviously was more familiar with zoological volumes than with close exposure to wild animals. "The black panther is the most dangerous beast there is! It is larger than the lion and the tiger! It kills from pure blood lust, not just from hunger. How old is it?"

"Only three years, sir, no more."

"Only? That's what you call 'only'? Then it is fully grown! My God! And such a beast is carried on board! Who is responsible for this?"

"I am, sir, I," answered the elegant stranger, at the same time bowing to the ladies and gentlemen. "Permit me to introduce myself, m'ladies, gentlemen! I am the famous menagerie owner Jonathan Boyler and for some time have stayed with my troupe in Van Buren. With this black panther having arrived for me in New Orleans, I traveled there with my most experienced beast trainer to pick it up. The captain of this good ship gave me permission against a high fee to load the panther; this under the condition that the passengers were, if possible, not to learn the company they were in. That's why I feed the panther only at night and have fed him, by God, always a whole calf, that he would be so stuffed he would sleep the entire day and barely be able to move. Obviously, if one hits the crate with one's fist, he wakes up and raises his voice. Now I hope that the honored ladies and gentlemen will not take any further notice of the little panther, who isn't the least trouble anyway."

"What?" protested the bespectacled one, his voice almost cracking. "Causing no trouble? Take no further notice? By the devil, I must tell you that such a demand has never been put to me before! I am to share this ship with a black panther? I might as well be hung if I manage to do that! He either goes or I go. Throw the beast into the water! Or take the crate to shore!"

"But, sir, there's truly no danger here," the menagerie owner assured him. "Just look at the strong crate, and --- "

"What crate? " the little man interrupted him. "I can bust this little crate; how much easier it would be for the panther!"

"Please, let me tell you that inside the crate is actually an iron cage, which even ten lions or panthers could not break open."

"Is that true? Show us the cage! I must convince myself."

"Yes, show us the cage, show us! We must know where we're at," shouted ten, twenty, thirty, even more voices.

The menagerie owner, a Yankee, took the opportunity to exploit the general wish to his advantage.

"I'll be pleased, very pleased!" he answered. "But, ladies and gentlemen, it is easy to see that one cannot look at the cage without also seeing the panther. That, however, I cannot permit without a certain return. To increase the attraction of this rare spectacle, I shall arrange for a feeding of the animal. We shall set up three tiers of seating, the front one at one dollar, the second for half a dollar and the third for a quarter dollar. But since here are only ladies and gentlemen, I am convinced that we can right away drop the second and third tier. Or is there anybody who would care to pay only a half dollar or even a quarter dollar?"

Naturally, no one responded.

"Well, then, only first row places. Please, ladies and gentlemen, a dollar a person."

Taking off his hat he collected the payments, while his beast trainer, whom he had summoned, made the necessary preparation for the show.

The passengers, mostly Yankees as such, were fully agreeable with the turn of events. Had most of them been angered that the captain had allowed the steamer to be used for the transportation of such a dangerous carnivore, they now felt appeased by the opportunity to view the panther and the welcome change this would bring to the ennui of shipboard life. Even the little scholar had overcome his fear and with great interest looked forward to the show.

The colonel used the opportunity to suggest to his companions, "Listen, boys, one bet I've won, the other I lost, since the red rascal didn't drink. That's a wash. The third bet we won't do for a round of brandy, but for the one dollar fee we have to pay. Are you agreed?"

Naturally his followers accepted his proposal, for the giant did not look as if he could easily be scared.

"All right," remarked the colonel, sure of victory by his plentiful imbibing of brandy. "Just watch how willingly and quickly this goliath will drink with me!"

He had his glass refilled and approached the hulking figure. And, certainly, the build of this man could only be called gigantic. He was even taller and huskier than the blackbeard, who had called himself Grosser, the German's play of word, meaning big. The giant certainly was no stay-at-home, for his face was tanned by the sun, and his handsome, manly features had a bold cut. His blue eyes had this hard-to-describe, peculiar look displayed by people living on great open spaces, not confined by a close horizon, as are seamen, desert dwellers and prairiemen. To be added is that his face was clean-shaven, that he was maybe forty years of age and that he wore an elegant travel suit. No weapons could be seen on him. He stood with several other men with whom he was talking engagedly about the panther.

The colonel arrived, stepping bumptiously in front of his assumed third victim saying, "Sir, I'm offering you a drink. I hope you won't refuse telling me, a veritable gentleman, who you are."

The other gave him a surprised look and turned away again to continue his conversation interrupted by the insolent fellow.

"Pooh!" the latter called out. "Are you deaf, or do you not want to hear me on purpose? I don't want to advise you of the latter, since I will not be pleased at having a drink refused. Take heed from the example of the Indian!"

The annoyed man shrugged his shoulders slightly and asked the captain, "You have heard what this lad just said to me?"

"Yes, sir, every word," the officer nodded.

"Well, then you are witness that I have not asked him to come here."

"What?" the colonel roared. " A lad you call me? And you refuse the drink? Are you to fare like the Indian, whom I ---"

He did not get any further, for at this moment the giant had boxed his ear so mightily that he fell down, sliding quite a distance across the floor, to finally even roll over. There he lay frozen for a moment, but then quickly rising, pulled his knife and raised it to stab at the giant.

This one had put both hands into his pockets, standing there very relaxedly as if not the least danger threatened him, as if the colonel didn't exist. The latter roared angrily, "Dog, boxing my ear? That calls for blood, yours for sure!"

Several other men as well as the captain wanted to intercede. However, the giant turned them away with a firm headshake. When the colonel approached within two steps, he raised his right leg and honored him with such a kick in the belly that the shocked man once again was downed and skidded across the floor.

"That's enough now, or ---" the goliath warned.

But the colonel jumped up again, screaming in anger, stuck the knife into his belt and pulled one of his pistols to point at his adversary. The giant, though, drew his right hand from his pocket where he had secreted a revolver.

"Away with the pistol!" he commanded, pointing the barrel of his small but excellent weapon at the right hand of his opponent.

One! Two! Three! Light but sharp reports --- the colonel screamed and dropped his pistol.

"So, lad!" said the giant. "You will not soon box anyone's ear again if he refuses to drink from the glass on which you have previously wiped your dirty mouth. I have mangled your hand. And if you still want to know who I am, so --"

"Damned be your name!" foamed the colonel. "I don't want to hear it. But you, you yourself, I must get. Get him, boys; go get him!"

Now this demonstrated that these characters were truly a gang, where all stood for one. Pulling their knives from their belts, they threw themselves at the giant, who seemingly would be lost before the captain could call his crew for help. The courageous man though stuck out a foot, raised his fists and called, "Come on then, those who dare to tackle Old Firehand!"

The sound of this name had an immediate effect. The colonel, who again had grabbed his knife with the unhurt left, stopped in his tracks and shouted, "Old Firehand! By the devil, who would have thought! Why didn't you say so before?"

"Is it perhaps only the name that protects a gentleman from your rudeness? Get lost. Sit down quietly in a corner and don't come face to face with me again or I shall give you all a good drubbing!"

"Well, we shall talk more later!"

The colonel turned and, holding his bleeding hand, went toward the bow. His comrades followed him like dogs having gotten a thrashing. There they sat down and bandaged their leader's hand, all the while speaking softly but urgently with each other, glancing at the famous hunter. Their looks, although not friendly, expressed nevertheless the mighty respect they had for him.

But not only they had been affected by the widely-known name. There probably wasn't a single one among the passengers who had not heard of this bold man, whose entire life was made up of dangerous deeds and adventures. Involuntarily, people stepped back deferentially, and now thoroughly looked him over, a tall figure, whose well-proportioned dimensions and means had been already obvious to everybody before.

The captain offered him his hand and said in the most pleasant voice a Yankee can offer, "But, sir, I should have been made aware of this! I would have offered you my own cabin. By God, what an honor for the 'Dogfish' to have your feet walk its planks. Why did you call yourself differently?"

"I did give you my true name. Only by frontiersmen am I called Old Firehand, because my rifle's fire, coming from my hand, is always ruinous."

"I heard you never miss?"

"Pshaw! There's no missing! Every good frontiersman can do as I do. But you see what an advantage it is to have a known warrior's name. Had mine not been so widely known, there would surely have been a fight."

"In which you most likely would have succumbed to superior force!"

"You think so?" asked Old Firehand, a self-assured but not at all proud smile flashing over his face. "As long as they come at me only with knives, I'm not worried. I would have held at least until your crew would have arrived."

"There would have been no shortage of them. But what am I going to do now with the rascals? I am master, lord and judge on board. Should I put them in chains and turn them in?"

"No."

"Or should I drop them off on shore?"

"Neither."

"But punishment there must be."

"I recommend you forego it. You're not going to make this steamer trip your last one, I suppose?"

"I wouldn't think of it! I intend to skipper up and down the old Arkansas for many a year yet."

"Well, then be careful not to rouse the vengeance of these people! It would surely be your downfall. They're capable of setting themselves up somewhere on the banks and play a trick on you that could not only cost you your ship but even your life."

"They would not dare!"

"They would surely try. It would be, by the way, not much of a risk. They would do it secretly and arrange it so that no one could lay it on them."

Now Old Firehand noticed the blackbeard, who had approached but had stopped nearby, his look expressing an obvious desire to talk to the hunter. He stepped toward him asking, "You want to talk with me, sir? Can I do you a favor?"

"A big one," answered the German.

"Tell me which!"

"Permit me to shake your hand once, sir! That's all I'm asking. Then I shall gladly leave and no longer bother you. But I shall happily remember this hour for the rest of my life."

From his open look and the sound of his voice it was obvious that these words came truly from his heart. Old Firehand held out his right hand and asked, "How far do you intend to travel on this ship?"

"On this ship? Only to Fort Gibson," replied Grosser, shaking the frontiersman's had enthusiastically.

"That's far enough!"

"Oh, then I want to go farther yet by boat. I'm afraid that you, the famous man who has never been defeated, will think me fearful."

"Why so?"

"Because I earlier accepted the drink of this so-called colonel."

"Oh, no. I can only commend you for having been so prudent. Certainly when he slapped the Indian, I intended to teach him a good lesson, which came to pass."

"I hope he'll take it as a warning. By the way, should he retain stiff fingers from your shot, he's finished as a frontiersman. Of the Indian, I rather don't know what to think."

"Why so?"

"He acted like a real coward with the colonel, although he didn't show the least bit of fright when the panther roared. I cannot reconcile the two behaviors."

"Well, I can explain it. It's not very difficult."

"So you know the Indian?"

"I've never seen him, though I've heard about him."

"I too heard his name when he spoke it. The word is a tongue-breaker. I was unable to commit it to memory."

"That's because he used his mother tongue, so that the colonel would not recognize who he was dealing with. His name is Nintropan-hauey, his son is Nintropan-homosch, meaning Big Bear and Little Bear."

"Is it possible? Of this father and son I have heard quite a bit already. The Tonkawa have degenerated. Only these two Nintropan have inherited the warrior spirit of their forebears and get about in the mountains and the prairie."

"Yes, they are two able fellows. Now you probably will no longer think that they didn't respond to the colonel out of cowardice, but rather in a way that would have been his due."

"Another Indian would have killed the ruffian immediately!"

"Maybe. But didn't you see the son reach for a knife or tomahawk under his blanket? Only when he saw his father's motionless face did he forego immediately to avenge the offense. I tell you, with these Indians a short glance suffices, where it takes a long speech for us whites. From the moment the colonel struck the Indian, his death was assured. The two Bears shall not cease following his tracks until they've killed him. You, though, gave him your name, which I recognized as being German. That makes us fellowcountrymen."

"What, sir, you too are German?" Grosser asked, surprised.

"That's so. My real name is Winter. I too will still travel a good distance on this ship, which in any case will give us the opportunity to talk some more."

"If you feel like doing it, I will be most honored, sir."

"Don't issue such compliments. I'm no more than you are, a frontiersman, nothing else."

"Sure, but a general too isn't worth more then a recruit, namely a soldier."

"Truthfully, do you compare yourself with a recruit? Then you must have been only for a short time in the West."

"Well," the blackbeard opined in a modest voice, "I've been here a bit longer than that. My name's Thomas Grosser. With the family name not used here, it's just Tom, and because I've such a black beard, I'm called Black Tom."

"How? What?" Old Firehand exclaimed. "You are Black Tom, the famous rafter?"

"Tom's my name, rafter I am, although famous I doubt."

"It is you, it's you, sir. Let's confirm it with a handshake!"

"Please, not too loudly, sir!" warned Tom. "The colonel there mustn't learn my name."

"Why not?"

"Because he would remember me by it."

"So you have had some dealings with him already?"

"A little. I'll tell you about it. You don't know him?"

"I saw him for the first time today."

"Now then, look at his beard and his red hair and tack on his name 'Brinkley'."

"What do you say? So he's the Red Brinkley who's committed a hundred dastardly deeds, with no evidence to tie any one to him?"

"It's him, sir. I recognized him."

"Then I shall keep a closer eye on him if he stays on board much longer. And I must get to know you better. You're the man I'm looking for. If you don't yet have any other commitments, I would have use for you."

"Well," Tom said, looking pensively at the floor, "the honor to be with you is worth more than anything else. However, I have made some arrangements with other rafters. They even have made me their leader, but I could resolve this easily if you can give me some time."

"Excellent. You must take a cabin then for us to be closer together. Any additional expense I shall gladly make up."

"Thank you, sir, but not necessary! We rafters too make a good bit of money if we are diligent. And presently my pockets are full, for I come up from Vicksburg where I presented our invoices for some cash. I can pay for the cabin myself. But look! I think the performance is about to begin."

From crates and packages the menagerie owner had set up a long row of makeshift benches and was now pompously inviting the public to be seated. The crew, if not otherwise occupied, was allowed to look on at no charge. The colonel and his companions didn't approach to watch; they had lost the desire for it.

The two Indians had not been asked whether they wanted to participate. Two Indians in the company of ladies and gentlemen, who had each paid a dollar, wasn't something the owner of the animal wanted to have anything to do with. They stood, therefore, at a distance and appeared to give not the least attention to the cage nor the gaggle of spectators, all the while their sharp yet covert glances missed not the least of what was happening.

The spectators were sitting in front of the still closed crate. Most of them had no true idea of what a black panther was like. The feline carnivores of the New World are substantially smaller and less dangerous than those of the Old World. The cowboy, for instance, catches the mountain lion, as the American beast is called, with the lasso and drags him behind his horse. That he would not dare do with the Bengal Tiger. The American lion, or cougar, flees from humans, even when hungry. One can easily picture the panther as being substantially smaller than a lion or tiger, and since the spectators here thought in terms of the mountain lion or cougar, most of them expected to see a barely two-foot-tall and respectively long and strong carnivore.

Since New Orleans, the panther had lain in the dark with the crate having been opened only during nighttime. For the first time now he saw daylight again, blinding his eyes. He closed them and stayed put, stretched out as long as the cage. Then he blinked a bit, noticing the people sitting in front of him. In a flash he was on his feet and let out a roar having such an effect that the majority of the onlookers jumped up and drew back.

Yes, he was a fully grown and beautiful specimen, surely more than three feet tall and without his tail twice that long. He took hold of the iron rods of the cage with his front paws and shook them so hard that the crate wobbled violently. At that, he displayed his terrible set of teeth. His dark coloration only increased his impact on the spectators.

"Yes, ladies and gentlemen," the menagerie owner explained, "the black type of panther is at home on the Sunda Islands. But these animals are small. The true black panther, which is becoming rare, is found in North Africa on the border of the Sahara. He is just as strong and much more dangerous than the lion and can carry a grown cow away in his jaws. What his teeth can accomplish you shall see shortly when he is fed."

The beast trainer brought the carcass of half a sheep and put it down in front of the cage. When the panther noticed the meat he went berserk. He jumped up and down, spat and roared, so that the more fearful of the spectators retreated even farther.

A Negro, employed in the ship's engine room, had been unable to resist his curiosity and had sneaked up on deck. The captain, seeing him, ordered him to return to work immediately. Since the black didn't obey at once, the captain grabbed a nearby rope end and lashed him a few times. Now the punished man quickly withdrew, but stopped at the hatch leading to the engine room. Behind the captain's back, he made a face and shook his fists at him. Since the spectators were watching only the panther, they hadn't observed the interplay. The colonel, however, saw it, telling his companions, "It looks like this nigger isn't fond of

13

the captain. He may be of use to us. Let's talk to him. A few dollars works wonders with a black."

The beast trainer now pushed the meat through the iron bars into the cage, gave the onlookers a searching look, then said something quietly to his boss. The latter, though, shook his head; the other kept talking to him and seemed to dispel his objections. The owner finally nodded and told the people sitting and standing in front of the cage, "Ladies and gentlemen, let me tell you of your great fortune. An untamed black panther has never before been seen, at least not here in the states. During our three-week stay in New Orleans, my beast trainer has taken the panther into schooling and just offered to publicly enter the cage and sit beside his pupil, provided you dispense to him some good compensation."

The beast trainer was a strong, extremely muscular man with an uncommon self-assured manner. In any case, he was fully convinced of the success of his plan, apparent from his present confident countenance.

Once the sheep carcass had been squeezed between the bars of the cage, the panther fell over his meal, whose bones were ground like cardboard between his great teeth. He seemed to pay attention only to his feed. Even a layman could, therefore, think that no great danger was involved in entering the cage right then.

None other than the fearful little bespectacled man responded enthusiastically, "That would be wonderful, sir! A stunt for which one could pay something. How much does the man want?"

"One hundred dollars!"

"Hmm! Isn't that a bit much?"

"No, far too little, sir. The danger into which he enters is not minimal since he isn't yet halfway sure of the animal."

"Okay! Well, I am not rich. Five dollars I will pay. Gentlemen, who else will contribute?"

So many responded that the sum was easily collected. Once having started this, everyone wanted to thoroughly enjoy the spectacle. Even the captain became excited and offered bets.

"Sir," warned Old Firehand, "don't make a mistake! I beg you not to take this risk. Especially since the man isn't yet fully assured of the animal's reaction, it's your duty to raise your objection."

"Objection?" laughed the captain. "Pshaw! Am I by chance the father or mother of the beast trainer? Do I have to give him orders? Here in this blessed land everyone has the right to risk his skin, just as he pleases. If he's eaten by the panther, then it is his and the panther's affair, but not mine. Well then, gentlemen, I maintain that the man isn't going to come out again as he will enter, and I bet one hundred dollars. Who is betting against it? Ten percent of the win is to go to the beast trainer as a bonus."

14

The example electrified everyone. Several more wagers for not insignificant amounts were agreed upon and, as it turned out, would net the beast trainer almost three hundred dollars should his stunt succeed.

Nothing had been said whether the beast trainer was to be armed for his stunt. He fetched his blackjack and hung from his belt a whip whose handle contained an explosive charge. Should the animal attack him, a powerful blow with it would kill the panther instantly.

"I don't even trust such a blackjack, " Old Firehand said to Tom. "A pistol would be more effective, since the animal could be frightened back by it without being killed. But everyone to his own pleasure. I shall praise the man but only once it's been accomplished."

The beast trainer now gave a short speech to the public and turned toward the cage. He opened the heavy bolts, then slid aside the narrow frame of the five-foot-high entrance gate. To enter, he had to bend down. For that he needed both his hands to hold the gate; then, when inside the cage, to close it again. He had, therefore, taken the blackjack between his teeth and was thus momentarily defenseless. Although he had often before been with the animal in the cage, this now took place under very different circumstances. Prior to today, the creature had been for days in the dark; not as many people had been close by, neither had there been the pounding of the engine nor the rushing of the wheels. These facts had neither been taken into consideration by the menagerie owner nor the beast trainer himself with the consequences to follow.

When the panther heard the noise of the gate opening, he turned. Just then the beast trainer stuck in his lowered head. In a lightning-like move of the carnivore, it had the head, from which the blackjack tumbled, in its jaws and with a single bite crunched it to splinters and pulp.

The shout of horror which erupted at this moment in front of the cage was beyond belief. All jumped up and ran clamoring away. Only three remained sitting: the menagerie owner, Old Firehand and Black Tom. The first wanted to slide the gate of the cage shut, but this was impossible since the beast trainer's body lay across the entrance, half in and half out. Then he tried to pull the corpse out by the legs.

"For God's sake, not that!" shouted Old Firehand. "The panther will come after it. Push the body in completely; he's dead anyway. Then close the gate!"

The panther lay in front of the headless body. With bone fragments still in his bloody, slavering jaws, he fixed his glittering eyes on his master. He seemed to divine his intention, for he roared angrily and crept forward on the corpse, holding it down by the weight of his body. His head was now only a few inches away from the open gate.

"Get away, away! He's coming out!" shouted Old Firehand. "Tom, your rifle! Your rifle! A revolver would only aggravate the situation!"

Black Tom ran for his rifle.

15

From the moment the beast trainer had tried to enter the cage to the present, barely ten seconds had passed. No one had found enough time to get to real safety. The entire deck was a confusion of fleeing and fearfully screaming people. The doors to the cabins and the lower deck were jammed. People took cover behind barrels and crates, then jumped up again, not feeling truly secure at all.

The captain had run toward the bridge, taking the stairs three and four steps at a time. Old Firehand followed him. The menagerie owner fled to the rear wall behind the cage. Black Tom, running for his rifle, suddenly remembered he had tied his ax to the stock and thus could not use it immediately. Instead, he stopped at the two Indians he was just passing and tore the rifle from the older Bear's hand.

"I shoot myself," said the Indian, his hand reaching back for the weapon.

"Let me!" the bearded one told him. "In any case, I shoot better than you!"

He turned around to the cage. The panther had just stalked out, lifted his head and roared mightily. Black Tom leveled the gun and pulled the trigger. The shot rang out, but the bullet didn't hit home. Hurriedly, Tom snatched the second rifle from the young Indian's hand and again fired on the animal -- with the same result.

"Poor shooting. Not know rifle," Old Bear said as if sitting quietly and safely over a roast in his wigwam.

The German paid no attention to these words. He tossed the rifle away and hurried farther up front where the rifles of the colonel's group lay. These gentlemen had not displayed any desire to take up the battle with the animal but rather had run quickly for cover.

At this moment close to the bridge a terrible scream arose. A lady had wanted to flee up there. The panther spotted her as his roar ended. He crouched down and then in long leaps bounded toward her. She was still well down on the stairs while Old Firehand stood already on the fifth or sixth step. He quickly took hold of her, swinging her up to him, his strong arms lifting her over his head where the captain could catch her. This had all happened in two eye blinks, but now the panther was also at the foot of the stairs. Putting his front paws onto one of the steps, he contracted his body to leap up and onto Old Firehand. Whereupon the brave fellow gave the beast a mighty kick on the nose, then fired the remaining three bullets from his revolver at the animal's head.

This kind of defense was actually ridiculous. With a kick of the foot and a few pea-sized revolver bullets, a black panther cannot be scared off. But Old Firehand had no more effective means of defense at hand. He was convinced the animal would now jump him; however that did not happen. The panther turned his head slowly aside as if thinking of something better to do, while maintaining his erect position on the stairs. Had the bullets fired from such close proximity, yet having barely dented his hard skull, somewhat stunned him? Or had the kick

16

on his sensitive nose been too painful? Whichever it may be, he no longer eyed Old Firehand but looked toward the foredeck where there stood a perhaps thirteen-year-old girl, unmoving and frozen in fright, both arms stretched out toward the bridge. It was the daughter of the lady Old Firehand had just rescued from the panther. The child, herself trying to escape, had seen her mother in danger, and shocked by it, stood stock still. She was wearing a bright, shining dress, which had caught the panther's attention. He withdrew his paws from the stairs, turned, and in six or eight leaps sprang toward the child who saw the terrible beast coming, but could neither move nor utter a sound.

"My daughter! My daughter!" the mother shrieked.

All who saw this screamed and hollered, but no one lifted a hand or foot to rescue the little girl. There was no time. None? And did really no one move? One did, and just the one no one anticipated would have possessed such attention, daring, and quick-wittedness. That is, the young Indian.

He had stood with his father about ten paces away from the girl. When he noticed the danger she was in, his eyes blazed lightning. Looking left and right as if searching for an escape route, he dropped the Zuni blanket from his shoulders, calling to his father in the Tonkawa language, "Tiakaitat; schai schoyana --- stay there; I shall swim!"

In two strides he reached the girl, grabbed her by her waist belt and holding her tightly vaulted onto the railing. There he stopped for a moment to look back. The panther was right behind them coiled to leap. Barely had the animal's paws left the deck when the young Indian sprang from the railing in a sideways jump so as to land in the river as far as possible from the animal. The waters closed over him and his burden. In the same instant, the panther shot over the railing unable to halt the force of his momentum.

"Stop, stop the ship immediately!" commanded the quick-witted captain through the mouthpiece down to the engine room.

The engineer slammed the engine into reverse; the steamer slowed then stopped and remained in place, its wheels catching only enough water to prevent back drift.

Since the danger to the passengers had now passed, they all came out from their hiding places to peer over the railing. The child's mother had passed out. Her father shouted excitedly, "A thousand dollars for the rescue of my daughter, two thousand, three thousand, five thousand, more, much more!"

No one listened to him. Everyone leaned over the railing, looking down at the river. There appeared the panther, an excellent swimmer, his paws spread wide on the water, looking for his prey -- but in vain. The brave boy and the girl were nowhere to be seen.

"They drowned, got into the wheels!" the father lamented, tearing his hair with his hands.

17

Reassuringly, the voice of the old Indian sounded from the opposite railing. "Nintropan-homosch smart. Swam under ship for panther not to see. He down here!"

Everyone ran to starboard, the captain calling for ropes to be thrown down. And truly, down there hard along the ship's side, Little Bear swam slowly on his back to avoid drifting away, with the unconscious girl draped across his body. Ropes were quickly found and lowered. One the boy attached under the girl's arms and while she was pulled up, swung himself nimbly aboard on the second one.

He was greeted with tumultuous jubilation, but walked proudly away without uttering a word. However, when he passed by the colonel who had also watched, he stopped in front of him, speaking so loudly that everyone could hear, "Well, is Tonkawa afraid of small, mangy cat? Colonel ran away with all his twenty heroes. But Tonkawa drew attention of great monster to save girl and passengers. Colonel will hear more from Tonkawa!"

The rescued girl was carried to her cabin. Meanwhile the helmsman, having the best view of the river, called out pointing to port: "Look at the panther; see the raft!"

Now everyone ran back to the opposite rail, where a new and nonetheless exciting spectacle was to unfold. All on board had been occupied watching the rescue events and had not seen a raft made of branches and rushes on which sat two figures intent on reaching the steamer from the riverbank's right side. They worked with improvised oars made of branches. One of them was a boy, the other seemed to be a peculiarly and strangely dressed female. She wore a head cover similar to an old balloon hat, from which peeked a round, red-cheeked face and a pair of small eyes. The rest of the figure appeared to be covered by a large sack whose cut and shape were indefinable, since the person was not standing but sitting. Black Tom, standing beside Old Firehand asked, "Sir, do you know this woman?"

"No. Is she so famous that I should know her?"

"Indeed. For she is no woman, but a man, a prairie hunter and trapper. There comes the panther. You shall see what a woman, who is a man, can do."

Leaning over the railing, he shouted: "Holla, Aunt Droll, watch out. He wants to eat you."

The raft was still approximately fifty paces distant from the steamer. The panther had swum back and forth beside the ship looking for his prey. Now he saw the raft and swam toward it. The make-believe woman looked up to the deck and recognizing the one who had called out, answered in a falsetto voice, "Good luck! It's you, Tom? Glad to see you, if it's necessary! What kind of animal is this?"

"A black panther which jumped off the ship. Get away. Quickly, quickly!"

"Oho! Aunt Droll doesn't run from anything, not even from a panther may it be black, blue or green. Can one shoot the animal?"

"Of course! But you can't do it. It belongs to a menagerie and is the most dangerous carnivore in the world. Flee to the other side of the ship."

No one but Tom knew this odd character, but all shouted warnings to flee. Yet this person seemed to find pleasure in playing games with the panther. He used the fragile oar like an expert and knew with amazing skill how to evade the animal. At the same time, he shouted in the same falsetto voice, "I shall finish this, old Tom. Where am I to shoot this creature, if it's necessary?"

"In the eye," answered Old Firehand.

"Well! Then let's have this wet rat come closer."

He pulled in his oar and reached for the rifle beside him. Raft and panther approached each other quickly. The carnivore faced his enemy with wide open, staring eyes. The hunter leveled his gun, aimed, and fired twice. To put down the rifle, grab the oar and push the raft forward was accomplished in the blink of an eye. The panther had disappeared. Where he had last been seen, a swirl indicated the place of his death struggle. Then he reappeared downstream on the surface, motionless and lifeless. For a few seconds he drifted there, then disappeared into the depths.

"Masterly shot!" Tom called down from the deck, the passengers agreeing enthusiastically. Only the menagerie owner remained silent, having lost both the expensive panther and his beast trainer.

"Those were two shots," answered the strange figure from the river. "One in each eye. Where's this steamer going, if it's necessary?"

"As far as it takes to find deep enough water," responded the captain.

"We wanted to come aboard, for which we built this raft over there. Will you take us?"

"Can you pay for passage, ma'am or sir? I truly don't know whether I am to invite you aboard as a man or a woman."

"As Aunt, sir. Because I am Aunt Droll, understand, if it's necessary. And what concerns the passage, I pay in good money, or even in nuggets."

"Then we'll lower the rope ladder. Come aboard! We must hurry to get away from this disastrous place."

The rope ladder was lowered. First the boy made his way up. He too carried a rifle. Then the Aunt threw up his rifle, rose, took hold of the ladder, pushed the raft away below him and, like a gymnast with squirrel-like agility, jumped onto the deck where he was greeted with very surprised looks.

Karl May – translated by Herbert Windolf

2. The Rovers

The United States of America is, because --- or rather as the result of --- its liberal institutions, the source of quite peculiar social calamities entirely impossible to occur in a European country.

An expert on those conditions would admit that these assertions of a later ethnographer have their good reasons. One could split the plagues he is talking about into chronic and acute ones. Belonging to the former, one could name primarily the quarrel-seeking loafers and rowdies, then the so-called "runners" who preferred to target immigrants. The runner, loafer, and rowdy situation has stabilized and will, as it appears, last a few decades more. It is different with the second kind of plague, which has evolved faster and will be of shorter duration. To the latter belonged the lawless conditions of the Far West, where due to this, gangs of robbers and murderers had sprung up which have been eliminated only by the most energetic application of Master Lynch. There are, furthermore, the Ku Kluxers to be mentioned, who during the Civil War and even thereafter played their evil games. However, it was the rovers who developed into the worst plague to the country as representatives of a most crude and brutal vagrant society.

When at a time that a heavy hand lay on trade and commerce, thousands of factories stood idle and tens of thousands of laborers went without work. These unemployed became migrants, who preferred moving in a westerly direction. The states on and west of the Mississippi were literally overrun by them. Soon there took place a separation process where the honest ones found work wherever possible even if it paid little and was strenuous. Most of them arrived on farms to help with the harvest and were, therefore, called harvesters.

Those averse to work, though, gathered in gangs, making their miserable living from robberies, murder and pillage. Their members quickly descended to the lowest level of moral depravity and were led by men in need of avoiding civilization since there the fist of the law could apprehend them.

These rovers usually appeared in large crowds, at times up to and over three hundred strong. They not only attacked individual farms but even small towns and plundered them completely. They dared to seize trains, overpowered the personnel and used the trains to get quickly to another area where they repeated the same crime. This disorder became so prevalent that the governors of several states were forced to call up the militia to literally conduct battles with these rovers.

As told earlier, the captain and helmsman of the "Dogfish" had thought this Colonel Brinkley and his followers were such rovers. This assumption, even if true, was no reason for immediate worry. Their group, only about twenty strong, was much too small to take on the other passengers together with the crew. But prudence and attention were still called for.

The colonel had, of course, also given his attention to the odd character approaching the ship on such a fragile raft and who had just in passing killed the mighty carnivore. He had laughed when Tom had attributed to him the odd name of Aunt Droll. But now, as the stranger stepped onto the deck where he was clearly recognizable, the colonel's brows knitted and he asked his people to gather around him. He led them to the very front of the foredeck and said to them, "This chap is not as ridiculous as he makes himself appear. I tell you, we better be careful with him."

"Why? Do you know him? Is it a woman or a man?" one of them asked.

"A man, of course."

"Why then this masquerade?"

"It's no masquerade. This fellow is truly an original, at the same time one of the most dangerous police spies there is."

"Pshaw! Aunt Droll a police spy! The man may be everything you believe; I'll believe many things but not that he's a police detective!"

"And yet he is," insisted the colonel. I've heard of Aunt Droll; he's just a half-crazed trapper who's on best of terms with all Indian tribes because of his gaiety. But now that I've seen him, I understand it better. This stout fellow is a detective par excellence. I've come across him up north at Fort Sully on the Missouri, where he pulled a comrade from our midst to deliver to the gallows, he alone, and us more than forty men!"

"That's impossible. Couldn't you have stabbed him forty times!"

"No, we couldn't. He operates more by cunning than force. Just look at his little, crafty mole's eyes! They don't miss even an ant in the grass. He approaches his victim with the most irresistible kindness and snaps the trap shut before one even realizes he's been taken."

"Does he know you?"

"I don't think so. He couldn't have paid attention to me then. It was a long time ago and in the meantime I've changed much. Nevertheless, I'm of the opinion that it's advisable for us to remain quiet and unaffected so as not to draw his attention. I think we can pull off a good trick here and wouldn't want him to interfere. Aside from Old Shatterhand, Old Firehand is the most famous hunter in the West. This Black Tom also demonstrated that he's one to reckon with; but more dangerous than either one is Aunt Droll. Watch out for him. Rather act as if you don't even notice him."

As dangerous as Droll had been described by the colonel, dangerous he was not. Actually those present had to make an all-out effort not to break into hurtful laughter at his appearance. Now that he stood on deck, it was possible to define the kind of garment he was wearing.

His headdress was neither hat, nor cap, nor bonnet, yet one could call it by any of these names. It consisted of five differently shaped and sewn-together leather pieces. The middle one on top of the head had the shape of an inverted bowl; another one shaded his forehead, supposedly as a kind of shade or brim; two others were broad flaps covering the ears.

The coat was very long and extremely wide. It was put together from nothing but patches, each sewn again and again over and beside the other. None of the patches was of the same age; one could rather picture them having come together little by little over time. Up front, the coat's edges were equipped with short straps tied together to take the place of the missing buttons. Since the garment's great length and width would have made walking difficult, the man had sliced it from the bottom seam upwards and had tied the two halves around his legs to form a pair of knickerbockers, giving the Aunt's movements a truly ludicrous appearance. The improvised leggings reached almost to his ankles.

The sleeves too were unusually wide and much too long for the man. At the front he had sewn them shut and farther back cut two holes through which he stuck his hands. In this way, the sleeves now formed two drooping leather pouches, which appeared to contain quite a few items. Two leather shoes completed the get-up.

With this kind of dress, the man's figure took on the appearance of shapelessness which, together with the full, red-cheeked, all-too-kindly face called downrightly for mirth. The little eyes seemed not to be able to remain still for even a second but were in continuous movement so as not to miss anything.

Such characters were not rare in the West. Whoever spends years in the wilderness has neither the time nor the money to replace his worn garments with anything other than what is offered him by the land. Thus one frequently meets there famous people whose dress is such that elsewhere children would run after them screaming and laughing.

In his hand the Aunt carried a double-barreled rifle, obviously of a very respectable age. Whether he carried any other weapons could be assumed but not seen, since the garment enclosed the figure like a tied sack in whose innards many an object could be hidden.

The boy in the company of this original fellow was maybe sixteen years old. He was blond, strong-boned and looked around very seriously, even defiantly, like one who already knows his own way. His dress consisted of a hat, hunting shirt, pants, stockings and shoes, all made of leather. Besides the rifle he carried a knife and a revolver.

When Aunt Droll stepped onto the deck, he offered his hand to Black Tom, exclaiming in his falsetto voice, "Welcome, old Tom! What a surprise! A real eternity that we haven't seen each other. Where are you coming from and where are you going?"

They shook hands in the most cordial way with Tom replying, "Up the Mississippi. Going into Kansas, where my rafters are waiting in the woods."

"Well, then all's fine. We're heading in the same direction. I'm going there too, even farther. We can be together for some time yet. But first and foremost:

the passage fee. What do we need to pay, myself and this little man here, if it's necessary?"

This question was directed to the captain.

"It depends on how far you want to go and what kind of accommodation you want," was the answer.

"Accommodation? Aunt Droll always travels first class, that's cabin, sir. And how far? For the moment, let's say Fort Gibson. We can lengthen the lasso any time. Do you take gold nuggets?"

"Yes, very readily."

"But how's your weigh scale? Are you honest?"

This question was asked in such a droll voice, the eyes simultaneously winking so merrily that no resentment was called for. Nevertheless, the captain gave the impression of being annoyed and answered, "Don't dare ask that again or I'll throw you overboard!"

"Oho! You think Aunt Droll can be kicked into the water so easily? There you are mightily mistaken! Just try it for once!"

"Okay, " the captain demurred, "To ladies one must be polite, and since you are an aunt, you belong to the fair sex. That's why I'm not going to take your question crosswise. And then there's no rush for payment. Talk to the officer some time!"

"No, I don't use credit, not for a minute; that's my principle, if it's necessary."

"Well! Then come along to the office."

The two departed and the others exchanged their opinions about this peculiar man. But the captain returned sooner than Droll. He said in surprise, "Gentlemen, the nuggets you should have seen. What nuggets! Droll retracted one of his hands into his sleeve and when he stuck it out of its opening, it was full of gold nuggets, pea-size, hazelnut-size, even larger. The man must have discovered a bonanza. I bet he is much, very much richer than he claims."

In the meantime, Droll paid for his passage at the office then looked around outside. First he noticed the colonel's people. Since he wasn't one to travel on a ship without knowing who his fellow passengers were, he slowly ambled to the foredeck and looked the men over. For a minute his eyes came to rest on the colonel, then he asked him, "Beg your pardon, sir, haven't we seen each other before?"

"Not that I know of," the other answered.

"Oh, I'm quite sure that we have met once before. Have you ever been up the Missouri?"

"No."

"Also not been at Fort Sully?"

"Don't even know it."

"Hmm! May I perhaps ask your name?"

"Why? What for?"

"Because it pleases me, sir. And once I've taken pleasure in someone, I can't have peace until I know his name."

"As it is, I like you too," the colonel responded in a sharp voice. "Still, I wouldn't want to be so impolite as to ask you for your name."

"Why? I don't think it impolite, and would answer your question at once. I have no reason to keep my name a secret. Only the one who doesn't have a clean conscience needs to conceal it, as I'm told."

"Is that meant as an insult, sir?"

"I wouldn't think of it! I never insult a decent human being, if it's necessary. Bye, sir, and keep your name to yourself! I don't care to hear it."

Turning, he walked away.

"To have that done to me!" grated the colonel. "And I have to take it!"

"Why do you suffer so?" laughed one of his companions. "I would have answered this leather bag with a fist."

"And drawn the short end of the stick!"

"Pshaw! This toad doesn't look like he has much strength."

"Yet a man who lets a black panther approach within arm's length, and then cold-bloodedly blows him away with his charge like a prairie chicken is not to be taken lightly. And it wouldn't have been he alone. Others would immediately have been against me, and we must avoid all attention."

Droll had gone aft and on the way came across the two Indians who had taken seats on a bale of tobacco. When he saw them, they rose like people expecting to be addressed. Droll slowed down then walked toward them quickly, exclaiming: "Mira, el Oso Grande y el Oso Chico --- look there, the Big Bear and the Little Bear!"

That had been in Spanish. Hence he had to know that the two red men were not fluent in English but understood and spoke Spanish much better.

"Que sorpresa, la tia Droll --- what a surprise, Aunt Droll," answered the old Indian, although he had seen him already when he was still on the raft.

"What are you doing here in the east and on this ship?" asked Droll, continuing in Spanish and offering both his hand.

"We visited New Orleans together with several red brothers to buy things and are now on the way home, while the others return with the purchases. Many moons have passed since we last saw the face of Aunt Droll."

"Yes, Little Bear has meanwhile grown to twice his size from when last I saw him. Do my red brothers live in peace with their neighbors?"

"We have buried our tomahawks in the ground and have no desire to dig them out."

"When will you return to your people?"

"We don't know. We thought to need half a moon but now it will take us somewhat longer."

"Well? What is the meaning of these words?"

"That Big Bear cannot return home before he has dipped his knife into the blood of the one who insulted him."

"Who is that?"

"The white dog over there with the red hair. He has slapped Big Bear in the face with his hand."

"By the devil! Has this chap been in his right mind! He must know what it means to slap an Indian, particularly Big Bear."

"He seems not to know who I am. I gave him my name in my people's language and now I ask my white brother not to translate it to him into English."

"If I ever translate anything, it would be something else but not my brother's name. Now I would like to leave for the others who would like to talk with me; yet I shall return to you to hear your voices."

He continued his interrupted walk aft. Farther on, the father of the rescued girl had come from his cabin to report that his daughter had awakened from her faint, felt relatively well and would now need only some rest to recover fully. The much-relieved man then hurried over to the Indians to thank the courageous boy for his bold action. Droll had heard his words and inquired about what had happened. When Tom told him, he said, "Yes, that was something I think the boy was capable of doing. He is no longer a child, but truly a man."

"Do you know him and his father? We saw that you talked to them."

"I've met them a few times."

"Met them? He called himself a Tonkawa. This almost extinct tribe never migrates but has become sedentary on its miserable reservation in the valley of the Rio Grande."

"Big Bear has not become sedentary but has remained true to the customs of his ancestors. He roves about like the chief of the Apaches, Winnetou. You might expect him to have a place of rest when he wearies of travel but he keeps it a secret. At times he talks about 'his own people' and whenever I meet him I ask him if they are doing well but who, what and where they are I have never found out. Now too, he wants to go to them but has been held up because of his need for revenge against the colonel."

"Did he speak of it?"

"Yes. He won't rest until the man has been killed. In my mind's eye, the colonel is a dead man."

"I said this too," Old Firehand commented. "The way I know the Indians, it wasn't from cowardice that he didn't react to the slap."

"So?" asked Droll, looking over at the giant. "Did you also come to know the Indians, if it's necessary? You don't look like you would even be a true goliath. I believe you would fit much better in a salon than on the prairie."

"Oh my, Aunt!" Tom laughed. "There you have gone way astray. Guess who this gentleman is!"

"I wouldn't think of it. Maybe you are so kind as to tell me."

"No. I'm not making it that easy. You ought to strain your mind at least a bit. This gentleman is one of our most famous frontiersmen."

"So. Not just famous but the most famous?"

"Yes."

"In my opinion, there would be only two of this kind, for no third one deserves such a superlative term."

He paused, shut one eye and with the other winked at Old Firehand. Letting go of a short laugh sounding like a 'hee, hee, hee" blown on a clarinet, he continued, "For those two are Old Shatterhand and Old Firehand. Since I know the former, if it's necessary, this good sir here could be none other than Old Firehand. Did I guess aright?"

"Yes, I'm the one," the hunter nodded.

"My word!" remarked Droll, stepping back two paces, once more looking Old Firehand over with his one open eye. "Are you truly the man before whom every crook trembles? Your figure's right as described, but --- maybe you're kidding me after all!"

"Well, is this too much of a joke for you?" asked Old Firehand, at the same time taking hold of Droll by the coat collar with his right hand, lifting him up, swinging him around three times, then putting him down on a nearby crate.

The face of the thus-reprimanded had gone dark red. Fighting for breath, he nevertheless protested in several stammered sentences, "Zounds, sir! Do you think me a pendulum or a centrifugal regulator? Have I been created to rotate about you through the air? It's fortunate that my garment is made of strong leather or it may have torn and you'd have tossed me into the river! But the test has proved okay, sir; I do see now that you are truly Old Firehand. I must believe it, if only for the reason that you'd be able to demonstrate to me once again the moon's rotation around the Earth. When hearing about you, I've often thought how happy I would be to meet you some time. I'm just a simple trapper but know for sure what a man of your kind can accomplish. Here's my hand. And if you don't want to sadden me immensely, do not reject it!"

"Reject it? That would be pure sin. I gladly shake hands with any brave man, particularly with one having introduced himself so splendidly."

"Introduced? How so?"

"By shooting the panther."

"Oh, that. That wasn't a feat one needs to brag about. The animal wasn't very happy in the water. It didn't do anything to me but wanted merely to rescue itself onto my raft. I haven't been too hospitable there, though."

"That was sensible of you, for truthfully the panther did have you in mind. He isn't afraid of water, is an excellent swimmer and could have reached the bank without much effort. What a calamity it would have been had he succeeded at it. By killing him you certainly have saved many lives. Let's shake hands and get to know each other better."

"My wish too, sir. May I suggest we have a drink to celebrate this new acquaintance. I haven't boarded this steamer to die of thirst. Shall we go to the salon?"

Following this suggestion, they departed. Tom had to pay his extra dues for the cabin in order to accompany them, but did so with pleasure.

When the gentlemen had left the deck, the Negro who had not been allowed to see the panther came up from the engine room. He had been spelled by another crew member and now looked for a shady spot for his afternoon siesta. As he walked slowly and sulkily up front, one could see from his face that he was not in a good mood. When the colonel saw this, he waved to him to come closer.

"What's the matter, sir, the black asked when he arrived. "If you have an order, call for the steward. I'm not here for the passengers."

He spoke English like a white man.

"I'm aware of that," the colonel answered. "I just wanted to ask you whether you would care to have a glass of brandy with us."

"If it's that, I'm your man. Down in the engine room, the throat and even the liver gets dry. But I don't see a single sip here!"

"Here, have a dollar; fetch yourself what you like over there. Then come join us."

Immediately the expression of displeasure disappeared from the Negro's face. Simultaneously he became much more animated. He returned with two full bottles and a few glasses and sat down beside the colonel who willingly made some room for him. After the first glass had gone down his gullet, the crewman poured a second one, emptied it, then asked, "This is a refreshment, sir, that one like me cannot afford often. But how come you thought of inviting me? You whites are usually not so obliging toward us blacks."

"With me and my friends, a Negro is worth as much as a white. I've noticed you work in the engine room. That's hard and thirsty work. And since I figure the captain isn't paying you in hundred dollar bills, I thought a good sip would be the right thing to offer."

"That was a great idea. Yes, the captain pays rather poorly; one cannot really afford a good drink, particularly since he doesn't give any advance. At least not me; he pays only at the end of the trip -- damn!"

"So he's picking on you?"

"Yes, me particularly."

"Why?"

"He claims I'm too thirsty. And while he pays the others daily, he doesn't pay me. It's no wonder my thirst gets greater and greater."

"Well, then it's entirely up to you whether you can quench it today or not."

"How so?"

"I'm prepared to pay you a few dollars if you can do me a favor."

"A few dollars? Huzzah! That would pay for a few bottles! Tell me your request, sir. I would happily do you the favor."

"It's not that easy. I'm not sure you're the right man for it."

"Me? If it's to earn brandy, I'm always the right man."

"Possibly. But it must be done craftily."

"Craftily? Is it something to bring harm to my back? The captain doesn't tolerate irregularities."

"Don't worry; nothing of that kind. You are only to listen a bit, eavesdrop some."

"Where? On whom?"

"In the salon."

"So? Hmm?" he mumbled thoughtfully. "What for, sir?"

"Well, anyway, I shall be truthful with you." The colonel pushed a full glass toward the Negro and continued in a confidential tone, "There's this big, gigantic fellow who's called Old Firehand, furthermore a dark-bearded chap by the name of Tom, and finally the joker in the long leather coat with the name of Aunt Droll. Old Firehand is a rich farmer, the two others are his guests whom he has invited to come along. By chance, we too want to get to this farm to find work there. It's only natural that this would be a good opportunity to find out what kind of people they are to deal with. I think they'll talk about their affairs, and if you keep your ears open it wouldn't be difficult to satisfy us. You can see that I'm not asking for anything improper or forbidden."

"Quite right, sir! No one has prohibited me to listen to what others say. The next six hours are mine; I'm off work and can do as I please."

"But how do you intend to do it?"

"That's the question I'm thinking about right now."

"Are you allowed in the salon?"

"I haven't been forbidden from entering it, but neither have I any place in there."

"Well, find a pretext to do so!"

"But which? I could carry something in or fetch something, but either would take so little time that I couldn't accomplish my task."

"Isn't there any work you could occupy yourself with for some time?"

"No --- yes, indeed! Something occurs to me. The windows are dirty. I could clean them."

"Wouldn't that draw attention?"

"No. The salon is always occupied, which is why this work cannot be done at a time when no one is present."

"But you're not the one who does this job."

"That doesn't matter. It's actually the steward's job, but I will be doing him the greatest favor if I relieve him of it."

"But he could become suspicious."

"No. He knows I have no money but like to have my brandy. I'll tell him I'm thirsty and would clean the windows for him for a glass. That should not arouse his suspicions. Don't worry, sir, I'll make it possible. Then --- how many dollars do you promise me?"

"I'll pay you by the value of the information you deliver to me, but at least three pieces."

"All right, I'll do it. Pour me another one, then I'll go."

When he had left, the colonel was asked by his comrades what he actually intended with the mission's information. He answered, "We are poor rovers and must see to our well-being. We have had to pay passage here and I would at least make the attempt to find out if we can recoup our money in some way. For the long trek ahead of us we must make preparations which will cost us a good bit of money, and you know our purses have become rather empty."

"Don't we want to fill them from the railroad pay office?" asked the one who fancied himself the group's speaker.

"Are you so sure we'll succeed at that plan? If we can make some money already here, it would be stupid to let the opportunity go by."

"Well. Let me tell you straight out: theft here on board? That's dangerous. It's not possible to get ashore right away and if the person concerned discovers his loss, there would be a terrible uproar followed by a search of all the people and every corner on board. We particularly would be the first to come under suspicion."

"You're the most childish fellow I've ever seen," the colonel scoffed. "Such a thing may be dangerous or not, depending on how it's done. And I'm not the one to approach it from the wrong side. If you follow me in everything, then we'll succeed even in the final great coup."

"The one up at Silver Lake? Hmm! Perhaps you've been sold a hoax."

"Pshaw! I know what I know. I wouldn't think of telling you yet all the details. When we get to the lake, I'll tell you. Until then you must trust me and believe what I tell you: that there are riches up there, which will last us a lifetime. Now, let's avoid all unnecessary prattle and instead wait to hear what the stupid nigger will report to us."

He leaned against the quarterdeck and closed his eyes as a sign that he didn't wish to hear anything else nor had he any more to say. The others too made themselves comfortable. Some of them attempted to sleep but without success. Others whispered quietly with each other about their big plan for whose outcome they had sworn life or death to each other.

The 'stupid nigger' seemed to be well up to his task. Had he found an insurmountable obstacle, he would surely have returned to report it. He first went to the service room to talk with the steward and then disappeared through the entrance of the salon without returning again. More than an hour passed before he showed up on deck. With several cleaning rags in hand, he put them aside then joined the awakening company. Sitting down, he never saw four eyes closely watching both him and the rovers. Those four eyes belonged to the two Indians, Big Bear and Little Bear.

"Well then?" the colonel asked anxiously. "Did you accomplish your task?"

The black responded sourly, "I made every effort but I don't think I've earned more than the agreed-upon three dollars for what I've heard."

"Why?"

Because my spying was in vain. You were mistaken, sir."

"In what?"

"Yes, the giant is called Old Firehand, but he is not at all a farmer and can, therefore, not have invited this Tom and this Aunt Droll."

"Can that be!" the colonel exclaimed, imitating a tone of disappointment.

"Yes, it's so," the Negro confirmed. "The giant is a famous hunter and is on his way far up into the mountains."

"Where to?"

"He didn't say. I heard everything, never missing a word of the conversation. The three men sat with the father of the girl that the panther had wanted to eat, as well as the others."

"Does he want to go up there by himself?"

"No. The father's name is Butler. He's an engineer. He too intends to come along."

"An engineer? What do these two want up there in the mountains?"

"Maybe a mine deposit has been found which Butler would investigate."

"No, Old Firehand could do it better himself than the smartest engineer."

"First, they want to visit Butler's brother who owns a splendid farm in Kansas. This brother is a very rich man. He's supplied cattle and grain to New Orleans, for which the engineer has collected the payment to bring to him."

The colonel's eyes lit up, but neither he nor any of the rovers betrayed by the slightest facial expression how important this information was.

"Yes, in Kansas there are immensely rich farmers," remarked the gang's leader in an indifferent voice. "This engineer, however, is a careless person. Is it a great sum?"

"Although he only whispered it --- about nine thousand dollars in paper --- I nevertheless understood it."

"One doesn't carry a sum like that around. That's what banks are for. If rovers got a hold of it, it would be lost."

"No, they would never find it."

"Oh, those are crafty fellows."

"But where he has it, they would surely never look."

"Then you know the hiding place?"

"Yes. He showed it to the others, although he did it surreptitiously because of my being present. I had turned my back to them so they thought I wouldn't catch his hints. But they didn't take into account the mirror into which I faced and in which I saw everything."

"Hmm, a mirror can deceive. Someone facing it sees his right side on the left and the left on the right, as is well known."

"I haven't observed that yet and don't understand it, but what I've seen, I've seen. The engineer has an old Bowie knife with a hollow shaft, inside of which he has hidden the notes. Rovers might rob him should he fall into their hands, but such an old, poor knife even the worst robber wouldn't take from his victim. He doesn't need it himself and would leave the victim at least a weapon, a tool, without which he would be lost in the West."

"That may be true. But where does he keep the knife? He doesn't wear a hunting coat nor a belt."

"He wears his belt underneath his vest and from it hangs the leather purse in which he keeps the knife. On the left side under the coat."

"So it is! Well, that doesn't really interest us. We're no rovers but honest harvesters. I'm sorry I was mistaken about the giant. His similarity with the farmer I was referring to is very great and he carries the same name."

"Maybe it's his brother. By the way, not only is it the engineer who carries so much money. The black-bearded one also spoke about a substantial sum he received and must share with his rafter comrades."

"Where are they?"

"They presently cut trees at the Black Bear River, which I do not know."

"I know it. It enters the Arkansas downstream from Tuloi. Is it a large group?"

"Close to twenty men, all good boys, he said. And the funny guy in the leather sleeping gown has a whole bunch of nuggets on him. He too is headed west. I wonder why he carries the gold. One doesn't carry it through the wilderness!"

"Why not? In the west people have needs too. There are forts, summer stores and traveling merchants with whom one can spend plenty of money or nuggets. Well then, these people are entirely of no concern to me. I just don't understand why this engineer intends to go to the Rocky Mountains with a little girl along."

"He only has this one child. The daughter loves him very much and didn't want to be separated from him. Since it's his plan to spend some time in the mountains for which it will even be necessary to build block houses, he decided to take her and her mother along."

"Block houses, he said?"

"Yes."

"A single block house would be sufficient for him and his family. One could surmise they are not going to be alone but will have company. I wonder what their purpose is?"

"Blackbeard wanted to know that too, but Old Firehand said he would tell him later."

"So they want to keep it a secret. Then it's probably a bonanza, a rich mineral deposit which is to be probed in secret and, if it should turn out favorably, be exploited. I would love to learn the place they are going to."

"Unfortunately that wasn't mentioned. As it appears, they intend to take Blackbeard and also Aunt Droll along. They've hit it off with each other, so much so that they have taken side-by-side cabins."

"Which ones?" Do you know?"

"Yes, because they discussed it loudly. The engineer sleeps in number one, number two is Old Firehand's, number three is Tom's, number four is Aunt Droll's, and in number five is little Fred."

"Who's that?"

"The boy the Aunt brought along."

"Is he Droll's son?"

"Not as far as I heard."

"What's his last name and why is he with Droll?"

"No word was spoken about this."

"Are cabins one to five on the right or on the left?"

"On the starboard side; that's left from here. Obviously, the girl and her mother sleep in a lady's cabin. But I don't need to tell you about it, for all this cannot be of interest to you."

"That's certainly true. Since I was mistaken about these people, I really don't care where they sleep. By the way, I don't envy them their narrow cabins where they must almost suffocate. We here on the open deck have as much air as we want."

"Well! But the men's cabins also have plenty of air since the windows have been taken out and replaced by screens. But the worst off are us workers. If we don't need to work at night, we're actually required to sleep down there." At that, he pointed to a hatch not far away leading below decks. "And it's a special favor if the officer allows us to sleep up here with the passengers. There's no air coming through the narrow hatch. Besides, a musty smell rises from the bilge below. On hot days, we could suffocate."

"Are your sleeping quarters connected to the hold?" the colonel asked urgently.

"Yes. Stairs go down there."

"Can you lock those?"

"No, that would be too awkward."

"Then you truly are to be pitied. But enough of these stories; we still have some brandy in the bottle."

"Right-o, sir! Talking dries the throat out too. I'll have one more drink, then look for some shade to take a nap. After my six hours off, it's back to the boiler. How about my dollars now?"

"I'll keep my word, although I'm paying you for nothing. But since it's my own error, it's not for you to suffer the consequences. Here then are the three dollars. You can't ask for more since your favor hasn't brought us any gain."

"I'm not asking for more, sir. These three dollars can get me enough brandy to kill myself. You're a noble gentleman. Should you come up with another wish, don't ask anyone else but talk to me. You can count on me."

He emptied another full glass, then turned away and lay down in the shade of a large package.

The rovers looked curiously at their leader. They basically knew what was going on, except that they could not properly connect some of his questions and inquiries.

"You're looking to me for information," the colonel said, his face assuming a superior, complacent smile. "Nine thousand dollars in bank notes --- cash --- not checks or drafts which could result in one's arrest upon presentation! That's a hefty sum and mighty welcome to us."

"Once we've got it!" the speaker for the others interrupted him.

"We will!"

"Not for a while yet!"

"Oho! When I say so, we do."

"Well, how are we going to get it?"

"I'll get it."

"From the cabin?"

"Yes."

"You yourself?"

"Of course. A big job like this I leave to no one else."

"And if you're caught?"

"Hardly likely. I've got a plan which will succeed."

"If true, we'll all be happy. But the engineer will miss his knife when he wakes up. There'll be a devil of a ruckus!"

"Yes, there will be a devil of a row, but we'll be gone."

"Where to?"

"What a question! Ashore, obviously."

"Are we to swim there?"

"No. I don't expect that, neither from me nor from you. I'm not a bad swimmer, but I wouldn't entrust myself to this wide river with its banks barely visible in the night."

"Do you plan then to seize one of the two boats?"

"That neither. It wouldn't be impossible to do without being noticed, but I would rather reckon in circumstances known to me, rather than with any that might arise unexpectedly."

"Then I don't see how we can get to land before the theft is discovered."

"That just proves what a child you are. Why do you think I inquired so urgently about the hold?"

"That I don't know!"

"Not know, but guess. Look around! What's that beside the anchor rope?"

"Looks like a tool box."

"You guessed it! I noticed that it holds hammers, files, pliers and several drill bits of which one has a diameter of one and one-half inches. Now put both together, the hold and the drill bit!"

"Thunder and lightning! By chance, do you intend to pierce the ship?" the other exclaimed.

"Indeed, I'm planning to do it."

"You'll have us all drown."

"Pshaw! Don't be ridiculous! No one's going to drown. I just want to force the captain to steer to shore."

"Okay! But is that going to succeed?"

"Absolutely. If the ship draws water, there must be a leak. And if there's a leak, you steer to shore to escape any danger and to check out the ship in peace."

"But if it's noticed too late?"

"Don't be such a worrywart. If the ship begins to sink, which will happen very slowly, the outboard waterline rises. This the officer or helmsman must notice if they're not blind. That will cause such an uproar that the engineer will at first not even think of his knife. When he finally notices it, we'll be long gone."

"But what if he thinks of his knife after all or if the captain steers to shore but lets no one debark? We need to think of everything."

"They won't find anything. We'll tie the knife to a string, drop it in the water, and attach the other end to the ship's outboard. Anyone who finds it there would have to be all-knowing."

"Not a bad idea. However, what happens if we get off the ship? Don't we want to travel by water as far as possible?"

"For nine thousand dollars, I'm prepared to walk some distance. Sharing it, there will be more than four hundred dollars per head. Then too, we shall not have to depend for too long on our legs. I figure we will soon come across a farm or Indian camp where we can 'buy' horses without having to pay for them."

"That sounds all right to me. And where do we ride from there?"

"First to the Black Bear River."

"By chance, to find the rafters the nigger talked about?"

"Yes. It shouldn't be difficult to scout their camp. Of course, we won't let ourselves be seen there but rather ambush the blackbeard and take his money. Once this is done, we'll have enough to outfit ourselves for our long ride."

"Then we're going to forget about the railroad pay office?"

"Not at all. There'll be many thousands of dollars there and we'll get this money as well. But we'd be fools not to pick up all kinds of things beforehand. And now you know what we're about. There'll be plenty to do tonight and we'll be short on sleep. Therefore, lie down now to be well rested and ready to march."

They followed his order. In any event, due to the oppressive heat there was an exceptional quiet on the ship. The landscape to the left and right offered nothing to attract the passengers' attention. Thus most travelers spent the time sleeping or at least dozing, that intermediate stage between sleeping and waking, a state offering neither body nor mind true refreshment.

Only toward evening when the sun approached the horizon did movement resume on deck. The heat had abated and a halfway fresh breeze had sprung up. The ladies and gentlemen came from their cabins to enjoy the freshness. The engineer too was among them. His wife and daughter were along, the latter having recovered from her fright and her involuntary bath. The three went to look for the Indians, since the two ladies had not yet expressed their gratitude.

Big Bear and Little Bear had spent the entire afternoon in true Indian fashion sitting quietly and immobile on the crate, the same one they had already occupied when Aunt Droll had greeted them. As the engineer, his wife and daughter approached, the father said to his son in Tonkawa, "He - el bakh schai - bakh matelu makik -- they will offer us money now."

His face darkened, since this way of expressing gratitude is offensive to an Indian. His son held his hand out in front of him with its back facing upward. He dropped it again quickly to indicate that he was of a different opinion than his father. With pleasure, his eyes took in the girl he had saved. In a few quick steps, she stood in front of him, took his hand between her own and pressing them together said, "You are a good and courageous boy. It's too bad that we do not live close. You would be very dear to me."

The boy looked earnestly at her rosy face and answered, "My life would be yours. If Great Manitou hears Little Bear's words, he knows they true."

"Then may I give you at least a keepsake to remember me by. May I?"

He only nodded. She pulled a thin gold ring from her finger and put it on his left little finger. It just fit. He looked at the ring, then at her, reached under his Zuni blanket, removed an object from his neck and gave it to her. It was a small, thick, squarish piece of leather tanned white and pressed flat with several symbols inscribed on it.

"Me, too, give you this as keepsake," he said. "It is totem of Nintropan-homosch, only leather, not gold. But when in danger with Indians, just show them, then danger is gone. All Indians know and love Nintropan-homosch and obey his totem."

She did not understand the meaning of a totem and what great value it could have under some circumstances. She understood only that he returned her gift of the ring with a piece of leather, but she didn't allow herself to look disappointed. She was too good-natured and kindhearted to offend him by rejecting his seemingly paltry present. She, therefore, tied the totem around her neck as the young Indian's eyes shone with pleasure and answered, "I thank you! Now I own something of you and you from me. It's a joy for both of us, although we would not forget each other even without these gifts."

Now the girl's mother also thanked him by means of a simple handshake. Then Butler, her father asked, "How am I to reward the feat of Little Bear? I am not poor, but all I have would not be enough for what you have vouchsafed to me. I must remain in your debt, but I will also be your friend. Only this memento can I give you with which you can protect yourself against your enemies, just as you defended my daughter against the panther. Will you take these weapons? I beg you."

He pulled two new, very well-worked revolvers from his pockets, whose handles were inlaid with mother-of-pearl, and offered them to the boy. The young Indian did not have to think twice. Stepping back a pace, he straightened up and said, "White man offers me weapons; this is great, great honor for me, for only men receive weapons. I shall accept them and use only to defend good people and shoot bad ones. Howgh!"

He took the revolvers and stuck them into his belt below the blanket. His father now could no longer contain himself. One could see from his face he was fighting with emotion. He said to Butler, " Me too thank white man that he not give money like to slaves or people with no honor. It is great reward we shall never forget. We always be friends of white man, his squaw and daughter. You keep well totem of Little Bear; it is also mine. I hope Great Manitou always send you sunshine and joy!"

The visit to express gratitude was now over; they shook hands once more, then parted. The two Indians again sat down on the crate.

"Tua enokh -- good people!" the father said.

"Tua - tua enokh! --- very good people," the son agreed. These were the only heartfelt expressions that Indian reserve permitted them to voice. The father felt particularly honored that it was not he but his son of whom he was so proud, who had been given such a gift.

That the engineer's gratitude had been expressed so appropriately was not entirely his own doing. Butler himself was not familiar enough with the views and customs of the red man that he could have known how to conduct himself in this case. Because of this, he had asked Old Firehand for advice and had received counsel. He now returned to find him sitting with Tom and Droll in front of their cabin and told them about the reception the presents had found. When he mentioned the totem, one could hear from his tone that he was unable to properly appreciate its significance. Old Firehand therefore asked him, "You know what a totem is, sir?"

"Yes. It is the mark of an Indian like our seal or signet. It may be different objects or consist of various materials."

"The explanation is correct but not quite complete. Not every Indian may carry a totem, only famous chiefs. That this boy already owns one, aside from its being also his father's, is proof of his having already accomplished feats considered exceptional even by red men. Then, depending on their purpose, totems may differ. In truth, a certain type is used only for the purpose of proof of identity and confirmation like our seal or signature. The one, however, of greatest importance to us palefaces acts as a recommendation of the one who received it. The recommendation can be a different one, depending on the degree of warmth and respect with which it was given. Let me see the leather again."

The girl gave it to him and he inspected it closely.

"Are you able to decipher these symbols, sir?" asked Butler.

"Yes," nodded Old Firehand. "I have been so often and long with the various tribes that I not only speak their dialects but understand their symbols. This totem is a very precious one rarely given as a gift. It is composed in Tonkawa and reads: 'Schakhe-i-kauvan-ehlatan, henschon-schakin hen-schon-schakin schakhe-i-kauvan-ehlatan, he-el ni-ya.' Translated, these words mean: 'His shadow is my shadow, and his blood is my blood; he is my elder brother.' And below it is the name symbol of Little Bear. The designation 'elder brother' is even more honorable than merely 'brother'. The totem carries a recommendation that cannot be expressed any more warmly. Whoever will hurt the owner of it must expect the worst revenge by Big Bear and Little Bear and all their friends. Wrap the totem well, sir, that it preserves the red-colored symbols. One cannot know of what great service it may be to you when you enter the area where the Tonkawa's allies reside. On this small piece of leather, the lives of many people might depend."

That afternoon the steamer had passed Ozark, Fort Smith and Van Buren, and had now reached the point where the Arkansas made a decisive turn to the north. The captain had announced that they would reach Fort Gibson about two hours after midnight, where he would dock until the morrow to inquire about the water level upstream. In order to be fresh upon arrival, most passengers went to bed quite early. The deck emptied entirely of the cabin passengers and a few people remained in the salon, engaged in chess and other games. In the adjacent smoking room sat only three people, Old Firehand, Tom and Droll who, undisturbed by others, talked about their experiences. The former was treated by the two others with the greatest esteem, which, however, did not prevent him from learning more closely of the circumstances and forthcoming intentions of

38

Aunt Droll. He now inquired how Droll had acquired the peculiar name of 'Aunt'.

Droll explained, "You know the custom of frontiersmen to give everybody a nickname or warrior's name which describes one of his exceptional characteristics. In my 'sleeping gown' I do look like a female, which is matched by my high voice. In the past, I spoke in a bass voice but a terrible catarrh once took my deeper notes away. And since I had the habit of taking care of every good soul like a good mother or aunt, I was given the name Aunt Droll."

"But Droll isn't your family name?"

"No. But I'm a merry fellow, maybe a bit droll too. Therefore my name."

"May we perhaps learn your real one. Mine is Winter, Tom's is Grosser. You have learned already that we are actually Germans. You, though, seem intent on keeping your origin in the deepest dark."

"I have, actually, reasons not to speak of it. However, not because I have to be ashamed of it. The reasons lie more in the --- nature of my business."

"Business? How am I to understand this?"

"Let's talk of it later. I understand that you wish to know what I'm going to do in the west and why I'm dragging along a sixteen-year-old boy. The time will come when I'll tell you. What concerns my name, a poet would take fright of it, for it is immensely poetic."

"There's no damage. No one's guilty of one's name. Out with it then!"

Droll closed one eye, hemmed and hawed, as if something were choking him, then exclaimed, "My name's --- Pampel."

"What, Pampel?" laughed Old Firehand. "Poetic this word is not, and if I laugh it is not because of the name but rather the face you're making. It looked almost as if it required a steam engine to force your name out. By the way, this name isn't even that rare. I did know a privy councilor by that name who carried it with great dignity. But this name is German. Are you also of German descent?"

"Yes."

"And born in the United States?"

Droll made his slyest and merriest face and answered in German, "Nee, das is mer damals gar nich eingefalle; ich habe mer e deutsches Elternpaar herausgesucht! --- Naw, I wouldn't have thought of it; I picked myself German parents!"

"What? A born German, a fellow countryman?" exclaimed Old Firehand. "Who would have thought that!"

"Das ham Se sich nich denke könne? Und ich habe gemeent, mer sieht mersch sofort an, dass ich als Urenkel der alten Germanen gebore bin. Könne Se vielleicht errate, wo ich meine erschte Kinderschtiefel angetret und abgelofe habe. - You couldn't figure that out? I had thought one could see from me that I was born a great-great-grandchild of the old Germanic tribes. Can you perhaps guess where I wore my first children's boots and scuffed their soles off?"

"Of course! Your dialect tells me that."

"Sagt ersch wirklich noch? Das kann mich ausserordentlich freue, denn grad off unsern schönen Dialekt bin ich schtets geradezu versesse gewese, was mer leider schpäter meine ganze Carriere verdorbe hat, wenn's nötig ist. Nu also, sage Se mal, wo bin ich denn gebore. --- Am I truly still talking this way? That pleases me immensely because of our beautiful dialect, which I have always been proud of, but which later messed up my entire career, if it's necessary. Now, tell me where I was born?"

"In the beautiful duchy of Altenburg, where they make the best quark, or cottage cheese, as it is called here."

"Right, in Altenburg; you guessed it immediately! And that about the cheese is true too. They're called quarkers and there are none better in Germany. You know, I had wanted to surprise you, which is why I didn't tell you right away about being a fellow countryman. But now while we all sit so nicely together, I couldn't keep it back any longer. Let's talk now about our beautiful homeland. I can't get it off my mind, although I've been in this country for a long time."

It looked very much as if a very animated conversation would develop now. Unfortunately, this was not to be the case, since some of the gentlemen in the salon had become tired of playing games and now entered for a good smoke. They engaged those already present in conversation so that they had to give up their desired subject. When they later separated to go to sleep, Droll said good-bye to Old Firehand. "It was a pity we couldn't continue our conversation, but tomorrow is another day to get back to our talk. Good night, fellow countryman, sleep well and fast because soon after midnight we must get up again!"

All cabins were now occupied and the lights were extinguished in the salons. On deck only the two lanterns burned as required, one at the bow, the other at the stern. The former illuminated the river so brightly and far ahead that the lookout could see and warn early enough of possible obstructions in the water. This man, the helmsman, and the officer walking back and forth on the bridge were the only people seemingly awake, except for the crew in the engine room.

The rovers lay on deck too as if asleep but some distance away from the crew, who also slept on the top deck because of the heat. Slyly, the colonel had placed his gang around the hatch leading to the hold so that no one could approach it without being seen. Of course none of the rovers slept.

"Damn thing!" the colonel whispered to the one lying beside him. "I didn't think that they would have a man standing up front here to watch for the navigable channel. The fellow's in our way."

"It's not as bad as you think. With this darkness, he can't see all the way here to the hatch. It's a dark night; there's not a star to be seen. Then, too, he has to look forward into the lantern's beam of light and he'll be blinded if he turns around. When do we start?"

"At once. We shouldn't lose any time. We need to be done before reaching Fort Gibson."

"First you're getting the money, of course."

"No. That would be stupid. If the engineer wakes up and notices the theft prior to the ship's needing to approach the river bank, all might fail. On the other hand, if we put against the bank before I have the money, nothing is lost yet. In the confusion of landing, it would be quite easy to wrest the knife from him and to disappear. I've got the drill already and will now climb down into the hold. Should you have to warn me, cough loudly. I should be able to hear it."

Favored by the darkness, the colonel crawled toward the hatch and put his feet onto the narrow stairs leading down. Quickly he descended its ten steps and checked the floor by touching it. He found the hatch leading farther down and descended the second stairs, which had more steps than the first. Having arrived there, he lit a match and shone it around. For better orientation, he had to move about and needed to light several more matches.

The space he was in was greater than a man's height and extended almost to the middle of the ship. With no center wall, it spanned the entire lower ship's body from one side to the other. A few small luggage pieces lay about.

The colonel then stepped over to the ship's hull and pressed the drill onto a board below the waterline. By the forceful pressure of his hand, the tool bit and quickly worked through the wood. Then there was some tough resistance -- the sheet metal with which the ship was clad below the waterline. This had to be punched through with the drill. Yet in order to fill the hold space quickly, at least two holes would be required. The colonel, therefore, drilled a second one as far back in the planking as possible, again only to the sheet metal. He then picked up one of the hard ballast rocks lying about and pounded the drill's handle until it penetrated the sheet metal. Water entered immediately, splashing his hand. When he pulled out the drill after some effort, a hard, strong jet of water erupted requiring a quick withdrawal. It was highly unlikely that his pounding could have been heard over the engine noise. He now penetrated the sheet metal at the first hole, which was closer to the stairs, then returned to the deck. He had retained the drill in his hand and only now tossed it away at the foot of the upper stairs. Why should he carry it up again?

Having arrived back with his companions, he was asked quietly whether he had succeeded. He answered in the affirmative and said that he would stealthily approach the number one cabin right away.

The salon and the adjacent smoking room lay on the aft deck with cabins on both sides. Each had its own door leading into the salon. The outer walls made of light wainscot had rather large windows, their openings now closed only by screens. Between each cabin's side and the respective shipboard was a small aisle for easier passage.

The colonel had to turn to the left, the starboard aisle. Cabin number one was the first, the corner location. He lay on the deck and carefully crept forward hard by the railing, the shipboard, so as not to be noticed by the officer walking back and forth. He easily made it to his goal. Through the first window's screen came a little glow. A light burning in the cabin? Was Butler still awake, maybe reading?

The colonel convinced himself that there was also light in the other cabins, which put him at ease. This illumination might even facilitate the execution of his plan, which would have been rather difficult in the dark. He pulled his knife and noiselessly cut the screen from top to bottom. A curtain had prevented him from looking into the cabin and he pushed it quietly aside. He could have jumped for joy at what he saw.

On the left wall above the bed hung a small lamp, covered underneath, so as not to disturb the sleeper. Below it, fast asleep, lay the engineer, his face turned toward the wall. On a chair lay his clothes. By the right wall stood a small folding table on which lay his watch, his purse, and --- the old Bowie knife within easy reach from outside. The colonel snatched the knife but left the watch and purse. He pulled it from its sheath and tested the handle. The latter opened like a pen case. That sufficed.

"By the devil, that was easy!" breathed the thief. "I might have had to enter and throttle him!"

Nobody had seen this event; the window faced starboard toward the water. The colonel threw the sheath overboard, stuck the knife in his belt and dropped to his knees to crawl back toward his gang. Luckily he made it past the lieutenant. A few feet farther, looking to the left, he thought he saw two faintly phosphorescent points, which quickly disappeared. These had been eyes, he knew. In a quick movement, he silently pushed himself forward, simultaneously rolling sideways. It was true! From where he had seen the eyes came a sound as if someone were about to jump him. The officer had heard it too and stepped closer.

"Who's there?" he asked.

"I, Nintropan-Hauey," a voice came back.

"Oh, the Indian. Why aren't you sleeping?"

"There crept man who did bad. I see him, but he go quickly."

"Where to?"

"Up front where colonel is; maybe was colonel himself."

"Pshaw! Why should he or anyone else creep about here! Go to sleep and don't disturb the others."

"I go sleep but then not guilty if bad happens."

The officer listened in the direction of the bow but heard nothing. Calmed, he convinced himself that the Indian had been mistaken.

A long, long time passed until he was called to the bow by the lookout.

"Sir," the man said, "I don't know the reason but water seems to be rising up the side of the hull. The ship must be sinking."

"Nonsense!" the officer laughed.

"Come here and look."

The officer looked down at the water, said nothing but hurried away to the captain's cabin. Two minutes later, the two returned together to the bow. They carried a lantern, shining it overboard. A second lantern was fetched. The lieutenant then climbed down into the hold by the rear hatch, the captain down the front one. The rovers had moved away from the hatchway. Within a short time, the captain came up and hurried back to the helmsman.

"He doesn't want to raise an alarm," whispered the colonel to his people. "But watch the helmsman steer toward the shore!"

He was right. The crew was quietly awakened and the ship changed course. This could not have been done without some disturbance. The deck passengers awoke and several cabin passengers came out.

"It's nothing, gentlemen. There's no danger," the captain called. "We've got some water in the hold and need to pump it out. We're going to the river bank. If anyone is afraid they can go ashore."

It was intended as a soothing effect but caused just the opposite. People screamed and cried out for life vests. The cabins emptied. Everyone ran about. As the light from the bow lantern fell onto the shoreline, the ship turned slightly to move parallel to the bank and dropped anchor. Two gangplanks turned out to be long enough. They were played out and the horde of fearful pushed toward land. In front of them all were the rovers, of course, who quickly disappeared into the night.

Except for the crew, only Old Firehand, Tom, Droll and Big Bear had remained on board. The former had climbed into the hold to check the situation. With the lantern in his right hand and the drill in his left, he returned and confronted the captain, who was busy procuring the pumps. "Sir, what's the proper location of this drill?"

"Over there, in the tool box," called out a crewman. "This afternoon it was still in there."

"It now lay on the between-deck. Its tip has been bent from the ship's sheet metal cladding. I'll bet the ship has been purposely pierced."

One can imagine the impression these words produced. The Negro joined them. Butler, the engineer who had first brought his wife and daughter ashore now returned to the ship to complete getting dressed. He came rushing from his cabin shouting for all to hear: "I've been robbed! Of nine thousand dollars! Someone cut through the screen and snatched it from the table!"

Big Bear shouted even louder, "I know! Colonel has stolen and pierced ship. I see him but officer not believe. Ask black stoker! He drink with colonel. He go in salon to clean windows. He come back and drink again. He must say all."

At once the captain, the officer, the helmsman and the Germans crowded around the Indian and the engineer in high excitement. From downstream came a sudden shout.

"That is Little Bear," said the Indian. "I sent after colonel who quickly go on land. He will tell where colonel is."

Little Bear came hurriedly across the gangplank, shouting while pointing at the river, illuminated far out by the many lanterns that by now were lit. "There rowing away! I not find colonel right away, but then see large boat they cut off in back to get to other bank."

Now the principal problem was known, although not everything was clear yet. The rovers cheered and shouted scornfully. The crew and most of the passengers returned the insults in a rage. In the general excitement, no one noticed that the two Indians had vanished. Finally, Old Firehand's mighty voice succeeded in returning quiet, but then abruptly another voice could be heard from the water. "Big Bear borrow small boat. He go after colonel to avenge. Small boat tie up over there. Captain will find. Chief of Tonkawa not let colonel get away. Big Bear and Little Bear must have his blood. Howgh!" The two had taken the bow boat and were now following the fleeing men. The captain cursed and railed but for naught.

The deck hands now pumped out the ship, and the black stoker was interrogated. Old Firehand cornered him with such pointed questions that he was forced to admit everything and recounted every word that had been spoken. This explained all. The colonel was the thief and had holed the ship's hull to get to land before the theft was discovered. The Negro was not about to escape his betrayal unpunished. He was tied up so that he could not escape and was to receive a number of lashings that the captain had yet to determine. Of course he could not be prosecuted by law.

It soon became apparent that the pumps could easily handle the water, that the ship was in no danger and could shortly continue its voyage. The passengers returned from the inhospitable bank to the ship and made themselves comfortable. The loss of time was of no concern to them; as a matter of fact many had even enjoyed the interesting interruption of the otherwise boring journey.

However, the interruption was of least interest to Butler. He had lost a substantial sum of money, which he would have to replace. Old Firehand comforted him by saying, "There's still hope to recover the money. By God's grace, continue your travel with your wife and daughter. I'll meet with you again at your brother's place."

"What? You want to leave me?"

"Yes, I'm going to follow this colonel to recover what he stole."

"But that's dangerous!"

"Pshaw! Old Firehand isn't a man to be afraid of these rovers, which they surely are."

"Nevertheless, I ask you to desist. I'd rather lose the money."

"Sir, it's not only your nine thousand dollars but much more. The rovers learned from the Negro that Black Tom too has money on him that his rafter companions are waiting for at Black Bear River. I would be mistaken if they're not traveling there to commit one more crime which could cost people's lives. The two Tonkawa are after them like good bloodhounds and by daybreak we'll be following their tracks. That's myself, Tom, Droll and his boy, Fred. Right, gentlemen?"

"Yes," Tom responded simply and seriously.

"True," Droll agreed. "The colonel must be ours, if not for others' sake. If we catch him, then may God have mercy on him, if it's necessary!"

3. Struggles in the Night

On the high banks of the Black Bear River burned a blazing fire. Although the moon had risen, its light was unable to penetrate the dense canopy of the trees below, where great darkness would have ruled but for the fire. The flames illuminated a kind of blockhouse, which peculiarly enough was not constructed of horizontally placed beams. Four trees stood in a square whose crowns had been cut off. Onto these poles crossbeams had been placed to support the roof, consisting of clapboards, boards rough-cut from knotless cypress or red oak timbers. Three openings had been left up front, a larger one for the door, two smaller ones to its left and right for windows. In front of this house burned the fire around which sat some twenty wild-looking characters which one could see had not been in touch with civilization for some time. Their clothing was threadbare, their faces not just tanned by sun, wind and weather but literally burned by it. Except for knives, they carried no weapons; those might lie in the blockhouse's interior.

From a strong tree branch above the fire hung a large iron kettle in which large pieces of meat were cooking. Alongside the fire stood two big, hollowed-out gourds containing fermented honey water, that is, mead. As men felt like it, they scooped a drink from them or ladled out a mug of broth and meat from the kettle.

At the same time, a lively conversation was going on. The group appeared to feel very safe for no one made any effort to speak softly. Had these people thought an enemy was close by, the fire would have been banked in the Indian way, leaving only a small flame, visible from not very far. Against the wall of the house leaned axes, large saws and other tools, which one could assume belonged to a group of "rafters", that is, lumbermen and raftsmen.

Rafters are a very peculiar type of backwoodsmen. They fit somewhere in between farmers and trappers. While the farmer is in closer contact with civilization and part of settled society, the trapper leads a nearly savage life, more like the Indian. The rafter, too, is not tied to the earth and leads a free and quite independent existence. He moves from state to state and county to county. He is not eager to associate with people or their habitations, since the activity he performs is actually illegal. The land on which he cuts trees is not his property, yet he has no concern whether the place he operates on is community land or belongs already to a private owner. He cuts down, saws and works the tree trunks, selecting only the best trees, ropes them together in rafts and floats them downstream where he can sell the pirated booty.

The rafter is not a welcome guest. Although it's true that the dense woods found by many a new settler makes life difficult for him and makes him wish they were less dense, the rafter does not thin them out. As already said, he takes only the best trunks, cuts off the crowns and leaves them to rot. Under and below these branches, new trees and bushes sprout, in time becoming tightly interconnected by vines and other creepers against which the ax, often even fire, can accomplish little.

Nevertheless, the rafter usually is not being bothered, for he is a strong and bold fellow --- not the sort one would tackle in thewilderness far from help. Obviously, he cannot work alone but usually works together with several others, often four to eight, even ten. At times considerably more gather to form a group. Then the rafter feels twice as secure, since no farmer or other owner would put up a fight with such a number of people who would not hesitate to risk their lives for possession of a tree trunk.

Of course, they lead a very hard and strenuous life, full of privations. However, in the end they have no mean reward. The rafter earns a nice piece of money, since the material costs him nothing. While most of them are engaged in cutting trees, one or two companions, or several depending on the size of the group, take care of the food supply. These are the hunters who, during daytime but also at night, range about "to make meat." Where game is plentiful, this is not difficult. But should game be rare, they have plenty to do. Then the hunter has no time to collect honey or to find other delicacies and the rafters must, by needs, eat those parts other backwoodsmen usually disdain, sometimes even intestines.

The group working here at Black Bear River appeared not to suffer from want, as the full kettle confirmed. Everyone was therefore in good spirits, with lots of joking going on after a hard day's work. They told each other funny stories or other interesting experiences and talked about people they had met in the past whose characteristics were laughable.

"You should get to know a fellow I once met up at Fort Niobrara," said an old graybeard. "The chap was a man, but was called 'aunt' anyway."

"Do you mean Aunt Droll?" another asked.

"Yes, precisely, the one and only. Did you meet him too, by chance?"

"Yes, once. It was in Des Moines at an inn, where his appearance caused such a stir that everybody was laughing about him. There was one chap in particular who wouldn't let up until Droll took him by the waist and tossed him out the window. That man didn't return."

"This I would truly believe of the Aunt. Droll likes a joke and doesn't mind people making fun of him; but go beyond a certain limit and he'll show his teeth. Then I too would show my fists to anyone who would seriously insult him."

"You, Blenter? Why?"

"Because I owe him my life. He and I were once captured by the Sioux. I tell you, at the time I truly thought they would send me to the eternal hunting grounds. I'm not the man to be afraid of three or five Indians; I also don't whimper when things turn bad for me, but at the time there seemed not the least ray of hope and I didn't know any way out. But this Droll is a slyboots without par; he socked the redskins with such humbug they couldn't peer out of their eyes any more. We escaped."

"How was that possible? How did that go? Tell us, tell us!"

"If it's okay with you, I'd rather keep my mouth shut. It's no pleasure to tell about an event in which I didn't play a laudable role but rather was duped by the redskins. It's enough to tell you that I'm sitting here today and enjoying this venison. I can't thank myself for it, but instead have to thank Aunt Droll."

"Then you must have been in deep trouble. You, the old Missouri-Blenter, known as a frontiersman, who surely finds an exit provided there is one."

"At the time I didn't. I was already standing right near the stake."

"Truly? That is, doubtless, a situation with poor prospects for escape. A devilish invention this stake! I hate those dogs twice as much just hearing the word."

"Then you don't know what you're saying! Those who hate the Indians judge them wrongly and haven't thought how much they all have suffered. If someone came now to chase us away from here, what would you do?"

"Defend myself, even if it would cost mine or the other's life."

"And is this place your property?"

"Don't know at all whose it is; but I've certainly not paid for it."

"Well then, all the land once belonged to the Indians. We took it from them. And when they defended themselves with a greater right than you, you condemn them?"

"Hmm! What you say is true, but the redskins must go, die out, that's their fate."

"Yes, they die out because we murder them," Blenter said ruefully. "It's said that the Indian cannot be civilized. But culture isn't fired like a bullet from the barrel; it takes time, lots of time. I don't really understand it, but it may take centuries. But are the redskins given any time? Do you send a six-year-old boy to school, then hit him over the head if after a quarter hour he hasn't made professor yet? But that's what is done to the Indians. I don't want to defend them, it doesn't get me anything, but among them I've met just as many good people as among whites, even more. Who do I have to be grateful to, the redskins or the whites, for the fact that I don't have a family or own a nice home but instead still wander the Wild West as an old, gray fellow?"

"How do I know? You've never talked about it."

"Because a man doesn't talk about such things, rather buries them within himself. I need to find only one more, the last of them who got away from me, their leader, the worst one!"

Gnashing his teeth, the old man spoke slowly, as if weighing each word. This increased the attention of the others; they moved more closely together, looking at him, but not uttering a word. For a while he stared into the fire, his foot kicking the burning wood, then he continued as if talking only to himself, "I didn't shoot them nor knife them, but whipped them to death one after the other. I needed them alive so they would die exactly as my family did, my wife and my two sons. Six of them they were. Five of them I killed within a short time, the sixth escaped. I hunted him through all the states until he managed to cover his tracks. I haven't found him yet, but he's still alive, for he was younger than I, much younger, and I think my old eyes will catch sight of him once more before I close them forever."

A deep silence pervaded the group now. Everyone felt the presence of something exceptional. After a long pause, one of the rafters dared to ask, "Blenter, who was that man?"

The old one rose from his reflections and answered, "Who was he? Not an Indian, no, but a white, a monster like none among the redskins. Yes, men, I'll even tell you that he was what we all are today; he was a rafter."

"What? Rafters killed your family?"

"Yes, rafters! You have no reason to be proud of your calling, particularly to feel superior to the redskins. As we sit here, we're all thieves and rascals."

Of course, this claim produced spirited opposition. Blenter, though, continued without acknowledging it. "This river at whose banks we camp, this forest whose trees we cut and sell, is not our property. We take something illegally, something, which belongs to a state, even a private owner. We would shoot anyone, even the rightful owner, if he intended to drive us away from here. Is that not theft? Even more, is that not robbery and murder?"

Looking around the circle without receiving an answer, he went on, "And with such robbers I had to deal at the time. I had come over from Missouri with a real purchase deed in my hand. My wife and my sons accompanied me. We brought cattle along, some horses, pigs and a large wagon with household goods. I can tell you, I was fairly well off. There were no other settlers nearby, but we didn't need anybody, for our eight arms were strong and diligent enough to get everything done quickly and by ourselves. In a short time, the blockhouse stood. We burned and cleared a field and began sowing. One day, I was missing a cow and went into the woods to find her. When I heard ax blows, I followed the sounds. I found six rafters cutting down my trees. Near them lay the cow they had shot for their meal. Now, gentlemen, what would you have done in my place?"

"Killed the bastards," one responded heatedly. "And that by all rights. By the laws of the West, a horse or cattle thief may be killed."

"That's true, but nevertheless I didn't do it. I spoke kindly to the people, demanded only that they leave my property and pay me for the cow. Was that too much?"

"No, no," resounded from the circle. "Didn't they do it?"

"No. They laughed at me. Yet I didn't return home immediately, since I wanted to shoot something for our supper. When I arrived at home, a second cow was missing. In the meantime, the rafters had decided to show their defiance and that they didn't give a fig for me. When I arrived the next morning, they had cut up my cow and hung the pieces to dry to make pemmican. My repeated, and now increased protests were just as much laughed off as the day before. I threatened to apply my rights and demanded money, leveling my rifle. One of them, the speaker and leader, also raised his rifle. I saw he was serious and shattered it with a well-aimed shot. I didn't want to hurt him but aimed only at his rifle. Then I hurried back to fetch my sons. In no way were we three afraid of these six, but when we returned they had disappeared.

"Obviously, caution was now called for, and for several days we didn't venture beyond the immediate surroundings of our blockhouse. On the fourth morning, our provisions were gone, so I went with one of my sons to hunt for meat. Of course we were careful, but didn't see any sign of the rafters. Then, when we slowly and quietly stalked through the woods, I suddenly saw the leader standing behind a tree, maybe twenty paces distant. He hadn't spotted me yet. So my son and I trained our rifles on him. Had I downed the rascal at once, as was my right, even my duty, I would surely not have become childless and a widower. But it has never been my passion to kill a human needlessly. I therefore quickly jumped him, tore the rifle from his hand, the knife and pistol from his belt, and punched him in the face, knocking him to the ground. He didn't lose his wits for a moment, and was rather faster than I. In a flash, he leaped up and ran before I could even reach out to catch him."

"By the devil! You were sure to suffer for such stupidity!" one of his comrades called out. "You can count on a man to avenge himself for having been struck like that."

"Yes, he did avenge himself," nodded the old one, getting up to pace back and forth. Obviously the memory upset him. Then he sat down again to continue. "We were lucky and had a good hunt. When we returned home, I went behind the house to deposit the game temporarily. It seemed to me that I heard a startled cry from my son, but unfortunately, didn't pay attention to it. Entering the blockhouse, I found my family tied up and gagged, lying beside the fireplace. At the same time, I was grabbed and pulled to the ground. During our absence, the rafters had come to the farm and overpowered my wife and my younger son, waiting thereafter for our return. When my older son entered the house ahead of me, they quickly subdued him too, giving him little time to shout out a warning. I didn't fare better or worse than the others. It happened so surprisingly and quickly that before I could think of offering any opposition, I was overwhelmed and tied up too. They then stuffed rags in my mouth to prevent me from screaming."

"It's your own fault! Why weren't you more cautious! Whoever makes enemies of rafters and has punched one of them must be on his guard."

"That's true. But then I didn't have the experience I have now. If today rafters would kill my cow, I would shoot the villains one at a time without allowing myself to be seen. But to go on! I want to make it short, because what comes now is difficult to speak of. They set up a monkey court. To have fired a rifle at them was construed as being a mortal crime. The rascals had also found my brandy. They guzzled themselves into such a drunkenness that they no longer were human beings, not even animals but beasts. They decided that we must all die. As an extra punishment for the blow the leader had received from me, he demanded that we be beaten to death. Two agreed, three were against, but the leader enforced his will.

"We were dragged out to the fence. My wife was the first. She was tied to the fence; then they beat her with clubs. One of them must have felt some pity for her, for he put a bullet in her head. My sons fared worse than she; they were literally cudgeled to death. I lay there and had to witness everything, since I was to be the last. People, I tell you, that quarter-hour became an eternity to me. It's impossible to describe to you my thoughts and feelings. The words 'rage' and 'fury' are meaningless; there is no word fit to utter. The blows I now received I didn't even feel. My soul had entered a state where no physical pain could be felt any longer. I only remember a sudden, loud shout from the cornfield and a shot ringing out when a command wasn't immediately obeyed. I fainted then."

"Oh, some people had come, by chance, who saved you!"

"People? No. It was only one. He of course didn't know what was going on and had thought a thief or other criminal was being punished. The way my head drooped, he could tell from afar that my life wasn't worth a penny if he didn't put a stop to the beating. Hence his shout and his shot. He had only given a warning shot into the air, not thinking he was dealing with murderers. When he hurried closer, he heard one of the rafters calling out his name in surprise. They had been able to commit cowardly murder, but the six of them did not have the guts to tackle this single man. For this, their courage failed them. They ran off, using the house as cover to disappear into the forest."

"Then the arrival must have been a very famous and feared frontiersman."

"Frontiersman? Pshaw! An Indian it was. Yes, people, I tell you, a red man saved me!"

"A redskin? One so feared that six rafters ran from him? Impossible!"

"Don't doubt it! Having a bad conscience, you too would turn tail to get away from him, for it was none other than Winnetou."

"Winnetou, the Apache? What luck! Yes, then it's certainly believable. But was he already so well known at the time?"

"Of course he stood only at the beginning of his fame, but the one rafter who had shouted his name, and then ran off had most likely made his acquaintance in a way that a second meeting was not considered desirable. Also, whoever has seen Winnetou but for a single time, knows the impression his mere appearance makes."

"But he let the rascals get away?"

"For the time being, yes. Would you have acted differently? From their hurried escape, he perceived they had a bad conscience, but the actual circumstances were at the moment still unknown to him. From afar he'd seen me hanging there, but not the corpses that had been untied and dumped on the ground. He now knew that a crime had been committed, but could not pursue the culprits since he needed to tend to me first and foremost.

"Nothing was lost by this, since someone like Winnetou knows for sure how to find his prey later. When I had somewhat recovered, he knelt beside me like the good Samaritan of the Holy Bible. He had freed me of my ties and gag but didn't permit me to speak. I truly didn't feel any pain and wanted to get away to take my revenge, but he would not allow it.

"He carried me and the bodies into the house, where I could defend myself in case the rafters returned. Then he rode to our nearest neighbor to seek a helping, caring hand. I tell you, this neighbor lived more than thirty miles away and Winnetou had never before been in this area. He found him, nevertheless, although he arrived there only in the evening and by morning brought him and a helper back to me. Then he left to follow the murderers' tracks.

"I had sworn solemnly not to act on my own since Winnetou assured me it would be useless. He was gone for over a week. By then I had buried my dead and asked the neighbor to sell my property. My beaten bones hadn't healed yet, while I waited impatiently for the return of the Apache. He had followed the rafters, and one evening had spied on them to discover that they were headed for Fort Smokey Hill. He had not shown himself, had done nothing to them, since revenge was to be mine alone. When he said his good-bye, I took my rifle, mounted my horse, and rode off. The rest you know already or can imagine."

"No, we don't know and cannot imagine it either. Keep talking, tell us! Why did Winnetou not accompany you?"

"Because he had other and better things to do. Had he not done enough already? And I shall not continue the story. You can imagine that it is no pleasure to me. The five have been eliminated, one after another. The sixth and worst got away. He was a rafter and may still be plying his trade. That's why I too became a rafter, thinking that this might be the surest means to come across him. And now --- behold! What kind of people are these?"

He jumped up, the others following his example. Two blanket-clad figures had stepped from the dark woods into the firelight. They were Indians, an older and a younger one. The first raised his hands soothingly and said, " No worry, we not enemies! Rafters work here know Black Tom?"

"Yes, we know him," answered old Blenter.

"He away getting money for you?"

"Yes, he was to collect payment and could be here within a week."

"He come earlier. We then found right people, rafters we look for. Now must make fire small or it seen far. And speak softly or heard far."

He tossed off his blanket, stepped to the fire, pulled the logs apart, extinguished some and left only a few burning. This done, he threw a look at the kettle, sat down and said, "Give us piece of meat. We ride far and not eat; very hungry."

His self-assured behavior naturally raised the rafters' astonishment. The old Missourian showed his surprise by asking, "But, man, what do you think? You dare approach us in the night, especially you, being a redskin! And act as if this place were yours!"

"We not dare anything," was the retort. "Red man must not be bad man. Red man is good man. Paleface will learn."

"But who are you? You certainly don't belong to one of the riverlands or prairie tribes. From your appearance I must assume you're from New Mexico, perhaps a Pueblo."

"Come from New Mexico, but be no Pueblo. Am Tonkawa chief. Name is Big Bear; this my son."

"What, Big Bear?" several rafters called out in surprise, with the Missourian adding, "So this boy is Little Bear?"

"This right!" the red man nodded.

"Well, that's different. The two Tonkawa Bears are welcome everywhere. Take meat and mead as much as you like and stay with us for as long as it pleases you. But what brings you to this area?"

"We come to warn rafters."

"Why? What danger is there to us?"

"Great danger."

"Which? Do speak!"

"Tonkawa first eat, then get horses, then talk."

He gave a sign to his son who left. He then pulled a piece of meat from the kettle, which he commenced to eat with as much calm as if sitting at home in his wigwam.

"You have horses along?" the old one asked. "At night in these dark woods? And looking for us, you found us! That is truly a masterpiece of work!"

"Tonkawa has eyes and ears. He know rafters always live by water, at river. You talk loudly and have big fire we see very far, smell even farther. Rafters very careless. Enemies have easy to find them."

"We have no enemies here. We're all by ourselves in this area and, in any case, are strong enough to fight possible enemies."

"Missouri-Blenter, err!"

"What, you know my name?"

"Tonkawa stand long time there behind tree and hear palefaces talk, so hear your name. If enemies not here, they now come. And if rafters careless, they be defeated by even few enemies."

They now heard hoofbeats on the soft ground. Little Bear brought two horses, hitched them to a tree, took a piece of meat from the kettle and sat down to eat beside his father. Big Bear had finished his portion, stuck his knife in his belt and said, "Now Tonkawa speak. Then rafters smoke peace pipe with him. Black Tom has much money. Rovers come, ambush, take money."

"Rovers? Here at Bear River? You must be mistaken."

"Tonkawa not wrong, but know right. Will tell you."

In his broken English, he reported the events on the steamer, but was too proud to mention his son's heroic deed, saying nary a word about this. His story was followed with the greatest attention by everyone. He also recounted what had happened after the rovers' escape. Close behind them, he and his son had reached the Arkansas' bank in the small boat and had remained there until first daylight, since they could not follow the rovers' tracks at night. By day the tracks had been very clear, bypassing Fort Gibson, leading west between the Canadian and the Red Fork, then swinging back to the north. During one of the succeeding nights, the rovers had attacked a camp of the Cree Indians to obtain horses.

By noon of the next day, the two Tonkawa had come across some Choctaw warriors from whom they bought two horses. However, due to the customary ceremonies involved with horse trading, such a long time passed that the rovers gained an entire day's lead. They had crossed the Red Fork and ridden to the Bear River across open prairie where the Tonkawa had succeeded in catching up with them. The rovers were camped in a small opening by the river, but the Tonkawas thought it wise to first locate the rafters in order to warn them.

The effect of this story was electric. Conversation now continued only in low voices and the fire was totally extinguished.

"How far from here is the rovers' camp?" the old Missourian asked.

"As much as the palefaces call half an hour."

"By gosh! Then they couldn't have seen our fire, but might have smelled the smoke. We truly felt too secure. And since when are they camped there?"

"A full hour before evening."

"Then they have surely scouted for us. Do you know anything about it?"

"Tonkawa not spy on rovers because still full daylight. Continue right away to warn rafters, because --- "

He stopped and listened. Then he continued in a more subdued voice, "Big Bear see something, movement at corner of house. Sit still, don't speak. Tonkawa crawl away to check."

He lay down on the ground, left his rifle, and crawled toward the house. The rafters listened closely. About ten minutes passed. Then a short, shrill scream rose, a scream every frontiersman knows --- the death shriek of a man. Shortly thereafter the chief returned.

"A scout of the rovers," he said. "Tonkawa give him knife from behind into heart. He not tell what have seen and heard here. But maybe second one here. Will return and report. Be quick, therefore. Maybe rafters want to spy on rovers."

"That's true," the Missourian whispered assent. "I shall go along. You lead, since you know the place where they're camped. As yet they're not aware that we know of their presence. They'll feel secure and will surely talk about their plans. If we leave right away, we may learn what they intend to do."

"Yes, but very quietly and secretly so if is second spy, he not see us leave. And not take rifle, only knife. Rifle in the way."

"What shall the others do here meanwhile?"

"Go into house and wait quietly for our return."

The advice was heeded. The rafters entered the blockhouse where they could not be observed. The Missourian, together with the chief, crawled some distance away, rising then and walking along the river in hopes of successfully spying on the rovers.

The Black Bear River may be said to be the border of that peculiar hilly landscape called the Rolling Prairie. Hillock beside hillock rises, one almost like the other, separated by depressions and valleys, all looking alike. This landscape stretches through the entire east of Kansas. The Rolling Prairie is well watered and wooded. From a bird's-eye perspective, one could equate these successive hillocks and depressions with the rolling, green-colored waves of an ocean. The name Rolling Prairie, therefore, shows that prairie need not mean a flat expanse of grassland. The waters of the Black Bear River have long eaten deeply into the soft, rich, hilly soil so that its banks, where they depart the Rolling Prairie, are mostly steep and covered by densely standing trees down to the waterline. This is --- or rather was --- true and rich game country, but in recent times the Rolling Prairie has been settled rather densely and has been robbed by gentlemen-hunters of its profusion of game.

Where the rafters had set up camp, the high bank dropped steeply to the water not far from the blockhouse. This was very advantageous for the building of slides, or chutes that the rafters used to get tree trunks to the water without great effort. Fortunately, the banks were free of underbrush. Nevertheless, it was not easy to move through them in the darkness. The Missourian was an old, agile and experienced frontiersman, yet he still marveled at the chief, who had taken him by the hand and was now noiselessly and confidently moving through the trees, avoiding them as if in broad daylight. From below, the rushing of the river could be heard, a fortuitous circumstance, since it covered any possible noises caused by their advance.

Blenter had been in this area for some time. He didn't work as a rafter but rather as a hunter and meat procurer and knew the area very well. All the more he had to acknowledge the assurance with which the Indian moved, being here for the first time and even then only since dusk.

After a quarter of an hour, the two descended into a depression to position themselves at right angles to the river's course. It, too, was densely covered by trees, with a softly murmuring brook flowing through it. Close to the point where the brook entered the river, there was a treeless clearing with only a few bushes growing. There the rovers had set up camp and lit a fire, whose glow became obvious to the two men when they were still under the forest's canopy.

"Rovers just as careless as rafters," whispered the Tonkawa chief to his companion. "Light big fire as if want roast entire big buffalo. Red warriors always make small fire. Flames not visible and very little smoke. We get to them easily and make us not seen."

"Yes, get there we will," the old one opined. "But to get close enough to hear what they say is questionable."

"We be very close, we hear. But support each other if rovers discover us. With knife kill attackers, then quickly into forest."

They advanced to the last trees before the clearing and now saw the fire and the men camped around it. Down here, there were more mosquitos then up at the rafters' camp, a common plague of the area's rivers. For this reason, the rovers were probably burning such a mighty fire. To one side stood the horses, which could not be seen, only heard. They were bothered so fiercely by mosquitos that their tails were in continuous movement to ward off the irritation. The Missourian heard the stamping of their hooves, the chief even the whipping of their tails.

Both now lay on the ground and crept toward the fire. For concealment, they weaved their way behind bushes growing in the clearing. The rovers were sitting close to the brook, whose bank was overgrown by a dense stand of bulrushes reaching close to the camp.

In the lead, the Indian turned toward the bulrushes, which offered the best opportunity for cover. He displayed absolute mastery of the art. The task was to get through the tall, dry stalks without causing noise in traversing them. Their fans, too, needed to be still so as not to allow discovery. Big Bear avoided this danger by simply slicing a trail through. With his sharp knife cutting down the rushes in front of him, he could still turn his attention to easing the Missourian's advance. The severing of the rushes occurred so silently that even Blenter could not hear the fall of the stalks.

They closed in on the fire and stopped only near enough so they could overhear the rovers' conversation, which was not being conducted quietly. Blenter had not held back, but had settled down beside the chief. He looked at the figures sitting in front of him and asked in a whisper, "Which of them is the colonel you were talking about?"

"Colonel not here, he away," the Indian whispered back.

"Probably also to look for us?"

"Yes. Must be so."

"Could he be the one you knifed?"

"No, not him."

"But you couldn't see that?"

"Palefaces see only with eyes, but Indians see also with hands. My fingers did know colonel."

"Then he wasn't by himself, but in the company of another man you killed."

"That true. Now wait for colonel come back."

The rovers talked very animatedly, chatting about everything except what would have been of interest to the two spies, until one of them said, "I'm wondering whether the colonel guessed right. It'll frustrate our purposes if the rafters aren't here."

"They're still around, maybe even close by," responded another. "The wood chips the water has carried here are very fresh. They were produced maybe yesterday, at most the day before."

"If that's correct, we better retreat if these fellows are so close that they could find us. They mustn't see us. They're of no concern to us. We only want to catch Black Tom with his money."

"And we won't get it," a third interjected.

"Why not?"

"Because we started so stupidly that it'll be impossible to succeed. Do you think the rafters won't notice our presence here, even if we go back aways? They would have to be blind. We've made tracks that can't be covered or eliminated. And once our presence is known, our plan too is given away."

"Not at all! We'll just shoot them!"

"They'll all line up for us to shoot them at our leisure? I gave my best advice to the colonel, but it was rejected. In the east, in the big cities, a victim of theft goes to the police and leaves it to them to find the thief. Here in the West, everyone takes matters into his own hands. I'm convinced that we've been followed at least for some distance. And who would be the ones hard on our tracks? In any case, only those of the passengers knowledgeable about it, that is Old Firehand, Black Tom and maybe this peculiar Aunt Droll. We should have waited for them and then it would have been easy to take Tom's money. But rather than do that, we took this long ride and now here we sit at the Bear River without knowing whether or not we're going to get it. And the colonel wandering around in the woods at night to look for the rafters is just as stupid. He could have waited until tomorrow and --- "

He stopped in his reasoning, because at that moment the one he was talking about stepped out from between the trees and toward the fire. Seeing the looks of his people, he took off his hat and tossed it on the ground saying, "I bring no good news, fellows. I've had bad luck."

"What kind? How so?" the round of men asked. "Where's Bruns? Hasn't he come back with you?"

"Bruns?" the colonel repeated, sitting down. "He won't come back at all. He's dead."

"Dead? Aren't you the devil's! Did he have an accident? He can't have been killed."

"How smart you are!" answered their leader. "Of course the poor devil had only an accident, but one by a knife stabbed into his heart."

This news caused great consternation. Everyone asked about the hows and whys, and because of all the questions, the colonel couldn't find an opportunity to answer. He therefore demanded silence. When this eventuated, he reported, "I took Bruns along because he, in particular, is or rather was the best tracker we had. He proved himself again, for his nose led us straight to the rafters."

"His nose?" asked the one usually acting as the speaker for the others.

"Yes, his nose. Of course, we thought the group was camped farther upstream and therefore took that direction. At that, we had to be very careful for we could easily be seen. For this reason, we advanced very slowly as darkness fell. I wanted to turn back, but Bruns wouldn't let up. We had seen several tracks from which he suspected we were close to the rafters' place. He thought we would 'smell' the rafters, for they would have a fire going to ward off the mosquitos. His surmise was correct, since soon we smelled smoke, and up above the bank, a faint light was coming which penetrated the trees and bushes. We climbed up and now could see the fire ahead of us. It burned in front of a blockhouse, the rafters sitting around it, about twenty of them, as many as we are. We crept close to spy on them. I stayed under cover of a tree and Bruns sneaked up behind the house. We hadn't yet had time to listen to their talk when suddenly two fellows arrived, not rafters but strangers. Just guess who they were! But no, you'll never guess right. They were the two Indians, Big and Little Bear, from the 'Dogfish'."

The rovers expressed great surprise about this information and didn't want to believe it. But they were downright perplexed about the chief's account of the rafters. The colonel continued, "I observed the redskin completely extinguishing the fire. They then continued speaking so softly that I could no longer understand anything. I would have preferred to leave then, but had to wait for Bruns of course. Suddenly I heard a scream, so terrible, so awful it cut through my bones and marrow. It came from the blockhouse behind where Bruns had taken cover. I became afraid for him and crawled from the camp toward the house. It was so dark I had to feel my way along. All at once my hand touched a body lying in a pool of blood. From the clothing I knew it was Bruns and grew greatly alarmed. I could feel a knife cut in his back, which must have directly penetrated the heart, and he was most certainly dead. What was I to do? I emptied his pockets, took his knife and revolver and left him there. When I came around front again, I noticed that the rafters had moved into the blockhouse and I quickly got out of there."

The rovers indulged in the coarsest terms of pity about the demise of their companion, but their leader put an end to it by telling them, "Quit that now! There's no time. We must leave."

"Why?" the question arose.

"Why? Haven't you heard that these redskins know where our camp is? They're going to attack us, of course, most likely in the morning. But since they can guess we're missing our dead comrade, they'll no doubt be suspicious. It's possible that they may come even earlier. If we let ourselves be surprised, we're done for. We must leave right away."

"But where to?"

"To the Eagle Tail."

"Oh, to raid the railroad pay office. Then we're going to forget about Black Tom's money?'

"Unfortunately. It's the smartest thing to do and --- "

He stopped, giving a sign of surprise that the others didn't understand.

"What's the matter? What have you got?" asked one of them. "Speak up."

Without responding, the colonel stood up. He had been sitting close to the place where the two spies were hidden. They no longer lay side by side as before. When the old Missourian's eyes had caught sight of the colonel, he was gripped by a great excitement, further increased by the tone of the speaker's voice. Instead of remaining still, he pushed farther and farther forward through the rushes. His eyes gleamed as if ready to pop out of their sockets. Filled with turbulent anger, he forgot all necessary caution and didn't notice that his head was protruding and was almost entirely exposed.

"Not be seen!" the chief whispered desperately, taking hold of him and pulling him back.

But it was too late, for the colonel had spotted the head of the intruder. He interrupted his conversation in order to render the listener harmless. He did this with great cunning, saying, "I just remembered something to do with the horses --- ah, the two of you come along!"

He waved to the two men who had been sitting to his left and right. They immediately stood as he whispered to them, " The horses are a pretense. Behind us in the bulrushes lies an eavesdropper, a rafter for sure. If he thinks I'm after him, he'll try to escape. As soon as I jump him, you follow suit. That way we get him pinned down so he can't fight back or injure me. So --- let's go!"

With these last two words, which he now shouted out, he turned lightning-fast and dived into the spot where he had seen the Missourian's head.

The Tonkawa chief was an extremely cautious, experienced and shrewd man. He saw the colonel rise and whisper to the two. He saw him make an involuntary move backward. As minute and almost unnoticeable as this

60

movement had been, it told Big Bear its reason. His hand touched the old one as he whispered, "Quick, away! Colonel see you, will catch you. Quick, quick!"

At the same time, he turned and jerked himself backward, away and behind the next bush, still keeping low to the ground. It was the work of at most two seconds, yet already there sounded the "let's go" of the colonel's. When Big Bear looked back, he saw the latter throw himself onto the Missourian, followed at once by the other two rovers.

Despite his famed presence of mind, old Blenter was totally taken by surprise. The three lay or knelt on him, holding down his arms and legs. The other rovers jumped up from the fire and came rushing over. The Indian had pulled his knife to help the old one, but realized that he could do nothing against these odds. For him there was nothing to do but observe what was happening to the Missourian and then report it back to the rafters. So as not to be discovered himself, he crawled away from the pathway cut through the rushes, far to the side, where he took cover behind a bush.

When the rovers saw the captive, they raised a clamor. But the colonel demanded silence, "Quiet! We don't know whether there are still others around. Hold him. I'll check."

He walked the fire's perimeter gun in hand, and finding no one, calmed down. He then ordered his captive brought to the fire. The latter had used all his strength to get free but to no avail. He knew now that he had to submit. His fate could not be too bad, he thought, since he had not really done anything to the rovers. The knowledge of the Indian's escape also consoled him. He would surely hurry quickly to fetch help.

While four men held the captive to the ground, the colonel bent down to look in his face. It was a long, long inquiring and thoughtful look. He then said, "Man, I must know you! Where have I seen you before?"

The old one was careful not to tell him, since his life would then have been forfeit. Hate boiled in his gut, but he made every effort to show an indifferent face.

"Yes, I must have seen you before," the colonel repeated. "Who are you? Are you one of the rafters working up there?"

"Yes," Blenter responded.

"Why did you sneak around here? Why are you trying to overhear us?"

"Odd question. Is it forbidden, here in the West, to look people over? I rather think it's a necessity. There are plenty of people one must be cautious of."

"Do you count us as being among them?"

"What sort of people you belong to remains to be seen. I don't know you yet."

"That's a lie. You heard what we said and know who and what we are."

"I didn't hear a thing. I was down by the river on the way back to our camp, when I saw your fire and crept up to see who was camping here. I didn't have time to hear what was spoken, because I was too careless and was seen and caught the moment I was ready to listen."

He hoped that only the knifed rover had seen him up at the blockhouse when he had faced him sitting there. But he was mistaken, for the red-haired man answered, "That's all bunk. I not only saw you earlier sitting with the rafters but also heard you speak. I recognize you. Will you admit it?"

"Wouldn't think of it! What I said is true; you're wrong."

"Then you were truly alone here?"

"Yes."

"And claim to really not have heard any of our conversation?"

"Not a word."

"What's your name?"

"Adams," the Missourian lied, having every reason not to give his true name.

"Adams," the colonel repeated, reflecting. "Adams! I never knew an Adams with your face. And still, I think, we have seen each other before. Do you know me? Do you know my name?"

"No," the old one insisted, again untruthfully. "But now let me go! I didn't do anything to you and hope you are honest frontiersmen who leave other honest people be."

"Yes, we are indeed honest men, very honest men," the colonel laughed, "but earlier your people knifed one of our men and, according to the laws of the West, that calls for revenge. Blood for blood, life for life. You may be whoever you are, but you're also a goner."

"What? You want to murder me?"

"Yes, the same way you murdered our comrade. It's only a question whether you will die like he did by the knife or whether we'll drown you in the river. No great ceremonies will be required. We mustn't lose any time. Men, let's vote. Gag him so he can't scream. Those of you for tossing him into the water, raise your arms."

That request was answered by the majority of the rovers, arms upraised.

"Then it's drowning!" the colonel confirmed. "Tie his arms and legs together firmly so he can't swim. Then dump him quickly into the river. After that, let's get away from here before his comrades show up!"

During the interrogation, the old Missourian had been held down by several men. Now he was about to be gagged. He knew it would be impossible for the Indian to have reached the rafters yet. Help could not be expected. Nevertheless, he did what every other man in such a situation would do: he fought back with all his strength and shouted for help. His call sounded far into the still of the night.

"Damn it!" the colonel cursed. "Don't let him scream like that. If you can't handle him, let me do it. Watch out!"

Grabbing his rifle, he held it butt down to strike Blenter on the head, but before he was able to deliver the blow ---

* * * * * *

Shortly before evening, four horsemen closely following the rovers' tracks, had paralleled the river upstream. They were Old Firehand, Black Tom and Aunt Droll with the boy Fred. The tracks wended their way between the trees and were reasonably visible, but it was difficult to determine how recent they were. Only when the riders crossed a grassy clearing did Old Firehand dismount to check more closely, since the grass blades gave better clues than the shorter moss. Having inspected the impressions closely, he said, "The rovers are about a mile ahead of us; these tracks were made approximately half an hour ago. We need to run our horses swiftly so we can get close enough to them before nightfall to learn where they plan to camp."

"Isn't that dangerous for us?"

"Not that I know."

"Oh, yes! They'll certainly make camp before dark, and if we're going to hurry, we can be sure to ride straight into their arms."

"I don't think so. Even if your assumption is correct, we couldn't catch up with them before dusk. From various signs, I conclude that we're in the vicinity of the rafters whom we have to warn first of all. In this connection, it would be to our advantage to know where the rovers are going to camp. What do you think, Droll?"

The two had spoken in German. Droll, therefore, answered in his dialect: "Se habe da ganz meine eegne Meening ausgesproche. Reite mer rasch weiter, so habe mer se eher; reite mer aber langsamer, so bekomme mer se schpäter und könne leicht eher und tiefer ins Dekerment gerate, als diejenige, welche mer rette wolle. Also, meine Herre, reite mer Trab, dass die Bäume wackle! --- You've spoken as if it were my own opinion. If we ride on quickly, we'll get to them earlier; but if we ride slower, we get to them later and can easily get more deeply into trouble than the ones we want to rescue. Therefore, gentlemen, let's trot to make the trees shake!"

Since the trees were not spaced too closely, they could follow this admonition even in the forest. But the rovers, too, had put daylight to good use and had stopped only when forced to by nightfall. Had Old Firehand not followed the rovers' tracks, and stayed closer to the river bank, he would have come across the tracks of the two Tonkawa Indians who had a very slight lead on them.

When it became so dark that the hoof prints were barely recognizable, he dismounted again to check. As a result of his inspection he said, "We've made a good half mile, but unfortunately, the rovers also rode very hard. Nevertheless, let's try to get close to them. Dismount. We must continue on foot and lead the horses!"

Unfortunately, while the distance to be covered was insignificant, it was now so dark that the tracks had become invisible. The four thereupon halted.

"What now?" asked Tom. "Are we forced to camp here?"

"No," answered Droll, "We're not going to camp, but let's continue on until we find them."

"Then they'll hear us coming!"

"We'll go quietly. They'll not hear us nor catch us. Don't you think so too, Mister Firehand?"

"Yes, I'm entirely of your opinion," he answered. "But prudence tells us to follow the tracks no longer. If we do, Tom would be right. The rovers would hear us coming. If we keep more to the right and away from the river, we get them between us and the water and will see their fire without their noticing us."

"And if they have no fire?"

"Then we'll smell their horses," answered Droll. "In the forest, one can smell horses much better than in an open field. My nose hasn't let me down yet. Let's traipse farther then, more to the right!"

Old Firehand walked ahead, leading his horse by the bridle, with the others following him. Unfortunately, the river made a rather wide turn to the left here. The result was that their course was taking them too far away from the water. Old Firehand noticed the difference from the reduced moisture on the ground and the changed environment. So he turned more to the left. It was too late to backtrack and return to where they had left the river without losing precious time. The four concluded that they had made a mistake and decided to return directly to the river from where they were. Not aware that they had bypassed the rovers' campsite, they were now between that point and the camp of the rafters. Luckily, Old Firehand smelled smoke and stopped to check the direction it was coming from. Behind him, Droll also sniffed the air announcing, "That's smoke. It's coming from our left. Let's get over there. But be cautious. I think it's brighter over there. It can only be coming from a fire."

He was ready to stride ahead but stopped because his sharp ears had heard footsteps approaching. Old Firehand heard them too and, simultaneously, the heavy breathing of an approaching person. Letting go of his horse's bridle, he stepped forward a few paces, his ears telling him that the man had to pass at this spot. In the dark of the night, barely recognizable to the eyes of the famous hunter, a figure appeared intent on moving through quickly. Old Firehand seized the man with both hands.

"Stop!" he demanded in a low voice, so as not to be heard over any distance. "Who are you?"

"Schai nek-enokh, schai kopeia -- I don't know, nobody," the man responded, at the same time trying to tear himself free.

Even the most fearless man will be alarmed if at night, thinking he's alone in the forest, he is suddenly grabbed by two strong hands. At the moment of such a scare, almost anyone will involuntarily speak in his native tongue, even if he can speak other languages. So too the man held by Old Firehand. The hunter understood the words and responded in surprise, "That's Tonkawa! Is it Big Bear before us? Are you --- say who you are!"

The man now ceased to struggle, having recognized the great hunter's voice, and quickly answered in his broken English, "I Nintropan-Hauey. You Old Firehand. That very good, very good! Have more men with you?"

"Big Bear then! What a happy coincidence. Yes, I'm Old Firehand. There are three more people with me and we have horses. What are you doing here? The rovers are very close. Beware!"

"Have seen them. They capture old Missouri-Blenter. Will probably kill him. I run to rafters for help. Old Firehand catch me."

"They intend to kill a rafter? We've got to stop it. Where are they?"

"There behind me, where light between trees."

"Is the red-haired colonel with them?"

"Yes, he there."

"Where are their horses?"

"If Old Firehand go there, then horses on right, before get to fire."

"And where are the rafters?"

"Farther up. Big Bear been with them and talk to them."

In a hurry, he told what had happened. Old Firehand answered, "If a rover has been killed, they'll want to kill the Missourian, and that immediately, so as not to lose time. They need to get away before their presence is discovered. We four will leave our horses here and hurry to the fire to prevent the murder. You, Big Bear, run to the rafters and fetch them! Although we're not afraid of the rovers, it's better if the rafters join us soon."

The Indian ran off. The four hitched their horses to trees, then moved as fast as possible towards the rovers' camp. It quickly became lighter ahead of them and soon they spotted the fire through the trees. To the right of the clearing they saw the horses.

Until now they had made no effort to avoid being heard or seen. Now, though, they dropped down to crawl toward the fire. Old Firehand turned to the boy, Fred, and told him in a low voice to crawl over to the horses and shoot any rover attempting a getaway. But barely had the first words crossed his lips when a loud, penetrating scream pierced the air in front of them. It was the old Missourian's cry for help.

"They're murdering him!" said Old Firehand, urgently, but still speaking softly. "Onto them, quickly, into their midst! No pardon to any who offer resistance!"

He rose and leaped toward the fire, tossing three or four rovers aside to get to the colonel, who had just begun to strike down the Missourian. He arrived just in time to knock away the attacker with his rifle butt. Two or three rovers who had been occupied with tying and gagging the Missourian fell under his furious blows. Tossing his still loaded rifle aside, he pulled out his revolvers and fired at the remaining enemies. No word passed his lips. It was his habit to be silent in battle, except when he needed to issue commands.

Louder, though, were the other three. Black Tom had also entered the fray, storming among the rovers and knocking them down with his rifle butt, simultaneously calling them abusive, derisive and menacing names. Sixteen-year-old Fred had first fired his rifle, then threw it aside and pulled out his own revolvers. He fired one shot after another, screaming at the top of his lungs to instill fear into his enemies.

Loudest of all was the shrieking falsetto voice of Aunt Droll. The amazing hunter screamed and stormed like a hundred fighters. His movements were so violent that no rover was able to keep him in his sights long enough to shoot at him. Moreover none was willing to try. The rovers were in such disarray from the unexpected attack that they attempted no resistance at all. By the time they recovered from their surprise, those not injured saw so many of their own either wounded, dead or unconscious on the ground that they thought only to escape. They ran off without taking time to count the number of attackers who, because of Aunt Droll and Fred's screams, they had thought were in much greater numbers. From the moment Old Firehand had issued his first blow to the flight of the uninjured rovers, barely a minute had passed.

"Follow them!" shouted Old Firehand. "I'll guard the camp. Don't let them get to the horses!"

Tom, Droll and Fred, shrieking maniacally, ran to the spot where they had seen the animals. Those rovers who fled there hoping to find their mounts could not, so great was their fright. They could only flee farther into the woods.

At this same moment, the rafters at the blockhouse were waiting for the return of their two scouts, the Missourian and Tonkawa chief. When they heard the shots downstream, they thought the two must be in mortal danger. Hoping to save them, they grabbed their weapons, left the house and ran as fast as the darkness permitted toward the area where the shots had come from. All the while, they joined the chorus of screams, hoping to scare the rovers from doing any harm. Ahead of all of them ran Little Bear, the only one who knew exactly the spot where the rovers were camped. From time to time, he called out to keep the rafters heading in the right direction. Before they had covered half the distance, a voice rang out ahead of them, that of Big Bear.

"You come quickly!" he called. "Old Firehand here shooting at rovers. Only four men. Help him."

Increasing their stride, everyone rushed downstream. The shooting had stopped. It was now unknown what the situation was. The rafters' shouting hadn't stopped the fleeing rovers, but actually accelerated their efforts to get away as far and fast as possible. The rafters were just as frantic with at least a few crashing into trees and getting bruised without, however, taking much notice of it.

"First, gentlemen," the hunter began, "give me your word of honor that you will not reveal what I am about to tell you …

4. Escape from Reprisal

When the sprinting rafters arrived at the battle scene, Old Firehand, Tom, Droll, the Missourian and Fred were sitting calmly beside the fire as if nothing unusual had happened. On one side lay the corpses of those killed, on the other the bound bodies of the wounded and captured rovers, among them the red-haired colonel.

"Thunder and lightning!" one of the first to arrive shouted to the old Missourian. "We believed you were in danger and there you sit like in Abraham's lap!"

"That was the case!" old Blenter responded. "I was almost sent to Abraham's lap. The colonel's rifle butt was already hovering above me, when these four gentlemen arrived and rescued me. Fast and good work! You can learn a bit from them, boys!"

"And --- is Old Firehand truly here?"

"Yes, there he sits. Look at him and shake hands with him! He's earned it. Just think, only four men jump twenty, kill nine and capture six, themselves not getting a single scratch. And that's not counting the bullets and blows the few escapees must have received! Actually, they are only three men and a boy. Think of it!"

With these words, he had risen from the fire. The others also stood up. The rafters remained standing respectfully at some distance, their eyes on Old Firehand who asked them to come closer and each shake hands. He particularly honored the two Tonkawa by telling them, "In the pursuit of the rovers, my red brothers have delivered a masterpiece of work, making it very easy for me to follow you. We, too, purchased horses from some Indians, trying to catch up with you prior to meeting the rovers."

"From white brother praise too much," Big Bear answered modestly. "Rovers made such track, deep and broad, like herd of buffalo. Who not see be blind. But where is colonel? Is dead too?"

"No, he's alive. My rifle butt only knocked him unconscious. He's come to again and we've bound him. There he lies."

His hand pointed to the spot where the colonel lay. The Tonkawa went over and pulling his knife said, "If not dead from blow, he then die from knife. He hit me. I now take his blood!"

"Hold it!" Blenter, the old Missourian cried, at the same time grabbing the chief's arm. "This man isn't yours; he's mine."

Big Bear turned, looked into his face gravely and asked, "You also revenge against him?"

"Yes, and a certain one!"

"Blood?"

"Blood and life."

"Since when?"

"Since many, many years. He ordered my wife and my two sons cudgeled to death."

"You not mistaken?" asked the Indian, for whom it was difficult to abandon his revenge which he was now forced to do by the laws of the prairie.

"No, no error is possible. I recognized him at once. Such a face I could never forget."

"You kill him?"

"Yes, without mercy or charity."

"Then I withdraw, but not all. He slapped me, but take life from you. Tonkawa not let him get away without some punishment; I take ears of him. You agree?"

"Hmm! And if I don't agree?"

"Then Tonkawa kill him right away!"

"All right, then take his ears! It may not be in the Christian spirit to allow it. But whoever has experienced the pain he has inflicted upon me must invoke the law of the prairie, not charity, which would spare even a villain like him."

"Who else maybe speak with Tonkawa?" the chief asked, looking around in case someone was set to oppose him. But since no one uttered a word, he continued, "Then, ears are mine, and I take them now."

He knelt beside the colonel to execute his intent. When the fallen man saw that the other was deadly serious, he screamed, "What's gotten into you, sirs! Is this Christian? What have I done to you that you permit this red heathen to mutilate my head?"

"About what you have done to me, we will talk later," Blenter answered, coldly and seriously.

"And what we others accuse you of, I shall show you right now," added Old Firehand. "We as yet have not checked your pockets. Let's have a look what they contain!"

He gave Droll a sign, who then emptied the captive's pockets. Among many other items was also the rover's money pouch. When it was opened, it was found to contain the entire sum of bank notes stolen from the engineer.

"Ah, so you haven't shared with your people yet!" Old Firehand smiled. "That's proof they have greater confidence in you than we do. You are a thief; most likely more than that. No mercy is owed you. Big Bear may do what pleases him."

The colonel shrieked loudly in terror. But the chief, not bothered by the screaming, took him by his hair and with two fast and sure cuts severed both ears and tossed them into the river.

"That it!" he said, "Tonkawa now avenged, now ride off."

"Now?" asked Old Firehand. "Don't you want to ride with me, at least spend this night with us?"

"For Tonkawa same, day or night. His eyes good but time short. Have lost many days pursuing colonel. Now me ride day and night to get to wigwam. Me friend of white men; big friend and brother of Old Firehand. Great Manitou always provide much powder and meat to palefaces who friendly to Tonkawa. Howgh!"

He shouldered his rifle and strode off. His son, too, tossed his rifle onto his shoulder and followed him into the dark of the forest.

"Where are their horses?" inquired Old Firehand.

"Up at our blockhouse," the Missourian answered. "The two will go there first, of course, to get them. But whether they find their way through the forest by night, I would --- "

"Don't worry," the hunter broke in. "They know the way, otherwise they would have stayed. Big Bear has purchased quite a bit, as he told us. These goods are on their way. He must meet up with his carriers, but has already lost so much time that his hurry is readily understood. Let them ride off and let us turn to our own matters. What's to happen with the dead and the captives?"

"The dead we just toss into the river. About the others, we will judge by our old customs. But let's make first sure that no danger threatens us from the ones that escaped."

"Well, with so few of them left, they're of little danger to us. They probably ran as far as they could. We can also post some guards, that should suffice."

The colonel lay with the other captured rovers and whimpered from pain, but no one took notice of him, at least not yet. Nothing was to be feared from the direction of the river; thus several guards were posted only on the forest's side. Old Firehand had his horse fetched, together with those of his previous three companions. Then the prairie court was convened.

First the common rovers were dealt with. It could not be demonstrated that any one of them had done harm to any of those present. For what they had intended, the wounds they had incurred and the loss of their horses and weapons were counted as punishment. During the night, they were to be closely guarded but then would be released in the morning. They were allowed to treat each other's wounds.

Now it was the main culprit's turn, the colonel. Until this moment, he had lain in the shadows but was now dragged to the fire. Barely had the firelight fallen on his face when the boy, Fred, uttered a loud shout, ran toward him, bent down and looked him over as if wanting to devour him. Turning to Aunt Droll, he cried, "It's him, it's him, the murderer. I know him. We've got him!"

Excited, Droll at once drew near and asked, "Are you certain? That can't be him. It's not possible."

"Oh, yes, it's him, it's him for sure!" the boy insisted. "Look at his eyes. Don't they show his fear of death? He's been discovered and now has no hope of deliverance."

"But if it's him, you should have recognized him already on the steamer."

"I didn't see him there at all. The other rovers, yes, but not him. He must have always been sitting in such a way that he was obscured by the others."

"That was the case, I recall. But something else: you described the perpetrator as black and curly-haired, yet the colonel here has stiff red hair."

The boy did not answer right away. His hand went to his forehead. He shook his head, stepped back a pace, then said in a tone of noticeable uncertainty, "That's really true! It's his face, but his hair is entirely different."

"It must be a mistake, Fred! People do look similar, but black hair cannot become red."

"Not red," Blenter chimed in, "but one can shave off dark hair and wear a red wig."

"Ah! could that be --- ? asked Droll, not completing his sentence.

"Of course!, I didn't let myself be confused by the red hair. The man I've been searching for so long, the murderer of my wife and my children, also had black, curly hair. This fellow here is a redhead. I nevertheless assert that he's the one I want. He's wearing a wig."

"Impossible!" said Droll. "Didn't you see the Indian holding him by the hair when he cut off his ears? If the fellow was wearing a wig, it would have been pulled off."

"Pshaw! It must be well made and very well attached. Let me confirm this right now."

The colonel lay stretched out on the ground, his arms and legs bound. He was still bleeding from the wounds where his ears had been, which caused him severe pain. His full attention was directed to the words of the two speakers. While before he had been gazing ahead rather listlessly, the expression on his face now changed entirely. Hope had replaced dread, disdain fear, and triumph despair. Blenter was totally convinced that the colonel was wearing a wig. He pulled the colonel into a sitting position, grabbed him by the hair and pulled sharply expecting to dislodge a wig. To his great surprise, this proved impossible. The hair held. It was truly the man's own.

"By the devil, the scoundrel truly has hair on his skull!" he exclaimed in dismay, at the same time showing such a stunned look on his face that the others would surely have laughed had the situation not been so serious.

The colonel's face contorted in a sneer and in a voice of boundless hatred he shouted, "Now, you liar and slanderer, where is the wig? It's easy to falsely accuse a person just because of the similarity he has to someone else. Prove that I'm the one you claim me to be!"

The old Missourian looked first at the colonel, then at Old Firehand, then said helplessly to the hunter, "Tell me, sir, what do you think of it? The one I remember had truly black and curly hair; this one, though, has straight red hair.

And still I would swear a thousand oaths that it's him. It's impossible for my eyes to deceive me."

"You could nevertheless be mistaken," answered the hunter. "It could happen that there's a similarity here which is deceiving you."

"Then I can no longer trust my old but good eyes!"

"Better open them!" sneered the colonel. "May the devil get me if I know anything about a mother with two sons being murdered anywhere, as you claim, leave alone cudgeled to death!"

"But you know me! You said so earlier."

"Must I be the man you think I am just because I saw you once before? The boy there is also mistaking me entirely. In any case, the man he's talking about is the same one you're speaking of; but I don't know the young boy and ---"

He suddenly stopped, as if frightened or surprised by something, but recovered quickly to continue in the same vein, " --- and I've never seen him before. Now I don't care if you accuse me, but deliver proof. If you intend to judge and execute me only because of an accidental similarity, then you are simply murderers. That's something I don't expect from the famous Old Firehand, into whose protection I herewith entrust myself."

For the colonel to have stopped in the middle of a sentence, he had to have a very good reason. He was lying right beside the corpses with his head on one of them. When the Missourian raised him to a seated position, the stiff, lifeless body had made a slight rolling movement, unremarkable to anyone else since it no longer bore the weight of the redheaded man. It now lay close behind him in the shadows opposite the fire.

But this man was by no means dead, not even wounded. He was one of those Old Firehand had downed with the butt of his rifle. The blood of his killed comrades had been splattered all over him, giving the impression that he too had been hit.

When he had regained consciousness some time before, he found himself lying among the dead who at that time had had their pockets emptied and their weapons removed. He would have liked to leap up and flee, seeing only four enemies, but the river didn't look inviting and from the other side came the sound of the approaching rafters. He decided to wait for a more advantageous moment. Covertly pulling his knife, he secreted it in his sleeve. A moment later the Missourian had approached him, turned him back and forth, thought him dead and took what he found from his pockets and belt. He then dragged him to the place where the corpses were being laid.

From then on, the rover had observed everything from below lowered lids. He hadn't been bound and could therefore leap up and run at an opportune moment. When the colonel was laid on top of him, the idea arose in him to also free his leader. When the red-haired rogue had been made to sit up, the

73

supposedly dead man rolled after him, coming to lie directly behind the colonel, whose hands were tied behind his back.

While the colonel was speaking, with all attention directed towards him, the uninjured rover pulled his knife from his sleeve and carefully cut the colonel's fetters. He then placed the knife's handle into the colonel's right hand, so that in a quick move the latter could rid himself of his leg fetters, then suddenly jump up to flee. Of course, the red-haired captive felt his hands being secretly released and felt the knife handle which he gripped instantly. He was, however, momentarily surprised, lost his composure and halted in his speech. But only for an instant; then he continued and no one noticed what had happened. And since he had entrusted himself to Old Firehand's honesty, the latter answered, "If I have something to say about it, no murder will take place, rest assured of that. But just as certain is that I will not be misled by the redness of your hair. It may be dyed."

"Oho! Can one dye hair red while it's still on one's head?"

"Indeed," the hunter nodded in affirmation.

"By chance with red ocher?" the colonel asked with a sarcastic laugh. "That would color up nicely!"

"Go on laughing; you won't mock us for long," answered Old Firehand in a quiet, firm voice. "You may fool others, but not me."

He stepped over to the weapons and articles taken from the prisoners and the dead, bent down and picked up a leather pouch which had hung from the colonel's belt. He continued talking while he opened it. "I checked this pouch once before and found several items in it whose purpose and use were not clear to me; now, though, I have a hunch I think may be correct."

He pulled out a small capped bottle, a small rasp, and a finger-length twig, still with its bark attached. Holding these three items in front of the face of the red-haired man, he asked him, "For what purpose do you carry these items on you?"

The colonel's face blanched by several shades. However, he responded quickly and in a confident tone, "Isn't it marvelous that the great Old Firehand bothers about such trifles! Who would have thought it! The bottle contains a medicine; the grater is an indispensable instrument for any frontiersman and the twig got into the pouch by accident, having no purpose at all. Are you now satisfied, sir?"

With this question, he threw a mocking yet anxious and questioning look at the face of the giant hunter who answered in his serious, firm way, "Yes, I'm satisfied, not by your words, but by my conclusions. A rover has no need for a grater, particularly one of such small size. A file would be of much greater use. This bottle contains shavings immersed in spirits and from the bark of this piece of wood I judge it to have come from a Celtis occidentalis tree. Now I know very well that one can dye even the darkest hair with shaved hackberry wood that's been soaked in spirits; therefore --- what do you say now to that?"

"That I didn't understand a single word of your entire learned lecture," the colonel responded angrily. "I'd like to see anyone who would color his beautiful black hair fiery red. Such a man would truly display a nice, admirable taste."

"Taste is of no consequence here; the purpose counts. A person who is pursued for having committed severe crimes would surely be glad to dye his hair red, if that would save his life. I'm convinced that you're the one being sought, and tomorrow morning in full daylight I shall check your head and the roots of your hair closely."

"We need not wait that long," Fred interjected. "There is an identification mark. When he dropped me to the ground and kicked me some time ago, I stabbed him in the calf, in one side and out the other, so deeply that my knife remained stuck. Let him bare his calf. If he's the right one, which I don't doubt, the two scars must still be visible."

Nothing could have been more convenient for the red-haired villain than this proposal. If it were done for him, he need not cut his leg fetters himself. He therefore answered quickly, "Well, my very smart boy. In this case, you will find that you're all mistaken. But with all your artfulness, I must wonder how you expect me to roll up my pants leg. For a man who has his hands and legs tied, it seems hardly possible."

"I know that, which is why I'll do it myself," cried Fred fervently.

Eagerness drove the boy to the captive. He knelt in front of him and fussed with the thongs tying his legs together at the calves. Once he had the knot opened, he intended to pull up one of the legs of the Nanking pants, but suddenly he received such a two-footed kick from the colonel that he tumbled a good distance away. In an eye's blink, the colonel was on his feet.

"Goodbye, gentlemen! We shall meet again!" he shouted, leaping through a gap between two of the rafters, brandishing his knife wildly. Then he dashed across the clearing into the woods and disappeared.

The escape of this man, thought to be well bound, came so unexpectedly to those present that they stood frozen --- all except two. The two exceptions were Old Firehand and Aunt Droll. The first possessed a keen presence of mind, on which one could rely even in the most unusual situations. The latter was close to him in this respect, despite his other characteristics, which permitted no comparison with the famous hunter.

As soon as the colonel sprang up from his seated position, raising his knife, Old Firehand had already begun a leap to catch him; yet an unexpected obstacle interfered. The rover who had been thought dead felt his time had come as well. Since all attention was focused on the colonel, he thought it now easy to escape himself. He also leaped up beyond the fire to break through the encircling rafters, just at the moment that Old Firehand, in a giant jump flew over the fire and collided with him. To grab, to lift, and to throw the rover down with a formidable whack was the work of only two seconds.

"Tie up this rogue who isn't dead!" the hunter shouted, turning toward the colonel who had gained time as a result of the two's collision. Old Firehand raised his rifle with the intention to cut him down with a bullet. But he saw the impossibility of his intent, for Droll was close behind the escapee and covered the latter's body in such a way that the bullet would have hit Droll.

The red-haired man ran like someone knowing he had to save his life. Droll followed him as hard as he could. He would certainly have caught him, had he not worn his famous leather 'sleeping gown'. This garment was much too heavy and a hindrance in such a pursuit. In desperation, Old Firehand dropped his rifle and raced in almost panther-like leaps after the two.

"Stop, Droll!" he called ahead.

The Aunt, though, paid no attention to the shout and ran on, despite the admonition having been repeated several times. The colonel now had the fire's illumination behind him and he vanished into the darkness between the trees.

"Stop, by heaven, stop, Droll!" Old Firehand shouted angrily for the fifth time, now being only three or four strides behind him.

"Must get him, must get him!" answered the excited Aunt in his usual falsetto voice, racing away through the trees.

Old Firehand, like a well-trained horse which even during full gallop obeys the reins, stopped in midstride, turned and returned slowly to the fire as if nothing had happened. There stood the others in various excited groups, looking toward the forest to await the result of the pursuit.

"Well. You return alone!" the old Missourian called to Old Firehand.

"As you see," he responded, quietly shrugging his shoulders.

"Could he not be caught?"

"Easily, had this devilish rover not come in between and collided with me."

"Terrible thing that the main culprit in particular had to get away!"

"Well, old Blenter, you should be the last to complain about this."

"Why I?"

"Because you alone are responsible for it."

"I?" the old one asked in wonder. "That I do not understand. Your word of honor, Sir, but do explain this to me!"

"That's easy. Who checked the rover who later revived?"

"I, certainly."

"And you believed him dead! How can this happen to such an experienced rafter and hunter like yourself? And who emptied his pockets and took his weapons?"

"Me, too."

"But you left him his knife!"

"No, he had none."

"He had hidden it. Then he lay there, playing dead all the time. Then he not only cut the colonel's bonds, but also slipped him the knife."

"Could it truly have been this way, sir?" the old one asked, embarrassed.

"Ask him yourself! There he lies."

Blenter kicked the tied-up rover and by threats forced him to answer. He learned that everything had happened as Old Firehand had guessed. The old fellow gripped his long, gray hair with both hands, twisting it vexedly and exclaimed angrily, "I could box my own ears. Such stupidity hasn't happened before in all the States. It's my fault, mine alone! And I would wager my life that he was the one I thought he was."

"It was him for sure; he would otherwise have allowed his leg to be inspected without a fuss. Had the two scars not been there, nothing would have happened to him. Even though he stole the engineer's money, we couldn't have punished him according to the laws of the prairie, since the victim isn't present."

Now, Droll returned slowly and hesitantly across the clearing. It was apparent from afar that he had not been successful. He had followed the escapee for quite some distance into the woods, but scratched his face on a number of branches. He stopped to listen then, but when he didn't hear the slightest noise, returned to camp.

Old Firehand had become fond of this peculiar man and therefore didn't want to embarrass him in front of the rafters. For this reason, he asked him in German, "But Droll, did you not hear what I asked you several times?"

"What you called about, yes, I certainly heard," the chubby one responded in German.

"And why didn't you acknowledge my request?"

"Because I wanted to catch the villain."

"And that's why you ran after him into the forest?"

"What else should I have done? Should I have asked him to run behind me?"

"Certainly not," laughed Old Firehand. "But to catch a man in the woods at night, one must be able to see him or at least hear him. By running yourself, the noise of the pursued's steps becomes inaudible. Understood?"

"That's easy to understand, of course. So, I should have stopped?"

"Yes."

"Oh, my God! Who's to comprehend this? If I stop, he runs away and I can then wait at that spot until Judgment Day! Or do you think he would have returned to throw himself into my arms?"

"Not like this, but similarly. I bet he was smart enough not to run too far. I suspect he ran into the woods for only a short distance, then hid behind a tree at his leisure and let you pass."

"'How? What? I passed him? If that's true, I couldn't experience a greater disgrace!"

"It was surely so. That's why I called for you to stop. Once in the dark forest, we could then have hugged the ground and listened. With our ears on the ground, we could have heard his steps and determined their direction. Had he stopped, we could have crept up on him. And sneaking up on someone is something you do very well, as I know."

"That's true!" answered Droll, pleased by the praise. "When I think about it, it seems you're entirely correct. I've been stupid, quite a bit stupid. Maybe I can compensate for it? What do you say?"

"It's possible to make up for the mistake, but it won't be easy for us. We must wait until tomorrow morning to find his tracks. Once we follow them, we can most likely catch up with him."

He also conveyed these thoughts to the rafters to which the old Missourian responded, "Sir, I will ride along. We've captured enough horses that I could ride one of them. This colonel is the one I've been seeking for too many years. I'm going to follow along his tracks; my comrades won't resent my leaving them. And it'll be no loss to me since I started work here only recently."

"I'd like that," answered Old Firehand. "Already on the way, I had decided to make all of you a proposal which I hope you'll accept."

"What kind?"

"About it, later. First, we have more urgent things to do. We must get back up to your blockhouse."

"Why not stay here until the morning, sir?"

"Because your property is in danger. You can expect anything from the colonel. He knows we're down here and can easily decide to head for your building."

"Zounds! That would be fatal! We have our tools and spare weapons in there, also powder and bullets. Quick, we must leave!"

"Very well. You go ahead, Blenter, and take two other men. The rest of us will follow with the horses and the captives. We'll light the way with torches from the fire here."

The shrewd hunter had judged the colonel properly. The latter had hidden behind a tree soon after he had entered the woods. He heard Droll rush past him and saw Old Firehand return to the fire. Since Droll didn't head in the direction of the blockhouse, it was obvious to the red-haired man that he could quietly slink away in that direction. So as not to run into a tree, he held his hands out in front of him and advanced up the sloping ground.

Suddenly the thought came to him of the advantages the blockhouse had to offer. Having been there before, he couldn't miss it. It was certain to hold most of the rafters' property; he could easily take his revenge on them. He therefore hastened his steps as much as the darkness permitted.

When he arrived there, he first stopped and listened. It was possible that one or even several of the rafters had remained. With everything quiet, he confidently approached the blockhouse, listened again and groped for the door. Just as he began to lift the latch, he was suddenly seized by the throat and pulled roughly to the ground. Several men came out of nowhere and knelt on him.

"At least we have one of them and he's going to suffer for it!" he heard one of the men say.

The colonel recognized the voice; it was that of one of his own rovers. He made a mighty effort to free his throat and could only hoarsely force out the words, "Woodward, by the devil, let me go!"

Woodward was the rovers' sub-leader. He recognized the red-haired man's voice and released him, pushing the others away as he responded, "The colonel! Truly the colonel! Where did you come from? We thought you'd been captured."

"I was," gasped the colonel, getting up at the same time, "but I escaped. Couldn't you have been more careful? You almost killed me!"

"We thought you were a rafter."

"So! And what are you doing here?"

"We happened to come together down here, only the three of us. We don't know where the others are. We saw the rafters sitting at our fire and got the idea to come up here and to turn the tables on them."

"That's good! The same thought brought me here. I want to burn this hut down."

"We also intended to do that, but not without first checking what the blockhouse holds. Maybe we'll find a few things we can use."

"For that we need some light. Those scoundrels have taken everything from me, even my fire lighter and we can look forever in there without finding one."

"You forget that we still have ours, since we weren't robbed."

"That's true. You still have your weapons?"

"Yes, all of them."

"And have you checked that there's no possibility for an ambush here?"

"There's not a soul here; the door unbolts easily and we were just about to enter when you arrived."

"Then let's be quick before the rafters get the idea to come up here!"

"Can't we find out from you what happened down there after we left?"

"Not now, later, when there's time."

Woodward lifted the latch and they entered. Having pulled the door shut behind them, he struck a light and shone it around the room. Above the beds were shelves on which stood elk-tallow lamps in the fashion frontiersmen pour them. Each of the four lit one, after which they hurriedly looked for useable items.

There were a few rifles, full powder horns, axes, hatchets, saws, knives, powder, cartons of bullets, meat and other provisions. Each took what he found necessary and liked. Then they stuck their burning lamps into the rushes from which the beds were made. At once the beds caught fire, sending the arsonists rushing outside. They left the door open to provide a good draft, then stayed outside to watch and listen. There was nothing to be heard but the crackling of the flames and the wind in the crowns of the trees.

"They're not coming yet," said Woodward. "What now?"

"We get away, of course," answered the colonel.

"But where to? We don't know the area."

"Tomorrow morning they'll hunt for our tracks wanting to follow us. Therefore we must to be careful not leave any."

"That's impossible, except in water."

"So we take to the water."

"How? With what?"

"In a boat, you fool. Don't you know that all rafter groups need one or more boats for their business? I bet they're anchored down by the timber slide."

"We don't know where that is."

"It's easy to find. Look over there where the lumber slide begins. Let's see if we can get down."

By then the flames had penetrated the roof and illuminated the entire area. At the edge of the woods toward the river, a gap in the trees was visible. The rovers raced over and saw that their leader had guessed correctly. A straight, steep and narrow slide led to the water, along which a rope had been fastened. Hand over hand, the four let themselves down.

At the river, they heard the distant mixture of voices originating from the old Missourian and his two companions as they hurried towards the blockhouse.

"They're coming," said the colonel. "Quick now, let's find a boat!"

The search was short, for right where they stood three boats had been tied up: canoes made of birch bark and caulked with tree resin in the Indian way, each able to carry four people.

"Tie the other two to the one we take," the red-haired man ordered. "We must bring them along so we can't be pursued. Later we'll sink them."

The men followed his instructions. Then all four boarded the first canoe, took the paddles lying in the bottom and pushed away from the bank. The colonel sat in the stern to steer. One of his fellows worked his paddle as if he wanted to head upstream.

"Wrong!" the leader told him. "We go downstream."

"But we were planning to travel farther west into Kansas for the big rovers' meeting!" the man protested.

"That's true. But this Old Firehand will find out about, extracting the information from his prisoners. He'll be looking for us upstream tomorrow; that's why to mislead him we must head downstream."

"A mighty detour."

"Not at all. We paddle until we reach the first open prairie we see tomorrow morning. There we'll sink the canoes and steal horses from the local Indians.

Then we'll ride hard to the north and make up for this little loss of time in one day, while the rafters will slowly and with great difficulty search in vain for our tracks."

They kept the canoes in the bank's shadow so as not to be visible in the glare of the inferno burning above. Then when they left this area behind, the colonel steered to the middle of the river, just at the moment when the rafters with their captives and horses reached the burning blockhouse.

The rafters, seeing this, sent up a great lament at the loss of their belongings. A hundred curses and angry wishes for the arsonists could be heard. Old Firehand calmed them by telling them, "I figured that the colonel would do something like this. Too bad we arrived too late. But don't take it to heart. If you accept the proposal I'm going to make you, you'll receive full compensation for your losses."

"How so?" asked Blenter.

"About that, later. First we must make sure there aren't any more of the scoundrels around."

The entire area was checked closely, but nothing suspicious was found. Then everyone settled down with Old Firehand by the light of the fire. The captives had been left some distance away so they couldn't overhear the conversation.

"First, gentlemen," the hunter began, "give me your word of honor that you will not reveal what I am about to tell you, even if you should not accept my proposal! I know you're all gentlemen on whose word I can rely."

He received the requested assurance from all, then continued, "Does any one of you know the big water up in the mountains called Silver Lake?"

"I do," answered only one, that being Aunt Droll. "Everybody knows the name, but none except myself has ever been up there, which I conclude from the silence of these gentlemen."

"Well, I know that up there are rich, very rich mines, old mines from the times of before the Indians, men who did not exploit the mineral deposits. I know of several of these deposits and I'm on my way up there with a competent mining engineer to look them over and see if they can be mined on a large scale. Also to determine if we can obtain the required hydraulic power from the lake itself. This enterprise is, of course, not without danger, which is why I need a group of able and experienced frontiersmen to accompany us. Let your work here rest for a while and ride to this lake with me, gentlemen! I shall pay you well!"

"That's the word then, yes, a beautiful word!" Blenter shouted enthusiastically. "That Old Firehand will pay well and honestly is without doubt, and for the participants to experience a hundred, even a thousand real adventures is just as assured. I would go along with it on the spot, but I cannot, I may not, for I must find the colonel."

"And me too, me too," Droll chimed in. "How much I would like to come along, very much indeed, not for the pay but for the adventure, and because I think it's a great honor to travel with Sir Firehand. But it cannot be because, I too, must not lose the track of the redheaded colonel."

A fine, superior smile swept over Old Firehand's face as he answered, "You two cling to a desire, which may very well be answered, if you stay with me. Why is it that Mister Blenter thirsts for revenge we all know. But why Mister Droll, with his brave Fred, wants to follow this colonel he has not told us yet. And it's not my intention to probe his secrets; he will doubtless open up yet. One thing, though, I may not keep from you. When we left that campfire to come here, we had to take along the bound rovers. I took one, the youngest, by the hand. He found the courage to address me, and I learned that he feels he doesn't fit in with these rovers, that he is sorry to have joined them, and that he only became a member because of his brother, who now lies among the dead men down there. He claims actually to have the intention of becoming a good and true frontiersman. Having heard my name, he's literally fired up to be one of my people, even if only the very least of them. He promised to tell me about the colonel's plans, and I would not like to reject the fellow, partly for humane reasons, partly from prudence. May I bring him over here?"

The others all agreed and Old Firehand got himself up to fetch the young man. The fellow was not much beyond twenty years old, of intelligent appearance and sturdy build. Old Firehand had removed his fetters and asked him to sit beside him. The other rovers lay some distance away where they could neither see nor hear the young man. Later on, they would not be able to report what was happening or that the boy was betraying them and the colonel.

"Now then," Old Firehand turned to him, "you see that I'm not averse to fulfilling your wish. You have been led astray by your brother. If you promise me with a handshake to be a honest person from now on, I shall set you free this very moment and you can become an able frontiersmen by my side. What's your name, actually?"

"My name is Nolley, sir," the lad answered, at the same time giving him his right hand while brushing away tears with his left. "I don't want to bother you with my life story; that you can learn later and on the by-and-by, but I do want you to be satisfied with me. I shall be grateful to you for the rest of my life if you will allow me two wishes."

"Which may they be?"

"Do not forgive me just seemingly, sir, but truly for being in such bad company. And secondly permit me to bury my dead brother tomorrow morning. He's not to rot in the water and be eaten by fishes."

"These wishes tell me that I have not erred in you; they're granted. From now on, you are with us and shall not be seen again by your earlier comrades.

They are not to know that you've joined us. You talked about the colonel's intentions. Do you know them?"

"Yes. He kept them to himself for a long time. Yesterday, though, he told us everything. He first wants to go to the big rovers' meeting which is to take place shortly."

"Hullo!" Droll exclaimed. "So I wasn't falsely informed when I learned that these vagrants intend to gather by the hundreds somewhere around Harper to make arrangements for a few en masse raids. Do you know the place?"

"Yes," answered Nolley. "It's actually located beyond Harper as seen from here and is called the Osage Nook."

"Haven't yet heard of this Nook. Odd! It had been my plan to get to this meeting too, perhaps find the one I was looking for, though I didn't have a clue that I traveled with him on the steamer. I should have grabbed him right on board! Then it's to the Osage Nook that the colonel is headed. Well then, we ride after him, right, Master Blenter?"

"Yes," the old one nodded. "Of course then we cannot accompany Old Firehand."

"That's not the case at all," the hunter responded. "My next destination is nearby -- that's Butler's farm -- belonging to the engineer's brother, who's expecting me. We can stay together, at least to there. Does the colonel have further plans?"

"Indeed," the converted young rover answered. "After the meeting, he intends to head for the Eagle Tail to attack the local railroad pay office for its money, of which there seems to be a plenitude."

"Good that we learned this! Should we not catch him at the meeting, we'll find him, sure enough, at the Eagle Tail."

"And if he gets away there," Nolley continued, "you can catch him later at Silver Lake."

These words caused a general consternation; even Old Firehand was so astonished that he quickly asked, "At Silver Lake? What does the colonel know about it and what does he want at that place?"

"To find a treasure."

"A treasure? Is there one there?"

"Yes, supposedly. Immense treasures are said to be buried or immersed there, dating to olden times and peoples. He has an accurate map of the place where one needs to look."

"Have you seen this map?"

"No. He doesn't show it to anyone."

"But we checked him over and took everything from him without having found any such thing!"

"He has it hidden very well. I believe that he doesn't even carry it on himself. I concluded from one of his remarks that he has buried it somewhere."

The attention of the listeners had been directed at the speaker, which is why no one paid any attention to Droll and Fred who, from what they had just heard, had become quite agitated. Droll stared at the former rover as if he not only heard his words, but intended to devour them as well. When the boy's account ended, Fred exclaimed, "It's the colonel! It's him! This map belonged to my father!"

Now all eyes turned to young Fred. Everyone assailed him with questions, but Droll energetically warded them off and said, "Nothing of it now, gentlemen! You'll learn all the facts later. The main thing now is, knowing the circumstances, that I and Fred will be absolutely at Old Firehand's service."

"Me too!" declared the old Missourian in a relieved tone. "We've got such a lot of secrets here that I'm wondering how we will ever disentangle them all. You're all coming along, right, comrades?"

"Yes, yes, of course!" it sounded from the circle of rafters.

"Well!" said Old Firehand. "Then we'll break camp tomorrow morning. We no longer need to bother tracking the colonel, since we know the places where he can be found. We'll hunt him through the forests and prairies, over mountains and through valleys, and if it must be, even up to Silver Lake. An eventful adventure lies ahead of us. Let's be good comrades, gentlemen!"

5. An Indian Masterpiece

The Rolling Prairie lay in the midday sun. Hillock upon hillock was covered by dense grasses whose blades billowed silently in the wind. It resembled an emerald ocean whose waves had suddenly been frozen. Every one of these arrested waves looked like the next with respect to its length, shape and height. And if one came out of such a wave trough into the next, it was easy to mistake the latter for the previous one. Nothing all around, nothing but wavy hillocks as far as the horizon. Whoever did not depend on the compass or guide himself by the sun would surely get as lost as a novice sailor in a small boat on the open sea.

In this green desert, there did not seem to exist a single living being; only high in the sky two black turkey vultures circled, rarely flapping their wings. Were they truly the only creatures around here? No, for just then a hearty snort could be heard, and from behind one of the wavy hillocks a horseman appeared, and at that a most curiously appareled one.

The man was of ordinary figure, neither too large nor too small, neither too heavy nor too gaunt, but seemed to be strong. He wore long pants, a vest and jacket, the outer garments made of waterproof rubber cloth. His head sported a pith helmet with a neck flap like those the English officers usually wear in East India and other such tropical countries. His feet were shod in Indian moccasins.

The man's bearing was that of an accomplished horseman; his face -- yes, his face was actually very peculiar. Its expression could be called that of a dullard, and not just because his nose looked very different from either side. On the left, it had a whitish cast and bore the slightly bent shape of the common eagle's beak; on the right side it was thick, as if swollen and of a color one could only call nondescript. The face was framed by a beard whose long, thin hair reached from above his chin to well below his throat. The beard was supported by a stand-up-collar whose bluish shine bespoke the fact that the rider preferred to wear rubber clothing on the prairie.

On the left and right, each stirrup held a rifle, attached to shoe-like braces beside the rider's feet. In front across the saddle hung a long tin metal container whose purpose was indecipherable. On his back the man bore a leather knapsack of medium size and attached to it several tin containers and oddly-shaped iron wires. His leather waist band was broad and appeared to be a money-belt. From it dangled several pouches. From up front peered the butts or handles of several revolvers and knives. In the back were attached two satchels that might have held cartridges.

The horse seemed to be ordinary, not too fine and not too decrepit for the toils of the West; there was nothing particular about him, but that his saddle cloth was a blanket which had surely cost a pretty penny.

The rider seemed to believe that his horse had more prairie-savvy than he himself. At least one could see that he did not direct it, but rather let it run where it liked. It ambled through several depressions, rose up on a hillock, descended its other side, fell into a trot, slowed again. In short, the man with the pith-helmet and the utterly dull face did not seem to have a definite destination, but rather had lots of time.

Suddenly the horse stopped and pointed his ears as his rider, simultaneously, showed a small sign of alarm. For in front of him, yet from no identifiable source, came a sharp, commanding voice, "Stop, not a step farther, or I shoot! Who are you, mister?"

The rider looked in front of him, behind, to the right and the left; no human being was visible. Without a change of expression on his face, he pulled the lid from the long metal container resting on the saddle in front of him and shook out a telescope. He pulled its sections apart to a length of nearly five feet, squinted his left eye, lifted the tube to his right one and held it toward the sky. For a while he inspected it quite seriously and intensely until the same voice rose again, laughing, "Put your telescope back together again! I'm not sitting on the moon, which isn't visible anyway, but down here on old Mother Earth. Now tell me where you're from!"

Obeying the command, the rider pushed his scope together. stuck it into its container and closed it slowly and conscientiously as if he were in no hurry at all. The he pointed behind him and said, "From there, old boy!"

"That I see. And where are you going?"

"Dash it! Over there!" responded the other impatiently, his hand now pointing carelessly forward.

"You are truly a precious character!" laughed the still invisible inquirer. "But since you find yourself on this beneficent prairie, I suppose you know its customs. There are so many questionable rabble carousing here that an honest man is forced to take every encounter seriously. Back you may ride, in God's name if it pleases you, but should you want to proceed forward as you appear to, you must give an account of your intentions, and that truthfully. Out with it then! Where do you come from?"

"Oh, my sainted aunt! From Castle Castlepool," answered the man in the voice of a schoolboy afraid of the stern face of a teacher.

"That I don't know. Where's that place?"

"On the map of Great Britain," explained the rider, his face becoming almost more doltish than before.

"God bless your brains, sir! What do I care about Great Britain. And where are you headed?"

"To Calcutta."

"Don't know that either. Where's that beautiful place located?"

"In East India."

"Oh, my God! Then, on this sunny afternoon you want to ride from Great Britain via the United States to East India?"

"Not all today."

"So! Wouldn't be easy anyway. Then you must be an Englishman?"

"Right-o."

"What's your profession?"

"I'm a lord of the realm if it should so please you, sir."

"Thunder and lightning! An English lord with a round chapeau on his head. Come on, Uncle, the man's not going to hurt us. I'm happy to believe him. He's either nuts or truly an English lord with a five meter craze or a hundred-liter liver ailment."

Over the rise from the next hillock appeared two figures who had lain there in the grass; a tall, lanky one and another very short one. Both were dressed alike, entirely in leather as it behooves true frontiersmen. Even their broad-brimmed hats were of leather. The tall one stood stiff as a pole on top of the hillock; the little one was hunchbacked and had a hawk-like nose, its ridge as sharp as a knife's. Their rifles were of the same design, old, very long weapons. The little hunchback had planted his rifle with its butt on the ground, but even then the barrel's muzzle towered above his head by several inches. He seemed to be the speaker for the two, since the tall one had not yet said a single word, so now he continued, "Stay put there fellow, or we'll shoot! We haven't finished yet with each other."

"I say, shall we bet?" the Englishman called up to them.

"What?"

"Tuppence or ten dollars or fifty or a hundred, whatever you like."

"What for?"

"That I shoot you before you shoot me."

"Then you would lose."

"You bloody well think so, do you? Well, then let's make it a hundred dollars."

Reaching behind him for his satchel, he pulled it in front of him, opened it and retrieved several bills. The two men on the hill looked at each other in astonishment.

"I think you are serious!" shouted the little one.

"What else?" asked the Englishman, surprised. "Wagering is my passion, that is, I jolly well like to bet and at every occasion."

"And carry a pocket full of bills across the prairie!"

"Could I bet if I had no money on me? A hundred dollars then, if you please? Or do you want to increase the stakes?"

"We have no money."

"That doesn't matter, chappie; I will advance it to you for the time being until you can pay me."

He said this with such seriousness that the tall one took a deep breath in amazement and the hunchback called out downright perplexed, "To lend us --- until we can pay? You are sure then to win?"

"Very much so!"

"But, sir, to win you must shoot us before we shoot you; but dead we couldn't repay you!"

"It's all the same! I would have won anyway and have so much money that I don't need yours!"

"Uncle," the short one opined to the tall one, shaking his head, "Such a boy I've never seen before nor heard about. We must go down to look him over more closely."

With quick steps he descended, the tall one following him in as stiff and bolt-upright position as if he had a bean pole in his body. Having arrived in the depression, the hunchback said, "Put your money away; the bet's off. And take my advice: don't let anybody see this satchel; you could live to regret it, and even pay with your life. I truly don't know what to think of you. You don't seem to be quite right in the head. We need to look you over a bit more seriously. Come forward a few paces."

His hand reached out to take the reins of the Englishman's horse, when suddenly two revolvers appeared in the lord's hands. He spoke in a short, stern voice, "Hands off, you blighter, or I shoot!"

The little one jumped back startled and started to raise his rifle.

"Leave off there. Do not move or I will damned well fire."

The bearing and face of Lord Castlepool had changed drastically. No longer was there the dull expression from before and from his eyes flashed an intelligence, which froze the two prairiemen.

"You blokes truly think I'm loony?" he continued. "And really consider me to be a chap with whom you can act as if the prairie were your sole property? There you are frightfully mistaken. Until now, you have asked me and I have answered you. Now I want to know what sort of rotters I am facing here. What is your name and who are you?"

The questions were directed to the short one, who was aware of the piercingly inquiring eyes of the stranger, which gave such a peculiarly different impression now. He therefore responded in a part angry, part embarrassed tone, "You're a stranger here; that's why you don't recognize us; but we're known from the Mississippi all the way to Frisco as honest hunters and trappers. We're on our way to the mountains to find and join a group of beaver trappers."

"Well! And your names?"

"Our actual names are of no use to you. I'm called Humpy-Bill since I'm unfortunately hunchbacked, about which I'm not worried enough to want to die from grief. My comrade here is known as Gunstick-Uncle, since he walks the world as if he had swallowed a ramrod. So now you know us. Tell us the truth about you without making dumb jokes about it."

The Englishman observed them with a penetrating look as if wanting to peer deeply into their hearts; then his features assumed a friendlier mien. He took a paper from the money bag, unfolded it, offered it to the two and answered, "I was not joking. Since I fancy you now to be good and upright folk, have a look at my passport."

The two looked at it and read it, faced each other, then the tall one opened both his eyes and mouth gapingly wide while the little one said, this time in a very polite voice, "Truly a lord. Lord Castlepool. But, sir, what do you want on the prairie? Your life is ---"

"Eh?" The lord interrupted him "What do I want? To get to know the prairie and the Rocky Mountains and then go on to Frisco. I have been all over the world, but not yet across the United States. So now that we have become introduced, we need not act beastly with each other. Go get your horses! I assume you have horses, although I have not seen them yet."

"Of course we do; they stand behind that hill where we stopped to rest."

"Jolly good! Then come along over there!"

From the tone of his voice, Lord Castlepool was now the one to give instructions instead of the other way around. He dismounted and strode ahead through the low area, then over the hillock where two horses were grazing. They were of the sort commonly called a nag or a hack. The Englishman's own horse followed him like a dog but when the other two approached, he neighed angrily and kicked out to drive them away.

"A malicious toad," opined Humpy-Bill. "He doesn't seem to be sociable."

"Oh, no," answered the lord. "He knows, though, that I am not yet well acquainted with you and has no intentions therefore to become friendly with your horses."

"Would he truly be that smart? I can't visualize it. Looks more like a plow horse."

"Gad, no! He is a veritable Kurdistan Husahn, a stallion, with your kind permission."

"So! And where is this country located?"

"Between Persia and Turkey. I purchased him there myself and brought him home."

He spoke this in such an indifferent tone, as if it were just as easy to transport a horse from Kurdistan to England and from there again to the United States, as to bring a canary from the Harz Mountains to the Thuringian Forest. The two hunters threw each other furtive looks. Lord Castlepool however, sat unceremoniously in the grass where the two had been sitting before. There lay a previously roasted and cut venison leg. The Englishman pulled his knife, cut off a hefty piece and began to eat, as though the meat were his own and not the others.

"That's the way!" said the hunchback. "Don't cause any inconvenience on the prairie."

"No intention to do so, dear boy," was the lord's reply. "If you shot some meat yesterday, I shall shoot some today or tomorrow, for you too, of course."

"So? You think then, your lordship, that we will still be together by tomorrow?"

"Tomorrow and much longer. Shall we bet? I'll wager ten to your one dollar, even more, if you care to."

He reached for his satchel.

"Keep your money there," answered Humpy. "We don't bet."

"Then do sit down here with me! I shall explain it to you."

They sat down opposite him. He once more studied them closely, then said, "I have come up the Arkansas River and disembarked at Mulvane. There I had intended to hire a guide or two, but found none I liked. Were all ruddy blighters, those fellows. I rode off telling myself that veritable prairie hunters could only be found on the prairie. I found you and you please me. Will you come then?"

"Where to?"

"Over to Frisco."

"You say this so offhand as if it were just a day's ride?"

"It's a bit of a ride. Whether a day or a year, it's all the same to me."

"Hmm, yes. But do you have any idea what one can come across on the way?"

"I have not thought about it, old sock, but hope to find out."

"Don't wish too much for yourself. By the way, we'll not come along. We aren't as rich as you seem to be, but live off hunting and can therefore not engage in a month-long detour to Frisco."

"Dash it, I shall pay you!"

"Really?"

"And pay well. We can talk about the matter. Can you shoot?"

It was an almost pitying look that the hunchback gave Lord Castlepool when he answered. "A prairie hunter not shoot? That's even worse than asking if a bear can eat. Both are just as obvious as my hunched back."

"I would like to see a proof of it even so. Can you bring down the turkey vultures up there?"

Humpy estimated the height at which the two birds circled and responded, "Why not? You, though, couldn't do it with your two only-on-Sunday rifles."

He pointed to the lord's horse where the rifles lay in their braces; they were polished and clean and looked like new, a horror to the frontiersman.

"Then shoot, old boy!" requested the lord, ignoring the gibe of the hunchback.

The latter stood, aimed his rifle and squeezed the trigger. They all could see that one of the vultures had been hit; it flapped its wings frantically attempting to keep itself aloft, but in vain; it began to lose height, first slowly, then faster; finally pulling its wings to its body, it plummeted straight to the ground like a stone.

"Now, Lord Castlepool, what do you say?" the little marksman asked.

"Not bloody bad," was the retort.

"What? Just not bad? Consider the height and that the bullet took the bird's life while it was still in the air! Any expert would have called it a masterly shot."

"Well, laddie, how about the second one!" the lord nodded to the tall hunter, without reacting to the protest of the little one.

Now Gunstick-Uncle rose stiffly from the ground, his left hand helping to support himself with his long rifle and raised the right like an orator. He lifted his eyes to the sky at the second vulture and spoke in the most pathetic tone, "The eagle travels in the fields of the sky - looks down onto hillocks and dales - longs for the carrion smellin' to heaven - I, though, shall shoot it dead before seven!"

While reciting these improvised rhymes, his pose had become as stiff as a scarecrow's pole. Until now, since he had not uttered a single word, the more impressive was this wonderful poet. So he believed. He therefore lowered his raised arm, turned to the lord, looking at him with proud expectation. The Englishman by now had resumed his dullard's face; it twitched as if he had to fight between laughing and weeping.

"Did you hear right, Lord Castlepool?" asked the hunchback. "Yes, Gunstick-Uncle is a fine chap. He was an actor and is still a poet. He talks little, but when he opens his mouth he speaks only in angel tongues, that means in rhymes."

"Well!" the Englishman nodded. "Whether the bloke speaks in rhymes or cucumber salad is his ruddy business, not mine. But can he shoot?"

The tall poet grimaced his mouth almost around to his right ear while jerking his hand forward, meaning to express his disdain. He then lifted his rifle to aim but set it down again. He had missed the right moment, he thought, since during his poetic effusion the female vulture, frightened by the death of its mate, had decided to fly off. The bird was already far distant.

"It's impossible to hit now," said Humpy. "Don't you think so too, Uncle?"

The one queried raised both hands, pointing in the sky where the vulture could still be seen. He then answered in a tone to raise the dead, "Carried away by its wings - over hillock and dale - and with much delight - it escaped from my might - any chance now is nil - one need fly after it still!"

"Stuff and nonsense! shouted Lord Castlepool. "You truly think it cannot be hit any longer?"

"Yes, sir," Humpy answered. "Not Old Firehand, not Winnetou and not Old Shatterhand could still down it now, and these are the three best shots in the Far West."

"I'll be dashed."

While Lord Castlepool mumbled this more than speaking it, a lightning-fast twitch passed over his face. Stepping quickly to his horse, he took one of the rifles from its support, released the safety, aimed and fired, all in a single brief instant. Lowering his rifle he sat down, reached for the venison roast, cut himself another piece and asked, "Now, laddies, was it possible to hit it or not?"

The faces of both hunters showed the greatest surprise, even admiration. The bird had been hit, and well at that, for with increasing velocity it fell to the ground in a tightening spiral.

"Wonderful!" Humpy shouted enthusiastically. "Sir, wasn't it a fluke?"

He caught himself. He had turned to the Englishman and saw him sitting on the ground with his back to the direction where the masterly shot had been aimed. Was it to be believed?

"But, your lordship," he continued, "turn around! You not only hit the vulture, but you truly killed it!"

"I did rather," the Englishman responded, and forbearing to turn around, he put another piece of meat into his mouth.

"But you didn't even watch it fall!"

"It was not at all necessary; I knew it. An Englishman's bullet never misses."

"But then you're a man who can readily equal the three famous hunters whose names I spoke of before! Isn't it so, Uncle?"

The grand Gunstick-Uncle once more put himself into his declamatory posture and answered, gesticulating with both hands, "Hit was the vulture - the shot was sure great - I must do without fame ---"

"My dear fellow, quit composing!" the Englishman interrupted him irritably. "What are these rhymes and blather all about? I just wanted to know what kind of shots you are. Now, sit down again and let us continue negotiating. So then, if you come along with me, I shall pay you for the trip. Agreed, chappies?"

The two prairiemen looked at each other, then confirmed their assent with a nod.

"Well! And how much are you asking?"

"Lord Castlepool, your question puts us on the spot. We have never before been in the service of another man, and it appears to us that one cannot talk about a so-called payment to scouts, which we are supposed to be."

"Jolly good! You are proud fellows, which I appreciate. Then we can only talk about a fee to which I shall add a bonus if I am satisfied. I have come here for experience, to meet famous hunters, and thus make you the following offer: I shall pay each of you fifty dollars for every adventure we experience."

"Sir," Humpy laughed, "that will make us rich, because there is no want of adventures here. Experience them we will, yes, but whether we survive them is another matter. You won't find us wanting in this respect, but for a stranger it is rather more advisable to flee those adventures than to seek them out."

"Egad! I do want them! Understood? Then, too, I want to meet famous hunters. Earlier you cited three names I have heard much about already. Are these three men now in the west?"

"There you ask me too much. These famous people are everywhere and nowhere. One can meet them only by accident, and even if one should come across them, there's the question whether one of these kings-of-frontiersmen deigns to take note of you."

"They ought to and surely will take note of me! I am Lord Castlepool, and what I want I shall have! For each of these three hunters we meet, I will pay each of you one hundred dollars."

"By the devil! Do you have that much money on you, your lordship?"

"I have what I need for traveling. Money coming to you will only be paid in Frisco at my banker's. Are you satisfied with that?"

"Yes, gladly. Here are our hands on it. We can't do anything better than accept your offer."

Both held out their hands to shake with him. The lord then pulled his second satchel from the back around to the front, opened it, and retrieved a book.

"This is my notebook into which everything is entered," he explained. "In it I shall create accounts for each of you and put your head and name at its top."

"My head?" asked Humpy much surprised.

"Right-o, your head. Sit still for a moment, like now!"

He opened the book and took out a pencil. They observed him looking alternately at each of them, then down at the paper, all the while working the pencil. After a few minutes, he showed them his sketches; they recognized their well-drawn heads with their names inscribed beneath.

"On these pages I shall record what I owe you by-and-by." he explained. "Should I have an accident, take the book to Frisco and show it to my banker whose name I shall later give you. He will pay you the respective moneys at once and without any wretched hesitation."

"That's a very nice arrangement, your lordship," offered Humpy. "But we don't want anything to happen to ---behold, Uncle, look at our horses. They twitch their ears and flare their nostrils. Something foreign must be nearby. The Rolling Prairie is a dangerous place. If one climbs a hillock, one risks being seen, and if one stays low, one may not be aware of the approach of an enemy, which may result in a bad surprise. I ought to climb up after all."

"Jolly good! I'll come along," declared Lord Castlepool.

"I'd rather you stay down, sir. You could mess things up."

"Piffle! I do not bloody well mess things up."

The two advanced then from the valley toward the top of the hill. When they had almost reached it, they dropped down and crept carefully to the crest. The grass covered their bodies and when they needed to look around, they raised their heads only as much as necessary.

"Hmm, you don't do badly for a novice, sir," Humpy said in a voice of praise. "I didn't do much better myself. But do you see the man there on the second hillock, straight ahead of us?"

"Yes, isn't the chap an Indian, as it appears?"

"Yes, it's a redskin. "Had I --- ah, sir, could you go back down and get your telescope so I could identify the man's face."

The lord acceded to his request.

Like themselves, the Indian was lying in the grass on top of the hill, looking attentively to the east, although there was nothing to be seen. A few times he raised his torso to increase his field of view, but always dropped it again very quickly. If he expected anyone, then surely only a hostile person.

The lord returned with his scope, extended it, and offered it to the hunchback. Just when he had the Indian in sight, the latter looked back for a moment so that his face became totally recognizable. Immediately Humpy put down the scope, jumped up so that his entire figure could be seen by the redskin, put his hands to his mouth and shouted at the top of his lungs, "Menaka schecha, menaka schecha! - My brother may come to his white friend!"

The Indian turned quickly, recognized the hunchbacked figure, and at once slid down from the hillock's top to disappear in a lower area.

"Now, your lordship, you will soon have to pay the first fifty dollars," said Humpy to the Englishman, as he ducked down again.

"Will there be an adventure?"

"Very likely, for the chief was certainly looking out for enemies."

"Is he a chief?"

"Yes, a clever Osage chief."

"And you know the fellow?"

"We not only know him, but have smoked the peace pipe with him and having sworn brotherhood, we are obligated to stand by his side as he to ours."

"Well, then, I wish for him not only to expect one but many foes!"

"Don't paint the devil on the wall! Such wishes are dangerous since they can all too easily come true. Come along down! Uncle will be glad, but also surprised by the chief's showing up here."

"I say! What did you call the redskin?"

"In Osage, 'Menaka schecha' means the 'Good Sun' or the 'Great Sun'. He's a very brave and experienced warrior and not really an enemy of the white man, although the Osages are counted among the tribes of the untamed Sioux."

Arriving at the bottom, they found Uncle in his stiff, theatrical position. He had heard everything and assumed this posture in order to greet his friend with as much dignity as possible.

In a short while, the horses began to snort. Soon thereafter they saw the Indian coming closer. He was in the best years of his life and wore the customary Indian leather dress, although torn in several places, in others stained by fresh blood. He carried no weapons. A tattoo adorned each of his cheeks; the skin on both his wrists was bloody. He appeared to have been bound and then sprung his bonds. In any case, he apparently escaped and felt himself pursued.

Despite the danger the Indian was threatened with and which might be very close, he approached very slowly, and without at first taking note of the Englishman, offered his right hand to the two hunters. He spoke in the quietest voice and in very good English, "I immediately recognized the voice and figure of my brother and friend and am pleased to greet you."

"We are glad too, you may believe it," answered Humpy.

The tall Uncle held both hands above the redskin's head as if he wanted to bless him and exclaimed, "Be welcome on this earthly vale - many, many a thousand times - great chief, most treasured - sit down with your friends - and consume very quickly - the remainder of this venison leg!"

With his final words, he pointed to the grass where lay the remains of the venison leg that the lord had left: bones with a bit of stringy meat that had resisted his knife's attack.

"Be still, Uncle." Humpy-Bill demanded, "There's truly no time for your poetry. Don't you see the condition the chief is in?"

"Bound, yet flee - he did to his friends - and escape he did - to you and to me," recited the other unabashed by the scolding.

The hunchback turned away from the actor, pointed to the lord while saying to the Osage, "This paleface, Lord Castlepool, is a master shot and a new friend of ours. I recommend him to you and your tribe."

At this the red man finally offered his hand to the lord saying, "I am the friend of every good and honest white man. However thieves, murderers and corpse profaners ought to be eaten by the tomahawk!"

"Have you met such horrible people?" inquired Humpy.

"Yes. My brothers can get their rifles ready, for those who pursue me may arrive at any moment, although I have not spied them yet. They will be on horseback, while I had to walk; but Good Sun's feet are as fast as the elk no horse can catch. I led them in arcs and circles, often even paced backward with my heels ahead to delay them and lead them astray. They are after my life."

"Then they far better should quit! How many are there?"

"I do not know, for when they discovered my escape, I was already far away."

"Who is it? What kind of whites dare capture Good Sun and seek to kill him?"

"These are many, many people, several hundred bad men, called 'rovers' by the palefaces."

"Rovers? What are they doing here and what do they want in this remote area? What place are they at?"

"At the corner of the forest you call the Osage Nook, but which we have named the Murder's Corner, because our most famous chief, together with his bravest warriors, were insidiously killed there. Every year when the moon has been full for thirteen times, some delegates of our tribe visit this place to perform the Dance of the Dead at the graves of our fallen heroes. This is why I, this year, together with twelve of our warriors, left our hunting grounds to go to the Osage Nook. We arrived there yesterday, and scouted the area to make sure no unfriendly people were present. Thus we felt secure and set up camp by the graves.

"Yesterday, too, we hunted for meat, and today we performed the celebration. I had been careful to post two guards. Nevertheless the white men succeeded creeping close to us unnoticed. They had followed the tracks we made while hunting and those of the horses' hooves as well.

"While we were dancing, they attacked us so suddenly that we had little chance to resist. They were several hundred strong. We killed some of them but they shot eight of us. I was overpowered together with the remaining four and all of us were bound. A court was convened and we were told that we were to be put to the stake, to be burned in fire.

"They camped by the graves and separated me from my warriors so that I could not speak with them. I was tied to a tree and they posted a paleface guard at my side, but the thongs holding me were too weak; I tore them. However, as you can see, they cut deeply into my flesh. But once I was free, I used the moment the guard stepped aside to slip away."

"And your four companions?" asked Bill.

"They are still there, I believe. Do you think I should have looked for them?"

"No, you would have only ended up being captured again."

"My brother speaks the truth. I could not have saved them, but would have perished with them. I decided to hurry to Butler's farm to get help there. The owner is my friend."

Humpy-Bill shook his head and protested, "Nearly impossible! From the Osage Nook to Butler's farm is a good six hours' ride, and with a bad horse it would take even longer. How could you have returned before evening when your comrades were to die?"

"Oh, Good Sun's feet are as fast as those of a horse," the chief asserted. My escape will cause them to delay the execution and to try to capture me again. Most likely help would arrive in time."

"Your assumption may be correct or it may not be. It's well that you came across us, for now it will not be necessary to seek Butler's farm; we shall accompany you to free your companions."

"Is my white brother truly going to do this?" the Indian asked in a joyous tone.

"Of course! What else? The Osages are our friends, while the rovers are the enemies of every honest man."

"But they are so many, so overwhelmingly many, and we here have all together only eight arms and hands!"

"Pshaw, you know me! Do you think I intend to assault them openly in their midst? But our clever heads can surreptitiously creep up on a horde of rovers and release their captives. What do you say, old Uncle?"

The stiff-necked fellow opened both arms, closed his eyes happily and exclaimed, "With pleasure I shall ride at once - where these white rascals camp - free with honor and without fear - all our red brothers from them there!"

"Good! And you, your lordship?"

The Englishman had retrieved his notebook to enter the chief's name. He now returned it to his satchel and answered, "Good show! I shall ride along. It is obviously an adventure!"

"But a very dangerous one, sir!"

"It is, rather! I will pay ten dollars more, that is to say, sixty. But if we are to ride, we will need to find a horse for Good Sun!"

"Hmm, yes!" the hunchback answered, glancing at him in surprise. "But from where would you get one, eh?"

"From his pursuers, obviously, who are probably close behind him."

"Very true, very true! You're quite a bright chap, sir, which makes me think that we'll all work pretty well together. It would also be desirable for our red friend to have a weapon."

"I shall give him one of my rifles. Here it is; I shall explain its use. And now let us not lose any more time. I propose to place ourselves in such a fashion that those blighters, when they arrive, will be surrounded on all sides."

The expression of surprise on the little one's face became even more intense. He measured the Englishman with an appraising look and replied, "You speak like an old, experienced hand, sir! How do you think we're going to do that?"

"Dear boy! Very easily. One of us stays on the hill, where the two of us just came from. He will spot the scoundrels just as you two earlier did me. The other three will go around in an arc so that their tracks are not visible, then climb up the three neighboring hillocks. When the blighters arrive, they will find themselves trapped between four occupied hills. We'll have them caught, since we have cover up there and can blow them away at will, while they will see only the smoke of our shots."

"You talk like you know it well, Lord Castlepool! Tell us honestly, are you truly on the prairie for the first time?"

"Yes, dash it! But I have been to other places where one has to be no less cautious than here. We talked about this already, dear boy."

"Well! I see that we won't have much in the way of trouble with you. I like that. I admit that I was going to offer the very same idea. Are you agreed, old Uncle?"

The stiff one made a theatrical arm movement, answering, "Yes, sir, ambushed they will be - and all together shot dead by me!"

"All right. Then I'll stay here to talk to them when they arrive. The lord goes to the right; you, Uncle, to the left, and the chief posts himself on the hillock ahead. In this way, we get them between us, and whether we kill them or not will depend entirely on how they conduct themselves."

"Egad! Don't kill them!" the lord cried out in a shocked tone.

"Quite right, sir! Normally I, too, would be against it. But, actually, these ruffians do not deserve any leniency, and if we spare them, what are we going to do with them? We cannot drag them along. Impossible! And if we set them free, they'll give us away. I'll talk with them in such a loud voice that you'll understand every word; then you'll know what to do. If I should down one, it will be a sure signal for you to shoot the others. None is to escape. Remember, they killed eight Osages without provocation! Gentlemen, I think we must not hesitate any longer."

He climbed the next hillock and lay prone in the grass where he, together with the Englishman, had previously observed the Indian. The others disappeared to the three sides along the depressions. The lord had taken his scope along. The horses remained where they stood.

A quarter of an hour passed uneventfully. The guard from whom the Good Sun had escaped must have been very careless and discovered the escape rather late. Then from the hillock that was the Englishman's post came the shout, "I say, watch out, they're coming!"

"Quiet!" Humpy warned him in a somewhat lower voice.

"Don't talk rot! They cannot hear me, they are still a mile off."

"Where?"

"Straight to the east. I saw two chaps through the scope, standing on a hill, looking in our direction to see if the chief might be visible. The buggers must have kept their horses down below."

"Be twice as careful to save the horses; we may need them all!"

Some time passed. Then came the thud of horses' hoofbeats. In the depression ahead of Humpy, two men riding side by side appeared. They were well-armed and mounted and kept their eyes closely on the chief's tracks. Right behind them came two more riders, then another, a total of five pursuers. When they had reached the middle of the valley and were between the four hidden companions, Bill shouted out, "Stop, gentlemen! Not a step farther or you'll hear my rifle talk!"

The five rovers halted in surprise, looked up and saw no one, since the hunchback lay deeply buried in the grass. But they obeyed his command, the foremost answering, "By the devil! What secretive highwayman is out there? Show yourself and tell us what right you have to stop us!"

"The right of every hunter who comes across strangers."

"We too are hunters. If you're an honest fellow, show yourself!"

The five rovers had taken hold of their rifles and did not seem at all peaceful. Nevertheless, the little one answered, "I'm an honest man and can surely show myself. Here I am!"

He jumped up so that his entire figure could be seen, yet kept his eyes so focused on them that not the least of their movements escaped him.

"Zounds!" one of them called. "If I'm not mistaken, that's Humpy-Bill!"

"That's what I'm called."

"Then Gunstick-Uncle must be close by, for those two never separate!"

"Do you know us then?"

"I'm sure of it. I must have had a word or two with you earlier on!"

"But I don't know you!"

"Possibly, since you spoke to me only from afar. Boys, this character is in our way. I believe he may even have joined up with the redskin. Let's get him off his perch!"

He aimed at the little one and fired. Bill dropped lightning-fast into the grass as if hit by the bullet.

"Great shot. That was well-aimed!" one of the others shouted. "Now there's only Gun ---"

He was unable to complete his sentence. Bill had dropped so quickly that the bullet whizzed over his head. Now his own rifle barrels quickly flashed twice, and not a second later cracked the rifles of the other three. Each mortally wounded, the five rovers fell from their horses as the four victors descended from the hillocks into the valley to prevent the five horses from fleeing. Then they examined the rovers.

"Not badly done," offered Bill. "Not a single bad shot. They died on the spot."

The Osage chief looked at the two men whose foreheads he had aimed at. He saw the two small bullet holes right above the bridge of their noses and turned to the lord. "My brother's rifle has a very small caliber but is a very good weapon one can rely on."

99

"I would bloody well think so," the Englishman asserted. "I ordered both rifles especially for the prairies."

"Will my brother sell this one to me? I will give you one hundred beaver pelts for it."

"Sorry, old chap, but it is not for sale."

"Then I offer you one hundred fifty!"

"Not then either!"

"Not even for two hundred?"

"No, even if these beaver pelts were ten times the size of our Indian elephants."

"Then I offer you the highest price possible. I will trade this rifle for the best riding horse of the Osages!"

From his face, one could see that Good Sun believed he had made the best offer he possibly could, but the lord shook his head and answered, "Lord Castlepool never trades or sells. What am I to do with a horse, since mine is at least as good as the one you offer me, laddie."

"No horse of the prairie excels mine. But since I cannot force my white brother to sell me his rifle, I shall return it herewith. Those dead have more weapons on them than I need."

He returned the rifle, but the expression on his face expressed his immense regret. The dead were relieved of all their useable possessions. As he went through their pockets, Bill said in a puzzled tone, "That fellow knew me. I, though, cannot recall ever having seen him. It may be! From his words, I must assume that I had nothing good to expect, neither from him nor the others. That's why we shouldn't grieve for the death of these people. Who knows how many infamies we prevented with our bullets. Now the chief has a horse and four more are left, just sufficient for the Osages we intend to free."

"Are we heading for those rotters right away then?" asked the Englishman.

"Certainly. I know this area. We won't arrive at the Osage Nook before evening, since we cannot take the straight route, but must approach in an arc that puts the forest behind them."

"And these beastly bodies?"

"We'll just leave them. Or would you like to build a mausoleum for these scoundrels? May they be buried in the bellies of vultures and coyotes; they don't deserve more!"

This may have been tough, un-Christian language, but the Wild West had its own kind of good sense. In a land where death and ruin threaten all around, human beings are forced, first and foremost, to take care of themselves, and to avoid everything endangering their personal safety. Had the four men decided to bury the bodies and to say a prayer over their graves, this would have been a loss of time for which the captured Osages might have easily paid with their lives.

The four, therefore, strung the free horses together, mounted their own, and rode off, first straight north only later to turn east.

Good Sun took the lead, since he knew the rovers' gathering place. The entire afternoon they spent crossing the Rolling Prairie. No tracks were sighted, nor any human. When the sun settled toward the horizon, they could make out a dark strip of forest in the distance, whereupon the Osage explained, "This is the far side of the forest. The nearer side turns inward and forms the corner or angle we call the 'Murder's Corner', where the graves of our slain warriors lie."

"How far might it be to reach the Corner, crossing the forest?" Lord Castlepool inquired.

"Once we have entered the forest, it is but a quarter hour to reach the rovers' camp," the red man explained.

At that Bill halted his horse, dismounted and without speaking a word, sat down in the grass. Uncle and the Indian followed his example as if they could read his mind. Consequently, the Englishman dismounted, too, but inquired, "I think we should not be losing any time. How can we free the Osages if we sit down here putting our hands in our bloody laps?"

"That's the wrong question, sir," Humpy responded. "Rather ask, 'How can we liberate the Osages if we've been killed?' "

"I say! Killed? Why?"

"Do you think the rovers stay quietly in camp?"

"Hardly, that's pure applesauce!"

"Correct! They must eat and will therefore go hunting. They'll rove the forest. It's where we intend to enter, only as little as a quarter hour's walk to their camp, and for certain, it can be expected that people will be right there to notice our approach. We must wait here until dark; then those rogues will all have retreated to their camp and we can approach the forest without being seen. Do you follow me?"

"Quite!" said the lord, looking rather abashed, and sitting down once more. "Didn't think I could still be so bloody naive!"

"Yes, you would have ridden right into the arms of those characters and I would have had to carry your notebook to Frisco without receiving a single dollar."

"Received nothing? Why?"

"Because we haven't yet completed our adventure."

"Dashed nonsense! We have done that! It's over and entered. Meeting the chief and shooting the five rovers has been a complete adventure, surely worth fifty dollars. It's noted in the book already. Liberating the Osages is another adventure."

"Also at fifty dollars?"

"Rather!" the lord nodded.

"Well, then keep noting, sir," Bill laughed. "If you divide each event into that many sub-adventures, we'll have ourselves such a payoff in Frisco that you won't know from where to take it all!"

The lord smiled quietly and answered, "It will be sufficient, old stick. I can pay you without having to sell Castle Castlepool. Wish to bet? I put up ten dollars. Who else?"

"Not me, sir. If I wanted to bet with you at every occasion, I'd lose everything I'm earning from you, and that, you may be sure, is something that the nephew of my uncle would not take kindly to."

The sun disappeared and the shadows of dusk brushed across the prairie depressions, rose higher and higher, flooded the hills and finally enveloped the entire earth in their shadowy enclosure. The sky, too, was dark and starless.

The four men mounted their horses and rode close, but not quite up to the forest's edge. Caution demanded they leave the horses in the open. Every frontiersman carries with him a wooden stake to secure his horse to the ground by the reins. Having thus staked their horses, the men advanced toward the forest in single file.

Good Sun was once more in the lead. His feet touched the ground so lightly that no ear could catch a sound. The lord, second in line, made every effort to be as inaudible. All around, nothing was heard but the wind moving through the crowns of the trees.

Then the Osage gripped Lord Castlepool's right hand and whispered to him, "My white brother should give his other hand to the next man in order that the three palefaces form a queue. I will lead so that none will bump into a tree."

Feeling his way forward by his one outstretched hand, he pulled the whites along, each behind the other. Time extended mightily for the lord, since minutes seem to stretch into hours in such situations. Finally the chief stopped and whispered, "My brothers may listen. I have heard the rovers' voices."

They all listened and found that the redskin had not been mistaken. One could hear voices, but so far distant that the words could not be understood. A few steps farther on, they could make out a slight glow, enabling them to differentiate the tree trunks.

"My brothers shall wait here for my return," said the Osage.

Barely said, Good Sun had already disappeared. A bit more than half an hour passed before he returned. They neither saw nor heard his arrival. He suddenly surfaced in front of them, as if he had risen out of the earth.

"Well, then?" asked Bill. "What can you tell us?"

"That even more rovers have arrived, many more."

"Thunder and lightning! Do these fellows intend to hold a mass meeting here? Then woe to the farmers and other people living in this area. Did you hear what they were talking about?"

"Several fires were burning; the entire place was very brightly illuminated by them. The rovers had formed a circle within which a paleface with red hair was giving a long and very loud speech."

"What did he talk about? Did you understand him?"

"I did understand him very well, since he spoke so vociferously. But my attention was turned toward discovering the whereabouts of my red brothers, so I remember very little of what he talked about."

"Then, the little? What is it?"

"He said that wealth was taken from the poor and one should therefore take everything from the rich. He claimed that the government should not levy taxes on its citizens and, for this reason, all moneys in its coffers ought to be recovered too. He spoke of all rovers being brothers who would become rich very quickly if they followed his proposals."

"Go on!" cried Humpy-Bill excitedly. "What else?"

"I did not pay further attention to his words. He kept talking about the money in the railroad pay office, that they ought to loot. But then I no longer listened to him because I had found the place where my red brothers are being held."

"Where's that?"

"Close to a small unattended fir. There they were standing tied to trees, and with each of them sat a rover guarding him."

"Then it's not easy to steal up on them?"

"It is possible. I could have cut them free; but it was better not to do so until I could fetch my white brothers to help me. Now it will go much more quickly. However, I was able to sidle up to one of my red brothers and whisper to him that they were going to be rescued."

"That's very good, for now they're forewarned and won't give us away by any movement of joy or surprise when we approach them. The rovers are no frontiersmen. It's tremendously stupid not to have taken the captives into their midst. In that case, we couldn't have freed them by cunning, but would have needed to leap into the circle to cut the Osages free while the rovers were still paralyzed from shock, even though we are only four men. Guide us to the place where your people are!"

With Good Sun leading the way, the four slipped from tree to tree making every effort to stay in the shadows. In this way, they quickly arrived at the rovers' camp where they could count eight fires. The smallest burned at the very corner, close to the trees where the chief now led them. At one point, he halted to whisper to them, "Now several palefaces are sitting by the fire. Earlier no one sat there. The man with the red hair is one of them. These people seem to be the leaders, the chiefs. Do you see my Osage brothers a few paces away in the trees?"

"Yes," Humpy responded. "Clearly the speech the red-haired one was giving is finished and the leaders are now sitting isolated from the others, probably to hold counsel. It may be very important to learn what they're planning, So many rovers didn't assemble for something small. Fortunately, there are bushes near the trees. I'm going to crawl over there and listen to what they're talking about."

"My brother may rather not do this," warned the chief.

"Why? Do you think I might get caught?"

"No. I know of my brother's ability to act covertly, but I fear he could nevertheless be seen."

"Seen, but not caught!"

"Yes, my brother has fleet feet and could get away, but then it would be impossible to free my Osage brothers."

"Not so. In an eye blink, we could cut down their guards and free the Osages; then fly like the wind to our horses. I should like to see the rover who could prevent this! So, now I'm going to creep over there. If I'm noticed, you jump for the prisoners. Nothing will happen to us. Take my rifle, Uncle."

So as not to be hindered by his firearm, he handed it to his comrade, then dropped to the ground and crawled toward the fire. His task turned out to be much easier than he thought. The rovers spoke so loudly that he stopped halfway there, yet could understand every word.

If the chief had been of the opinion that the four men sitting by the fire were the ranking rovers and their leaders, he had not erred. One of them, the redhead, was Colonel Brinkley, who had arrived with his few escaped gang members toward evening. He was just now talking and Humpy-Bill could hear him say, "... so I promise you great success, because the main pay office is right there. Are you agreed?"

"Yes, yes, yes," the other three promptly answered.

"And how about Butler's farm? Shall we take it too? Or shall I do it myself and hire three score of the guys from the gathering?"

"Of course we'll come along," one of them declared. "I don't see why we should let all that money go into your pockets! It's just a question, though, whether the cash has already arrived there."

"Not yet. The rafters didn't have horses at first, while I 'found' a few good ones the next morning. They cannot have arrived at the farm yet. But Butler is rich in any case. We can attack the farm, rob it, then wait in hiding for the arrival of the rafters and the rascals leading them."

"Do you know for sure they will go there?"

"I know it very well indeed. This Old Firehand has to go there because of an engineer who must have arrived already."

"What engineer? What's the matter with him?"

"Nothing, really. That's a story, which means nothing to you. Maybe I'll tell you about it some time. And maybe I'll engage you in yet another coup where a lot of money is to be had."

"You speak in riddles! Honestly, I'd rather have nothing to do with this Old Firehand. I've heard much about him."

"Are you afraid?" sneered the colonel.

"Not afraid, but I have a very sound dislike for this kind of people."

"Nonsense! What could he do to us? Think! We have four hundred men who together could tackle the devil!"

"Are they all coming to Butler's farm?"

"Obviously! It's in our direction anyway. Would we rather return here?"

"No, that's right. And when do we leave?"

"Tomorrow afternoon so that we reach the farm by evening. It's large and will make a nice fire where we can prepare many a good roast." Delighted with his own plan, Brinkley laughed uproariously.

Humpy-Bill had heard enough. He crept back to his companions and told them it was time to free the Osages. His idea was for each of them to come up behind one of the captives, but Good Sun interrupted him, saying, "I only brought my white brothers for quick assistance should I not succeed in freeing my Osage brothers by myself. What is to be done now is not a matter for palefaces, but for red men. I shall go alone and you may only come to my aid should what I am about to do be discovered."

Like a snake, he crawled away on the ground.

"What's the bloke planning?" the Englishman asked softly.

"A masterpiece," Bill replied. "Be so kind as to stay put and watch closely where the captives are standing. If things go wrong, we'll rush over there to help. We only need to cut their bonds and dash to our horses."

The lord and the others followed Bill's advice. The fire by which the four rovers were sitting was perhaps ten paces distant from the edge of the woods. Standing erect, their captives had been tied to trees both hand and foot. Beside each captive sat an armed guard. The Englishman strained his eyes to see Good Sun, but in vain. He only saw one of the guards who had been sitting up suddenly lie down, but so quickly it appeared he had fallen over. The other three guards made identical moves, one after the other, so strangely that their heads came to rest in the shadows of the adjacent trees. With all that happening, not a sound, not the softest noise was to be heard.

A few moments later, the lord suddenly saw the chief reappear, lying prone between him and Bill.

"Finished?" the latter asked.

"Yes," the red man replied.

"Good show!" whispered the lord. "But your Osages are still tied up!"

"No, they just remain standing until I have spoken with you. My knife struck the guards directly into their hearts, then I took their scalps. I will now return and go with my brothers to the horse compound where there are also our own. Since everything went so well, we will not leave without getting our horses, too."

"Why head back into danger once again?" warned Bill.

"My white brother is mistaken. There is no danger any longer. As soon as you see the Osages disappear from the trees, you can leave too. You will soon hear the hoof-pounding of the horses and the screams of the rovers who are guarding them. You will find us at the place where we dismounted earlier. Howgh!"

With these last confirming words, Good Sun wanted to indicate that any objection would be useless; then he suddenly vanished once more. Lord Castlepool stared at the captives, who leaned stiffly against their trees, then were suddenly gone as if the earth had swallowed them.

"Oh, my sainted aunt," he whispered to Humpy. "Just like I've read in American novels!"

"Hmm!" the little one answered. "You'll experience many a novel yet with us. Reading about it, though, is of course easier than participating in it."

"Shall we dash off now?"

"Not yet. I want to see the look on these fellows' faces when they find their captives gone. Wait a few moments yet."

Only a short time passed when from beyond the camp came a shrill, frightened shout followed by a second. Then several more shrill screams could be heard, seemingly coming from Indian throats --- then a snorting and pounding, a neighing and thunder of hooves from which the earth seemed to shake.

The rovers jumped up. Everyone shouted, yelled and demanded to know what was happening. Only the red-haired colonel's voice could be heard over the din, "The Osages are gone! By the devil, who has ---"

Shocked, he stopped in mid-sentence. As he spoke, he ran over to the guards, grabbed the closest one and started to lift him up. He saw the glazed-over eyes and the hairless, bloody skull. He pulled the second, third and fourth into the fire's light and shouted in horror, "Dead! Scalped! All four! And the redskins are gone! How the devil --- "

"Indians, Indians!" someone shouted at that very moment from the direction where the horses were kept.

"Take your rifles! To the horses!" the red colonel roared. "We've been attacked. They're trying to steal our horses!"

There arose a scene of indescribable confusion. Everyone ran hither and yon, but no enemy was to be seen. After a period of time when some quiet returned, it was established that only the captured Indian horses were missing. Only then, once disaster had struck, were guards posted and the camp's environs searched, but without result. The rovers could only conclude that other Osages must have been in the forest and had liberated their comrades. In doing so, they had knifed the guards from behind, scalped them, then taken the horses. Inconceivable though to the rovers was that the murder of the guards had been achieved without a sound. They would have been even more surprised had they known that only a single man had accomplished this "Indian masterpiece."

When the leaders gathered once more by the fire, the colonel said, "These events are not a real disaster for us, but they force us to change our plans for tomorrow. We must set out earlier."

"Why?" came the question.

"Because the Osages have heard everything we said. It's fortunate that they don't know anything about our plans for the Eagle Tail, since we didn't speak of that, only earlier at the big fire over there. But our intentions for Butler's farm they know about."

"And you think they'll pass on what they've learned?"

"Doubtlessly!"

"Could these wild scoundrels be in cahoots with Butler?"

"Friends of his or not, they'll report it just to get even and prepare a warm reception for us."

"That's of course to be expected and it makes it highly advisable for us to break camp and get moving." The rover shook his head agitatedly. "I'd just like to know where the five chaps are we sent after the escaped chief?"

"I don't understand that either," Brinkley said pensively. "If he'd taken cover in the woods, he would have been difficult or impossible to find, but his tracks led straight into the open prairie, and he had no horse. That should have made him easy to catch!"

"Right! But our men may have been overtaken by nightfall on their return and may have gotten lost. Or they may have camped so as not to become lost, and will return tomorrow morning. In any case, we're sure to come across their tracks since they went in the exact direction we're taking tomorrow."

But here the rover was mistaken. The sky, or actually, dark clouds took care of obliterating the tracks, since later a light but persistent rain of several hours wiped out all hoof and footprints.

6. A Hard Ride in the Dark

When the screams at the horse corral had arisen, it was high time for Bill, Uncle and the Englishman to make it to safety. As quickly as the darkness permitted, they hurried through the forest to their mounts. That they didn't bypass them was due only to the two hunters' superior sense of orientation. Lord Castlepool would not have found his way as readily, since by night hillocks and depressions of the Rolling Prairie look even more alike than by day. The three unhitched their horses, mounted up and led the extra horses by their reins.

Barely on their way, they heard the Indians coming. Good Sun had found the place as readily as if it had been daylight.

"The rovers were blind and deaf," he remarked. "We could not kill more of them, for if we wanted to get our horses, we could not remain there much longer. But many of them shall yet enter the eternal hunting grounds to serve the spirits of the Osages.

"You want to take revenge?" asked Bill.

"Why does my white brother ask such things? Have not eight Osages been slain whose deaths must be avenged? Were not the remaining four to be put to the stake and murdered? We shall ride to the wigwams of the Osages to bring many warriors. Then we will follow the tracks of these palefaces to kill as many as Manitou has given us hands."

"Where are the herds of the Osages grazing now?

"To the west from here."

"Then you would have to pass by Butler's farm?"

"Yes."

"And from there how far is your ride to reach your people?"

"The first Osage herds can be found in half a day if one has a good horse and rides like the wind."

"That's very good. We must hurry to save Butler's farm."

"What is my brother saying? Butler is the friend and protector of the Osages. Is he threatened?"

"Yes." replied Bill. But let's not talk about it here and now. We must get away from the rovers' proximity. They plan to attack the farm tomorrow and we must get there to warn Mr. and Mrs. Butler."

"Uff! I shall come to help you! My red brothers meanwhile can follow with the extra horses so that we four can make the best speed to the farm."

Obeying the chief's command, the Osage braves gathered the reins of the captured horses and moved out at a fast trot. For their part, Good Sun and the whites quickly passed them at a dead gallop, heading into the low hills, not following the tracks made at their approach, for that would have led them to the north. Instead they took the tracks of the chief and his pursuers from that afternoon. These led straight as an arrow in the direction of Butler's farm.

At a full gallop! In the darkness! Even by daylight only an experienced frontiersman is able to find his way across the Rolling Prairie without getting lost; by night it bordered on a miracle. When the Englishman riding alongside Bill remarked on this, the latter replied, "Yes sir, while I've noticed that you do have brains, you're going to see, hear and experience quite a few things yet that you would have thought impossible before."

"Then you too would not get lost here, old bean?"

"Me? Well, to be honest, I must tell you that I'd never have thought of racing like this between these hillocks. I would ride real slow and check the bend of each valley very carefully. Nevertheless, I would still probably arrive at a very different place than the one I had intended."

"Then this could happen as well to the chief."

"No. A redskin like him practically smells the way and can sense the direction. The main thing is that he has his own horse again. This animal will surely not diverge, even by a step, from the tracks his master has made today, you can rest assured. The sky is as black as a sack of soot, and of the ground I can't see even a fingernail's full. Nevertheless, we gallop along as if it were a clear day and on an even road. I bet we'll halt our horses directly in front of the gates of Butler's farm before six hours have passed."

"Oh, I say! What? Lord Castlepool questioned cheerfully. You'd like to bet? Wonderful! So you claim it will be six hours? I assert the opposite and stake five dollars, even ten. Or do you want to bet any higher? I'm for it!"

"Thanks, your lordship! Mentioning betting was just an expression. I repeat: I never bet. Keep your money! You'll need it for something else. Remember what you have to pay me and Uncle already for today!"

"One hundred dollars. Fifty for the killed rovers and fifty for the freed Osages."

"And soon it will be even more."

"Very true, since the attack on the farm, which we're going to repulse, is another adventure, for which I will happily pay fifty dollars."

"Whether we'll succeed in repelling the attack is uncertain. And even if we don't win, it will still be an adventure, which will pay us fifty dollars, provided we stay alive. But how was it, actually, about Old Shatterhand, Winnetou and Old Firehand? How much did you say you would pay if you should get to see one of these three men?"

"A hundred dollars, if that's all right."

"Very much so, because it's very likely that we'll meet Old Firehand tomorrow or the day after."

"Jolly good! Truly?"

"Yes. He also is expected to arrive at Butler's farm."

Good Sun, riding ahead, had overheard this conversation. He turned around in the saddle without slowing his horse's pace and asked, "Old Firehand, this famous paleface will come?"

"Yes. The red-haired colonel said so."

"The man who gave the long speech? How does he know? Has he seen the great hunter, even talked to him?"

Maintaining his position behind the chief, Bill recounted what he had overheard.

"Uff! the Osage exclaimed. "Then the farm is saved, for the brain of this paleface is worth more than the weapons of a thousand rovers. I will be very glad to see him again!"

"Do you know him?"

"All chiefs in the west have seen him and smoked the calumet with him. Why should I alone not know him? Ah, do you feel it? It is beginning to rain. This is good; the rain will give the trampled grass the strength to rise again. Tomorrow morning the rovers will be unable to find our tracks."

They now ceased their conversation. The speed of the ride and the attention required to maintain it safely made talk difficult. Sometimes rain itself makes people less talkative.

As it was, the path they followed was not difficult. No rocks, no ditches, no other obstacles slowed their advance, and the depressions were so wide that several horses could run comfortably side by side. The ground beneath their feet was soft grassland. Only the darkness had to be dealt with.

From time to time, the horsemen allowed their animals to walk, so as not to tire them too much, then they resumed trotting, even galloping. After a few hours had passed, Bill's earlier confidence appeared to waver a bit and he asked the chief, "Is my brother convinced we're heading in the right direction?"

"My white brother need not worry," Good Sun responded. "We have made haste and will soon arrive at the place where I met you and Uncle today."

Was it from practice or born of instinct that this Indian could speak so confidently? Bill couldn't believe they had covered such a significant distance already. However, with the rain came a strong wind from behind which made the horses run much more easily.

Shortly after Bill's inquiry, the chief's horse suddenly slowed from its gallop into a light trot, then halted without having been reined in by its rider. The animal vented a slight snort.

"Uff!" the red man grunted in a low tone. "People must be ahead of us. Listen, my brothers, do not move but inhale sharply through your noses."

The group had stopped and could hear Good Sun sniffing the air for any revealing odor.

"A fire!" he whispered.

"There's nothing visible!" Bill declared.

"But I smell smoke which seems to come from around that hillock. My brother could perhaps dismount and climb the hill with me to find out what is hidden behind."

The two left their horses with the others and approached the hillock side-by-side. But not ten paces farther along two hands abruptly seized the Indian by the throat. He was jerked to the ground flailing with arms and legs and unable to utter a sound. Simultaneously, another pair of hands gripped the hunchback's throat, forcing him too to the ground.

"You got him good?" asked the one who had taken the Indian, speaking German in a very low voice.

"Yes, I have him in such a grip that he can't even speak," was the equally muted response.

"Then quickly, behind the hill! We must learn whom we've encountered here. Or will your man be too heavy to carry?"

"Not at all! The fellow weighs less than a fly that hasn't eaten nor drunk for three weeks. My God, he seems to have a hump on his back, what's called a lopsided backbone! It wouldn't be ---"

"What?"

" --- my good friend, Humpy-Bill?"

"We'll decide that when we get back to the fire. At the moment, we need to make sure that no one will follow us. I figure the group must have at least a dozen men who won't stir for a while, since they're waiting for the return of these two."

All this had happened so lightning-fast and noiselessly that the companions of the two captured men had no inkling of it, despite their close proximity. Old Firehand, since it was so easy for him, carried his captive in his arms, while Droll pulled his along on the grass around the hillock. Beyond rested the tired horses, where a small fire burned. By the firelight, more than twenty people lay ready with aimed rifles to greet with hot lead any possible enemy.

When the two men brought their captives to the fireside, words of wonder escaped from many of them.

"By gosh!" voiced Old Firehand. "This is Menaka schecha, the Osage chief. We have nothing to fear from him."

"Hell's bells!" Droll joined in. "It is truly Bill, Humpy-Bill! Chap, friend, beloved human child, couldn't you have told me before I went for your throat? Now you lie there and can neither pant nor talk! Get up, brother-mine, and fall into my arms! Oh, curse it, you don't understand German. For Droll, in his upset state, had spoken in his mother tongue. "Don't you die on me! Jump up, then, treasure of my heart! I really didn't want to throttle you, if it's necessary!"

The good Altenburger experienced a greater fear at this very moment than did the one he had throttled who lay there with his eyes closed, gasping urgently for breath. Then Bill finally opened his eyes, threw a long, ever more aware look at Droll, who was bent over him, and asked in a hoarse voice, "Is it possible? Aunt Droll!"

"Thank God I didn't kill you!" the other exulted, now in English. "Of course it's me. Why didn't you tell me that it was you?"

"Could I have spoken? I was grabbed so fast and without warning that I --- heavens, it's Old Firehand!"

Seeing the hunter standing there returned Bill's ability to function. But the pressure of Old Firehand's hands had been much stronger than that of Aunt Droll. As a result, Good Sun still lay unmoving on the ground with his eyes closed.

"Is he dead?" asked Bill nervously.

"No," the giant answered, offering the little one his hand. "He's only unconscious and will soon come to. Welcome, Bill! This is a pleasant surprise. How come you have the chief of the Osages along?"

"I've known him for many years."

"So. Who's with you then? Presumably Indians from the chief's tribe?"

"Yes, four of them. They've been following us and probably have caught up by now."

"Only four? Then you have extra horses with you?"

"That's right. There's also Gunstick-Uncle, whom you probably know, and an English lord."

"A lord? Aristocratic company then. Have these people come over. They've nothing to fear from us or we from them."

Bill ran off. When he had covered half the distance, he shouted, "Uncle, come on over! We've found friends. Old Firehand and Aunt Droll are here."

Both Uncle and the Englishman responded to this invitation, the Osages who had indeed arrived following closely behind. The rafters who where still lying at the ready in the grass rose to welcome the arrivals. What a surprise it was for the newcomers to find the chief unconscious and to learn what had happened. Having dismounted, the Osages stood at a distance and looked at the famous hunter respectfully. The lord's eyes were wide open as he slowly approached the giant. He was sporting such a dazzled expression that one could die laughing just to see it. Old Firehand noticed, it as well as the lord's one-sided, thickly swollen nose. He offered his hand and said, "Welcome, your lordship! You must have traveled in Turkey, in India, maybe even in Africa?"

"I say! How do you know that?" asked the Englishman, astonished.

"I only presume it because you still carry the remains of the 'bouton d'Alep', the Aleppo boil on your nose. Whoever has journeyed that far will eventually find his way around here too, although ---"

He stopped with a smile, seeing the Englishman's equipment, particularly a roasting device attached to the backpack. At this moment Good Sun came to. To open his eyes, take a deep breath, leap up and draw his knife was the work of an instant. But when his eyes fell on the hunter, he lowered his blade and exclaimed, "Old Firehand! Was it you who took me?"

"Yes. It was so dark that I couldn't recognize my red brother."

"Then I am glad. To have been defeated by Old Firehand is no disgrace. Had it been someone else, the shame would have rested on my head until I had killed him. My white brother is on the way to Butler's farm?"

"Yes. How did you know?"

"Palefaces said so."

"I want to go to this farm later. Right now my destination is the Osage Nook."

"What is my famous brother looking for there?"

"A white renegade by the name of Colonel Brinkley and his associates, all villains."

"Then my brother can confidently ride with us to the farm. The red-haired one will arrive there tomorrow to attack it."

"How did you find that out?"

"He said so himself. Bill overheard it. The rovers had attacked me and my Osages yesterday, killed eight, and captured me with the rest of my warriors. But I escaped and came across Bill and Uncle who, together with the Englishman, helped free my brothers."

"You were pursued here by five rovers?"

"Yes."

"Bill and Uncle camped here?"

"That is so."

"And the Englishman had met these two just before?"

"You describe it perfectly, but how could you know about it?"

"We rode up to Black Bear River and left it early this morning to get to the Osage Nook. Here we found the bodies of five rovers and ---"

"Sir," Humpy-Bill interrupted, "tell us how you discerned that the men were rovers? No one could have told you."

"This piece of paper told me," he answered. "If you searched these characters, you left this paper in the pocket of one of them."

He pulled out a piece of newspaper, held it toward the firelight and read, "Something either forgotten or overlooked and impossible to comprehend has now been brought to light by the Bureau of Lands Commissioner of the United States. This official directed the attention of the government to the surprising fact that there is within the United States a piece of land, larger than several states, which is distinguished by not being governed and administrated at all. This peculiar piece of land is a rectangle of 40 miles width and 150 miles length and includes almost 4 million acres of land. It is located between the Indian territory and New Mexico, north of Texas and to the south of Kansas and Colorado. As it turned out, this land was overlooked during the public survey, its cause being a mistake in the definition of the borders of the neighboring territories. It was, therefore, not assigned to any state or territory; it is without government of any kind and also not subject to the jurisdiction of any court of justice. Law, order and taxes are unknown there. The commissioner's report describes this land as one of the most beautiful and fertile areas of the entire west, very well suited for ranching and agriculture. However, the few thousand free Americans living there are not peaceful farmers and ranchers, but gangs of riffraff, rabble, horse thieves, desperadoes and escaped criminals, who coming from all directions have found refuge there. They are the terror of the neighboring territories, where ranchers especially suffer much from the robberies of these people. These troubled neighbors urgently demand to see an end put to this robber estate and its lawless practices, that is by the establishment of a functioning government authority."

The redskins who had heard these words remained indifferent; the whites, though, looked at each other in surprise.

"Egad! Is that true? Is it possible?" asked the lord.

"I think it's true," answered Old Firehand. "Whether this report is false or not is beside the point. The main thing is that only a rover would carry such a piece of paper on him for so long and so far. This scrap of paper is the reason why I thought these people were rovers. When we arrived here and saw the bodies, we obviously knew that a fight had taken place. We checked out the bodies and all the tracks and figured out the following facts: two white men had camped here, a big and a little one. Then arrived a third white man who joined them and finished the remains of their meal. They undertook a test shooting, downing two vultures. The third white man proved to be a good shot and was accepted into the company of the two others.

"Then an Indian approached them on the run. He was fleeing, coming from the Osage Nook and pursued by five rovers. He turned out to be a friend of the whites, who stood by him and killed the five pursuers. The three palefaces and Good Sun then mounted their horses to proceed by a detour to the Osage Nook where they wanted to attack the rovers. I decided to help them. But since nightfall had come by then, I had to wait until daybreak; I couldn't follow the tracks by night."

"Why did my white brother attack us?" asked the chief.

"Because I was led to believe that you were rovers."

"For what reason?"

"I knew there are many rovers at the Osage Nook. Five of them had left to pursue an Indian. They had been shot here, therefore never returned. This had to raise concern among the others and it was highly probable that help would be sent after them. Accordingly, I posted guards who reported a group of horsemen approaching. Since the wind was blowing from the direction of the Osage Nook, we were able to hear your approach quite early. I had my people take to their weapons while Droll and I prepared to ambush you. When two of you dismounted to sneak up on us, we took you captive to see your faces by firelight. The rest you know."

"Again my brother has shown himself to be the most skillful hunter among the palefaces," said Good Sun admiringly. "What does he plan to do? Are the rovers his personal enemies?"

"Yes. I'm pursuing the red-haired one to capture him. But in order to make a decision, I need to know first what the situation is at the Osage Nook and what has happened there. Will you tell me, Bill?"

Humpy-Bill answered this request with an extensive report. At its conclusion, he added, "You see, sir, that we must act quickly. Will you mount up immediately and ride with us to the farm?"

"No. I will not," Old Firehand replied in a firm tone.

"Why not? Would you prefer to attack the rovers on the way?"

"Wouldn't think of it. No, I'm going to remain here, although I know the danger is even greater than you think."

"Greater. How so?"

"You think these fellows will break camp only by afternoon?"

"Yes."

"Then I tell you that they will already ride out by early morning!"

"But the colonel said afternoon!"

"He's changed his mind in the meantime, Bill."

"How did you arrive at that conclusion, sir?"

"Where had the captured Osages been tied up?"

"Not far from the fire where the red-haired one sat."

"Did you hear what was said?"

"Yes."

"Also that Butler's farm was to be attacked?"

"That too."

"Well, and in the meantime the Osages have escaped. Must not the colonel then have gotten the idea that they're hurrying to Butler to warn him?"

"By the devil! That's true, Firehand! That speaks for itself!"

"Of course. To limit the damage this may cause, they'll set out earlier. I'll bet they've decided to mount up by daybreak."

"Did I hear bet?" Lord Castlepool called out. "Well, you are my man, sir! You'll bet that they will ride out that early? Right-o then, I assert that they will leave the Osage Nook only by tomorrow night. I stake ten dollars, even twenty or thirty. Or do you prefer fifty?"

He pulled his satchel back up front and opened it to draw out some money. A quiet wink of Humpy-Bill's that the Englishman did not notice told Old Firehand that he had an impassioned wagerer in front of him. He therefore answered, "Close your satchel again, sir; it's not my intention to take the word 'betting' seriously. Such important issues do not lend themselves to wagering anyway."

"But I am fond of betting!" insisted the lord.

"But not I!"

"Dashed nuisance! Such a pity! I have heard so many good and admirable things about you, sir. Every real gentleman bets. That you do not almost forces me to change my opinion about you."

"Go ahead if you like! It's very possible that you will soon resume your previous views. Now we have other and better things to do than to enter into wagers. Life and property of many people is at risk and it's our duty to prevent this disaster. This won't be accomplished by betting."

"Correct, sir. I only wager on the side. When it comes to action, you will surely find me in the ranks, maybe just as firmly and calmly as you. Bodily strength, though, is insufficient by itself. You bloody well ought to remember that!"

He had become angry and measured the Herculean figure of the hunter with an almost insulting look. For a moment the latter didn't seem to know what to think of the Englishman; his face darkened, but quickly brightened again for he had guessed the lord's thoughts. He therefore answered, "Take it easy, Lord Castlepool. Until we get to know each other, we don't want to trade any rudeness. You're still new in this country."

The word 'new' did not miss its mark, for the lord shouted even more angrily than before, "Dammit, who says so? Do I look new? At least I'm equipped with what the prairie calls for. But you, fellow, sit there as if you had just left a private club or even a ladies' shop!"

That was the reason then! Old Firehand still wore the elegant travel suit he'd worn on the steamer. He hadn't been able to change since his hunting gear was waiting for him at Butler's farm. The suit had suffered much from the ride to the rafters and then back here, but appeared still quite new in the glow of the small fire that was fighting the rain. The famous man wasn't taken as a real frontiersman by the Englishman. Smiling he nodded and said, "You're not entirely mistaken, sir; but I will yet outfit myself in the western style; in any case, let's remain friends."

"If you are serious, do not speak so about betting, because by the amount staked one recognizes the true British gentleman. By the way, I do not understand why you intend to stay here and not ride to the farm right away. This was the first thing that puzzled me about you."

"I have my good reasons for it."

"Will my white brother tell me the reasons?" asked Good Sun.

"Yes. It's sufficient if you ride to the farm and notify Butler. He's quite the man to make the right preparations. I'll remain here with my rafters to harass the rovers and delay them so they will surely not arrive at the farm before the defenders are ready to receive them."

"My brother has always the best ideas. And this would also be the case today except that Butler is not in his wigwam."

"He's not?" Old Firehand asked surprised.

"No. On the way to the Osage Nook, I passed by the farm and stopped, hoping to smoke the calumet with my white brother Butler. But he was not home. His brother had arrived with his daughter and the three had departed for Fort Dodge to purchase clothing for the daughter."

"Then his brother has already arrived! Do you know how long Butler intends to stay in Fort Dodge?"

"A few more days."

"And when were you at the farm?"

"In the morning, the day before yesterday."

"Then I must absolutely go there," cried Old Firehand, jumping up. "How long will it take for your Osages to come to help?"

"If I leave right now, we can be at the farm by next midnight."

"That's much, very much too late. Are the Osages presently on good terms with the Cheyenne and Arapaho?"

"Yes. We have buried the tomahawk of war in the ground."

"These two tribes live on the other side of the river and can be reached in four hours. Will my brother leave right away to carry a message from me to them?"

Without a word, Good Sun strode over to his horse and mounted up.

"Ride hard," Old Firehand continued, "and tell the two chiefs of my request to come to Butler's farm with one hundred warriors each, as quickly as possible!"

"Is that the entire message?"

"Yes."

The Osage clucked his tongue, let the horse feel his heels, and in a moment had disappeared in the dark of the night. The lord looked on in wonderment. Did a tribal chief obey so unconditionally and unquestioningly a man dressed in a salon suit? But Old Firehand too was already in his saddle.

"Gentlemen, we are not to lose a minute," he said earnestly. "Although our horses are tired, they must hold up until we reach the farm. Get ready then!"

The fire was extinguished and the troop formed up quickly. Ahead was Old Firehand with his close friends and hunters, then the rafters, finally followed by the few Osages with the horses.

They rode slowly at first, then moved into a trot, and as soon as their eyes became accustomed to the dark, went to a full gallop. Lord Castlepool overtook Bill and asked, "I say, is it possible that Old Firehand might get lost?"

"No, even less so than the Osage chief. Some say he can see like a cat at night."

"And wears a formal suit. What a strange bloke!"

"Just wait until you see him in his buffalo coat! He makes a very different figure then."

"Well, figure he has enough of. But who, actually, is this frightful woman who has attached herself to you?"

"Woman? Oh, this lady is a man."

"Who would believe that she's a ruddy bloke!"

"Go ahead. Believe it!"

"But she was called 'aunt'!"

"That's only for fun, because of his falsetto voice and since he dresses so peculiarly. His name is Droll and he's a very good hunter. Also as a trapper he has an excellent reputation. Beavers and otters literally rush into his traps. He seems to have a secret way about him like no one else. But let's quit talking now. On such a ride we need to keep our minds on the task."

He was right. Old Firehand in the lead rode like the devil, with the others forced to follow him whether they wanted to or not. The lord was a passionate chase rider and had risked his head many a time, but a headlong ride like this he had never experienced before. They were all enveloped by utter darkness, as in a tunnel; none of the hills could be discerned, not even the ground pounded by the horses' hooves. It was as if the animals were racing through a lightless abyss and yet there was no misstep, no stumble! Each horse precisely followed the one in front with everyone depending on Old Firehand. His horse had never been in this neck of the woods and was only a common nag that he had had to accept, since none better was then available. The lord once more gained respect for this man.

It continued like this for half an hour, a full hour, and another, with only short breaks for the horses to catch their breaths. The rain continued to fall, but so lightly that it didn't bother these hardened men in the least. Then came Old Firehand's shout from up front, "Watch out, gentlemen! It goes downhill here, then through a ford. But the water will reach only to the horses' bellies."

They slowed down. The rushing of the river's waters could be heard and despite the Stygian darkness they could still make out the phosphorescent surface. During the crossing, the riders' feet became immersed in the water, then swiftly the opposite bank was attained. Another short ride of a minute. They stopped and Lord Castlepool was surprised to hear the ringing of a bell. It was still as dark as ever in front of his eyes.

"What is that? Who is ringing, where are we?" he asked Humpy-Bill.

"At the gates of Butler's farm," he was told.

"Do you see anything of the farmstead?"

"No. But come closer a few paces and you'll be able to feel the wall."

Dogs barked. From their deep, harsh voices one could imagine their size. Then there sounded a voice, "Who's ringing, who wants to enter?"

"Has Master Butler returned yet?" the hunter inquired.

"No."

"Then fetch the key from his lady and tell her Old Firehand has arrived!"

"Old Firehand! Well, sir, just a minute. Ma'am isn't asleep and neither is anyone else. Passing by here, the Osage chief stopped and reported your coming."

"What kind of people must live hereabouts!" pondered the lord. "Then Good Sun must have ridden even faster, much faster than us!"

After a while, commands could be heard calling back the dogs. Then a key clattered in the lock, wooden crossbars groaned, hinges creaked, and finally the lord spied several lanterns whose dim light made the darkness of a seemingly vast yard even more impenetrable. Farmhands approached to take the riders' horses, then the visitors were led into a high, gloomy-looking house. A woman servant asked Old Firehand to come upstairs to see the ma'am. The others were invited into a large, smoke-stained room on the lower floor, from whose ceiling hung a heavy petroleum lamp. A number of tables, benches and chairs filled the room. The men quickly sat down at the tables where lay an assortment of foods, bottles and glasses, a welcome result of Good Sun's early announcement of the group's coming.

The rafters, together with the Osages, immediately dug in. While frontiersmen don't like to give or accept unnecessary compliments, it happened as if by itself that the 'elite' of the group had assembled at a table away from the others. There the lord had first taken a seat and had beckoned Humpy-Bill and Gunstick-Uncle to sit beside him; then Aunt Droll, Fred Engel and Black Tom had joined them, and finally Blenter, the old Missourian, had ventured over as well.

Everyone now partook of the food and drink as if they were starving. The lord seemed to have come to the conclusion that being among wolves, he had to howl with them. Thus he dropped all pretense of gentlemanly behavior and performed no better nor worse than his voracious neighbors.

Later, Old Firehand entered the room with Mrs. Butler who welcomed her guests in the most amicable way. She told the Englishman that a separate room had been reserved for him, but he rejoined that he was content to do without any privileges not accorded to his comrades, since he considered himself nothing other than a frontiersman. His manner delighted the others so much that they expressed their appreciation in a highly boisterous and honest way.

Old Firehand then announced that they were not required to accomplish any task for the remainder of the night, but should get some rest to be fresh in the morning; there was enough farm help to make the necessary preparations.

Lord Castlepool could not take his eyes off the famous hunter who by now had changed from his 'civilized' suit into his hunter's attire. He wore fringed leggings reaching down to his knees, both sides richly embroidered. High boots, a vest of soft, white-tanned deer leather, a short elk-leather hunting jacket, and over it a massive coat made of buffalo hide completed the outfit. His powerful waist was enclosed by a broad leather belt from which jutted his short weapons. His head was adorned by a beaver hat with a wide brim and a beaver tail hanging down behind. The latter seemed less intended to give the giant man an adventurous appearance than to protect his neck from a cunning enemy's attack from behind.

Around his neck hung a long chain made of grizzly bear teeth, and from it a peace pipe with a masterly carved head. All the seams of his coat were trimmed with grizzly claws, and since a man like Old Firehand would surely not use someone else's bounty, it was very clear from these adornments and the pipe chain how many of these terrible animals had fallen victim to his bullets and strong hands.

As he left with the lady, the Englishman remarked to the others, "I now rightly believe what is said about him. This chap is a true giant!"

"Pshaw!" answered Droll. "Not by his figure alone does a frontiersman want to be judged; a good mind is of greater value. It's rare for such giants to be so brave. But with him, both come together. Old Shatterhand is not as tall and sturdy, and Winnetou, the Apache, is even less so. But both are equal to him in every respect."

"Also with regard to bodily strength?"

"Yes. I've seen Old Shatterhand pull a mustang down with only one hand. Who knows whether Old Firehand could duplicate that. Little by little, a frontiersman's muscles become like iron with tendons of steel, even if he doesn't possess the figure of a giant."

"Then you too, Master Droll, must be of iron and steel?"

It sounded somewhat like a challenge, yet the funny one answered with a friendly smile, "Would you like to find out, sir?"

"Oh! I say, yes, very much so."

"But it seems you doubt it?"

"That's so! An 'Aunt' with muscles and tendons of steel! Shall we bet?"

"What and how?"

"Who is stronger, the Englishman or the German."

"Why not?"

Finally Lord Castlepool had found someone who didn't reject his offer to wager. His eyes sparkling, he jumped up and exclaimed, "But Aunt Droll, I have thrown down many a bloke who would have to bend to even notice you! Do you really dare?"

"Of course!"

"For a quid, that's to say, five dollars?"

"Well!"

"I will lend it to you."

"Thank you. But Droll never borrows."

"Then you have money?"

"For what you might win, it's enough, sir."

"Even ten dollars?"

"That too."

"Or twenty?"

"Why not!"

"Maybe even fifty?" the lord exclaimed joyfully.

"Agreed! But no more. I don't want to take too much of your money, sir."

"What? To take Lord Castlepool's money? Are you daft, Aunt? Out with your money! Here are my fifty dollars."

Pulling one of his satchels hanging from his strong belt to the fore, he withdrew ten five dollar bills and laid them on the table. For his part, Droll inserted his hand into the dangling sleeve of his 'sleeping gown' and produced a small bag. When he opened it, it appeared to be filled with hazelnut-sized gold nuggets. He put five of them on the table, returned the bag to its former place and said, "You have paper money, your lordship? Fie! Aunt Droll deals only in true gold. These nuggets are worth more than fifty dollars. Anyway, we can begin, but how?"

"You show me whatever you wish to demonstrate and I will copy it; then we shall do it in reverse."

"No. I'm only an Aunt, but you're a lord. You have precedence."

"Good show! Stay put, then, but defend yourself. I'm going to lift you onto the table!"

"Try it!"

Droll spread his legs widely. The lord grabbed him by the waist to lift him, yet the Aunt's feet never left the floor by even an inch. It was as if Droll had been made of lead. The Englishman tried again and again in vain and finally had to admit that he was incapable of accomplishing his purpose. He comforted himself by saying in a loud voice, "If I didn't get you up there, chappie, then you will succeed even less so."

"We'll see," Droll laughed, looking up at the ceiling where, just above the table, a strong iron hook had been inserted for hanging a second lamp. The others, noticing this, watched the droll Aunt, who they knew possessed exceptional strength, and punched each other surreptitiously.

"Have at it then!" the lord urged.

"Then only onto the table?" asked Droll.

"Do you fancy getting me even higher?"

"As high as possible. Watch out, your lordship!"

Despite the encumbrance of his dress, a single leap brought Droll onto the table from where he seized the lord beneath his armpits. The latter flew high above the table so fast that he never understood how it was possible. A moment later, he hung by his belt from the ceiling hook, much to the general hilarity of all the men in the room. Droll bounded from the table and asked laughing, "Now then, sir, are you up there?"

The Englishman, arms and legs thrashing madly, shouted, "By gosh, where am I? Woe to me; on the ceiling! Get me down. Take me off! If the hook comes loose, I will break my neck!"

"Say first who's won!"

"You, you blighter, you!"

"And the second part of the bet I was to exercise, where I was supposed to suggest what to do?"

"I release you from it. Just get me down! By my sainted aunt! Please!"

Droll once more jumped on the table from which the dishes had earlier been removed. With both hands he took the Englishman by his waist, lifted him up so the belt could come free of the hook, placed him first alongside himself on the table, then dropped him on his feet onto the floor. Having followed him down, he now laid his hand on the lord's shoulder and asked, "Now, sir, what do you think of the Aunt."

"A bit much, not to say a bit too much!" was the breathless response, the Englishman's look still directed at the hook he had been hanging from.

"Then into my bag go these old bills!"

He put the bills and nuggets into his bag and continuing with a triumphant grin proposed, "Please, your lordship, whenever you wish to bet, come to me! I will always be your man."

Droll returned the dishes, bottles and glasses to the table, during which he received congratulatory cheers from all sides. Much abashed, the lord sat down and felt his arms, legs and waist to see if perhaps a screw might have come loose. Once he convinced himself that everything was in order, he offered the Aunt his hand and said, smiling happily, "Wonderful bet. Right? Good chaps these frontiersmen. One just needs to treat them rightly!"

"Well. I think that, on the other hand, I did 'treat' you, sir."

"Too true. You are frightfully strong. But the reason must be that you are from Old England?"

"Oh, no, sir. I'm a German," answered the Aunt.

"A German? Then surely from Pommerania?"

"A wrong guess! There everyone grows taller and broader than I. I'm from Altenburg."

"Hmm! Perhaps some wretched little hamlet?"

"A German duchy, sir! The best goat cheese comes from there."

"No offense meant, chappie, about the cheese. I didn't know."

"That's too bad!"

"Doesn't make me shed any tears. You are a fit fellow, Aunt, and you have piqued my interest. But you haven't been a frontiersman forever? Or are there also trappers in Altenburg?"

123

"Not in my time. Maybe some have found their way there by now."

"What did your father do, and what brought you to the United States?"

"My father was no lord, but much, much more."

"Really? More than a lord? How is that possible?"

"Very much so! You're a lord, and probably nothing more, but my father was many things."

"Eh? What then?" the Englishman pressed, expecting to hear an interesting life story.

"He was a wedding and baptism chaplain, an undertaker, bell-ringer, church warden, waiter, gravedigger, scythe-grinder, orchard guard and at the same time a home-guard sergeant. Isn't that enough?"

"Surely, more than enough!"

"Right, for if I sum it up: he was a good man."

"Is the poor fellow dead?"

"A long time already. I have no other relatives."

"So then out of grief you crossed the big ocean?"

"Not out of grief. My dialect caused me to leave."

"Your dialect? How do you mean?"

"To understand this, you'd have to be a German, or at least speak German. There's a saying that every human being has an angel and a devil inside. Now, my devil was the Altenburg dialect. At home it drove me from one house to another, one street to the next, from one village to another and finally across the ocean. Then, finally, I was relieved here of this Satan by people speaking English. I long for my fatherland, have also the means to retire over there, but, unfortunately, I cannot go back, because in Hamburg or Bremerhaven this very same devil would be waiting for me as soon as I debarked and began speaking this dialect again."

Lord Castlepool gazed around the room in chagrin. "I don't understand this fellow at all."

"But I do," Black Tom interjected. "You know, Droll speaks such a horrible German that he couldn't let himself be heard over there."

"Then should he not learn it better?"

"Won't work! He's been pummeled from all sides for this weakness but without success; he only became ever more confused. Let's talk about other things. He doesn't enjoy the subject."

Old Firehand had returned to remind the men that it would be better to get some rest, since everyone would have to be up bright and early the next day. The troop readily followed his urgings and retired to an adjoining room, where hide-covered wooden frames served the farmhands as hammocks or beds. Comfort was provided by soft foundations and blankets. In these truly western beds, the men slept at their best.

7. The Battle for Butler's Farm

In the early morning hours, the farm's defenders were awakened. The dawn seemed to portend a warm, even hot and sunny day and in the pleasant morning light, the farm building, which last night had appeared so gloomy, looked quite different today. It had been built to house many occupants. Very long and broad, it was built of bricks and had a lower and upper floor with a flat roof. Its very high windows were so narrow that no intruder could crawl through. This precaution was necessary in an area frequently traveled by rapacious Indians. Hereabouts it had often happened, and still might, so that a lonely house or farmstead could well have to be defended for several days against such interlopers.

Just as useful was the large, open yard enclosed by a high adobe wall with built-in embrasures. Between the embrasures were broad masonry benches on which to stand if shooting over the parapets became necessary.

Not far from the house flowed the river that the newcomers had forded the day before. The fording spot could be comfortably defended with rifle fire from the farm's wall, and overnight, on Old Firehand's orders, it had been made impassable by obstacles. As a second and very important precaution, the hunter had also had Butler's cattle driven overnight to the nearest neighbor. Likewise a messenger had also been sent in the direction of Fort Dodge to warn the Butler brothers should they already be on their way home, so that they wouldn't walk into a rover trap.

Old Firehand led his companions onto the roof of the building from where there was an excellent view across the hilly prairie to the east and north, and extensive, well-tended fields of corn and grain to the south and west.

"When do you expect the Indians you summoned will arrive?" asked Droll.

"According to the chief's calculations yesterday, they should be here soon," Old Firehand answered.

"I don't think so. The redskins must first be gathered, maybe from far away, and won't go on the warpath before they have performed their ancient rites. We'll be lucky to see them by noon. By then the rovers could be already close. I don't much trust these Cheyenne and Arapahoe."

"Me neither," Bill chimed in. "Both tribes are very small and have not handled a tomahawk for a long, long time. We cannot rely on them; worse yet, there are no other strong neighbors. We should be prepared for an extended siege."

"No need to worry about that. The cellars hold plenty of provisions," Old Firehand told them.

"But water will be our main concern!" cautioned Droll. "With the rovers outside, we cannot get to the river to fetch any!"

"It won't be necessary. In one of the cellars is a well with good, potable water for people, and the animals are provided for by the canal."

"There's a canal?"

"Yes. Everything here has been built and arranged for defense. Behind the house is a wooden trapdoor, with steps leading to the vaulted canal which connects to the river."

"Is it deep?"

"Man-high. The water almost reaches to one's chest."

"Is its intake open to the river?"

"Oh, no. An enemy should not know about it, which is why the opening has been concealed with thickly planted bushes and vines."

There had not been any particular reason for Droll to make such a detailed inquiry about the canal, but later this knowledge would turn out to be invaluable.

The lady of the house had not come out yet. All night long she had worried and planned with Old Firehand and had gone to her room to sleep only at daybreak. However, none of the guests had reason to complain, since everything had been prepared to satisfy their desires. The tables, chairs and benches they had sat on the previous night were carried into the yard so breakfast could be taken under the open sky. Then all available weapons and ammunition were distributed and checked for their readiness.

Later, Old Firehand and Mrs. Butler sat on the roof and peered southward in the direction from which the Indians were expected to arrive. Finally, not long after noon, a long, long line of redskins approached Indian-file, Good Sun on horseback in the lead.

As they entered through the gate, Old Firehand counted more than two hundred warriors. Unfortunately, only a very few were well armed. Most of them didn't even have a horse, and many others had refused to bring their mounts along. They would prefer to be wounded themselves, or perhaps even killed, than lose their animals. But then riders were not really required for the defense of the farm.

Old Firehand descended from his rooftop perch and divided these proud but somewhat ill-prepared redskins into two groups. The first was to remain near the farm, the second was to position itself under the leadership of the Osage chief at the border of the farm's neighbor to protect the cattle that had been sheltered there. Both warrior teams had the task of repelling the expected rover attack. To spur them to be attentive and brave, a prize was promised for each killed rover, then Good Sun headed out with his detachment.

Within the walls there were now more than a hundred Indians, twenty rafters and the company of hunters. Against so great a number of rovers, this was surely not many, but a hunter or rafter certainly was the equal of several rovers, and the protection that the house and wall afforded was not to be underestimated.

Specific orders could not be issued as yet since it was unknown how the rovers intended to attack.

Nothing further could now be done except to await the rovers' arrival. It was very well that Mrs. Butler took the coming danger in stride. It was not her fashion to upset her employees by lamenting. Instead she summoned them to promise each a substantial reward for faithful and brave behavior. There were about twenty farmhands who knew how to use weapons and Old Firehand was sure he could count on them.

The preparations completed, Old Firehand returned to the roof together with the woman and the Englishman. Using Lord Castlepool's telescope, he searched the horizon in the direction where the rovers were expected. After long, fruitless observation, he finally spied a large contingent of horsemen so far distant that an unaided eye would not have been able to detect them. It had to be the rovers. At one point three figures separated from the main group and moved in the direction of the farm, not on horseback, but on foot.

"Aha, they're sending scouts!" said Old Firehand. "Maybe they're even so insolent as to ask to be invited in."

"That would be bolder than I credit these ruffians," remarked the lord.

"Why not? They send here three men that no one knows. They enter by some pretense. Who would do anything to them? Let's go down so they don't notice us on the roof. We can still observe them through the telescope from one of the windows."

The horses had been hidden behind the building so that they could not be seen by the invaders. All the defenders needed to conceal themselves as well. Upon their arrival, the three rovers were to get the impression that the farmstead had little defense.

The trio approached the wall slowly. Old Firehand noticed that one of them boosted up the second to peer through one of the embrasures into the yard. Quickly, the hunter issued several more orders he found necessary, then walked out into the yard. The bell rang. He went to the gate and unconcernedly inquired what was wanted.

"Is the farm's owner at home?" a voice asked.

"No, he's away," the hunter responded.

"We're looking for work. Do you need any farmhands?"

"No."

"May we ask at least for some food. We come from far and are hungry. Please, let us in!"

This was said in a plaintive voice. In the west there is no farmer who would turn a hungry man away. With all primitive races, and in all regions where there are no inns, this deficit is compensated for by the wonderful custom of hospitality as is also true in the American West. Not only would it be harsh to the needy but also a disgrace to the farm, or rather its owner, to deny a stranger asked-for sustenance.

Therefore the three men were admitted and, after the gate had been locked again, were assigned seats at the side of the building. However, the latter arrangement did not seem to be to their liking. Although they projected unaffectedness, it could not escape attention that they observed the house and its environs with probing looks, following which they gave each other significant glances. One of them said, "We're poor miserable folks who don't want to inconvenience you. Permit us to stay near the gate where we would have more shade than here. We'll get ourselves a table."

Their wish was granted, although it was a malicious one. They wanted, of course, to be near the gate so they could open it for their fellow rovers. The three men carried a table and some chairs to their desired location, then a maidservant brought them an ample meal. Not one of the farmhands was now to be seen on this side of the courtyard, all having withdrawn into the house.

The pretended farm workers now expressed satisfaction about their situation, as Old Firehand discerned from watching their gestures. They had arrived at the conclusion that the farmstead had so few defenders that those they did have could be easily overcome. After a while, one of the rovers got up and very innocently walked to the closest embrasure to peer outside. This was repeated several times, a certain sign that the rogues expected the arrival of their fellow rovers.

Once more Old Firehand stood at an upper window to scan the area from which the rovers would be coming. Having dispatched their three scouts, they had withdrawn so that they could no longer be seen. Now they reappeared and approached at a full gallop to cover the distance to the farm as quickly as possible.

It was evident that several of them had to know this locale since the attackers headed straight for the ford. Arriving there and finding it blocked, they stopped in puzzlement. Now the moment had come for Old Firehand to act. He strode to the gate. Just then, one of the three supposed farmhands again ventured over to the embrasure to search for his comrades. Finding himself observed, he stepped back, startled.

"What are you doing? Why are you looking through that hole?" asked Old Firehand in a gruff voice.

With an embarrassed look, the rover gazed up at the giant hunter and stammered, "I --- I wanted --- to see where we should go from here."

"Don't lie. You know your way already. It leads out to the river and those riders there."

"What riders are you referring to, sir?" the man asked with feigned surprise. "I didn't notice anyone."

"If that were the case, you would have to be blind. You must have seen the horsemen."

"Not a single one! Who are they?"

"Pretending ignorance is contemptible. You belong to the group of rovers from the Osage Nook who plan to attack us. And you've been sent to scout us out."

At this, the fellow assumed an expression of deep offense and exclaimed in a tone of wounded indignation, "What? You claim that we're rovers? Sir, we're honest and diligent workers and have nothing in common with any itinerants who might be around here. We're looking for work and since we can't find any with you, we'll look elsewhere. To count us as belonging to such riffraff is a serious insult. Think about it! If it were true that rovers intended to attack you and we were part of their gang, what would be the use of our coming here prior to the attack? It would mean a risk which would surely backfire."

"It had a very definite purpose," Old Firehand responded. "With our walls being so high, you came to us under the pretense of looking for work, when your true purpose was to be able to open the gate for your companions. That's the reason you wanted to sit so close to it."

"Sir!" the man roared angrily and reached into his pocket.

But Old Firehand already had his revolver in his hand and threatened, "Keep your weapons tucked away! The moment I see one, I'll fire. Yes, your coming here was a risk, since I could seize you now and call you to account. But you're of such little threat that I'll let you go. Leave, and tell your rabble that every one of you who attempts to cross the river will get a bullet. That's it; now get moving!"

He opened the gate. The rovers looked as if they still wanted to say something, but thought better of it, seeing the revolver pointing at them. As they stepped outside, Old Firehand heard one mutter, "What a blockhead! Why is he letting us go if he thinks we're rovers? Just count how many we are. We'll make short work of these few people. They'll all hang in less than a quarter of an hour."

"And you'll be the first to fall by our bullets," the hunter called after them. Thereupon he gave the planned signal to the hidden defenders to come out from behind the house and to take their posts at the embrasures. He too chose a location at one of the openings to observe the enemy's movements.

The ejected scouts had now reached the near bank of the river and shouted words across, which could not be understood back at the farm because of the distance. Hearing the encouraging cries, the entire band of rovers entered the water, urging their horses across the river.

"When they attack, get the scouts first, as I promised," Old Firehand said to Droll and Black Tom, who stood nearby. "I'll shoot the first two arriving on our side of the river. After I fire, Bill, Uncle, Blenter, the lord and the others will fire in the order they're lined up along the wall. This way each of you gets to shoot at a different man, not two or more at the same rover. And we'll save ammunition."

"Very well!" answered Humpy-Bill. "I'll fire in the sequence."

And his sidekick, the Gunstick-Uncle chimed in, "As soon as they cross - they will be made dross - aimed at one by one - to hell they be gone!"

The first of the horsemen had now reached the near bank, the second right behind. As they arrived at the place where the fake workers waited, Old Firehand gave the sign. His two shots rang out a split second ahead of Tom's and Droll's. The two riders spun off their horses just as the three mortally wounded scouts hit the ground. The rovers, seeing this, raised holy hell, furiously screaming and hollering, and drove forward to get to the near bank. The ones behind pushed those ahead into certain ruin, for as soon as one of the horses made the bank, a bullet took its rider out of the saddle. In a time span of maybe ten minutes, there milled some twenty to thirty riderless horses on the farmstead's side of the river.

The rovers had not expected this kind of reception. The scouts' information shouted across the river had told them of the laughably poor defense of the farm. And now shot after shot had rung out from the embrasures. None of the bullets had missed its target. The rovers' original outburst of fury now changed into fearful screams. At the sound of their leader's command, the riders still in the river turned their horses to return frantically to the far bank.

"Repulsed!" rejoiced Blenter. "I'm curious what they'll do now."

"No question what that'll be," Old Firehand answered. "They'll cross the river at a spot where our bullets can't reach them."

"And then?"

"Then? That's too early to tell. If they act smartly, we're in for a difficult time."

"And what do you consider smart?"

"They must not come massed but need to disperse. If they leave their horses at a distance and race on foot towards the wall from all four sides and find cover behind it, we'd be forced to disperse our forces as well. We'd be too few to repulse such a horde. If the rovers then suddenly massed together, they'd be able to vault over the wall."

"That's true, but many would be blown away. Then we too would have to face them without much cover."

"On the contrary, we could retreat to the building and would have enough men to force them back over the wall. It's fortunate that the yard is so wide and open, with the building standing in its center. I'm not worried; let's wait and see what they do. They seem to be deliberating."

The rovers had assembled in a tight grouping from which four had separated, probably the leaders. Faces were unrecognizable from such a distance, but from the vivid gestures, it was apparent that the discussion was very animated. Shortly thereafter, the entire group headed upstream to a point farther north, outside the farmstead's range of fire. There they crossed the river. Once assembled, they formed a close rank and rode hell-for-leather toward the wall. Until now, the defenders had massed on the eastern side of the barrier. Now Old Firehand shouted, "Quick! All of us to the north side! They intend to force the gate."

"They can't crash it," cried Blenter.

"No. But once they reach it, they can quickly jump the gate or vault the wall from horseback. Then they can squash us inside the yard."

"But many will die first."

"Perhaps so, but too many will remain alive. Don't shoot until I command it, then all of us at the same time. Two salvos from the double-barreled rifles, right into their midst!"

Quickly the north face was manned. Some of the defenders took their places behind the embrasures; others stood on the stone benches in between, from where it was possible to shoot over the top of the wall. Those on the benches kept their heads down so as not to be seen too early by the attackers.

It now became clear that old Firehand had guessed right. The group galloped straight for the gate. Only when they approached within some eighty paces did Firehand give the order to commence firing. Two salvos rang out, a first volley followed quickly by the other; so fast, actually, that the two sounded almost like one. The outcome corresponded with Old Firehand's expectations. It seemed as if the rovers had been stopped in the midst of their gallop by a rope stretched across their way.

A messy cluster of horsemen and riderless horses resulted which could not be quickly disentangled. The lord, who had two rifles, squeezed off two more shots; the others gained time to reload, even if only one barrel, and now fired not in salvos but continuously and freely into the melee.

The rovers were unable to take this; they scattered, leaving their dead and wounded behind. It would have been far too dangerous to attend to them in the midst of the fire-fight. The riderless horses instinctively ran towards the farmstead where the defenders opened the gate to allow them inside.

When, somewhat later, the rovers attempted to attend to their previously abandoned casualties, they were not prevented from doing so out of a sense of humanity. They carried their dead and wounded to a distant group of trees where they could tend to the injuries.

Food and drink was issued to the brave defenders. Then the rovers' departure was observed. They had left their casualties in the shade of the trees and ridden off westward.

"Are they retreating?" wondered Humpy-Bill. "They've been given a good lesson that they would be wise to take to heart."

"No way," answered Aunt Droll. "Had they really abandoned their plans, they would have taken their wounded along. I figure they now intend to go after the farm's herds. That's where they're headed for. There, look up on the roof! There's Old Firehand with the telescope. He's keeping tabs on those guys, and I expect to hear his orders soon."

"Which?"

"To go to the aid of the farmhands and Indians."

The Aunt's speculation proved to be correct. The rovers had now gained such a distance that they thought they could no longer be seen from the wall, but with his telescope Old Firehand had them still in sight. Now he called from the roof, "Saddle the horses! The rovers have turned south and are headed for Good Sun and his people."

In less than five minutes, the horses were saddled and ready. The men all mounted except for a few farmhands who remained behind to open the gate quickly should it become necessary. With Old Firehand in the lead, the group exited the gate, turned the wall's corner and headed south. After crossing several fields, they came upon the prairie, a greenish pasture, its sameness here and there broken by bushes.

From there the naked eye could not discern the rovers, but Old Firehand with his telescope could pick them out. This made it possible to parallel their course, yet remain invisible to them. A quarter hour later, Old Firehand stopped since the rovers had also come to a halt. They had arrived at the border of the neighboring farmstead where they could now see not only the grazing cattle but also their defenders.

Old Firehand examined the various bushy growths dotting the grassland and selected several that offered cover to his men. Moving from one to another, they approached the area where they expected the attack to take place. They then left their horses behind and in a crouching position advanced toward a broad grove of bushes where the rovers were most likely to pass during the upcoming fight. Careful not to be noticed, they took their posts and kept their rifles at the ready. From their vantage point, they could see both the attackers and the attacked with the naked eye.

The former seemed to be astounded to find such a great number of Indians delegated to the protection of the animals. How was it possible to find redskins for something like that and in such numbers? The rovers, at first startled, soon noticed that the Indians were poorly equipped, that is, they had bows and arrows but no rifles. This seemed to comfort them.

The leaders conferred briefly, then issued the order to attack. From their approach, it was clear that they had no stomach for an extended fight from a distance but planned simply to run the redskins down. In closed array and with loud, threatening screams, the horsemen galloped towards the Indians.

Now it became evident that Good Sun was up to his task. Upon his command, his closely packed warriors dispersed so they could not be overrun. As the rovers became aware of this stratagem, they executed a turn to come upon the redskins' right flank and roll them up towards the left. The Osage chief perceived their intent and again issued a command. For an instant, his people gathered in a milling cluster then flew apart, again totally rearranging their positions. Their previous line had been one facing east-west; it had now become one pointing north-south. The Osages had made this maneuver not because he knew the proximity of allies behind the bushes, but rather to offer the enemy not his flank but, like a bison, the armored, horn-equipped forehead.

This, by itself, had been a tactical masterpiece. In addition, it had the unexpected result that the bandits were now placed between the Indians and the whites. Seeing their plans frustrated, the rovers stopped short, a carelessness they were to suffer for immediately. They were mistaken in their estimate of the range of the Indians' weaponry and felt safe from mere arrows.

One of the rovers' leaders was talking to his people, seemingly to give new orders. Good Sun put the pause to good use. Seeing his upraised hand, his warriors ran forward, halted, let loose a flight of arrows, and just as quickly retreated. The arrows found their targets, leaving dead and wounded not just among the riders, but among the horses. Many animals reared up, trying to break free and were hard to keep under control. This produced a chaos Old Firehand took swift advantage of.

"Let's do it!" he ordered "But shoot only the riders, not the horses!"

His companions stepped from behind the bushes and being at the enemy's rear, they were not immediately sighted. But when their shots rang out and their bullets struck home, the rovers turned toward them, right into the face of the second salvo. They screamed in terror.

"Away!" a voice boomed. "We're surrounded. Break through the Indians' line!"

The remainder of the rovers immediately wheeled about, leaving their casualties behind and galloped toward the Indians, who readily opened up for them, but followed them, voicing a triumphant howl.

"Look how they run away!" old Blenter laughed. "They won't come back. Do you know who ordered their flight?"

"Of course!" answered Black Tom. "That voice we know by now. It was the red-haired colonel. Satan himself seems to protect him from our bullets. Aren't we going to pursue the bandits, sir?"

He had directed his question to Old Firehand who answered, "No. We're too few to take them on in hand-to-hand combat. They may also guess that we weren't hiding here long, but came from the farmstead to the aid of the redskins. If they figure that out, it's highly probable they'll ride back there to attack the farm during our absence. We must get back quickly."

"And what's to happen to the wounded rovers and the riderless horses?"

"We must leave that to the Indians. Let's not lose any time. To the horses and let's ride!"

The men waved their hats and shouted a resounding hurrah to the redskins, who responded with shrill victory screams. They then mounted their steeds to rush back to the farmstead.

When they arrived, no rover could be seen in the vicinity, except for the dead and wounded left under the distant trees. Old Firehand immediately went up to the roof to scout around.

Up there still standing guard was Mrs. Butler, whose great concern was now happily relieved by the knowledge that the rovers' attack on the herds had been successfully repulsed.

"Then we're saved now?" she asked taking a deep breath. "Since the rovers have incurred such severe losses, can we not assume that they've lost the courage to continue their attacks?"

"Maybe," the hunter said, reflecting.

"Only maybe?"

"Unfortunately, yes. Most likely they won't attempt to attack the herds again, since they have to assume they're well guarded, not only by Indians, but also by a sufficient number of whites. But it's different with the farmstead. While the bandits must realize that nothing can be accomplished in daytime, they may figure they can accomplish something in the dark of night. We must be prepared for a possible nighttime attack."

"Then they surely won't show up again by day?"

"I'm afraid they will. Out there by the trees lie their wounded they must take care of. I'm convinced we'll see them there shortly. They took flight in a westerly direction and from that direction they'll appear again."

He pointed his telescope to the west and shortly thereafter continued, "Just so, here they come! They arced around and are returning now to their casualties. We must assume that ---"

He stopped. Still looking through his scope, he had swung it in a northerly direction.

"What is it?" asked the lady. "Why did you stop, sir? What's the reason for your suddenly concerned look?"

For a moment longer Old Firehand looked through the scope, put it down and answered, "Because something is likely to happen now which will not improve our situation."

"What do you mean? What's to happen?" the lady asked anxiously.

He considered whether he had to tell her the truth. Fortunately, his decision was made easier by the sudden appearance on the roof of Lord Castlepool who wanted to find out whether the rovers were yet visible. Old Firehand used the interruption to assure Mrs. Butler, "It's nothing of major concern to us, ma'am. Not to worry; you may go down to get our people some refreshments, please."

Calmed somewhat, she acceded to his request, but as soon as she disappeared, the hunter turned to the lord, who had brought his big telescope up top. "I had good reason to ask the lady to leave," he said. "Take your scope, your lordship, and look straight to the west. What do you see there?"

The Englishman peered westward, then answered, "Those wretched rovers. I see them clearly. They are coming."

"Are they really coming?"

"Eh? What? Of course! What else would they do?"

"Then my scope is better than yours, although it's much smaller. Do you see the rovers on the move?"

"No. They have stopped."

"And in what direction are they facing?"

"North."

"Then turn your scope in that direction! Maybe you'll see why the devils have stopped."

"Right-o, sir, will do!" A moment later he said, "Three horsemen are approaching. They haven't noticed the rovers."

"Horsemen? Truly?"

"Yes! But no! One of them seems to be a lady. I see her long riding dress and the wafting veil."

"And do you know who these three are?"

"No. How can I know --- oh dear, they would not be ---?"

"That's correct," Old Firehand nodded. "It's the farmer, his brother and his daughter. The messenger we sent to warn them must have missed them."

The lord collapsed his scope and exclaimed, "We must jolly well get to them; otherwise they will fall into the rovers' hands!"

He rushed to leave. But before he could, the hunter seized his arm saying, "Stay, sir, and don't raise any alarm! The lady need not learn anything right now. We can neither warn nor help the three; it's too late for that. Look!"

The lord took up his scope again and saw that the rovers were now galloping toward the three.

"By George!" he exclaimed. "They will kill them!"

"They wouldn't think of doing that! These fellows recognize an advantage when it comes their way and will make good use of it. What would they gain by the death of these three people? Nothing! On the contrary, that would only make us more determined to oppose them. If they keep them alive, the three will be hostages they can use to extort concessions from us we otherwise would not agree to. Watch! It's happening! The three are surrounded. There's nothing we could have done. First, time was too short, and second, even now we're still too few to oppose the rovers in the open."

"Well, that's true, sir," the lord responded. "But woe to the rascal who will not treat the captives decently! But shall we really allow ourselves to be blackmailed for concessions? We should actually be ashamed to enter into negotiations with such ruffians!"

135

Old Firehand shrugged his shoulders in his characteristic way, and a confident, almost contemptuous smile played about his lips, as he answered, "Just leave it to me, sir! I've never done anything I later had to be ashamed of. And even if the rovers were a thousand strong, Old Firehand would not accept blackmail. When I tell you that the three captured people out there are in no danger, you can believe my words. Nevertheless, I urge you not to say anything to Mrs. Butler about what's happened. I myself almost gave it away in my moment of surprise. But telling her would not do any good, and would only frighten her."

"Is no one else to know about it?"

"Those close to us we'll tell so they'll at least know where they are. Would you take on this task then, please? Go down to them now, but urge them not to talk about it. I'll continue to observe the rovers from up here and, depending on their actions, make my provisions."

Lord Castlepool descended to the yard to inform his companions of what had transpired. Old Firehand directed his attention to the rovers who had forced their three captives to ride with them to the group of trees where they had left their wounded. There they dismounted and settled in. The hunter could see that a very lively conversation or deliberation was taking place. He thought he knew what its result would be, and reflected on how he should respond. In this task he was interrupted by Droll who, in a rush, had leaped up the stairs, then asked in German, "Is it really true what the lord told us? The two Butlers have been taken captive and the girl too?"

"That's so, " nodded Old Firehand.

"Who would have thought it possible! Now the rovers will think they're riding high and dry. They will surely come with great demands. And us? How are we going to answer?"

"Well, what do you think?" Old Firehand asked, giving the little man a pleasant but probing look.

"You even ask!" the latter responded. "Nothing, absolutely nothing shall we concede. Or should we pay them ransom?"

"Will we not be forced into it?"

"No, no and no again! These bandits cannot do a thing. What are they to do? Kill the captives? They wouldn't risk it since they'd fear our revenge. They'll threaten to do it, but we shouldn't believe it and can simply laugh at them."

"But we must have consideration for the family; their situation is highly compromised. Even if they're kept alive, the rovers may apply pressure and do all kinds of things to make them miserable."

"That won't hurt them; they'll have to live with it. Why did they have to approach so carelessly anyway? It should be a warning for the future --- and, by the way, I'll be hornswoggled if we won't find ways and means to get them out of this dilemma."

136

"How are we going to do it? Do you have an idea?"

"No, not yet; it's not necessary yet. First we must wait to see what will eventuate; only then can we act. I'm not at all afraid, at least not for myself, whom I know very well. Come the right moment, we'll surely get the right ideas. Let's wait for night and watch where they set up camp. Then perhaps I can slip in to free the captives."

"I have confidence in your doing so, but it would be a highly dangerous enterprise!"

"Poppycock! You and I have accomplished much more dangerous feats. Neither one of us is soft in the head. An old Altenburger saying goes like this: 'If we can do it, than we have done it'. That's how it's here, too. If one has the brain, the native intelligence, the execution won't be difficult. No, we aren't going to be afraid of such rascals as the rovers, who haven't the faintest idea how Adam met Eve.

"Hold it, I think --" he interrupted himself. "Watch it! They're coming now! Two fellows, straight for the house. They're waving flags for us to see that they're to be treated as parliamentarians. Will you talk with them?"

"Of course! For the captives' sake, I need to learn what their demands are. Come along!"

Quickly they descended to the yard where their people stood anxiously by the embrasures to observe the two emissaries. The pair remained outside rifle range, waving their flags. Old Firehand opened the gate, stepped out and gave them a signal to approach. When they arrived, they greeted him politely and made every effort to appear confident.

"Sir, we come as emissaries," one of them said, "to present our demands."

"So!" the hunter answered in a stern voice. "Since when do prairie rabbits dare to come to the grizzly bear to issue commands?"

The comparison he used was not far off the mark. Broad and forceful, he towered over them, his eyes dominating them so sharply that involuntarily they stepped back a pace.

"We are no rabbits, sir!" declared the rovers' speaker.

"No? Well then, maybe cowardly prairie wolves content to feed on carrion? You pretend to be emissaries. Bandits you are, thieves and murderers who have placed themselves outside the law, the sort that any honest man should feel free to shoot on sight!"

"Sir," the rover objected, "I need not listen to such insults ---"

"Be quiet, scoundrel!" thundered Old Firehand. "Rogues you are, nothing else! I should actually be ashamed of myself even to talk to you. I permitted your approach only to find out how insolent characters like you might dare to be. You're the ones who need to listen to what I'm going to tell you and not to object to any of it. Say another word I don't like and I'll smash you to the ground. Do you know who I am?"

"No, not exactly" answered the man, intimidated and abashed.

"I'm called Old Firehand. Tell the others who have sent you; they may know that I'm not a man to trifle with. They should already have found that out today. Now to the point: what's your message?"

"We're to report that the farmer with his brother and niece are in our hands."

"I know that already!"

"These three people will die ---"

"Damned if they will!" the hunter interrupted.

"--- if you do not agree to our terms," the emissary continued.

"Old Firehand never accepts terms, least of all from people of your ilk. Besides, you're the defeated ones, so if anyone can present conditions, it is I."

"But, sir, if you won't listen to me, the captives will be hung from the trees over there in front of your eyes!"

"Go right ahead! There are enough ropes at the farm to hang you too."

That the rover had not expected. He was well aware that his gang would not dare to execute their threat. Embarrassed, he looked at his feet, then ventured to say, "Consider, three lives!"

"I am considering this very well --- only three lives! As compensation, we shall wipe you all off the face of the earth! We have the advantage."

"But you can easily prevent the death of your friends!"

"How so?"

"By pulling out and delivering the farmstead to us."

At this, Old Firehand laid his fist so heavily onto the other's shoulder that the man winced. Then the hunter shouted at him, "Fellow, are you mad? Do you have anything more to say?"

"Uh, no, not exactly."

"Then get away from here as quickly as you can, or I shall think you an idiot in need of being rendered harmless."

"Are you serious, sir?"

"Totally serious. Away with you, right here and now, or it will be your end!"

He pulled his revolver. The two withdrew precipitously. However, one of them dared ask once at a safe distance, "May we come back if we get other instructions?"

"No."

"You're rejecting all negotiations?"

"Yes. I'll only talk to the red-haired colonel, and he only briefly."

"Do you promise him safe return?"

"Yes, provided he doesn't insult me."

"We will tell him."

They ran off so swiftly that all could see they were very glad to have escaped from the presence of this dangerous man. Firehand did not return to the yard, but instead strode purposefully in the direction of the rovers until he had covered half the distance to them. There he sat down to await the colonel whom he expected to come soon.

Those who did not know Old Firehand would have thought it an exceptional risk to separate himself so far from his companions; at least he might carry a rifle. But the hunter knew very well what he could or could not dare.

Soon events showed that he had not been mistaken. The circle of rovers opened as the colonel walked slowly towards Old Firehand. He was intent on producing an elegant bow but failed miserably in its execution. Recovering awkwardly, he said, "Good day, sir! You wanted to speak with me?"

"Not at all!" the frontiersman exclaimed. "I only said that I would not talk to anyone else; I would even have preferred it had you not shown up."

"Mister, you speak with a very proud voice!"

"I've every reason. But I advise you not to assume the same tone."

They faced each other eye to eye. The colonel lowered his first and answered with barely suppressed anger, "We seem to be facing each other on equal terms!"

"The rover in front of the honest frontiersman, the vanquished in front of the victor --- and you call that equal?"

"I'm not vanquished yet. We shall prove to you that your previous successes were only temporary. It's in our hands to turn the tables on you."

"Just try it!" Old Firehand laughed contemptuously.

This annoyed the colonel and he angrily responded, "We only need to take advantage of your own incaution."

"Oh! How so? Where have I been careless?"

"By exposing yourself this far away from the farmstead. Had we wanted to, you would have already become our prisoner. And without you, I suggest, the others behind the walls amount to nothing."

Old Firehand's face lit up in a cheerful laugh, like that of an adult who has just been told something stupid by a child.

"You must not believe your own words," he responded. "You! Catch Old Firehand! Why didn't you try? The fact that you haven't tried is the best proof that you didn't believe the attempt could succeed."

"Oho! Although everyone knows you are a good frontiersman, you're not by a long shot as invincible as you're thought to be. It would have taken only a few of my men on horseback to cut off your retreat, and you would have been our captive."

"You truly think so?" Old Firehand retorted scornfully.

"Yes. Even if you were the fastest runner, a horse is faster still. I suppose you'll admit this. You would've been surrounded before you could reach the building."

"Your calculation is correct except for two points. First is the supposition that I wouldn't have fought back; I'm not afraid of a few of you. And second, you forget that the ones set to catch me would've been in the range of my people's rifles. My friends would have killed them on the spot."

"No, that's not at all the point, sir. I've come to offer you the opportunity to save the lives of our three captives."

"Your effort has been for naught since the lives of these people are in no danger."

"Indeed?" the colonel offered with a malicious grin. "There you are mightily mistaken, sir. If you don't agree to our demands, sir, they will hang."

"I relayed already the information to you that all of you shall then hang."

"Ridiculous! Have you counted how many we are?"

"Very much so; but do you know how many I can put into the field against you?"

"We know precisely."

"Pshaw! You have no way of evaluating us."

"That's not necessary. We know how many farmhands are usually present on Butler's farm; there will be no more now. To those, we add at most the rafters you brought along from the Black Bear River."

With a sideways look, he measured the hunter expectantly, since he was certainly in the dark as to how many men Old Firehand had available. From the hunter's expression, he hoped to see whether his guess was correct. But Old Firehand was alert to this ploy. With a disparaging gesture, he answered, "Count your dead and wounded. Then tell me whether a few rafters could have accomplished this. Besides, you've seen our Indians and the other whites that came at you from the rear."

"The other whites?" the rover laughed. "These were none other than the rafters. I admit that you outfoxed us there. It was you who came to the aid of the Indians from the farmstead. Unfortunately, I didn't think of that earlier. We should have ridden at once to the farmstead. Then it would have been ours. No, sir, you can't impress us with your numbers. If we kill the captives, it would be impossible for you to avenge them."

Once more the colonel watched Old Firehand from beneath lowered lids. The latter shrugged his shoulders deprecatingly and suggested, "Let's not squabble about it. Even if we were only the few people you mistakenly assume us to be, we would be far superior. Rovers, rovers, what kind of people are you? Lazy workers, itinerants, tramps! Over there, though, behind the wall, stand the most famous hunters and scouts of the Wild West. A single one of them is worth ten of your rovers. Were we only twenty frontiersmen, and you'd dare to harm the captives, we would stay on your tracks for weeks and months to kill you to the very last man. You know that very well. That's why you won't harm even a hair on the heads of that good family."

Old Firehand had spoken these words in such a threatening and confident tone that the colonel averted his eyes. He knew that the hunter was the kind of man who turns his words into deeds. It was well known that once a single man had pursued an entire gang to avenge a misdeed, and that his rifle had put to death one after another. And of all man, certainly Old Firehand could be expected to accomplish such a feat. However, Brinkley was careful not to admit that. He looked up and with a sneering look said, "Let's wait and see! Were you sure of your position you wouldn't be standing here. Only apprehension must have driven you out here."

"Don't blabber such garbage. I was willing to speak to you, only with you, but not from fear, only to once more properly memorize your face and your voice for the future. That's the only reason. You're now sufficiently imprinted on my mind that we can separate. We are finished."

"Not yet, sir!" asserted the colonel. "I must first learn what kind of answer you have for me."

"You've received it already."

"No, because I have a new proposal for you. We're no longer asking to occupy the farm."

"Oh, that's very kind of you! And what else?"

"You return to us our horses you captured. To this you add all your weapons and munitions. Furthermore, the necessary cattle to provision us and, finally, twenty thousand dollars. That much should be on hand at the farmstead."

"Only that? Nothing more? Very nice! And what do you offer us in return?"

"We'll turn our captives over to you and move off after you have given us your word of honor to desist in any effort to pursue us. Now you know what I want and I request your decision. We've talked already far too long and to little use."

He said this in a voice as if he had the greatest moral right to his demands. Old Firehand pulled his revolver and answered, not angrily, but very quietly and with the most contemptuous smile, "Yes, prattle on you did enough, all of it crazy stuff, to which I now tell you only one thing: get lost at once, or you'll get a bullet in your head!"

"What? Is that ---"

"Away! Now!" the hunter interrupted in a far more intense voice, at the same time raising his weapon and pointing it at the colonel's head. "One --- two ---"

The rover decided not to wait for the "three"; he turned, shouted a threatening curse, and hastened quickly away. He had interpreted from Old Firehand's mien that the latter would truly have fired upon the count of "three".

The hunter watched the colonel's departure to make sure that he wouldn't catch a bullet from behind. Then he returned to the farmstead where the meeting had been observed with intense attention. Asked about its result, he gave a brief report, which was received with tumultuous approval.

"You acted very properly, dear boy," declared the lord. "One must not make the least allowance to such blighters. I believe they fear us and will avoid harming the captives. What do you think they will do now?"

"Hmm!" answered the hunter. "The sun is setting. I guess they'll wait until dark for another attempt at the wall. If they don't succeed, they still have the captives for another blackmail attempt."

"Would they truly force another attack?"

"Probably. They know they have far superior numbers. We must prepare our defenses and must carefully observe our enemies. Once it's dark, some of you must go outside, approach them covertly and afterwards inform me of all their moves. Who will volunteer for this dangerous task?"

Practically all offered to go. Old Firehand selected the ones he deemed most accomplished: Aunt Droll, Humpy-Bill and Gunstick-Uncle. The three were very happy with his expression of confidence.

The sun now touched the horizon. Its beams, like liquid gold flooding the wide expanse of the prairie, outlined the rovers in such a way that every single figure could clearly be distinguished from the farm. They were making neither preparations for departure nor for setting up a night camp. From this the defenders at the farmstead assumed that they had no intention of leaving the area, nor did they have any plans to stay where they presently were.

Old Firehand ordered wood to be brought to the yard's four corners, as well as coal, which is plentiful in Kansas. Then also several barrels of petroleum.

Once it had become totally dark, the scouts departed. Since there was a risk of discovery and pursuit, several lassos were attached at various spots on the outside of the wall so the three could quickly regain the protection of the yard without having to wait for the gate to be opened.

Logs were soaked in petroleum, lit and thrown over the wall. More logs and coal were heaped on top creating four blazes outside the wall's four corners. The fires illuminated the approach so well that one could readily spot any rover advance not only in groups, but by any individual man. The flames continued to be fed but only through the embrasures so that no one would be exposed to enemy fire.

More than an hour passed; nothing seemed to be moving outside. Then Gunstick-Uncle came bounding over the wall. He looked up at Old Firehand to tell him in his original way, "The trees the rovers left behind - for a very different place to find."

"Thought so. But where to?" the hunter asked, smiling about the rhyme.

Uncle pointed to the corner at the right of the gate and answered in a somber tone, "Out there, in the bushes by the river - we now must look for them to quiver."

"They dared to come that close! Shouldn't we have heard their horses?"

"Wisely did they take them out -- to graze the prairie or thereabout -- but I do not know the very place -- there was no light for me to gaze."

"And where are Bill and Droll?"

"They stayed behind the bandit rovers -- to watch and guard these awful loafers!"

"Good! I must know exactly where the rovers are located. Be so kind as to get back to Droll and Bill. As soon as the rovers have settled down, Droll is to come and inform me. Those bandits probably think they acted very cleverly, but they've entered a trap we only have to close."

The Uncle departed, and the lord who had listened intently to the conversation asked what trap Old Firehand was referring to. The hunter answered, "The enemy is down there by the river. He has the water behind him and the wall in front; if we block the two sides we have them."

"I say, that's quite ripping! But how do you propose to block them?"

"By getting the Indians to position themselves on the south; we, then, will leave here and attack them from the north."

"Then you're willing to leave the walls bare of any defense?"

"No, the farmhands will remain; that should suffice. However, we'd be in trouble if the rovers hit on the idea of attacking the wall; but I don't expect them to be smart enough to figure out that we've left this primary area unprotected. I'm also going to have the horses' location scouted out. If we find them, the few guards could easily be overcome. Once we're in possession of their horses, the rovers have lost, since any that escape tonight we can pursue tomorrow and destroy them."

"Well, a daring and excellent plan. You're truly a brave fellow, sir!"

Without delay Black Tom and the smart old Blenter were dispatched to search for the horses. Meanwhile, two of the farmhands who knew the area very well were sent to Good Sun to deliver explicit instructions. Prior to these peoples' return, nothing more could be initiated.

A long time passed before anyone reappeared. Finally the farmhands showed up. They had found the Indians and had led them close by, hiding now by the river only a few hundred paces from the rovers. Upon hearing the first shot fired, they'd be ready to attack.

Then Droll, Bill and Uncle returned.

"All three of you?" Old Firehand asked disapprovingly. "At least one of you should have stayed outside."

"I wouldn't know what for, if it's necessary," answered Droll, using his peculiar phrasing.

"To keep watching the rovers, of course."

"Would be superfluous! I know where I'm at. I got so close that I could overhear everything. They are very annoyed about our fires, which make an attack impossible. It's their intention to wait us out and see how long our supply of wood and coal will last. They're of the opinion that our supply will be exhausted in a few hours, because they think that the farmer was never prepared to withstand a long siege. Then they intend to launch their assault."

"That works very much to our advantage, since it'll allow us time to close the trap."

"What trap?"

Old Firehand explained his plan.

"That's wonderful, he, he, he, he!" laughed Droll using his usual undertone when something gave him pleasure. "This will and must succeed. The rovers believe we think they're still over there beneath the trees. But, sir, there's something else of great importance to consider."

"What?"

The captives' condition. I'm afraid they may be killed as soon as hostilities begin."

"Don't you think I've thought of that? Fortunately, I'm not worried about what you're suggesting. Although I too am convinced that the captives would be the first to perish, we can prevent it. Three of us will sidle up close to where they're being kept to protect both Butlers and the young lady. Are they bound?"

"Yes, but not very securely."

"Well, then they must be quickly freed from their ropes and ---"

"And then into the water with them," Droll inserted quickly.

"Into the water?" Old Firehand asked in surprise.

"Of course."

"You're being facetious, dear Aunt."

"Facetious? Not for a moment!" When he saw the questioning looks from all the other men, he continued with a snicker, "Yes, into the water with them. He, he, he, he, that's the cutest trick we can play. Just imagine what astonished faces the rovers will have! And how they will wonder what happened!"

"They won't have time for that since we're going to bash in their skulls."

"Not immediately, not right away; that will come later," Droll continued.

"Later? How so? Are we going to give them time to escape?"

"Not at all; we'll simply free the captives before our attack."

"Do you think that's possible?"

"Not only possible, but very much necessary. During the battle it'll be very difficult to protect the captives; we must remove them from danger beforehand. It won't even be that difficult."

"Not difficult?" marveled Old Firehand. "Well, then, how do you expect to accomplish this? I know you're a sly fox. You have already fooled many a smart fellow and safely extricated your head from a tight noose when all seemed lost. What wild idea have you come up with this time?"

"A good one, I'm certain!"

"Well, then tell us!" Old Firehand demanded.

"Doesn't need much shrewdness. I'm surprised you didn't hit on it yourself. Remember the canal behind the house leading from the yard to the river? It's subterranean, or rather covered, and the rovers have no knowledge that it exists. I crept past them to the river's bank, and despite the dark, was able to see where the canal enters. The large rocks there form a small dam that directs the water into the canal. And, think about it, gentlemen! Close to the canal's entry is where the rovers are waiting. They've formed a semicircle by the bank where the captives are being kept. They think they have them secure there. Yet it's precisely the setting which will enable us to get them out."

"Ah, I'm following you!" Old Firehand responded. "You intend to enter the canal from inside the yard and follow it to the river?"

"Yes. But not by myself. Two others have to come along, so there's one for each of the captives."

"Hmm! An excellent idea. But let's check first whether the canal is passable."

Old Firehand asked several of the farmhands and learned to his satisfaction that the canal was free of mud and held clean air. It would be easy to pass through and -- by a fortunate circumstance -- a small boat was hidden at the entrance large enough to carry three men. The boat was moored there to protect it from raiding Indians or other marauders.

The crafty Aunt's plan was thoroughly discussed and it was agreed that Droll, Humpy-Bill and Gunstick-Uncle would execute it. When their preparations were almost finished, Tom and Blenter returned. They had searched the area in a wide arc but had not found the horses. The rovers were wily enough to have taken them well away from the farm.

Then Old Firehand, together with a knowledgeable farmhand, went over the wall and sought out the Osage chief to make sure that he had received the proper instructions. This accomplished, they returned to find that Droll, Bill and Uncle had removed some of their clothing preparatory to entering the canal, which they proposed to light with a lantern they took along. The water reached only to their chests. They carried their rifles on their shoulders and tied their knives, revolvers and munition bags around their necks. The tall Gunstick-Uncle led the way, holding the lantern high. Once they disappeared, Old Firehand and his people moved away too.

The hunter opened the gate very quietly and, once outside, left it partly ajar so he and his companions could enter quickly should they be forced to retreat. A farmhand was assigned as gate guard, ready to close it should the rovers

145

approach. The other farmhands and women were posted at the wall facing the river and ordered to defend against any possible attack as best they could.

The rafters, and particularly the accompanying frontiersmen, were expert in covert approaches. Under the famous hunter's lead, they first veered north so as not to be seen by the light from the fires. When they reached the river, they crept back along the bank towards the south until they were sure to have come close to where the rovers were gathered. Old Firehand stole still closer until, despite the darkness, his sharp eyes could make out the semicircle where sat the waiting bandits. Knowing now from where his assault should come, he returned to his people to instruct them and await the signal from the three men assigned to free the captives.

Droll, Uncle and Bill had by now traversed the canal, whose water, fortunately, had not been cold enough to encumber them very much. Just before the canal's mouth, they found the little boat tied to an iron hook in the wall. Uncle extinguished their lantern and hung it on the hook. Droll then asked the two others to wait at that spot. He wanted to enter the river by himself to reconnoiter. It took a quarter of an hour before he returned.

"How about it? Humpy-Bill asked anxiously.

"It wasn't easy," the Aunt answered. "The water is no hindrance since the river isn't any deeper than the canal, but the darkness in the bushes was a problem. I couldn't see anything so I had to literally grope my way forward. But now that I've orientated myself, the darkness will be our best ally."

"Looking from the direction of our fires, it must be possible to see clearly!"

"Not from the water, only from the bank. Once again, the rovers are sitting in a large semicircle, its center point being at the river. And within the circle, close to the water, well away from the rovers sit the three prisoners ---"

"What carelessness!" Bill scoffed. "In such a fashion they cannot be properly watched in the darkness. If only they could free themselves from their bonds, how easy it would be for them to reach the water and get away. Surely the two men at least must know how to swim."

"Not as easy as you think! There's a special guard beside them watching them closely."

"Hmm! He must be dealt with. But how?"

"We eliminate him. There's no other way and we should not feel sorry for the ruffian."

"Then you have a plan?"

"Yes. The prisoners need not enter the water. We'll bring the boat to them."

"That will surely be noticed. Certainly its shape will be visible against the shimmering water."

"There's no shimmer at all! The water is so muddy from yesterday's rain that it seems barely different from the adjacent ground. Let's get the boat over there and tie it up. You stay with it at the water's edge and I'll go alone on land to knife the guard and untie the captives. I'll bring them to you. They in turn will row into the canal to be safe. We then can cheerfully take the place where they'd been sitting. Once ready, we'll give the signal, the vulture's call. Then the dance can begin. Agreed, Bill?"

"Well, I can't think how to plant it any better."

"And you, Uncle?"

"Exactly as you had in mind --- we aim to leave this task behind," answered the poet.

"All right then, let's go!"

They untied the boat and pushed it into the river. Droll, knowing the terrain, played guide. Keeping hard to the bank, he advanced it slowly and carefully. Then he grounded the little craft and the two others stepped out to tie it up.

"We've arrived," he whispered, "wait here until I return!"

The bank was not very high. He crept up quietly. Beyond the bushes he saw the fires at two of the wall's corners against which the rovers' outlines were reasonably visible. At most ten paces from the bank sat four people, the captives with their guard. Farther back, the little man could barely make out the dark shapes of the rovers in various positions of rest. With his rifle held close, he moved surreptitiously, step by step, until he had arrived just behind the guard. Only then did he gently lay his rifle aside and silently reach for his knife. The rover had to die without uttering a sound.

Droll pulled in his knees, rose, and grabbed the rover by the throat with his left hand and with his right stabbed the blade so savagely into his back that it penetrated through his heart. Quickly lowering himself, the Aunt rolled the rover onto his side. This had all happened so quickly that the prisoners had not even been aware of it. Only after a while did the girl say, "Pa, our guard is gone!"

"Really? Yes. I'm surprised," her father replied. "But stay put; he may be testing us."

"Quiet, quiet!" Droll whispered to them. "No one is to hear a sound. The guard is dead here in the grass. I've come to rescue you."

"Rescue? Heavens! Impossible! You must be the guard after all!"

"No, sir, I'm a friend. You know me from Arkansas. I'm Droll, they call me the Aunt."

"My God! Is it true?" the man exclaimed.

"Hush! Hush, sir! Old Firehand is also here, and Black Tom and many others. The rovers wanted to loot the farm, but we repulsed them. We saw them take you into captivity. I've come here with two good men to get you out. And if you still don't trust me, since you cannot see my face, I'll prove the truth of my words by cutting you loose. Let me feel your bonds!"

A few cuts and the three regained the use of their arms and legs.

"Now I do believe you, sir," whispered the farmer, who until now had remained silent. "I shall soon show you how grateful I am. But what now?"

"Go down to the river bank silently. We came through the canal and brought the boat here. You get in and make for the canal. You're familiar with it. There you wait for the dance to finish."

"The dance? What dance?"

"The one that begins right now. The rovers have the river to their back and the farmstead's wall in front, two obstacles in their way. To the right of us Old Firehand is positioned with a number of rafters and hunters. To the left the Osage chief, Good Sun, waits with a group of redskins for my signal. As soon as I give it, they'll know you're safe and will attack the rovers. Those villains will have to fight on two sides, while being hemmed in by the river and the wall. Even if we cannot entirely destroy them, they'll encounter such losses that they'll be unable to continue any more depredations."

"So that's how it is. And we're to get to safety by boat?" Butler asked.

"Yes. We feared the rovers would lay hands on you the moment we attack them. That's why we came here first to rescue you."

"That was very brave of you and earns our highest gratitude. But do you really think we're such cowards that my brother and I would fold our hands and let others fight for us and risk their lives? No, sir, there you're mistaken!"

"Well, fine! Glad to hear that! That's two more men on our side. Do as you please, but the little miss must not remain here when the bullets fly. She must be taken to safety."

"That's true. Be so kind as to take her to the canal! How about weapons, though? Ours have been stolen by the rovers. Can you leave us at least a knife or a revolver?"

"No need for that, sir. What we have, we need ourselves. But here lies the guard with enough weaponry for at least one of you. For the other, I'll provide by sneaking up on a rover and ---" He stopped in midsentence. "Pssst, quiet, someone is coming! Most likely one of their leaders to make sure you're being well guarded. Let me take care of him!"

Looking against the fires they could see a man approaching to check the rovers' position and to ascertain that all else was in good order. Coming closer, he halted in front of what he thought were the captives and asked, "Well, Collins, is everything all right?"

"No," answered Droll, being mistaken for the guard.

"Well! Keep your eyes open! It'll cost you your head if something happens. Understood?"

"Yes. But my head is more secure than yours. Watch out for your own!"

He spoke these threatening words in a purposely undisguised voice. He wanted the man to bend over him. The ploy succeeded. The rover stepped a pace closer, lowered his head and demanded, "What's that supposed to mean? What's come into your head? Aren't you Collins ? ---"

He was unable to continue for Droll's hands were suddenly like iron clamps around his throat. The Aunt pulled him to the ground and dug his thumbs into his windpipe so deeply that no sound escaped. There was a spasmodic kicking of the rover's legs, then all was quiet. Droll whispered, "So, now he's delivered you the weapons you need. That was very obliging of him, wasn't it?"

"Do you have him securely?" asked Butler.

"How can you ask? He's dead. Take his rifle and whatever you need. Meanwhile I'll bring the little miss to the boat."

Droll stood up, took Ellen Butler by the hand and led her to the water, where he informed his waiting companions how things stood at the moment. Bill and Uncle took the girl to the canal and tied up the boat, then waded back to join Droll and the Butler brothers. The latter had meanwhile armed themselves with weapons from the two rovers. In a hushed voice, Aunt Droll said earnestly, "Now it can begin. We 're expecting the rovers to rush here first to secure the prisoners. That could become very dangerous for us. Let's move some distance to the right where we can avoid them."

The five crawled stealthily along the river bank until they found some suitable cover. There they rose where they could conceal themselves behind some tall bushes. While they themselves were in complete darkness, they had the rovers clearly visible in front of them as easy targets. Droll put his hands to his mouth and produced a short, tired croak like that of a raptor briefly woken from its sleep. This sound, so frequently heard on the prairie, went unnoticed by the rovers, even after it was repeated twice more. For a moment deep silence ruled. Then came Old Firehand's shouted command, "Fire!"

From the right the rafters' rifles barked. The hunter and his men had approached so close that each of them had a single man for a target. Then from the left sounded the shrill war cries of the Indians, who first let loose a rain of arrows on the rovers, then attacked them with their tomahawks.

"Us too, now!" ordered Droll. "First with bullets, then with rifle butts!"

It was a true Wild West melee that now developed. The rovers had felt so secure that the sudden cross fire stunned them deeply. Like rabbits pursued by eagles overhead, they at first crouched terrified and offered no resistance. Then, when the attackers were in their midst working them over with rifle butts, tomahawks, revolvers and Bowie knives, their brief shock dissolved and they sought frantically to defend themselves. They were unable to count the number of their enemies, but in the confusion and the poor illumination it seemed to be larger by a factor of two or three times than it truly was. This increased their terror and flight seemed to be their only salvation.

"Away, get away to the horses!" a voice was heard shouting.

"That's the colonel," Droll raged. "Get him! Don't let him get away!"

He rushed to the area from where the voice had come, others following him, but in vain. The colonel had been clever and experienced enough to quickly hide in the bushes and observe developments from there. Like a snake, he crept from bush to bush, staying in the deepest shadows not to be seen. The victors made every effort to let few escape, but the rovers' numbers were so great that when they finally realized the hopelessness of their situation, they grouped together and broke through to flee northwards.

"After them!" ordered Old Firehand. "Don't let them catch their breath!"

His intention had been to reach the rovers' horses at the same time as the bandits, but this turned out to be impossible. The farther they got from the farm, the dimmer the fires' illumination became, until they all were surrounded by such darkness that it was no longer possible to differentiate friend from foe. Some of the former almost came under friendly fire.

Old Firehand was finally forced to call his men to rally. It took several minutes for all of them to gather, giving the fleeing rovers an even greater head start which, since they could no longer be seen, was impossible to overcome. Although the pursuers pressed on in the direction the bandits had headed, they soon heard the mocking cries of the rovers and the hoofbeats of many galloping horses, which meant that further attempts at pursuit were useless.

"Return!" Old Firehand commanded. "Nothing else is left to do except prevent the wounded from hiding so they could escape later."

This concern proved unnecessary. The Indians had not taken part in the pursuit. Greedy for the whites' scalps, they had remained behind, had carefully searched the battle field and the adjacent bushes for any living rovers and had killed and scalped them all.

When in the light of the fires the bodies were counted, it turned out that, including the dead from the daytime attack, there were two dead rovers for every live victor, a terrible number! Notwithstanding, the number of the escaped was so great that they could only congratulate each other for having taken flight.

Of course, Ellen Butler was immediately brought from her hiding place. The young girl had not shown any fear but rather had shown surprising calm and levelheadedness from the moment of her imprisonment. When Old Firehand learned about this, he told her father, "Until now, I had thought it would be very risky to take Ellen along to Silver Lake, but now I no longer object to it. She's convinced me that she's not going to be a problem for us."

Since there was no longer any danger that the rovers would soon return, the Indians spent the rest of the night in a victory celebration. They were given two steers, which were butchered and divided. Soon the heady scent of roasting beef rose from the fires. Later, the booty was also shared out. The weapons and other abandoned possessions of the rovers were given to the Indians, which pleased them exceedingly. They expressed their satisfaction in their customary ways by giving long speeches and performing war dances. Only at daybreak did the noise abate. The rejoicing ended and the redskins wrapped themselves in their blankets to finally fall asleep.

As for the rafters, they had bedded down immediately after the pursuit in order to be in good shape for the morning. Fortunately, none of them had died in the battle, although some of them had suffered wounds. With their help, Old Firehand intended to pursue the rovers at dawn to determine where they had fled.

When sunrise came, the rafters found tracks leading back to the Osage Nook and followed them there only to find the place deserted. Old Firehand examined the ground closely. He was able to determine that earlier, additional groups of rovers had arrived. The remnants from the fight had joined them and together they had swiftly departed in a northerly direction, fearing to be hunted down. It looked, therefore, as if they had abandoned their plans for the farm. But they were totally unaware that Old Firehand knew very well their future intentions.

However, unknown to Old Firehand, the colonel, with two volunteers, had separated from the band of rovers to ride ahead and scout the environs of Sheridan where his next heist was to take place.

8. A Drama on the Prairie

A man was slowly and wearily plodding across the prairie, a rare sight where even the poorest man owned a horse since its maintenance cost nothing. It was difficult to define the man's background. His dress had an urban look but was threadbare. He gave the appearance of a peaceful fellow to which, however, the old, very long rifle he carried on his shoulder stood in striking contrast. His face was pale and drawn, possibly due to the hardship of a long march on foot.

At times he halted as if wanting to rest, but his hope of finding people drove him quickly to renewed effort. Again and again he scanned the horizon for a long time in vain, until finally his eyes shone with relief -- he had spied a man on the horizon, like himself on foot, who approached from the right, and whose direction had to intersect his own. New strength seemed to flow into his limbs; his pace increased and he soon saw that the other had noticed him as well and had stopped to await him.

The newcomer was dressed oddly. He wore a blue tailcoat with yellow buttons and a red standup collar, velvet knickerbockers and top boots of a yellowish color. A bow tie made from a blue silk neckerchief covered his breast. A broad-brimmed straw hat completed his outfit. From his neck hung a large shiny wooden box on a leather strap. The man was tall and lean; lean too was his clean-shaven face. Whoever saw his features and looked into the small, cunning eyes knew at once that he was facing a true Yankee, a Yankee of the sort whose craftiness has become proverbial.

When the weary man had closed to hearing distance, the box carrier lifted his hat to greet the other, "Greetings, comrade. Where do you hail from?"

"From Kinsley down there," the fatigued one answered, pointing backwards with his hand. "And you?"

"From just about everywhere. Last from the farm behind me."

"And where are you headed?"

"Everywhere. Now to the farm ahead of us."

"Is there one?"

"Yes. It's no more than half an hour's walk."

"Thank God! I wouldn't have lasted much longer!" This was said with a deep sigh. By now the nearly exhausted fellow had bridged the distance to the other and, tottering, had stopped.

"Why couldn't you have lasted much longer?"

"Because of hunger."

"By the devil! Hunger? Here, I can help you. Sit down on my box. I'll give you something to put between your teeth."

He set the box down and pushed the stranger onto it. Then he produced two huge slices of bread from a chest pocket of his tailcoat, from his lap pocket a large piece of ham. He offered both to the hungry man and said, "Here, eat comrade! While these are no delicacies, they'll do for your hunger."

The famished man reached for the food. He was so starved that he wanted to take an immediate chunk out of the bread, thought differently, hesitated and said, "You're very kind, sir. But this food is for you. If I eat it, you'll go hungry."

"Oh, no! I tell you. At the next farm I'll get as much to eat as I want."

"Are you known there?"

"No. I've never been there. But don't talk now. Eat!"

The hungry fellow swiftly acted on this invitation. The Yankee sat down on the grass, watched him and was pleased how quickly giant bites disappeared behind the man's healthy teeth. When the bread and ham were gone, he asked, "You're not satiated yet, but for the time being satisfied, I presume?"

"I'm like a newborn child, sir. Consider, I've traveled for three days without a bite to eat."

"Is it possible? You haven't eaten anything from Kinsley to here? Why? Why didn't you bring any provisions?"

"I couldn't. My departure was too sudden."

"Then why not stop at a farm?"

"I had to avoid farms."

"Oh, that's it. But you carry a rifle; could you not have shot some game?"

"No, sir, I'm no rifleman. I would more likely hit the moon than a dog standing in front of me."

"What then is the rifle for?"

"To scare away red- or white-skinned vagrants."

The Yankee looked the man over then suggested, "Listen, mister, something isn't quite right about you. You seem to be fleeing from something, yet appear to be a most harmless individual. What's your destination?"

"Sheridan, the railroad stop."

"That far and without any provisions! You'll end up a wreck. You don't know me, but when in trouble it's better to show some trust. Tell me what's wrong. Maybe I can help you."

"It's easily told. You're not originally from Kinsley; I would otherwise know you and you can therefore not be one of my enemies. My name is Haller; my parents were German. They came from the Old Country to get ahead in the States but didn't make it. Roses didn't bloom for me either. I worked and did a lot of things until I became a railroad clerk. My last employment was in Kinsley.

"Sir, I'm a fellow who isn't hurt easily but when one is utterly insulted, the bile rises and calls for a response. I had a quarrel with the local newspaper editor which resulted in a rifle duel. Never before did I have such a murder weapon in my hands! A rifle duel at thirty paces! Just hearing it made all shades of color appear before my eyes.

"To make it short, the hour came. We took positions. Sir, think of me what you will but I'm a peace-loving man and didn't want to become a murderer. Even the thought that I could kill my adversary gave me goose bumps. When the command was issued, I aimed several feet to one side.

"I squeezed the trigger; he did too. The shots rang out --- just think, I wasn't hit but my bullet had entered his heart. In horror, I ran away holding onto the rifle, which wasn't even mine. I think its barrel is crooked; bullets fired from it seem to travel three feet to the left. The worst was that the editor has numerous and influential friends, something very important here in the west. I had to flee, flee immediately, and only took time to say goodbye to my superior. For my well-being, he suggested I go to Sheridan and wrote a letter of recommendation to a local engineer there. You may read it to convince yourself that I tell the truth."

He got up from the box, pulled a letter from one of his pockets, opened it and handed it to the Yankee.

"Dear Charoy," it read.

"I'm sending you Mister Joseph Haller, my previous clerk. He is of German descent, an honest, loyal and diligent chap who has had the bad luck to shoot around a corner and, precisely because of that, dropped his adversary in the dirt. He must take a leave from Kinsley until grass has grown over this situation. Until then, please, do me the favor to employ him in your railroad office.

Yours,

Ben Norton."

To authenticate this letter, a signet had been affixed below the name. The Yankee folded the letter, returned it to its owner and said with a half ironic, half pitying smile, "I believe you, Mister Haller, even without the letter. Whoever sees and hears you knows he's facing a totally honest human being who wouldn't twist another's hair. I'm in the same boat. I'm neither a great hunter nor rifleman, before the Lord. That isn't a shortcoming for man does not live only by gunpowder and lead. But as afraid as you've been, I wouldn't have been. I believe you've taken the situation much too seriously."

"Oh, no. It was truly a dangerous situation."

"Are you sure you were pursued?"

"Certainly! That's why I avoided all farms so that my direction would remain unknown."

"And you're convinced you'll be welcomed in Sheridan and will get a position?"

"Yes, because Mister Norton and Mister Charoy, the engineer in Sheridan, are good friends."

"Well, then, what salary do you think you'll get there?"

"In Kinsley, I received eight dollars a week and hope to get the same in Sheridan."

"So! I know a job paying twice that much --- sixteen dollars and free board."

"What? Really?" the clerk exclaimed in surprise and delight. "Sixteen dollars? That's enough to get rich!"

"Maybe not that, but you could save some."

"Where's this position to be had? With whom?"

"With me."

"With .... you?" Haller sounded disappointed.

"Indeed. You probably didn't expect that from me?"

"Hmm! I don't know you."

"That can be remedied right away. I'm Master of Arts Doctor Jefferson Hartley, physician and veterinarian."

"You are a people and horse doctor?"

"A people and horse doctor," nodded the Yankee. "Would you like to become my assistant? I shall pay you the salary I just mentioned."

"But I don't know anything about medicine," Haller declared modestly.

"Nor do I," confessed the self-titled doctor.

"You don't?" Haller asked, surprised. "But you must have studied medicine?"

"No need for that!"

"But if you're a Master of Arts and a doctor ---?"

"That I am! These titles and degrees I know very well because I've conferred them on myself."

"You --- you, yourself?"

"Indeed! I'm very candid with you since I expect you to accept my offer of employment. I'm actually a tailor. At other times I've been a barber, later a dance instructor, then I opened a teaching institute for young ladies. When this ended, I took up accordion-playing and became an itinerant musician. After that, I excelled in at least another twenty or thirty different trades and activities. I've learned about life and people and have come to the conclusion that a smart fellow need not be a blockhead. People want to be deceived; yes, you even do them a favor and they're very grateful when you make them believe an X is a U. It's especially important to flatter their shortcomings, their mental and physical deficits and handicaps. That's why I've specialized in this field and became a doctor. Here, look at my medicine collection!"

He arose from the grass, unlocked his box and opened its lid. The interior was elegantly arranged in fifty compartments, which were covered by velvet and ornamented with golden lines and arabesques. The compartments held vials containing colorful liquids in varying shades.

"These are your medicines?" Haller ventured to ask. "Where do you obtain them?"

"I prepare them myself."

"I thought you didn't know anything about medicine!"

"Oh, but I do know about it! It's easy as pie. What you see here is nothing but a bit of color and a lot of water called 'aqua'. This last word constitutes my entire knowledge of Latin. All other descriptions I've made up myself. They need to sound very impressive which is why you read here: Aqua salamandra, Aqua peloponnesia, Aqua chimborassolaria, Aqua invocabulataria and others. You wouldn't believe what cures I have already accomplished with these waters. Never mind if you don't believe it, because I don't either. The main thing is not to wait for the cure but rather to collect the fee and then get away quickly. The United States is large, and before I cover it, many many years will pass. In the meantime, I'll have become a wealthy man. Life doesn't cost me anything because wherever I drop in, I'm offered more than I can eat, and upon leaving I have my pockets stuffed with more food. I don't have to be afraid of the Indians since, as a medicine man, I'm sacred and inviolable. Shake hands with me! Will you become my assistant?"

"Hmm," murmured Haller, scratching his ear and declining the proffered hand. "This is a delicate proposition. It's not a very honest one."

"Don't be ridiculous! Faith moves mountains! My patients believe in the medication's effect and grow healthy. Is that deception? At least give it a try! You've fortified yourself and since the farm I'm headed for is on your way, no damage is done in trying."

"Well, try it I will, already from gratitude, but I've no skill in making people believe in something."

"You don't need to. I'll take care of that. You simply maintain reverent silence and your entire labor will consist of retrieving the vial I specify from the box. Let's go then!"

He hung the box around his neck again and the two began their journey towards the farm. Half an hour later, they could make it out on the horizon; it didn't appear to be large. Now Haller was assigned to carry the box since it wasn't proper for the principal, the doctor and Master of Arts, to carry it.

The farm's main building was of timber construction. On each side was a well-tended orchard and a vegetable garden. The barn stood a distance away. In front of it, three horses had been tied up, a sign that strangers were present. These visitors were sitting in the living room drinking home-brewed beer. They were by themselves since only the farmer's wife, Mrs. Rafferty, was home and she was working in the small stable. Through the open door the three drinkers observed the charlatan and his assistant approaching.

"Hell's bells!" called one of them. "Do I see aright? I know one of this pair. If I'm not totally mistaken, it's Hartley, the accordion musician!"

"An acquaintance of yours?" asked the second, a wily rogue named Smitty. "Did you have anything to do with him?"

157

"Indeed. Some time ago, the fellow had done some good business and had his pockets full of money. Of course, I did just as well by emptying them during the night."

"Does he know it was you?" inquired Smitty.

"Hmm. Probably. It comes in very handy that I just dyed my red hair black. Under no circumstance call me Brinkley nor Colonel! This fellow could upset our plans!"

Just as the two newcomers reached the main building, Mrs. Rafferty came out of the stable. She extended a friendly greeting and asked their desires. When she learned that one was a doctor and the other his assistant, she appeared very pleased and invited them to enter her living room.

"Gentlemen," she announced to the previous company, "here comes a learned doctor with his assistant. I suppose these gentlemen's company will be a pleasure to you."

"Learned doctor?" murmured the colonel under his breath. "Insolent character! I'd love to tell him what I think of him!"

The newcomers said their hellos and without ceremony took seats at the table. To his satisfaction, the colonel noticed that Hartley didn't recognize him. Brinkley pretended to be a trapper and explained that he and his companions were on their way to the mountains. During the ensuing conversation, their hostess made herself busy at the fireplace. Above it hung a kettle in which lunch was simmering. When it was ready, she stepped out in front of the house and blew a horn, her customary method of calling in her people.

They arrived from the surrounding fields, the farmer, his son and daughter and a farmhand. They all shook hands with the visitors, the doctor's with particular friendliness. Then they joined the rest at the table to partake of the meal. Before and after, a prayer was spoken. They were simple, unaffected and pious people who were no match for the cleverness of a duplicitous Yankee.

Farmer Rafferty remained taciturn during the meal. Once he finished, he tamped some tobacco into his pipe, laid his elbows on the table and remarked in an expectant tone to Hartley, "After a while, doctor, we must get back to the fields. Right now we have a little time to talk to you. Maybe I can use some of your know-how. What illnesses are you familiar with?"

"What a question!" answered the quack. "I'm a physician and veterinarian and treat all human and animal ailments."

"Well, then you're the man I need. I hope you're not one of those cheats who travel about claiming to be doctors. They make promises and claim to know everything without ever having studied."

"Do I look like such a scoundrel?" Hartley responded bridling up. "Had I not studied, I wouldn't have been issued my doctor's and master of arts' certificates. Here sits my assistant. Ask him and he'll tell you that thousands of people owe their lives and health to my ministrations, not counting the animals."

"I believe it, I believe it, sir!" Rafferty assured him. "You have come at the right time. I have a cow in the stable. You know what that means. Hereabouts, a cow is kept in the stable only when she's ill. She hasn't eaten anything for several days; her head's hanging very low. I've given up on her."

"Pshaw! I give up on a patient only after he's died! Your helper can show her to me. Then I'll give you my opinion."

He was taken to the stable to look at the cow. On his return, he professed great concern and suggested, "It's high time I treated her or your cow might have died tonight. She's eaten locoweed. Fortunately, I have a surefire antidote. Tomorrow morning she'll be as healthy as she was before. Fetch me a bucket of water and you, assistant, pull out the Aqua sylvestropolia!"

Opening the box, Haller found the required vial from which Hartley poured several drops into the bucket of water. The cow was to be given half a gallon every three hours.

Then it was the turn of the human patients. Sarah Rafferty had the beginnings of a goiter and was given Aqua sumatralia. Her husband suffered from rheumatism and was administered Aqua sensationia. The daughter, healthy as a horse, was nevertheless urged to take Aqua furonia against her freckles. The farmhand limped a bit since boyhood, but used the opportunity to take care of this condition by applying Aqua ministeralia. As for Rafferty's son, the boy refused all efforts to treat him with Aqua florescia. Lastly Hartley inquired of the three strangers whether he could also be of service to them. The colonel shook his head and answered, "Thank you, sir! We're very healthy. And if I ever feel indisposed, I help myself by the Swedish method."

"And that is?"

"By using healing gymnastics. I dance to lively accordion music until I break out in a sweat. This is a wonderful treatment. Understood?"

He gave Hartley a meaningful look. Perplexed, the charlatan turned away from the colonel to ask his host for the location of the nearest farm. According to the information offered, the closest one was located eight miles to the west, another one fifteen miles to the north. When the Master of Arts announced that he wanted to leave right away for the nearer one, the farmer asked him about his fee. Hartley asked for five dollars which was gladly paid. He then took his leave; his assistant hung the box around his own neck.

Far enough away that they were no longer visible from the farm, Hartley explained, "We've come west but shall now turn north. It's not a good idea to go to the closer farm. That cow was so sick that she'll probably die within the hour. Should the farmer think of riding after me, I could do badly. But lunch and five dollars for ten drops of colored water, isn't that great? I hope you see the profit that may come to you and have decided to enter into my service."

"You're mistaken, sir," Haller answered. "You're offering me lots of money, but for that I would have to exercise even more mendacity. Don't take it badly! I'm the honest man that I want to remain. My conscience won't allow me to accept your offer."

Haller had said this so earnestly and firmly that the Master of Arts realized that further attempts at persuasion would be useless. Shaking his head pityingly, Hartley responded, "I meant well for you. Too bad your conscience is so tender!"

"Thank God he hasn't given me a different one. Here's your box. I'd like to reciprocate for what you've done for me but I'm unable to do so."

"Well, a man's will is his heaven. I don't want to urge you any further. But we need not separate right away. Our paths are the same to the next farm. Until we get there, we can stay together."

He took his box back. From his ensuing silence, it was clear that the clerk's integrity had made an impression. In this fashion, they walked side by side, their eyes straight ahead until they heard hoofbeats behind them. Turning, they were surprised to see the same three men they had met at the farm.

"Woe is me!" Hartley exclaimed. "They're after me. These fellows said they were heading for the mountains! Why would they not ride westward? I don't trust them; they're more likely hoodlums than trappers."

To his regret, he was soon to find that his premonition was correct. The horsemen halted as they came up to the two and the colonel sneeringly addressed the quack. "Mister, why did you change direction? Now the farmer won't be able to find you."

"The farmer find me? Why should he want to?"

"Yes. Once you were gone, I not only thanked Rafferty for his hospitality to us three weary travelers, but I also happened to tell him about your wonderful titles. He left in a rush to follow you and get his money back."

"Nonsense, sir!"

"Not nonsense, the truth. He headed for the farm you intended to bless with your next presence. We, though, were smarter. Knowing how to read tracks, we followed you to make you a proposal."

"I wouldn't know of what kind. I don't know you and want nothing to do with you."

"All the more we want something to do with you. We know you. By permitting you to cheat these honest farmers, we've become accomplices and it's only right that you pay us part of your fee. While you are two, we are three, and therefore demand three-fifths of the amount. You see that we act justly. If you don't agree, look at my two comrades!"

He pointed at his companions whose rifles were now aimed at Hartley, making it clear that any further argument would be dangerous. Convinced he was dealing with real hoodlums, Hartley was glad to get away so cheaply. Pulling three dollars from his pocket, he offered them to the colonel, suggesting, "You must have mistaken me for someone else and be in dire circumstances to require part of my well-earned fee. I take your demand as a jest and agree to it. Here's the three dollars, yours according to your calculation."

"Three dollars? Are you joking?" laughed the colonel. "Do you think we rode after you for such a pittance? No, no! I didn't mean only your today's take, but our share of everything you've made so far. I presume that you're carrying a nice little sum on you."

"Sir, that's not the case," Hartley protested, greatly afraid.

"Let's see! Since you deny it, I must check you out. I figure you'll allow that to be done without giving me any trouble since my companions don't fool around with their rifles. The life of a poor accordion player isn't worth a penny to us."

He dismounted and stepped toward the Yankee. The latter went through various verbal contortions to prevent the coming disaster, but for naught. The threatening rifle muzzles forced him to submit. He silently hoped that the colonel wouldn't find anything since he believed his cash was well hidden.

The now black-dyed red-haired colonel searched all of Hartley's pockets but found only a few dollars. He felt every inch of the man's suit to check if anything had been sewn in, but without success. Hartley now thought he had escaped danger, but Brinkley was too clever for him. He had the Yankee open the box and examined it closely.

"Hmm!" he ventured. "This velvet pharmacy is so deep that the compartments don't go all the way to its bottom. Let's see if they cannot be removed."

Hartley paled, for his adversary was on the right track. Using both hands, the colonel took hold of two compartment walls and pulled --- and sure enough, the pharmacy lifted from the box. At its bottom lay several envelopes. Opening them, he found them filled with bank notes of various denominations.

"Ah, here's the hidden treasure," he laughed triumphantly. "That's what I thought. A physician and veterinarian earns a heap of money. It had to be here."

He prepared to pocket the envelopes, which sent the Yankee into a rage. Incautiously, Hartley threw himself at the colonel to snatch back his money. A shot rang out. The bullet would surely have killed the charlatan had he not just then made a sudden sideways movement. As it was, it hit his upper arm, damaging the bone. With a shriek, the injured man sank to the grass.

"Rightly so, scoundrel!" the colonel shouted. "Get up or say a wrong word, and the second bullet will hit better than the first. Now let's also check your assistant."

Putting the envelopes in his pocket, he strode over to Haller.

"I'm not his assistant. I met him just before getting to the farm," the poor man explained nervously.

"So? Who or whatever are you then?"

Haller answered truthfully. He even handed the colonel his letter of recommendation to prove the truth of his statement. Brinkley read the paper, and returning it, said disparagingly, "I believe you. Whoever sees you can tell at once that you're a truly honest fellow who, however, has surely not invented gunpowder. Run over to Sheridan; I've nothing in mind for you." Turning once again to the Yankee, he continued, "I had spoken of our share of your loot, but since you lied to us, you ought not to complain if we take it all. Go ahead, make every effort to do some new business. Next time we meet, we shall share again."

Hartley had learned painfully that resistance would be fatal. He pleaded for getting at least part of his stash back, but only with the result that he was laughed at. The colonel mounted his horse and together with his two rogue companions and the spoils rode northward, leaving no doubt that he was no trapper and that it had never been his intention to head west to the mountains.

As they cantered along, the three hoodlums discussed their profitable adventure and agreed to divide the loot without telling their fellow bandits. When after some time, they reached a suitable spot where they couldn't be seen nor disturbed, they dismounted to count their take. When each had pocketed his share, the rover named Smitty turned to the colonel and said reprovingly, "You should have checked the second fellow. I wouldn't be surprised if he also had some money on him."

"Pshaw! What can you find on a poor clerk? At most a few dollars, not worth the effort."

"The question is: did he tell the truth and is he really just a clerk? What did the letter say that he showed you?"

"It was a letter of recommendation to an engineer by the name of Charoy at the railroad office in Sheridan."

"What? Really?" Smitty reacted. "And you returned it to him!"

"Yes. Of what use would that scrap of paper have been to us?"

"Much, very much! You even ask? Isn't it clear that this letter could have been of immense help in the execution of our plan? It's really strange you didn't see or think of it yourself. We kept our people away from Sheridan so we could surreptitiously investigate the location ourselves. First we must get to know the place, but we also need to know the amount kept in the railroad pay office. This could have been done unobtrusively if we had taken the man's letter. Then one of us could have gone to Sheridan claiming to be the clerk. He could have found employment at the office and received insight into the books. This would have enabled him to obtain all the necessary information for us within a couple of days."

"By the devil!" the colonel shouted. "That's true. Why didn't I hit on the idea myself! You, Smitty, as a matter of fact, are experienced with such bookkeeping and could have assumed his role."

"And I'd have done it right. That would have taken care of all our difficulties. Maybe there's still time to make up for our neglect."

"Sure there's still time! We know where the two are headed. The directions the farmer gave them leads right past here. We just need to wait for them to show up."

"That's right, let's do it! But it's not enough just to take the clerk's letter. He'd continue on to Sheridan and spoil everything. We must prevent him as well as the quack from doing that."

"That's understood. A bullet in both heads, then we bury them. Afterwards, you present the letter in Sheridan, find out everything there is to know and pass the information on to us."

"But where and how?"

Brinkley thought about the problem for a few seconds, then made his decision. "We two will ride back and bring the others. You'll find us in the area where the railroad crosses the Eagle Tail. It's difficult to specify the exact spot beforehand. I'll post some of our guys near the part of Sheridan that you'll be traversing as you head out of town."

"Fine. But if my departure is noticed and causes suspicion?"

"Hmm, that we must consider. Perhaps we can circumvent this problem by your taking along our friend Faller here to bring us the payroll information. You can say that you met him on the way and that he's also looking for work with the railroad."

"Excellent!" agreed Faller, the third rover who had been listening intently to the conversation. "I bet I'll find work, and if not it'll be even better, because that will give me time to carry Smitty's message to you at the Eagle Tail."

The three discussed their plan further and decided on its execution. Then they waited for the approach of the quack and his companion. But hours passed with no sign of them. Perhaps, Smitty suggested, the two changed their original direction so as not to cross the rovers' path again. The bandits finally decided to backtrack and try to find the new tracks of the Yankee and his companion.

In the meantime, Hartley had had his wound dressed by Haller. The upper arm was seriously injured and would require getting to a place where Hartley could get some rest and care for a few days. They hoped to do that at the farm where the two had been heading. But since the rovers had taken the same direction, the Yankee cautioned, "We might come across them again. They may regret not having killed us and should we meet again, correct the omission. My money they got, but I see no need to throw my life away. Let's find another farm!"

"It may take a long time to find one," Haller said. "Can you hold up for such a long walk?"

"I think so. I'm a sturdy fellow and think that we'll get to a farm before wound-fever occurs. In any case, I hope you'll stay with me until we get there."

"Certainly. If you collapse on the way, I'll go on ahead for help. Now, let's not lose any time. Which way shall we go?"

"North, like before, but a bit more to the right. On the horizon, I see a stretch of darkness that may be trees or bushes. And where there are trees, there's water which I need urgently to cool my wound."

Haller picked up the box and the two left their place of misfortune. The Yankee's surmise proved correct. After a while, they arrived at an area of green shrubbery with a small body of water where the first dressing could be replaced. Hartley dumped his colored waters and filled the vials with clear water to moisten his new bandage during the long walk ahead. Then the two set out again.

They now crossed a section of prairie where grass grew so short that their tracks were barely visible. It would have taken the sharp eyes of a frontiersman to determine whether the footprints made by the two were caused by one or two people. After some time, they again saw a dark strip on the horizon, a sign they were approaching a more heavily wooded area. At that point, the Yankee happened to turn around and spied several moving dots, in fact three of them. He at once arrived at the conclusion that the rovers were pursuing them. Now their lives were clearly in danger. Someone other than the Master of Arts would have called his observation to the clerk's attention, but not Hartley. He only increased his pace and when Haller expressed surprise, Hartley satisfied his curiosity with the next best plausible explanation.

One can see horsemen from farther away than people on foot. The distance to the riders was such that Hartley could assume that he and his companion had not yet been spotted by the rovers. On this, he based his plan for escape. He knew that outright resistance would be futile. If caught, they'd both be lost. One of them might have a chance of survival, he thought, although unfortunately the other would have to be sacrificed. Obviously this was to be the clerk, not he. Therefore Haller was not to to be warned of the danger approaching from behind. The Yankee cleverly kept his own counsel. In no way did his conscience bother him that he was delivering his companion to ruin, since he figured the man was lost anyway.

More and more swiftly they proceeded until they entered the woods with its densely growing bushes above which towered the crowns of some hickory, oak, walnut and elm trees. The growth was not very deep but stretched some distance to the right. When they had crossed it, the Yankee stopped and proposed very casually, "Mister Haller, I've been thinking about how much trouble I am to you. You need to get to Sheridan but because of me had to detour from a direct path. Who knows if and when we'll find a farm in the direction we're headed. You might have to trouble yourself for days to attend to me. There's an easier way out of this situation and to make such a sacrifice unnecessary."

"So? What way?" Haller asked unsuspectingly.

"You go on, in God's name, and I'll return to the farm I came from before I met you."

"I can't permit you to do that; it's too far."

"Not at all. I've walked west, then north with you, that's at a right angle. If I cut this angle it'll take me no more than three hours to get to the farm and for that long I can surely hold up."

"You think so? All right, but I'll come along. I did promise not to leave you."

"And I must release you from your promise since I don't want to expose you to any danger."

"What danger?"

Thinking quickly, Hartley came up with a plausible lie. "There's a possibility of it. The farmer's wife told me that she's the sister of the sheriff of Kinsley. If your pursuers get there, I would bet one hundred to one that the sheriff will stop by the farm. You'd be a sitting duck."

"That I would surely like to avoid," Haller said anxiously. "Do you really want to go there?"

"Yes, it's best for me and also for you."

Hartley had explained the advantages of his proposal in such a sincere and reasonable manner that the poor clerk finally agreed to their separation. They shook hands, offered each other mutual best wishes and took their leave. Haller continued out across the open prairie. Hartley looked after him and told himself, "I feel sorry for the chap, but there's no other way. If we stayed together, both our lives would be forfeit. Now it's high time for me to take care of myself. When they catch up with him and ask for me, he'll tell them that I've gone to the right in the direction of the farm. Instead, now I'll turn left and find a place to hide."

The Master of Arts was no hunter or trapper, but he knew that he shouldn't leave any tracks. He had heard in the past how best to cover them. Making his way into the shrubbery, he looked for places that didn't leave signs. If he produced a footprint, he reached back to smooth it out with his hand. His wound as well as the box he carried were quite a hindrance and he could advance only slowly. To his good fortune, he soon found a place where the bushes grew very thickly, too densely for eyes to penetrate. He carefully worked his way inwards, put down his box and sat on it. Soon afterwards, he heard both the voices of the three riders and their horses' hoofbeats. The men passed without noticing that the tracks were now only those of one person.

The Yankee cautiously lifted some branches to look at his pursuers out on the open prairie. There walked Haller. The rovers saw him and spurred their horses to a gallop. When Haller heard them, he turned and stopped, terrified. Soon they reached him; a conversation ensued. He pointed eastward, indicating that the Yankee was walking in the direction of the farm. Then there was the sound of a revolver being fired. The doomed Haller collapsed on the ground.

"It's happened," murmured Hartley to himself resignedly. "But wait, you bandits! Maybe I'll meet you again; then you'll pay for this murder! But what are they doing now?"

He saw all three riders dismount and do something to the man they had shot. Then they conferred, after which they mounted their horses, with the colonel putting the murdered Haller across the front of his saddle. To the Yankee's surprise, Brinkley returned to the woods while his two companions rode onwards. When the colonel reached a deep thicket, he forced his horse into the bushes, located not too far from Hartley's position. He dropped Haller's body where it couldn't readily be seen from outside. He backed his horse out of the thicket and rode off, but to where Hartley could not ascertain from his position. For a while he heard hoofbeats; then silence returned.

Regret and horror now befell the Yankee and he felt some guilt not to have warned the clerk. He had been an unwilling witness to the terrible deed and felt partly responsible, now that the body lay so very close to him. He would have preferred to get away from his hiding place but didn't dare, since he was certain Brinkley was still looking for him. A quarter of an hour passed, then another before he felt safe to leave. Before doing so, he once more scanned the prairie, suddenly noticing something that caused him to quickly crouch back in his hiding place.

A horseman, leading a second riderless horse, was approaching from the right across the prairie. He arrived at the tracks of the two rovers, stopped and dismounted. After carefully looking in all directions, he bent down to examine the tracks. With the horses following him on their own, he walked over to the spot where the murder had taken place. There he stopped again to investigate. Some time elapsed before he stood upright again. With his eyes on the ground, he followed the colonel's tracks. About fifty paces from the brushy area, the man stopped and produced a peculiar throaty sound, while pointing with his arm toward the bushes. This was meant for his saddle horse. The animal walked away from him approaching the bushes in an arc, then trotted along the perimeter, its wide nostrils testing the air. Since it gave no sign of alarm, the rider seemed satisfied to approach as well.

Hartley now realized that he was watching an Indian. The redskin wore fringed leggings and his embroidered hunting shirt was similarly fringed at its seams. His small feet were shod in moccasins. Long black hair was kept in a helmet-like bob but no eagle feather adorned it. A threefold necklace of bear claws, a peace pipe and medicine bag hung from his neck. He carried a double-barreled rifle whose shaft was studded with many silver nails that glittered in the sun. His face, a soft bronze, had an almost Roman shape, and only the slightly raised cheekbones made obvious that he was of Indian descent.

The proximity of a redskin was all it took to raise hackles of fright in the Yankee, not having been born to be a hero. However the longer he observed the Indian, the more he thought he had nothing to fear from him. By now the red man had approached within twenty paces. His saddle horse had come even closer, while the second animal followed tightly behind the Indian. It had already lifted one of its forelegs for the next step when it rose up, snorted loudly and stepped back; it had caught Hartley's scent or perhaps that of the dead man. In a sideways panther-like leap, the Indian disappeared and with him his second horse. Hartley could no longer see either one.

For a long time the Yankee remained motionless, until he heard a barely suppressed sound, "Uff!" the Indian's expression of surprise. When he turned in his direction, he saw the redskin on his knees beside the clerk's body, examining him with both eyes and hands. Then he crawled away and was not seen for almost a quarter of an hour. All at once, the Yankee gave a frightful start, for from close beside him came the words, "Why is the paleface hiding here? Why does he not come out and show his face to the red warrior? Does he not want to tell where the three murderers of this other paleface have gone to?"

When Hartley turned toward the voice, he saw the Indian kneeling beside him, a large Bowie knife in hand. The redskin's words showed that he had read and evaluated the signs correctly. He didn't think the Yankee was the murderer, which sufficiently calmed Hartley so that he could answer, "I hid from them. Two rode out onto the prairie; the third dropped the body here. I stayed in hiding since I wasn't sure whether the third villain had left or not."

"He is gone. His tracks cross the woods then lead eastward."

"Then he's gone to the farm to try to catch me. Is he truly no longer here?"

"No. My white brother and I are the only human beings alive here. He may come out of hiding and tell me what happened."

The Indian spoke excellent English. What he said and how he spoke gave Hartley enough confidence to crawl from the shrubbery. Once out there he saw the two horses staked a distance away. The redskin examined the white man with a penetrating look, then said, "Two men on foot came from the south. One of them hid here; that was you. The other continued out onto the prairie. Then came three horsemen who followed this lone walker. They killed him with a revolver bullet. Two rode off. The third put the body on his horse, rode to the bushes and dropped it here. Then he galloped eastward. Is that correct?"

"Yes, exactly," nodded Hartley.

"Would you tell me then why your white brother was killed. Who are you and what are you doing in this place? Was it also the three men who wounded you?"

The friendly tone in which these questions were asked convinced the Yankee that the redskin was well-meaning and bore no suspicions against him. He answered each of the questions. All the while, the Indian was facing away from him. Suddenly, though, he looked at Hartley penetratingly and remarked, "Then your companion saved your life by paying with his own?"

The Yankee dropped his eyes and answered haltingly, "No. I begged him to stay and to hide with me, but he refused."

"Then you mentioned to him that the murderers were following you?"

"Yes."

"And told him that you intended to hide here yourself?"

"Yes."

"Why then did he direct the murderers eastward to the farm when they asked him?"

Hartley thought fast and found an inspired reply. "To deceive them."

"Then he wanted to save you and was a gallant comrade. Are you worthy of his deed? Only Great Manitou knows everything; my eyes cannot enter your mind. If they could, you might be ashamed before me. I shall remain silent. Your God will be your judge. Do you know me?"

"No," Hartley answered, much ashamed of his own deception and cowardice.

"I am Winnetou, chief of the Apaches. My hand is against all evil men and my arm protects all those of good conscience. Let me look after your wound. But it is even more urgent to learn why the murderers came to follow you. Do you know why?"

Hartley had often heard about Winnetou. Knowing now that he was in the presence of the famous chief, he answered in an increasingly polite tone, "I've told you already. They wanted to kill us so we couldn't tell others that they had robbed me."

"No. Were it just that, they would have killed you at once. It must be something else they only thought about later. Did they search you closely?"

"Yes."

"And took everything from you? Also from your companion?"

"No. He told them he was only a poor fellow fleeing from something. He proved it by showing them a letter."

"A letter? Did they keep it?"

"No, they returned it."

"Where did he put it then?"

"In his coat's breast pocket."

"It is no longer there. I searched all pockets of the dead man and found no letter. They took it from him. Then it is this letter which made them turn and follow you."

"Hardly!" responded the Yankee in a puzzled tone, shaking his head.

The Indian did not explain his reasoning. He pulled the body from the bushes and examined it again. Its terrible aspect was not because of the bullet wound, but because his face had multiple slash wounds to make it unrecognizable. His pockets were empty. Of course his rifle had also been stolen.

The Indian looked pensively into the distance, then said in a tone of utter conviction, "Your comrade wanted to get to Sheridan. Two of the murderers rode north in the direction of this town as if it were also their destination. Why did they take his letter? Because they need it; they intend to misuse it. Why did they make the dead man's face unrecognizable? So that he cannot be identified. They don't want it known that Haller is dead. He is meant to be thought alive so that one of the murderers can impersonate him."

"But to what purpose?"

"That I don't know but I shall learn it."

"Then you intend to follow them?"

"Yes. My destination is the Smoky Hill River near Sheridan. If I ride to Sheridan, my journey will not be much longer. These palefaces are planning something terrible in Sheridan. I may be able to prevent them from doing it. Will my white brother come along?"

"I was thinking of heading for a nearby farm to have my arm taken care of, but Sheridan might be preferable. There I may even get my money back."

"Then you will ride with me?"

"But what about my wound?"

"I will look after it. On a farm my white brother would find care but no doctor. There is one in Sheridan. I also know how to treat wounds. I can treat your hurt arm and have an excellent remedy against wound fever. Show me the place!"

The clerk had cut the coat sleeve open earlier so it presented no difficulty for Hartley to bare his arm. Winnetou checked it and advised him that the wound was not as bad as it appeared. Fired from close range, the bullet had not shattered the bone but had penetrated it cleanly. The redskin took a dried plant from his saddlebag, moistened it and placed it onto the wound. Then he cut two wooden splints and dressed the arm so skillfully that a true doctor could not have done better with the means at hand. He explained, "My brother can safely ride with me. There will be no fever, at least not before he reaches Sheridan."

"But don't you want to find out first what the third murderer is up to?"

"No. I know he is looking for you. Once he finds your tracks, he will turn to follow the other two. But then perhaps not, since there may be other accomplices to meet before they all ride to Sheridan. I have come from settled areas and have learned that many palefaces, called rovers, have gathered in Kansas. It is possible that the murderers belong to these people and that the rovers plan an attack on Sheridan. We must not lose any time to get there and warn the white townspeople."

"But if this third man returns here, he'll find our tracks and see that we've followed his friends. Must he not become suspicious?"

"We will not follow the two paleface tracks. Winnetou knows where they are headed and doesn't need their tracks. We ride another way."

"And when do you think we'll arrive in Sheridan?"

"I do not know how my brother rides."

"Well. I'm no steeplechaser. I've not been riding very much, but I won't let myself be thrown."

"Then we cannot ride hard but must gain by steadiness. We shall ride through the night and will be at our destination by the morning. Anyone following us will bed down for the night and arrive after us."

"And what happens to poor Haller's body?"

"We shall bury him and my brother may speak a prayer over his grave."

The soil was loose, and although only their knives could be used for digging, they soon had a deep enough pit into which the two placed Haller's body, covering it with the removed soil. Then the Yankee took off his hat and folded his hands. Whether he truly prayed was doubtful. The Apache gazed gravely toward the setting sun. It was as if his eyes looked beyond the western horizon to find the Eternal Hunting Grounds. He was a heathen, but he surely prayed. Then they went over to the horses.

"My white brother may take my horse," the redskin offered. "It has a soft stride like a canoe in the water. I take the other."

They mounted and rode off, first a distance to the west, then swinging northward. The horses seemed to have come a long way already but trotted along as lively as though they had just left their pasture. The sun sank lower and lower as they rode and finally disappeared below the horizon. The brief dusk passed quickly and deep night fell. Hartley became concerned.

"Won't we get lost in the darkness?"

"Winnetou never gets lost, neither by day nor by night. Like a star in the sky, he is always at the right place and knows the country as well as a paleface knows the rooms of his house."

"But there are so many obstacles that can't be seen!" Hartley protested.

"Winnetou's eyes see also by night. And what he does not notice his horses will. My brother must not ride beside me, but behind. That way his animal will not make a misstep."

The security with which horse and rider traveled was truly amazing. In a walk, sometimes in a trot, often even galloping once Hartley had become more comfortable with the ride, they covered the distance hour by hour, avoiding all obstacles. There were boggy places to bypass and creeks to be waded. They passed farms, and always Winnetou knew their location. Not for a single moment did he appear to be in doubt. This calmed the Yankee immensely.

He had worried very much about his arm, but the plant dressing had a wonderful effect. He felt no pain and couldn't complain about anything except the discomfort from his unaccustomed jouncing. A few times they stopped to water their horses and to moisten the dressing.

After midnight, Winnetou produced a piece of meat that Hartley was glad to eat. No other break was taken, and when the increasing chill told of the morning's approach, the Yankee figured that he would be able to stay a while longer in the saddle.

Dawn rose, but the contours of the terrain could not be made out since a heavy fog lay on the land.

"It is the fog from the Smoky Hill River," explained the chief. "We will soon be there."

It sounded as if he had wanted to continue speaking, but stopped both speech and horse to listen to his left from where a regular hoofbeat could be discerned. It had to be a galloping horseman. Through the fog and gloom a rider approached, passed and disappeared like a phantom. The two observers had neither seen the horse nor the rider himself. Only his broad-brimmed hat became briefly visible above the dense ground fog. A few seconds later, the hoofbeats could be heard no longer.

"Uff!" Winnetou said, surprised. "A paleface! Only two white men ride the way this man rode. One is Old Shatterhand, who is not in this area since I am to meet him at Silver Lake; the second is Old Firehand. Could he be in Kansas? Could it have been him?"

"Old Firehand? Hartley asked. "That's a very famous frontiersman."

"He and Old Shatterhand are the best and bravest and the most experienced palefaces Winnetou knows. They are my friends."

"The man seemed to be in quite a rush. What may be his destination?"

"Sheridan! Our directions are identical. To the left of us is the Eagle Tail and ahead of us is the ford. We will reach it in a few minutes. In Sheridan, we will learn of the rider's identity."

The fog began to dissipate. The morning winds dispersed it and soon the two saw the Smoky Hill River ahead of them. Here, too, the Apache's extraordinary local knowledge proved to be a boon. At the river, they arrived unerringly at the ford. The water barely reached the horses' bellies, making passage easy.

On the opposite bank, the riders had to force their way through bushes growing along the river, but thereafter had open grassland all the way to Sheridan.

9. Ruse and Counter-Ruse

At the time of these events, Sheridan was nothing like a town but rather a temporary settlement of railroad workers. Most of its buildings were of a primitive construction, some of rock, some of sod, others of wood, yet their doorways often featured the proudest inscriptions. There were hotels and salons wherein the lowliest laborer in Germany would not have cared to live or to frequent. There were also wooden dwellings, which were designed so they could be taken down at a moment's notice, to be reassembled in another place. The largest of these designs stood on top of a rise and bore the widely visible sign: 'CHARLES CHAROY, ENGINEER'. The building was Winnetou and Hartley's destination. They dismounted in front of it and noticed another horse that was tied to a hitching rail.

"Uff!" exclaimed Winnetou, admiring the horse. "This animal is worth a good rider. It surely belongs to the paleface who hurtled past us."

They tied up their horses. There was no one around. Looking over the settlement, they saw only three or four people yawning and looking up at the sky for what weather might be in store. The building's door stood open so they stepped inside. A young Negro greeted them and asked their desires. Before they could answer, a side door opened and through it stepped a youthful white man who gave the Apache a surprised but friendly look. He was the engineer. His name and his skin tone, as well as his dark curly hair, made it appear that he was of French descent.

"Who are you looking for this early, gentlemen?" he inquired, making a respectful bow to the redskin.

"We're looking for the engineer, Mister Charoy." Winnetou answered in his excellent English, pronouncing even the French name correctly.

"Well, that's me. Please come in!"

He stepped back into the room from which he had come. It was small and simply furnished. The drawings on the desk showed it was the engineer's office. He pushed two chairs towards them, then waited with obvious interest for what they had to say. Hartley sat down at once, the Indian remained politely standing for the moment, nodded his head and began his story:

"Sir, I am Winnetou, the chief of the Apaches ---"

"I know, I know it already!" the engineer broke in.

"You know already, sir?" asked the redskin. "Then you must have seen me before?"

"No, but someone arrived who knows you and watched your approach through the window. I'm very pleased to make the acquaintance of the famous Winnetou. Sit down, won't you, and tell me what brings you to me. And, please, be my guest."

173

The Indian sat down and continued, "Do you know a paleface by the name of Ben Norton, down in Kinsley?"

"Yes, very well. The man is one of my best friends."

"You know also the paleface Haller, his clerk?"

"No. I haven't visited my friend since he moved to Kinsley or had an opportunity to meet any of his employees."

"This clerk will arrive here today, together with another white man. The first will present to you a letter of recommendation from Norton asking you to employ him in your office and to find work for the second. If you do this, great danger threatens you."

"No! What danger?"

"That I do not precisely know. The two palefaces are murderers. Once you have talked with them, and provided you are wise, we will be able to figure out their intentions."

"To perhaps murder me," Charoy replied doubtfully.

"Maybe!" Winnetou nodded earnestly. "Not only you but also others. I think they are rovers."

"Rovers?" the engineer responded quickly. "Oh, that's somewhat different. I just learned that a horde of rovers is on the way to Sheridan via the Eagle Tail to rob us. The gang is after our cash desk."

"Who did you learn that from?"

"From --- well, I think it best if I don't name the gentleman, but instead introduce him to you."

Charoy's face showed pleasure that he could present the redskin with a pleasant surprise. He opened the door to an adjacent room from which Old Firehand appeared. Had the engineer believed the redskin would break out in words of delight he was mistaken, showing that he was unused to Indian customs. No red warrior will express his joy or pain in the presence of others. But the Apache's eyes brightened. Then he stepped towards the hunter and offered his hand. Old Firehand pulled him close, hugged him, kissed him on both cheeks and in an emotional voice addressed him enthusiastically, "My friend, my dear, dear brother! How surprised I was to see you coming and dismount! For how long have we not seen each other?"

"I did see you at dawn today," the Indian responded, "when you flew like an arrow past us in the fog by the river. The fog enveloped you so that I could not really identify you. Then like a storm across the plains, you were gone."

"I had to ride fast to arrive ahead of the rovers. The issue at hand is so important that I didn't want to entrust it to anyone else and had to ride here myself. More than two hundred rovers are approaching."

"Then I was not mistaken. The murderers are their scouts."

"May I ask what's the situation with these scouts?"

"The chief of the Apaches is no man of words but of action. Here stands a paleface who can explain everything to you."

He pointed to Hartley who had risen from his chair upon Old Firehand's entry and was now watching the giant man in wonder. Yes, these were heroes, Old Firehand and Winnetou. The Yankee felt small and paltry. A similar feeling appeared to have overtaken the engineer as well; at least it seemed so from his facial expression and the respectful posture he had taken.

Hartley recounted yesterday's experiences after everyone had sat down again. When he had finished, Old Firehand briefly described his encounters with the red-haired colonel on the steamer, at the rafters' place, and on Butler's farm. Then he asked for a description of the leader of the threesome that had killed the clerk and who had then separated from the other two. After the Yankee had succeeded in painting a vivid picture of the outlaw, the hunter said, "I'm certain it's the colonel. He's dyed his hair dark now. I hope I come across him soon!"

"That would be the end of his miserable deeds!" the engineer remarked angrily. "More than two hundred rovers! What a carnage and burning this would have been! Gentlemen, you're our saviors and I don't know how to thank you! This colonel must have somehow found out that I've got the money to distribute to my colleagues farther along the tracks. Now that I've been warned, let him come with his rovers; we'll be ready."

"Don't think yourself safe," warned Old Firehand. "Two hundred desperadoes are not to be discounted!"

"That may be. But within a few hours, I can have a thousand railroad workers together."

"All well armed?"

"Every one of them will have some kind of weapon. And, in the final event, even knives, spades and shovels will do."

"Spades and shovels against two hundred rifles? That would result in the kind of bloodshed I wouldn't want on my conscience."

"Well, then I can also get up to one hundred soldiers from Fort Wallace."

"Your courage is admirable, sir, but cunning is usually better than brute force. If I can render an enemy harmless by a ruse, why should I then sacrifice lives?"

"What kind of ruse do you have in mind, sir?" Charoy asked. "I'll gladly follow your advice. You're just the man for this venture, and if you wish, I'll immediately cede command to you over this place and my people."

"Not so fast, Charles! Let's think about it first. First, the rovers mustn't learn that you've been warned. They also cannot know of our presence. Neither should our horses be seen. Can you find a hiding place for the animals?"

"I'll have them concealed at once, sir."

"But somewhere that we can readily get to them!"

"Yes. Fortunately, you arrived early enough that few of my workers saw you. The scouts might have learned about you from them. My Negro, who is loyal and discreet, will hide the horses and take care of them."

"All right then. Give him your instructions! And, please, take care of Mr. Hartley. Give him a bed to lie down in. But no one is to know of his presence, no one except you, your Negro and a doctor. I suppose a doctor is available here?"

"Yes. I'll have him called at once."

He led the Yankee out, who followed gladly since he felt pretty fatigued by now. When Charoy returned after some time to tell them that the wounded Hartley as well as the horses were being well taken care of, Old Firehand said, "I wanted to avoid any discussion in the presence of this quack. I don't trust him. There is a dark smudge in his story. I'm convinced that he purposely sent the poor clerk to his death to save himself. I don't want anything to do with such a betrayer. Now we're among ourselves and know that we can trust each other."

"Are you going to explain your plan to us?" Charoy asked inquisitively.

"No. We can come up with a plan only after the arrival of the rover's scouts and your talk with them."

"That's true. We must be patient for the time being."

At this point, Winnetou raised his hand as a sign that he was of a different opinion and suggested, "Every warrior can fight two ways. He can attack or he can defend himself. If Winnetou does not know how to defend himself, he prefers to attack. That is quicker, safer and also more brave."

"Then my red brother doesn't want to learn the rovers' plan?" asked Old Firehand.

"I will learn it eventually. But why should the chief of the Apaches have to respond to their plan if it is easy for him to force them to react to his own?"

"Oh, then you have a plan already?"

"Yes. It came to me during my nighttime ride and was confirmed when I heard what the rovers had done before. These ruffians are not warriors that one fights honorably but are mangy dogs one ought to club to death. Why should I wait for such a dog to bite me if I can batter him before or catch him in a trap!"

"Do you know of a trap for the rovers?"

"I do know of one and we shall prepare it. These coyotes have come to rob the railroad pay office. If its money chest is here, they will come here; if it is somewhere else, they will go there. And should it be on a firehorse, they will mount it and ride to their ruin without the least injury to people hereabouts."

"Ah, I begin to follow!" marveled Old Firehand. "What an idea! Only Winnetou could have come up with it! You think to lure the fellows onto a train?"

"Yes. Winnetou does not understand the firehorse and how it is driven. He has given you his idea; now my white brothers may think about it further."

"Lure them onto a train?" asked the engineer. "But what for? We can wait for them here and destroy them in the open!"

"But many would die!" countered Old Firehand. "However, if they board a train we can take them to a place where they must surrender without doing any harm to us."

"They wouldn't think of getting on a train."

"They will if we lure them with the money chest."

"Then I'm to put the chest on a train?" asked Charoy.

No one would have expected this question from the otherwise ingenious engineer. Winnetou made a disdainful movement with his hand, but Old Firehand continued to explain. "Why would you do that? The rovers only need to be convinced that there's money on the train. You employ the scout as your clerk and pretend to trust him completely. You tell him that a train will stop here with a money chest. That will doubtlessly draw them. They'll all crowd onto the train. Once they're aboard, we drive it away."

"That doesn't sound bad, sir, but it isn't as easy as you think."

"So? What difficulties does it pose? Don't you have a train available that we can use for this purpose?"

"Oh, yes. You can have as many coaches as you want! And I'd gladly assume responsibility, if I could fully believe in it. But there are a number of questions yet. We can't be certain that the train's engineer and his stoker wouldn't be killed by the rovers."

"Don't worry!" Old Firehand responded. "I suppose we can find a driver and I'll be the stoker. If I offer my services for this job, that should prove that there'll be no danger. Let's talk about the details first. The main thing is that we mustn't wait too long. I figure the rovers will arrive today at the Eagle Tail, their first destination. So we can time our ruse for tomorrow night. Then we need to establish a place where we can transport the bandits. Let's look for one this morning, since the scouts are expected to arrive only by afternoon. Do you have a handcar available, sir?'

"Of course."

"Well, then we two will take that ride. Winnetou cannot come along. He needs to stay in hiding since his presence would give our plan away. I also mustn't be recognized as Old Firehand. I expected this and brought an old linen suit along that I usually carry with me."

The engineer's face became ever more confused. "Sir, you talk about this like a fish in water. But to me it doesn't look that simple. How do we get word to the rovers? How do we get them to come when we want them to?"

"Easy questions. The new clerk will sound you out, and whatever you tell him he'll convey as absolute truth to his fellow rovers."

"All right! But what if they get the idea to not board the train? If they decide instead to sabotage the rails at some point and derail it?"

"You can prevent that by telling the clerk that such an important money-bearing train is always preceded by a security locomotive. That'll stop them from trying a derailment. If you're smart, everything will work out fine. You must engage the clerk with so much work and such friendliness that he cannot -- will not -- leave the house before bedtime or be able to communicate with anyone else. Then you assign him a room upstairs with only one window. I'll climb up, and with the flat roof just half a foot above the window, I'll hear every word spoken."

"You think he'll talk to someone through the window?"

"I'm sure of it. This substitute Haller is supposed to spy on you, with Faller accompanying him, as the messenger. There's no other possibility; you'll soon see. The other rover will also ask for work as an excuse to stay here, but he'll find some reason not to accept it so he can leave at will and play messenger. He'll try to speak with the clerk to get the news, but you'll make it impossible to get close to him before bedtime. We can expect him to loiter close by. Smitty, which is the real name of the fake clerk, will open the window right below the spot where I'll be lying on the roof. I'll hear everything. Right now this sounds difficult and highly adventurous since you're no frontiersman. Once you begin, everything will follow as a matter of course."

"Howgh!" the Indian affirmed. "My white brothers may now look for a place to close the trap. Once you return, I shall leave so that I will not be seen."

"Where is my red brother going?"

"Winnetou is at home everywhere, in the forest and on the prairie."

"No one knows that better than I, but the chief of the Apaches can have company if he wants to. I've ordered my rafters and the hunters who are with them to go to a place an hour's ride south of the Eagle Tail. They're to spy on the rovers from there. Aunt Droll is with them."

"Uff!" the Apache exclaimed, his usually serious face showing an amused expression. "The Aunt is a good, brave and smart paleface. Winnetou will join him."

"Very good! My red brother will find other good men there: Black Tom, Humpy-Bill and Gunstick Uncle, all men whose names he'll at least have heard. In the meantime, have my room until we return."

Prior to the Apache's arrival, Old Firehand had been assigned a room by the engineer. Winnetou went there to change from his conspicuous hunting outfit to a simpler one, so that he would be considered simply a newly-hired comrade by the railroad workers. No one was yet to know what unusual events were about to transpire.

Soon the handcar was ready. Old Firehand and Charoy took its front seats with two workers providing the propulsion of the vehicle. They rolled through the settlement where by now many people were at work, out onto the open track which had been extended as far as the settlement of Kit Carson. During their trolley excursion, Firehand completely won the confidence of the engineer and explained everything so precisely to him that a mistake should be highly unlikely.

Meanwhile the Apache made himself comfortable. He had traveled all night and used the opportunity to take a nap. When the two inspectors returned, he was awakened. Old Firehand had found a highly suitable spot for the trap, and when he described it to Winnetou, the Indian nodded in satisfaction and remarked, "That is well. The dogs will shiver from fear and howl from terror. Their salvation will be to fall into our hands. Winnetou now rides to Aunt Droll and the rafters to tell them to get ready."

He left the house inconspicuously to go where the horses were hidden.

The shrewd chief had not been mistaken about the arrival of the scouts. Barely was the noon break over when two horsemen slowly rode up from the river. From Hartley's description, there was no doubt that these were the expected rover scouts.

Quickly Old Firehand went to the Yankee, who was still sleeping, to have him verify the identity of the men. Once it was confirmed, the hunter went into the room adjacent to the office through a door, which had been left ajar. He stationed himself behind it, ready to eavesdrop on the ensuing conversation.

Charoy was in his office when the two men entered. They greeted him politely, then one of them handed him the letter of recommendation without at first explaining its purpose. The engineer read it, then responded in a friendly voice, "You were employed by my friend Norton? How is he?"

After the usual questions and answers, which followed this introduction, the engineer inquired about the reason that had forced the clerk to leave Kinsley. Smitty, impersonating the murdered Haller, told a sad story congruent with the letter but which he had totally invented. The engineer listened carefully, then replied, "This is truly pitiful and I'm very sorry to learn it, particularly since I gather from this letter that you had Norton's trust and good will. I'll honor his request and give you a job here. Although I have a clerk, for some time now I've been looking for a man to whom I can entrust confidential matters. Can you assure me of your loyalty and good work?"

"Sir," the impostor responded unctuously, "Try me. I promise you, you'll be satisfied with me."

"Well. Let's give it a go. We'll talk about your salary in a few days when I get to know you a bit better. The more able you are, the better you'll be paid. Right now I'm very busy. For the time being, have a look around the settlement and come back at five o'clock. By then, I'll have come up with some work for you. You'll live with me in this house, eat at my table and must comply with the rules of the household. I don't want you to associate with the common workers. At ten o'clock, the door to the house will be locked."

"That's fine by me, sir. That's how it was handled in Kinsley," the man assured him, feeling great satisfaction at having been hired. Then he added. "One more request, please. Would you also have some work for my traveling companion here?"

"What kind of work?"

"Any," answered the other modestly. "I'd be glad for any kind of work."

"What's your name?"

"It's Faller. I met Mister Haller on the way and accompanied him when I heard that there may be work here on the railroad."

"Haller and Faller. A curious similarity of names. I hope you're similar in other respects. What have you done so far, Mister Faller?"

"I was a cowboy on a farm near Las Animas. It was hard and dirty work that I didn't want to do any more. So I left. On my last day as a cowboy, I got into a fight with another ranch hand, a really coarse fellow, who knifed me in the hand. The wound hasn't quite healed yet. It would be very kind of you to keep a job open for me for a few days until my hand has healed."

"Well, work you can have any time. Stay around then, take care of your hand, and once it's healed report back. You can go now."

The two men left the office. When they passed by the open window where Old Firehand stood, he heard one of them say in a low voice, "All's well! If only the end will be like the beginning!"

Charoy stepped into Old Firehand's room and said excitedly, "You were correct, sir! This Faller made sure he doesn't have to work, but has the time to ride to the Eagle Tail. He had his hand bandaged."

"We can assume it's very healthy. Why did you ask the clerk to come only at five o'clock?"

"Because you asked me to keep him working until bedtime. If he started earlier, it would tire us both and might look somewhat peculiar."

"That's good reasoning. The five hours until ten o'clock is a long time and it may not be easy to prevent him from any contact with the other rover."

The initial part of the ruse had been accomplished. The next could be entered into only after the conspiracy between the two scouts could be overheard later that night. Old Firehand used the time for some sleep. When he woke up, it was almost dark. The Negro brought him dinner. Around ten, the engineer came to tell Old Firehand that the clerk had eaten his meal some time ago and would now be going to his room.

Old Firehand stealthily climbed the stairs to a trap door leading onto the roof. Once there, he crept silently to the edge beneath which the rover's window was located. It was so dark that he had to reach down with his hand to verify its location.

Lying there for a while, he heard a door open in the room below. Footsteps led to the window and a light shone from it. Because the roof consisted only of thin clapboard with nailed-on zinc sheeting, Old Firehand could hear the steps inside the room just as he himself could be heard by the clerk. Caution --- and absolute stillness --- was essential.

Now the hunter squinted closely into the dark below, and not in vain. There, faintly illuminated in the window's light, stood a figure. Then he heard the window open.

"Smitty, you ass!" whispered an angry voice. "Turn off the light; I could be noticed."

"Ass yourself!" hissed the clerk. "Why did you come so soon! They're still awake in the house. Come back in an hour."

"All right. But tell me if you got the information."

"And how!"

"Good!"

"Wonderful news! Much, much better than we expected. But go now, before you're seen!"

The window was shut quietly and the figure below disappeared from the vicinity. Old Firehand was obliged now to wait for an hour or more without being able to move. Yet this was little effort for him since a frontiersman is used to far more difficult tasks. Time passed slowly but steadily. Lights were still on in the houses and huts of the settlement down the hill. Up here at Charoy's house, deep darkness ruled. Old Firehand heard the window open again; this time the light in the room was extinguished. Smitty was waiting for his fellow conspirator. Before long came the soft crunch of feet.

"Faller?" the clerk whispered from the window.

"Yes," the other confirmed.

"Where are you standing? I can't see you."

"Close to the wall, below your window."

"Is the house dark now?" asked Smitty.

"Yes. I went around twice. No one's awake any more. What can you tell me?"

"There's no money at this pay office. They pay every two weeks and yesterday was payday. We'd have to wait two more weeks, which I think the colonel would reject out of hand. Right now there's less than three hundred dollars in the kitty, not worth our effort."

"And that you call wonderful news? Blockhead!"

"Shut up! While there's nothing to be had here, tomorrow night a train with forty thousand dollars is coming through."

"Not so!"

"It's true. I've seen the notification with my own eyes. The train comes from Carlyle heading for the settlement of Kit Carson, where the money is needed to build the railroad extension."

"Are you sure of that?"

"Yes! I've read the letter; also other telegraph messages relating to it. This foolish engineer trusts me like himself."

"But what good is that to us? The train is passing by here!"

"No! It's stopping here for five minutes!"

"Is it?!"

"And the two of us are going to be riding in the locomotive."

"By golly! I think you're fantasizing."

"Not a bit of it! A railroad official needs to board the train in Carlyle and to stay on the locomotive through Sheridan and on to Fort Wallace where he's supposed to hand over the train to army soldiers."

"And this official is to be you, Smitty?"

"Yes. And you're to come along, or rather you may."

"How so?"

"Mr. Charoy gave me permission to take a second man along with me when I ride to Carlyle to board the train. When I asked who this could be, he responded that he would put no requirement on me; whoever I selected would be all right with him. It was obvious that I'd pick you."

"Look. Isn't such quick and total trust suspicious?"

"Actually, yes. But from all I've learned, he needs a confidant and has never had one. The letter of recommendation worked wonders. Then, too, this rather too swift trust doesn't trouble me since it includes a big 'but'."

"And that would be?"

"The job isn't without danger."

"Ah well! That really eases my worry. Have the tracks been built sloppily?"

"No, although it's presently only a preliminary track, as I found from viewing the books and design plans. But Faller, you can imagine the shortage of truly professional people on a project this big. There are drivers who are insufficiently known and stokers whose background and behavior is suspect. Just think, a train carrying that much money driven by such an engineer and stoker. Should the two come to terms, they could abandon the train somewhere along the tracks and abscond with the money. That's why an official must accompany them, and since there are two to deal with, he needs an assistant. Understand, it's kind of a police job. Each of us will have a revolver to shoot the two if they should start anything crooked."

"Hey, that's a laugh. Us watching the money! Let's just force the two to stop along the way and help ourselves to the money."

"That won't work, because in addition to the engineer and stoker, there'll also be a conductor aboard and an administrator from Kansas City who actually will be transporting the money in a large chest. No, it must be done differently. We must attack with a superior force and at an unexpected place, that's to say, right here in Sheridan."

"And you figure that'll succeed?"

"Of course! There's nothing to worry about. Nothing will go wrong, I'm sure. Now go inform the colonel."

" You should know that a ride like that is impossible in the dark, Smitty, particularly since I don't know the territory."

"Well, then wait until morning, but that's the latest. I need the colonel's answer by noon. Ride your horse hard even if it kills him."

"And what am I to say to the colonel?"

"What you just heard. The train arrives here at exactly three o'clock in the morning. The moment it stops, the two of us on the locomotive will tackle the driver and the stoker. If need be, we'll have to shoot them. Brinkley must hide our men alongside the track and immediately spring aboard the coaches. With such a superior force, the few workers still awake in Sheridan and the three or four officials on the train will be so shocked they'll be incapable of fighting back."

"Hmm. Not a bad plan. And for what a sum of money! If we share equally, that's two thousand dollars per man. I hope the colonel will go for it."

"He'd be crazy not to. Tell him that if he doesn't, I'll quit our gang and go for it myself. The risk would be much greater of course, but if the heist succeeded, I'd get the entire sum of money."

"Don't worry! I don't want to miss this great opportunity either. I'll recommend the plan in such glowing terms that Brinkley won't hesitate. I'm sure I'll return with his agreement. But how do I transmit it to you?"

"Yes, that'll obviously be difficult. We must avoid anything that might raise suspicion, any thoughts that we have secrets together. It's imperative not to meet face to face. I also don't know whether we'll have time and a suitably inconspicuous opportunity for a meeting. You'll have to leave me a note."

"Wouldn't that be even more conspicuous? Why not send a messenger ---"

"A messenger? Ridiculous!" interrupted Smitty. "That would be the most stupid thing we could do. I'm not sure whether I'll be able to leave the house at some point; you must write everything down and hide the note nearby."

"But where?" Faller demanded.

"Hmm! It'll have to be a place I can get to without needing much time and drawing any attention. I know that I'll have to work hard in the morning; long salary lists must be completed, Mr. Charoy told me. I ought to be able to find a moment to come to the entrance. Right beside it stands a rain barrel, behind which you can hide the note. Put a rock on it so it can't be seen by a casual a glance."

"How will you know when the note's been deposited? You can't go out to the barrel over and over."

"That, too, can be arranged. I haven't yet told you officially that you're to come along on the train. That I'll do tomorrow morning. I'll have someone look for you when you return from the colonel. Once you've learned that you need to come to the office, and as you arrive hide the note and I'll know that it's there. Agreed?"

"Yes. Are we done or do you have any other messages?"

"There's nothing else. Just put the pressure on to have my plan accepted and preferably without changes, because that would require more preparations for which we have no time. And ride hellbent! Good night then!"

Faller responded in kind and scurried away. The window was quietly closed. Old Firehand remained stock-still for a while, then pushed himself quietly toward the trap door to descend the stairs. As he came down, a whispered voice inquired, "Is that you, Firehand? It's me, Charoy."

Old Firehand had the man follow him to his own room. Once there, the engineer asked if the hunter had been able to overhear the rovers' plans. Old Firehand recounted the story and expressed his conviction that everything would fall into place. After a few reassuring remarks, they separated to go to bed.

Old Firehand awakened early. Used to movement and action, it was difficult for him to secrete himself quietly in his room but that's how it needed to be. It may have been towards eleven o'clock before Charoy joined him. He told the hunter that the clerk was deeply involved in his assigned work and was making every effort to appear to be a solid fellow. A messenger had been sent to look for Faller but of course had not found him. Accordingly, the workers around the settlement had been told to send the fellow to the office as soon as he showed up. Just as this instruction was given, Old Firehand saw a small humpbacked chap walk up toward the office. He wore a leather hunting shirt and carried a long rifle.

"That's Humpy-Bill!" Old Firehand said, perplexed. As an explanation to the engineer he added, "This is one of my men. Something unexpected must have happened, otherwise he wouldn't have come here. I hope it's nothing serious. He knows I'm here incognito and will ask for me only from you. Would you bring him in here, sir?"

Charoy stepped out just as Bill entered the office.

"Excuse me, sir," the hunchback said. "From the sign out there, I take it the engineer lives here. May I talk to this gentleman?"

"Sure. I'm Mr. Charoy. Come in, please."

He escorted Bill to Old Firehand's room who received the little man and questioned him sharply why he had come here against his instructions.

"No need to worry, sir. It's nothing bad," Bill responded. "It may be even something good; in any case it's something you need to know. That's why I came myself to deliver the message. I've had a hard ride along the railroad tracks, figuring the rovers will stay away from there. I don't think I was noticed by anyone. I hid my horse in the woods, and came here so surreptitiously that probably not even any of the workers out there saw me."

"That's good," Old Firehand nodded. "Now, what's happened?"

"As you're aware, Winnetou arrived last night. The meeting was a delight for the Aunt. The others, too, were intrigued and proud to meet the chief ---"

"If he found you so readily, you must not have been hidden very well."

"Don't think that, sir! We mustn't be seen by the rovers, so we chose a place where none of these characters is likely to find us. But who can escape Winnetou's eyes! Prior to coming to us, he had sought out the rovers' camp. After dark, he went there to hear what was being discussed. When he had not returned by daybreak, or even several hours afterwards, we became worried, but unnecessarily so. Nothing had happened to him. Once again, however, he had accomplished one of his masterpieces by approaching the rovers so closely that he was able to hear everything they said. By the way, their conversation was much more screaming and hollering than talking. A messenger had arrived whose information roused the entire group to wild excitement."

"Ah, that was Faller!"

"Yes, Faller was his name. He spoke of forty thousand dollars to be carried aboard the train."

"That's correct!"

"So! The Apache also talked about it. That means you want to lure these rapscallions into a trap. Faller told the group exactly what you wanted them to believe. And you knew that he went there to report it?"

"Yes, that was part of our plan."

"But you also ought to know what's been decided by the rovers!"

"Obviously! We've made arrangements to learn about it as soon as Faller returns here."

"Well, you don't need this fellow's information because Winnetou heard everything. The bandits hollered so loudly that one could hear them for miles. Faller's horse is a nag; he won't get back at best until past noon. It may work to our advantage that Winnetou sent me here."

"That's correct, because the sooner we know the rovers' plan the quicker we can act on it. But first I need to tell you about our own plan."

Old Firehand described to the little man all of the scheme from start to finish. Bill listened carefully, then said, "Excellent, sir! I think everything will develop as you propose. The rovers agreed immediately to this Smitty's suggestions and are not making any changes, except for one."

"And what's that?"

"The location for the attack. Since there are many laborers in Sheridan and such a money train is sure to draw attention, the rovers speculate that some workers might come out of their huts hoping for a look at all that cash. That could raise a ruckus. The rovers want the money, but they don't want to see their own blood spilled. Therefore Smitty and Faller are to remain on the train out of Sheridan well beyond the settlement, and only then force the driver and stoker to stop it out in the open."

"Did they mention a place?"

"No. But the rovers intend to build a bonfire alongside the tracks where Smitty will order the locomotive to be stopped. If the driver and stoker won't obey, they are to be killed. You may not like this change, sir?"

"No, actually I don't mind it at all. This eliminates the potential danger of a fight between the workers and the rovers. Did Winnetou tell you where you're to position yourselves?"

"Yes, ahead of the tunnel, just beyond the bridge."

"Correct! But you're to remain hidden until the train has entered the tunnel. The rest will fall into place."

Everything was clear now and preparations could be completed. Carlyle was contacted by telegraph to assemble the required train and Fort Wallace to request soldiers. In the meantime, Humpy-Bill was given a meal and shortly thereafter disappeared as inconspicuously as he had come.

By noon, word arrived from both places that all requirements would be met. Some two hours later, Faller returned. Old Firehand, sitting with the engineer in one of the rooms, observed the rover busying himself briefly behind the barrel.

"Receive him in your office," Old Firehand counseled, "and keep talking to him until I join you. In the meantime, I'll read the note."

Charoy went to his office and as soon as Faller entered Old Firehand stepped outside. Behind the barrel lay a rock. Lifting it, he found the note, unfolded it and read the colonel's reply. Its content squared with Humpy-Bill's report. He returned the note underneath the rock and entered the office where Faller stood in front of the engineer. The rover did not recognize the hunter in his linen suit, but was quite alarmed when the latter placed his hand on his shoulder and asked in a threatening tone, "Do you know who I am, Mister Faller?"

"No," was the shaky response.

"Then you didn't keep your eyes peeled at Butler's farm. I'm Old Firehand. Are you carrying any weapons?"

Having said this, he jerked the rover's knife from his belt and the revolver from his holster before the shocked man could make a move. Then he told the engineer, "Please, Charles, go tell the clerk that Faller has returned, nothing else. Then come back."

Charoy left. Old Firehand pushed the rover onto a chair and tied him to the backrest.

"Sir," objected the fellow, recovering somewhat, "why this treatment? Why do you tie me up? I don't know you!"

"Be quiet now!" demanded the hunter, pointing the revolver at him. "If you make a sound before I permit it, I'll put a bullet through your head!"

The man paled and didn't dare open his mouth any longer. Charoy returned. Old Firehand asked him to stand by the door. He himself stepped to the side of the window where he could not be seen from the outside. He was sure curiosity would quickly drive the clerk outside. Barely two minutes passed when a hand and forearm appeared reaching behind the barrel. The arm's owner was not visible since he stood so close to the doorjamb. Firehand nodded to the engineer who opened the door just as the clerk scampered by.

"Mister Haller, would you come in for a moment?" Charoy requested.

The bogus Haller, note still in his hand, quickly pocketed it and entered with visible embarrassment. But what a look of astonishment crossed his face when he saw his co-conspirator tied to a chair! He quickly composed himself though and managed to produce an unaffected expression.

"What kind of a note did you just pocket?" Old Firehand asked him.

"Oh, just an old paper bag," was the offhand response.

"Well, then let's see it!"

The clerk gave him a surprised look and retorted, "It's not your business to make such a demand. Who are you? I don't know you. Are my pockets your property?"

"Don't you know who this is?" Charoy interjected. "It's Old Firehand."

"Old Fi ---!" the rover almost screamed. The last two syllables stuck in his mouth. His wide open eyes were fixed on the hunter.

"Yes, it's me," confirmed the frontiersman smoothly. "You didn't expect to find me here, did you? And concerning the contents of your pockets, I think I have a greater right to them than you do. Let's have a look!"

First Old Firehand relieved the rover of his knife and revolver without encountering any resistance, then he retrieved the note.

"Sir," the unmasked Smitty inquired doggedly, "by what right are you doing this?"

"First and foremost, by right of the stronger and the more honest, and then by police authority transferred to me by Mister Charoy here."

"In what connection? What I carry on me is my property. I haven't done anything illegal and demand to know why you're treating me like a thief?"

"Thief?" Pah! It would be well if that's all it was. We're not dealing with theft here but murder, and secondly with something worse than a single killing, that is, an attack and robbery of a train, which probably would cost the lives of more than one man."

"Sir, do I hear you rightly?" Smitty asked in well-feigned surprise. "Who's told you such wild lies?"

"No one. We know very well that such a raid has been organized."

"By whom?"

"By you!"

"By me?" the rover laughed. "Don't take me wrong, sir, but whoever insists that I, a poor clerk, all by myself with no help, is to stop a train and rob it, must be crazy!"

"That's quite true! But first you're no clerk and second you're not alone as you would like to have us believe. Your real name is Smitty and you're one of the rovers who assaulted the Osages at the Osage Nook, then attacked Butler's farm, and now want to rob forty thousand dollars from a train."

Observing the two rovers, it was easy to see that they were becoming terrified. But Haller's impostor pulled himself together long enough to answer in the voice of a totally innocent man, "I don't know a thing about this!"

"You came here only to reconnoiter the place and then inform your confederates!"

"Me? I never left the house for even a moment!"

"Quite true, but your comrade here played messenger. What did you talk about last night through your window? I lay above you on the roof and heard every word. This note contains the response from your colonel. I know its contents. Your rovers are camped near the Eagle Tail. During this coming night, they intend to pass by Sheridan to position themselves by the railroad tracks and light a bonfire. That fire is to tell you the spot where you're supposed to force the engineer to stop the train so your pals can rob it."

"Sir," Smitty exclaimed, no longer able to contain his fright, "if there are truly people intent on this adventure, it's a series of circumstances unknown to me that seem to associate me with this crime. I'm an honest man and ---"

"Shut up!" demanded Old Firehand. "An honest man does not kill."

"Are you claiming I murdered someone?"

"Yes. You and your friend here are both murderers. Where's the quack and his assistant that you and the colonel pursued? Has the real clerk not been killed to obtain his letter of recommendation, so you could present yourself here as Haller to facilitate your spying? Did you not steal all the quack's money?"

"Sir, I don't -- know -- anything about this!" stammered the rover, now in a state of full panic.

"No? I've proved it to you already! So you don't get any ideas about escaping, we're going to tie you up too. Mister Charoy, go ahead and tie this fellow's hands behind his back. I'll hold him."

When the rover heard these words, he whipped about and raced for the door. But Old Firehand was too quick for him. He grabbed Smitty's arm, jerked him back, and held him despite the man's frantic resistance so the engineer could bind his hands without too much trouble. Then Faller, hands still bound, was freed from the chair and together with his co-conspirator was led to the room where the wounded Hartley was lying in his bed. When the fake doctor saw the two men, whom he recognized immediately, he raised himself to a sitting position and shouted, "By God, these are the villains who robbed me and killed poor Haller! Where's the third one?"

"We haven't got him yet, but he'll become ours eventually," answered Old Firehand. "These two deny the offense."

188

"Deny it? I recognize them and swear a thousand oaths that it's them. I hope my word is worth more than their denials!"

"It doesn't require your assurance, Mister Hartley. We have enough proof to know where we stand with them."

"All right! But how about my money?"

"That will be found too. We only took their weapons, and this note."

Old Firehand unfolded and read the document, then handed it to the engineer. The note contained exactly what Winnetou had overheard and Bill had reported, also what Old Firehand had learned listening to the two rovers in the night. The two rogues no longer said a word, recognizing that further protestation of innocence was useless.

Now their pockets were emptied. Their share of the loot was found and returned to Hartley. They confessed that the colonel had the remainder. Then their feet were bound and they were deposited in a nearby room since there was no basement or other secure facility near the office. Hartley was so enraged that he made the best possible guard. He was given a revolver and instructions to shoot both men at once if they made any attempt to break free.

Up to now the ruse had succeeded, and instead of riding the train, the two rovers had been apprehended.

In the course of the afternoon, a message from Fort Wallace arrived confirming that a detachment of soldiers was on its way and would arrive before midnight at the assigned rendezvous.

10. At the Eagle Tail

The laborers at Sheridan were mostly Germans and Irishmen. Until now, they had not been given any information about the forthcoming events so that they would remain unaffected and give nothing away should the colonel send additional scouts. But when evening came, Old Firehand and Charoy filled in the work boss and told him to let the laborers know what they could expect and what was expected of them.

The work boss was a New Hampshire man who had had an eventful prior life. For a number of years, he had worked in the architectural business but had not succeeded in becoming independent. He had dabbled in other fields which, for a Yankee, is nothing to be ashamed of, but luck had not been with him there either. So he had said goodbye to the east and crossed the Mississippi hoping for better times, but experienced similar failures. Here in Sheridan, he had finally found a place where he could apply his previously acquired knowledge. However, he was not quite happy after all. Whoever has breathed the air of the open prairie finds it difficult to settle back into ordered conditions.

This man, Watson by name, was extremely delighted to learn what was to transpire.

"Thank God, finally a break in this daily humdrum!" he said. "Far too long my old rifle has stood in a corner and longed for action. I guess it may get some today. But about the name you mentioned, sir. The red-haired colonel? And his name's supposed to be Brinkley? I once met a fellow named Brinkley who had dyed red hair when his original color was actually black. That encounter almost cost me my life."

"Where and when did this happen?" asked Old Firehand.

"Two years ago at Grand River. I had been at Silver Lake with a German friend by the name of Fritz Engel. We were on the way to Pueblo to head east via the Arkansas to acquire tools for a venture that would have made us millionaires."

Old Firehand's ears pricked up.

"Your friend's name was Engel?" he inquired. "And you thought the venture would bring you a few millions? May I ask you for details?"

"Why not! We had sworn each other to maintain silence about the project. But the millions vanished into nothing since our plans never came to fruition. I think I'm no longer bound by our oath. The project was about raising a tremendous treasure that's hidden in Silver Lake."

Despite the engineer's brief skeptical laugh, Watson continued, "It may all sound like a wild story, sir, but it's true nevertheless. You, Mister Firehand, are one of the most famous frontiersmen the West has ever known and will have doubtlessly experienced a few things which, if told, no one would believe. Maybe you won't laugh at my story."

"Not at all," the hunter answered seriously. "I do believe you, and have good reason for it. I too have learned that a treasure is hidden at the bottom of the lake."

"Truly? Well, then you won't think me a fraud. I can swear that the treasure is there. The fellow who told us about it certainly didn't lie to us."

"Who told you?"

"An old Indian. Never before had I seen such an old person. He was nearly as thin as a skeleton and told us that he had seen more than a hundred summers. He called himself Hauey-kolakakho, but then claimed that his original name was actually Ilhatschi-tatli. I do not know the meaning of these Indian names."

"But I do," Old Firehand broke in. "The first name is of the Tonkawa language, the second is Aztec, and both mean the same, that is 'Great Father'. Go on, Mr. Watson. I'm most curious how you got to know this Indian."

"There's nothing special or adventurous about it. I had miscalculated, stayed on too long in the mountains, and was trapped by the first snow, so I had to stay up there and find a place to winter. I was all by myself in very deep powder. It was no fun. Fortunately I made it to Silver Lake. There I came upon a stone hut from which smoke rose. I was saved. The owner of the hut was this old Indian. He had a grandson and a great-grandson by the name of Big Bear and Little Bear, who ---"

"Ah! Nintropan-hauey and Nintropan-homosch!" Old Firehand interrupted.

Yes. These are the Indian names. Do you know them, sir?"

"Yes. But go on, continue!"

"The two Bears had gone to the Wasatch Mountains. But winter had come much too early that year and they were unable to return to Silver Lake through the deep snow. They knew the old man was in trouble, being all by himself, and that he might die. Fortunately, I found him and when I arrived there another man had already taken shelter with him, the German fellow named Fritz Engel I mentioned earlier.

"I want to make it short, just tell you that the three of us spent the entire winter together. We didn't starve; there was enough game. But the cold had been too much for the old man. When the first warm breezes wafted through the mountains, we had to bury him. He had become fond of us and to express his gratefulness he told us the secret of Silver Lake. He had an ancient piece of leather on which was shown the treasure's exact location. He allowed us to make a copy from it. Engel was lucky to be carrying some paper with him so he could make the copy, since the old man wouldn't let us have the leather piece. He wanted to save it for the two Bears and he buried it the day before his death --- where we do not know and didn't seek out, because we respected his desires. Today only Big Bear and Little Bear know where that spot lies. Once the old man he lay beneath his grave mound, we left. Engel sewed his copy of the map into his hunting coat."

"You didn't wait for the return of the two Bears?"

"No."

"That was a big mistake!"

"That may be, but we had been snowed in for months and longed to see people. We soon met others, but not the kind we'd hoped for. We were attacked by a group of Ute Indians who robbed us of all our possessions. They would surely have killed us, but they knew the old Indian up at the lake. They held him in high esteem, and when they learned that we had taken care of him and had buried him after his death, they let us live and at least returned our clothing. However, they kept our weapons, a dire loss for us, since without arms we were exposed to manifold dangers including death by starvation. Fortunately -- or maybe unfortunately -- we met a hunter by the third day who gave us meat. When he heard of our intention to get to Pueblo, he claimed to have the same destination and allowed us to accompany him."

"That was the red-haired Brinkley?"

"Yes, that was the man, but he called himself by a different name. I only learned his true name later. He pumped us about our experience. We told him most things except let on nothing about the treasure and the Silver Lake drawing, since his manner didn't inspire trust. I can't help it but I've always had reservations about red-haired people, although I think there are no more villains among them then with people of other hair color. However, our not telling him about the treasure turned out to be useless. Since only he had weapons, he was the one to go hunting.

"During those times, Fritz and I sat by ourselves and often talked about the treasure. At one time, Brinkley must have returned secretly, crept up behind us and listened to our talk. When he left for another hunt, he made me come along, claiming that two sets of eyes could spot game better than one. After an hour's walk, he told me that he had overheard everything and would punish us for our mistrust by appropriating our map. He pulled out his knife and attacked me. I fought back but he stabbed me in the chest and my strength failed me."

"Infamous!" Old Firehand exclaimed. "Then he was also planning to murder Engel and get sole possession of the map."

"Of course. Fortunately he didn't strike me in the heart, but still he thought I was dead. When I came to, I was lying in a pool of blood and my head was being cradled by an Indian. It was Winnetou, the Apache chief."

"How lucky you were! You found yourself in the best of hands. It seems this man is everywhere."

"Yes, I was in good hands, that's true. The redskin had already dressed my wound. He gave me drink and I tried to tell him what had happened as much as my weakness permitted.

"Then he left me to follow Brinkley's tracks. When he returned two hours later, he told me that the colonel had headed straight back to our camp, probably to kill Engel.

Fritz, though, had become suspicious when Brinkley forced me to accompany him and had followed us. From the tracks Winnetou had seen, he deduced that Fritz had observed from a distance Brinkley's attempt to kill me, but he had been too far away to help. My friend knew then that his own life was in danger, but since he wasn't armed, thought it best just to slip away. Brinkley started to return to camp but when he found Engel's tracks, he followed my friend. As I learned later, Fritz managed to escape."

"Yes, he did get away," Old Firehand confirmed.

"How?" Watson asked. "You're sure of it, sir?"

"Yes. I'll tell you later. For now, please continue!"

"Winnetou was on a ride north. He had no time to take care of me for any long period so he took me to a camp of Timbabatsche Indians with whom he was on friendly terms. They nursed me until my wound healed, then guided me to the closest settlement where I later found work. For half a year I did all kinds of jobs there to earn money for my return east."

"Where did you want to go?"

"To find Fritz. I assumed he'd gotten away. I knew he had a brother named Otto in Russelville, Kentucky, whom we had intended to visit, and where we could make preparations for our Silver Lake adventure. When I arrived there, I was told that this brother had moved to Arkansas, but no one knew exactly where. He had left a letter for Fritz with a neighbor. When my friend arrived in Russelville, he obtained the letter, which must have included Otto's new address, and then had left to find him. Unfortunately for me, the neighbor had since died.

"I traveled to Arkansas and searched almost the entire state but with no luck. However, Fritz had spoken of our experience while he was in Russelville, and had even mentioned that the name of the would be murderer was Brinkley. I don't know how he learned his name. So, gentlemen, that's what I can tell you. If the name of the rovers' leader is Brinkley, I'm looking forward to meeting this scoundrel. I've a debt to settle with him."

"There are others with the same intention," remarked Old Firehand. "One thing though isn't clear to me yet. You said earlier that Brinkley's red hair is fake. How do you know that?"

"Very easily. When he attacked me, I grabbed his hair in defense. I would surely have been able to pull him to the ground and overcome him had his hair been firmly attached. But I held a wig in my hand and in my surprise Brinkley had time to stab me with his knife. At that moment, I was able to see that his real hair was black."

"Well! Then there's no doubt that you were dealing with the colonel. This fellow's life seems to consist of a series of murders and other crimes. Let's hope we can put an end to it today."

"I too wish it with all my heart. But you haven't told me yet how we're going to defend ourselves against the coming attack."

"You don't need to know that yet, but you'll be told at the appropriate time. Most important is that the workers remain quiet. They should be prepared to get little sleep tonight. Ask them to put their weapons in good order. Before midnight, they are to board a train which will bring them to the location we've selected for our countermove."

"Well, I suppose I'll have to live with that for the time being. I'll make the required arrangements."

When Watson had left, Old Firehand checked with Charoy whether he knew of two workers who resembled the captured rovers in build and facial features. They should also posses the courage to take the places of Brinkley's men on the locomotive. The engineer gave it some thought then sent his Negro helper to fetch two men he thought would be suited for the job.

The two arrived and Old Firehand agreed that Charoy's choice had been a good one. Their build was very much like that of the rovers and what difference there was in facial features would barely matter in the dark of the night. Now they still had to make sure that the voices would not sound too different. For this, Old Firehand took the two workers to Hartley's room, and in appearing to interrogate the rovers, enabled the two replacements to hear the rovers' voices so they could attempt to copy them.

With this much accomplished and dusk come, the hunter decided to scout once more for any additional spies the colonel might have sent. Leaving the house, he searched the area in the direction of the Eagle Tail from which direction spies would need to come.

An experienced frontiersman, not knowing where an enemy may be hiding, will not randomly search an area but rather consider which place would be most expeditious for a spy. Old Firehand too followed this routine. If spies had come, they'd be found at a place from where the laborers' settlement could most safely and advantageously be observed. Such a location was not far from the engineer's house. An escarpment had been cut for the placement of the railroad tracks. Above this slope stood several trees, offering some cover. This would be the place where scouts might be hiding.

At a distance, Old Firehand cautiously climbed the rise. On top, he found his assumption was well-founded. Underneath the trees sat two men talking quietly so that they could not be heard or seen from below. The daring hunter approached so closely that his head pressed against the tree trunk next to where the two were resting. He could have touched either of them. His approach was made possible by his gray coat which even to the sharpest eye blended in with the ground. Now his task was to hear what the rover scouts were discussing. Unfortunately, a pause had ensued in their conversation and some time passed before one of them said, "Did you find out what's going to happen after we're finished here?"

"Nothing definite," the other responded.

"There are all kinds of rumors, with probably only a few of us in the know."

"Yes. The colonel keeps it secret and has few confidants. I think only those who were his companions on the steamer know his actual plans."

"Do you mean Woodward, who escaped with him from the rafters? Well, isn't he the one who's talking with you quite a bit? Didn't he tell you anything?"

"Nothing but hints."

"But surely you drew some conclusions from his hints?"

"Certainly! That's why I conclude that the colonel has no intention of keeping our group together. Our great number appears to be a hindrance to his future plans. And I agree with him on that. The more we are, the smaller the share for each of us will be. I figure he'll pick the best of us, then suddenly disappear."

"By the devil! Are the others to be cheated then?"

"Why cheated?"

"Well, for instance, if the colonel disappears with his group tomorrow after the heist."

"That wouldn't be so bad. I'd be delighted."

"Would you now? I'd very much object to it!"

"You? You blockhead! I'd have thought you were a bit smarter."

"How so?"

"It's self-evident that you wouldn't be one of those cheated."

"Can you prove that? If not, I'll keep my eyes peeled and sound an alarm."

"It's not difficult to prove it to you. Didn't he send you here with me?"

"So what?"

"Only able and reliable fellows get such a job. By delegating us to spy on the settlement, he's shown us the best testimony of his trust. From this we can conclude that if he truly intends to shake off a bunch of our group, it won't be us. More likely we'll be part of those he intends to take along."

"Hmm! You make a good argument and I suppose it satisfies me. But if you think I'll be one of those selected, why hold back from telling me what Woodward told you about the colonel's plans?"

"Because I'm not clear on it. It's about a trip into the mountains."

"Why the mountains?"

"Hmm! I'm not sure it's wise to talk about it; but I guess I'll tell you after all. Up there in the mountains, once lived an ancient people whose name I don't recall. These people either moved south or were exterminated but before that happened, they deposited an immense treasure in a lake."

"What poppycock! Whoever possesses treasure takes it along!"

"As I told you, they might have all been killed."

"What is this treasure? Money?"

"That I don't know. I'm not a learned man and cannot tell you whether early people coined or printed money. Woodward said it was a heathen people who had enormous temples filled with massive gold and silver idols and innumerable vessels of the same materials. These treasures are now at the bottom of Silver Lake; that's why the name."

"Are we to drink its waters to the last drop in order to find the treasure at the bottom?"

"Don't talk so absurdly! The colonel will know what to do. He's supposed to have a drawing that shows the exact location of the treasure."

"So! And where's this Silver Lake?"

"That I don't know. I suppose the colonel won't talk about it until he's selected those he wants to take along. It's pretty obvious he won't reveal his secret and his plans beforehand."

"Of course not! But I figure this thing will be dangerous."

"Why so?"

"Because of all the Indians."

"Pshaw! Only two Indians live up there, the grandson and great-grandson of the Indian whose drawing it was. And these two can be blown away with just a couple of shots."

"If that's so, I'll go along. I've never been up in the mountains and I'll have to rely on those who know them. But I think we must pay attention to today's business. Do you think it'll be successful?"

"It will be. Look how quiet it is in the settlement! Not a soul down there has the slightest glimpse of our presence or our plan. And two of our best, most cunning people are already in the engineer's office to prepare for it. Who could speak of failure here?"

"Well! If only all the laborers are smart enough not to become involved. We would be forced to use our weapons against them."

"Nothing to worry about since they don't know anything that's going to happen. The train arrives here, stops for five minutes, then continues. An hour's drive from here, it comes to our fire where the colonel and our whole gang will be waiting. There our two pals on the locomotive pull their revolvers and force the engineer to stop the train. Our men surround it, the colonel gets on and takes ---"

"Wait a minute!" the other interrupted. "Who gets on? The colonel himself? With only a few of his men and then he comfortably steams away? Later, he stops the train, gets off, and the money disappears. And the rest of us are left with nothing except our perplexed faces. No, that's no bet I want to take!"

"What is it with you?" came the angry retort. "Didn't I tell you that if the colonel truly had such intentions the two of us wouldn't be aboard the train."

"You're so sure about that. I wish I could believe it and could see what's going to happen. I've heard what others are saying. They don't trust the colonel. I'm also convinced that once the train stops, everyone will try to get on."

"So be it! It isn't my style to take advantage of my comrades and I'll warn the colonel not to cheat us. If this Silver Lake thing is going to bring us such wealth, there's no need for dishonesty against our own people. We share equally. Then the colonel can take his pick of those he wants to lead to the mountains. That's it! Let's quit talking about it! I'd much rather know what they're going to use that locomotive down there for. It's been put under steam and is ready to go. But where to?"

"Maybe it's a security engine they plan to run ahead of the money train?"

"No. They wouldn't get it ready this early. The train isn't expected until three o'clock this morning. I don't feel good about this engine's being there and would like to know what it's all about."

The man voiced a suspicion, which had to be taken into account. Old Firehand understood that the locomotive should not remain. It was a common small construction engine with a number of attached wagons normally used to transport dirt. They were intended now to carry the workers to their destination. It wouldn't be wise to wait until midnight. If they were going to disperse the scouts' suspicions, it should be done as soon as possible.

Old Firehand quickly withdrew from his listening post to return to the engineer's house where he told Charoy what he had overheard.

"Well!" exclaimed Charoy. "Then the workers must leave right away. But the spies will see them get aboard!"

"Not necessarily. Order your workers to leave as inconspicuously as possible. They should walk along the tracks for about a quarter of an hour, then wait for the train to catch up with them. The track's curve will shield any sound or view when the train stops and the workers board."

"How many people should we leave here?"

"I think twenty is enough to protect your house and secure the prisoners. You can make these arrangements in the next half hour; then the train has to leave. I'm going back to the two scouts again to listen to what else they say."

Soon he was hidden once more behind the two spies who had fallen silent. Like the scouts, Old Firehand could view the terrain below and made an effort to detect the workers' departure, but happily to no avail. The men left so secretly and covertly that the two spies were not even aware of it. Then too the lights in the buildings and dwellings were so dim that they illuminated little of the surroundings in a way that would clearly define people.

A man with a powerful lantern walked from the engineer's house to the tracks shouting so it could be heard everywhere, "Take the construction train to Wallace! The empty wagons are needed there."

It was Charoy. Without Old Firehand's having told him, he'd been clever enough to invent an idea that would alleviate the scouts' suspicions. He had shared his ruse earlier with the train driver who responded now just as loudly, "Well, sir! I'm glad to finally get going and not burn my coal for nothing. Is there anything to report in Wallace?"

"Nothing but a 'good night' to the local engineer who will probably be playing cards by the time you arrive. Safe travels!"

"Good night, sir!"

A shrill whistle and the train got under way. When its noise had abated, one of the spies suggested to the other, "Now you know the reason for the locomotive."

"Yes, it's all right. The wagons are needed in Wallace. My suspicions were unfounded. Suspicion is foolish anyway. Our plan is so well designed that it's sure to succeed. We could actually leave right now."

"No. The colonel ordered us to wait until midnight. We must follow his orders."

"Okay! But if we're to hang around here for that long, I don't see why I should strain my eyes any longer. I'm going to lie down and catch some sleep."

"Me too. It's probably the smartest thing to do. There'll be no time for it later and in all likelihood also too much commotion for it."

Old Firehand withdrew quickly since the two men were moving to find a more comfortable place to rest. He returned to the engineer and complimented him on his ingenious scheme. Over some wine and the smoke of cigars, they passed the time until it was the moment to leave. As planned, twenty workers remained in the settlement for its protection, a number quite sufficient since no attack was now anticipated.

The laborers who had departed earlier had assembled outside Sheridan, then followed the tracks to the agreed-upon pick-up point. There they waited, then boarded the arriving train to take them to the Eagle Tail. The rovers would be unable to observe them even though they must have left their camp already. The river would force them to keep a distance from the tracks so they could neither see nor hear what was happening down there.

Old Firehand had selected a completely suitable terrain for his plan. Here the river narrowed, enclosed by high banks. The tracks crossed it on a temporary bridge and immediately entered an eighty-yard-long tunnel on the far side. A few yards from the bridge, the train stopped. Rather than being empty, the last two wagons had been loaded with dry wood and coal. No sooner had the train halted when from out of the darkness stepped a small stout fellow who asked the locomotive's engineer in a falsetto voice, "Sir, what are you doing here? Have you brought the workers already?"

"Yes," was the answer from the surprised engineer who watched the peculiar figure, illuminated by the engine's fire. "Who are you?"

"I?" laughed the stout fellow. "I'm Aunt Droll."

"An aunt! Heavens! What are we to do here with women and aunts!"

"Now, now, don't be scared so easily! It's bad for your nerves. I'm Aunt in name only. You'll understand that later. So, why have you come so early?"

"It's by orders of Old Firehand who covertly listened to two rover spies at Sheridan. They were getting suspicious, so we left sooner. Are you one of this famous hunter's men?"

"Yes. But don't run away now; they are all uncles. I'm the only Aunt."

"No way will I run from you, Miss or Mrs. Where are the rovers?"

"Off and away. They already left three quarters of an hour ago."

"Can we unload the coal and wood then?"

"Yes. Have your people board again. Then I'll give you the necessary instructions."

"You, giving instructions? Have you been made the general here?"

"Yes, that I am, with your kind permission, and here I am," Droll said, having jumped into the cab of the locomotive. "And now have your iron horse cross the bridge nice and slow, and stop when the last coal wagon reaches the entrance to the tunnel."

With Droll and the workers back on the train, the engineer gave the Aunt one more baleful look that said it was not easy for him to follow this questionable person's directions.

"Well! How about it?" asked Droll.

"Are you really the man whose instructions I'm supposed to follow?"

"I sure am! And if you don't immediately do as I say, I'll help out a bit. I'm not in the mood to stay on this bridge until doomsday."

He pulled his Bowie knife and pressed its point against the engineer's belly.

"By the devil! You're a hot aunt!" the man complained. "But precisely because you point the knife at me, I think you must be a rover, not an ally. Can you prove yourself?"

"Stop this nonsense now," Droll told him in a serious tone, slipping his knife back into his belt. "We're going to stop over there at the tunnel. My coming across from the other side of the bridge should prove to you that I knew about your coming and that I cannot be one of the rovers."

"All right. I guess I believe you. Let's get over there."

The train crossed the bridge and entered the tunnel, the last wagon remaining outside. The workers now jumped off and dumped the wagon's contents beside the tracks. Then the train pulled forward to the far end of the tunnel and stopped where the second-to-last wagon's contents could be dumped.

When this was done, the workers gathered both heaps of coal and wood into two easily-lit piles alongside the tracks but prepared to protect the rails from the heat which would ensue. In the meantime the engineer had moved the train a quarter-mile down the tracks, stopped the engine, and walked back to where the action was.

His distrust had disappeared. What he saw told him he was with the right people. Beyond the tunnel burned a fire invisible to the rovers camped in the river valley on the opposite side. Near the fire, the rafters and other members of Old Firehand's group had set up camp. Two solid forked tree trunks were rammed into the ground to the left and right of the fire. From a strong branch laid across them both hung large pieces of buffalo meat spitted for roasting. When the train exited the tunnel, these men had all risen to welcome the workers.

"Now do you believe I'm no rover?" asked Droll when the engineer returned and joined them at the fire.

"Yes, sir, you're an honest chap after all."

"And a good one too! I'll prove it to you by inviting all of you to eat with us. We've shot a nice buffalo cow and would like to introduce you to steak à la prairie. It's enough for all of us and I hope your people will be finished soon and can join us for the meal."

Not much later, everyone had come to eat, although there were too many to sit by the fire. Several groups had formed, which were served by the hosting rafters. In addition to the buffalo cow, there was some smaller game so that there was plenty for everybody despite the large number of railroad workers.

Prior to the train's departure from Sheridan, when Charoy was issuing his instructions to his work boss, Watson, he had told him, "I'm also going to pass along some information from Old Firehand. If you wish to learn more about your former companion and friend Engel, ask for a German by the name of Pampel, whom you will find with the rafters."

"What does this Pampel know? Has he heard of Engel?"

"Most likely. Otherwise Old Firehand wouldn't have asked you to talk to him."

Watson now remembered these words and tried to determine from the rafters' conversation whether one of them had an accent and was the German in question. Once he had listened to them all, he had to admit that none of them had an accent and that all of them spoke pure Yankee English. Being one of the few who had found a place by the fire, he decided to ask directly. Beside him sat Aunt Droll and Humpy-Bill whom he asked, "Pardon me, sirs, is there a German among you?"

"Several actually," responded Bill.

"Really? Who are they?"

"First of all, Old Firehand is German. Then I can point out that stout fellow Aunt Droll here and Black Tom over there. Maybe little Fred you see sitting there can be counted as one of them too."

"Hmm. The one I'm looking for doesn't seem to be among them."

"So? Who are you looking for?"

"A man by the name of Pampel."

"Pam-pam-pampel?" Bill called out, breaking into raucous laughter. "Heavens, what a name! Who can pronounce it? Pam-pam-pam- how does it go? Did you say 'pample'? Or was it 'pimple'? Let me hear the name again."

"Mr. Pampel," Watson repeated, causing everyone around the fire to join in Humpy-Bill's laughter.

The name was picked up from one group to the next, followed by uproarious hilarity until there was not a serious face at the camp any longer. Not a single one? Oh, yes. Droll's face showed no expression. He had taken a large piece of buffalo meat, cut off huge pieces, put one after the other in his mouth, chewed with eagerness and concentration as if he had neither heard the name nor the mocking laughter. When things finally quieted down, Bill piped up again, "No, sir, you must have been misled. There's none among us by the name of Pampel."

"But Old Firehand's message told me so!" answered Watson.

"You may not have heard the name correctly or do not remember it aright. I'm sure every one of us would rather put a bullet in his head than ridicule a man by such a name. Don't you think so too, old Droll?"

Droll stopped chewing and responded, "A bullet? No, I shouldn't think so!"

"It's easy for you to say that since your name isn't Pampel, but Droll. If it were Pampel, I'm sure you wouldn't even associate with people."

"But I'm doing just that!"

He emphasized his last words in such a peculiar manner that Bill eyed him sideways and asked, "You don't laugh about this name then?"

"No. I don't, because I wouldn't want to insult a comrade who's indeed among us."

"What? Really? This Pampel is truly one of us?"

"That's right!"

"By the devil! Who is it then?"

"It's me!"

At this, Bill jumped up and shouted, "You, you are this Pam-pam-pampel!"

Renewed laughter prevented him from continuing as most of the others were unable to control themselves. The hilarity was heightened because Droll remained so serious and engaged in consuming his meat as if totally disengaged from the laughter and its cause. After he swallowed his last bite, he stood up, looked around and said loud enough for all to hear, "Gentlemen, your fun has come to an end! No person is guilty of the name he carries and whoever finds mine laughable may tell me so now to my face. Then he should take his knife and step aside with me into the dark. We'll see who is still laughing when we're done!"

A deathly silence suddenly descended on the group.

"But Droll," Humpy-Bill begged, "who would have thought that this is your name! The name's just too cute. We didn't mean to insult you and I hope you'll forgive us. Come on, sit down again with me!"

"Well. That I will do. I'm not even angry because the name is truly kind of 'pampish'. But now that you know my name, I want you to keep quiet about it."

"Obviously! That's understood. But why did you keep it secret all this time? You must really be a fellow who doesn't like to talk of his earlier days."

"Doesn't like to? Who says? I love to remember times from my past, but haven't had any opportunity to reminisce about them."

"Well, then make up for it. You know all about us, what and who we are. We became almost brothers on the ride here and needed to know each other. But about you we know very little, almost nothing."

"Because there's not much to learn. And my home town you know already."

"Yes, Langenleuba in Altenburg County. What did your father do? Will you tell us?"

"Why not?" smiled Droll. "He did many more jobs than most other fathers. Since we must wait here until three a.m. for the rovers, that gives me enough time to name all his professions and titles. He was a bell ringer, waiter, sexton, gravedigger, wedding and baptism chaplain, an undertaker, scythe-grinder, orchard guard and home-guard sergeant. That's it!"

Everyone looked at him to see whether he was serious or joking.

"You can believe it, fellows!" he assured them. "My father was all that, and anyone who knows the conditions over there knows also that he was churchmouse-poor but nevertheless an honorable man enjoying the respect of his fellow citizens. There were almost a dozen children in my family and we starved and had to live in a miserly fashion, but we made it honorably through our lives. Of that I can tell you later --"

"Stop now, please!" interrupted the work boss. You acceded to the wishes of the others and talked about yourself, but you didn't respond to my question. Old Firehand gave me your name ---"

"Yes, he's the only one who knew my real name."

"He gave it to me," Watson continued, "so I could learn what happened to your fellow countryman Engel."

"Engel? Which Engel do you mean?"

"Fritz, the hunter and trapper who was up at Silver Lake."

"Fritz? He's the one you're referring to?" Droll exclaimed. "Do you know him?"

"Like myself! Is he still alive?"

"No. Unfortunately, he died."

"Are you certain of that?"

"Absolutely. Where did you get to know him?"

"Up at Silver Lake. We had to spend an entire winter together there. We were snowed in ---"

"Then your name must be Watson?" Droll interrupted.

"Yes, sir, that's my name."

"Watson, Watson! What a coincidence! But no, there's never a coincidence! It's God's providence! Mister, I know you like a friend, yet I've never seen you before."

"Then you were told about me? By whom?"

"Your comrade Engel's younger brother, Otto. Look! This boy, here with us, is Fred Engel. He's the nephew of your companion from Silver Lake and travels with me to find his father's murderer."

"His father was murdered?" Watson asked incredulously and with a friendly nod shook hands with the boy.

"Yes, for a drawing which ---"

"The drawing again!" Watson interjected. "Do you know the murderer? It must have been the colonel!"

"Yes, it's him, sir. But ... he's reputed to have killed you too!"

"He only wounded me. His thrust missed my heart. I would have died from loss of blood had not a rescuer appeared, an Indian, who dressed my wound and led me to other redskins. I stayed with them until I had recovered. My rescuer is the most famous of Indians. His name is ---"

He did not complete his sentence, but slowly got up and stared at the rock outcropping as though he was seeing a supernatural apparition. From out of the shadows, Winnetou approached slowly. He had been out scouting.

"There he is, there he stands, Winnetou, the chief of the Apaches, " the work boss cried. "It's him, he's here! What luck! Winnetou! Winnetou!"

He dashed towards the chief, took his hands and held them to his chest. The Apache looked at his face, his features brightening with a soft friendly smile as he said, "My white brother Watson! I passed by the warriors of the Timbabatsche and learned that you had recovered and gone back to the Mississippi. Great Manitou must have loved you very much to heal your wound, one which was more severe than I admitted to you. Sit down and tell me how your days have passed to the present!"

No one thought the rovers' actions more important at the moment than the work boss's account. Winnetou knew what he was doing when he directed everybody's attention to Watson's story. His scouting had convinced him that they were secure and could talk about an issue other than the rovers.

Of course, everyone was curious to hear the tale of a man whose life had been saved by Winnetou. Not a sound could be heard as Watson now recounted his adventure, just as he had reported it to Old Firehand and the engineer Charoy. At the end of his story, he hesitated for a moment to ask, "And now, Mr. Droll, can you tell me what happened to my friend Fritz?"

"Yes, that I can," the Aunt responded. "He became a dead man."

"Then the colonel murdered him?"

"No, but he wounded him, just like he did you. From this grave wound, the poor devil died."

"Keep talking, keep talking, sir!"

"After the colonel made you leave the camp with him, Engel began to wonder about it, thinking that without weapons you would be of little use in the hunt. So why take you along? It had to be for some purpose other than hunting. Both of you had distrusted the colonel, and Fritz, who had come to like you very much, feared for your life.

"His fear would not diminish, so he decided to follow your tracks. His concern speeded his pace and after about an hour, he had nearly caught up with both of you. Just when he stepped around some bushes, he spotted you, but what he saw made him hastily leap back. In shock, he peered through the bushes and saw the colonel stabbing you. Then he saw the villain kneel beside you, seemingly to make sure you were dead. Brinkley stood up then and remained there as if contemplating something.

"What was Engel to do? Attack the well-armed murderer when he had no weapon? It would have been sheer madness. Or should he wait for the colonel to leave, hoping you were still alive? Not that either! You were surely dead; otherwise the villain would have made sure with a second thrust. Then, too, if the colonel had killed you, it was surely his intent to kill Engel as well. Only a quick escape would save his life.

"He turned away and hurriedly retraced his path, and once the terrain looked advantageous headed eastward. But only too soon did he discover that the colonel had not lingered where your body lay. He had looked around, found Engel's tracks and was following.

"Engel climbed a rise and looking back saw his pursuer in the valley below, not more than ten minutes behind. Ahead stretched a prairie. Engel raced to the prairie as swiftly as he could. Not until a quarter of an hour had passed did he dare stop and look back. To his horror, he saw that his pursuer was overtaking him and was even closer than before.

"The chase continued for another hour until Fritz located a grove of bushes ahead of him. He believed he was saved, but when he got closer he realized that the bushes grew far apart with lush grass in between which revealed tracks very well. While the fleeing man was actually a good runner, the privations of the hard winter had sapped his strength; his pursuer drew ever closer. Once when he glanced over his shoulder, he saw the colonel at most a hundred paces behind him. This spurred his legs to ever greater effort.

"Engel saw water ahead. It was the Orfork branch of Grand River. He headed for it, but before he could reach it, a shot rang out. Fritz felt as if he had been hit by a fist in his right side but kept on running and dived into the water intending to swim to the opposite bank. But when he saw a tributary entering the river to his left, he turned towards its mouth and swam a short distance upstream. Despite his wound, he reached a thicket whose dense branches hung down to the water level, made even more impenetrable by flotsam that offered concealment from even the keenest eyes. He pushed his way in and stood still in the water, shivering mightily from his agitation."

"And from fatigue and fear!" Watson added. "But, please continue!"

"The colonel had also reached the river bank. Since he didn't see Engel and the river was narrow, he figured that his prey must have swum across. He also entered the water but had to do it carefully to protect his weapons and munitions from getting wet. This took some time as he had to swim on his back, holding his weapons in the air. Once on the other side, he disappeared into the bushes."

"He must have returned." opined Humpy-Bill. "When he didn't find tracks on the far side, he had to assume that Engel was still on the near bank."

"That's true," nodded Droll. "First he searched a stretch of river bank. Then he crossed the river again to recheck the far side. But there were no tracks on that side either which must have confused him. Examining the entire area, he passed Fritz's hiding place twice but didn't see the concealed man. Your friend kept listening for a long time without seeing or hearing the colonel. He continued standing in the water until dark. Then he crossed the river and ran all night long to get as far away as possible from his pursuer."

"But he was wounded!"

"Indeed, by a glancing shot under his arm. Because of the excitement and the cold water, he had not paid much attention to it, but on his subsequent run, the wound started to burn. He padded it as well as he could until he found some cooling herbs the next morning, a dressing he replaced from time to time. Totally exhausted, he tried to still a gnawing hunger by eating some roots, even though he was not familiar with them. He dragged himself along until evening whereupon poor Fritz came to a remote cattle camp where he was received with hospitality. By that time, he was so weak that he couldn't even tell the people what had happened to him. He simply collapsed unconscious.

"When he awoke, he found himself lying in an old bed, unable to recall how he got there. Soon he learned from the rancher that for two weeks he had had a horrific fever during which he had mumbled about murder, blood, escape and water. Only now was he able to recount his adventure.

"One of the cowboys mentioned to Engel that he had met a red-haired man who was inquiring whether a stranger had shown up at their camp. This cowboy had once seen the red-haired man in Colorado Springs and knew his name was Brinkley. Since he didn't think him trustworthy, he denied the presence of any such visitor. In this way, Engel learned the name of the murderer, who had earlier given a different sobriquet.

"The wound finally seemed to be healing and at the next opportunity, Engel was taken to Las Animas."

"Then he never got to Pueblo?" questioned Watson. "Otherwise I would have heard about him when I was there. Where did he go after that?"

"He joined a company of traders," Droll replied, "as a driver traveling on the Arkansas Trail to Kansas City. Once he received his pay there, he had enough money to seek out his brother in Russelville. However, when he arrived, he found Otto gone. A neighbor handed him a letter his brother had left for him, from which he learned that Otto could be found in Benton, Arkansas."

"Oh, there! Benton is one of the few places I missed in my search!" said Watson. "What happened to the drawing he had on him?"

"It had suffered from the waters of the Orfork River and Engel had to recopy it. In Benton, when he had finished telling his story, he gave the drawing to his brother for safekeeping. Excited, Otto was prepared to ride immediately with him to Silver Lake. But it soon turned out that Fritz's experiences had not remained without consequences. He began to cough, and rapidly lost weight. A doctor diagnosed him with rapid consumption and eight weeks after arriving at his brother's place; Fritz was dead. Standing in the cold water for such a long time must have pushed his system over the edge."

"Then his death is the colonel's doing after all."

"If only that were all!" Droll said ruefully. Among us here are several who are ready to settle accounts with him. But listen to what happened later! Otto Engel was a well-off man who tended several fields and pursued a profitable trade on the side. He was married and had two children, a boy, Fred, and a girl, Frieda. A hired man helped out with the chores on the property.

"One day a stranger showed up at Engel's residence and offered him a lucrative opportunity which greatly delighted Otto. The stranger gave his profession as a ship operator who had made his fortune as a gold prospector. In the ensuing conversation, it was mentioned that he once met a hunter named Engel, also a German. The remark obviously referred to Otto's dead brother. Following this, much needed to be said and the entire afternoon and evening passed without the stranger's showing any desire to leave. He was invited to spend the night with the Engels which, following a bit of urging, he accepted. Engel had finally told his guest about Fritz's death and its cause, and had fetched the Silver Lake drawing from a small wall chest to show to the stranger. Once he returned it back in the chest everyone retired.

"The family slept upstairs in a room at the back of the house, with their helper in an adjacent small side room. The guest had been given the best room, facing the front of the house. Downstairs the doors had been locked and Engel as usual had taken the keys upstairs with him. As it happened, young Fred had celebrated a birthday a couple of days before and had received a two-year-old foal as a gift. Because of all the interesting stories that had been told that evening, the boy had forgotten to feed his horse. Only remembering after having already gone to bed, he rose and quietly left the room to tiptoe down the stairs. Down below, he retrieved a key from behind the back door, unlocked it and crossed the yard to the stable. He hadn't found it necessary to take a lantern along; besides, the kitchen where the lantern was kept had been locked. Thus he had to feed the foal in the dark, which took longer than usual.

"He was not quite finished when he thought he heard a scream. Rushing from the stable into the yard, he saw a light in his parents' bedroom. It disappeared only to reappear in the helper's room. A great commotion arose from there. The helper was screaming and furniture seemed to be breaking. Fred ran to the house and climbed a vine trellis to the lighted window. When he looked in, he saw their helper lying on the floor, the stranger kneeling on him, throttling him with his left hand and holding a revolver to his head with his right. Two shots rang out. Fred wanted to scream but couldn't utter a sound.

"In his shock as the shots were fired, the boy lost his hold on the trellis and fell to the cobblestone yard. He hit his head and momentarily lost consciousness. When he came to, he agonized about what he should do. Most likely the murderer was still in the house, which was a reason not to enter. Yet he had to help. He ran into the kitchen, grabbed a knife, and when he entered the living room was surprised by the villain, who knocked him to the floor. In the tussle Fred managed to stab the intruder in the calf. In the dark the man disappeared. Fred got up, ran out of the house, and shrieking loudly to scare the murderer and hoping to prevent him from harming his parents and sister, jumped over the fence and ran to a neighbor located some distance outside the village.

"When these people heard his cries for help, they quickly arose and hurried outside. Hearing what had happened, they armed themselves and followed Fred. Before reaching the house, they saw fire engulfing the upper story. The stranger surely had set the house afire and then escaped. The flames spread so quickly that no one was able to get upstairs. Only the downstairs possessions were able to be retrieved. The wall chest that had contained the Silver Lake drawing stood open and empty. The four bodies upstairs -- parents, sister and helper -- had to be left to burn."

"Horrible! Terrible!" It sounded from the round of men when the story teller paused. Young Fred Engel sat by the fire, his face in his hands, sobbing fitfully.

"Yes, horrible!" Droll nodded. "The event was a sensation and resulted in a search in all directions, but without avail. The brothers Engel had a sister in St. Louis, wife of the rich owner of a freight firm. She put up a bounty of ten thousand dollars for the apprehension of the murderer, which has not yet led to his capture. Then she thought of contacting the private detectives, Harris and Blother, and this finally brought some results."

"What results?" asked Watson. "The murderer is still on the loose! I assume it turned out to be the colonel?"

"Yes, it was, and he's still free," Droll responded, "but he's as good as dead. I went to Benton to do a really exhaustive search, much greater than others had…."

"You? Why?"

"To earn five thousand dollars."

"Wasn't it ten thousand?"

"The amount's to be split," explained Droll. "Half goes to Harris and Blother, the other half to any detective who finds Brinkley."

"Oh, are you a policeman then?"

"Hmm! I think you're all decent people with none among you who might need to be chased some time in the future. Let me tell you then what I've kept secret until now: I'm a police agent for certain districts of the far west. I've delivered many a man to the gallows and intend to continue to do so. Now you also know why I don't talk much about myself. Old Droll whom many have laughed about, is, once you get to know him, not such a ridiculous guy. But that's not important here. I'm talking about a serial killer."

If everyone had laughed about the Aunt's peculiar name, he was now seen in a far different light. His revelation of being a police detective put a whole new aspect on his personality and onto his assumed oddities. He hid behind his droll behavior in order to put his hands with greater certainty onto those he was out to apprehend.

"Well then," he continued, "I looked up Fred in St. Louis, questioned him and learned what all had been talked about prior to the murders. When everyone had gone to bed, the little wall chest was opened by the colonel to pilfer the drawing. The noise awakened the others, which ended up in their deaths. I assumed that the murderer was preparing to go to Silver Lake to retrieve the treasure. So I followed him and took Fred along who had seen him and would certainly recognize him again. Already on the steamer, I was fairly sure that he was one of the rovers, and my certainty has grown with every passing day. I hope to get my hands on the man today."

"You?" asked old Blenter. "So! What are you going to do with him?"

"What I consider best at the time."

"Take him to Benton, by any chance?"

"Maybe."

"Don't even think of it! There are plenty of other people here with greater rights than yours. Just think of the account I myself have to settle with him!"

"And me!" called Watson.

"And also us rafters!" it sounded in a chorus.

"Don't get excited everyone. We don't have him yet!" responded Droll.

"We're about to have him!" insisted Blenter.

"He'll be the first to board the train," a rafter shouted.

"That may be," returned Droll. "But I don't eat buffalo loin until I've shot the buffalo. It also doesn't matter to me who gets him. It's not necessary for me to drag him to Benton. If I bring proof of his death and that I assisted in it, the bounty is mine as certain as my 'sleeping bag' gown. Okay, I've talked enough and now I need to get a few winks of sleep. Wake me when it's time!"

He got up to find a dark, quiet place. The others could not even think of sleep. The story they had just heard filled their minds, and the forthcoming encounter with the rovers was an excitement all by itself.

Winnetou did not participate in the ensuing conversation. He leaned against a rock and closed his eyes. Yet he did not sleep. From time to time, his lids rose, and with a probing look he surveyed the area.

* * * * *

Meanwhile back in Sheridan around midnight, the twenty workers had come to create a protective circle around the engineer's house. Just before 2:30 A.M., Old Firehand went to Hartley. He was in bed fast asleep. But beside him sat Charoy's Negro, revolver in hand. He had taken his place next to the wounded man who needed his rest. Old Firehand saw that he need not be concerned. Satisfied, he went to the engineer to tell him that he would now depart to meet the train.

"Then the hour of truth is coming," remarked Charoy. "Are you not afraid, sir?"

"Afraid?" the hunter asked, surprised. "Would I have taken on this task of my own free will if I were afraid?"

"At least concerned?"

"My only concern is that the colonel will get away."

"But it's possible, even likely, that you'll be fired on!"

"It's even likelier that I will not be hit. Don't worry about me; just see that everything here stays in good order during my absence. It's not impossible that the colonel will send some of his people to Sheridan to see that everything works out right. If he does so, he'll arrange with his men to send a messenger telling him what's happening. So, act as if everything is normal."

Old Firehand now called for the two workers who were to act out the role of the two rovers on the locomotive. At Charoy's insistence, the workers had been dressed similarly to rovers. Together they headed off along the tracks so that any arriving spies would not notice their departure.

It was totally dark, but the workers knew the line and took the hunter between them. As they continued away from Sheridan and in the direction of Kit Carson, Old Firehand instructed them how to react to whatever possible event he could envision. When they reached the arranged meeting place, well up the line from the settlement, they sat in the grass to await the train's coming.

Shortly after three o'clock, it arrived and chugged to a stop. The train consisted of the engine and six large coaches. Old Firehand boarded and inspected each of them. All were empty. In the first coach stood a large locked suitcase partially filled with rocks to simulate the weight of forty thousand dollars. There was no conductor; the crew consisted only of the driver of the locomotive and the stoker. When Old Firehand had finished his inspection, he approached these two men to issue his instructions. He had barely begun when the stoker burst out, "Hold it, sir! I don't need to hear your orders. I'm not willing to do this job."

"No? Why not?"

"I'm a stoker. My job is to feed the engine's fires; that's what I'm paid for, not to get myself killed."

"Who's talking about getting killed?"

"Not you, maybe, but I."

"No one will shoot."

"All right, but how about stabbing or clubbing? There's no difference. It's all the same whether I'm shot, stabbed, clubbed or throttled. I don't want to depart from my job by any of these means."

"But didn't your superiors order you to follow my commands here?"

"No. They can't do that. I have a family and do my duty, but to fight with rovers is not part of it. I was told that I was to come here and listen to what would be required of me. What I choose to do was left to my discretion. And I'm not prepared to do it."

"That's your final word?"

"You can be sure of it!"

"And you, sir?" Old Firehand asked the engineer, who had listened quietly.

"I will remain at my post," the brave man responded.

"You're a good man!" the hunter exclaimed. "What's your name?"

"Brocker, Sir," came the response.

"Well, Mr. Brocker, it's my duty to tell you that you could experience some mishap through unforeseen circumstances."

"You too, sir."

"Indeed."

"Well then! What you the stranger dares, I as an employee may dare too."

"Right! You are an upright fellow. The stoker can walk back to Sheridan and wait for our return. I shall take his post."

"Well, I'll go then and wish you good execution!" grumbled the frightened man as he walked away.

Old Firehand with his two rover actors climbed onto the locomotive and finished his instructions to Brocker. Then he blackened his face and clothing with soot. In his plain linen shirt and pants, he now looked the perfect picture of a stoker. The train got under way.

The coaches were built and arranged in the American way. One had to board the last car to get to the first. All were lighted. The locomotive was of a tender design with high and strong protective walls of sheet iron. This was very fortunate since the walls almost completely hid the people on the command platform and had sufficient strength to withstand revolver or rifle bullets.

Under full steam, the train headed in the direction of the rendezvous with the rovers.

By this time, the two spies Old Firehand had overheard earlier in the evening above the settlement had arrived at the spot where the colonel and his gang were waiting, close to the tracks where the highjack would occur. They reported that no one in Sheridan had any idea what was to happen, which generated a joyful reaction among the rovers. With this accomplished, they took the colonel aside and told him of the mutual concerns they had discussed earlier. Brinkley listened to them quietly then answered, "I'm aware of what you're telling me. But I wouldn't think of keeping all these good-for-nothings, most of whom are useless characters, neither will I give a single dollar of this forty thousand to anyone I don't need. They don't get anything."

"Then they'll just up and take it."

"Wait and see! I have my plan."

"But they'll board the train!"

"Let them! I know that everyone will greedily push and shove to be the first to get to the money chest. I, though, will remain outside until the chest has been brought out by Woodward through the front door of the first coach. Once the train has left, we'll see what happens."

"What about us two?"

"You stay with me. By sending you to Sheridan, I demonstrated my trust in you. Now go to Woodward. He knows my plan and will tell you the names of those who are to stay with me."

They obeyed his order and joined the colonel's special group, most of whom apparently were his lieutenants. It was still dark. As it approached four o'clock, the rovers started a blazing fire beside the tracks.

All these rogues had no idea that this early morning hour had been chosen for their downfall. By the time the train reached the Eagle Tail, dawn would be on the way and the defenders' shooting could be deadly accurate.

It was quarter past four when the colonel and his gang heard the distant rumbling of the train and shortly thereafter saw the headlights of the engine. Aboard the locomotive, Old Firehand kept the fire gate closed so that the four people in the locomotive's cab were hardly visible. A hundred paces from the rovers' fire, Brocker gave reverse steam. The whistle sounded, wheels screeched and the train coasted to a stop.

Up to now the rovers had worried whether Faller and Haller would be able to force the engineer and stoker to follow their orders. Once the train stopped, they rejoiced and jostled each other in a wild effort to clamber aboard. Each and every one wanted to be first into the rear coach to search for the money chest. In their excitement, none of them wondered why there were no railroad officials on the train.

But the colonel knew what to do. He climbed up onto the first steps of the locomotive's cab, looked around and asked, "Everything all right, boys?"

"Looks like it," responded one of Charoy's workers who was holding a revolver to Brocker's chest. "They had to obey. Look, colonel! The slightest move and I fire."

As if afraid, Old Firehand stood pressed against the water tank, the second worker with a gun in front of him. The colonel was totally deceived. He said, "Very good! You did your job well and you'll get a bonus. Stay up there until we're done and when I give the signal, jump off so that these good employees don't die of fear and can continue their trip."

Brinkley retreated from the engine into the dark. He was convinced he had been speaking with his two rover spies, particularly since the worker had answered in a well-imitated voice of the clerk Smitty. When he was gone, Old Firehand leaned out to have a look along the length of the train. He could see nothing except coaches full of people. He could hear that they were fighting over the chest.

"Away, away!" the hunter ordered Brocker. "And don't drive slowly, pour on the steam! The colonel seems to have boarded too. We mustn't wait any longer or they'll all disembark again."

The train started to move without its usual warning whistle.

A window opened in one of the coaches and a furious shout rang out, "There's no money in the chest, just rocks!"

"Stop, stop!" shouted a second agitated voice. "Kill those dogs in the cab! Kill them! Shoot, shoot!"

The words were recognizable but not the voice itself. Old Firehand had no way of knowing that the cry had come from the colonel and that the villain had indeed not boarded the train.

Brinkley's plans had been different, and he, together with a select group, had actually waited alongside the tracks. He knew now that his heist had gone badly awry, that he had been fooled, but as much as he wished to pursue the train, he stood impotent; his horses had been staked some distance away.

The rovers in the coaches became terrified when the train lurched forward. They wanted to leap off but dared not because of the speed the train had already attained. Old Firehand was vigorously stoking the fires as the flames illuminated him and his helpers. Suddenly, the door of the first coach was wrenched open and Woodward appeared. Looking across the tender car to the cab in front of him, he could make out the clearly defined face of the hunter, the replacement rovers standing motionless by his side.

"Old Firehand!" he screamed so loudly that it could be heard even over the noise of the wheels and the engine. "You dog! Go to the devil!"

Pulling a revolver from his belt, he fired wildly. Firehand dropped to the floor of the cab, ducking the shot. But in the blink of an eye, his own revolver rang out and Woodward fell back into the coach, struck in the heart. Others appeared in the opening but were hit by a barrage of the hunter's bullets. The two workers also fired into the doorway until they had a moment to wedge a panel crosswise between the engine and the coach. Now the rovers could shoot as much as they wanted; the engine crew was fully protected.

The train rushed along. Brocker kept his eyes on the tracks ahead. Half an hour passed and the sky in the east brightened. The engineer sounded the whistle, not in short bursts but in a continuous shrill scream. He was approaching the bridge and the tunnel and wanted to alert the waiting men.

The welcoming party had long since taken their posts. Shortly before midnight, soldiers from Fort Wallace had arrived and positioned themselves below the bridge on both sides of the river to catch any rover who might try to escape. At one end of the bridge, Winnetou stood with the rafters and hunters. Beyond, on both sides of the tracks leading into the tunnel, stood three-quarters of the armed workers, the rest waiting at the tunnel's end. One of them was the work boss, Watson, who had the dangerous task of disengaging the engine from the train inside the tunnel. Hearing the shriek of the whistle, he ordered his people to light the first fire, just alongside the tracks at the far end of the tunnel.

While the coal and wood stacks were being ignited, Watson stepped inside the tunnel and pressed himself against the wall to await the train.

As the locomotive slowed down to cross the bridge, Old Firehand shouted from the engine to the men waiting by the tunnel entrance, "Now light the fire behind us!"

A moment later, the train came to a dead halt. The locomotive stood exactly where Watson had expected it, its cowcatcher just at the tunnel's exit.

"Hang on!" Watson shouted. "It'll just be a moment!"

With these words, he crawled between the locomotive and the first coach, disengaged the coupling and raced out of the tunnel. The locomotive, belching steam and smoke, followed ponderously. Only the coaches remained inside the tunnel.

Swiftly, the rafters now protected the rails at both ends of the tunnel by piling rocks on them, so the raging fires of wood and coal could be shoved on top of the tracks by means of makeshift push-beams.

This had happened very quickly, much too quickly for the rovers to recognize the dire straits they were in. They had become fearful and distraught during the breakneck ride knowing that Old Firehand was aboard the locomotive.

Although they knew their plan was doomed, they expected that once the train came to a halt, they could still gain their freedom. Being so many and so well armed, they expected no opposition.

Now the train was stopped, the moment the rovers had waited for. But looking out, they saw only the deepest darkness. Those rovers who had pushed their way into the last coach climbed down but found themselves in a narrow, dark hole from which they could only stare into a roaring, smoking fire. The ones in the first coach were horrified to discover that the locomotive had disappeared, replaced by a mighty inferno. That's when the awful truth of their predicament became clear.

"A tunnel, a tunnel!" one of the rovers cried in fear, with others carrying the exclamation forward, "It's a tunnel; we're in a tunnel! What'll we do? We've got to get out!"

Push came to shove, so that all the frantic men at the exits, front and rear, were literally tumbling out. Before the first rovers could get up, more fell on top of them. A chaos of bodies, arms and legs ensued, accompanied by cries, curses and inevitable injuries. There were even some men reaching for their weapons to fight off those on top of them.

Heavy smoke from the coal and wood fires was now drifting into the tunnel. "By the devil! They want to suffocate us," a terrified voice screamed. "Out! Out of here!"

Ten, twenty, fifty, a hundred voices echoed the cry and, caught in mortal dread, everyone pressed, shoved, pushed and jostled toward the two tunnel exits. But there the fires burned, their expanse and high-blazing flames permitting no passage. Anyone wanting to get through would have to jump through the flames, certain that his clothing would catch fire. The men up front, recognizing the enormity of their trap, turned and pushed back. The rovers in the back pushed forward or would not give room. Those close to both fires quickly engaged in a terrible fight with those who had until now been their friends or at least compatriots in evil. The tunnel walls amplified the screams and frenzy so that on the outside it sounded as if every wild animal on earth had been let loose inside.

Old Firehand climbed down from the locomotive and walked around the rocky outcrop where the tunnel cut through to get to its opposite side near the bridge. "We need not do a thing," one of the workers called out to him. "The beasts kill each other off, sir! A better plan than yours couldn't have been devised."

"Yes, they really fell on each other," Firehand answered. "But they're still human beings and we must help them. Clear the entrance for me!"

"You want to enter?"

"I do."

"By God, no! They'll fall on you and kill you, sir!"

"No, they'll be relieved when I tell them how they can save themselves."

Old Firehand helped push the blazing coal pile aside, just far enough that one man could pass between it and the tunnel wall. He leaped into the tunnel, he alone facing the throng of raging men. Never before in his life had his boldness shown itself so clearly as at this very moment. But Old Firehand had often seen how the courage of a single man can fascinate, even paralyze a crowd.

"Rovers! Silence!" his mighty voice roared. It drowned out the screams of a hundred throats and a sudden hush fell. "Listen to what I tell you!"

"Old Firehand!" Voices echoed back and forth, coughing and choking, but full of surprise at this incomparable fearlessness.

"Yes, it's me," he answered. "Have you learned now that wherever I am, resistance is useless? If you don't want to suffocate, drop your weapons and come out one by one. I'll stand beside the fire and give orders. Whoever jumps out without waiting for my command will be shot. And anyone still carrying a weapon will also get a bullet in his gut. There are many of us, workers, hunters, rafters and soldiers, enough to make my threat credible to you. Think about it! Then throw a hat out to us as a sign of compliance. If not, we have a hundred rifles aimed at the tunnel's mouth to prevent you from coming out."

Because of the dense smoke, he had been able to speak the final words only with great effort. So as not to provide a target for a bullet, he quickly leaped outside again, an appropriate caution but in the final analysis, not really needed. The impression he had made on the rovers had been so powerful that none would have dared to aim a weapon at him.

He now ordered the workers to sight their rifles at the tunnel entrance, ready to repel the rovers should they try to break out en masse. They could be heard debating, many voices talking at once. Conditions in the tunnel didn't permit them much time, since the smoke entering the tunnel was becoming more dense and impaired their breathing more and more. They had lost all courage, facing a man like Old Firehand; they knew he would make his threat stick. Death by suffocation was coming so close that they saw no other alternative but to surrender. A hat flew out of the tunnel across the fire. Pleased to see the capitulation, Old Firehand ordered the first rover to come out. The man leaped and was made to cross the bridge at once where he was received by the rafters and hunters. In expectation of the successful ending of their plan --- actually, Winnetou's --- a goodly supply of ropes had been brought along and the first man was quickly tied up. The same happened to each of his companions who followed him.

Their escape from the tunnel was staggered so enough time was available to bind one man after the next. Yet it all happened so quickly that after a quarter of an hour all the rovers were in the hands of the victors. However, to Firehand's great dismay and anger, the worst of the lot, the colonel, was missing. Some of the captives said that he had not boarded the train, nor had twenty others. With the fires now pushed aside the tunnel and the coaches could be searched but to no avail. The rovers had not lied.

Should this unspeakable criminal be allowed to get away, he, the one most wanted? No! The captives were entrusted to the soldiers and workers. Then Old Firehand, Winnetou, the rafters and other hunters rode back to where the rovers had boarded the train, in an effort to pick up the tracks of the missing thugs. From there, Old Firehand sent four rafters on to Sheridan to fetch his horse and hunting gear, as well as the two captive rovers and bring them to Ft. Wallace. He didn't want to return to Sheridan but intended to continue with his comrades the fort, where the captive rovers could be held in military custody. The four messengers were also told to report back to engineer Charoy to describe the success of their mission insofar as it had been accomplished.

The group, led by Old Firehand, found the burned out fire where the rovers had been waiting to ambush the train, not far from the spot where they had staked their horses. After a long search and critical examination of the many foot and hoof prints, it was established that indeed the twenty men had escaped from here. They apparently had taken the best horses and released the others who had scattered in all directions.

"This colonel is a smart one," Old Firehand acknowledged ruefully. "If he had taken all the horses, it would have been a major undertaking for his small troop, and his tracks would have been easy enough for a child to follow. But by chasing off the majority of the horses, he has made our search much more difficult and has gained considerable time. And since he seems to have selected the best animals, he has quite a head start on us that we'll have difficulty making up."

"My white brother may be mistaken," offered Winnetou. "This paleface will not have left the vicinity without checking what has happened to his people. If we follow his tracks, they will surely lead us to the Eagle Tail."

"Perhaps my red brother's suggestion is correct. Brinkley rode from here to spy on us. By now he knows the situation and has fled. Our having come here to look for him has cost us precious time."

"If we make haste, we may still be able to catch up with him!"

"No. My brother must understand that we cannot follow him right away. We must get to Fort Wallace to give depositions against the rovers. That'll take the entire day. We can only follow the rovers' tracks tomorrow."

"Then they will be more than a day ahead of us!"

"Yes, but we know where they're going and need not lose any time in tracking them. We'll head directly to Silver Lake."

"Does my brother think they will still go there?"

"Yes, I'm sure of it."

"Even though they were badly beaten here?"

"Yes. Despite that."

"But they had no success here," Winnetou pointed out. "You don't think that will affect their plans?"

"Certainly not," rejoined Old Firehand. "They wanted to get the money from the train to make some major purchases. But these purchases are not absolutely necessary. They can live off the land from the game they shoot. Weapons and ammunition they already have. And should they run short of the latter, there's plenty of opportunity to acquire it by honest or dishonest means. I strongly believe they're on their way to Silver Lake."

"Then let's follow them at least a short way to find out where they rode from here."

Twenty horses leave plenty of tracks, but even fewer would not have escaped the sharp eyes of such experienced hunters. The tracks led to the river, then upstream from there, and were so obvious that the riders could move at a gallop without losing sight of them.

At the Eagle Tail, not far from the bridge and the tunnel, the rovers had halted. One of them, most likely the colonel, had crept up to the tracks under cover of trees and bushes and must have witnessed the capture of his gang. After he rejoined his small group, the rovers had swiftly ridden off.

The hunters and rafters continued to follow the tracks for another half hour, but once they saw the direction the gang was taking, they turned back and returned to the bridge. Clearly, the rovers were heading to Bush Creek, a sure sign that they intended to ride to Colorado and Silver Lake.

Not long afterwards the four rafters returned from Sheridan. They also brought Hartley and Charoy along to accompany them to Fort Wallace, since their testimony would also be required. The laborers returned to Sheridan on foot, having received all the rovers' weapons as a reward. There were more than enough coaches to transport the captive rovers to Fort Wallace; the soldiers returned on horseback.

Before the train arrived, word of the events reached Fort Wallace and the locals were all astir to learn the details. As the train pulled in, everyone crowded close to give the rovers a preview of the treatment they would receive after sentencing. Had there not been so many rovers and had their escorts not protected them, some lynchings might well have taken place on the spot.

The rovers had already suffered so many losses by their own hands that a quarter of them were found dead in the tunnel. To this day, people in the area still talk about the famous smoking-out of the rovers in the tunnel of the Eagle Tail and the exploits of Old Firehand and Winnetou, chief of the Apaches.

11. In a Jam

Beyond the Cumison River toward the Elk Mountains, four men rode across a high plain covered by short grass bare of any brush or trees. Although exceptional characters abound in the Far West, the four horsemen would have been conspicuous anywhere.

The most distinguished-looking of them rode a splendid black horse, the sort bred only by some Apache tribes. The man was built neither too tall nor too broad, yet gave the impression of possessing great strength and endurance. His suntanned face was framed by a full dark-blond beard. He wore leather leggings and a hunting shirt. High boots reached up over his knees. His broad-brimmed felt hat was adorned with ear tips of the grizzly bear. The broad braided leather belt appeared to hold a goodly supply of cartridges, two revolvers and a Bowie knife. From it also dangled a pair of clamp-on horseshoes and four nearly circular woven thick straw pads with attached straps and buckles. These items seemed to be meant to attach to a horse's hooves to mislead pursuers.

From his left shoulder to his right hip hung a lasso, and from his neck, suspended on a strong silk string, was a peace pipe decorated with hummingbird skins. In his right hand he held a short-barreled rifle, its bolt of a unique design. On his back he carried a long, heavy double-barreled rifle rarely seen nowadays but formerly called a "bear killer" which fired bullets of enormous caliber. This man was Old Shatterhand, the famous hunter, who owed his honorary nickname to his ability to down an enemy with a mere blow of his fist.

Beside him rode a slender, beardless little chap dressed in a blue tailcoat with polished yellow buttons. His head was covered with a large lady's hat, also called an Amazon hat, adorned with a huge feather. His pants were too short and on his stockingless feet he wore old leather shoes with large Mexican spurs. This rider carried a whole arsenal of weaponry but whoever saw his good-natured little face had to think that such an impressive collection's sole purpose was to frighten away possible enemies. The little man was Mister Heliogabalus Morpheus Franke, commonly called Hobble-Frank by his companions since he limped from a long-ago injury.

He was trailed by a more than six-foot-tall scrawny fellow riding an old, low-slung mule, which barely seemed to have the strength to carry his rider. The man wore leather pants obviously made for a much shorter but heavier person. His bare feet were also stuck in a pair of heavily patched leather shoes, each of which must have weighed five to six pounds. The man's torso was covered by a buffalo-leather shirt which, having neither buttons nor other fastening devices, left his chest bare. Its sleeves reached barely past his elbows. His neckerchief's original color could no longer be divined. On his pointy head sat a contraption one could have called a cylinder many years before. Perhaps it once adorned the head of a millionaire. Then it had degenerated lower and lower to end up at last

219

on the prairie in the hands of its present owner, who had found its brim useless, had ripped it away, except for a token stub he used as a handle for doffing the indescribably bent and rumpled headdress.

A short rope serving as a belt held two revolvers and a scalping knife as well as an assortment of bags containing various items a frontiersman cannot do without. From his shoulders hung a rubberized coat, but such a garment! Its exposure to the first rain had shrunk this glorious piece to the size of a Hussar's jacket, never again to fulfill its original purpose. Across his infinitely long legs, the man had placed one of those rifles with which the experienced hunter never misses his target. The man's age, just like that of his mule, was impossible to divine. At most, one could say that both man and beast knew each other well and had lived through quite a few adventures together.

The fourth horseman of this diverse entourage sat on a very high and strong nag. He was very, very corpulent but so diminutive that his short legs were unable to surround his horse's flanks. Although the sun offered sufficient heat, he wore a fur coat that suffered, however, from extreme hairlessness. Collecting its remaining hairs would have barely sufficed to furnish fur for a mouse. He wore a much too large Panama hat and from underneath his furless coat protruded two giant cuffed boots. With the coat's sleeves being much too long to expose his hands, one could only see the man's rosy, fat, good-natured but crafty face. He carried a longrifle; what other weapons he might have had was impossible to tell since his coat covered all.

These last two men were David Kroners and Jakob Pfefferkorn, known everywhere only as Long Davy and Fat Jemmy. They were inseparable and no one had ever seen the one without the other. Jemmy was a German and Davy a Yankee. Through the years of their companionship, Davy had learned enough German from his friend to converse in his language. Just as inseparable as the two riders were their mounts. They stood always side by side, grazed together, and when they were obliged to share the company of other horses at a camp site, they moved at least a bit aside from the others to press against each other and comfort themselves by snorting, sniffing and licking.

Although it was not far past midday, the four horsemen had already traveled a significant distance and traversed not only soft grasslands but arid terrain since they and their animals were covered in dust. Yet neither showed any signs of fatigue. Had they been tired, it could only have been detected from their silence. The quiet was broken by Hobble-Frank riding beside Old Shatterhand, as he addressed his friend in their hometown dialect. "Are we then to stay overnight at Elk Fork? How far is it still?"

"We'll get to the river by evening," Old Shatterhand answered.

"Only by evening? Oh my! Who's to bear this! We've been in the saddle since five o'clock this morning. Mustn't we stop at least once to let the horses rest? Don't you think so?"

"That's true. Let's wait until we reach the end of this prairie. There we'll find some woods and also a small brook."

"Good! The animals can get water and grass too. But what are we going to eat? Yesterday we consumed the last of the buffalo meat and this morning we had only bones. Since then not even a sparrow, much less larger game, has come in sight. I'm hungry and need something to gnaw on, otherwise I'll croak."

"Don't worry! I'll provide a roast."

"Perhaps, but what kind? This old meadow here is so forlorn, I think not even a beetle's wandering around here. Where's a decently hungry frontiersman to get a roast?"

"I see one already. Here, hold my horse and keep on riding slowly with the others."

"Really?" asked Frank, shaking his head while looking around. "You already see a roast? I'm not seeing a thing."

As the hunter dismounted, Frank took the reins of Old Shatterhand's horse and continued alongside Davy and Jemmy. Old Shatterhand walked toward a number of mounds where he had spotted a colony of prairie dogs, some of whose abandoned burrows were often occupied by rattlesnakes and owls. Prairie dogs are inquisitive little critters who straighten up when someone or something approaches, then dive lightning-fast into their burrows once they perceive danger. Every hunter disdains the meat of these animals if he can catch larger game, not because it's inedible but because he finds it distasteful. Should he nevertheless want to hunt prairie dogs he mustn't try to sneak up on them -- they're far too vigilant -- but must trigger their curiosity and hold their attention until he has come into firing distance. He can do this only by assuming the most ridiculous positions and acting out the most idiosyncratic movements. Then, hopefully, the prairie dog won't know what to make of the approaching man.

Old Shatterhand was familiar with this lore of the prairie. As soon as he had been spotted by the animals perched on their mounds, he commenced a series of sideways leaps, ducked down, rose up, turned himself about and whirled his arms like a windmill with only one purpose in mind -- to get ever closer.

Hobble-Frank, riding beside Jemmy and Davy, saw this odd behavior and remarked in a concerned tone, "Oh my God, what's happened to him? Has he gone mad? He looks like he drank Bellamadonna!"

"You mean Belladonna," Jemmy corrected.

"Oh, be quiet!" commanded the little one. "Belladonna doesn't make sense. It's Bellamadonna; I, who was born in Moritzburg ought to know. At home, Bellamadonna grows wild in the forest and I've seen it there a thousand times. Listen! He's shooting."

Old Shatterhand had fired a quartet of shots that sounded almost like one. He ran a short distance and bent over repeatedly, each time to pick up a small furry animal. He had killed four prairie dogs, made his way back to the waiting

221

group, put them in his saddle bag and remounted. Hobble-Frank made a rather doubtful face and inquired, "Is that to be our roast? I'd rather cease and desist!"

"Why so?"

"I don't eat stuff like that!"

"Have you tried it before?"

"Naw! Wouldn't dream of it!"

"Then you can't judge whether a prairie dog is fit food or not. Did you ever taste young goat?"

"Kid goat?" answered Frank, smacking his tongue. "Of course I've eaten it. Listen, that's something totally different!"

"Really?" Old Shatterhand responded with a smile.

"Honestly! It's a delicacy without par."

"And thousands of people snicker about it!"

"Yes, but those thousands are stupid. I tell you, us Saxons are bright and know real culinary treats like no other European nation. A young goat into a pan, a toe of garlic and some twigs of marjoram, roasted nicely brown and crisp, is true ambrosia for the lords and ladies of Mount Olympus. I do know it, for around Easter, when there are young goats, Saxons eat nothing but kid roast on Sundays and holidays."

"Very well! Now tell me, have you ever eaten lapin?"

"Lapin? What's that?"

"Domestic hare. Actually rabbit."

"Rabbit? Delicious! That's something very expensive. While I lived in Moritzburg, we always had rabbit during the parish fair. The meat is tender as butter and virtually melts on the tongue."

"Yet many would laugh about it if I recounted it to them."

"They aren't right in their heads. Rabbits fed only the best and finest herbs must have the most delicious meat, that speaks for itself. Or don't you think so?"

"I believe you. But now I request that you don't profane my prairie dogs. You'll see that the meat tastes just like kid goat and almost like rabbit."

"Never heard that!"

"You did today and shall taste it. I'll tell you that --- hold it, are those horsemen over there?"

He pointed to the southwest where movement could be seen. It was still too far to distinguish whether it was animals, buffalo or horsemen. The four hunters slowly rode on keeping their eyes on the group. After awhile, they recognized them as riders and soon it became apparent that they wore uniforms. They were soldiers.

The troop was actually headed in a northeasterly direction but when they caught sight of the four riders, they changed course and approached at a gallop. They halted at a distance of maybe thirty paces. There were twelve of them, commanded by a very young lieutenant. The officer examined the four with a scowl and asked, "Where you coming from, boys?"

"By the devil!" mumbled Hobble-Frank. "Shall we have ourselves addressed as 'boys'? This chap should see that we belong to the better classes!"

"What's there to whisper about?" the lieutenant rebuked him. "I want to know where you come from?"

Frank, Jemmy and Davy looked at Old Shatterhand to see what he would do or say. The hunter responded in the calmest voice, "From Leadville."

"And where are you headed?"

"To the Elk Mountains."

"That's a lie!"

Old Shatterhand urged his horse on until it stood beside the officer and asked in the same calm tone, "Do you have a reason to call me a liar?"

"Yes!"

"What is that?"

"You're not coming from Leadville, but from Indian Fort."

"You're mistaken."

"I'm not mistaken. I know you."

"So? Then who are we?"

"I don't know your names, but you'll tell them to me right off."

"And if we don't?"

"Then I'll take you along under arrest."

"And if we object, sir?"

"Then you'll have to suffer the consequences. You know who and what we are. If any of you reaches for a weapon, I'll shoot him dead."

"Really?" smiled Old Shatterhand. "Have a look whether you can match this. See!"

Already he had his rifle in his right and revolver in his left hand pointing at the officer. Just as quickly Frank, Davy and Jemmy had their weapons at the ready.

"By the devil!" shouted the lieutenant while reaching towards his belt. "I --"

"Hold it!" thundered Old Shatterhand. "Hands off your belts, all of you! And hands up or we'll shoot!"

In situations like this, provided they are meant seriously -- which was not the case here -- everything depends on who is ready to shoot first. The one who has the advantage demands that his adversary raises his arms to keep them as far away as possible from weapons thrust into belts or holsters. If the adversary does not obey at once, a bullet may well be the response. The lieutenant and his men knew that all too thoroughly. Assured by their superior number, they had missed their opportunity to have their weapons at the ready and now were looking into the muzzles of eight rifles and revolvers. Convinced they were dealing with criminals, they immediately complied with Old Shatterhand's order and raised their arms high.

It was actually a funny sight to see that many well-armed cavalrymen astride their horses with their arms held skyward. Old Shatterhand smiled faintly as he addressed the lieutenant, "So, my good sir, what do you think we're going to do now?"

"Shoot us!" answered the officer. "But revenge will follow you everywhere until you are caught."

"Pshaw! What's the use wasting good bullets on people who are intimidated by four miserable chaps like us. That's sure no glory! I only wanted to teach you a lesson. You're still young and can use it. Always be polite, sir! A gentleman doesn't take it lightly being addressed as 'boy' by the first chap he comes across. And never accuse men of lying unless you have proof. You might come across the wrong people, as the present situation demonstrates. And thirdly, when you meet riders in the west that you don't plan to treat gently, have your rifles at the ready. You may otherwise be forced to assume the same schoolboy position you're presently in. You've been mistaken. We are neither 'boys' nor liars. And now put down your arms. It's not our intention to drill holes in your skins!"

He put his own revolver away and lowered his rifle, his three companions following suit. The soldiers lowered their arms. Shamed and angered, the officer exclaimed, "Sir, you dare play such comedy with us! You must know I have the power to punish you!"

"The power?" Old Shatterhand asked, laughing. "The desire, yes, but not the power as I just demonstrated. I'd love to know how you'd punish us. You'd only make a fool of yourself as you did before."

"You think so? Look, now who has the revolver in his hand first ---"

He was unable to continue. Once again he had reached for his belt but found himself unceremoniously jerked from his saddle and thrown across the front of Old Shatterhand's horse. Lightning-fast, the hunter pressed his knife against the man's chest and, laughing again, suggested, "Keep talking, sir! What were you going to say? It all depends who has the other in front of his saddle, isn't that so? If one of your people moves, you get my knife in your chest! Just try me!"

The soldiers remained stiffly on their horses. They would never have anticipated such bodily strength and speed. Perplexed and startled, they entirely forgot their weapons and their superior numbers.

"By the devil!" the lieutenant screamed, yet out of fear did not dare to move a limb. "What do you think you're doing? Let go of me!"

"My only thought is to tell you that you've tackled the wrong man. We're not afraid of how many men you have. And were it an entire platoon we would still not be concerned. Step away now and listen politely to what I'm going to tell you."

Grabbing the humiliated lieutenant by his collar, he hoisted him off the horse and put him down on the grass. Then he continued, "Have you ever seen any of us before?"

"No," the lieutenant responded, catching his breath. Although boiling with anger, he didn't dare express it. He saw himself humiliated in front of his men and would have loved to pull his saber and run Old Shatterhand through, yet he was convinced that any attempt would backfire again.

"No?" repeated the hunter. "But I'm convinced you know us. At least you've heard our names. Has someone told you about Hobble-Frank? There he is before you."

"I neither know the man nor his name," grunted the officer.

"But you must have heard about Long Davy and Fat Jemmy?"

"Yes. Are those two supposed to be them?"

"Indeed."

"Pshaw! I don't believe it!"

"Are you again calling me a liar? Leave off, sir. Old Shatterhand has the habit of proving every word he utters."

"Old Shat ---" exclaimed the lieutenant, stepping back a pace, eying the hunter in utter surprise. The last syllables had become stuck in his throat.

The soldiers too expressed their astonishment and awe, stammering a few loud "ahs".

"Yes, Old Shatterhand," the hunter repeated smoothly. "You know the name?"

"I know it; we all know it only too well. And you claim to be this - this - man, sir?"

His wide-eyed expression still showed doubt. But when his eye fell on the short-barrelled rifle with its peculiar round bolt, his face immediately changed and he asked, "Behold! Isn't that a Henry repeating rifle, sir?"

"That it is," nodded Old Shatterhand. "You know this type of firearm?"

"I've never seen one before but I've had it described to me. Its inventor is supposed to have been a unique character who produced only a few such carbines. He was afraid it would speed the demise of both Indians and buffalos if his repeating rifle found general distribution. The few pieces he made are thought to be lost and I've heard that only Old Shatterhand still owns one, the very last."

"That's correct, sir. Of the eleven or twelve Henry carbines ever made, only mine is still around; the others have disappeared in the Wild West, together with their owners."

"Then you are truly -- truly Old Shatterhand, that famous frontiersman who can push a grown buffalo's head to the ground and can down the strongest Indian with his bare fist?"

"I've already told you that it's me. If you still doubt it, I'll be happy to give you proof. I give my fist not only to Indians but also to whites if required. You wish me to demonstrate?"

From his saddle, he bent towards the officer raising his fist as if to strike him. The young man quickly stepped even farther back and called, "Thanks, no thanks, sir! I'd rather believe you without proof. It's my only head and I wouldn't know where to get a replacement. Forgive me if I wasn't polite! I've every reason to look at people cautiously. Would you be kind enough to accompany us? My men would not only be glad but consider it an honor if you would ride with us as our guests."

"Where to?"

"To Fort Mormon, that's our destination."

"Then I cannot accept your invitation. We are headed in the opposite direction to meet friends at a prearranged moment."

"I'm truly sorry. May I ask where you're headed, sir?"

"First to the Elk Mountains, as I told you already. From there over to the Book Mountains."

"Then I must warn you," suggested the officer, speaking now politely as if facing a superior.

"Why? Of what or about whom?"

"The redskins."

"Thank you! I need not fear Indians and don't understand what danger threatens us from that quarter. At present, the redskins are at peace with the whites. The Utes we are dealing with here haven't done anything for years to cause suspicion."

"That's correct. But just because of that, they're now all the more aroused. We know for certain that they've taken up their tomahawks requiring us to ride patrol between the Mormon and Indian Forts."

"Really? We know nothing about this."

"I believe you, since you come from Colorado where perhaps the news hasn't traveled yet. Your path leads you straight through the Utes' territory. I know that Old Shatterhand's name carries great weight with redskins of all nations, but don't take things too lightly, sir! The Utes have great reason to be angry with the whites."

"Why?"

"A party of white gold prospectors attacked a Ute camp in an attempt to steal horses. It happened during the night but the Utes awoke and defended themselves. Many of them died at the hands of the better-armed whites. The robbers escaped with horses and other goods but the redskins followed them the next morning. They caught up with the villains and another fight ensued, again costing many more lives on both sides. Sixty Indians supposedly died in the two battles and of the whites only six are believed to have gotten away. The Utes are now on the warpath trying to find the six who escaped. They also sent a delegation to Fort Union to demand compensation, a horse for a horse, the sum of a thousand dollars for the stolen goods, and two horses and a rifle for each of the Indians killed."

"I don't find that excessive. Have their demands been accepted?"

"No. The authorities refused every one of the redskins' demands. The delegation returned home unsuccessful and, therefore, tomahawks have been taken up. The Utes have risen in large numbers and since we don't have enough troops in the territory to put them down alone, allies have been sought. Some of our officers went to the Navajos to solicit their help against the Utes and they seem to have succeeded."

"And what was offered the Navajos for their help?"

"Plunder from the Utes."

Hearing this, Old Shatterhand's face darkened. Shaking his head, he summarized the situation, "First the Utes are attacked, robbed and many of them killed by whites. When they demand punishment of the perpetrators and compensation, they are rebuffed and now that they have taken the matter into their own hands, the Navajos are incited against them, to be paid by the booty they are to take from the insulted Utes! Is it surprising then if the Utes feel pushed to the limit? Their embitterment must be horrendous and woe to any white or Navajo who falls into their hands!"

"I must obey my orders and have no right to judge this situation," responded the lieutenant. "I gave you this information as a warning, sir. My views cannot be the same as yours."

"I do understand that. My thanks for your warning. And when you report our meeting at the fort, tell them also that Old Shatterhand is no enemy of the redskins and regrets very much that a richly-endowed family of Indian nations is being cruelly destroyed. They are not being given time to develop naturally according to the rules of human culture; instead it's expected that a hunting people transform itself overnight into a modern civilization. With the same logic, one should kill a schoolboy because he isn't quick enough to develop the knowledge and skills of a general or a professor of astronomy. Goodbye, sir!"

Wheeling his horse about, he rode off, followed by his three companions, without giving the soldiers a further look. After some perplexed glances, the troop continued its interrupted ride. His fury at such injustice had induced Old Shatterhand to useless speech, as he well knew. Now in enraged silence he rode on. Half an hour passed before he retreated from his pensiveness. His attention was now focused on the horizon where a dark line had become ever wider. Pointing ahead, he said, "There's the forest I spoke of earlier. Put the spurs to your horses and we'll be there in five minutes."

The foursome urged their horses to a gallop and soon reached the dense fir forest, which seemed impenetrable on horseback. But Old Shatterhand knew his way, directing his horse to a certain spot and pushing through bushes to enter an Indian trail only some three feet wide. He dismounted to check for any tracks and when he found none signaled his companions to follow.

Not the slightest breeze stirred in the forest and except for their hoofbeats no sound was heard. Old Shatterhand had his carbine in hand and his eyes on the path ahead, ready to be first in aiming his weapon at an enemy, although he thought it probably unnecessary. If the Utes were passing through the area on horseback, they would be doing it in large numbers and would not use a narrow trail like this. There was little visibility and the woods' density made progress difficult. There were even very few places along the trail where a rider could turn his horse. A group of Indians could fall easy victim to a few adversaries on foot.

After some time, the trail opened into a glade where rose a rock outcropping. Overgrown by mosses, a few bushes had taken hold in some gaps and cracks. Here Old Shatterhand stopped and suggested, "This is the place where we can give our horses some rest and roast our prairie dogs. There's water, too, as you can see."

A small spring gurgled among the rocks and a streamlet wound its way across the meadow to lose itself into the woods. The men dismounted, set the horses to grazing and began collecting dry wood for their fire. Jemmy took on the job of skinning and gutting the prairie dogs while Old Shatterhand scouted the vicinity to assure their safety.

The forest was only three-quarters of an hour's ride in width, with the glade roughly in its center.

Before long, the meat roasting over the fire gave off a most pleasant odor. Old Shatterhand returned. He had quickly walked the trail to the opposite edge of the forest from where one could see across the entire wide open prairie. He had located nothing suspicious and assured his comrades that no surprises lay in store.

It took an hour for the roast to be done after which Old Shatterhand sampled a piece.

"Hmmp!" grumbled Hobble-Frank. "Eat roast dog! Had I been told before that I would ever eat man's best friend, I would have answered him in no uncertain terms. But I'm hungry and must try it."

"But it isn't dog," Jemmy reminded him. "Didn't you hear that this rodent is mistakenly called by the name prairie dog because its voice is like a bark?"

"That doesn't change anything. It makes it even worse. A rodent roast! What a man must eat sometimes! Well, let's see."

He took a small piece and tasted it carefully. But then his face brightened. He put a larger piece in his mouth and remarked, "Not so bad, honest! It tastes almost like rabbit, although not as good as kid goat. Boys, I don't think much is going to be left of these four dogs."

"We must keep some for tonight," Davy suggested. "We don't know if we'll be able to shoot anything else."

"I don't worry about later. When I'm tired, I'll just fall into Orpheus' arms and be content."

"It's Morpheus," Jemmy corrected him.

"Oh, be silent! Must you put an M before my Orpheus! I know better. In my village of Klotsche near Moritzburg, there was a singing club known as Orpheus in the Upper World. These fellows sang so lovely that they soothed their audience into the most pleasant slumber. That's why the term 'To sink into Orpheus's arms' originates from Klotsche. So don't quarrel with me; rather eat your prairie dog in silent contemplation. Then the food will sit better with you than arguing with a man of my experience. You know I'm a nice fellow, but if someone wants to put a Morpheus on me while I'm eating, I get rather unhappy!"

Old Shatterhand gave Jemmy a sign to leave off so their meal could be consumed in peace. However, another disturbance not caused by Hobble-Frank was in the making, one that he was powerless to prevent.

If the four men were feeling secure, they were very much mistaken. Unbeknownst to them, two groups of horsemen were fast approaching the forest.

One of these groups was small, consisting of only two horsemen, coming from the north and crossing Old Shatterhand and his companions' tracks. They stopped and dismounted to investigate in a way that showed they were experienced frontiersmen. They were well-armed but their clothing had suffered and gave some indication that they had not had the best of times lately. Their horses were well-fed and lively but equipped with only a halter, lacking both saddle and bridle, Indian fashion.

"What do you think of those tracks, Knox?" asked the first rider. "Are there redskins ahead of us?"

"No," the other answered with clear certainty.

"Then whites! How do you know?'

"The horses are shod and the men didn't ride single file like Indians but alongside each other."

"And how many are there?"

"Only four. We have nothing to worry about, Hilton."

"Except if they're soldiers!"

"Pshaw! Not in that case either. However, we can't show ourselves near a fort; there would be too many eyes and questions that would give us away. But four cavalrymen wouldn't get anything out of us. They also wouldn't make the connection that we belong to the rovers who attacked the Utes!"

"I think so too. But it's a devil's game sometimes and one never knows in advance what may happen. We're in a miserable position. Hunted by the redskins and pursued by soldiers, we wander the Utes' territory. We were stupid to let this colonel and his rovers paint such rosy pictures for us."

"Stupid? Not us! To get rich quick will be wonderful and I'm not getting desperate yet. Before long, the colonel will be along with his gang and we won't need to be concerned any longer."

"But a lot can happen by then."

"Sure. We need to get out of this quandary --- and I think I just found a way."

"And that is?"

"We must attach ourselves to other whites. In such company, we'll be thought of as hunters and no one will connect us with the raiders who got the Utes to dig up their tomahawks."

"And you think the men ahead of us might serve the purpose?"

"Why not? They were headed for the forest. Let's follow them."

They continued on Old Shatterhand's tracks. On their ride, they talked about their experiences and intentions from which any eavesdropper could tell they were willing confederates of the colonel.

The group that escaped from the Eagle Tail had consisted of only twenty men. Subsequently it had occurred to the colonel that his gang might be whittled down by Indian attacks in the mountains so he thought to add additional gunmen. On the ride through Colorado, he had engaged everyone who showed an interest in his venture. Obviously, these were all people of doubtful morality in the first place. Among them were Knox and Hilton, now heading for the woods.

The enlarged gang of rovers had quickly grown to a size where finding food supplies had become more and more difficult. This caused the colonel to split up his men. Half of them were to cross the Rocky Mountains in the area of La Veta; the other half was to do the same, but taking the Morriso and Georgetown route.

Knox and Hilton as experienced outdoorsmen led the second group, a task they had accepted gladly. Without much trouble, they crossed the mountains and stopped near Breckenridge. There they had the misfortune to encounter a herd of horses that had escaped from a hacienda. Their own horses broke free and followed the runaways. To acquire new horses, they attacked a camp of the Utes but were hunted by the Indians and later badly beaten. Only six had escaped. The redskins pursued the remaining six, four of whom had lost their lives yesterday, leaving only the two leaders, Knox and Hilton.

Talking about their predicament, they neared the forest, found the Indian trail and followed it. They arrived at the glade at the very moment when the little dispute between Jemmy and Hobble-Frank had come to an end.

When the rovers sighted the small group of men at the fire, they halted for a moment but could tell at once that they had nothing to fear.

"Remember we are hunters!" whispered Knox to Hilton.

"Yes," Hilton responded, "but they will ask where we come from!"

"Let me do the talking."

Now Old Shatterhand caught sight of the two. Someone else would have been alarmed, but not he. Taking his carbine in hand, he looked at them expectantly as they approached.

"Good afternoon, gentlemen!" Knox greeted. "Will you permit us to rest with you for a while?"

"We welcome every honest man," answered Old Shatterhand, observing first the riders, then the horses.

"I hope you don't think us dishonest!" protested Hilton, withstanding Old Shatterhand's examination without flinching.

"I judge my fellow men only after I get to know them."

"Well, then permit us that opportunity!"

The two dismounted and sat down by the fire. They were hungry and threw longing looks at what was left of the roast. The good-natured Jemmy offered the last pieces, for which they didn't need a second invitation. While they ate, silence was maintained.

The second group approaching the forest from the opposite side consisted of nearly two hundred Indians. Although Old Shatterhand had scouted this side of the woods and had looked far out onto the prairie he had been unable to see the approaching redskins who, at that time, were still hidden behind a wall of projecting trees.

The Indians too seemed to know the area. They headed straight for the exit of the forest trail.

The redskins were on the war path, as the bright painted colors on their faces clearly demonstrated. Most were armed with rifles, only a few with bows and arrows. They were led by a giant man, obviously their chief, since he wore an eagle feather in his bun. With his face painted in black, yellow and red lines, it was impossible to determine his age. When the group arrived at the trail, he dismounted to check for tracks. The foremost warriors observed him with close attention. A horse snorted; the chief raised his hand in warning and its rider held his hand over his horse's nostrils.

Since the chief had required silence, he obviously had discovered something suspicious. Slowly, he advanced a few paces along the trail into the woods, bent low over the tracks. When he returned, he spoke quietly in Ute, a dialect of the Shoshone division of the Sonora language family. "Palefaces have passed here a short while ago. Have the warriors hide behind the trees. I, Ovuts-avaht, will go to look for the palefaces."

Ovuts-avaht, Big Wolf, was a man almost taller, more broadly built, and stronger than Old Firehand. He silently advanced into the woods along the trail. When he returned after nearly an hour, none of his people was visible any longer. A low whistle and his men stepped from the woods, leaving their horses behind. Upon a hand signal, five or six of his sub-chiefs stepped closer.

"Six palefaces are camped at the rock," he told them. "They may be some of those that escaped yesterday. They eat meat and their horses graze nearby. My brothers must follow me to the glade. There we split; one half goes to the right, the other to the left to surround the opening. When I give the signal, the warriors will attack. The white dogs will be so frightened they will quickly surrender. We shall grasp them in our hands and take them to our village to put them to the stake. Five braves stay here to watch the horses. Howgh!"

With their chief in the lead, the redskins silently took the trail into the woods, so noiselessly that not the least sound could be heard. Closing on the glade, they split to surround the unsuspecting palefaces. No rider could have penetrated the woods; however on foot the agile Indians had little difficulty.

The whites had just finished their meal. Hobble-Frank shoved his Bowie knife in his belt and addressed the two newcomers, "We have eaten and the horses have rested. Let's head out so we can get to our destination before nightfall."

"Yes," Jemmy assented. "But before that we must get to know each other a little better and find out where everyone's headed."

"That's true," confirmed Knox. "May I ask what destination you have in mind today?"

"We're headed for the Elk Mountains."

"Us too. Excellent! Then we can ride together."

Old Shatterhand did not offer a word. He gave Jemmy a covert signal to continue his examination. He wanted to talk only when the time was right.

"Fine by me," the stout Jemmy responded. "But where are you headed from there?"

"That's open yet. Maybe over to the Green River to look for beaver."

"You won't find many there. For beaver you must head farther north. Then you're both trappers?"

"Yes. My name's Knox and my companion is Hilton."

"But where are your beaver traps, Mister Knox, without which you can't catch any?"

"Ours were stolen at the San Juan River, possibly by Indians. Maybe we'll come upon a camp where we can buy some. Is it all right then to accompany you to the Elk Mountains?"

"I don't mind, if my comrades are agreed."

"Fine, mister! May we learn your names then?"

"Why not? I'm called Fat Jemmy; my neighbor to the right ---"

"Must be Long Davy?" Knox broke in.

"Yes. You guessed it."

"Indeed! You're known far and wide. And where you find Fat Jemmy, Long Davy isn't far. And who's the little gentleman to your left?"

"We call him Hobble-Frank. A fine little chap you'll get to know soon."

Frank gave the speaker a grateful look. Fat Jemmy then continued, "And the last name to mention to you must be even better known to you than mine. I suppose you've heard of Old Shatterhand?"

"Old Shatterhand?" Knox exclaimed in pleasant surprise. "Really? Is it true you're Old Shatterhand?"

"Why shouldn't it be true?" the hunter answered.

"Then permit me to express my delight in getting to know you, sir!"

He offered his hand to the hunter and threw Hilton a look as if to tell him, "Hey, be glad. Now we're safe! Being with this famous man, we've nothing to fear any more." However Old Shatterhand ignored the proffered hand and responded in a cold voice, "Are you truly glad? Then it's too bad I cannot share your pleasure."

"Why not, sir?"

"Because you are people one cannot be glad to meet."

"How do you mean?" asked Knox, perplexed by this frankness. "I suppose you're joking, sir."

"I'm totally serious. You are two cheats, maybe even worse."

"Say! Do you think we'll tolerate such an insult?"

"Yes, that's exactly what I think, since there's nothing else for you to do."

"Do you know us then?"

"No. It wouldn't be an honor anyway."

"Sir, you're getting more insulting by the minute. One doesn't castigate a man one has just shared a meal with. Prove to me that we're cheats!"

"Why not!" Old Shatterhand responded calmly.

"That'll be impossible for you. You just admitted that you don't know us. You've never seen us before. How are you going to prove your words are truthful?"

"Pah! Don't think Old Shatterhand is stupid enough to have people like you try to paint a coyote for a buffalo! From my very first look at you, I knew who and what you are. So, down at the San Juan River, you had your traps. What then?"

"That was four days ago."

"Then you come directly from there?"

"Yes."

"That's from the south and is surely a lie. You arrived shortly after us and we would certainly have seen you out on the prairie. To the north, the forest projects out somewhat and behind that tongue of woods you were concealed when I took a final look before entering the trail. You came from the north."

"But, sir, I've told you the truth. You simply didn't see us."

"I? Not see you? If I had such bad eyes, I would have been lost many times. No, you don't fool me! Now go on: where are your saddles?"

"They were also stolen."

233

"And the bridles?"

"Those too."

"Fellows, don't think me such a stupid child!" Old Shatterhand snorted disdainfully. "You must have set out your saddles and bridles --- together with your traps --- into the river so that everything got stolen at once. What hunter takes off his horse's bridle? And where are the Indian halters from?"

"We traded them from a redskin."

"The horses too?"

"No," answered Knox, who realized that one more lie would be too much and too impudent.

"Then the Utes trade in halters! I didn't know that. Where did you get your horses?"

"We bought them at Fort Dodge."

"As far away as that! I don't think so. I would bet these animals have been grazing for weeks until recently. A horse that has carried his rider from Fort Dodge to here looks very different. And how come yours have no shoes?"

"There you must ask the fellow we traded them from."

"Nonsense! From a trader? These horses have not been bought!"

"What else?"

"They were stolen!"

"Sir!" shouted Knox, reaching for his knife. Hilton too reached for his.

"Keep your knives where they are or I'll fell you like timber!" Old Shatterhand threatened. "Don't you think I know that these horses have had Indian training!"

"How can you know? You haven't seen us ride! Only that short distance from the trail to the rocks could you see us on horseback. That's not enough for a judgment."

"But I did notice that they avoid our animals, that they keep together. These horses have been stolen from the Utes and you belong to the people who attacked the poor redskins."

Knox was stymied; he no longer knew what to say. He was no match for the shrewdness of this man. As is common for people of his kind in such situations, he resorted to rudeness.

"Sir, I've heard much about you and thought you were a different kind of person. You talk as if in a dream. Whoever makes assertions like you do must be crazy. Our horses have Indian training? I could kill myself laughing if it weren't so absurd. I see that we're no congenial match and am leaving so I no longer have to listen to your fantasizing."

He rose together with Hilton. But Old Shatterhand rose too, put his hand on the man's arm, telling him, "You stay!"

"Us stay, sir? Are you giving us an order?"

"Indeed."

"You have no right to demand this."

"Yes. I'm going to deliver you to the Utes for punishment."

"Oh, really? That would be even crazier than the Indian horse training!"

He spoke this in a disdainful tone, yet his lips quivered. It was apparent that he was far from possessing the confidence he tried to project.

"But it'll be the same as the Indian training," the hunter responded. "The fact that your horses belong to the Utes is shown by the --- by the devil, what's that?"

As he spoke of the Utes' horses, he had looked in their direction and something had caught his eye. Their nostrils flaring, the horses turned in all directions, then trotted, neighing happily, towards the glade's edge.

"Yes. Watch out!" cried Jemmy. "There are redskins close by!"

In the blink of an eye, Old Shatterhand grasped the danger. He whispered, "We're surrounded by Utes whose presence has just been given away by the horses. They may attack at any moment."

"What are we to do?" asked Davy."

"First, let's demonstrate to them that we have nothing to do with these thieves and murderers. That's the most important thing. Down with them!"

His fist hit Knox's temple, dropping him like a log, and before Hilton could defend himself, he received the same treatment.

"Quick, up into the rocks," ordered Old Shatterhand. "There we have some cover. Then we must wait to see what happens." The rocks were not easy to climb, but in situations like this, men's abilities multiply. In a few seconds, the four hunters had clambered up and disappeared behind rocks and bushes. From the moment when the horses began to neigh, barely a minute had passed.

The chief, Big Wolf, ready to issue his order to attack, had hesitated when he saw one of the palefaces knock down two others. This had confused him temporarily, giving the four enough time to take cover in the rocks.

Big Wolf was now faced with the dilemma of what to do. He had missed his chance to surprise the whites. Hidden up there on top, they were poor targets for his bullets and arrows. But from that perch, the palefaces were able to cover the entire glade. Two hundred redskins against four whites! Victory would surely belong to the Indians. But how were they to accomplish it? By storming the rocks? Many lives would be lost in the attempt.

When he must, the redskin is brave, bold, even audacious, but when he can accomplish his goal by cunning without exposing himself, he won't put his life needlessly in danger.

A whistle of the chief called his lieutenants together. The result of their deliberations was soon evident. From the glade's edge, his loud voice rang out. With the glade only some fifty paces in diameter, the chief's words could readily be understood. Standing behind a tree, he shouted, "You palefaces are surrounded by many braves. Come down!"

This was so naive that no response was given. The redskin repeated his demand twice more and when he received no response either time he added, "If the white men do not obey, they will all be killed."

To this Old Shatterhand responded, "What have we done to the red warriors that they have surrounded us and want to attack us?"

"You are dogs who killed our men and stole our horses."

"You are mistaken. Only two of the bandits are here. They arrived shortly before you did, and when I suspected them to be enemies of the Utes, I knocked them unconscious. They are not dead and will awaken soon. If you want them, come get them."

"You want to lure us to them so that you can kill us!"

"Not so."

"I don't believe you."

"Who are you? What is your name?"

"I am Ovuts-avaht, chief of the Utes."

"I know of you. Big Wolf is strong in body and mind. He is the war chief of the Yampa Utes who are brave and just and do not avenge the sins of the guilty on the innocent."

"You talk like a squaw. You beg for your life. You call yourself innocent because you fear death. I despise you. What is your name? It must be the name of an old blind dog."

"Is Big Wolf not blind himself? Has he not seen our horses? Do they belong to the Utes? There's a mule among them. Has it been stolen from you? How can Big Wolf think we are horse thieves? Look at my black mustang! Has a Ute ever owned such a horse? It is of blood that only Winnetou, the chief of the Apaches, and his friends breed. Does Big Wolf not realize from this that I'm a friend of this famous man? Can he then accuse me of fear and cowardice? Hear my name, warriors of the Utes. It is not the name of a dog. The palefaces call me Old Shatterhand. In the Ute language, I'm called Pokai-mu, the Killing Hand."

The ensuing silence was a sure sign that the hunter's name had made an impression. The chief did not respond immediately. Finally he replied, "The paleface pretends to be Old Shatterhand, but we think he speaks with forked tongue. You know that this great white hunter is highly respected by all red men and you take on his name to deceive us, hoping to escape death. From your conduct, we know that this name is not yours."

"How so?" asked the hunter.

"Old Shatterhand does not know fear, but such courage has failed to show itself."

"If that were the case, then the warriors of the Utes show more fear than I. You count many warriors, but you and they stay hidden from only four men. Who has greater fear, you or I? Let me demonstrate that I'm not fearful. You shall see me."

Old Shatterhand rose from cover and climbed to the highest point of the rock outcropping. Looking around, he stood there as unconcerned as if a bullet was powerless to harm him.

"Ing Pokai-mu, ing Pokai-mu, howgh!" sounded several voices. "It is the Killing Hand; it is the Killing Hand, indeed!"

The voices came from men who knew him or had seen him in the past. Old Shatterhand fearlessly remained standing and shouted to the chief, "Have you heard your warriors' confirmation? Do you now believe that I'm Old Shatterhand?"

"I believe it. Your courage is great. Our bullets travel much farther than where you stand. One of our rifles could easily kill you!"

"That will not happen, because men of the Utes are brave warriors, not murderers. And if you killed me, my death would be severely avenged."

"We are not afraid of revenge!"

"It would catch and eat you, not asking whether you are afraid or not. I have acceded to Big Wolf's wish and shown myself. Why is he still hiding? Is he still afraid or does he think me an assassin?"

"The chief of the Utes is not concerned. He knows that Old Shatterhand will reach for his weapon only when attacked. I shall show myself."

Stepping from behind the tree, Big Wolf's mighty figure became fully visible.

"Is Old Shatterhand satisfied now?" he asked.

"Not yet."

"What else do you want?"

"I want to talk with you face to face to better learn your wishes. Come closer to half our distance. I shall climb off this rock and meet you there. Then we can sit and talk as is proper for warriors and chiefs."

"Will you not rather come to us?"

"No. Both of us will honor the other by approaching half the distance."

"Then I would sit in the open glade exposed to your men's bullets."

"I give you my word that this will not happen. They will shoot only if your warriors fire at me. But then your life would be forfeit."

"If Old Shatterhand gives his word, it can be trusted. It is as sacred to him as the greatest oath. I shall come. How will the great white hunter be armed?"

"I shall leave all my weapons up here; you may do as you wish."

"Big Wolf will not disgrace himself by showing less courage and trust. Come down then!"

Where he stood, the chief dropped his weapons into the grass, then waited for Old Shatterhand.

"You dare too much," warned Jemmy. "Are you sure you should do this?"

"Yes. Had the chief stepped back into the woods to talk to his men or given a covert signal, I would've distrusted him. Since he did nothing like this, I must dare all."

"And what are we to do?"

"Nothing. Without letting anyone notice, line him up in your rifle sights and kill him at once if I'm attacked."

He climbed down and chief and hunter approached each other slowly. When they stood in front of each other, Old Shatterhand offered his hand to the chief and said, "I have never seen Big Wolf, but heard much about him, that he is the wisest in counsel and the bravest in battle. I am glad to see his face and to greet him as a friend."

The Indian ignored the white's hand, instead closely examined the other's form and face. Then he answered while pointing to the ground. "The warriors of the Utes were forced to take up tomahawks against the palefaces. There's not a single white I can greet as a friend. Let us sit and parley."

He sat down, Old Shatterhand following suit. The hunters' campfire had gone out. Beside the ashes lay Knox and Hilton, who were either completely stunned or dead, since they hadn't moved.

Old Shatterhand's mustang had smelled the Indians long before the chief's voice had sounded and, snorting, had moved close in to the rock outcropping. Davy's mule, with a similar fine nose, had followed his example. Frank and Jemmy's horses had taken the cue from these two and had joined them. The four animals now stood hard by the rocks, their posture and behavior demonstrating how aware they were of the danger their masters were facing.

Neither one of the two men facing each other seemed ready to converse. With a patient look Old Shatterhand waited and gave the appearance as if nothing could happen to him. The redskin, though, could not avert his probing looks from the white's face. The thickly-applied war paint obscured any expression, but the lowered corners of his mouth indicated that he had had a different image of the vaunted hunter, not confirmed by the man now sitting across from him. This was expressed when he finally made the ironic remark, "Old Shatterhand's fame is great, but his stature did not grow with it."

While Old Shatterhand's build exceeded normal height, he was no giant. In the redskin's imagination, he must have assumed him a true Goliath. The hunter answered with a smile, "What's the connection between build and fame? Am I to respond to the chief of the Utes, "Big Wolf's build is enormous, but his fame, his courage hasn't grown with him?"

"That would be an insult," declared the redskin, his eyes flashing, "after which I would leave at once to order the attack!"

"Well, why then do you permit yourself such a remark about my stature? Although your words cannot offend someone like Old Shatterhand, they contain a slight that I cannot permit. I'm a chief at least as great as you. I shall speak politely to you and expect the same from you. I must tell you this before we begin our conversation, or it will not come to any good conclusion."

It was his responsibility to his comrades to reprimand the redskin. The more forcefully he presented himself, the more he impressed his adversary. From whatever impression he now made would the shape of their situation be determined.

"There is only one conclusion, no other," declared Big Wolf.

"Which?"

"Your death."

"That would be murder, for we did nothing to you."

"You are in the company of the murderers we are pursuing!"

"Do you think I was in their company when they attacked you?"

"No. Old Shatterhand is no horse thief; he would have prevented them from attacking."

"Well. Why do you treat me as an enemy then?"

"You rode with them."

"No, that's not true. Send one of your men back to study our tracks. He'll see that these two men arrived later and stumbled upon our tracks."

"That does not change anything. The palefaces attacked us when we were in deepest peace, stole our horses and killed many of our braves. Our rage was great, our consideration not less so. We sent wise men to the soldiers to demand punishment of the guilty and replacement of our losses, but we were laughed at and sent away. That is why we have taken up the tomahawk and sworn that every white falling into our hands will be killed until we have completed our vengeance. We must keep this oath, and you are a white."

"Who is innocent!"

"Were my warriors guilty of anything when they were killed? Do you demand us to be more merciful than our adversaries and murderers?"

"I deplore what's happened. Big Wolf must know that I'm a friend of the red man."

"I do know this, but you must die nevertheless. When the unjust palefaces who did not listen to our grievances learn that their behavior caused the death of many just men, even Old Shatterhand's, they will take this as a lesson to act more judiciously and sensibly in the future."

That sounded highly dangerous. The Indian talked in all seriousness and the conclusion he drew was not entirely illogical. Nevertheless, Old Shatterhand answered, "Big Wolf thinks only of his oath, but not of its consequences. If you kill us, a cry of indignation will echo across the mountains and prairies, and thousands of palefaces will gather against you to avenge our deaths. Their vengefulness will be even greater since we were always friends of the red man."

"All of you? Not just you? You speak of companions? Who are they? Palefaces?"

"One of them is Hobble-Frank, you may not know. The other two names you've heard often enough. It is Fat Jemmy and Long Davy."

"I know them. One is never seen without the other, and I've never heard their being enemies of the red man. But it is precisely their deaths that will teach the chiefs of the whites how unwise it was to send our delegates away. Your fate is sealed, but it will be an honorable one. You are brave and famous men and shall suffer the most painful deaths we can devise. You shall suffer it without crying out in anguish and its message will ring out across the land. Your fame will be even greater than before; so too will be your esteem in the Eternal Hunting Grounds. I hope you appreciate our respect for you and will be grateful!"

Old Shatterhand was not overly delighted by the offered respect. He did not let on, however, and answered, "Your intent is good and I praise you, but those who will avenge us won't be grateful."

"I laugh about them; let them come!"

"Do you think you'll win, with their being so many?"

"Ovuts-avaht does not have the habit of counting his enemies. And do you not know how many we will be? The warriors of the Weaver, Uinta, Yampa, Sampitsche, Pah-vant, Wiminutsche, Capote, Pas, Tasche, Muatsche and Tabequatsche will gather. These are all members of the Ute nation and they will crush the white warriors."

"Then go east and count the whites! And what leaders they have! Avengers will rise so powerful even a single one will make up for many, many Utes."

"Who would that be?"

"I name only one. Old Firehand."

"Yes, he is a hero. Among palefaces, he is like a grizzly to prairie dogs," the chief admitted. "But is he the only one? Can you not name a second?"

"Oh, many more I could name, but I'll mention only one, Winnetou, whom you know."

"Who does not know him? But were he here, he would also have to die. He is our enemy."

"No, he's not. He willingly risks his life for any of his red brothers."

"Do not mention it! He is chief of the Apaches. The whites are too weak against us, which is why they have incited the Navajos against us."

"You know about that?"

"The eyes of Big Wolf are sharp and no words on the wind escape his ears. Are the Navajos not part of the Apaches? Must we not consider Winnetou our enemy? Woe to him if he falls into our hands!"

"Woe also to you! I warn you. Not only would the white soldiers be against you but also the thousands of warriors of the Mescalero, the Llanero, the Xicarilla, Taracone, Navajo, Tschiriguami, Pilanenjo, Lipan, Copper, Gila and Mimbrenjo, all belonging to the Apache tribe. They'd all rise against you while the whites would have nothing to do but watch the Utes and Apaches slaughter each other. Do you really want to give your white enemies this pleasure?"

The chief pensively looked down and after a while responded, "You have spoken truth. But the palefaces press against us from all sides. They choke us. The red man is sentenced to die a slow and painful death by suffocation. Is it then not better to do battle, to die more nobly? The view you offer me of the future does not prevent me, but rather strengthens my resolve to use the tomahawk without mercy or consideration. Make no further effort; all will remain as I said."

"That you want to see us die at the stake?"

"Yes. Will you accept your fate as I have described it?"

"Yes," answered Old Shatterhand in such a quiet tone that the redskin called quickly, "Then tell your friends to lay down their weapons!"

"That I will not do!"

"But you said you would surrender!" Big Wolf exclaimed, astonished.

"That's so. We'll surrender to our fate as described by your own words. What was it you said? That you'll kill every paleface who falls into your hands. Is that not so?"

"Yes. These were my words," the redskin nodded, anxious to hear Old Shatterhand's reasoning.

"Well, then kill us once we've fallen into your hands --- which hasn't yet happened."

"Uff! Do you think you can escape?"

"Indeed."

"That is impossible. Do you know how many warriors I have? I have two hundred!"

"Only two hundred! Haven't you been told yet that greater numbers have tried to catch me in vain?"

"But two hundred against you four! There is no way out for you!"

"We'll make a way!"

"You will be killed trying!"

"Possibly! But how many of your warriors will die? For each of my companions, I reckon twenty of your braves will die. I alone will surely kill more than fifty before you get your hands on us!"

Old Shatterhand spoke with such conviction that the redskin looked at him in utter surprise. Big Wolf produced a nervous laugh and rocking his hand disdainfully up and down responded, "Your thoughts are becoming confused. You are a brave hunter, but how can you kill fifty warriors?"

"Easily! Haven't you heard what kind of weapon I have?"

"You are supposed to have a rifle which shoots forever without reloading. That is impossible; I do not believe it."

"You want me to show you?"

241

"Yes, show me!" the chief exclaimed, excited by the idea of seeing this mysterious rifle to which so many legends were attached.

"Then I'll have it handed down to me and will give it to you."

He rose and walked towards the rock outcropping to collect the carbine. As things stood, he had to make every effort to intimidate and dismay the Indians, a task for which this rifle was ideally suited. He knew how many legends coursed among the redskins. They thought it a magic rifle the Great Manitou had given the hunter to make him invincible. Jemmy handed it down from above. Old Shatterhand returned to the chief, held the weapon out to him, and told him, "Here's the rifle. Take it and look it over!"

The redskin had already reached out to take the rifle but retracted his hand, asking, "Is anyone but you permitted to touch it? If it is truly a magic rifle, it must bring danger to anyone else who touches it."

Old Shatterhand had to exploit this superstition. If he and his companions were to surrender to the redskins, they'd have to hand over all their weapons. In that case, it would be important to keep this particular rifle. Although Old Shatterhand preferred not to tell a direct lie, he answered, "I'm not allowed to tell the secrets of this weapon. Take it and try it yourself!"

The hunter held the carbine in his right hand, and while speaking to Big Wolf, slid his thumb surreptitiously onto the hair-trigger mechanism, setting it so that a shot would be released at the slightest touch. His sharp eyes had noticed a group of redskins who had left their cover out of curiosity and now stood at the edge of the glade. This group made such an easy target that an even roughly fired bullet would likely hit one of them.

All now depended on whether the chief would take the rifle. Although he was less superstitious than the other redskins, he didn't quite trust it either. The question "Should I or should I not?" could be seen flickering across his face even as he coveted handling the rifle. Old Shatterhand now took it in both hands and held it closer to him, but in such a way that the barrel aimed at the group of Indians. The chief's curiosity was greater than his apprehension; he accepted the rifle. Suddenly the gun went off. Where the group of Indians stood a shout of dismay arose and, startled, Big Wolf dropped the rifle. One of the redskins cried out that he had been shot.

"Was I the one who wounded him?" the chief asked, dumbfounded.

"Who else?" responded Old Shatterhand. "That was only a first warning. When next you touch the rifle, it'll be more serious. You have my permission to take the rifle once more, but let me warn you, the bullet would ---"

"No, no!" the redskin protested in great agitation, both hands warding off the offer. "It is a truly magic rifle and only for you. If another takes it, it will fire, hitting one's own friends, maybe even myself. I don't want it; take it away!"

"That's very wise of you," Old Shatterhand suggested sententiously. "Be glad that it fired only once. You've learned a small lesson; next time it could be different. Now I'll show you how often it fires. Look at the small maple tree over there by the brook. Its trunk is only two fingers wide. I'll fire so that ten holes will be precisely spaced the width of your thumb."

He lifted the repeating rifle, aimed at the maple and fired once -- three times -- seven times -- ten times. Then he said, " Go and look! I could shoot many times more, but I think it suffices to demonstrate to you that I could target fifty of your warriors' hearts in a minute if I'm provoked to."

Awestruck, the chief approached the little maple. Old Shatterhand saw that he measured the distance of the holes with his thumb. Several redskins came out of hiding, driven by curiosity to join their chief. The hunter, unnoticed, used this opportunity to quickly reload.

"Uff, uff, uff!" he heard them grunt in amazement. If it was a miracle for the Indians to see so many shots fired without reloading, they were twice as surprised to see the accuracy of the weapon. Not a single bullet had missed. Each had penetrated the thin trunk exactly a thumb's width above the other.

The chief returned, sat down, indicating with a sign of his hand that the hunter should do the same. Staring down for some time he finally said, "I see that you are favored by the Great Spirit. I have heard about your rifle, but did not believe it. Now I know that truth has been told."

"Then be careful and consider well what you do!" advised Old Shatterhand. "You want to attack and kill us? Try it; I don't mind. When afterwards you count the warriors killed by my bullets, great lament for the fallen will rise in your village from the squaws and children. Do not blame me for it!"

"You think we will permit you to shoot us? You must surrender without a shot being fired. You are surrounded and have nothing to eat. We will besiege you until hunger forces you to lay down your weapons."

"Then you'll wait a long time. We have water and meat aplenty. Our animals there, four horses, we could live off for many weeks. But it won't come to that, because we'll force our way out. I'll walk ahead, the magic rifle in my hand, and will send bullet after bullet towards you; and you have seen how well I hit."

"We shall stand behind the trees!"

"Do you think that will protect you from my magic rifle? Beware! You'll be the first I will sight on. I'm a friend of the red man and would be very sorry to have to kill so many of you. You've already suffered heavy losses and once the battle with the white soldiers and the Navajos begins, many more of your men will die. Therefore, you should not force us, your friends, to send death among you."

These serious words had a powerful effect. The chief once more stared ahead pensively, unmoving as a statue. Then, in an almost regretful tone, he mumbled reluctantly, "Had we not sworn to kill all palefaces, I might let you go; but an oath must be kept."

"No. One can retract an oath."

"But only after a grand council permits it."

"Then gather for council!"

"How can you say this! I am the only chief here; who I am to counsel with?"

Now Old Shatterhand had the chief exactly where he wanted him. If he was already talking of counsel, the greatest danger had passed. The hunter knew this redskin's mentality. He had achieved his intention and knew enough not to pursue it immediately. He fell silent and waited for what Big Wolf might have to say now.

The chief's eyes swept the glade, obviously contemplating whether it might be possible to overpower the four whites despite the dangerous repeating rifle. Only after the silence had lasted too long did Old Shatterhand give an indication that he would rise, saying, "The chief of the Utes has heard everything I have to say. There's nothing more to consider. I'm going to return now to my companions. Big Wolf may do as he pleases."

"Wait!" the redskin responded quickly. "Will you think us cowards if we forbear to battle with you?"

"No. A chief must not only be brave and courageous, he must also be smart and cautious. No leader will sacrifice his people for nothing. I, myself, have always attacked an enemy only when I was sure of victory. Everybody knows Big Wolf is a brave warrior. But if you allowed more than half of your warriors to be killed by only four whites, talk at the campfires would consider that you had acted senselessly and are not fit any more to lead the warriors of the Utes in battle. Consider that the whites and the Navajos are already on their way against you and that you will need all your warriors against these enemies. It would be folly to have them killed here."

"The paleface is right," the redskin answered with a deep sigh, deploring circumstances that forced him to give in to only four men. "Yet I, myself, cannot retract my oath. It can only be released by the council of elders. This is why you must accompany us as our prisoners to learn the result of our powwow."

"But if we refuse to do so?"

"Then we will be forced to fight you and overcome you with bullets."

"Not a single one will hit. The rocks afford plenty of protection. We, however, from up there can fire very well on all sides; every one of our bullets will reach its target."

"Then we will wait until dark when you cannot see. We will crawl up the rock outcropping carrying wood to light dense and smoky fires. In the morning, we shall see whether you are still alive or have suffocated."

He announced this with a very confident air, but unfazed, Old Shatterhand responded with a smile, "That's not as easy as you might think. As soon as darkness falls, we'll climb off the rocks. One of us will lie on each side and woe to the red warrior who dares to approach! He will be shot. You can see that we have the advantage. But precisely because I'm a friend of the red man and don't wish to kill a single one, I'm prepared to waive all those advantages. I'm also your friend and don't want you to remain in the bad position you find yourself in. I'll talk with my comrades. They may be willing to come with you. It now depends on your conditions. One can only be a captive if one has been seized. If you wish to capture us -- and I invite you to try -- I don't mind. But it would be just the battle you want to avoid."

"Uff!" the chief exclaimed ruefully. "Your words hit as accurately as your bullets. Old Shatterhand is not only a master in battle but also of words."

"I not only speak to my advantage, but also to yours. Why should we be enemies? You have taken up the tomahawk against the white soldiers and the Navajos. Would it not be to your advantage if Old Shatterhand were your ally instead of your enemy?"

The chief was wise enough to see that the hunter was correct. But his oath bound him. This restriction forced him to proclaim, "I must treat you all as enemies until the council has spoken. If you do not agree, our rifles must speak."

"I agree. I'll talk with my companions and see if they are prepared to come with you --- but not as prisoners."

"As what then?"

"As escorts."

"Then you will not surrender your weapons and allow yourselves to be tied up?"

"No. On no account!"

"Uff! I will give you my final word. If you do not agree, we shall besiege you in spite of your magic rifle. You will come with us now to our camp. You will keep your weapons and your horses and you will not be bound. We shall act as if we were at peace. For this, you swear to submit to the decision of the council. I have spoken. Howgh!"

His last word was confirmation that he would no longer yield, but Old Shatterhand was completely satisfied by the result of the conversation. If the redskins were truly prepared to do battle, it would be impossible to escape with their skins intact. It was very fortunate that the Utes had such respect for the repeating rifle. Old Shatterhand had achieved everything he could. He expected this respect would also transfer to the council of elders. He proposed, "I want to prove to Big Wolf that I'm his friend. I won't even talk with my companions, but give you my word and, speaking for them, theirs. We'll submit to the council's resolution without fighting back."

"Then take your calumet and swear by it that you will act so."

Old Shatterhand removed the peace pipe from its string, tamped a bit of tobacco into its head and lit it by means of a punk. He blew the smoke to the sky, to the earth and the four directions and confirmed, "I promise that we will not fight you!"

"Howgh!" the chief nodded. "It is good; all is now finished here."

"No. You too must seal your promise," Old Shatterhand demanded, offering him the pipe.

The redskin might have hoped to escape any commitment on his side. In that case, he would not have felt bound by his promise and could have acted at will, once the whites had come down from the rock outcropping. But outflanked once again, he submitted without argument, took the pipe and, following Old Shatterhand's example, blew its smoke in all directions, then said, "The four palefaces will be safe with us until the council of elders has decided their fate. Howgh!"

He returned the calumet to Old Shatterhand and walked over to where Knox and Hilton still lay.

"My promise does not extend to these two," he said. "They are murderers, because we recognize their horses as being ours. Their punishment will be severe. It would have been well if your hand had taken their lives. Even now they seem to be dead."

"No," Old Shatterhand answered, whose sharp eyes had noticed that during the conversation each of them had once raised his head to look around. "They're not dead. They're not even unconscious. They're only playing possum and may think we'll leave them here."

"Then the dogs must rise or I shall crush them with my foot!" the chief shouted, simultaneously giving each of them such a mighty kick that the rovers gave up feigning unconsciousness. They stood up hastily. Their fear was so great that it prevented them from even thinking of defending themselves or trying to escape.

"You fled from my warriors this morning," the chief told them furiously. "But now Great Manitou has delivered you into my hands and you shall shriek at the stake for your murderous deeds, that all palefaces may hear."

The two understood every word the redskin spoke, and quaked visibly.

"Murders?" asked Knox, intending to rescue himself by denying everything. "We don't know anything about that. Who are we supposed to have murdered?"

"Be silent, dog! We know you, as do these four palefaces, who have fallen into our hands because of you!"

Knox was a cunning fellow. He saw Old Shatterhand standing unhurt beside the redskin. The Indians had not dared lay hands on the famous man. Whoever was under his protection must be just as safe as he himself. An idea arose in the rogue that might be his only salvation. Old Shatterhand was white, therefore, he surely would take the side of other whites against the redskins. At least that's what Knox assumed and therefore answered, "Indeed, they know what we've done, since we've been riding with them for weeks."

"Do not lie!"

"I'm telling the truth. Ask Old Shatterhand. He'll explain to you that we cannot be the men you think we are."

"Don't expect me to support your falsehood," objected Old Shatterhand, "so that you can escape your well-earned punishment. I won't lower myself to your level. You know what I think of you and my view has not changed."

He turned his back on both men.

"But, sir," Knox called after him, "Are you abandoning us? We're talking about our lives!"

"Indeed! But how about the lives of those you murdered? You've earned your death and I've no reason to object to it. May justice be done."

"By the devil! If that's what you're thinking, I know what I must do. If you don't save us, you'll perish with us!" He turned from Old Shatterhand to the chief, telling him, "Why don't you also apprehend these four? They also took part in the horse theft and fired on your braves. It's their bullets that killed most of the Utes!"

This was impudence without par. Old Shatterhand made a move as if to assault the impertinent fellow, but thought better of it and remained at his place. But punishment followed at once and brutally. The chief's eyes widened, flashing like lightning, as he thundered at Knox, "Coward! You do not have the courage to accept the guilt for your deeds but try to include others, compared to whom you are a stinking toad. For that, your punishment will not begin at the stake but right here. I shall take your scalp, and you shall live to see it hang from my belt. Nani witsch, nani witsch!"

He shouted these two Ute words, meaning "my knife, my knife," to the Indians standing at the glade's edge.

"My God, no!" the threatened man screamed. "To be scalped alive. Please, no!"

He made a leap to escape but the chief was too quick for him. He went after him, grasped him by the neck, and with mighty pressure of his hand soon left Knox hanging limp. An Indian hurried over to bring Big Wolf his knife. He took it, tossed the barely conscious Knox to the ground, knelt on him, made three quick cuts, a pull that brought a terrible scream from the prone man, and the redskin rose holding the bloody scalp in his left hand. Knox did not move. He had fallen unconscious, his head a horrible sight.

"This will happen to every dog who falls on the red man and then intends to destroy other innocents!" proclaimed Big Wolf, attaching the scalp to his belt.

Hilton had watched with horror what happened to his companion. Fright froze all movement; he slowly sank beside the scalped Knox and sat there without uttering a word.

The chief gave a sign for his warriors to approach. Quickly the glade swarmed with them and in a trice Hilton and Knox were tied fast.

When Big Wolf had mentioned scalping, Old Shatterhand had turned and climbed the rocks so as not to be witness to the horrible scene and to tell his comrades of the powwow's conclusion.

"This doesn't look good," answered Jemmy. "Couldn't you have gotten us free entirely?"

"No. That was impossible."

"It might have been better to fight!"

"Not hardly. It would surely have cost us our lives."

"Ho! We would've fought back. And with the fear and respect the redskins have for your carbine we wouldn't have despaired. They wouldn't dare to come close."

"Most likely. But they would've starved us out. Although I talked about eating our horses, I would rather die from hunger than kill my mustang."

"You'd have had no need to do that. Upon opening of hostilities, the first thing the redskins would do is shoot the horses."

"But precisely that would rob us of any chance of escape."

"Yes, on horseback! But we could escape on foot. Two hundred men surrounding the glade! The redskins wouldn't stand side by side. Under cover of darkness, we could sneak away, all four of us, towards a single point --- some gap in their lines that we could slip through. We'd have to deal with only one or two redskins --- two knife stabs and we could break through."

"But what then? You see the situation very differently from what would really happen. The redskins already plan to light fires all around the glade and they'd notice at once our attempt to escape. Even if we broke through their lines, we wouldn't get far without their being on our tracks. We'd have to kill many of them without the least prospect of our being spared."

"That's quite true," agreed Hobble-Frank. "I don't understand how Fat Jemmy Pfefferkorn can try to sound smarter than Old Shatterhand. You're always the goose's egg trying to be smarter than the goose. Old Shatterhand has done his best and I give him the highest grade point, a one with a star attached. And I'm sure Davy's of the same opinion."

"That's sure," was Davy's response. "A fight would mean the end of us."

"But what'll happen if we follow them?" asked Jemmy. "Don't we have to assume that the council of elders will treat us as enemies?"

"I wouldn't advise them to do that," growled Frank. "I've a word or two to add to that story yet. No one is getting me to the stake that easily. I'll fight tooth and nail."

"You're not allowed. It was sworn to. We must let everything happen to us."

"Who says so? Don't you see, you poor soap boiler, that this oath has its buts, ifs and whens? It doesn't take a reflecting telescope to see that our famous Shatterhand has left a most sweet back door ajar. Nothing's been written that says we must accept everything. It promises only, as you've heard, that we won't fight back. Well, that we won't. Let them decide what they want; we won't smash everything up with steam engines. But cunning, a ruse, that's the veritable thing; that's not fighting. If the elders condemn us to die, we'll just disappear through some curtains and rise beyond the theater with twice our grandiflora."

"You mean grandezza," corrected Jemmy.

And once again the two friends were back to sparring about the proper meaning of words. And while Frank and Jemmy's arguments were by no means in jest, the four hunters' situation was serious enough. Old Shatterhand put an end to their squabbling by saying, "Frank understood me well. I renounced fighting back, but not cunning. However, I'd prefer not to resort to such a sophist interpretation of my promise. I hope we'll find other more honest means for our rescue. But let's look at the present first."

"Then the first thing is," Davy interjected, "can we trust the redskins? Will Big Wolf keep his promise?"

"That's one thing sure. Never has a chief broken his oath once he smoked the calumet. Until the council, we can trust the Utes in our sleep. Let's mount up; the redskins are getting ready to depart."

Knox and Hilton had been tied to their horses. The former, still faint, lay forward on his animal, his arms secured around its neck. The Utes followed one behind the other down the narrow trail. The chief waited until last. He held back so he could escort the whites. That was a good sign, since it demonstrated a lack of enmity. The hunters had expected to be herded into the middle and heavily guarded. They could now assume that Big Wolf held no mistrust for them but believed fully in Old Shatterhand's promise.

When they arrived where the trail exited the woods, the redskins had already retrieved their horses and remounted. The troop headed out. Together with the chief, the four whites remained last; the point was taken by Indians with Knox and Hilton in between. Old Shatterhand was pleased by this arrangement. The redskins riding single file made a line so long that the agonized wails of the revived Knox could not be heard at such a distance.

On the open prairie, the Elk Mountains could be seen rising in the distance. Old Shatterhand didn't inquire of the chief but assumed that today's destination must be the mountains. Not a word was spoken. Even among themselves the whites observed silence, since talk would have been useless anyway. They had to wait for their arrival at the Ute camp. Only then could a plan for their escape be devised, should it become necessary.

"Intsch ovomb." …'To yonder spruce'

12. Dead or Alive

The redskins appeared to be in a hurry. They kept their horses at a trot and did not show the least consideration for their captives, even the one with a life-threatening injury. Occasionally, a man who has been scalped escapes to tell his fate, but these are rare exceptions since it takes a robust constitution to survive such an injury.

The war party came closer to the mountains and towards evening reached the foothills. The riders headed for a long narrow valley with forested slopes. Subsequently, several side valleys were crossed, the direction leading always up-slope. Despite the darkness that had descended, the Indians found their way as if it were broad daylight.

A bright moon rose, illuminating the densely wooded rock faces between which the riders rode silently and steadily. Towards midnight, their destination seemed to be closer. The chief issued orders to several men to ride on ahead and announce their impending arrival. Without a word, the braves cantered off on their task.

The party reached a wide stream. Following it, they watched its high banks part farther and farther apart until they were no longer visible despite the moon's bright light. The forest, at first close to the river, retreated too, opening to a valley meadow. In the distance, fires were burning.

"Ugh!" the chief exclaimed, his first word directed at his captives since the beginning of the ride. "There are my tribe's teepees where your fate will be decided."

"Still tonight?" inquired Old Shatterhand.

"No. My warriors need rest and your death struggles will last longer and bring us greater joy if you have fortified yourself with sleep."

"Not bad!" exclaimed Fat Jemmy in German so that the redskin would not understand. "Our death struggles! He acts as if there was no getting away from the stake. What do you say, old Frank?"

"Not a word at this time," answered the little Saxon. "I'll only talk later when the time for it has come. Nobody dies before his death and it's not my intention to make an exception from this well-known rule. Just let me say that I really don't feel in the mood to die yet. Let's wait and see what happens. But should brute force prematurely send me into the company of my forefathers, I'll defend my skin and make sure that at my gravestone many Ute widows and waifs will mourn the passing of their kinfolks whom I surely will have expedited to Elise."

"You mean Elysium?" asked Jemmy.

"Don't talk nonsense! We're talking German and Elise is purely Germanic. I'm a good Christian and don't want anything to do with the heathen Roman

Elysium. Why is it that people with the most smarts always have the least brains? Well, it's forever been the case that the largest potatoes have been the sappiest."

He would have continued in this vein venting his anger about the correction had he the time. But their arrival was imminent. The camp's residents were approaching to welcome the returning warriors. Up front were the men and boys, followed by the squaws and young girls, all of them screaming at their loudest and sounding like a herd of wild animals.

Old Shatterhand had expected to arrive at a normal teepee camp but was disappointed that his assumption was mistaken. A large number of fires indicated that many more warriors must be present than the teepees could hold. Members of many other Ute camps had assembled here to attend the powwow of vengeance against the whites. The messengers Chief Big Wolf had sent ahead had told about the capture of the six palefaces. The redskins expressed their delight at this feat as only wild tribes are capable of doing. Shaking their weapons above their heads and screaming with all their force, they uttered the most terrible threats.

The center of the gathering formed a large circle consisting of buffalo hide teepees and quickly- erected wigwams made from branches and bark. Knox and Hilton were untied from their horses and tossed to the ground. The terrible moaning of the wounded Knox was totally lost in the redskins' howling. Then the four frontiersmen were led into the center as well. The warriors formed a large ring around the six whites and in the space between, squaws and girls began to dance and shriek.

This constituted the greatest possible insult. It is an accusation of cowardice and dishonor to have women dance around captives. Whoever allows this to happen is thought to stand lower than a dog. The four hunters still retained their weaponry. Old Shatterhand shouted instructions to his companions upon which they knelt and aimed their rifles. He himself fired his bear killer into the air with a report even louder than the howling; then he leveled his rifle. Immediately the dancing stopped and a deep silence fell.

"What does this mean?" he shouted loudly enough for all to hear. "Have we been forced to ride with you or did we come of our own free will? How can the red man treat us like prisoners? I've smoked the pipe-of-council with Big Wolf and agreed that the council of the Utes might discuss whether to treat us as foes or friends. Even were we captives, we wouldn't tolerate your squaws and girls dancing around us as if we were cowardly coyotes. We are only four warriors facing Utes who count in many hundreds, but I ask who of you dares to insult Old Shatterhand? May he step forward and fight me if I shall not think him a coward! Beware! You've seen my magic rifle and know that it speaks in a voice of thunder! If the women resume their dance-of-insult, we'll let our rifles bark and this place will be reddened with the blood of those perfidious enough to disrespect the pipe-of-council which stands sacred to all brave red warriors!"

These words made a deep impression. That the famous hunter dared to speak these threats in the face of vastly superior numbers did not appear irrational behavior to the redskins, rather it impressed them. They knew he had not spoken idly but that he would make his words count. The squaws and girls meekly withdrew without being told. The braves whispered to each other; the clearest words heard were "Killing Hand" and "the killing rifle."

Some warriors adorned with feathers approached Big Wolf and spoke briefly with him.

Although the four hunters were still aiming their rifles, the chief courageously approached them speaking in Ute, the same language Old Shatterhand had used, "The chief of the Yampa Utes is not perfidious. He respects the calumet of council and knows what he has promised. Tomorrow at daylight, the fate of the four palefaces will be decided. Until then, you will stay in the teepee I assign you. The two others, though, are murderers and do not fall under my promise. They will die as they lived -- dripping blood. Howgh! Is Old Shatterhand agreed?"

"Yes," the hunter answered, "but I request our horses be staked by our teepee."

"I shall permit this too, although I do not understand the reason for Old Shatterhand's wish. Do you think of escaping? I tell you, several rings of warriors will encircle your teepee to make escape impossible."

"I've promised to await the result of your council; you need not put up guards. But if you prefer to do so, I don't object."

"Then come with me."

As the four followed the chief, the Indians opened a passage giving Old Shatterhand abashed and respectful looks. The assigned teepee turned out to be one of the largest. Several spears, adorned with three eagle feathers, were planted on either side of its entrance, showing it to be Big Wolf's own sleeping place.

A large hide, used to close the entry, was flipped back. Barely five paces away a fire burned, which also illuminated the inside of the tent. The hunters bent low to enter, put down their rifles and sat down to rest. Big Wolf left, but soon enough several redskins appeared, who placed themselves around the teepee at an appropriate distance so that none of its sides were unobserved.

A few minutes later, an Indian maiden entered, put two vessels in front of the whites and withdrew without a word. One was an old pot containing water, the other a large iron skillet with meat.

"Oho!" smiled Hobble-Frank. "That must be our supper. A pot of water, that's noble. The Utes are really putting one on. Are we to clap our hands in admiration at their civilized kitchen utensils? And buffalo meat, at least eight pounds. Maybe they rubbed it with rat poison?"

"Rat poison!" Fat Jemmy laughed. "Where would they get such stuff? And besides it's elk meat, not buffalo."

"Here you go again knowing something better than I do. Whatever I say and do, you always cross me. There's nothing better I can expect. But I won't quarrel with you today, only throw you an extemporaneous look from which you can see how infinitely superior my personality is compared to your pigment figure."

"It's pygmy figure," corrected Jemmy.

"Will you be still for twelve six-eighth measures!" the little one exploded. "Don't make my gall bladder swell pneumatically, but rather devote to me the respect I by all rights can claim, based on my exceptional course of life! Because only under that condition can I make myself so popular as to bestow my undeniable culinary skills to bless this roast."

"Yes, roast along," suggested Old Shatterhand, to deflect the little one's outrage.

"That's easily said. But where are the onions and bay leaves to come from? Then, I don't know whether they'll let me take the skillet to the fire out there."

"Try it."

"Yes, I'll try! If those redskins don't like it and put a bullet into my belly, it's all the same whether the meat's come from below an elk's or a buffalo's hide. But fear not, as long as one is of a hearty mind. Veni, vidi, vici -- I'm going outside!"

He carried the skillet to the fire and began applying his culinary abilities without being bothered by the guards. The others remained in the teepee watching the activity of the Indians through the open door flap.

The risen full moon lit up the entire campground. Opposite Big Wolf's teepee it illuminated a wooded hillside from which a broad mountain stream descended like a shimmering silver snake, tumbling from up high and forming a small lake at its bottom. Its flow shaped the stream alongside whose banks they had come to the camp. No trees or bushes grew in the vicinity; the lake's surroundings were flat and open.

Each fireside was occupied by a group of Indian braves watching their squaws prepare meat. From time to time, one of the redskins rose to pass slowly by and throw a glance at the whites. Nothing could be seen or heard of Knox and Hilton, but certainly their condition was less accommodating than that of Old Shatterhand and his friends.

After an hour, Hobble-Frank returned to the teepee with the steaming skillet, sat down with his companions and told them in a self-assured tone, "Here's the splendor. I'm curious what expressions I'll get. Although the spice is missing, my inborn talents easily overcame the deficits."

"By what means?" asked Jemmy, holding the skillet under his small nose. Not only did the meat simmer, it smoked, and that not a little. Within a few minutes, the teepee was pervaded by a sharp burnt odor.

"I accomplished it by such simple means that the result is a miracle," the little man responded. "I once read that charcoal not only substitutes for salt, which is lacking here, but will also remove a meat's ripe odor. Our roast was blessed by such a dissident scent that I resorted to the aforementioned additive and roasted it in wood ash, available since we have a wood fire. Although the fire did jump a bit into my pan, my ingenious kitchen know-how tells me that it must have produced a wonderful crispness, a delight for every sensitive and appreciative human palate."

"My stars! Elk roast in wood ash! Are you out of your mind?" exploded Jemmy.

"Don't talk apple sauce! I'm always of right mind! You ought to know this by now. Ash is the chemical enemy of all alchemist uncleanness. Enjoy this elk with all necessary reason, that it'll sit well with you and bestow on you the physical and mental strength without which a man's constitution is bound to suffer immensely."

"But," Jemmy protested, shaking his head, "you said yourself that the fire jumped into your skillet. The meat is burned; it's ruined."

"Stop talking and eat!" Frank expostulated. "It's very unhealthy to talk or sing while eating, since food may go down the wrong opening in the throat and end up in the spleen instead of the stomach."

"Eat! Eat this? Who can chew this stuff! Look! Is that still meat?"

He speared a piece with his knife, lifted it and held it under the little man's nose. The meat was charred black and coated with a fatty layer of ashes.

"Sure it's meat. What else could it be?" answered Frank.

"But it's black as Chinese ink!"

"Go bite into it! It'll taste wonderful!"

"I believe it," Jemmy said, with heavy irony. "The ashes too?"

"Wipe it off."

"First you have to show me how to do it!"

"With royal ease!"

From the pan, Hobble-Frank fingered a piece and rubbed it back and forth on the teepee hide until the ashes had been transferred onto the hide.

"That's how it's done," he said with smug satisfaction. "You're always short of the necessary dexterity and presence of mind. Now look how delicious it is when I cut myself a little bite and let it melt on my tongue. You ---"

He suddenly stopped. He had taken a bite, opened his mouth again and gazed totally stricken at one after the other of his companions.

"Well," Jemmy reminded him, "keep chewing!"

"Chewing -- I can't! By the cuckoo, this piece crackles like a -- like -- well, a roasted scrubbing brush. Who would think it possible?"

"That was to be expected. I think the old skillet is probably more tender than the meat. Go ahead, you can consume your intellect's creation all by yourself!"

"Never! Nobody can say that you had to starve because of me. How about if we pound it?"

"Give it a try!" Old Shatterhand laughed. "I'll have a look whether all of it is spoilt."

"Maybe there's a piece that hasn't quite become hard of character. Let me test some and remove the ash."

Fortunately there were a few pieces which were still edible and sufficient for the four men. But Frank had become quite dejected. He retired to a dark corner and pretended to be asleep, but in fact he heard everything that was spoken and happening in and outside the teepee.

Despite all the hilarity and animation inside the teepee, a serious situation was brewing outside.

Knox and Hilton were to die at the stake the next morning. The four others might well share the same fate. This could mean a great festivity for the redskins for which they wanted to be ready. Following their late meal, the whole camp settled down to sleep. All the fires were allowed to burn down except two, the one at the teepee of the four hunters and the second in front of Knox and Hilton. Around the first, a threefold circle of redskins had arranged themselves, with additional guards posted at the camp's periphery. An escape, while not totally impossible, would have been very difficult and certainly dangerous.

So the redskins could not have their eyes on them the entire night, Old Shatterhand lowered the teepee's entry flap. The frontiersmen now lay in the dark but all attempts at finding sleep eluded them.

"How's it going to be with us tomorrow at this time?" Davy wondered aloud. "By then the redskins may have already sent us to the Eternal Hunting Grounds."

"Maybe one, or two or three of us," responded Jemmy.

"Why so?" questioned Old Shatterhand.

"I don't think they'll touch you."

"Only you three? Hardly! What do you think of me! We all belong together and none of us is excluded from the fate of the others. Should your death be decided, I won't let myself be spared. In that case we'll fight to the last man."

"But you promised not to fight."

"Indeed, and I'll keep that promise literally. But I didn't promise not to flee. We'll at least make an attempt and whoever gets in our way will be responsible for his own death. By the way, my concern is not that the redskins will decide to kill us."

"What then? That they'll let us go?"

"No, not that either. Embitterment against the whites is so deep and, I must confess, justified, that they cannot willy-nilly grant any captured paleface his freedom. But they respect our names; in addition, they're afraid of my repeating rifle, afraid to the extent that they don't dare to touch it. I not only think it's possible but even probable that they'll make an exception for us. They won't grant us life and freedom, but make us struggle for it."

"By the devil! That would be wonderful. It's tantamount to murdering us right away. They would set conditions to assure our slaughter."

"Perhaps so. But let's not lose courage. We whites have gone to school with the redskins and know just as much cunning and cleverness as they do, but when it comes to perseverance, we're superior to the red man. We've all had experience and it'll be the same here. To sum it up, I say that in open close combat, three whites can take on four Indians if the weapons are the same, also their relative strength. The redskin's pride will prevent them from confronting us with too great a numerical superiority. If they do it, however, we would make a mockery of it, causing them to back away."

"But," objected Hobble-Frank, who had remained silent until now, "the perspective you describe here is by no means a blessing. The Utes will make our lives as sour as possible. Yes, for you, with your physical strength and elephant power, it's easy to laugh. You'll punch and strike and push your way through, but we three unhappy mushrooms will have enjoyed the pleasures of existence for the last time."

"In the form of an elk roast?" Jemmy inquired.

"Are you starting again? I thought our situation is dire enough that you'd abstain from annoying your best friend and fighting buddy so close to his ascension. Don't splinter my intellectual powers! I'm concentrating all my thoughts on our escape. Or do you find it immensely noble and heroic to kill a doomed man by mocking hippological expressions four hours before his complimentary demise?"

"Hippocratic, not hippological, " remarked Jemmy.

He couldn't resist the correction which drove the little one into such a rage that he shouted, "Listen, that's just too much! You're becoming impossible! I can only smack you down, and I shall, by quoting Heinrich Heine's 'Singer's Curse', that goes like this:

'You truculent man of diabolic nature,
Impudent to God, to man and beast,
The woe and grief of every creature,
Sees the police take you, the bold,
Before the local district court.'

"There, now you know my opinion. Take it to heart and mull it in your mind until you've understood and can repent."

"But old Frank, this wasn't meant maliciously. It's just that being your friend, I feel it's necessary to draw your attention to where you're mistaken. I don't want you to make a fool of yourself."

"So? Can I -- I -- I, my very self, Hobble-Frank from Moritzburg, really ever err and compromise myself?"

"Like any other human being. The rhyme you just said proves it. First of all, there's no mention of the police or a district court in the original; second, the poem isn't Heine's, but Buerger's, and third its title isn't the 'Singer's Curse', but 'The Wild Hunter'.

Frank could not feature himself elaborating further on the subject and finally declared vehemently and unequivocally that he would no longer talk to Jemmy. He lay down and closed his eyes. From the other side, a faint snicker could be heard; he paid no attention to it. The others no longer spoke either. A deep silence ensued, broken only by the occasional crackling of the fire.

Sleep finally took hold of the fatigued men who did not awaken until loud shouts sounded outside. The teepee flap opened, a redskin looked in and announced, "The palefaces are to rise and come with me."

They rose, took their weapons and followed him. The fires had gone out and the sun had risen over the mountains. Its beams caused the falling water on the hill to sparkle like liquid gold and the lake's surface to shine like polished metal. The view now extended farther than the previous evening. The plain, at whose western end lay the lake, was about two miles long and half as wide and was surrounded by forest. Towards the south was the camp consisting of some two hundred teepees and wigwams. Horses grazed at the lake's shore; those of the four hunters, as agreed, had been staked near their teepee.

Among the dwellings, Indians stood or walked, all daubed in war paint to celebrate the impending death of at least the two captured murderers. Wherever necessary, they politely made an opening for the passage of the four hunters, their looks resting on them with expressions more probing and appraising than hostile.

"What's the matter with these fellows?" asked Frank. "They look me over as if I were a horse they'd like to purchase."

"They're checking our build," answered Old Shatterhand. "It confirms my surmise. Our intended fate is known to them. We'll have to fight for our lives."

"Fine! Mine will not be sold cheaply. Are you scared, Jemmy?"

His anger at Fat Jemmy had vanished. From the tone of his question, he was more concerned for his friend than for himself.

"I'm not scared, but concerned, obviously. Fear would hurt us. We must now be as composed and calm as possible."

Outside the camp, two wooden posts had been rammed into the earth. Close by stood five warriors decorated with feathers, among them Big Wolf. He approached to within a few paces of the whites and declared, "I have brought you here to witness how Ute braves punish their enemies. The murderers will now be fetched to die at the stake."

"We don't care to watch this," answered Old Shatterhand.

"Are you cowards, terrified by flowing blood? Then we must treat you as such and I need not keep my promise."

"We are Christians. We kill our enemies if we need to, but we don't torture them."

"Perhaps. But now you are here with us and must abide by our customs. If you do not wish to do this, it is an insult that will be punished by death."

Old Shatterhand knew that the chief was serious and that he and his companions would be in mortal danger if he didn't agree to observe the executions. He therefore declared, "All right then. We'll stay."

"Sit down with us! If you comply, an honorable death will be yours."

Big Wolf settled onto the grass facing the stakes. The other chiefs followed suit and the whites were obliged to do the same. Then Big Wolf's voice rose in a long loud cry answered by hundreds of voices in a triumphal howl, the sign for the gruesome spectacle to begin.

The braves approached from all sides, forming a semicircle around the stakes, with the chiefs and the whites inside. Then the squaws and children lined up in an arc opposite the men to close the circle.

Now came Knox and Hilton, bound so tightly that they had to be dragged at times. The straps cut so deeply into his skin that Hilton groaned. Knox was quiet. He was suffering from wound fever and had stopped hallucinating only moments before. He looked terrible. Both men were tied to the stakes in an upright position, using wet straps which, as they dried, would shrink and cause the victims of this gruesome justice the most terrible pain.

Knox's eyes were half-closed and his head hung low to his breast. He had lost consciousness and didn't know what was happening to him. Hilton threw panicked looks in every direction. When he saw the four hunters, he cried out, "Save me, save me, gentlemen. You are no heathens. Have you come to watch our terrible death and to gloat over our suffering?"

"No," answered Old Shatterhand. "Our presence here is under duress and we cannot do anything for you."

"You can, you can, if you only want to. The redskins will listen to you."

"No. You alone are guilty of your crimes. Whoever has the courage to sin must also have the courage to suffer the consequences."

"I'm innocent. I didn't kill any Indians. Knox did it."

"Don't lie! It's cowardice to pile guilt onto him alone. Rather repent so that you will find forgiveness in heaven!"

"But I don't want to die, I don't want to! Oh, help, help, *help!*"

He screamed so loudly that it echoed across the plain, pulling so hard at his bonds that blood gushed from his flesh. Big Wolf rose and gave a sign that he wished to speak. All eyes focused on the chief. In brief, powerful, yet flourishing words he eloquently recounted what had happened. He described the treacherous behavior of the palefaces with whom they had formerly lived in peace and who had suffered no insult from the Utes. His words made such an impression on the redskins that they started to rattle their weapons. Then he declared that the two murderers had been sentenced to die at the stake and that the execution should begin. When he had finished, Hilton once more raised his voice to beg Old Shatterhand to intercede.

"Well, I'll try," he answered. "If I cannot prevent your death, I may be able to obtain a swifter and less painful one."

He turned to the chief, but before he could open his mouth Big Wolf angrily bellowed at him, "You know that I speak the palefaces' language and I understood what you just promised this dog. Have I not done enough by extending you favorable conditions? Are you to speak against our sentence and anger my warriors so that I may be unable to protect you from them? Be silent then; don't say a word! You have plenty to think about yourself and ought not to be concerned with others. If you take the side of this murderer, you put yourself on his level and will suffer the same fate."

"My religion demands intercession," was the sole excuse Old Shatterhand could think of.

"By what religion are we to judge here? Yours or ours? Did your religion stop these dogs from attacking us while we were at deepest peace, to steal out horses and to kill our warriors? No! Then your religion will not have any influence on the punishment of these perpetrators."

He turned away and gave a sign, whereupon a dozen braves stepped forward. Once more Big Wolf turned to Old Shatterhand, telling him, "There stand the relatives of the murdered victims. They have the right to begin the punishment."

"What's that to be?" demurred the hunter cautiously.

"Many torments. First knives will be hurled at them."

If a redskin's enemy is to die at the stake, he will try to prolong the torment as long as possible. The first wounds inflicted will be light, gradually becoming more and more severe. Usually, various body parts and members are specified which are to be struck by knives. The target areas are selected so that little blood is lost and the tortured man does not die prematurely from blood loss.

"The right thumb!" ordered Big Wolf.

The captives' arms had been tied in such a way that their hands hung freely. The dozen braves split into two groups, one for Hilton, the other for Knox. At a distance of twelve paces, they lined up one behind the other. The first took his knife between his first three fingers, aimed, threw, and pierced the thumb. Hilton screamed. Knox had been hit too, but he was still unconscious.

"The index finger," the chief called.

In sequence, both men's fingers were struck with stunning accuracy. If Hilton had first shouted a single scream, he now howled continuously. Knox awoke only after his left hand had become a target. He first stared ahead vaguely, then closed his bloodshot eyes and commenced an entirely inhuman wailing. He comprehended what was happening to him. His fever was affecting him, and both delirium and mortal dread tore sounds from his throat one would not have thought possible for a human.

Punctuated by the incessant screams of the two villains, the execution continued. Hurled knives penetrated the back of their hands, their wrists, their upper and lower arms, then continued to their legs. This lasted for about a quarter of an hour and constituted the lightest part of the torture, which was meant to last for hours. Old Shatterhand and his comrade averted their faces. They were unable to watch the scene. The screams they had to suffer.

From early childhood, an Indian is trained to endure physical pain. This leads him to the point where he can suffer the worst of punishments without showing anguish. Perhaps redskins' nerves are also less sensitive than those of whites. In any event, an Indian sentenced to die at the stake suffers the pain inflicted on him smilingly, sings his death song, interrupts it only to insult his tormentors and to laugh at them. To be a wailing man at the stake is an impossibility for redskins. He who whines in pain is despised, and the louder the wails the greater the contempt. It has happened that tortured whites were released when they showed by their wailing that they were cowards not to be feared and whose killing would shame any warrior.

One can imagine the impression Hilton and Knox's laments produced. The redskins turned away with shouts of indignation and scorn. When the relatives of the murdered Utes had been given sufficient satisfaction and others were asked to continue the torture by other means, not a single brave stepped forward. No one wanted to touch such dogs, such coyotes, such toads. One of the chiefs rose and said, "These palefaces are not worthy of laying hands on by a proud warrior. My red brothers surely see this. We shall leave them to the squaws. When a man dies at the hands of a squaw, his soul takes on the body of a woman in the Eternal Hunting Grounds and must work for all eternity. Howgh!"

Following a brief council, the proposal was accepted. The wives and mothers of the murdered Utes were summoned. They were given knives to cut the two men in a sequence Big Wolf prescribed.

A civilized European will be hard-pressed to believe that a female can descend to such cruelty. But the redskins are not civilized, and in this case revenge for multiple murders banished all mitigating circumstances. The women, mostly old wenches, began their work. The shrieks and wails of the two whites rose anew to the extent that it became intolerable even to the redskins. Big Wolf put a stop to the torture and said, "These cowards are not even worthy of becoming women upon their deaths. No red man will set them free. Their guilt is too great. They must die now and enter the Eternal Hunting Grounds as coyotes who are chased and pursued without cessation. Give them to the dogs. Howgh!"

Now a second council began whose outcome Old Shatterhand anticipated and awaited with horror. He was bold enough to dare another intercession but was rebuffed so harshly that he was glad nothing worse had happened. The council concluded by accepting Big Wolf's proposal. Some of the redskins left to fetch the dogs. The chief addressed the four whites, "The Utes' dogs are trained to attack palefaces. They will not attack on their own, only when they are incited to do so, then they will tear apart any white they see. I shall have you led away and guarded in a teepee until the animals have been tied up again."

On his command, the four hunters were taken to a nearby tent guarded by several Indians. The situation affected them as deeply as if they themselves were destined for the jaws of the beasts. The two murderers deserved death, but to be torn apart by dogs was too gruesome to envisage.

Outside the teepee tent silence reigned for about ten minutes, broken only at times by the whimpering of Hilton, who was not yet aware of what was to come. Then loud, fierce barking could be heard, changing to a bloodthirsty howl. Two human voices rose in horrible mortal fear. Then a terrible silence. Almost silence.

"Listen!" said Jemmy. "Do I hear the crunching of bones? Do they let the dogs eat them?"

"Possibly, but I don't think so," answered Old Shatterhand. "The crunching exists only in your imagination. Mine too is very active. We're blessed that we weren't forced to watch that hideous scene."

Now the four hunters were taken from the teepee and returned to the place of execution. Farther to the center of the camp, four or five redskins were leading the dogs away, who were attached to strong leather thongs. One of the animals caught the scent of the whites and refused to be pulled along. He turned, saw the four palefaces, and with a violent jerk tore free. A general shout of dismay arose. The dog was big and strong, far too much for a human being to tackle. Yet none of the Indians wanted to shoot him since the animal was very precious. Jemmy leveled and aimed his rifle.

"Stop, don't shoot!" demanded Old Shatterhand. "The redskins will take even further offense if we kill this splendid dog. I want to show them what the fist of a white hunter can accomplish."

His words had come quickly. Everything happened much faster than it can be told. The dog covered the distance in panther-like leaps in no more than three or four seconds. Old Shatterhand faced him, hands at his sides.

"You are lost!" Big Wolf shouted.

"Just wait!" responded the hunter.

The dog sprang at Old Shatterhand, jaws agape. The hunter's eyes focused firmly on those of the animal. With the dog already in mid-leap, Old Shatterhand lunged toward him, arms wide apart --- a mighty crash of dog and man. Old Shatterhand locked his arms behind the creature's neck and pressed the dog's head so tightly against his chest that the animal was unable to bite. An even firmer pressure and the dog was unable to breathe, his scratching legs suddenly hanging limply. With a quick jerk, the hunter tore the beast's head aside --- a blow to the nose --- then he tossed him away.

"There he lies," he called, turning to the chief. "Tie him up so he cannot cause mischief when he awakes."

"Uff, ugh, ugh, uff!" came from the amazed redskins. None of them would have dared what they had just witnessed and would not have even thought possible. Big Wolf issued the order to carry the animal away, stepped towards Old Shatterhand, saying to him with sincere admiration, "My white brother is a hero. He stopped the bloodhound's attack and smashed him to the ground. No feet of an Indian would have stood as firmly and no chest of another man could have borne the collision. His ribs would have been crushed. Why did Old Shatterhand not allow the dog to be shot?"

"Because I didn't want you to lose this splendid animal."

"What fearlessness! What if he had torn you apart!"

"Pah! Old Shatterhand will not be rent by a dog! What now is the intention of the braves of the Utes?

"They will sit in council over you; the time for it has come. Will the palefaces ask for mercy?"

"Mercy? Have you lost your wits? Rather ask whether I will have mercy on you!"

With a look of surprise and admiration, the chief led the hunter to where the whites were to sit, far enough outside the redskins' circle that they couldn't hear what was said in the council. Then he returned to sit with the other chiefs.

The hunters' looks inevitably went to the two stakes. There hung the lacerated bodies of the murderers dangling from the straps that the dogs had torn: a truly gruesome sight.

Now began the decisive tribal council, held in true Indian fashion. First Big Wolf stood to speak for a long time, then one after another the rest of the chiefs did the same. Then Big Wolf again, followed by the others. Common braves were not permitted to speak; they stood listening respectfully. The Indian is taciturn, but during council he speaks plenty. There are redskins who acquired great fame as tribal orators.

The council took two hours to complete, a long time for those whose fate depended on its outcome. Suddenly a general and loud exclamation of "Howgh!" proclaimed its end. The whites were fetched and made to step into the inner circle to hear the council's decision. Big Wolf rose to announce it. "The four palefaces have already heard why we have taken up the tomahawk; I do not wish to repeat it. We have sworn to kill all whites who fall into our hands. We cannot make an exception for you. You agreed to follow me here for us to sit in council over you and you promised not to fight us. We know you are friends of the red man, which is why you are not to suffer the fate of other palefaces we intend to capture. Those will be killed at the stake --- but you will be allowed to fight for your lives."

He paused, which gave Old Shatterhand time to ask, "With whom? Us four against all of you? All right, so be it. My Rifle of Death will send many of you to the Eternal Hunting Grounds!"

He raised his carbine. The chief was unable to entirely hide his fright. Warding off the weapon with a quick movement of his hand, he answered, " Old Shatterhand is mistaken. Each of you will face only one adversary, and the victor has the right to kill the vanquished."

"I am agreed. But who has the right to select our adversaries? Us or you?"

"We do. I shall issue an invitation for volunteers."

"And how and with what weapons will we fight?"

"As determined by those of us who fight you."

"Oho! You won't respect our wishes?"

"No."

"That's not just."

"Yes, it is just. You must consider our power over you, allowing us to demand an advantage."

"You have power over us? How so?"

"So many against four."

"Pshaw! What are your weapons against my Rifle of Death! Only those who have fear in their bellies seek an advantage over the other."

"Fear?" cried Big Wolf, his eyes flashing. "Do you try to insult me? Are you saying we are cowards?"

"I didn't speak about you personally, great chief, but in general terms. If a poor runner runs against a better one and bets on the outcome, he usually asks for a handicap. By putting us at a disadvantage, you've given me reason to believe that you think we're better warriors than you. That I would not do, being chief of the Utes."

Big Wolf stared ahead for awhile. He could not find a flaw in the hunter's reasoning, but had to be careful not to agree. He finally responded, "We have already shown you much consideration; you cannot demand any more. Whether we are afraid of you, you will learn in battle."

"All right, but I demand honest conditions."

"How do you mean?"

"You said that the victor has the right to kill the vanquished. What then when I defeat one of your braves and kill him? Will I be allowed to leave this place freely and safely?"

"Yes."

"No one will prevent me?"

"No. Because you will not win. None of you will be victorious."

"I understand you. You'll make your choice from among your braves and determine the kind of fight in such a way that we are certain to be defeated. Don't make a mistake! It may all turn out differently from what you think."

"How it will end I know so well that I shall add one more condition, that is, that the victor will receive all of the loser's property."

"This new condition is very important," Old Shatterhand spat contemptuously, "since otherwise no one would be willing to fight us."

"Beware!" the chief raged, "Your only right is to say whether you agree or not."

"And if we don't?"

"Then you break your promise, for you said that you would not oppose us."

"I keep my promise, but I want your word that if any of us emerges the victor, he will be treated as your friend."

"Done! You have Big Wolf's word."

"Are we going to smoke the peace pipe over it?"

"Do you not believe me?" roared Big Wolf incredulously.

Old Shatterhand was keenly aware that he ought not to be too insistent if he was not to lose the advantages he had already gained. He therefore declared, "All right, I believe you. Ask your warriors who is willing to fight us."

A great commotion arose among the Indians. They shouted and milled about. Old Shatterhand whispered to his companions, "Unfortunately I couldn't tighten the string too much with Big Wolf; it would otherwise have snapped. I'm not at all satisfied with the conditions we were given."

"We must be content, since we couldn't get better ones," Long Davy said.

"Yes. As it concerns myself, I'm not worried," said Old Shatterhand. The redskins have such a respect for me that I'm curious whether an opponent will be found."

"Indeed, one will."

"Who?"

"Big Wolf himself. Since no other will come forward, he will have to save the tribe's honor. He's a giant, a real elephant."

"Pah! I don't fear him. But you! They'll pick the most dangerous opponents and determine for each of us the type of contest where they think we have the least experience. None of them will enter into a fist fight with me, for instance."

"Let's just wait and see," suggested Jemmy.

"Right now all the worry and concern won't help us. Let's tense our muscles and keep our eyes open."

"And our minds bright and clear," added Hobble-Frank. "Myself, I'm as quiet as a milestone at the roadside. I don't understand it, but it's true: I'm not the least worried. Today these Utes will get to know a Saxon Mortitzburger. I'll fight so sparks fly all the way to Greenland."

Order returned among the Indians. The circle reformed and Big Wolf announced the three braves who had volunteered to battle the whites.

"Pair up the men," requested Old Shatterhand.

Big Wolf pushed the first towards Long Davy and said, "Here stands Pagu-angare, Red Fish, who will swim for his life against the paleface."

The choice was an excellent one for the Indians. It was obvious that the long, lean Davy would not be the swifter competitor in water. The redskin, though, was a fellow with round hips, broad meaty chest and strong arm and leg muscles. In any case, he was certainly the tribe's best swimmer. If his name had not given it away, the contemptuous looks he gave Davy spoke volumes.

Next the chief introduced a tall, broad-shouldered man with bulging muscles to the short Fat Jemmy and said, "This is Namboh-avaht, Big Foot, who will wrestle with the fat paleface. They will be tied together back to back. Each will receive a knife in his right hand and whoever wrestles the other underneath himself may put his opponent to death with the knife."

Big Foot's name was greatly justified. He had gigantic feet, on which he stood so firmly that little Fat Jemmy might well think of running away in desperation.

The third redskin remained now, a bony chap, almost six feet tall, lean, but with a wide chest and preternaturally long arms and legs. Big Wolf pulled him to Hobble-Frank and declared, "And this is To-ok-tey, Leaping Elk, who is prepared to run for his life against this paleface."

Poor Hobble-Frank! While Leaping Elk with his seven-mile-legs made two strides, the little one would require six! Yes, the redskins were very much out for their advantage.

"And who fights me?" asked Old Shatterhand.

"I," answered Big Wolf proudly, straightening his gigantic stature. "You thought we were afraid; I'll demonstrate that you are mistaken."

"I like that," the white responded gently. "I've always sought my adversaries among chiefs."

Both men now dueled verbally with overweening bravado.

"You will succumb!"

"Old Shatterhand will not be defeated!"

"And Ovuts-avaht won't either! Who can speak of ever having defeated me?"

"I'll do so today!"

"And I shall be lord of your life!"

"Big Wolf, let's not fight with words but with the rifle!"

Old Shatterhand said this in a somewhat sardonic voice; fully aware that the chief would never agree. And indeed the other responded quickly, "I will have nothing to do with your Rifle of Death. The knife and the tomahawk will decide between us."

"I'm also satisfied with that."

"Then you will shortly be a corpse and I shall take possession of all your property, including your horse!"

"I believe that you covet my horse, but the magic rifle is even more precious. What will you do with that?"

"I do not want it and no one else desires it. It is too dangerous, since whoever touches it wounds his best friends. We shall bury it deep in the earth where it may rust and rot."

"Then whoever touches it in the process should be very cautious, or it will bring calamity to the entire tribe of the Utes. Now tell me, when and in what sequence are the individual fights to take place?"

"First the swimmers. But I know that whites perform special customs before their death. I shall allow you the time you palefaces call an hour to prepare yourselves."

The redskins had closed the circle around the whites, expecting to see how frightened the palefaces would be at the sight of their assigned opponents. Not having observed anything of the sort, they dispersed again, thoroughly disappointed. No one seemed to bother about the hunters, yet it was all too clear that they were being kept under close surveillance. The four sat together to discuss what chances they had. Being first, Long Davy faced the primary danger. While he didn't look desperate, he wore a very serious face.

"Red Fish!" he grumbled. "Obviously this rascal got his name for being a champion swimmer."

"And you?" asked Old Shatterhand. "I've seen you swim, but only when bathing or crossing a river. How's it with your ability?"

"Not too good."

"Oh my!"

"Yes, oh my! I can't help it if my body is made up of heavy bones. In fact, I believe my bones are heavier than any other human being's."

"Then speed's out. How's your endurance?"

"My stamina? Pah! As much as you like. I've strength galore, but there's that lack of making headway. It looks like I may lose my scalp."

"Let's not be so sure about that yet, nor give up all hope. Have you swum on your back before?"

"Yes. That seems to be easier."

"It is. Experience has shown that lean and inexperienced people swim better on their backs than on their bellies. So! Lie on your back, keep your head low and your legs up. Push strongly, make full use of your feet and take a breath only when you throw your arms over your head."

"Well! But all that will do no good because this Red Fish will overtake me regardless."

"Maybe not, if my trick will work."

"What trick?"

"You must swim with the current and he against it."

"Oh, if that were only possible. Is there a current?"

"I suppose there is. If not, then indeed you will lose."

"We don't even know yet where I'm to swim."

"Obviously in the lake, which is actually only a pond. It's somewhat elongated, about five hundred paces long and three hundred wide, I might guess from here. Look! The mountain stream tumbles into it from some height and, as it appears, in the direction of the left shore. That must produce a current along the shore, three quarters of the way around the lake to its outlet. Let me work on it. If at all possible, I'll arrange it so you'll beat your opponent by using the current."

"That would be a blessing, sir! And should I succeed, am I to kill the chap?"

"Would you want to?"

"He wouldn't spare me, leastwise my few belongings."

"That's true. But apart from our being Christians, it'll be to our advantage to be charitable."

"Fine! But what will you do if he outswims me and comes after me with his knife? I'm not permitted to defend myself!"

"In that case, I shall force the issue so that all killings will have to wait until the individual battles have been completed."

"Well, that's a worst case comfort; I'm relieved. But, Jemmy, how about you?"

"Not much better than you," answered the fat one. My opponent's name is Big Foot. You know what that's supposed to mean."

"What?"

"He stands so firmly on his feet that no one's in a position to topple him. And I, shorter by two heads, am supposed to do that? Besides, the muscles this guy has are like those of a hippopotamus. What's my fat against that?"

"Not to worry, my dear Jemmy," comforted Old Shatterhand. "I'm in the same position. The chief's substantially taller and broader-built than I am, but I expect he's wanting in agility. And finally, I may even be the stronger of the two."

"Yes, your strength is phenomenal, a veritable marvel. But me against this Big Foot! I'll try to defend myself as long as possible, but in the end he'll surely prevail. Yes, if there were only such a current for me, another trick!"

"There is one!" Hobble-Frank interjected. "If I had to deal with this character, I wouldn't be worried."

"You? You're even weaker than I!"

"Bodily, yes, but not in mind. And you must win with your mind. You understand?"

"What am I to do with my mind against such a muscle man?"

"You see, that's you. Always and ever you know everything better than I. But when it comes to your life and scalp, you sit like a fly in buttermilk. You struggle, hands and feet, and don't get out after all."

"Then fire away if you have an idea!"

"An idea! What's that again? I don't need an idea; I'm brainy without needing ideas. Just picture yourself in your situation! You two stand back to back, tied together at your buttocks, just like the nice constellation of the Siamese twins in the Milky Way. Each gets a knife, then the fight begins. Whoever gets the other underneath him has won. But how can you get your opponent underneath from such a position? Only by removing the grip of his feet, which can be done by kicking his calves from behind or by wrapping your foot around his, trying to break its hold. Am I right or not?"

"Yes. Go on."

"Easy, easy! It must all be done with finesse and without hurry. If the maneuver succeeds, Big Foot will tumble on his nose and you get to lie on top of him, unfortunately with your back against his, an easy position for losing your balance. You actually should be tied together face to face. I don't know whether the redskins have a trick up their sleeves with that reverse position. I haven't thought this through yet, but if that's true, then their ruse can only be to your advantage."

"How so? Make your point!" pressed Jemmy.

"My, oh my, oh my! Here I've been talking already for a quarter of an hour! Then listen! The redskin will kick you from behind to unhinge and unbalance you. That will not do you any harm, because of the exceptional resilience of your calves. You'll feel his kicks only fourteen months later. Now you must wait a moment and when he kicks again, he'll be standing on only one leg. You then bend forward with all your strength and lift him onto your back. You cut the strap that ties you together and toss him over your head. Then, in an eye blink, you take hold of the fellow's throat and put your knife to his heart. Did you understand, you old snow sifter?"

Old Shatterhand offered the little man his hand and said, "Frank, you're a man of substance! I couldn't have figured this out any better. Your advice is excellent and will surely save our friend."

Frank's honest face shone with delight as he shook the proffered hand and responded, "Okay, okay, master hunter! But I can't pride myself about something so obvious. My merits and asters bloom somewhere else entirely. But it's the best proof that a diamond is often seen as a piece of coal by unreasonable people. That's why I think ---"

"It's carbon, not coal," interrupted Jemmy. "Heavens, what kind of diamond would it be if it were a lump of coal!"

"Oh, be silent, you old, incorrigible brawler! I save your life through my mind's superiority and you throw a lump of coal at my head as a thank you! What a nice fellow to be so capricious! Have you ever found a diamond?"

"No."

Then don't talk about such things!"

"Have you found one?"

Hobble-Frank could not resist answering Jemmy, this time in German. "Yes. A Moritzburg glazier had lost his diamond and I found it on the street. I was a young fellow then and was rewarded with a gift of tremendous value for my honesty. The glazier was also a merchant and gave me a clay tobacco pipe worth two pfennigs and half a packet of tobacco worth three. I've never forgotten this generosity and you see that I can certainly discuss diamonds. If you don't soon quit rubbing me the wrong way, it may easily happen that I'll terminate our friendship. Then you'll have to find out how to get through life without me. Don't you see: it's neither the time nor the place to quarrel. We're all facing the end of our lives and have a holy obligation to assist each other with advice and in deeds instead of angering each other. If we're to be butchered in an hour, why should we injure our health now and shorten our lives even more by being rude. I think it's time to finally smarten up."

"That's entirely correct," Old Shatterhand agreed. "Let's think only about the fight we are each facing. Jemmy will do as you've suggested. I can see him being saved. But what will you do, good Frank?"

"Good Frank!" the little man repeated. "What nice acoustics! It's really much better to communicate with educated gentlemen! What am I going to do? Well, I'm going to run. What else?"

"That I know, but you'll be left behind!"

"I know that quite well!"

"You need to take three steps to his one!"

"Unfortunately, yes!"

"There's the question though of what distance you're to run and how long you can last. How is it with your breathing?"

"That's fine. I've got lungs like a bumble bee. I buzz and hum all day without losing my breath. Run I can. I had to learn it as a royal Saxon forestry assistant."

"But you can't keep up with such a long-legged Indian!"

"Hmm! That remains to be seen!"

"He's called Leaping Elk. Speed is his best skill."

"I'll give a hoot for his name only if I finish first."

"But that you won't!" Old Shatterhand remonstrated.

"Oh? Why not?"

"I told you already and you admitted it. Compare your legs with his!"

"Oh, the legs! You think the legs matter?"

"Of course! What else would matter in a run for life or death?"

"The legs too, sure, but they're far from being the most important thing. Most of it is decided by the head."

"But the head isn't doing the running!"

"Sure, it runs along. Or am I to have my legs run and wait for my head to catch up? That would be dangerous. No, no, my head must come along; it's to do the main job."

"I don't understand you!" Old Shatterhand exclaimed, much surprised by the little man's unconcerned demeanor.

"Me neither, at least not yet. At the moment I only know that a single good thought is worth more than a hundred paces or leaps that don't get you to the goal."

"Then you have an idea?"

"Not yet. But I think if I could give Jemmy some good advice, I'll not leave myself in the lurch. I don't know yet where we're going to run. When that's decided, I'll see the picture better. Don't get worried about me! My inner tenor voice tells me that I'm not going to leave the world just yet. I'm born for greatness, and world-historic personalities never die before they've achieved their success, especially so far from civilization."

Before any further plans could be conceived, Big Wolf appeared with his other chiefs demanding the whites to follow them to the lake. There it teemed with people of all ages and of both sexes, all ready to watch the swimming contest.

When they arrived at the shore, Old Shatterhand saw from the rippling water that he had assessed the situation correctly: there was a considerable current. The lake's shape was like a long ellipse with almost straight sides. Upstream, at the distant narrow side, the mountain brook entered, the current following the left shoreline for almost three quarters of its circumference to the outflow. If Davy could utilize it, he might be saved.

The squaws with their papooses and older children spread out along the shoreline. The braves settled at the lower point where the contest was to begin. All eyes focused on the two contestants. Red Fish proudly and self-confidently looked across the water like someone totally sure of his success. Davy too seemed to be calm, but he swallowed frequently, his larynx constantly bobbing up and down. Those who knew him well saw it as a sign of internal turmoil.

Finally, Big Wolf turned to Old Shatterhand, "Is your man ready to start?"

"Yes, but under what conditions?"

"You will hear them. Right in front of me, both enter the lake. When I give the sign by clapping my hands, they push off. A circuit of the lake must be completed and the swimmers must always maintain a man height's distance from the shore. Whoever tries a shortcut will be considered vanquished. The one returning here first kills the other with his knife."

"Accepted! But in which direction shall they swim? To the right or the left?"

"To the left. They shall return here from the right."

"Are they to swim side by side?"

"Indeed!"

"My comrade on the outside and Red Fish on the shoreside?"

"No. The other way around."

"Why?"

"Because the one swimming on the shoreside would be closer to land and would have to swim a longer distance."

"Then it's wrong and unjust for both to swim in the same direction. You don't wish to cheat and will admit that it is fairer if they swim in different directions. From here, one swims along the right shore, the other along the left. They meet somewhere near the other end of the lake, pass each other, and return along the opposite shoreline."

"You are right," declared the chief. "But who is to swim to the right and who to the left?"

"To also be just in this matter, we'll draw lots to decide. See, I'll take two blades of grass for both swimmers to pick from. Whoever draws the longer one swims to the left, the other to the right."

"All right, let it be so. Howgh!"

Unknowingly, Big Wolf's last word was spoken in Davy's favor, for it confirmed that nothing could change the decision. Old Shatterhand had picked two grass blades, both of the same length. He first stepped towards Red Fish to let him choose. Then he gave the other blade to Davy, but surreptitiously snipped off a little piece before handing it to him. The blades were compared. Davy had the shorter one and was to swim to the right.

His opponent wasn't concerned about the choice; he had no idea yet of the disadvantage he had been handed. But Davy's face shone. Looking at the lake, he whispered to Old Shatterhand, "I don't know how I got the shorter straw, but it'll be my salvation. I surely hope to arrive first. The current is strong on the left and will make it difficult for him."

He took off his clothes and leaped into the water. Red Fish followed suit. Now the chief clapped his hands -- and in a flash both men raced off in opposite directions, the redskin to the left, Davy along the right shoreline.

"Go, Davy, go! Go!" Hobble-Frank shouted after his friend.

Not much of a difference was noticeable at first between the two. The Indian slowly but powerfully reached out like someone totally at home in the water. He looked straight ahead and took care not to check the white's progress. Davy, unused to swimming, had yet to find the right rhythmic stroke. When it didn't come, he turned on his back. Now it went better. With the current aiding him, he was able to stay apace of the redskin. They both had now reached the beginning of the lake's long shores.

By now the Indian realized that the harder task had fallen to him. He had to swim upstream the entire length of the lake up to the mountain brook's inflow, and with every stroke felt the current intensify. He still husbanded his strength but it was evident that he was having to exert himself. His lunges were so difficult that with each one his breast rose above the water. It cost him time.

On Davy's side, the downstream current carried him along. Adding to this, he had more and more found his pace. He was more settled and deliberate. Observing the result of every stroke, he learned quickly to avoid wrong moves. His speed increased and soon he was ahead of the redskin, causing the Ute to exert himself even more, instead of saving his strength for his ever-increasing difficulties.

Davy now approached the outflow point. The current became stronger, pulling him from his path towards the outflow and away from the lake. He battled valiantly but began to fall behind the redskin. This was the moment everything depended on.

His companions at the shore watched in suspense.

"The redskin is overtaking him," Jemmy said anxiously. "He's going to lose."

"If he fights on for another five feet," answered Old Shatterhand, "he'll be past the outflow and be safe."

"Yes, yes," Frank agreed. "He seems to realize it. Look how he struggles! There, right so, he's going ahead, he's over it. Hallelujah!"

Davy had conquered the pull of the outflow and entered still waters. Now his smooth backstrokes propelled him in a straight line towards the far end of the lake. Before long, he had the right shoreline behind him well before the redskin could complete the left, and Davy could turn into the narrow side towards the mountain brook's inflow.

The red man saw this and worked like a madman, knowing his life depended on it, but no stroke, not even the most powerful, furthered his advance much more than a foot, while Davy achieved twice that. At last, the Indian fought his way to the inflow point, just as Davy reached it from the opposite direction. Battered by the turbulent waters gushing from the brook, both men shot past each other.

"Hurrah!" Davy could not resist shouting in his elation. The redskin answered with a far and widely audible cry.

The brook's waters now caught Davy and carried him along. It was no longer an exertion but a pleasure to swim. He needed only gentle strokes to stay in his appointed course. Little by little, aided by the current, he applied greater force, but it went so easily now as if he had been swimming all his life. He arrived at the starting point and clambered out of the water onto the shore. When he turned, he saw that his feckless opponent had only just reached the outflow of the lake and was once more fighting the current.

Loud, bone-chilling shrieks of disbelief rose from the redskins ranged along the shore, horrified that Red Fish had lost and was doomed to die. Davy quickly donned his clothes again, then rushed to his comrades to greet them, glorying in his newfound life.

"Who would have thought it!" he glowed, shaking both of Old Shatterhand's hands. "I've beaten the Utes' best swimmer!"

"By a blade of grass!" the hunter answered smiling.

"How did you do it?"

"About that later. A little trick, but it wasn't cheating, since it was done to save your life without hurting the redskins."

"So it was!" Frank joined in, always happy for a victory by his friend. "Your life didn't hang by a hair but by a blade of grass. So may it be with the run! My legs alone aren't going to do it. Who knows what grass blade will save me? Yes, I need the legs, but even more, the head. Look, here comes Bad Luck Fish."

The dejected Indian arrived from the right, more than five minutes behind the victor. He climbed onto the land and sat down, mournfully facing the lake. None of the redskins looked at him, none moved; they waited for Davy to strike the death blow.

A squaw hesitantly came up to Red Fish, a child on each hand. He drew one of his children to his left, the other to his right. Then he gently pushed them away, shook hands with his wife and gave her a sign to leave. His eyes fastened on Davy as he called out, "Nani witsch, ne pokai -- your knife, kill me!"

Tears almost came to Davy eyes. He took hold of the squaw and her children, pushed them back toward Red Fish and said in half English, half broken Ute, "No witsch - not pokai!"

He turned and walked back to his comrades. The Ute watched and listened wonderingly. Chief Big Wolf demanded, "Why do you not kill him?"

"Because I'm a Christian. I give him his life."

"But had he won, he would have killed you!"

"He didn't win and therefore didn't do it. He may live."

"But you'll at least take his property, his weapons, his horses, his wife and his children?"

"I wouldn't think of it! I'm no robber. He may keep all he has."

"Uff! I do not comprehend your action! He would have been wiser."

The other redskins too did not seem to understand. The looks they sent Davy showed clearly how shocked they were by his behavior. None of them would have given up his right even if a hundred lives were at stake. Red Fish slinked away. He too could not understand why the paleface did not scalp and kill him. He was ashamed of having lost and thought it best to make himself invisible.

There was gratitude after all. The squaw approached Long Davy and shook his hand, raised also her children's hands and stammered a few barely audible words whose meaning Davy did not catch but could easily divine.

Now Namboh-avaht, Big Foot, approached the chief and asked whether he could begin his contest against his white opponent. Big Wolf nodded and together they walked to the designated location near the two stakes. A new circle formed; into its midst the chief led Big Foot. Old Shatterhand accompanied Fat Jemmy. He had his reasons for doing so: to watch that no cunning came to bear against his friend.

The two fighters bared their upper torsos and stood with their backs pressed against each other. Jemmy's head did not quite reach the redskin's shoulder. Big Wolf used a lasso to tie the two together. The strap went around the redskin's hips but around Jemmy's chest. By accident but to Jemmy's advantage, the lasso's ends happened to come together at the fat one's chest where the chief had to make a slip knot.

"Now you don't need to cut the strap, only to release the knot," Old Shatterhand whispered to Jemmy in German.

Each received a knife in his right hand and the drama could begin. When the chief stepped back, Old Shatterhand did so too.

"Stand fast, Jemmy, and don't let yourself be thrown!" shouted Hobble-Frank, also in German. "You know that if he kills you, I'll be forever widowed and waifed, and you wouldn't want to do this to me. Let yourself be kicked, then flip him right over!"

Big Foot too received encouraging words. His response was, "My name is not Red Fish, the loser. In the blink of an eye, I shall crush the little toad hanging on my back."

Jemmy said nothing. Serious in his gaze, he actually looked puny behind the big redskin. Cautiously, he looked backwards to see his opponent's footwork. It was not in his interest to begin the contest but rather to wait for the Indian's first move.

The redskin stood silent and motionless for some time. Counting on a sudden attack, he was hoping to take his opponent by surprise. This strategy did not succeed. When he finally and quite casually thrust a foot backwards to trip Jemmy, he received such a kick against his other leg that he nearly toppled.

Attack and counterattack followed. The redskin was stronger, but Jemmy was more wary and deliberate. Because of his failures, the Indian became ever angrier. But the more he raged and kicked backwards, the calmer Jemmy appeared. As the fight became drawn out longer and longer, the spectators began to lose interest since neither man seemed to have the least advantage over the other. But the end was soon to come because of a prearranged trick of the Ute's.

Big Foot had intended to make his opponent less wary by demonstrating predictable behavior. Jemmy was supposed to think that there would be no other type of attack. Suddenly, the Indian reached for the lasso, pulled hard so that he gained some room in front of him for a turn --- but not quite.

Had his plan succeeded his front would have faced the white's back and he could have forced Jemmy to the ground. But Jemmy, the slyboots, was prepared. Hobble-Frank, too, had noticed the cunning intent of the redskin and shouted to his friend, "Throw him, he's turning!"

"I know!" answered Jemmy breathlessly.

The moment he spoke these words, and while the Indian was in the middle of his turn with no firm hold, Jemmy swiftly bent down, pulled his opponent onto his back and released the slipknot. The lasso gave way. The redskin, completely off guard, somersaulted onto the ground and lost his knife. Lightning-fast, Jemmy knelt on his foe's chest, his left hand gripping the Indian's throat, the knife in his right hand poised above Big Foot's heart.

Although Big Foot never intended to surrender, the somersault had so knocked the wind out of him, and Jemmy's eyes sparkled so close and threateningly in front of his face, that he could only remain motionless. Jemmy turned triumphantly to the chief asking, "Do you concede he has lost?"

"No! Never!" answered Big Wolf, stepping closer.

"Why not?" inquired Old Shatterhand, also approaching.

"He has not been defeated."

"I claim the opposite; he has been defeated."

"That is not true, the lasso opened."

"That was Big Foot's own mistake. He turned and opened the lasso."

"Nobody saw such a thing. Let him up! He is undefeated and the fight must continue."

"No, Jemmy, don't do it!" demanded the hunter. "As soon as I order it or if he moves, kill him!"

In a tone of utter outrage, the chief straightened up to ask, "Who is in command here, you or I?"

"You and I; both of us."

"Who says so?"

"I do. You're the chief of your people and I the leader of mine. You and I, both of us, entered into an agreement on the conditions of the fight. Whoever does not respect them has broken the contract and is a liar and a cheat."

Nearly apoplectic, Big Wolf screamed, "You dare talk to me like this in front of all my braves?"

"It's not a question of daring. I'm telling the truth and demand your faithfulness and honesty. If I'm no longer permitted to speak, my Rifle of Death will talk."

The butt of his rifle had been resting on the ground. He now lifted the repeating rifle in a very threatening way.

"Then say what you want," muttered the chief, suddenly subdued.

"You agreed that the two were supposed to fight back to back?"

"I said it."

"But Big Foot lifted the lasso and tried to turn. Is that correct? You must have seen it!"

"Yes," the chief admitted reluctantly. His braves, after all, had witnessed the same thing.

"And the one who would lie beneath the other was to die," Old Shatterhand continued inexorably. Do you remember the rule?"

"I know it."

"Well then, who is underneath?"

"Big Foot, but he ...."

Old Shatterhand pressed on. "Who, then, is the defeated?"

"Sadly, it must be the brave," the chief answered under compulsion, since Old Shatterhand held his carbine's muzzle close to his chest.

"Do you object to anything?"

With these words the famous hunter's eyes focused so sharply and intensely on the chief that despite his giant build, Big Wolf felt small and gave the response that Shatterhand demanded. "No, the vanquished belongs to the victor. Tell your man that he can kill mine."

"I need not tell him that. He knows it already, but won't do so."

"Is he also giving him his life?"

"On that score, we'll decide later. Until then, Big Foot is to be tied with the same lasso he tried to free himself from."

"Why tie him up? He will not escape."

"Will you answer for it?"

"Yes."

"With what?"

"With my entire property."

"That's sufficient. He may go where he wishes, but must return to his victor after the next two fights are over."

Jemmy now got up and put on his shirt and jacket. Big Foot too jumped up and pushed through the circle of redskins, who were unsure whether to show him contempt or not.

The Utes had never before experienced how a paleface, not even in possession of his complete freedom, could deal with their chief as Old Shatterhand did. The hunter was in their power, yet they did not dare refuse his demands. Such was the strength of Old Shatterhand's personality and the effect of the prestige with which history and legend had surrounded him.

In any case, the chief was frustrated and angry that two of his best warriors had been defeated by opponents who had appeared far inferior. His look now fell on Hobble-Frank and his mood began to improve. This little fellow would surely be unable to keep up with Leaping Elk. In this instance, the redskins would certainly gain a victory.

He signaled Leaping Elk to approach, led him to Old Shatterhand, and said, "This warrior has the speed of the wind and has never been beaten by another runner. Do you wish to advise your companion to concede without humiliating himself?"

"Most certainly not!"

"He would die quickly and without shame."

"Isn't it a greater shame to concede without a fight? Didn't you also think Red Fish invincible and didn't Big Foot brag that he would squash his opponent, the little toad, in the blink of an eye? Do you expect Leaping Elk to be more fortunate than those who began so proudly and slinked away so humbly and miserably at the end?"

"Pah!" exclaimed Leaping Elk, unfazed by all the talk. "I run as fast as the deer!"

Old Shatterhand looked him over more closely. Yes, he had the build of a good runner. His legs were certainly strong enough to cover long distances without tiring. But the volume of his brains did not appear to be in accord with the length of his legs. He had veritably ape-like features, but apparently without any of the smarts of these animals.

Hobble-Frank also approached to peer at Leaping Elk.

"What do you think of him?" Old Shatterhand asked, sotto voce.

Frank answered in like fashion. "This is one true dumb bub of Meissen, who stands in front of the grease drops and can't find the broth," the little one answered.

"You think you can take him on?"

"Well! Concerning his legs, he's three times better than I. But I hope my head's better than his. Let's find out first where we're going to run. I may run better with my head than he with his legs."

Old Shatterhand once more turned to Big Wolf. "Has it been decided where the run is to take place?"

"Yes. Come along. I shall show you."

Old Shatterhand and Hobble-Frank followed him through the circle of redskins. Leaping Elk remained behind. He already knew the terms of the contest. The chief pointed south and said to Frank, "Do you see the tree halfway between here and the forest?"

"Yes."

"You must run to the tree, circle it thrice, and whoever returns first is the winner."

Hobble-Frank measured the distance, also the southern terrain behind, then asked in English, which he spoke more purely than German, colored by his Saxonian dialect, "But I expect honesty on both sides!"

"Are you saying we are dishonest?" the chief responded sharply.

"Yes."

"Beware! Another such impudence and I will knock you down."

"Try it! My revolver's bullet is far faster than your fist. But consider. Earlier, didn't Big Foot turn although it was forbidden? Was that honest?"

"It was not dishonest, but cunning."

"Ah! Then such cunning is permitted?"

The chief contemplated his reply. If he said yes, he defended Big Foot's behavior, and just maybe there might be a reason for Leaping Elk to need a ruse as well. These palefaces were performing better than they had been given credit for. Maybe the little chap was a good runner after all. Maybe it was advisable to keep a ruse as a last resort for his Ute champion. His answer came. "Cunning is not cheating. Why should it be forbidden?"

"Does it release me from meeting all the other conditions?"

"No. Those must be exactly maintained."

"Then I'm in agreement and ready for the run. Where do we start?"

"I shall push my spear into the ground to mark the start and finish of the run."

He left to fetch his spear, leaving the whites standing by themselves.

"You have an idea?" asked Old Shatterhand.

"Yes. Does it show?"

"Indeed, because you're wearing this smile."

"It's actually a big laugh. The chief wanted to hurt me by allowing the option of a ruse. But to the contrary, he did me a great service."

"How so?"

"You'll see in a moment. What kind of tree is it we're to run around three times?"

"A beech, I believe."

"And look farther to the left; there's another tree, but nearly twice as far. What kind is that?"

"A spruce."

"Fine. Then to which tree are we to run?"

"To the beech."

"Ah! But I'll run toward the spruce."

"Frank! Are you becoming unhinged?"

"No. I'll run with my head to the beech, but with my feet to the spruce, although it's twice the distance."

"For what purpose?"

"You''ll see and be happy about it. I think I'm not mistaken in my expectations. Looking at this Leaping Elk's upstairs compartment, I don't think I'm making a mistake."

"Be careful, Frank! It's your life."

"Well. If it were only my life, I wouldn't even exert myself. If I lost, I might nevertheless stay alive. Since Big Foot is condemned and you'll put the chief down. I could be traded for them both. But I'm not afraid for my life; it's honor and reputation I'm talking about. Is there to be written in the fourth quarter of the nineteenth century that I, Hobble-Frank from Moritzburg, was overcome by such an Indian Merino face? That I will not accept!"

"But tell me your intentions. Maybe I can give you some additional advice!"

"Thanks, but no thanks! Advice I've given myself aplenty and shall exploit the invention myself. But tell me only one thing: what's the word for 'spruce' in the Ute language?"

"Ovomb."

"Ovomb? Funny name! And how would one say the short sentence: 'To yonder spruce'?"

"Intsch ovomb."

"That's short. Only two words. I'm not going to forget those."

"What's has 'intsch ovomb' got to do with your plan?"

"It's the guiding star for my run. Quiet now, the chief's returning!"

Big Wolf returned, pushed his spear into the soft grassy ground and declared, "The death run is to begin from here!"

"How are we to be dressed?" asked Hobble-Frank.

"As you like."

Frank dropped all of his clothing except for his pants; Leaping Elk wore only his loincloth. The Ute looked at his adversary with a face intended to express disdain, but presented only the image of God-given feeble-mindedness.

"Frank, make an effort!" warned Jemmy. "Remember that Davy and I both won!"

"Don't you fear!" the little man comforted him. "If you don't yet know that I have legs, you'll now see their protuberance."

The chief clapped his hands. Sounding a shrill scream, Leaping Elk flew away, leaving Frank as expected well behind him. The entire camp population had gathered once again to watch the race. Everyone's opinion was that after only three or four seconds, the run had been decided. Leaping Elk was already far ahead and with each stride opening the gap between them. The redskins were jubilant. It would have been madness for anyone to suggest that Frank could catch up and overtake the red man.

It was marvelous how the little one moved his legs. They were almost not visible so fast was he, and yet to the close observer, it seemed as if he was not running at his best but could do better if he wanted to.

The Indians became unruly, shouting exclamations of disdain and schadenfreude, laughed and truly thought they had good reason for it. The reason was this: the beech stood alone in the midst of the grassland, not quite two thousand feet distant. To the left of it, but at least another thousand feet farther on, stood the aforementioned spruce. Now that the two runners had put some distance between themselves and the spectators, it was clear that the little man was not running towards the beech, but had taken the spruce as his destination. He ran as fast as his short legs permitted, which looked so ridiculous that one could forgive the Indians their self-assurance.

"Your companion misunderstood me," said the chief to Old Shatterhand.

"Not at all."

"But he is running for the spruce!"

"Yes, indeed."

"Then Leaping Elk will win twice as fast!"

"No. As a matter of fact, he's going to lose!"

"Lose?" Big Wolf asked, astounded.

"It's a ruse and you allowed it yourself."

Uff, uff! Uff, uff!" the other redskins shouted in dismay when the chief explained Old Shatterhand's remarks. Their laughter fell silent and their suspense doubled, no, increased tenfold.

In short order, Leaping Elk reached the beech. He had to circle it three times. On his first turn, looking back, he saw his opponent running in an entirely different direction three hundred paces away. He stopped, befuddled, and stared at the Moritzburger.

The whole tribe could see from their vantage point that the little one was pointing to the distant spruce, but could not hear what he was shouting.

"Intsch ovomb, intsch ovomb - to the spruce, to the spruce!" he called to the Indian.

Leaping Elk considered if he had heard right. His thoughts did not extend further than the directions given by his chief. Had he misunderstood Big Wolf that the halfway mark was not the beech but the spruce? Already the little one was ahead, far ahead. There was no time for further consideration or hesitation. This run was for life! The redskin left the beech and sprinted towards the spruce. In a moment, he flew past his adversary without looking back.

This caused quite a stir among the Utes. They kicked up a row as if everybody's life were at stake. Greater though was the whites' joy, particularly Fat Jemmy's, who saw his comrade's ingenious trick working out so well.

As soon as Leaping Elk had passed him, Hobble-Frank spun around and raced towards the beech. Arriving there, he circled it three, four, five times, then speedily resumed his return run. Four-fifths of the distance to the spear he covered at high speed, then stopped to look back toward the spruce. There stood Leaping Elk, unmoving. Obviously, it wasn't possible to see his face at this distance, but it was clear enough that he was standing there like a statue. He wasn't sure what had happened and his mind wasn't bright enough to guess how gloriously he had been led by the nose.

Hobble-Frank was satisfied to the utmost and continued at a stroll for the rest of the race. The Indians greeted him with dark scowls, which perturbed him not at all. He walked up to Big Wolf, clapped him on the shoulder and asked, "Now, old house, who's won?"

"Whoever completed the conditions," the redskin answered between his teeth.

"That's me!"

"You." Big Wolf said, glowering.

"Yes. Haven't I been at the beech?"

"I saw it."

"And was back first!"

"Yes."

"Did I not circle the tree five times instead of only three?"

"Why two more?"

"For the love of Leaping Elk. After he had circled the beech once, he ran away and I completed the missing circuits for him, so the beech can't complain."

"Why did he leave the beech to run towards the spruce?"

"I meant to ask him, but he passed me so quickly that I didn't have time. When he returns, you can ask him yourself."

"Why did you run at first toward the spruce?"

"Because I thought it was a fir. Old Shatterhand had called the tree a spruce and I wanted to find out who was right."

"Then why did you not run all the way to it?"

"Because Leaping Elk ran there. I can just as well learn from him who's wrong, Old Shatterhand or me."

He said all this in the most unctuous and unaffected tone possible. The chief's innards boiled. The words came hissing from his lips, as he demanded, "Did you cheat Leaping Elk?"

"Cheat him? Beware! I will knock you down," the little man exclaimed angrily, using the chief's own words.

"Or did you use a ruse?"

"A ruse? What for?"

"To divert Leaping Elk from the beech to the spruce."

"That would've been an unworthy ruse that I'd have been ashamed of. A man running for his life wouldn't let himself be led so far from his assigned destination. If he did such a thing, it would show that he had no brains and that members of his tribe ought to be ashamed not to have trained and educated him better. Only a fool would choose such a man to fight for his life. I can't comprehend your presumptions, since by them you insult your own honor."

Big Wolf's hand itched to lunge for the knife at his belt. In his fury, he would have liked to knife his own witless brave and the cunning, scheming Hobble-Frank simultaneously. However, the little man's words did not truly offer him sufficient provocation for such a deed and he had to swallow his rage.

Hobble-Frank walked to his companions where he was greeted and congratulated with quiet but hearty joy.

"So, I also have won. Are you satisfied with me?" he asked Jemmy, referring to the fat one's earlier exhortation.

"Indeed! You did really well. It was a true masterpiece."

"Really? Then put it into your memory at page one hundred thirty six and always open it when doubts arise in you with regards to my mental facility! Ah, here comes Leaping Elk at last, but skulking, not leaping. He seems to have a bad conscience and keeps to one side as if expecting a thrashing. Look at his face! And I was supposed to measure myself against this Confucius! Yes, it's not the legs that make it in a competitive run but mostly the brains."

Leaping Elk wanted to melt into the landscape, but the chief called him over and bellowed, "Who has won?"

"The paleface," was the tremulous response.

"Idiot! Why did you run for the spruce?"

"The paleface lied to me. He said the spruce was the goal."

"And you believed him? I told you the beech!"

Old Shatterhand translated to Hobble-Frank that Leaping Elk had called him a liar. Turning to the chief, the crafty little man explained everything in a most disingenuous manner. "I'm supposed to have lied? That I told Leaping Elk the spruce was the goal? That's not true. I saw him standing by the beech. He gazed at me in surprise and seemed to fall apart worrying about what I might have up my sleeve. I felt pity for the poor devil and shouted at him 'Intsch ovomb!' By that, I made him know that I was on my way to yonder spruce. Why he then ran in my place to the spruce I can't imagine. He may not know why himself. Howgh!"

Old Shatterhand smirked inside at how the ironic little conjurer employed the Indian expression of 'howgh' -- I have spoken. It only increased the chief's choler and he shouted, "Yes, you have spoken and are finished, but I am not yet finished with you and shall deal with you later. But in spite of all, I must keep my word. Life, scalp and property of Leaping Elk are yours."

"No, no!" Frank parried. "I don't want anything. Keep him. You may need him again should it come to another race for a white man's life."

Among the redskins, one could hear an angry rumble as the chief hissed at him, "You paleface who speaks with forked tongue may now still spit poisonous words. Later, though, you will beg for mercy that will echo to the sky. Each member of your body shall die a separate death and your soul will part piecemeal. Your death will take many moons."

"What can you do to me?' laughed Frank. "I've won and am free."

"There is still one who has not been victorious -- Old Shatterhand. Just wait; soon he will lie in the dust before me begging for his life. I shall trade his for yours; then you are mine."

"Err not!" warned Old Shatterhand. "I'm yet to lie at your feet. And should you succeed at the deed no other has yet accomplished, I would not trade my life for that of any other."

"Just bide your time until later!" counseled Big Wolf between clenched teeth. "Presently you are not injured. But when you feel the pain that now is awaiting you, your pride will be humbled and your courage will disappear. Then, yes then, you will offer a thousand lives for your own if you had them! Come along; we will now have the last, greatest and most decisive conflict of all!"

The redskins accompanied their chief in a disorderly fashion. The whites followed slowly.

"Did I provoke him too much?" asked Hobble-Frank, concerned.

"No," responded Old Shatterhand. "It's well that their warrior's pride must bend for once even to a little fellow like you. Obviously, if Big Wolf should kill me, you would also be lost, for they would attack you at once. But neither can we trust them in the more likely event that I win. Without any specific reason to think so, I'm convinced that the Utes won't let us go peacefully. They decided on the individual fights because they were certain we'd all fall to their braves. Now that this has proved faulty, they'll think of something else. The main thing is to impress them. For now, that's kept them in line and will continue to be useful to us. That's why I'm happy that you talked so fearlessly to Big Wolf, you, the midget to the Goliath. Although he ranted and raged, he's learned that even the smallest of us doesn't show the slightest fear. It will now be important to make him small before his own people. And that'll be my task. It looks to me as if they want to keep us as hostages, an intention we must thwart, since our lives wouldn't be safe for a single moment."

During Old Shatterhand's explanations, the foursome had continued along until they arrived at the circle formed by the teepees and wigwams. At its center, preparations had been made for the forthcoming, most long-awaited duel.

From between a pile of many hundredweight of rocks a strong pole rose, to which two lassos were attached. The camp's entire population had gathered around this setting to witness the spectacle. Old Shatterhand noticed that the braves were all fully armed, a situation not conducive to calming his concerns. He decided to object to this and stepped into the circle where Big Wolf was waiting, cockily posed as if sure of victory. The chief pointed to the two lassos and said, "You see these lassos? Do you know what they are for?"

"I can imagine," the hunter responded. "We're to be tied to them for the fight."

"You perceived it then. One end of each lasso is attached to the post; its other end will be tied around each of us."

"Why?"

"So that we move only in a narrow circle and cannot flee."

"An unnecessary precaution for I'll not flee. I know its actual reason though. You think I have greater agility and dexterity than strength, compared to you, and by tying me you can prevent me from applying this superior capability. Let it be so; it's all the same to me! What will be our weapons?"

"Each will get a knife in his left hand and a tomahawk in his right. We will use these weapons until one of us is dead."

Clearly the chief had chosen this type of duel believing that fighting Indian-style with Indian weapons put all the advantage on his side. But the hunter responded quietly, "I am agreed."

"Agreed? With your death? I am certain to win."

"Time will tell!"

"First, let us compare our strength. See whether you can do this!" Big Wolf said.

He swaggered over to one of the huge rocks, bent down, seized it and lifted it high. Possessing an enormous strength, he knew that none of his braves could have done the same. Old Shatterhand bent down to lift it too, but seemed unable to raise it for more than a few inches off the ground despite a mighty effort. A contented 'ahh' sounded from the circle of Indians. But the little Saxon said to Jemmy, "He's just putting one over on them to make the chief feel secure. I know for sure that he could lift that rock above his head and toss it ten paces away. Let's just wait for the perplexion. The redskin will get the shock of his life."

Big Wolf was of a different opinion. He had wanted to intimidate the famous hunter with his demonstration of strength and was convinced he'd succeeded. Indulgently he said, "You see what you can expect? The palefaces pray when they face sure death. I permit you to speak with your Manitou before we fight."

"That's not necessary," answered Old Shatterhand. "I'll speak with him when my soul will meet him. You're a strong man and for this duel I hope you'll only rely on your strength!"

"I shall do that. Who else would help me?"

"Your warriors. It looks as if they think you may fall victim to me. Why otherwise did they arm themselves as if girding for battle?"

"Are your companions not armed?"

"They are. But we'll deposit all our weapons in our teepee. That's the paleface custom. White warriors' pride doesn't allow the smallest of cunning acts. Am I to believe you're not equally brave?"

285

"You insult me!" the redskin shouted angrily. "I don't need others' assistance. My warriors will take all weapons to their dwellings if yours do the same."

"Well! You'll see us do it at once. I'll keep only my knife."

He handed his rifles to Hobble-Frank; Jemmy and Davy did the same. During the exchange, he said to Frank in German, "Show that you're carrying everything into the teepee, but then shove the weapons out under the back when nobody's looking. Being focused on the duel, the braves will pay no attention to you. Then crawl under the back of the teepee yourself and get our horses ready."

"What are you saying to this man?" demanded Big Wolf. "Why do you talk with him in a language we do not understand?"

"Because it's the only language he's fluent in."

"What did you tell him?"

"That he is to carry these items into the teepee and guard them."

"Why guard them? Do you expect us to steal them?"

"No. But I don't like to leave my magic rifle unprotected. A misfortune might easily occur. You know it can easily discharge and hit a red man."

"Yes, I did see that. Then have it guarded. Once I have killed you, I shall bury it deeply or toss it into the lake to render it harmless."

On their chief's orders, all the warriors handed their weapons to the squaws to carry to the dwellings. Hobble-Frank left too. Big Wolf took off his shirt so as not to be hindered by it. Old Shatterhand did not. If he won, having to dress again would mean a loss of time that could easily turn disastrous. The women returned quickly, not wanting to miss anything. All eyes were on the inside of the circle, no one thought of little Frank.

"Your condition is met," Big Wolf said. "Shall we begin?"

"One more question. What will happen to my companions if you defeat me?"

"They will remain our prisoners."

"But they fought for their freedom and should be free to go where they want!"

"They shall. But first they must stay as hostages."

"That's contrary to our agreement, but I won't waste another word on it. So now, Big Wolf, what happens if I kill you?"

"That cannot happen," the redskin shouted arrogantly.

"But we must nevertheless consider this a possibility."

"Well then! If you defeat me, you are free to go."

"And no one will prevent us?"

"Not even a single brave!"

"Then I'm satisfied and we can begin."

"Yes, begin. Let us be tied. Here is your tomahawk."

Two tomahawks had been retained when the other weapons were removed. The chief, already equipped with a knife, took one of them and passed it to Old Shatterhand. The hunter took it, examined it, then tossed it in a high, wide arc far away from the circle.

"What are you doing?" the chief asked in perplexity.

"I discarded the tomahawk because it's no good. Yours, I can see, is well made, the other one would've broken at the first blow."

"Are you saying I gave it to you treacherously?"

"I'm saying that it would've hurt me more than it helped, nothing else!"

However, Old Shatterhand knew very well that he had intentionally been given an inferior weapon. Despite the thick coat of paint covering the chief's face, the sneering wrinkles were evident when the Ute remarked, "It was your right to toss the tomahawk away but you will not receive another one."

"That won't be necessary. I'll fight with my knife. This I can rely upon."

"Uff! You are insane! My first blow with the tomahawk will kill you. I have it and my knife, and you are not as strong as I."

"Big Wolf, did you take my earlier jesting behavior seriously? I simply didn't want to intimidate you. But since you persist in your bragging, judge now who's the stronger."

Old Shatterhand bent down and selected a boulder far larger and heavier than the one Big Wolf had lifted. He raised it first to his midriff, swung it overhead, held it there for a few moments, then tossed it effortlessly a distance of nine or ten feet.

"Do the same!" he challenged the redskin.

"Uff, uff, uff!" all the Utes marveled. The chief did not respond right away. He looked from the hunter to the rock and back again. He was more than surprised and it took him some time to regain his composure. "Do you think you can frighten the chief of the Utes? Do not! I shall kill you and take your scalp, even if the duel will last until the sun sets in the west!"

"It won't take that long. Realistically, it'll be over in a few minutes," responded Old Shatterhand smilingly. "But my scalp you will not take!"

"I will, because the scalp belongs to the victor. Tie us!"

The order was issued to two braves who now tied one lasso around the chief's waist and the other around Old Shatterhand's, then both braves quickly stepped back. Tied to the post the combatants could circle only in a narrow radius. Big Wolf gripped his tomahawk in his right hand, the knife in his left. Old Shatterhand's Bowie knife was in his right fist.

Big Wolf's plan was to drive his opponent around the circle and come close enough to deliver a blow or a slash. He had to admit to himself that he wasn't superior in strength to his adversary. But the weapons were unequal in his opinion and he was fully convinced he had the upper hand, particularly since the hunter was holding his knife totally wrong. Old Shatterhand had grasped the knife so that the blade faced up instead of down. This made it impossible to stab downwards from above. The redskin gloated secretly about this mistake but watched his opponent's every move so that nothing would escape him.

Shatterhand too watched closely. He had no intention of allowing himself to be chased around the circle. Attack was not on his mind, but to await attack. The first encounter would decide everything. It all depended on how Big Wolf was planning to use his tomahawk. If he held it in his hand to strike a blow, nothing was to be feared. If he threw it, however, maximum attention and caution was called for. The two of them were standing too close together for Old Shatterhand to evade a throw.

Fortunately, the chief did not intend to risk a throw. If he missed, his tomahawk would be lost to him as a weapon.

Thus they stood, stock still for minutes --- five, then ten, neither moving, bodies twitching, each eying the other. The redskin audience tried to fire up the opponents, some even voicing disapproval of the standoff.

Impatiently, Big Wolf began shouting insults, hoping to provoke his enemy to attack. Old Shatterhand said nothing. His response, when it came, was astonishing. He simply sat down on the ground in an unaffected manner as if he were in the most peaceful company. However, his muscles and sinews were tensed and ready to leap into action.

The chief viewed this behavior as an act of disdain, an insult, while in fact it was nothing but a tactic meant to distract him into carelessness. It served its purpose well. Big Wolf decided he could easily finish off his sitting opponent if he took advantage of the opportunity quickly. Shouting a war cry, he threw himself on Old Shatterhand, tomahawk raised for a deadly strike. Already the excited Indians visualized the strike hitting home; already their lips opened to shout out exclamations of joy. But their joy was short-lived.

Old Shatterhand sprang up sideways, the deliberately wrongly-held knife flung upwards to knock Big Wolf's blow awry. The chief's descending fist was impaled on the flashing blade; his tomahawk fell impotently to the ground. A quick smash by Old Shatterhand against the redskin's left arm shocked the knife from his hand as well. Then the hunter, in a blindingly fast movement, delivered a devastating blow with the handle of his Bowie knife just above the heart of his enemy. The redskin dropped like a stone and lay inert and unmoving. Old Shatterhand brandished his knife in the air and shouted, "Now the paleface asks the Ute braves, 'Who is the victor?' "

Awed and stunned, no onlooker dared say a word. Even those who had thought their chief's defeat possible had not imagined how quickly it could happen. The tribe was frozen motionless.

"Big Wolf himself said that the loser's scalp belongs to the victor," Old Shatterhand continued. "His scalp is therefore my property, but I disdain it. I'm a Christian, a friend of the red man and give your chief his life. I may have crushed one of his ribs, but he's not dead. My red brothers may look after him; I shall go to my teepee."

He cut himself free from the lasso and strode away. No one attempted to prevent him nor Davy and Jemmy from leaving. The Ute braves wanted to determine Big Wolf's condition and everyone pressed forward. The hunters reached their teepee undisturbed. Behind it lay their weapons, with Hobble-Frank holding the horses.

"Mount up quickly and let's be off!" Old Shatterhand said urgently. "We can talk later."

Seizing their weapons, they all swung into their saddles and rode off, at first slowly, finding cover behind the wigwams and teepees. But outside the camp, posted guards spotted the riders and raised a great war cry. Shots rang out, whizzing past the heads of the escapees. The hunters spurred their horses into a full gallop, realizing that the guards' shouting and rifle fire had drawn the attention of the whole camp. Redskins literally flowed from between the camp dwellings, sending out a satanic howl that echoed again and again from the surrounding mountains.

The hunters galloped in a straight line across the plain towards the point where the mountain brook debouched into the lake. Old Shatterhand was familiar enough with the area to know that the brook's valley offered the best chance of escape. He knew too that the Utes would immediately take up the pursuit, so he and his companions needed to find a rocky area where it would be difficult for the redskins to track them.

13. Old Shatterhand's Noble-Mindedness

It was morning when a group of horsemen advanced along the brook which the Utes with their captives had followed the previous evening. At its head rode Old Firehand and Aunt Droll. Behind came Humpy-Bill and Gunstick-Uncle with the English lord and the other whites, fresh from their adventures at the Eagle Tail. They had made their way to the mountains heading for Silver Lake. In Denver, Butler, the engineer, had joined them with his daughter Ellen. He had traveled directly there from his brother's farm, since he didn't want to expose her to a renewed encounter with the rovers. The girl had not wanted to be separated from her father and insisted on accompanying him into the wilderness. She sat in a kind of chair carried between two small but tough Indian ponies.

Winnetou was not to be seen, riding ahead as scout, a task he excelled in. By coincidence, their path led them to the forest and glade where Old Shatterhand and his companions had encountered the Utes. The two leaders were experienced and knowledgeable enough to read their tracks. They had deduced that some whites --- not knowing they were Old Shatterhand and his group --- had been taken captive by the Indians. They decided to follow in case help was needed.

None of Old Firehand's party was aware that the Utes had taken up the tomahawk. Both Winnetou and Old Firehand thought that peace reigned with this tribe and both were convinced that they would receive a friendly reception. Perhaps they would even be able to put in a good word for the captives.

Where the redskins had set up camp was unknown to them, but they knew the lake, and since its surroundings were very well suited for a campsite, they expected to find the Utes there. Despite their expectation of a welcoming reception, it would have been against western caution to show themselves without having reconnoitered a little beforehand. Accordingly, Winnetou had scouted ahead. Just as the group reached the place where the brook's banks widened and expanded into a plain, the Apache returned. He arrived at a full gallop and waved from afar for them to stop. This was not a good sign. When Winnetou arrived, Old Firehand asked, "My brother is warning us. Has he found the Utes?"

"I saw them and their camp."

"And Winnetou couldn't show himself?"

"No, because they have taken up the tomahawk."

"How could you tell?"

"By the colors they were painted with; also by their numbers. That many red warriors assemble only for war and great hunts. Since it is not the time for the buffalo hunt, it can only be the tomahawk which has called so many together."

"How many are there?"

"Winnetou could not see clearly. Three hundred may have been standing by the lake, and the teepees may have held many more."

"At the lake? That many? What was going on there? Was there perhaps an execution? Did they throw the whites into the lake and drown them?"

Old Firehand's presumption wasn't too far off the mark. The Apache had observed the Utes at the moment that the swimming contest got under way. Winnetou responded confidently as if he had stood by the lake and observed everything. "No, no one was to be drowned, but a life-or-death swimming contest was in progress."

"You have reason to think so?"

"Yes. Winnetou knows his red brothers' customs; Old Firehand is also familiar with them so he will agree. The Utes bear war colors and consider the whites who are in their midst as enemies. They are out to kill them. But the red man will not let his foe die quickly; he slowly tortures him to death. He will not cast him into the water to drown him, but confronts him with a superior adversary against whom he has to swim for his life. Since the Ute can swim faster than the paleface, the white is doomed to lose. They let him swim only to delay his dying and to prolong his dread of death."

"That's correct and I agree. We identified the tracks of four whites and later two more, making it six altogether. They won't all swim but each will be forced to fight in a different way. We're going to have to hurry if we're to save them."

"If my white brother attempts such a thing, he will only speed up his own death."

"We must dare to try. I bank on the fact that I was never an enemy of the Utes."

"You cannot rely on that. Once they have taken up the tomahawk, they treat even their best friend as an enemy and they will make no exception for you."

"But the chiefs would protect me!"

"No. The Utes are loyal and honest, but cannot be deterred once they are on the war path. Not even a chief of theirs has the influence to protect you from his braves. We cannot show ourselves."

"But you may show yourself!"

"No, because I do not know whether they have not also taken up the tomahawk against other red nations."

"Then there is no hope for the lives of the six whites!"

"My brother should not believe this. I have two reasons for speaking differently."

"The first is?"

"First, I said that the captives of the red men will only die slowly. It is still morning and we have time to observe the camp. We may learn more than we know now and can then make a better decision."

"And second?"

The Apache's face took on a sly expression as he answered, "There is a man among the palefaces who will not allow himself and his companions to be killed easily."

"Who is it?"

"Old Shatterhand."

"What?" the hunter exclaimed. "Old Shatterhand, whom you wanted to meet at Silver Lake? Could he be here already?"

"Old Shatterhand is as punctual as the sun or a star in the sky."

"Did you see him?"

"No."

"How can you know he's there then?"

"I have known it since yesterday."

"Without telling me?"

"Silence is often better than talk. Had I mentioned yesterday whose rifle had spoken at the glade, you would not have remained calm and would have rushed ahead."

"His rifle spoke? How do you know?" demanded Old Firehand.

"When we searched the glade and its environs, I found a small tree peppered with bullet holes. The bullets were from Old Shatterhand's magic rifle. I know this for certain. He wanted to frighten the red men who now have respect for his rifle."

"You should have shown me the tree! Hmm! If Old Shatterhand is among the whites, we need not fear for them. I know him. I know what he's able to accomplish and what respect the Indians have for him. What shall we do? What are you suggesting?"

"My friends must follow me now in single file so that the Utes cannot count how many we are if they discover our tracks. Howgh!"

He turned his horse to the right and rode off without asking whether Old Firehand agreed and without looking back to see if he was indeed being followed.

The creek's banks had broadened. Hills on both sides enclosed the valley plain and the lake. The forest descended from the hilltops to the plain, petering out to open brush at the sloping bottom. Taking cover behind the bushes and trees, Winnetou followed the right slope bordering the northern side of the plain to arrive at the mountain from which the brook flowed.

Close behind, Old Firehand's group bypassed the plain from its eastern to its western point until they reached the brook a few hundred paces upslope from the lake. From under the trees they could observe all the camp events. They dismounted but kept the reins of their horses in hand until Winnetou had searched the area and reported nothing suspicious. No Ute had come to this place. Now the animals could be hitched to nearby saplings and everyone could rest on the soft moss. The place was literally made for watching the camp in comfort from above.

They could see the Utes standing outside the camp to the south. Then they noticed that two men had separated from the crowd and were sprinting southward. Old Firehand took his scope and said excitedly, "It's a race -- between a red and a white man! The redskin's far ahead and is going to win. The white is a very small fellow."

He handed the scope to the Apache. Barely had Winnetou spied the smaller runner in the scope when he exclaimed, "Uff! That is Hobble-Frank! This little hero has to run for his life and will never be able to overtake the red man."

"The Hobble-Frank you told us about?" asked Old Firehand. "We cannot just put our hands in our pockets but must come to some kind of decision!"

"Not yet," the Apache countered. "There is no danger yet. Old Shatterhand is with them."

Trees obstructed the view of some of the terrain below so that the watchers could not follow every part of the contest. The two runners had disappeared to the right. Everyone waited for their reappearance, convinced that the redskin would show up first. What a surprise it was when instead the little man appeared, walking leisurely as if on a stroll.

"Frank is first!" Old Firehand said. "How's that possible?"

"By cunning," answered Winnetou. "He has won and we will learn how he accomplished it. Listen to the Utes' angry screams! They are leaving in a fury to return to camp. Look, there are now four palefaces and I know them all."

"Me too," said Droll. It's Old Shatterhand, Long Davy, Fat Jemmy and little Hobble-Frank."

The mention of these names caused a stir. Some knew one or several of the four men personally; others had heard plenty about them to pique their interest. Comments flew back and forth until Winnetou said to Old Firehand, "Does my brother understand now that I was right? Our friends down there still carry their weapons. They cannot be in danger yet."

"For the time being, yes, but it can change quickly. I suggest we ride in openly."

"My brother may do so, but Winnetou thinks it is not a good idea. I, however, will stay here," the Apache answered firmly. "Old Shatterhand knows the situation, also what he is doing. We, though, do not and may disrupt the execution of his plans. Better my brother stays here. I shall approach the camp as closely as possible to find out what is going on."

Retaining the telescope, he disappeared between the trees. After half an hour, he returned and reported, "There is a duel going on in the midst of the camp. The Utes were surrounding it, so closely that I could not see the combatants but I saw Hobble-Frank. He has covertly brought their horses behind a teepee and has saddled them. The palefaces plan to escape."

"To escape secretly?" asked Old Firehand. "Then let's post ourselves on their route to welcome them or even ride with them."

"None of it," responded the Apache, shaking his head.

"Today, my views seem to constantly find objections from my red brother."

"Old Firehand should not be angry but think about it. What will the Ute warriors do when the whites escape?"

"They will pursue them."

"Pursuing four or six men will take how many warriors?"

"Well, perhaps twenty to thirty."

"Good! We can easily defeat such a number, but if we show ourselves to the Utes, all their braves will pursue us and much blood will flow."

"You are wise, Winnetou. But we cannot blind the Utes. They'll soon learn our numbers from our tracks."

"They will find tracks ahead of them, but not those behind."

"Oh, you're suggesting we follow them?"

"Yes."

"Without showing ourselves to Old Shatterhand?"

"We shall speak with him, but only you and I. Listen! What is that?"

A cacophony of shouts arose from the camp as four horsemen could be seen galloping away. It was Old Shatterhand and his companions. They took the direction to the upper end of the lake, seemingly intending to reach the brook and ride upstream.

"There they go," said Winnetou. "Old Firehand may come with me. My other white brothers must enter farther into the woods with their horses to wait there for our return. Take our horses too."

Pulling Old Firehand by the hand along the brook's bank, he led the way under cover of the trees to a point where they could observe the camp without being seen. And there they waited.

Old Shatterhand and his three friends approached swiftly keeping close to the brook. When they arrived where Winnetou and Firehand were hidden, they heard a voice call out from above, "My white brothers may halt where they are."

The four quickly reined in their horses and looked up.

"Winnetou!" they exclaimed in unison.

"Yes, it is Winnetou, chief of the Apaches," he assured them. "And here stands another friend of my white brothers."

He pulled the giant hunter out from behind a tree.

"Old Firehand!" shouted Old Shatterhand. You're here too! I must come up and greet you! Or you come down!"

Despite the danger he was in, he prepared to dismount.

"Stop! Stay there!" With a gesture, Old Firehand warded him off. "We shouldn't meet now."

"Why not?"

"The Utes following you must not learn of our presence."

"Oh, are you by yourselves?"

"No. We're about forty hunters, rafters and other frontiersmen. You'll find good friends among them. But there's little time for talk now. Where are you intending to ride?"

"To Silver Lake."

"We too. Ride on then. As soon as the Utes have passed, we'll follow and put them between us."

"Right-o!" called Old Shatterhand. "What a pleasure and what luck to meet you here! But even if we cannot talk for long, you should learn what happened. Can you see the camp from up there?"

"Yes," replied Old Firehand.

"Then be on the lookout so we won't be surprised. I'll tell you what's necessary."

The two men's joy at meeting was certainly great, but conditions did not allow it to be put into words nor to waste time. Quickly and briefly, required information was transmitted, readily complemented by both men's quickness and presence of mind. When they were done, Winnetou asked, "Does Old Shatterhand know the deep gorge that the palefaces call the Night Canyon? It can be reached in five hours from here. In the middle, it widens to a round place with walls that no one can climb rising to the sky. Does my white brother remember the place?"

"Very well."

"Then Old Shatterhand must ride there and take a position beyond it. There the gorge is so narrow that two horsemen can scarcely pass. He will not need his companions' help but can deter several hundred Utes with his magic rifle. Once the red men arrive there, they will neither be able to advance nor return because we will be blocking their retreat. Their only choice will be to surrender or be killed to the last man."

"Very well. We'll follow your advice. But tell me one thing: why are so many of you riding up to Silver Lake?"

"I'll explain," answered Old Firehand hurriedly, watching for any sign of the pursuing Utes. "Up there is a very rich silver mine, but in such a dry area that its exploitation is impossible because of insufficient water. I hit on the idea of diverting the waters of Silver Lake. If we succeed, we'll get many millions from the mine. I have an engineer along to investigate its technicalities and, if it's feasible, to execute them."

Old Shatterhand responded with an indefinable smile, "A mine? Who discovered it?"

"I was involved in it."

"Indeed! Well, if you can direct the lake to the mine, you'll have twice the business."

"How so?"

"The lake's bottom holds uncounted treasures against which your silver mine is pure poverty."

"Ah! You're referring to the Treasure of Silver Lake?"

"Exactly."

"What do you know of it?"

"More than you think. You'll learn about it later when there's more time. But you too mentioned the treasure. From whom did you learn about it?"

"From --- no, later. Hurry off! I see Indians coming from the camp."

"Heading this way?"

"Yes, on horseback."

"How many?"

"Five."

"Pah! We needn't fear five. But don't let yourselves be seen. It's only the advance guard; the main group will be following shortly. Off we go! See you in Night Canyon!"

Old Shatterhand spurred his horse and rode off with his three companions. Old Firehand and Winnetou ducked down to watch the five approaching Utes. They were peering closely at the escapees' tracks and didn't notice the men watching from above.

Once the Indians passed from sight, the two left their concealment and returned to their group who had moved deeper into the woods and were now close to where the brook flowed into the lake. Just as Old Firehand was about to report what he had discussed with Old Shatterhand, he noticed several Ute squaws heading to the lake carrying fishing equipment. He pointed them out to Winnetou and suggested, "If we could spy on the squaws, we might find out the plans of the warriors."

"Winnetou will give it a try should they come close enough," the Apache answered.

Fortunately, the squaws did come close, intending to fish at the mouth of the brook, and not in the lake itself. There they sat among the bushes, threw out their lures, and began to converse. They did not seem to mind talking during an activity which actually called for silence. Winnetou snaked down the slope toward them and chose a position behind the bushes to listen. For the men still above, it was very satisfying to simultaneously observe the observer and the observed. After a quarter of an hour, Winnetou returned to say, "If these squaws do not learn to be quiet, they will never catch trout. But they spoke of everything we need to know."

"And that was?"

"The five braves have been sent to add to Old Shatterhand's tracks and make them easier to follow. Shortly, fifty more will follow, led by Big Wolf."

"Then he's unhurt?"

"More or less. Old Shatterhand's blow paralyzed his right hand and stopped his breath momentarily, but it has returned. The hand does not prevent him from leading the pursuit. They are planning to kill Old Shatterhand and his friends so they cannot tell the Navajos of the Utes' intentions. The warriors below will spread out today to hunt and 'make meat'. Tomorrow the camp will be abandoned."

"Where are they going to relocate?"

"To be safe, the women and children will move to the mountains where the old people dwell. The warriors are to follow Big Wolf to gather at the meeting place of all Ute tribes."

"Where is that?"

"That the squaws did not know. There was nothing more to learn, but it is enough for our plans."

"Then we cannot do anything until Big Wolf and his people have passed. That he takes fifty-five warriors along shows the respect he has for Old Shatterhand. Such a superior force against just four whites!"

"Old Shatterhand is my friend and student," Winnetou responded. "He need not fear fifty-five."

The large group of rafters and hunters who had stayed behind now lay in wait for an hour until Big Wolf and his braves had passed by. The Indians proceeded without looking into the trees. Their appearance was most warlike, and without exception they carried rifles. The chief's right hand was bandaged. His face was now painted even more fiercely than in the morning. From his shoulders the feather-adorned war coat hung over the back of his horse, but he no longer wore the eagle headdress. Defeated, he would not wear this mark of distinction until he had avenged himself. He had his best warriors along riding the tribe's best horses.

Ten minutes later, bold Winnetou alone followed them, the others picking up the trail not long afterwards.

In reality there was no true trail. They rode alongside the brook whose banks had been worn down somewhat during spring flooding. Rocks and branches had been torn away and washed down, which slowed their ride, particularly since the chair carrying Ellen between the two ponies was difficult to get over these obstructions. Once they were past the mountain slope, progress became easier. The steepest rise was past and the lower the brook dropped, the less it had damaged its surroundings.

The tracks they followed could not have been more obvious. Since Old Shatterhand had found allies, he did not see any necessity to keep his tracks to a minimum. The five Utes pursuing him had intentionally made their tracks very obvious, and since Big Wolf did not expect an enemy from the rear, he had not thought to maintain caution either.

The route to Night Canyon crossed the Elk Mountains at their narrowest point. Once Old Firehand and his troop reached the crest, they left the creek behind. Their path led through a tall forest bare of underbrush. The crowns of the widely-spaced trees made a canopy through which barely a ray of sunlight penetrated. The moldy ground showed tracks clearly.

A few times they glimpsed the Apache ahead of them. He appeared quite unconcerned, knowing that the Utes' attention was directed forward.

It was ten o'clock when Old Firehand and his troop had departed from the lake. Until one o'clock they traversed the forest until they reached a prairie well interspersed with bushes, which pleased the men very much. If it were an open prairie, they would have had to maintain greater distance. The undulating grassland led them up and down, and alternated with forested areas. Once they crossed one type of growth, they soon reached another. Finally, coming out of a patch of woods, they saw Winnetou waiting for them. He explained the reason, not by words but by pointing directly ahead.

A unique view presented itself to the whites. The Elk Mountains lay behind them and the area of the Grand River with its canyons straight ahead. From the right, the left, and from where the riders had stopped, three slanted black rock flats descended, at their bottom coming together as giant slate plates. Their slope was so steep and their surface so smooth that the riders had to dismount. It was almost vertiginous to look down to the bottom, which was their destination. From two sides where the giant slopes met, brooks descended but without nourishing tree or bush, not even a blade of grass. Down below, the two creeks joined to disappear in a narrow rock cleft.

"This is Night Canyon," announced Old Firehand, pointing to the cleft. "It got its name from being so deep and narrow that sunlight cannot penetrate its depths. Even in full daylight, it's almost dark down there. Look below!"

He pointed to where the waters disappeared in the cleft. Small figures were moving at the bottom, horsemen so small that they seemed to be only knee-high. It was the Utes just now disappearing into the slot canyon.

The canyon seemed to be cut vertically into a gigantic rock wall forming a wide plateau, which terminated in the distant fog-enshrouded Book Mountains. Aunt Droll, looking into the depths, said to Black Tom, "We're supposed to get down there? Only a slate roofer could do that! That's life threatening, if it's necessary! If you sit down and I give you a push, you'd slide all the way to the bottom."

"But we must get down," Old Firehand told them. "Dismount and hold your horses on short bridle. Since it's so steep and we have no brakes, we must descend by zigzagging down."

Following his advice, without which they would surely have encountered misfortune, they reached bottom after more than half an hour of tortuous descent. It was fortunate that the Utes had been so unsuspecting. If they had noticed their pursuers and positioned themselves at the canyon's mouth, they could have easily, and without danger to themselves, picked off one after the other of the group as they descended the steeply slanted wall.

Finally all made their way down and readied themselves to enter the floor of the canyon, so narrow here that only two horsemen found space to ride side by side next to the brook. Winnetou took the lead followed by Old Firehand, accompanied by Lord Castlepool. Then came the hunters just ahead of the rafters who had taken the engineer and his daughter into their midst. The group had grown after the events at the Eagle Tail since Watson, the work boss, and several of his fellow workers had decided to come along.

No talking was permitted now since every sound in the slot canyon carried much farther than in the open. Even the hoofbeats of the animals might become a giveaway. Winnetou had therefore dismounted, handing his horse to a rafter, and had gone ahead shod in his soft and silent moccasins.

It became a ride through Hades one might think. Ahead and behind the narrow cleft, bordering the rock-strewn ground and the dark sinister water, on both left and right the straight ascending rock walls loomed so high and overlapping that the sky was invisible most of the time. The air became colder the farther they advanced and daylight turned to dusk.

And long was the canyon, eternally long! At times it widened a bit to accommodate five or six riders. Then the walls closed in again, causing claustrophobia to the faint-hearted. Even the horses were uneasy. They snorted fearfully and were in a hurry to get out of their confinement.

A quarter of an hour passed, then another. Suddenly, involuntarily, everyone stopped --- there was a loud boom as if ten cannons had been fired.

"By God! What was that?" asked Butler. "Did a wall collapse?"

"The report of a rifle reverberating off the canyon walls," answered Old Firehand. "The moment has come. Enough men to watch three horses each will remain here; the others dismount and come forward!"

In a moment, more than thirty men were ready to follow him, rifles in hand. After only a few paces, they found Winnetou, his back towards them, his Silver Rifle aimed straight ahead.

"Lay down your weapons or my magic rifle will speak!" roared a mighty voice from ahead but which seemed to come from everywhere.

"Drop your weapons!" it thundered again in Ute, the slot canyon's acoustics converting the few words into a thunderous rumble.

This was followed by three quickly fired shots, all from the same rifle, Old Shatterhand's repeating rifle, whose report in the canyon's confines sounded more like artillery than a mere rifle. Soon after, Winnetou's Silver Rifle boomed out. The Ute warriors who were hit yelled, followed by a massive howl as if all hell had broken loose. The redskins had not dropped their weapons immediately upon Old Shatterhand's demand, which resulted in the shots being fired. Four

Utes lay dead or dying, the others unable to think of defense, being fully engaged in trying to rein in their horses who had been spooked by the shots.

Old Firehand by now had reached the Apache and could see what was going on. The slot canyon widened and had formed a high-walled theater. It was large enough to accommodate about a hundred horsemen. The brook meandered along its left side.

The five warriors had made a major mistake by stopping here to await the arrival of their main party. Had they continued, they would have met the four whites posted at the opposite end of the theater and could have fled back to warn their own. However, since they had waited, the entire group was now trapped in the opening. On one side stood Old Shatterhand with his repeating rifle. Beside him Hobble-Frank knelt so Davy and Jemmy could shoot over his head.

"Put down your weapons or we'll shoot again!" thundered Old Shatterhand.

From the opposite end another shout rose, "And here stands Old Firehand. Surrender if you want to save your lives!"

Beside him, the Apache called out, "You know Winnetou, chief of the Apaches. Raise your rifles and you lose your scalps. Howgh!"

The Utes who thought they were only facing an enemy ahead now found their retreat blocked. There stood the mighty figure of Old Firehand and the proudly slender one of the Apache chief. Beside these two stood Aunt Droll in the brook, since there was no more space, and in between, three other muzzles pointed menacingly.

Not a single Ute dared raise his rifle. They gazed wildly ahead and back not knowing how to react. To offer resistance would have meant their deaths, but to surrender that swiftly without any negotiations was repugnant to them. During this frozen moment, Droll stepped from the water, walked up to Big Wolf, held the muzzle of his rifle against the chief's chest and demanded, "Throw down your rifle or I'll fire!"

Big Wolf stared down from his horse at the heavyset foreign figure as if a ghost had risen before him. The fingers of his left hand uncurled and the rifle fell to the ground.

"Also the tomahawk and your knife!"

The chief reached to his belt, took the two weapons and dropped these too.

"Give me your lasso!"

With a look of loathing, Big Wolf also obeyed this command. Droll used the lasso to tie the chief's feet together on either side of his horse's belly. Then he grabbed the horse's reins, led it aside and called to Gunstick-Uncle who was standing behind Old Firehand, "Come here, Uncle, and bind his hands!"

Gravely and stiffly Uncle advanced, declaring, "To his belt behind his back -- I'll tie his hands for safety's sake."

He swung himself onto the horse behind Big Wolf to complete his task, then jumped off again. It looked as if the chief was not even aware of what was happening. He appeared to be in a trance. His example had a paralyzing effect on his people; they simply surrendered to their fate. All were disarmed and tied like their chief, with the whites out to quickly accomplish whatever was necessary.

Hobble-Frank would have loved to greet Winnetou. Davy and Jemmy had the same wish, but such desires had to wait for a later time. The first requirement was to leave the canyon. As soon as the last Utes had their weapons confiscated and their hands bound, the ride resumed, first the hunters, then the Utes followed by the rafters.

Winnetou, Old Firehand and Old Shatterhand took the lead. They had all quietly shaken hands, the only greeting they found appropriate under the circumstances. Ahead of the captives rode two men who had more in common than they could know: Aunt Droll and Hobble-Frank. At first neither spoke a word to the other. After a while, Droll removed his feet from the stirrups and without reining in his mount, reversed his position in the saddle.

"Heavens! What's that to mean?" asked Frank. "Are you starting a comedy, sir? Have you been engaged as a clown in the circus?"

"No, mister," answered Droll. "It's just my habit to enjoy holidays as they fall."

"What on earth do you mean?"

"I've turned around in case something goes wrong. Think! Behind us ride fifty redskins. Something might happen that we haven't thought of. In my new position I can keep them in sight and with my revolver in hand can send them a pill if it's necessary. If you're smart, you'll do so too."

"Hmm! What you say is true. I don't think my horse will mind my turning around."

A few seconds later he too was astride his saddle in reverse to watch the redskins. It did not take long for the two riders to examine each other from time to time, their looks becoming ever more curious. They obviously seemed to be drawn to each other. For a while not a word was spoken, until Hobble-Frank could not keep silent any longer. He began, "Don't mind if I ask your name. The way you sit there beside me makes me think I've seen you already."

"Where?"

"In my imagination."

"That's peculiar! Who would think of me living in your imagination! How much rent did I have to pay and how's it with giving notice?"

"As you like. But as of today my imagination is satisfied since I'm seeing you now in person. If you're the one I think you are, I've heard lots of funny things about you."

"Well, then, who do you think I am?"

"I'd wager you're Aunt Droll."

"And where did you hear about the Aunt?"

"At various places I've been with Old Shatterhand and Winnetou."

"What! You rode with these famous men?"

"Yes. We were up at the national park, also at the Estacado."

"My, oh my! Then you must be Hobble-Frank?"

"Yes. Do you know of me?"

"Indeed! The Apache spoke often of you and just this morning when we spied on the Utes from above the lake, he called you a little hero."

"A -- little -- hero!" Frank repeated, a contented smile crossing his face. "A -- little -- hero! That I must write down! Well, you guessed right about me, but did I guess right about you?"

"Tell me again. Who do you think you're addressing?"

"Aunt Droll, as I said before."

"You're right. I'm indeed he."

"So! That's a real pleasure."

"How did you arrive at the conclusion that I'm the Aunt?"

"Your clothing tells me, also your behavior. I've often been told that the Aunt is an extremely courageous character, and when I saw you confront the chief of the Utes and plant your rifle in his chest, I thought right away, He and no other is the Aunt!"

"I'm honored! Well, we're probably both fellows who do their job. The main thing for me was to learn that you're a fellow countryman of Old Shatterhand."

"That's correct."

"A German then?"

"Yes."

"From where?"

"Straight from the center. I'm a Saxon."

"Really! What kind? Kingdom? Altenburg? Koburg-Gotha? Meiningen-Hildburghausen?"

"Kingdom, the kingdom! But you know these names all too well. Are you also German?"

"Obviously!"

"From where?" Frank asked delightedly.

"Also from Saxony, that is Sachsen-Altenburg."

"Oh my, oh my!" the little man fell into his native dialect. "Also a Saxon, and at that an Altenburger! Is it possible? From the city of Altenburg or from the countryside then?"

"Not from the Residence but from Langenleube."

"Langen -- leube?" asked Frank, his mouth agape. "Langenleube-Niederhain?"

"Yes! Do you know it?"

"Why should I not? I've relatives there, close ones; I've been to the carnival twice with them. Listen, there are real carnivals in Altenburger land! They bake cakes two weeks in advance. And when a carnival is over in one place, it continues at the next. That's why they talk only over there about the Altenburger country feasts."

"That's true!" nodded Droll. "As we say in Altenburg, 'If we can do it, we've done it'. Do you have relatives in our neck of the woods? What's the name of your folks and where are they from?"

"Close relatives. It's like this: my father had a godfather whose late daughter-in-law remarried in Langenleube. Her stepson had a brother-in-law, and he's the one I'm talking about."

"So! What did he do?"

"Lots of things. He was every inch a man who did everything. He was a waiter, a sexton, then a home-guard sergeant, later a wedding chaplain, then ---"

"Stop!" Droll demanded, while reaching across to take Frank's arm. "What was his name?"

"I don't remember his first name, but his last was Pampel. I always called him cousin Pampel."

"What? Pampel? Do I hear aright?" Droll exclaimed. "Did he have children?"

"Quite a few!"

"Do you remember their names?"

"Not any more. But I do remember the biggest one very well; we liked each other. His name was Bastel."

"Bastel, that's short for Bastian?"

"Yes. Bastian in the Altenburger dialect is called Bastel. I think another one of his names was Melchior, a name quite common in Altenburg."

"Right, quite right! It fits, it all fits very well! Sebastian Melchior Pampel. Do you know what happened to him?"

"No, unfortunately not."

"Then have a look at me, look closely!"

"Why?"

"Because it's me."

"You --- you?" the little man asked.

"Yes, I! I'm Bastel, and I remember very well who came to our carnival. It was cousin Frank from Moritzburg, who later became a forestry assistant."

"That's me in person! Cousin, here we find each other, close relatives in the middle of the wilderness! Who would have thought it! Come here, brother mine, let me hug you to my heart!"

"Yes, I too. Here I am!"

They both took hold of each other, which posed some difficulties, due to their sitting on their horses backwards, but determination overcame all obstacles.

The somber-looking Indians could make no sense of the peculiar behavior of the two who didn't seem to care about the captives. They rode side by side holding hands, backs turned forward, chatting about their long-past youth. They would have happily continued had the procession not come to a stop. The end of the slot canyon had been reached but became now a much wider, open terrain.

Although the sun had sunk low so that its rays no longer reached the canyon floor, there was better light than before and clearer, fresher air. The riders breathed relief upon entering the opening, but not before checking for any unfriendly presence.

At this spot the canyon was about two hundred paces wide, with its small shallow brook meandering through. There was grass by the water as well as some bushes and trees.

The redskins were pulled from their horses and were set on the ground after their feet had been retied. This was the moment when the real welcome was enjoyed by everyone. Those who did not yet know each other learned to do so very quickly.

Old Firehand's group brought food and all sat down to eat. Afterwards the fate of the Indians needed to be decided, about which several different opinions were presented. Winnetou, Old Firehand and Old Shatterhand were prepared to set them free. The others demanded some severe punishment. Lord Castlepool explained his view. "I do not consider their actions before the duels as punishable. But when you all won your contests the blighters were obligated to give you your freedom. Instead, dash it they took up pursuit in order to kill you. I do not doubt the beastly fellows would have done so if they had the opportunity."

"That's very likely," answered Old Shatterhand, "but they didn't get the opportunity and therefore didn't do it."

"Well! Then at least the intent is punishable, don't you think, old stick?"

"How do you want to punish their intent?"

"Hmm! That is a rum go!"

"Not by death?"

"No."

"By imprisonment?"

"Gad! Let's just give them a good thrashing!"

"That would be the worst thing we could do. For an Indian, there's no worse punishment than being struck. They'd chase us across the entire continent."

"Then issue a monetary punishment!"

"Do they have money?"

"No, dear fellow, but they have horses and weapons, don't they?"

"You suggest we take these? That would be heartless. Without horses and weapons, they'd starve and be defenseless against their enemies."

"Dashed nonsense, sir! The more lenient we are with these rotters the less grateful they'll be. You in particular should not be so easy on them since it was you who bore the brunt of the offenses."

"And it's because they committed offenses against me, Frank, Davy and Jemmy, that we four should decide their fate."

"Do as you like, chappie, but I think you're barmy," the lord responded, stepping aside to show his annoyance. A moment later though, he turned back and asked, "I say! Shall we bet?"

"What about?"

"That this wretched tribe will repay you badly if you treat them leniently."

"No."

"I wager ten dollars!"

"Not I."

"I wager twenty against your ten!"

"And I will not bet at all."

"Oh, my sainted aunt! Never?"

"No."

"I say, all you fellows have gone potty! On the entire long ride from the Osage Nook to here, I was never able to make a single bloody wager. From everything I heard about you, I thought you were a true gentleman, but now you too tell me that you never bet. I repeat: do as you wish!"

Lord Castlepool was now thoroughly vexed. He had entered readily and well into western habits, but that no one would bet with him was simply intolerable.

Old Shatterhand's statement that he, Frank, Jemmy and Davy had the sole right to decide the redskins' fate had a strong influence on the rest of the men. After a lengthy debate, everyone agreed to delegate the decision to these four. They were urged to make their decision in such a fashion that no further hostility by the redskins would occur. Therefore a firm agreement with them needed to be made. For this, it was insufficient to confer solely with the chief; his tribe members should also hear what was discussed and what Big Wolf would promise. This setting might compel his honesty and force him to maintain his promises, if only to assure the tribe's good opinion of him.

Old Shatterhand and the other three who were to judge conferred briefly. The redskins and whites then formed a wide circle. Two rafters each stood guard upstream and downstream. Big Wolf sat in front of Winnetou and Old Shatterhand. He did not face them, possibly from shame, possibly from obstinacy.

"What does Big Wolf think we're going to do with him?" Old Shatterhand asked in Ute.

There was no response.

"Is the chief of the Utes so afraid that he doesn't answer?"

Big Wolf lifted his head, his scowling look drilling into the hunter's face, and said, "The paleface is a liar if he claims I am afraid!"

"Then answer! You're not to speak to me of lying, for you yourself have spoken falsehoods!"

"That is not true!"

"It is! When we were still in your camp, I asked you whether we would be free to leave if I were victorious. What did you answer?"

"That you could leave."

"Was that no lie?"

"No, because you left."

"But you pursued us!"

"No."

"You deny it?"

"Yes, I deny it."

"For what purpose then did you leave camp?"

"To travel to the Ute gathering place, not to pursue you." Big Wolf was nothing if not wily.

"Why then did you set five of your braves onto our tracks?"

"I did not do that. We have taken up the tomahawk and once this is done we must be extremely careful. When I promised you your freedom, I did not even know in which direction you would be heading. We promised to let you go and Big Wolf has kept his word. You, however, have attacked us, taken our belongings and killed four of my braves. Their bodies still lie in the canyon."

"You know only too well the contempt in which I hold your words. Why did your guards shoot at us when we rode off?"

"They did not know what I had promised you."

"And why did your other braves shout war cries? They knew your promise very well."

"Their shouts were not for you but for the guards, so they should not shoot at you. This was precisely a well-meant action that you construe as evil."

"I must admit, Big Wolf," said Old Shatterhand, shaking his head, "that you know how to defend yourself very astutely, but you're failing to prove your innocence. Let's see if your braves have the courage to be more truthful than you."

He asked several of the redskins the purpose of their ride and all of them -- unanimously and in accordance with their chief -- denied that they had had any murderous intentions against the palefaces.

"Your people don't wish you to have to own up to a lie," Shatterhand continued in an accusing tone. "But, Big Wolf, we have incontrovertible proof. We spied on your camp and overheard some of your people. We know you intended to kill us."

"You merely assume this!"

"No, we heard it. We also know that you'll break camp tomorrow and that all your braves are to follow you to the gathering place of the Utes. The women and children will join your old people in the mountains. Isn't that true?"

"Yes, that is so."

"Well, then everything else we heard is true too. We're convinced you were after our lives. So, what kind of punishment is to be yours?"

The redskin was silent.

"We had done nothing to you and you took us along to kill us. Now a second time you tried to take our lives. You've earned worse than death. But we're Christians. We'll forgive you. You shall be freed and your weapons will be returned to you. In exchange for that, you and your braves must forswear any attempt to ever harm any of us in the least way."

"Is your tongue speaking or your heart?" the chief asked in disbelief.

"My tongue never speaks differently from my heart, chief. Are you willing to make the required promise?"

"Big Wolf will give his word!"

"That all of us here, red and white men, shall be brothers from now on?"

"Big Wolf says yes, before all my braves!"

"Who will assist each other in need and danger?"

"Yes."

"And are you willing to swear this by smoking the peace pipe?"

The Ute chief drew a long hard breath, then replied, "I am ready."

That Big Wolf had answered without delay led everyone to conclude that he was serious about his promise. The expression on his face, however, was hidden under the thick layer of paint.

"Then let's pass the pipe around," Old Shatterhand continued. "I'll say the words and you'll repeat them."

"It is good you say them. I shall repeat them!"

His willingness was seen as a good sign. The well-meaning hunter was very appreciative but could not help issuing a final warning, "I hope you're truthful this time, Big Wolf. I've always been a friend of the red man and take into account that the Utes have been brutally attacked. Were this not the case, you wouldn't have gotten away so cheaply. If you're dishonest once again, you'll surely pay for it with your life. I assure you this and I always keep my word!"

The chief stared down, never looking up at his adversary. Old Shatterhand took off his calumet and packed it with tobacco from his pouch. When he had it lit, he undid Big Wolf's bindings. The hunter stood up to blow smoke to the six directions and to say, "I am Big Wolf of the Yampa Utes. I speak for myself and for my braves who are with me. I speak to the palefaces I see here: Old Firehand, Old Shatterhand and all others, also Winnetou, famous chief of the Apaches. All of these warriors and white men are forever our friends and brothers. They shall be like us and we shall be like them. They shall never experience harm from us and we will rather die than have them think us their enemies! This is my oath. Howgh!"

Now it was Big Wolf's turn to honor the agreement. The chief stood, took the peace pipe from Old Shatterhand and puffed deeply, following the age-old ritual. Slowly, and deliberately, he repeated the substance of the hunter's oath.

He sat down again.

Now the other braves were freed and the pipe went from mouth to mouth being filled and refilled until everyone had taken part in the ceremony. Even little Ellen Butler had to take her six puffs. In order to be included in the oath, no exception was made.

Then the redskins' weapons were returned. This constituted no risk if one could trust their oath. Nevertheless, the whites were cautious and each of them kept his hand close by his revolver. The chief fetched his horse then asked Old Shatterhand, "My brother has given us complete freedom?"

"Entirely."

"Then we may leave?"

"Yes, to wherever you want."

"We shall return to our camp."

"Oh! Didn't you want to ride to the Utes' gathering place? Are you admitting now that you were pursuing us?"

"No. You took away the time for our journey; we would arrive too late. We shall return to camp."

"Through the slot canyon?"

"Yes. Live well!"

He shook hands with Old Shatterhand, then mounted and rode off stiffly without looking back. His people followed him after each of them had waved a friendly farewell.

"The fellow is a rascal after all!" declared Old Blenter. "Had the color not been thick as a finger on him, one could have read falsehood all over him. A bullet to the head would have been better."

Winnetou heard these words and responded thoughtfully, "My brother may be quite right but it is better to do good than bad. We shall stay here for the night but I will follow the Utes to spy on them."

He disappeared into the slot canyon, not on horseback but on foot, his preference for such a task.

Everyone was relieved at last. What should they have done with the Utes anyway? Kill them all? Unthinkable! Drag them along as prisoners? Just as impossible! Now the Indians had been obligated to maintain peace and friendship, and the hunters were rid of them. A solution better than any alternative.

The day drew to its close with the canyon gradually becoming darker. Some of the men went to collect firewood. Old Firehand rode downstream for a distance reconnoitering the canyon while Old Shatterhand went upstream following Winnetou and the Utes. Finding nothing suspicious, they both soon returned.

No one had camped here in the canyon for some time. Although there was no forest here, there was nevertheless plenty of firewood. Spring floods had carried a multitude of branches and logs downstream. Happiest of all for the fire was Lord Castlepool; it gave him a wonderful opportunity to demonstrate his culinary skills with his roasting kit. There was still a small but sufficient supply of meat, preserved goods, flour and such from Denver. Everyone licked their lips over the meal.

Much later Winnetou reappeared. Despite the dark, the Apache had found his way safely back through the slot canyon. He reported that the Utes had picked up their dead and continued on their way home. He followed them to the slot canyon's entrance and watched them ascend the steep rock face, disappearing into the forest high above.

The hunters nevertheless posted guards in the narrowest part of the slot canyon to make any attack from there unlikely to succeed. Others stood guard downstream and upstream from the camp to provide additional safety.

There was much to be talked about but it was past midnight and everyone needed rest. Old Firehand checked that all the guards were awake, and reminded others to spell each other in a defined sequence. The fires were extinguished. Silence and darkness finally descended.

14. Captured and Ready

Winnetou had observed correctly that the Utes had entered the forest at the top of the slope. However, they had not crossed the forest but had stopped just inside. Transporting their dead had not been difficult since they had the horses of the dead braves to carry them. Now the chief ordered the bodies taken down from the horses. He walked to the forest's edge and looking back down into the slot canyon, said, "They are watching us. One of the white dogs is surely standing down there to make sure we are returning to our camp."

"Are we not returning?" asked one of his braves. He had distinguished himself through bravery or some other distinction to dare ask such a question.

"Do you have as little brains as the jackal of the prairies?" Big Wolf bellowed at him. "We must take revenge on these pale toads."

"But they are now our friends and brothers!"

"Never."

"We smoked the peace pipe with them!"

"Whose pipe was it?"

"Old Shatterhand's."

"Well, than it is his oath, not ours. He was stupid not to use my pipe! Do you see that?"

"Big Wolf is always right," the brave answered, agreeing with the chief's sophistry. His perfidious excuse had to satisfy every Ute brave.

"Tomorrow morning the souls of the palefaces will enter the Eternal Hunting Grounds to serve us in later times," the chief continued.

"You intend to attack them?"

"Yes."

"For that our numbers are too few and we cannot attack through the slot canyon. They will have guards posted."

"Then we will take a different route and call on as many warriors as we need. Are there not many over there at the P'a-mow, the Forest of Waters? And is there not another trail farther down the canyon that the palefaces do not seem to know? The bodies of our fallen braves shall stay here with two guards. We others shall ride north."

Obediently, the warriors accepted his decision. Although the forest here was relatively narrow, it took an hour's ride for the Utes galloping alongside it, until a slope descended into a second canyon which cut through the same rocky plateau as the first. The canyon ahead led to the one where the whites were camped three miles downstream.

The Indians rode on, but instead of heading directly for the whites, they took a wider side canyon where several riders could canter side by side. Big Wolf seemed to know his way very well and led his braves confidently through the rocky wilderness in spite of the dark.

The canyon they were passing through was dry and slowly rose again to a plateau crisscrossed by a whole network of canyons. Here on the plateau the moonlight illuminated the ground well. The Utes galloped across the plain which, half an hour later, gently descended to a broad depression. To the left and right, protective rock walls remained, rising higher the farther the troop progressed into the valley. Finally a rich forest rose ahead of them where many Indian fires burned.

This was P'a-mow, the Forest of Waters, the chief's destination. It was a substantial forest, protected in its depression from the storm-swept and sun-dried height of the plateau. The forest's existence was due solely to this valley and the collection of rains and snow which had created a small lake whose waters penetrated the ground and made the forest's growth verdant.

No moonlight would have been required to find the way from here because of the multitude of camp fires. The aspect was that of a war gathering. There were no teepees, no wigwams. Many braves lay around the fires, either on their blankets or on the bare ground. Between them stood or reposed just as many horses. This was the Utes' assembling place to ready themselves for the war path.

When Big Wolf arrived at the first fire, he dismounted, signaled his braves to wait and called to one of the seated warriors to take him to Nanap-neav. The brave rose and led Big Wolf to the lake where a crackling blaze burned, somewhat apart from the others. Four Indians sat there, all adorned with eagle feathers. One of them was far more conspicuous than the others. His face was not painted and was crisscrossed by innumerable deep creases. His white hair hung down his back.

The man was at least eighty years old but sat as straight, proud and strong as if carrying fifty years less. This was Nanap-neav, whose name meant Old Chief, the paramount chief of all the Ute tribes. He looked sharply at the new arrival without uttering a word of greeting. The others also remained silent. Big Wolf sat with them and stared silently ahead. Many minutes passed until the ancient one said, "The tree drops its leaves in the fall, but if it does so before, it is not worthy and ought to be chopped down. Three days ago, he still wore them. Where are they now?"

This question was referring to Big Wolf's missing war bonnet. To any brave the question was a depressing accusation.

"Tomorrow the bonnet will adorn me again, together with the scalps of ten or twenty palefaces!" Big Wolf asserted hotly.

"Has Big Wolf been defeated by palefaces that he may no longer wear the symbol of bravery and dignity?"

"By one paleface only, the one whose fist is heavier than the hands of a hundred whites."

"That can only be Old Shatterhand!"

"It was he."

"Uff!" exclaimed the ancient chief and "Uff!" the others chimed in. "Then Big Wolf has encountered this famous hunter?"

"He and many others. Old Firehand, Winnetou, the tall and the fat hunters, a whole group about five times ten heads strong." Big Wolf's voice was raised in repressed fury. "I have come here that I may soon bring you their scalps."

The Indian is expected to hide his feelings, particularly old ones and chiefs. What these four leaders heard shocked their self-control, resulting in exclamations of astonishment and disbelief. The old one's face became so tense that almost no creases were visible any more.

"Big Wolf must tell us!" he demanded.

The chief responded to their request but his report departed sharply from the truth. He took pains to put himself and his actions in the best possible light. The others sat motionless, listening to the story teller with great attention. When he was finished, Old Chief asked, "And what does Big Wolf intend to do now?"

"Give me another fifty warriors and together with mine, we will attack these dogs. Their scalps will surely hang on our belts before sunrise."

The old one's creases returned. His brows contracted and his eagle's nose seemed to become even more thin and pointed.

"Before sunrise?" he asked. "Are these the words of a Ute warrior? Palefaces have attacked us, robbed and killed our men. Now they come to spill our blood and gather as allies even the hordes of the Navajos. They are intent on our destruction and now that the Great Spirit has delivered these most famous and distinguished men into our hands, you would have them die quickly and painlessly like a child in its mother's arms? What do my red brothers say to Big Wolf's words?"

"The whites must be put to the stake," asserted one of the chiefs.

"We must catch them alive," suggested the second.

"The more famous, the greater their torment should be," added the third.

"My brothers have spoken well," grunted the old one approvingly. "We shall capture the dogs alive."

"Perhaps our old chief might consider what kind of men are among them!" warned Big Wolf. "Old Shatterhand can force down the head of a buffalo and Old Firehand is just as powerful. Bad spirits dwell in their weapons. And Winnetou is a great warrior ---"

"But he is an Apache!" the old one interrupted. "Do the Navajos warring against us not belong to the Apaches? Winnetou is our mortal enemy and must be tortured far more than the whites. I know what powers and skills rest with these famous palefaces, but we have warriors enough to overcome them. You shall have first right of reprisal and I appoint you leader. I will also give you three hundred braves and you shall bring me the palefaces alive."

"May I take the scalps of Old Firehand, Old Shatterhand and Winnetou once they are tied to the stake?"

313

"They are yours, but only if no white is killed beforehand. The premature death of any one of them will deprive us of the pleasure of watching his torment. Your troop is already fifty men strong; together with my three hundred this will make ten braves for each paleface. If you approach them silently, you will succeed in surrounding them and can bind them before they can resist. Take enough straps along! Now come, I shall select those who are to accompany you. Those who must remain behind will begrudge my choice, but they shall be the foremost at the stakes."

Together, Old Chief and Big Wolf rose for a walk around the fires to select the braves. Before the moon was high, three hundred warriors had been chosen, plus another fifty to guard the horses, which could not be taken all the way to the whites' camp. Big Wolf explained everything to his people, describing the situation as precisely as possible, including his plan for the attack. Then the Utes mounted up for their ride, which was to become so fateful for the whites. The names Old Firehand, Old Shatterhand and Winnetou rose from many throats. What glory to capture such heroes and put them to the stake!

They returned the same way Big Wolf had come, but only as far as the main canyon. There they dismounted to leave their horses under the protection of the fifty guards. With such a superior force, the venture was surely without risk. Yet its success was not guaranteed. Big Wolf knew only too well that the whites' horses could readily smell his forces as they approached and would react by snorting and restless stomping, a strong likelihood considering the large number of his troop. What could he do about it? The chief posed this question not just to himself, but aloud so that others around him could hear. One of the more experienced braves bent down, tore off a piece of a plant, held it up to Big Wolf and said, "Here is a sure means to cover our scent."

The chief recognized the twig. It was sage. There are areas in the far west with many square miles covered with this herb. In this canyon too, where the sun reached to the bottom, sagebrush grew profusely. The brave's advice was good and it was immediately followed. The redskins rubbed sage all over their hands and clothes. They now exuded such an odor that there was promise it would deceive the whites' horses. Big Wolf also noted the faint breeze blowing against them, which would be to their advantage.

Because of their numbers, the Indians had chosen not to arm themselves with rifles but only knives. Their intent was to surprise the whites and overcome them so quickly that it would never come to a fight.

They now advanced on foot for nearly three miles. At first, they could progress quickly and without much caution, but after two miles had been covered far greater care was called for.

Only now did it occur to Big Wolf that the whites, as a precaution, might have moved their camp to a different location, a possibility that threw him into to a feverish unrest. On they went, silently and pantherlike. Seven hundred feet with not the slightest noise to be heard. No pebble dislodged, no twig cracked. Then -- - Big Wolf, in the lead, stopped abruptly. He had spotted guard fires, just at the moment when Old Firehand was checking the guards. The chief saw that a sentinel each had been posted above and below the camp. They had to be silenced first.

He commanded a stop and ordered two braves to follow him. Flat to the ground, they advanced farther. Soon they reached the upper guard who, looking after the departing Old Firehand, had unknowingly turned his back to the redskins. Suddenly, Big Wolf's hands wrapped around his neck and the two braves seized his arms and legs. Breath left him and consciousness failed. When he came to, he was bound and gagged. Beside him sat an Indian holding the tip of a knife against his chest.

By then, the main camp fire had burned low. Big Wolf called on two more braves to accompany him. Now they were seeking out the second guard and had to circle around the camp on the near side of the brook so that they could cross unnoticed to the far side. The three cautiously waded across and crept on. The Utes assumed that both guards had been posted equidistant from the camp, which enabled them to estimate the distance they had to cover. Yet the phosphorescent water and what little splashing they might cause could easily give them away. Because of this, the redskins continued for a distance farther, crossed, then crept back on their bellies towards the guard.

A few moments later, they saw him standing six feet away, his face turned sideways. Quick steps, a leap, a brief thrashing about and he was taken. Two redskins remained with him while Big Wolf traversed the brook again to return to his warriors for the main assault.

The whites' horses stood in two groups between the camp and where the two guards had been posted. Until now, they had remained quiet, but this was unlikely to continue. Once the Indians came closer, the horses would become suspicious, sage scent or not. Big Wolf, therefore, found it good strategy to have his braves cross the brook as well. This was accomplished in masterly silence. On the far side, they dropped down to cover the distance of a hundred paces on hands and knees until they arrived opposite the camp site. Their greatest obstacle was the many men cramped together in so small a space, and that it had to be done in total silence. Although the Utes were lying prone and motionless, the horses were becoming nervous after all. Speed was now called for. There could be no thought of crossing the water silently.

"Attack!" hissed Big Wolf in a suppressed but nevertheless audible voice.

The Utes sprang across the brook. None of the whites was still awake, all were in their first sleep. The developing scene was indescribable. The palefaces lay so closely together that there was no room for action by three hundred Indians. Five or six of them threw themselves onto each white, jerked him upright and tossed the sleep-drugged man to other braves waiting behind, then immediately grabbed a second, a third and a fourth. This all happened so swiftly that the sleeping men were in the Indians' power before they were fully awake.

Much against Indian custom of accompanying every attack with a war cry, these Utes worked in almost total silence. Only after the whites began shouting in alarm did they explode into triumphant yells that reverberated through the night and reflected manifoldly from the canyon walls.

The mix of arms, legs and bodies resulted in such confusion that in the darkness man could not be differentiated from man. Only three groups could be distinguished in the gloom, not far apart from each other and pressed hard against the canyon wall. At their centers were Old Firehand, Old Shatterhand and Winnetou, surrounded by Utes. These hunters, because of their superior presence of mind and experience, had not been taken by surprise like the others. They had leaped up and sought protection against the rock wall. Now they defended themselves with knives and revolvers against the overwhelming enemy, who were powerless to use their blades and tomahawks, having been ordered to capture the whites alive. Despite their famed agility and strength, the three hunters had to succumb eventually. The Utes were pressing so tightly against them they were finally unable to lift their arms any longer. They were overpowered and bound like their companions. A bone-chilling war cry from the Indians announced that their attack had succeeded.

Big Wolf ordered the fire to be stoked. Once its flames illuminated the area of the battle, it turned out that twenty redskins had been either wounded or killed by the three hunters.

"The dogs will suffer a tenfold death for this!" raged Big Wolf. "We will cut off their skin in strips. They shall all die a dreadful death and not one will see the stars of tomorrow's night. Collect the dead, the horses and weapons of the palefaces. We must return."

"Who is to touch the white hunter's magic rifle?" asked one. "It discharges by itself and kills the one holding it, even others."

"We will leave it here and build a cairn over it that no red warrior will put his hand on it. Where is it?"

They searched without finding it; it had disappeared. Big Wolf's question to Old Shatterhand as to its whereabouts received no answer. When the hunter had leaped up in the heat of battle, the carbine had been torn from his hand and tossed far aside. Torches were used to penetrate the clear waters of the brook so that every pebble on the bottom was visible, but the rifle had disappeared.

All during the day the Yampa Utes had seen the rifle in Old Shatterhand hands and could not now comprehend how it could have vanished. Maybe it lay in the slot canyon. That too was searched for a short distance but to no avail. The result was that the redskins, who so far had doubted that Old Shatterhand's rifle possessed supernatural powers now joined the ranks of the believers. The magic rifle might, if they stayed here too long, turn its incomprehensible powers against them. Big Wolf, finding this much too sinister, ordered, "Tie the captives to the horses and let us get away from here! An evil spirit made this rifle. We must not stay at this place where it might send us its bullets."

His command was quickly obeyed. When the redskins left, not much over an hour had passed since the beginning of the battle.

"Not one will see the stars of tomorrow's night," the chief had promised. He was certain he had captured every one of the palefaces. But that was not the case. Old Firehand had posted an additional guard deep in the slot canyon to warn of an attack should the Yampa Utes return. The guard was Droll, who was supposed to be relieved in two hours. Hobble-Frank had accompanied him cheerfully to chat about their common homeland. Fully armed, they had sat in the darkness and conversed in whispers, from time to time listening in the direction of the canyon should anyone approach. They felt not at all fatigued. There was so much to talk about that they found no lack of subjects.

Suddenly, Frank heard sounds coming from the canyon's entrance.

"Listen!" he whispered to his cousin. "Did you hear that?"

"Yes, I did," answered the Aunt just as quietly. "What was it?"

"Several of our people must have gotten up."

"No, that's not it. It must be many, many people. It sounds like the footsteps of hundreds of men!"

He stopped in alarm, because at this moment the sleepers had been brutally awakened and were crying out in dismay.

"Thunder and lightning, there's a battle going on!" Hobble-Frank exclaimed. "I think we've been attacked for the most part!"

"Yes. We've been attacked!" Droll agreed excitedly. "It must be the red scoundrels, if it's necessary!"

A moment later his surmise was confirmed as the redskins raised their war cry.

"God help us; it's truly them!" cried Frank. "Let's help our comrades! Hurry!"

He took Droll's arm to try to pull him along. But this cunning hunter held Frank back, and shaking in excitement said, "Stay! Not so quick! If the Indians are raiding by night, they're doing it with so many braves that we must be as careful as possible. First let's see what happened, then we'll know what to do. Let's get down and crawl to the canyon entrance."

On hands and knees they approached the mouth of the canyon. Despite the darkness, they could tell that many of their friends were captive. The redskins' numbers had been too great. To their left, the fight was still raging. Shots cracked from Firehand, Shatterhand and Winnetou, but not for long. Then rose the hundred-fold victory yell from the redskins.

In front of the two hunters the way was clear. "Quick! Follow me across the brook!" Droll whispered to his cousin.

As fast as he could, he snaked across the ground. Frank followed. Droll's hand suddenly touched a hard, long object. He realized it was Old Shatterhand's Henry rifle and quickly grabbed it up.

The two reached the brook and crossed to the far side. There Droll took Hobble-Frank's hand and guided him along downstream, southward. Their departure from the scene of battle succeeded because of the darkness and because their footsteps couldn't be heard over the Indians' raucous screams. Soon the space between brook and canyon wall became so narrow that Droll said, "We must cross to the brook's other side again. I think it's wider there."

They waded across. Fortunately, they had already come far below the point where Firehand's guard had been captured. They walked -- no they ran -- sometimes banging into the canyon wall, sometimes stumbling over rocks until they no longer could hear the Indian voices. At length Hobble-Frank stopped to ask his companion reproachfully, "Hold it finally, you runaway! Why did you dash off and disgracefully seduce me to come along? That's against all duty and comradeliness! Don't you have any courage in your body?"

"Courage?" Droll answered, breathless due to his bodily circumference. "I've got that for sure, but if I'm to keep it, I must save that body first. That's why I ran."

"But that wasn't really proper!"

"So? Why shouldn't it be proper?"

"Because it was our duty to save our friends."

"So! And how were you going to do it?"

"By throwing ourselves on the redskins, clubbing them and cutting them down."

"Hehehehe! Clubbing and stabbing!" laughed Droll in his peculiar way. "We wouldn't have accomplished anything except they would have captured us too."

"Captured us? Do you think our companions were only captured, not shot, stabbed or clubbed to death?"

"No. They weren't killed, that's sure. I know it."

"That would ease my conscience!"

"All right. Calm yourself. Did you hear the shots?"

"Yes."

"And who fired? The Indians, by chance?"

"No, what I heard were revolvers being fired."

"There you have it! The Indians didn't use their weapons. It was their plan to capture our companions alive so they could put them to the stake. That's why I fled off. Now the two of us are saved and we can do more for our people than if we had been captured."

"You're right there, cousin, you're right! A big stone just rolled off my heart. I don't want it said of world-famous Hobble-Frank that he ran like a rabbit when his comrades were in mortal danger. Not at all! I'd rather dive into the thick of battle and strike out like a raging Roland. It's awful! Who'd have divined in his quiet, peaceful temperament what was to happen! I'm really out of myself!"

"I'm also shocked, but I won't let myself be discouraged. One shouldn't give up on people like Winnetou, Firehand and Shatterhand unless they're truly lost. And they aren't alone. There are fellows with them who've got hair on their teeth. So, let's see what happens!"

"That's easily said. What kind of Indians might they have been?"

"Utes naturally. I don't think Big Wolf returned to his camp, but recruited other Utes in the area to help him."

"That rascal! And before that he smoked the peace pipe with us! Where do you think he came from?"

"If I knew that, I'd be smarter than before. He isn't going to stay at the camp but he'll certainly take the captives away. Since we don't know which direction he'll be heading, we mustn't stay here, but continue on farther until we can find a place to hide."

"And then?"

"Then? Well, we'll wait for daylight. Then we'll check for tracks and follow the Indians until we know what we can do for our friends. Now, let's head out. Come on!"

He again took Frank by his arm but this time happened to touch the Henry repeater.

"What's that?" he asked. "You've got two rifles?"

"Yes. I found Old Shatterhand's carbine when we crossed the brook at the slot canyon entrance."

"That's good, that's excellent. It'll come in handy. But do you know how to shoot it?"

"Sure! I've been with Old Shatterhand for so long that I know his rifle like he does. But let's go now! If the redskins should think of riding downstream, they'll catch up with us and we'll be goners. I must protect my precious life so I can sacrifice it for the rescue of my friends. Woe to these Indians and woe to the whole Wild West if one of our people has even a single hair pulled! I'm a good-natured chap. It's been said I'm two souls with one thought, but when I get into a rage I'll pound the entire world into a pan. You'll get to know me yet. I'm a Saxon. You understand we Saxons have always been a strategically amusing people and in all wars, and in diatonic squabbles, dispensed the worst thrashings."

"Or received!" corrected Droll with a chuckle, drawing Frank away.

"Be quiet!" was the response. Frank had become livid, words spilling from him in his sudden anger. "You Altenburgers are just Cheese Saxons, but we from the Elbe are the real ones. As long as lips will be talking of cultural events,

319

Moritzburg and Perne will be the Symplegade centers of all kalospinthechromokrene greatness and decency. Napoleon was beaten at Leipzig, and in Räcknitz near Dresden, Moreau lost his only two legs. At the Weissernitz lies the same seminal place of boldness and bravery that I've taken into my breast. I thus advise the redskins not to raise in me a Berserker's rage. I'm astringent in my wrath and impossible in my fury. Tomorrow I shall talk more with you, tomorrow when the first beams of the sun do ... do shine their last rays, plunging the bloody grounds into darkness!"

He made a fist and shook it threateningly over his shoulder. Never before in his life had he been so enraged and uncontrolled. This not only showed in his words, but also in the way he stormed forward into the night as if to threaten the enemy behind him.

The direction the two had taken was the right one after all and best suited to find the redskins, as they would discover to their surprise. So that the Indians wouldn't catch up with them, they increased their speed as far as that was possible in the dark of the night. With the brook to their right and the canyon wall to their left, they hurried south until after about an hour the canyon made a turn to the east. As they came around the curve, the moon became visible high on their right due to a side canyon, which opened the view skyward. Droll stopped and said, "Hold it! We must decide which way to go. To the left or the right?"

"That cannot be in doubt," Frank declared. "We must enter the side canyon."

"Why so?"

"Because we can assume with absolute consecration that the redskins will remain in the main canyon. If we hide in this side canyon, they'll pass us and tomorrow morning we can attach ourselves to their heels with most obligatory hypnology. Don't you think so?"

"Hmm! Not a bad idea, particularly since the moon's right above the side canyon and lights our way."

"Yes. Luna beams comfort into my heart and kisses away the streams of my tears from my rage-dried soul. Let's follow these sweet beams! Maybe this beloved shine will lead us to a place where we can hide, which is the most important thing in this imponderable situation."

They jumped across the brook and entered the dry side canyon. Yet there were plenty of signs that at other times of the year water flowed deeply here. Their direction was now due west. They had to walk far into the canyon so that the Indians would not discover them. After half an hour's march, they suddenly stopped in the most pleasant surprise. The canyon wall to their right fell away to form a sharp corner, with a wall coming from the north. Ahead of them lay not open terrain but forest, real forest, the sort no one would have expected here. Above a sparse undergrowth, the crowns of the trees were matted so densely that moonlight penetrated only in a few places. It was the Forest of Waters where the Utes had set up their camp.

The depression or valley, which it covered, extended in a line from north to south, parallel to the main canyon not more than half an hour away. There were two connectors between the main canyon and the forest, a northern one, which had been used by Big Wolf, and a southern one through which Droll and Frank had passed. The two side canyons leading east to west, together with the main canyon and the forest, created a rectangle in whose interior was formed a high, rocky plateau into which water had carved many hundred-foot-deep pathways.

"A forest, a real forest with trees and bushes, as if planted by a royal Saxon forester!" Frank enthused. "We couldn't have done any better. This is the best possible hiding place. Don't you think so?"

"No," answered Aunt Droll. "This forest looks suspicious to me, even threatening. I don't trust it."

"Why so? Do you think bears might have set up their nightly domicile here?"

"Not that. Bears need not be much feared really, but other creatures who are just as dangerous."

"What kind?"

"Indians."

"That would be rotten, real rotten!"

"I would be happy if I were wrong, but I think I'm on the right track."

"Would you be so kind as to logically present your thoughts, cousin."

The two stood at the canyon's corner in the shadows, their eyes fixed on the moonlit forest edge. Droll asked, "Who will know better that there's a forest here, us or the Utes?"

"The Utes, certainly."

"Would they also know that one can hide best in a forest?"

"Obviously."

"Haven't I explained to you yet that the Indians must be near?"

"Yes. Because Big Wolf got his help from here."

"Where might these fellows be hiding? In the bare canyon or the pleasant forest?"

"In the latter."

"All right. Then we must be very careful. I'm convinced of it."

"Do you think we should avoid the forest?"

"No, but we must be on guard. Do you see anything suspicious?"

"No, nothing at all."

"Neither do I. Then let's try it; let's get across quickly and duck behind those bushes. Then we'll listen to hear if something's moving. Let's go!"

They dashed across the moonlit opening. Under the trees and behind the bushes they squatted down to listen. Nothing could be heard, not even a leaf was moving. Droll took a deep breath and asked softly, "Frank, sniff the air! I smell smoke! Don't you?"

"Yes," Frank confirmed, "but the smell's very faint. Mine's a half-guess of a quarter-trace of smoke."

"Because it comes from quite a distance. We need to check it out and sneak up on it."

They clasped hands and threaded their way ahead slowly and quietly. It was so dark below the canopy that they had to rely more on their sense of touch than sight. The farther they advanced the more noticeable the smoke became. But progress was very slow. In Hobble-Frank arose the question whether their ongoing enterprise wasn't too dangerous after all. He asked in a whisper, "Wouldn't it be better if we left the smoke to itself? We're entering uselessly into danger we know nothing about."

"Sure it's dangerous," answered Droll, "but we must try it. Maybe it'll help us rescue our friends."

"Here?"

"Yes. If Big Wolf doesn't remain at our camp site, he'll come up here."

"That would be great!"

"Great? Who knows? It could cost us our lives!"

"That wouldn't matter to me if we could save our companions' lives. I'm not thinking any longer of turning back."

"Right-o, cousin, you're a good guy. But cunning is better than force. So, be careful, very careful!"

They went on and only halted when they saw the light of a fire. Undefinable sounds could also be heard that seemed to be human voices. The forest now stretched farther to the right. They followed in this direction and soon saw several more fires.

"A big, big camp," whispered Droll. "They must be the Ute warriors who've gathered to move against the Navajos. There's got to be hundreds of them."

"That doesn't matter. We need to get closer. I must know what's happening to Old Shatterhand and the others. I want to ---"

He was interrupted. Suddenly, ahead of them rose a many-voiced cry not of pain or rage, but of joy.

"Ah! They're bringing the captives," Droll said, lowering his voice. "Big Wolf comes from the north and we came from the south. We must find out what they intend to do with them."

They had been walking erect; now they had to crawl forward. Before long they reached the seemingly sky-high rock wall which formed the eastern extreme of the forest. They snaked alongside it side by side. Now the fires were to their left and soon they saw the small lake where the chiefs' fire crackled and flamed.

"It's some kind of pond or lake!" whispered Droll. "I thought so. Where there's a forest, there must be water. We can't go any farther; the lake reaches right up to the rock wall. We must stay more to the left."

They were at the lake's southern end. The fires were burning on the western shore where the chiefs had been sitting. Crawling along the shoreline, the cousins arrived at a tall tree whose lower branches could easily be climbed. Meanwhile the Utes were throwing additional wood on the fires. The flames leaped up and illuminated the faces of the captured palefaces who had just been led in.

"Watch out, cousin," said Droll. "Can you climb?"

"Like a squirrel!"

"Then up we go into the tree. From there we'll have a much better view than from down here."

They swung themselves up and found a place in the foliage where even the most sharp-eyed Indian could not spot them.

The captives had been forced to walk so their legs were not tied. They were led over to the fire where the tribal leaders, among them Big Wolf, squatted cross-legged, The chief had retrieved his war bonnet and put this mark of distinction on again as behooved a victor. His eyes rested on the whites with the expression of a hungry puma. He kept silent for the time being since the eldest chief had the right to speak first.

Nanap-neav's gaze moved from one of the whites to the other, coming to rest on Winnetou.

"Who are you?" he asked. "Do you have a name? And what is the name of the mangy dog you call your father?"

He had not expected the proud Apache to answer him, but Winnetou answered calmly, "Whoever does not know me is a blind worm living in the dirt. I am Winnetou, chief of all the Apaches."

"You are no chief, no brave, but carrion of a dead rat!" the old one taunted him. "The palefaces will die an honorable death at the stake. You, however, we will cast into the lake for the frogs and crayfish to feed upon."

"Nanap-neav is an old man. He has seen many summers and winters and experienced much. But he seems not to have learned that Winnetou will not be derided without revenge. The chief of the Apaches is prepared to suffer all torments, but will not let himself be derided by a Ute."

"What do you expect to do to me?" laughed the old one. "Your hands are bound."

"Nanap-neav should consider that it is easy for a free and armed man to be uncouth to a bound captive! But honorable it is not. A proud warrior disdains to speak such words. If Nanap-neav will not adhere to this, he shall have to suffer the consequences."

"What consequences?" the old one snorted contemptuously. "Did your nose ever smell the stinking jackal that even the vulture will not touch? You are such a jackal. The odor you ---"

He was interrupted in mid-sentence. A shout of terror rose from the throats of the Utes standing nearby. Winnetou had taken a mighty leap onto Nanap-neav, toppled him backwards and with his heels had struck a succession of murderous blows and kicks to his chest and head then returned to his previous position, all before the onlookers could spring up to stop him.

The general outcry was followed by a moment of utter silence broken by the Apache's loud voice, "Winnetou did warn him. Nanap-neav did not listen and will never again insult an Apache."

The other chiefs had jumped up to examine the old one. His skull was broken on the right side and his chest had been crushed. He lay dead. The braves pressed in, hands at their knives, casting vengeful looks at Winnetou. One might have thought that the Apache's deed would have incited the Utes to a murderous fury, but that was not the case. Their rage remained silent, the more so because Big Wolf had raised his hand and ordered, "Back away! The Apache killed our old chief hoping that he might then die quickly and without pain. He thought you would rush and kill him swiftly. But he is mistaken. He will die a worse death than any other man has ever suffered. We shall confer about it. Carry Old Chief away in his blanket so the eyes of the white dogs no longer will take pleasure in seeing his corpse! They shall all be sacrificed at his grave. We shall bury Old Firehand and Old Shatterhand -- alive -- with him."

"You will not live long enough to bury me!" Old Shatterhand said in a voice of quiet menace.

"Be silent, dog, until you are asked to speak! How can you know the days I still have to live?"

"I know them. There will not be another one, for tomorrow at this time your soul will have departed from your body."

"Are your eyes so keen that you can see the future? If so, I shall have them pecked out!"

"To know when you will die, Big Wolf, does not require keen eyesight. Have you ever heard Old Shatterhand not speak the truth?"

"All palefaces lie, and you are one."

"It's the redskins who lie and you've proved it. We were four whites and fought four redskins for our lives. If victorious, we were to kill our opponents and than be free. We defeated them and gave them their lives. You, nevertheless, would not give us our freedom. You pursued us and fell into our hands. We could have taken all your lives. You had surely earned death, but we didn't make you pay the price because we are Christians. We smoked the peace pipe with you and you swore to be our friends and brothers all your lives. We freed you and in thanks you attacked us and dragged us here. Who lies? You or us? But do you remember what I told you before we separated last night in the canyon?"

"Big Wolf is a proud warrior. He never notes the words of a paleface."

"Then I'll help you recall them. I warned you that if you didn't keep your word this time, it would mean your death. You broke your promise and you shall die."

"When?" grinned Big Wolf.

"Tomorrow."

"By whose hand?"

"By mine."

"Your head has a hole through which your brains have run out!"

"I've told you your fate and that's how it will happen. Twice I held your life in my hands, twice I granted it to you, but you spoke to me with forked tongue nevertheless. It won't happen a third time. The red men shall learn that Old Shatterhand is lenient, but that he also knows when to punish."

"Dog, you shall never punish another man. You will be surrounded and guarded all night. We shall sit in council over you and by daybreak your mortal suffering will begin and will last many days."

The captives were brought to a small clearing where a fire burned, an Indian named Running Deer sitting by it to replenish it. Now their feet were tied as well and they were shoved down. Twelve armed warriors stood between the trees during the night to guard them. Escape was utterly impossible; at least it seemed so.

Droll and Frank had seen everything clearly from their high perch. The tree they occupied stood about a hundred and fifty paces from the camp fire of the chiefs, so that they had been able to understand most of what had been said there. Now they had to reconnoiter the place where the prisoners had been taken and try to approach them.

As they descended from the tree, the captured weapons and other possessions of the whites were being brought to the chiefs. Since these items didn't attract much attention, the hunters concluded that they would only be distributed in the morning, a fact that pleased Aunt Droll immensely.

Only the chiefs were still sitting by their fire. There must be a reason for the rest of the Utes to have abruptly disappeared. Soon Droll and Frank were to find out why. Peculiar, mournful sounds arose. For a while, a solo voice could be heard, followed by a chorus. This continued without a break, sometimes softer, sometimes louder.

"You know what this means?" Droll asked his Moritzburger cousin.

"It must be the funeral chant for the old chief."

"Yes. The Utes begin their songs even before the corpse is cold."

"That's good for us, because with all this wailing, the Indians will have difficulty hearing us. We absolutely must get to our friends."

"But what do we do when we've found them? We can't get them out!"

"That's not even necessary, because they'll go by themselves. The main thing for us is to untie or cut their bindings. If the place where they're kept isn't too far from where the weapons are deposited, we've won. It's really fortunate that it's so dark between the trees. The fires aren't a disadvantage for us, they're even useful since we can detect where the redskins are and avoid them."

"That's true. So, let's get going. I'll crawl ahead."

"Why you?"

"Because I've been in the west longer than you have and I know covert approaches better than you do."

"Oh, don't talk such nonsense! Don't fancy such big raisins! I'm experienced in all details of western know-how. The immense capability with which I comprehend the most difficult things is child's play. It's brought my perceptive faculties to such a high level that there's nothing I'm not at once a master of. But because you are my dear cousin, I shall give you precedence. But watch out! Should a rascal want to stab you dead in front of my eyes, just let me know so I can help you from behind. I'll not forsake you!"

The little Saxon soon showed that his schooling by Old Shatterhand had been excellent. He did extremely well, crawling agilely and noiselessly despite having to carry two rifles. Obviously the forward man had the more difficult task of looking out for twigs that might crack while at the same time looking for available cover.

They avoided the chiefs from a distance of about fifty paces and turned in the direction of the next fire which, serendipitously, turned out to be where the captives were being guarded. Slowly but surely they came closer, an approach with no little danger. Several times a redskin passed very close by. Once Frank had to quickly roll sideways so he wouldn't get stepped on. A bit later the foot traffic subsided. The Indians who had earlier taken up the funeral song now sat by the corpse; the others had stretched out for an hour's sleep.

Droll and Frank took cover behind two massive trees. Running Deer, the redskin delegated to maintain the fire, had left once to join the funeral dirge; some of the twelve guards had done the same. The fire had burned down somewhat and now provided so little light that the shapes of the prisoners could barely be discerned. Droll crawled a short distance to the right, then a bit to the left without seeing a guard. When he returned to Frank, he whispered, "This is the opportune moment. Can you make out Old Shatterhand?"

"Yes. He's the nearest one to us."

"Crawl over to him and remain still as if you were also tied up!"

"And you?"

"I'll get to Old Firehand and Winnetou, lying over there."

"That's dangerous!"

"Not more than here. Old Shatterhand will be happy to get his rifle back! Get moving!"

Hobble-Frank had at most eight paces to bridge. Just then, the flames died down to the point that it looked as if the fire was going out completely. It became so dark that it wasn't possible any longer to differentiate between the captives. The Ute guard had added wood, but before it caught, Droll and Frank took advantage of the blackness.

Frank was now beside Old Shatterhand. He stretched out his legs as if they were tied, laid the Henry rifle next to his neighbor and quickly pulled back his arms for the guards to think they were tied behind his back.

"You, Frank?" whispered Old Shatterhand, not at all surprised. "Where's Droll?"

"Over there with Old Firehand and Winnetou," replied Frank in a hushed undertone.

"Thank God you found the tracks and got here before daybreak!"

"Did you know we'd come?"

"Indeed! When the Utes stoked up the fires, I could see you weren't among the prisoners."

"We could've been caught in the slot canyon!"

"Pshaw! When the redskins looked in there for my rifle, I was afraid they might find you. But they returned empty-handed, and my rifle had disappeared. That told me everything. I was so convinced of your not forsaking us that I threatened Big Wolf with death."

"That was daring!"

"My dear Frank, the world belongs to the daring!"

"Yes, to the daring and to Hobble-Frank. Haven't I done grandly? Haven't we followed our comradely obligations very pizzicato?"

"You've done very well!"

"Yes, without us you'd have been a sausage!"

"Well, not quite yet. You know that I don't give up the game until it's truly lost. But here we not only have the cards stacked in our favor, but even hold the trumps. Had you not come, we would have helped ourselves in another way. Have a look!"

Frank looked over and watched the hunter very slightly raise his unbound right hand.

"I got my hands free already," he continued. In a secret back pocket I have a tiny knife which would have traveled from man to man so that we all would have been free before dawn. Then some quick leaps to the weapons over there by the chiefs ---"

"You know about that too?"

"I would be a poor frontiersman had I missed that. Without weapons there would be no escape for us. That's why I watched for them right from the start. First I need to know how you got here. Did you follow the redskins?"

"No, we didn't. We left ahead of them."

"To spy on them, then to follow?"

"Not that either. We just hiked down the canyon until we found a side canyon, which led this way. We intended to look for the redskins' tracks, hoping we could help you."

"Oh! Then it's actually not to your merit that you found this forest?"

"No, we really didn't deserve the forest. But chance put it in our path and I hope you won't take it crosswise that we paid you this nighttime visit."

"You're waxing ironic, Frank."

"Not really. I just want to make it clear that it wasn't easy to assimilate with you through the forest and all these redskins."

"I know enough to appreciate it, old friend. You risked your neck, and rest assured I'll not forget it. But pull your rifle closer; it could easily be spotted. And give me your knife so I can free my neighbor. He can pass it on."

"What are we going to do once everyone's bindings are off? First run for the weapons, then the horses, and off we go merrily?"

"No, we stay."

"By the devil! Are you serious? Stay here! Do you call this a rescue?"

"Yes."

"Thanks a million! This will be some fine business for the redskins, because once the sun comes up, it'll shine on two more captives than the night before."

"We won't be prisoners. If we run for the weapons and horses, it would have to be done so fast that total chaos would result, with everyone trying to find his own rifle, knife and other gear. The redskins would be on us before we could get to the horses. And who knows whether the horses are still saddled. No, what we must do is hide immediately behind our shields."

"Shields? I'm no knight in shining armor and I've no shield. So, might you give me an explanation of what you mean by a shield."

"The chiefs."

"Chiefs? Oh! Marvelous! What a great idea!"

"Not marvelous, but obvious. We'll take the chiefs hostage assuring thereby that nothing will happen to us. Quiet now. The fire's burning so low again that the guards won't see us moving."

He cut the bonds on his feet and then freed his neighbor, who passed the knife on. Droll's knife was already making its rounds. Then Old Shatterhand's order went quietly from mouth to mouth that everyone was to rush the chiefs as soon as the fire was extinguished.

"Extinguish the fire?" growled Frank. "How are we going to do that?"

"Watch. You'll see! It must be extinguished or the guards will start shooting."

At length, everyone lay ready for action. Old Shatterhand waited until Running Deer stood up to heap on fresh wood, an act that choked the flames briefly. Instantly, the hunter leaped over to the man, hit him with his fist and threw him onto the fire. Rolling the body back and forth a few times killed the flames. This happened so quickly that it was pitch-black before the guards comprehended what was happening. Their warning cries came too late; already the whites were racing through the forest toward the lake, Old Shatterhand in the lead, Winnetou and Old Firehand close behind.

The chiefs were still sitting around their fire. It was a most pleasant task for them to conceive and discuss the most exquisite tortures for the whites and the Apache to endure before they died. Although they heard the guards' warning shouts, they only had time to stand up in alarm; already the whites rushed them. In a few seconds, they were thrown back down, disarmed and tied securely hand and foot.

The hunters quickly found and grabbed up their rifles, not questioning who owned what. When the guards appeared, they saw their leaders lying on the ground, whites kneeling beside them with knives at their hearts. Behind them stood other palefaces, rifles aimed. Frozen in shock, the redskins let forth a furious baying which quickly brought more Utes on the run.

Old Shatterhand had to prevent a mass attack. His voice boomed out, threatening to kill all the chiefs on the spot. He demanded the redskins withdraw so he could peacefully negotiate with their leaders.

This was a decisive moment, suspended between life and death, not only for a few but for many. The Indians stood under protection of the trees. The whites were fully illuminated by the blazing fire. There was no doubt that the first rifle shot would see the knives find their targets in the hearts of the chiefs.

"Stay back!" Big Wolf called to his people. "Let me talk with the palefaces."

"We've nothing to negotiate with you," Old Shatterhand told him. "The others may talk."

"Why not me?"

"Because your mouth is full of lies."

"I shall speak only truth."

"You promised that before, then didn't keep your word. You ordered me earlier to speak only when asked. I'm no longer your prisoner, but you're mine and I give you the very same order now. Should you speak without being asked, a knife will enter your heart without pity!"

Old Shatterhand turned to the eldest of the chiefs. "What is your name?"

He answered, "Kunpui, Fire Heart is my name. Set me free and I shall talk with you!"

"You shall be free, but only when we're done speaking and you've agreed to our terms."

"What do you demand? Freedom?"

"No, because that we have already and it won't be taken from us ever again. First, call five of your most honored braves!"

"What for?"

"You'll learn soon enough. Call them quickly or the knives hovering over you may get impatient!"

"I must think whom to choose."

He said this only to gain time to consider whether it was truly necessary to follow Old Shatterhand's commands. The ensuing pause gave the whites the opportunity to sort out and gather their belongings. None of them was totally happy since everyone was missing one item or another.

Finally, Fire Heart named five braves who were ordered to approach without weaponry. They sat down to await what was to ensue, expecting to hear what was demanded of them, but instead saw something entirely different. Old Shatterhand had dropped his Henry rifle when the chiefs had been struck down. He now picked it up. Big Wolf's eyes fell on the rifle and forgetting the risk to his life, he shouted in terror, "The magic rifle, it has returned. The spirits delivered it to him through the air. Do not touch it, do not touch him either or it may cost you your life!"

"The magic rifle, the magic rifle!" the petrified Yampa Utes wailed from between the trees.

Shatterhand again demanded silence from Big Wolf and turned to Fire Heart. "We require the following: we're still missing items belonging to us; we want these. Upon daybreak, we'll ride out and take you chiefs and these five men along as hostages. Once we're convinced that there's no further danger threatening us, we'll set you free and permit you to return."

"Uff! That is asking too much," responded Fire Heart. "We cannot permit this. No courageous Ute is prepared to come along as a hostage to white men."

"Why not? What is worse? To be a hostage who'll be released, or a prisoner who was so careless as to let himself be captured? The latter, for sure! We were captured by you but it did no damage to our fame nor our honor. We even gained in both by demonstrating that we don't give up even when overcome by such a superior force. There's no shame for you to ride with us for a day and then be allowed to return."

"It is a shame, a great shame. You were in our hands. At daybreak, the stakes would have been ready, and now we are the captives and you give us ultimatums!"

"Is that made any better by refusing to accept our demands? Will the shame be less if we enter into battle in which you chiefs, sitting here, will be killed, not to mention many more of your braves. You chiefs and these five honored warriors will go to the Eternal Hunting Grounds from our first shots and our rifles will then eat many more. Remember also my magic rifle!"

This last admonition in particular seemed to have an impact since it prompted Fire Heart to ask, "Where do you want us to come with you? Where are you going to ride?"

"To be cautious, I could tell you a lie," answered Old Shatterhand, "but I disdain that. We're heading for the Book Mountains, up to Silver Lake. If we find you to be honest, we'll keep you with us for only a day. I now give you a quarter of an hour to consider. If you accede to our demands, nothing will happen to you. If you refuse, our rifles will begin to speak after the time I've given you. Howgh!"

Emphasizing his last word left no doubt that he could not be diverted from his conditions. Fire Heart lowered his head. It was outrageous that these few whites were now in a position to make such demands when only shortly before they faced the most gruesome death. Suddenly his attention was drawn to the trees from where a voice called, "Mai ive!"

These two words meant 'Look here!' They had not been shouted but spoken very softly and could have been directed at anyone and would have no meaning to the whites. But Old Shatterhand, Firehand and Winnetou looked surreptitiously to the spot from where the voice had come. What they saw was quite significant. Two redskins stood there holding a blanket by its upper corners between themselves. They moved this curtain in quick but specific intervals up and down. Behind them a fire burned. The two were speaking to Fire Heart in signals.

Indians use a sign language different from tribe to tribe. At nighttime, they employ a fire and blanket. During the day a large skin or blanket is held over a fire to collect smoke. Removing the cover permits a smoke cloud to rise which, depending on its timing, emits a signal not much different from Morse code. Tribes change the signs frequently so that outsiders cannot readily decipher their communication.

The two redskins thought their attempt to communicate secretly with Fire Heart had gone unnoticed. They were mistaken. As soon as the blanket began to move, Winnetou quite casually stepped a few paces aside to stand in the shadows behind Fire Heart.

Old Firehand and Shatterhand knew at once what was going on, but acted as if they had noticed nothing, leaving the deciphering to Winnetou who, as a redskin, was more experienced in these matters.

The messaging took about five minutes, during which Fire Heart didn't avert his eyes from the two for an instant. The two messengers then left, certain that only Fire Heart had seen their signals. But now the old chief realized that Winnetou was standing behind him. Alarmed, he turned to see which direction Winnetou was facing. The Apache was smart enough to have quickly turned his

331

back and was acting as if the lake's moonlit surface attracted his entire attention. This eased Fire Heart's concern.

A bit later, Winnetou walked slowly over to Old Shatterhand and Old Firehand. The three stepped aside a few more paces, then Winnetou said quietly, "The two redskins spoke to their chief. Did my brothers understand their words?"

"I saw them, but didn't understand all of it," was Old Firehand's answer. "But its meaning is clear, for what I didn't understand, I can easily complete in my mind."

"Well, what did they say?" Old Shatterhand asked urgently.

"The two redskins are young chiefs of the Sampitsche Utes." replied the Apache. "Their warriors are also gathered here. The young chiefs want Fire Heart to accompany us."

"Are they being honest? I'd be surprised," remarked Old Firehand.

"They are not honest. To get to Silver Lake our path will first lead us across the Grand River and into the Teywipah, the Elk Valley. There, many warriors of the Tasch, Capote and Wihminutsche Utes are camped, gathering for their drive against the Navajos and waiting for the Yampa Utes here to arrive. They expect us to encounter this group where they can overcome us and free the hostages. Right now, some messengers are being sent to alert them to our coming. And to prevent us from escaping the trap, the Utes camped here are to follow us so that we will be caught between the two armies and crushed by both."

"By the devil!" exclaimed Old Firehand. "That's not a bad plan. What's my red brother's opinion about this?"

"I agree that it is well-devised. But it contains a big mistake."

"What's that?"

"That I know about it. Now we all know and can respond to it."

"But we must cross the Elk Valley or we'll have to take a four-day detour."

"We shall not make a detour but ride to this valley without falling into the Utes' hands."

"Will that be possible?"

"Yes. Ask my brother, Old Shatterhand. I have been with him in the Elk Valley. We were by ourselves and were being hunted by a large number of Elk Utes. We escaped because we found a rocky trail, which may never have been traveled before us and never after. It is somewhat dangerous to cross, but if it comes to a choice between it and death, there is no doubt which to choose."

"All right, let's take that trail. What shall we do with the hostages?"

"We will not release them until we have crossed the Elk Valley."

"But shall we also set Big Wolf free?" asked Old Shatterhand.

"Do you want to kill him?" inquired Winnetou.

"He's earned death. Down in the canyon, I told him that it would cost him his life if he was treacherous once more. And again he broke his word. I'm of the opinion that he shouldn't get away scot-free. It's not for us only. If he's not punished, he'll think there's no need to keep his word to any white, and a chief's example is an example for other red men."

"My brother is right. I do not like to kill a man, but Big Wolf has betrayed his sacred word several times and has earned death. If we let him live, it will be construed as weakness. Punish him, and his warriors will learn that a promise may not be broken without retribution. In the future they will not dare to act in such a faithless manner. But of this, we need not speak to the Utes at this time.

The quarter hour had passed and Old Shatterhand asked Fire Heart, "Your time is up. What has the chief of the Utes decided?"

"Before I can tell you," Fire Heart answered, "I need to know exactly where you want to drag us hostages?"

"We won't drag you; you'll ride with us. You'll be tied, but no pain will be inflicted. We are riding to Teywipah."

"And from there?"

"Up to Silver Lake."

"And we hostages must ride with you up there? Those Navajo dogs may have already arrived and will kill us."

"We're not going to take you that far, only to the Elk Valley. If nothing's happened to us by then, we'll assume you've kept your word and shall set you free."

"Is that the truth?"

"Yes."

"Will you smoke the peace pipe with us to confirm this?"

"Only with you, because you speak and smoke in the name of all others."

"Then take your calumet and light it."

"We'd rather take yours."

"Why? Is not your pipe as good as mine? Or will yours emit only clouds of untruth?"

"The reverse is true. Mine always speaks truth, but a red man, smoking a paleface's pipe, one cannot trust."

This was a serious insult causing Fire Heart to shout, his eyes flashing, "Were I not tied, I would kill you. How dare you insult the Indian peace pipe oath!"

"I've the right. Big Wolf, smoking my pipe, lied to us repeatedly, and you're just as guilty by allowing your warriors to attack us. No. Only your calumet will be used, Fire Heart. If you don't agree, we can only assume that you won't be honest. Decide quickly! I don't wish to waste any more words."

"Then untie me so I can smoke the pipe!"

"That's not necessary. You are a hostage and shall remain tied until you're set free in the Elk Valley. I shall service your calumet and hold it to your lips."

Fire Heart preferred not to answer. He had to accept this insult as well. Old Shatterhand took the pipe from around the chief's neck, stuffed and lit it. He puffed the smoke to the sky, the earth and the four compass points, declaring in a few words that he would keep his promise to the Utes if they would desist from all hostilities. Fire Heart was put on his feet and turned to the four compass points. Glowering, he had to take the same six puffs from his pipe and confirm what he had promised for himself and his people. This concluded the ceremony.

Now the Utes returned the whites' missing belongings. They did it without qualms since they believed they would get them back soon enough, as they had learned meanwhile from the plans of the two young Sampitsche chiefs. Finally, the whites' horses and those for the hostages were produced. This all happened as dawn began to break. The whites thought it best to depart as quickly as possible and with great caution so as not to give the redskins any opening for a reprisal.

The five chosen braves and the chiefs were tied to their horses. Each was compelled to ride between two whites whose revolvers were at the ready should any of the redskins attempt to violate their oath. The group set off at a canter to the side canyon Droll and Hobble-Frank had taken earlier. The redskins kept silent; only the scowls on their faces told of their feelings.

15. An Indian Battle

No one was more pleased with the happy ending and proud of this adventure than Droll and Hobble-Frank, whose judicious intervention had made it a success, or at least contributed much to its speedy conclusion. They rode behind the hostages. Once they left the camp, Droll said with his unique giggle, "Hehehehe, it sure was a pleasure for my old soul! The Indians must be verily annoyed that we've upset their apple cart like this. Don't you think so, cousin?"

"They sure are!" Frank nodded. "This has been a genius pela de toros like none better. And you know who were matadors?"

"Who?"

"You and I, us two. Without us, the others would still be tied up like Prometheus who year after year had to eat nothing but eagle's liver."

"Well, you know Frank, I think they would've made it out by themselves. People like Winnetou, Shatterhand and Firehand won't let themselves be tied to the stake that easily. They've been in deeper trouble already and are still alive."

"I think so too, but it would've been a bit more difficult for them. Without our incomparable pluck, it wouldn't have been as easy to counterpoint themselves from this devilish trap. While I'm not outrageously proud of it, it's nevertheless a rousing feeling if one can tell oneself that aside from outstanding mental facilities, one possesses also such swift intelligence that can't even be overtaken by a horse. Once I enter retirement and am in good ink, I'll write my memoirs like all famous men. That's when the world will truly learn to what hallucinations a human spirit has the capability. You too are such a highly-endowed and honored man of the world. We can remind ourselves with our imitated self-confidence that we aren't only German countrymen but also configured cousins and relatives."

The group had arrived at the side canyon and followed it, not turning into the main canyon. Winnetou, who knew the trail best, rode ahead followed by the hunters, then those rafters who had the hostages between them. Behind came Ellen, sitting in her chair, her father riding by her side, and at the end rode the rest of the rafters.

Ellen had handled herself very well yesterday. She had not been mistreated by the redskins as severely as the men had been. During the assault on the chiefs sitting by the fire, she had stayed there all alone. Fortunately, the redskins had not thought to take her hostage and force a trade.

The narrow canyon rose rather steeply and after an hour's ride terminated in a wide open plateau which, in the far distance, seemed to be bordered by the massive range of the Rocky Mountains. Halting there, Winnetou turned and said, "My brothers know that the red warriors are following us. Let us ride at a gallop to put as great a distance as possible between them and us."

They spurred their horses as much as Ellen's ponies permitted. Later their run was interrupted by a gratifying event. They came across a herd of pronghorns and succeeded in hunting two. That fortunate happenstance provided food for the day with plenty to spare.

They drew closer to the mountains where the plateau seemed to reach to the foothills. However, this was an illusion, since the valley of the Grand River lay in between. By noon, when it had become uncomfortably hot, they arrived at a narrow gash in the plateau that dropped downward.

"This is the entrance to a canyon leading to the river," Winnetou explained as he descended the slope. It was as if a giant had used a plane to cut a deeper and deeper path leading through the solid rock. The walls on both sides, at first barely noticeable, rose to a man's height, then to that of a house, higher and higher, until they seemed to close in above their heads. It became dark and cool in the confine. At some spots, water dripped from the walls, collecting on the canyon floor and was soon a foot deep, a boon for the thirsty horses. Oddly enough, the canyon was a straightaway with not a single turn. It was cut so precisely through the rock that long before they reached its end they could see a bright line ahead, which became broader the closer they came. It was the end of the several hundred-foot-long giant-planed canyon.

When the riders arrived there, an almost overwhelming view presented itself. They were entering the Grand River valley. It was perhaps half a mile wide with the river flowing through its middle, leaving a broad strip of grassland left and right, bordered by vertical cliffs on both sides. The valley ran from north to south as if drawn with a straightedge. Overhead hung the burning sun which had, despite the depth of the valley and the river's water, dried out the grasses. Did the opposite cliff face have an opening?

It did! Almost opposite the group, a rather wide gap in the rock face presented itself from which a substantial creek tumbled. Winnetou pointed to it and said, "We must follow this creek upstream. It will take us to the Elk Valley."

"And how do we cross?" asked Butler, concerned for his daughter. "The current doesn't appear to be strong, but the river itself seems deep."

"Upstream from the creek's entry, there is a ford so shallow that at this time of the year the water will not even reach to Ellen's chair. My brothers may follow me!"

They crossed the grassland to the ford. On the other side, they also would have to cross the creek where footing for the horses would be easier. Winnetou drove his horse into the river, the others following. He had been right; the water reached barely to his boots. He had not yet attained the other bank when he suddenly stopped and called out a warning as if he had spied some danger.

"What's the matter?" asked Old Shatterhand, riding behind him. "Did the riverbed change?"

"No, but men rode over there!"

He pointed to the low bank. Old Shatterhand urged his horse several paces forward so he too could see the tracks. They were broad, made by many horsemen. The grass had not yet recovered.

"That's significant!" said Old Firehand, who had also approached. "We must check the tracks. You others," he called back, "wait in the water for the time being."

The three rode up to the bank, dismounted and inspected the tracks with expert eyes.

"These tracks were made by palefaces," Winnetou stated.

"Yes," Old Shatterhand affirmed. "Indians would have ridden single file and wouldn't have left such broad obvious tracks. I suspect these people aren't true frontiersmen. Experienced hunters would be more circumspect. I estimate the group to be thirty to forty men."

"Me too," added Old Firehand. "But whites, here, under the present conditions! They must be novices, heedless people, in a hurry to get up to the mountains."

"Hmm!" growled Old Shatterhand. "I think I know whom we're facing here."

"Well. Whom?"

"The colonel and his band."

"Thunder and lightning! It's possible. By my calculation, that crowd could have made it here by now. And that conforms with what you learned from Knox and Hilton. We must follow ---"

Winnetou interrupted him. He had walked to the creek and pointing to the shallows, said, "My brothers may come here. It is certainly the colonel."

The two walked over and peered into the crystal-clear water. At its bottom, one could clearly recognize a series of impressions close to the point where the horsemen had crossed the river and then continued across the creek.

"Before they crossed the creek," explained the Apache, "one of them dismounted to check the water's depth. They must be foolish people, for anybody can see that the water does not reach above the knees here. And what did the man check the depth with? May my brothers tell me?"

"With a hoe, easily recognizable by the impressions," answered Old Firehand.

"Yes, with a hoe. These people do not intend to hunt but to dig. It was the colonel."

"I'm of the same opinion," Old Firehand offered, "but we cannot exclude that others came by here as well."

"Only prospectors could have passed here," said Old Shatterhand, "and that I doubt."

"For what reason?" asked the other.

"First, prospectors are experienced people who would not be so incautious, and second, we can subtract maybe ten pack horses from the forty tracks, which leaves thirty riders. Prospectors don't wander the mountains and canyons in such large groups. No, it's the colonel with his men. I'd swear to it."

"I don't doubt it either. But where are they headed? They didn't follow the Grand River. No, they turned here to follow the creek upstream to the Elk Valley. They'll be riding directly into the Utes' hands."

"That's their fate and their own doing. We can't help it."

"Oh, no!" called Old Firehand. "We must intervene."

"Must? Why? Did they earn it?"

"No. But we need to get our hands on the drawing that the colonel stole. If we don't, we'll never learn where the treasure's located in Silver Lake."

"True enough. Do you intend to follow the scoundrels to warn them?"

"Not to warn them, but to capture them ourselves."

"That's hardly likely," Old Shatterhand said doubtfully. "Consider the lead they have!"

Old Firehand bent down once more to check the grass, then said in disappointment, "Unfortunately you're right! They came through here about five hours ago. How far is it to the Elk Valley?"

"We won't reach it before evening."

"Then I can forget about my plan. They'll be in the redskins' hands before we've covered half that distance. But what about the messengers the Yampa Utes sent to the Elk Valley? They must have left before us but we haven't seen any of their tracks."

"Those men probably did not ride but ran," Winnetou explained. "On foot the distance is much shorter, since a moccasin can cross areas a horse and rider may break their necks on. My brothers may no longer think of the colonel, but instead that we must efface these tracks."

"Why efface them?"

"We know the Yampa Utes are following us. Later, we will leave in the direction they expect us to follow. We must try deception if we want to lose them. We must lead them to think the colonel's tracks are our own, leading directly to the Elk Valley. Then they will follow them and will not imagine us turning off to the side to escape. They must not learn that there were horsemen here before. My two white brothers know how to blot out tracks. Hobble-Frank, Droll, Humpy-Bill and Gunstick-Uncle have learned it too, also Watson and Black Tom. These men must raise the grass, and water it from their hats. Once wet, the sun will straighten it. This must be done for a distance as far as the eye can see. When the Yampa Utes arrive, the grass will be upright again and depressed only where we have been riding."

It was an ingenious tactic. The hunters were called as the others finally crossed the river, then the creek, to wait for the tracks to be obliterated for some considerable distance. The hunters walked back along the tracks of the colonel's party for several hundred paces, sprinkled the grass with water --- making innumerable replenishing trips to the creek --- straightened it up, and drew their blankets across the ground while stepping slowly backwards. The rest the sun had to accomplish and that it would do without doubt. Whoever had not witnessed this stratagem and arrived just an hour later would assume the tracks were only those of Old Firehand and his companions. Once done, the "effacers" waded across the creek and remounted.

The hostage redskins had watched all this in silence. None had said a word since the departure from the camp. What they were now observing looked suspicious. Why had the palefaces blotted out the other tracks? Why did they waste precious time instead of following the tracks as quickly as possible? Fire Heart could not remain silent any longer and asked Old Firehand, "Who are the men who rode here before? Where did they go?"

"Am I supposed to know?" replied Old Firehand.

"Why do you blot out the tracks?"

"Because of your warriors."

"Our warriors? What have they got to do with the tracks?"

"They won't see them."

"They will not see them because our braves are camped at the Forest of Waters."

"They aren't camped there, but are on our trail."

"Do not believe this!"

"I don't just believe it; I know it."

"You are mistaken. Why would my people follow you?"

"To get us between your warriors and the Utes camped in the Elk Valley."

One could see that Fire Heart was becoming frightened. But he quickly regained his composure and said in what he hoped was a convincing tone, "My white brother must be dreaming. I do not know anything that he is talking about."

"Don't lie! We saw the signals the two young chiefs sent you using the blanket. We understood their meaning as well as you. We also know that you spoke with forked tongue while we were smoking the calumet."

"Uff! My words were not false!"

"We shall see. Woe to you if the Yampa Utes are pursuing us! I've nothing more to say. We must go."

The interrupted ride was continued up the creek. The tracks they followed were widespread, requiring them to ride in similar fashion so that their pursuers wouldn't realize they were following two different tracks.

If the redskins were quiet before, they now hung their heads even lower. They knew they had been unmasked and that their lives weren't worth a plugged nickel any longer. They would have tried to escape but their bonds were tight and the whites surrounded them so closely that a breakout was far from possible.

The creek meandered uphill. The valley broadened and was more and more covered by bushes and trees. Side valleys branched off from which small brooks descended to become part of the creek they were following. Winnetou led the way up the widest of the brooks to a valley which kept its breadth for about a fifteen minute ride, narrowing to a rocky constriction, then once more opening to a rich green meadow. After they crossed the narrows, Winnetou stopped and said, "This is an excellent place to rest and eat. Our horses are tired and hungry and we need rest too. My brothers may dismount and roast the antelopes."

"But then the Utes will catch up with us!" warned Old Firehand, somewhat alarmed.

"What does it matter? They will see that we know their intent. If we post one man at the narrows who can see them coming and signal us, they will realize that it is impossible to attack the place we have chosen to camp and will have to withdraw."

"But we'll lose much time!"

"We will not lose a minute. Eating and drinking will restore the strength we are going to need. And allowing our horses to graze and drink will later enable them to run faster. I have chosen this place. My brother may do as I suggest without concern."

The Apache was right and the others agreed to rest here. They posted a guard where the valley was narrowed by rock cliffs. The hostages were tied to trees, the horses began to graze and on two fires the game was roasted. Soon they were able to enjoy fragrant steaks, with the Indians also receiving their share along with water from Lord's Castlepool's cup.

The lord was in an excellent mood. He had come to America for adventure and had found more than he thought possible. He now pulled out his notebook to tally up the liabilities he owed to Bill and Uncle.

Repeating his favorite refrain, he asked Humpy-Bill, "Shall we bet, old sod?"

"Bet on what?" came the rejoinder, Bill being much on his guard.

"That I owe you already a thousand dollars or even more?"

"I don't bet."

"Egad! What a pity! I would have won that ruddy bet."

"Fine by me. You'll have to enter some more in your notebook today, your lordship, because it's likely we'll see more action."

"Jolly good! As long as we survive it, let it come. Look, it's begun already!"

Their guard was signaling them with a suppressed whistle. He waved and the leaders ran to him. Hidden behind the narrow gap and looking down the valley, they saw the Utes approaching, still half a mile away.

Old Shatterhand ordered their best sharpshooters to take cover beyond the narrow defile and behind some bushes. They were to commence firing as soon as they heard his first shot. But at the horses only, not their riders.

The redskins approached quickly, their eyes keenly on the tracks. They were sure the whites would be so happy to have escaped that they would be careless. In fact, they imagined themselves secure to the point that they had not even sent scouts ahead. The Utes were caught completely unawares when a shot rang out; ten, twenty and more followed. Wounded horses fell or reared, throwing off their riders and creating total disorder in the advance. A penetrating outcry of anger from the stunned Indians was followed by a general retreat. All at once, the defile was empty.

"So!" announced Old Shatterhand. "Now they've learned that we're prepared and know their intentions. But we must leave. They may try to approach us through a side valley. Let's go!"

In a few minutes, the group was ready and rode out swiftly. The redskins would probably follow only slowly now and with great caution, giving the whites a more than sufficient lead.

Farther up the meadow they went at a canter, crossing a ridge into a labyrinth of canyons and valleys which originated from various directions but all seemingly tending towards the same point. The point was the entrance to a wide, long and bare canyon where not a single blade of grass grew. Rocks of all shapes and sizes lay about, some singly, others piled on top of each other. It looked as if a tunnel from ancient times had collapsed.

In this rock-strewn environment, it was difficult to pick up a continuous track. Only here and there did a dislodged or horseshoe-scratched rock indicate that the rovers had passed this way. Winnetou pointed ahead and said, "In two hours' ride, this rocky passage will lower into the big green Elk Valley. But we will turn off here to the left. Old Shatterhand and Old Firehand may dismount, have their horses led by someone and follow us to erase any tracks we may leave, so the Yampa Utes will not notice that we turned here."

He reined his horse left and rode into the jumble of rocks. All the others followed except the two hunters who disguised all the tracks including their own before remounting once the group was well ahead.

The Apache displayed an incomparable memory of the terrain. It looked as if no man could find his way through this rocky chaos and although years had passed since he had come through, he remembered every slope and turn, never a moment in doubt about the direction to take.

Together once again, they followed a steep ascent until a broad and bare plateau was reached. They traversed it at a gallop. Already the sun had disappeared behind the Rockies when it looked as if they had reached the end of the plateau. Winnetou stopped, pointed ahead and said, "Only five hundred paces ahead, the plateau drops vertically into the depths, just as it does on its far side. In between lies the Elk Valley with plenty of water and a fine forest. It has only one known entrance, through which we have come, and an exit leading up to Silver Lake. Old Shatterhand and I are the only ones who know of a second entrance. We discovered it some time ago by accident when we were faced with danger. I shall show it to you."

He approached the plateau's edge. Piles of rock formed a balustrade there as if to protect travelers from falling into the terrible depths below. Winnetou disappeared between two such rock mounds. Everyone else followed him one by one.

And lo and behold, there was a path. To the right yawned the abyss into which they had to descend. But the path swung left along gaps and openings of the plateau so steep that everyone preferred to dismount and lead the horses. The immense mile-long, mile-wide rocky colossus had cracked here, creating a ravine leading ever farther down.

Despite the path's steepness, the horses picked their way securely because the ground was not of smooth rock but rather of rugged boulders. The lower they descended, the darker it became. Old Firehand put Ellen on his horse and supported her as he walked alongside.

It seemed as if they had been descending for hours when suddenly the steep trail ended, flattened out, and the ravine became so wide that it formed a broad open theater. Here Winnetou stopped and said, "We are almost in the valley. We will stay here until darkness permits us to pass by the Utes. Take the horses to the rear where there is water to drink. And gag the captives so they may not give us away."

For the descent the redskins were allowed to dismount which required freeing their legs. They were now tied again and their mouths gagged. Dusk ruled in this place, but these men, able to see in the night almost like owls, easily found their way about. In a far corner, moisture seeping from the rocks formed a small pool from which a tiny rivulet exited.

Winnetou took some of the hunters along to show them the locality. What they saw left them awed. Up front where the rocky theater narrowed again was an exit, so narrow that two men could barely pass through it side by side. The opening also led down, but not far. After a few turns, the men stood in front of a dense curtain of vines, below which the rivulet disappeared. Winnetou pushed the curtain somewhat aside, after which they saw a forest ahead, tree after tree, tall and strong and so dense with foliage that the day's final light could not penetrate.

The Apache stepped outside to reconnoiter. When he returned, he reported, "To the right many fires burn between the trees. The Utes are camped there. Up the valley it is dark. That is where we must go. Maybe no red men are posted there. If there are, it will be at most two or three at the Elk Valley's exit, and they can easily be taken care of. We could leave the valley without encountering much danger if the colonel were not somewhere in here. We must learn what his situation is. This is why I will approach the fires to listen when it has become even darker. Before this happens, we cannot leave. Until then, we must remain totally quiet."

He led the men back to show them some other essential places, since in case of danger everyone needed to know where he was and where there was an escape route.

The hostages' bonds were checked thoroughly; in addition each had his own personal guard. Since the whites had been able to slip their bonds the night before, the redskins were scrupulously watched to make sure they could not accomplish the same.

Winnetou wished to reconnoiter alone but neither Old Shatterhand nor Old Firehand would allow it. His task was highly dangerous and a single spy might not return, after which it would be unknown what had happened to him or how help could be provided. The two insisted on accompanying him.

They waited for almost two hours, then all three walked the fifty paces down to the vine curtain and departed through it. Entering the forest, they stopped to listen for any enemy that might be in the neighborhood. Nothing could be seen nor heard. A multitude of campfires burned some distance away. From their number, one could estimate the great horde of Utes camped there.

Now they advanced from tree to tree, Winnetou in the lead. The closer they approached to the fires, the easier their task became, since looking away from the flames made every person in front easily recognizable.

They moved along the valley's right side. The fires were located towards the middle. Maybe the redskins did not trust the cliff. That pieces had broken off could readily be seen from the many rock falls and rubble, which had crushed several trees, leaving rocks deeply imbedded in the soil. The three men advanced quickly. Already they had come parallel to the foremost fires. To the left and farther back burned a far brighter bonfire, separate from the others. By it sat five chiefs, recognizable from the eagle feathers in their buns.

One of them rose. He had tossed off his war coat. His bare chest, face and arms were streaked with thick, bright yellow paint. "It is Tab-wahgare, Yellow Sun," whispered Winnetou. "He is the chief of the Capote Utes and possesses the strength of a bear. Look at his body! What thick, strong muscles and what a powerful chest!"

The Ute waved to a second chief who also rose. He was taller than Yellow Sun, but certainly no less strong.

"I know this one. He is Tsu-in-kuts, Four Buffalo," muttered Old Shatterhand in a low voice. "He carries this name because he once killed four buffalo bulls with just four arrows."

The two chiefs exchanged a few words, then left the fire. Maybe they intended to check the guards. In any event, they avoided the other fires and approached the rock wall.

"Ah!" breathed Old Shatterhand. "They'll pass quite close here. What do you think, Firehand? Shall we take them?"

"Alive?"

"Obviously!"

"That would be a coup! Down on the ground; you take the first, I'll take the second!"

The two Utes came closer, one walking behind the other. Suddenly two figures rose up behind them. Two mighty fist blows and both men dropped without a sound.

"Well done!" whispered Old Firehand. "We got them. Now quickly to our hiding place with them!"

Each carried his victim over his shoulder. Winnetou was asked to wait while the two made their way to the hidden rock theater. They delivered their new captives, had them tied and gagged, then returned to Winnetou. But first they gave strict orders that no one was to leave this refuge before they returned, no matter what might happen.

Winnetou was still at his place. It was less urgent now to listen to what the chiefs had to say; better to locate the colonel and his gang. To find them the entire camp had to be reconnoitered. The three courageous men walked along the rock wall keeping the fires always on their left.

Where the flames illuminated the area they could see clearly, but ahead it was dark and that required caution. Where the eye failed, a touch of the hand was required. As usual, Winnetou scurried ahead. Suddenly he halted and voiced an almost too loud "Uff!" The two others stopped too and listened tensely. When all remained silent, Old Shatterhand asked urgently, "What is it?"

"A man," the Apache responded.

"Where?"

"Here, where I am, in front of me, under my hand."

"Hold on to him. Don't let him cry out!"

"No. He cannot cry out. He is dead."

"Did you throttle him?"

"He was dead already; he hangs from a stake."

"Oh, my God! A torture stake?"

"Yes. His scalp has been taken. His body has many wounds. He is cold and my hands are full of his blood."

"Then the whites have been killed already. This must be where the torture took place. Let's look around!"

They felt their way as they went and within ten minutes had found twenty horribly mutilated bodies tied to stakes and trees.

"Shocking!" groaned Old Shatterhand. "I thought it would be possible to save these people, at least from such suffering! Usually the redskins wait for the next day, but here they didn't waste any time."

"The drawing!" Old Firehand said. "It's lost now."

"Not yet," responded Old Shatterhand. We've got the captured chiefs. Maybe we can trade them for the drawing."

"If it still exists and hasn't been destroyed."

"Destroyed? Hardly! The redskins have learned the importance of such papers. An Indian nowadays would rather destroy other things than any paper he might find on a white, particularly if it's not printed but handwritten. Let's not give up hope. By the way, I think I know why these fellows were murdered so quickly."

"Why, then?"

"To make room for us. Our arrival had been forewarned. We didn't arrive; therefore they expect us to come tomorrow morning. Should we not arrive by then, they'll send scouts to look for us."

"The messengers must have arrived but not the full force of the Yampa Utes," Winnetou suggested.

"Right! The full force won't be here yet. It must have taken some hours before they dared approach that narrow defile again and to pass through it. They may come only by tomorrow morning since the last part of the trail is so difficult at night --- no! Listen, they're coming now!"

Up from where the three stood, a clamorous and happy cheer could be heard, which was echoed from farther down. The Yampa Utes had come despite its being night and despite the precipitous trail, which actually was well-known to them. The bellowing and yelling rose to a crescendo. Torches were lit from the campfires, and brandishing them the resident Utes ran towards the new arrivals. The forest became bright everywhere and so lively that the three scouts were in danger of being detected.

"We must get away," Old Firehand said. "But where? In front and ahead it teems with people."

"Up into the trees," answered Old Shatterhand. "We can wait in the dense foliage until things have settled down."

"All right! Up we go. Winnetou's already up there."

The Apache hadn't waited but lithely sprang into the branches of a large oak. The other two swung themselves up into different trees and disappeared in the foliage. They thought it no disgrace to hide when the odds were that great.

In the glow of the fires could now be seen the Yampa Utes, together with the reception committee. The new arrivals dismounted, their horses were led away and they then inquired whether Winnetou and the whites had come and been captured. The answer was received with great surprise. The Yampa could not believe that the whites had not yet arrived since they had been following their tracks all the way. Questions flew back and forth but the facts remained an enigma.

For the local Utes it was electrifying to learn that Old Firehand, Old Shatterhand and Winnetou were believed to be only hours away. From the exclamations and jubilation this news produced, the three men realized the reputation they had with these redskins.

But when the Yampa Utes learned that twenty whites had already been put to the stake, they thought it could possibly be their quarry after all and demanded to see them. The resident Utes used firebrands to illuminate the executed whites that, in the flickering light, displayed an even more hideous aspect to the three hidden hunters. When the Yampas saw that the corpses were not the ones they sought, they vented their anger on them in the most terrible ways. Fortunately, this carnage did not last long. It found an end no Ute would have expected.

From the lower end of the valley rose a long drawn-out cry, a scream once heard one never forgets, a human death scream.

"Uff!" one of the chiefs exclaimed in alarm. "What was that? Yellow Sun and Four Buffalo are down there!"

A second, similar scream arose; then shots were fired.

"The Navajos! It must be the Navajos!" the chief shouted. "Winnetou, Shatterhand and Firehand have called them to seek revenge. Forward, braves, throw yourselves on the dogs! Destroy them! Leave the horses behind and fight on foot from behind the trees!"

For a moment everyone ran helter-skelter through the camp. Weapons were fetched and wood was thrown on the fires to make the enemy more visible. The forest resounded with the war cries and shouts. Shots rang out, closer and closer. Invading dark figures rushed from tree to tree firing rifles.

The Utes responded, first singly and disorganized, than in assembled defensive groups. There was no real battle area --- the struggle encompassed the entire valley --- but around each fire the fighters seemed to gather in force.

Yes, it was indeed the Navajos. They had intended to take the Utes unawares, but had failed to silence the guards at the valley's entrance. The death cries had raised alarms throughout the forest and it now meant fighting man to man without the element of surprise, depending only on bravery and superior numbers.

The red man prefers to attack towards morning when sleep is deepest. Why the Navajos had departed from this tradition was difficult to understand. They may have thought they could approach unnoticed, then quickly fall on the enemy while they were trapped at the fires. When this failed, their honor would not permit them to withdraw. They had continued their attack and now fought on, sustaining great losses.

The Utes, it turned out, had the greater numbers. They also knew the terrain better than their enemies, and although, the Navajos fought bravely, they were pushed back little by little. The two sides battled both from afar and close in, using rifle, knife and tomahawk. It was a most spectacular scene for the three hidden spectators, wild men against wild men fighting in the most savage manner! Here, two battled with brutal yells; there, several butchered each other in unbroken silence. Where one was killed, the victor was quick to take his scalp, possibly to lose his own a moment later.

Of the three chiefs who had been sitting at the fire, two battled hand-to-hand, courageously firing up their braves by example. The third took a position near a tree to follow the course of the battle closely, shouting his orders right and left. He was the commander-in-chief, chosen to lead the defensive arrangements. Even as the Navajos were pushed back farther and farther, he remained at his post, leaving pursuit of the enemy to the other fighting chiefs.

The battle became more distant. Now the three involuntary witnesses could make it to safety. The path to their hiding place lay open. Should there be a turnaround in the battle, or when the Utes returned victorious, it would be impossible to return unnoticed to their companions.

Winnetou climbed down. Despite the darkness, the two others saw him and followed suit. The commander-in-chief still occupied his post. The battle noise sounded far away.

"Back now!" urged Winnetou. "Later they will light more fires to celebrate; then it will be too late."

"Shall we take this chief too?" asked Old Shatterhand.

"Yes," responded Old Firehand. "We can easily grab him --- he's alone. I'll ---"

He stopped. What he saw gave cause for great surprise and left his words stuck in his mouth. Out of the darkness leaped a little fellow swift as lightning, swinging his rifle and downing the chief with a well-aimed blow. He then grabbed the redskin under the arms and dragged him quickly into the dark. Meantime, one could hear his softly spoken, but audible words, "What Old Shatterhand and Old Firehand can do, the Saxons for the most part know also how to do!"

"That's Hobble-Frank!" Old Shatterhand said in astonishment.

"Yes, it's Frank!" confirmed Old Firehand. "The little chap's crazy! We must follow him quickly so he doesn't do anything stupid."

"Crazy? Certainly not! He's a funny hop-o'-my-thumb, that's true, but he's got his heart in the right place; and reckless he's not at all. I've schooled him and can tell you that I've enjoyed it. But let's follow him; our paths are the same.

They hurried after the little man when suddenly a shot rang out in front of them.

"He's come across a redskin! Quickly, let's ---" Old Shatterhand asked, but then fell silent, for ahead of them they heard Frank's laughing voice, "Blockhead, watch out where you aim! If you want to hit me, don't aim at the moon! Here's the return and 'Good night!' now."

The sound of a heavy blow, then silence. The three pressed forward to meet the little man.

"Back!" he demanded. "There's shooting and stabbing going on here!"

"Stop! Don't shoot!" warned Old Shatterhand. "What are you looking for out here?"

"Is that you, Shatterhand? Looking for? Nothing, nothing at all. I've already found two. Thank God you opened your mouth! Had I not recognized you by your conglomerate voice, dear sir, I'd have shot you to pieces. I've two bullets in my rifle and with my presence of mind it would have been highly unpleasant for you. I seriously warn you never again to first, blindly rush into danger and second shout at me, or you might, thirdly, speedily as the wind, meet your forefathers and patriarchs!"

Despite the seriousness of the situation, the two white hunters couldn't help laughing at this admonishment. At the moment, no enemy was nearby so Old Shatterhand could unconcernedly inquire, "But who gave you permission to leave the hide-out?"

"Permission? Who's to give me permission? I'm my own lord and master. Only worry for you drove me out here. You'd barely gone when all this ruckus started outside, as if the Cimbers had encountered the Teutons. I could've stood the noise since my nerves have been marinated in tar and cod liver oil. But then all that shooting started and I veritably feared for you. My childlike mind is concerned for your soul's existence with paternal attachment, and I really can't let the redskins deliver you from your wonderful life. That's when I took my rifle and scurried away without the others noticing my disappearance act in that Stygian darkness.

"To the right, there was shooting. To the right, you had gone. Therefore I went right. There stood that chief against the tree like a marinated idol. That annoyed me. So I gave him a little tap from the top to put him into the horizontal position. Naturally, I wanted to get him quickly into successive security and dragged him away. But he turned out a bit heavy for me. So, for a moment, I sat down on his corpus delictus to rest a bit.

"Then this red interloper crept up and saw me against the light. He pointed his rifle at me. I slapped it aside and his bullet took off for the Milky Way. I then engaged the fellow by means of my rifle butt with such endearment that he collapsed beside the chief. Now the two fellows lie there without sense and reason and don't know what to make of it. There's sure trouble in this world!"

"Be glad that no greater misfortune arose! Had you come earlier, you'd have been lost!"

"Not to worry! Hobble-Frank never comes before he hasn't got victory by its tail. What are we going to do with these charming fellows? I cannot take care of them myself."

"We'll help you. Up there now! Quickly! The shooting has stopped and we can expect the Utes to return at any time."

The two unconscious Indians were carried to the hiding place and tied and gagged like the others. Thereafter Winnetou and Old Firehand took up positions at the vine curtain to observe what was going on outside.

The Utes returned as the victors. They started more fires and in their light and with torches they searched the woods for the dead and wounded. The Navajos had taken theirs along, as is customary for Indians.

Each time a dead Ute was found, a mourning and angry wail went up. Sorrowfully, the bodies were gathered for an honorable burial. Several men were missing who must have been taken captive. Among those were the three chiefs who had disappeared without a trace. When this was discovered, the forest once more resounded with the dismayed cries of the infuriated braves. The two remaining leaders called their most distinguished warriors for a council at which loud, angry declamations were made.

This gave Winnetou the opportunity to slip up on them once again to learn the Utes' intentions. It turned out not to be difficult. The redskins were convinced they were alone after having driven off their foes. The beaten Navajos would surely not attempt to return and even should this happen, guards had been posted at the valley's entrance. That more serious enemies lurked in the valley's middle they couldn't know. With this advantage, Winnetou heard everything that was planned.

The Utes intended to bury their dead during the night; mourning dirges were to be sung later. First they wanted to find and free their captured chiefs. They thought this more important than awaiting tomorrow's arrival of Winnetou and his famous white companions. Since the three were headed for Silver Lake, they were certain to fall into the Utes' hands anyway. If they were to save the chiefs, the Indians had to depart quickly. All necessary preparations were made to leave for Silver Lake at daybreak.

Winnetou withdrew slowly and carefully. Close to the whites' hiding place, he came across a number of ponies, five animals who had shied during the battle and separated from the others. The Apache thought of the four new captives who also needed transportation. No one was around. Being Indian steeds, the animals did not shy from him. He took the first one by its lead rope and led it through the vine curtain where Old Shatterhand took charge of it. In this way, one by one, the other three ponies were brought in. Although they snorted a bit, Winnetou was able to keep them calm.

Within their hiding place, time passed quickly. There was much to talk about and listen to. In the darkness, Hobble-Frank had settled down at his cousin's side. Before he had found Droll, Frank had never parted from Fat Jemmy and, despite all quarrels, the two had always been one heart and soul. But this had changed since he met the Altenburger. Droll didn't insist on being learned and he let the little man talk without ever correcting him. This produced a powerful force that tied him to his cousin. Then again, Droll, as an experienced frontiersman, didn't think poorly of the little man. Just the opposite; he appreciated his good character traits and was honestly pleased at his recent heroic accomplishment. That Frank could first overcome the chief and then the Indian brave was not the work of foolhardiness but of agility and presence of mind. The deed had found general respect and all had expressed praise, except for one, Lord Castlepool. He now caught up with his omission. Sitting on Frank's other side, he returned to his favorite subject and asked, "Shall we bet, my dear fellow?"

"I don't bet," came the response.

"Ah, but why not?"

"I haven't got money for it."

"I would be delighted to lend you some."

"Lending means bending, we say in Saxony. Then isn't it un-Christian and contra-social to first lend a poor schlemiel money and afterwards take it away from him in a bet? That's approaching me slap-dab backwards. I keep my money, even if I don't have any."

"But, dash it, you might win!"

"I wouldn't have a prayer of it! I'll not get rich by betting. There's no blessing in it. I've my basic principles and counterpoints from which I won't let myself go astray."

"That's bloody sad. This time I purposely intended to lose, old blister, as a reward for your heroic exploit."

"Every heroic deed rewards itself within oneself. One carries the accusative recognition around within one's own holiest heart. To the merit be the crown, to the other just a frown! Isn't it also a duplicitous custom to reward princes and heroes by a wager? Who wants to give ought to give, not by a false bet, but straightforward with the hand in the mouth. That's how it's done in all high-cultured countries, and the opposite isn't going to be introduced in the vicinity of my very own person."

Scarcely at all chastened, the lord declared, "Then you would not take it crosswise if I made you a present?"

"Very much so! Hobble-Frank won't let himself be given anything. For that he has far too many majestic ambitions --- but a memento, what the conscientious Frenchman calls a souvenir and cataplasm --- I can readily be given without becoming afraid to decompose the lyre chords of my disposition into dissonances."

"Well, then you shall have a memento. I hope you will be happy with it. I have two and can spare one."

He pressed one of his excellent rifles into Frank's hands, who quickly handed it back saying, "Listen, your lordship, let's not joke! Don't tackle me to the point where I become ruinous! I love to smile and laugh but I can also make a cannon face if one comes too close to my unguarded interference. A little pleasantry is all right and easily digested, but to pull my nose I can't let happen. For that I think too highly and diagonally of myself!"

"But I'm not jesting, old bean; I'm entirely serious!"

"What? You really want to dismiss this rifle from your possession?"

"Right-o," Castlepool confirmed with a broad smile.

"And to make it a bona immobilia present to me?"

"So it shall be."

"Then quickly, hand it to me, before regret overcomes you! Delusion is short like Jemmy, but remorse is long like Davy, sings the poet. This rifle is my property, my incontrovertible and concentrated property. It's like Christmas today! I'm expostulated from joy! I'm totally complexed and overcome! Lord Castlepool, if you ever need a good friend who goes through thick and thin for you, just whistle and I shall be right there! How am I to thank you? Is it to be a friendly handshake, a lucrative kiss or an intimate embrace before the whole wide world?"

"Bless me, a handshake will do."

"Good! Then here's my hand. Press it, press it for as long as it brings you pleasure. From now on, I'll make it available daily as long as I don't need it myself, for gratitude is a decor and Frank does owe you that and additional. Droll, cousin of Altenburg, did you hear what Fortuna granted me this day with all requisite esteem?"

"Yes," Droll answered. "Anyone else but you I would envy. But since you're my cousin and friend, I'm pleased from the bottom of my heart. Congratulations!"

"Thanks, and back to you! Hurray, will there be shooting from now on! With that rifle, I'll put my millennium to its bounds without advocate and protocol. Here, Castlepool, my hand once more. Press it again, just go ahead, I'll gladly have it happen. You Englishmen have always been splendid fellows. I'll gladly confirm that with my very own signature. As of today, count me as one of your most intimate house and family friends. As soon as I come to London, I'll visit you. You need not feel troubled; I'm pure modesty and take everything as it comes."

Frank's delight knew no bounds. He indulged in more idioms and profuse expressions to the amusement of the others. It was fortunate that he could not see their faces in the dark.

Since considerable exertion was expected the next day, lots were drawn for the posting of guards and everyone else attempted to sleep, which posed no little difficulty. It was past midnight before slumber could come to the group, but they were abruptly awakened at first daylight by the noisy departure of the Indians.

When everything had turned quiet outside, Winnetou slipped out to check whether they could leave their hiding place. It had been ample but not very comfortable due to the horses and ponies' presence. When he returned, he reported all safe. Not a single Ute remained in the valley.

For safety's sake, a guard was first posted both at the valley's entrance and its exit. Then the entire valley was searched thoroughly. They found a mass grave with a huge cairn piled on top of the bodies. There were also several horses that had been hit by errant bullets. The redskins had left them lying unburied; the whites were smarter. If they wanted to avoid the Utes, their path to Silver Lake would lead them through bare tracts of land, bare of plant and animal life, where it would be difficult to find food. Horse meat would come in handy. Frontiersmen are not picky; they'll eat horse flesh if there's nothing better to be had. And it's not unusual when one is a guest of Indians for a festive roast of fattened dog to be presented!

The best pieces of the horses were taken and distributed. Then several fires were started and everyone roasted his share to better preserve it.

This didn't amount to much loss of time since they could not follow the redskins too closely anyway. It was also wiser to prepare ready-to-eat portions now than waste precious time later. Their own horses were well-watered and had plenty of time for grazing.

Shortly after the Utes were gone, the captives' gags had been removed. They could now breathe more easily and speak freely once again. Yellow Sun was first to put the opportunity to use. He had lain still and observed the whites, each and every one, a scowl darkening his face. Now he turned to Old Shatterhand, asking, "Who of you knocked me down? How dare you to take us captive and bind us although we have done nothing to you!"

"Do you know who we are?" the hunter asked him.

"I know Winnetou, the Apache, and know that Old Shatterhand and Old Firehand are with him."

"I'm Shatterhand, and it was my fist that smote you."

"Why?" the Indian asked disingenuously.

"To render you harmless."

"Are you saying that I intended to harm you?"

"I'm saying exactly that."

"That is a lie!" burst out Yellow Sun in a pretense of outrage.

"Make no effort to deceive me! I know everything. We were to be slaughtered here by you, although we've smoked the peace pipe with the Utes. The Yampas sent you messengers yesterday, than joined you in force. Every untruth you say is in vain. We know where we stand with you and won't believe a single duplicitous word."

The chief turned away his face and fell silent. In his place, Wild Horse, the common brave that Hobble-Frank had captured spoke up, "Are the palefaces now enemies of the Utes?"

"We are friends of all red men, but defend ourselves if we are treated as enemies."

"The Utes have taken up the tomahawk against the palefaces. You are famous warriors and are not afraid of them. Do you know that the Navajos have risen to aid the palefaces?"

"Yes, I do."

"The Navajos are Apaches and the most famous chief of theirs, Winnetou, is your friend and companion. I see him standing over there by his horse. Why do you subdue a brave of the Navajos and tie his arms and legs?"

"Are you referring to yourself?"

"Yes. I am Wild Horse, a Navajo."

"Then why aren't you painted with the colors of your tribe?"

"To take revenge."

"And why were you still around when your people had already withdrawn?"

"Because I wanted to avenge myself. My brother fought at my side and was killed by a chief of these dogs. I carried him to safety so the Utes could not take his scalp. When I gave his body to our warriors, I wiped off my war paint so that the Utes would not immediately recognize me as an enemy. Then I returned to avenge his death, although my brothers had by then departed.

"I crept past my enemies without being seen. Because a chief had slain my brother, so a chief was to give me his scalp. I knew that one remained in the valley and I wanted to find him. Then I spotted two men in my path, one struck down and the other standing. I tried to shoot the erect man but he was faster and I was knocked unconscious. When I came awake, I lay in darkness, bound hand and foot. Call Winnetou! He does not know me, but when I talk with him I can prove that I am no Ute, but Navajo.

"I believe you, Wild Horse. You are Navajo and will be freed."

Unexpectedly, Yellow Sun rose up in protest, "He speaks with forked tongue! He is Ute, one of my braves and a coward who tries to save himself with lies!"

"Silence!" Old Shatterhand commanded. "Were he truly one of your braves you wouldn't betray him. That you intend to ruin his chances confirms that he's speaking truth. You're a chief, but your soul is that of a common coward one must despise!"

"Dare not to insult me!" the other roared. "I have the power to destroy you all. If you take off my bonds, you shall be forgiven. If you do not, you can expect a thousand indescribable pains!"

"I laugh at your threats. You're totally in our power and we'll do with you as we please. The more you accept your situation, the more bearable it will be. We are Christians and do not delight in making our enemies' suffer."

While saying this, he freed the young Wild Horse from his bonds. The youth jumped up, stretched his limbs and demanded, "Hand these dogs over to me that I may take their scalps! The more charitable you are with them, the more they will deceive you."

"They're not yours," Old Shatterhand told him. "You may travel with us, but if you dare to attack any of our captive Utes, I shall kill you with my own hands. Only if we keep them alive will they be of use to us. Their deaths would be greatly to our disadvantage."

"Of what use can they be?" the redskin asked disdainfully "These vermin are good for nothing."

"I need not give you an answer. If you wish to return to your people, you'll have to follow our orders."

From the look on the Navajo's face, it was apparent that he disliked having to relinquish his revenge, but he had no choice but to submit. To satisfy him somewhat, Old Shatterhand assigned him to guard the captured Utes and promised him the scalp of any who tried to escape. This calmed the young man and at the same time was a wise arrangement, since no better or more tireless guard could be found who was also so hungry for their scalps.

The first task now was to inspect the rovers who had died at the stake, a sight better left undescribed. They had died with great suffering. Looking at the corpses, the whites who had seen and experienced much already, could not help but shudder as they stared horrified at the mutilated and disfigured bodies. The rovers had harvested what they had sown. The colonel had suffered most. He hung upside down on the stake. Like his companions, he was totally naked. The redskins had shared the clothing among themselves; not the least item could be found.

"That's too bad!" said Old Firehand. "Had we only come earlier and prevented these peoples' murder!"

"Pah!" said Old Blenter. "Do you have pity on these scoundrels? Had we come at the right time and succeeded in saving their lives, Brinkley would have died anyhow. My knife would surely have had a talk with him."

"That wasn't what I meant. I don't regret their deaths, although I wish it had been less gruesome. But the drawing the colonel was carrying! That I wanted, that we need! And now it's gone, lost!"

"Maybe we'll find it yet. In any case, we'll certainly meet the Utes again. It might be possible to find the colonel's clothes which we could then search."

"Hardly! We don't know who was wearing what; the pieces probably didn't stay together either, but were shared among several redskins. How are we to put the puzzle together? The drawing's lost, and the old chief Ikhatschi-tabli, from whom Fritz Engel received it, is dead. Another copy isn't available any more."

"You're forgetting," interrupted Watson, the former work boss from Sheridan, "that this chief had a son and grandson who, while not present at the time, live at Silver Lake. They'll know the secret and can surely be induced, freely or by force, to tell about it."

"An Indian cannot be forced to reveal something like that, particularly when dealing with gold and silver. He'd rather die than help the hated whites to acquire wealth."

"But the question is whether they count us among the hated. Maybe the two Bears are friendly toward whites."

"The two Bears?" Old Firehand asked. "Are those their names?"

"Certainly! Big Bear and Little Bear."

"Thunder and lightning! How could I've missed that! Yes, I now recall their names. How could I not have thought immediately of the two Tonkawa we met on the paddle-wheeler! Nintropan-hauey and Nintropan-homosch, Big Bear and Little Bear!"

"The two Nintropan live up at Silver Lake," confirmed Winnetou. "I know them. They are my friends and have always been well disposed towards palefaces."

"Is that true? That's good, very good! Then perhaps not all hope is lost to locate Ikhatschi-tabli's map. Unfortunately, there's fighting going to occur and the Utes are between us and the lake. We may not be able to get past them."

"We need not get past the Utes," the Apache replied. "I know a path no white or Ute has ever taken. It is difficult, but if we leave here soon, we will arrive even ahead of them, even before the Navajos."

"Then let's waste no time," urged Old Firehand. "We've nothing more to do here other than bury the rovers. We cannot leave them hanging like that. We can do it quickly if we lay them side by side and pile rocks on top. After that we can leave. Let's hope for the best, particularly since we have several hostages which should enable us to induce the Utes to accept peaceful proposals."

16. At Silver Lake

A grand scenery presented itself to the hunters and their troop when they approached the destination of their troublesome ride. They rode up a slowly ascending canyon, its mighty walls shining with almost blinding colors. Colossal sandstone columns, beside or in front of each other, strove skyward in a variety of hues, layers and stories. At times they manifested themselves in straight walls, at others in pillars, sometimes with protruding corners, points and edges, giving the traveler the impression of castles or fantastic citadels. The sun stood above these grandiose formations producing an indescribable splendor of color. Some rocks shone in opalescent blues, others in reddish gold; between lay yellow, olive-green and fiery copper layers, while in clefts a saturated deep blue shadow reposed. But all this glory, impressive to the onlooker, was dead, missing any signs of life. Not a drop of water could be seen among the rocks. No blade of grass found nourishment down here and the rugged walls offered no hold for any greenery to please the eye.

But that water flowed at times, and in huge quantities, was evidenced by the traces left on the canyon walls by these deluges. At flood times, the now dry canyon formed the bed of a river, which emptied its rushing waters into the Colorado. For weeks at a time, the canyon was impassable on foot and unlikely to be crossed even by a daring frontiersman or an Indian in his canoc.

The canyon floor was formed of a deep layer of large rounded rocks, their interstices filled with sand. This made for difficult travel since the round boulders all too often gave way under the hooves of the horses and tired the animals so that frequent rest stops were required.

Old Firehand, Old Shatterhand and Winnetou rode in the lead, the rest following. Firehand looked around with conspicuous attention. It was obvious he was seeking a location of some importance. Finally, where two rock columns leaned against each other, forming a passage at their bottom barely ten feet wide, and seemingly narrowing farther in, he reined in his horse, looked at the spot critically and said, "This must be the place where I came out after I'd found the vein. I don't think I'm mistaken."

"And there you want to enter?" asked Old Shatterhand.

"Yes. And you too."

"Does the opening continue? It seems to end soon."

"Let's see. Maybe I'm mistaken after all."

Just as Old Firehand began to dismount to check the place, the Apache veered his horse over to the rock narrows and said in his quiet and assured voice, "My brothers may follow me. Here begins the trail by which we can shorten our remaining travel distance substantially. It is also easier on the animals than the rubble-strewn floor of the canyon."

"You know this cleft?" Old Firehand asked in surprise.

"Winnetou knows all mountains, valleys, canyons and passages. And you are aware he is never mistaken."

"That's true. But that you exactly know this place and insist it's the beginning of a trail is peculiar. Do you know where it'll lead us?"

"Yes. First the cleft will narrow even further; then it widens again, not into a narrow canyon, but into a smooth rocky surface which slowly rises."

"That's true. That's it! It's the right place! This slope leads several hundred feet upward. And what comes then?"

"At its highest extent, the edge of the slope suddenly drops off into a large basin from which a winding canyon leads up into the wide and beautiful valley of Silver Lake."

"Yes, I remember. Have you been to the basin?"

"Yes."

"Did you see anything unusual there?"

"No. There is nothing, nothing at all to find. No water, no grass, no animal. Not even a beetle or an ant crosses the eternally dry rock."

"Then I'll show you something there more precious than water and grass."

"Do you mean the silver vein you discovered?"

"Yes. Not only silver, but gold as well. The rocky basin is the destination of our long ride. Let's proceed!"

They entered the gap, one behind the other, since there was insufficient space for more. Soon, though, the walls opened further and further, the gigantic columns receded and in front of the riders lay a huge triangular rocky slope, its pointed end at their feet, broadening slowly from the parting walls. Its upper edge formed a straight line against the bright sky.

It was as if the horses had to climb an immense roof. Fortunately, its rise was gentle so that it did not pose any difficulty to the animals even though it took an hour for the group to arrive at the top. Ahead of the men, a mile-wide rock-flat extended to the west. Carved into it was the deep basin of which Old Firehand and Winnetou had talked. At its left, one could see a dark streak leading southward: the canyon leading out to Silver Lake.

Now they had to descend. The slope was so steep that everyone had to dismount and lead his horse, sometimes past highly dangerous spots. The captives, too, had to walk, which meant their legs needed to be untied. The young Navajo, Wild Horse, stayed hard at their sides, not letting them out of his sight. Once at the bottom, they were compelled to remount their horses, and their feet were again tied together below the horses' bellies. At this point the basin had a diameter of at least one mile with a flooring of deep sand mixed with pebbles the size of a man's fist.

Old Firehand wanted to show his find to his companions without the Utes learning about it. The hostages were therefore led a distance away, with some rafters and Wild Horse to guard them. None of the others remounted. The knowledge that they had arrived at the long wished-for location had caused keen excitement among them.

Two of the men were of key importance now. Old Firehand, who knew the vein, and Butler, the engineer, who was to investigate the find and check into the feasibility of its exploitation. Butler examined the area with probing looks then suggested, "It's possible we've got a bonanza. If there are truly precious metals here we can expect to find them in large quantity. This enormous basin was created over thousands of years by the waters that washed in through the canyon from the south and formed --- since it could not continue --- a huge whirlpool, loosening the rock and grinding it to gravel and sand. The floor on which we stand was configured by these waters and will contain the washed-out metals which, because of their weight, sank the deepest and must lie below the sand. Let's dig down a few feet and find out whether our journey was successful or in vain."

"We don't need to dig. Isn't it sufficient to prove that the walls contain these minerals?" asked Old Firehand.

"Of course. If there's gold and silver in the walls, then the same metals will also be found at the bottom of this basin."

"Then come on! I'll deliver your proof."

He walked straight to a spot he seemed to know precisely. The others followed, filled with suspense.

"Cousin, my heart's a-beating," Hobble-Frank confessed to Droll. "Should we find silver here, or gold, I'm going to fill my pockets and head for home in Saxony. There, I'll build a so-called villa at the banks of the lovely Elbe and from morning to evening stick my head out a window to show the people what a distinguished and splendid gentleman I've become."

"And I," answered Droll, "will buy myself a farm with twenty horses and eighty goats and do nothing but make quark and goat cheese. That's all that matters in Altenburg country."

"But what if we don't find anything?"

"Well. If there's nothing there, we can't help that either. But I figure we'll be in luck, because it speaks for itself that there must be silver in the vicinity of Silver Lake."

Their confidence was not in vain. Old Firehand arrived at the wall, which had been washed out at this location and was rather fragmented. He pulled away a loose rock, another and then another. A hole appeared, probably created by natural causes, but artificially widened as was clearly evident then covered again by these rocks. Old Firehand reached in, saying, "From what I found here, I took along a sample and had it tested. Now let's see whether Mister Butler's opinion is the same."

When he retracted his hand, it held a whitish, brown-tarnished, wire-like object that he handed to the engineer. Barely had Butler looked at it when he called out loudly, "Heavens! That's pure, genuine silver! And that comes originally from this crevice?"

"Yes. The entire fissure was filled with it. The crevice seems to extend farther into the wall and likely is very rich in the metal."

"Then I think I can guarantee that we'll have a very rich yield here. There must be more crevices like this one."

"Also solid veins, as I'll show you in a minute," smiled Old Firehand.

He pulled a second, much larger piece from the opening and handed it to the engineer. It was a twice fist-size piece of mineral. Butler inspected it carefully then declared, "A chemical analysis would certainly be much better, but I'd swear that we're dealing here with silver chloride, horn silver, or ceragyrite!"

"That's it! The chemical analysis showed it was silver chloride."

"Of what percentage?"

"Seventy five percent pure silver."

"What a find! And indeed, horn silver is most often found in Utah. Where's the vein this piece came from?"

"Over there, on the basin's other side. I've covered it high with rubble, but I'll show it to you. And now, what's this?"

Once again he pulled a handful from the crevice, this time hazelnut-size kernels.

"Nuggets! Gold!" the engineer erupted. "Also from here?"

"Yes. At one time we hid here and couldn't escape because redskins were waiting for us. We had run out of water and I dug in the sand, hoping to find some moisture. There was no water, but I found several such nuggets instead."

"Then there must also be gold veins, as I surmised before! Old Firehand, here lie millions, and its discoverer is a rich man, an extremely rich man!"

"Only the discoverer? You all shall have part of it. I as the discoverer, Butler as engineer and the others who will help exploit it. That's the reason I took you along. The condition under which we'll work together and each one's share we've yet to determine."

His words caused general jubilation, a jubilation that showed no signs of subsiding. Old Firehand now revealed the vein of silver ore, which was very substantial. It could be expected not to be the only one. Most of the men were enthusiastic enough to want to begin exploration immediately, but Old Shatterhand put a stop to it, warning, "Not so fast, gentlemen! There's something else to think of first. We aren't all by ourselves up here!"

"But we're bloody well ahead of the redskins, aren't we?" remarked the lord who, although he did not stake any claim to the find, was just as excited as the others.

"We've arrived before them, yes, but not by much. Our Navajo brave here knows his people's line of retreat very well. He's estimated that they'll arrive at the lake just a few hours later than we, and the Utes won't be far behind. We mustn't lose any time preparing for this."

"That's true," affirmed Old Firehand. "Nevertheless, I'd like to learn whether the exploitation here will be difficult. It will probably take Mister Butler only a few minutes to tell us. Well then, Mister Butler, what are you saying?"

With a long look, Butler surveyed the surroundings, then answered, "It's water, first and foremost, that we'll need. Where's the closest place we can obtain it?"

"From Silver Lake."

"How far is that from here?"

"An hour's ride."

"Is its elevation higher than here?"

"Substantially."

"Then we have the necessary gradient. There's only the question of how we can channel it here."

"The canyon, the only direct access to the basin, leads up to the lake."

"That's important and leads me to believe that conducting the water here won't present insurmountable obstacles. But we'll need a sluice, also pipes made of wood; later we'll need iron pipe. Are there trees near here?"

"Lots of them. Silver Lake is surrounded by trees," Old Firehand confirmed.

"Excellent! We may not need to construct a sluiceway for the entire distance. We'll build a reservoir farther up. From the lake to the reservoir the water can run freely. But, farther down, we'll need pipes to obtain the required pressure."

"For squirt guns?"

"Yes. We won't have to work the rock with pickax and shovel, just break it using water pressure. Only where water pressure fails we'll have to use powder. The metal-bearing basin floor can also be worked using water."

"But then we'll need drainage. Otherwise the basin will fill up and we won't be able to work it."

Butler considered this problem for a moment. "Yes, the discharge! There's none here, yet we must arrange for it. At first, a pump or paternoster will suffice to get the water to the top. From there, it'll run down the slope into the canyon beyond. When we ride up to the lake now, I'll see how all this can be accomplished. Of course, we'll need machinery, but that doesn't pose much difficulty. Within a month, we can gather everything. There are only just two items that concern me."

"And these are?"

"First of all, the Indians. Shall we let ourselves get butchered little by little?"

"We don't need to worry about that. Old Shatterhand, Winnetou and I are on friendly terms with the respective tribes and we can easily come to an agreement with them."

"All right! But the rights to the property? Whose are those?"

"The Timbabatsches. I believe that Winnetou's influence can convince them to sell to us."

"And will the government recognize the sale?"

"I'd like to see the man who'll dispute my rights! I'm not worried about that."

"Then I'm satisfied, too. The main issue is how to get the lake's water here, which I'll check on our forthcoming ride. Let's go!"

The crevice in the rock that Old Firehand had opened was sealed up again and the ore vein covered with rubble. Thereafter, everyone mounted up to continue the ride.

It was like a defile, or sunken road, where the captives with their guards were waiting, a water-eroded, winding gully at most ten to twenty feet wide, leading upward. It, too, was totally bare of any growth. The seasonal water course had entirely dried up and carried only a trickle during spring rains, insufficient to promote any growth.

Almost two hours passed when the former water course suddenly broadened to open into a rock-enclosed basin holding a still pond. Here there was grass for the first time on the long ride. Due to the heat, the lack of water and the poor footing, the mounts had suffered. They were no longer responding to the reins, but wanted to graze. The riders dismounted to allow the animals to disperse. In small groups, the party gathered to discuss the riches they hoped to gain in the near future. They didn't fear hostile Indians here, and since they intended to rest only briefly, no guards were posted.

During the ride, the engineer had given the surroundings his full attention and now commented on his observations. "Up to this point, I'm extremely satisfied. The canyon we traversed not only provides enough space for a pipeline but is wide enough to transport whatever equipment we'll need. If our further requirements are satisfied like that, I can say that nature is accommodating us in the most friendly way."

"Droll!" chuckled Hobble-Frank, giving his cousin a punch in the ribs. "Did you hear? Looks more and more like there'll be a villa in my future."

"And my farm as well! Well, look forward, Altenburg, for your sons to arrive with a money bag twenty feet long! Cousin, come here, let me give you a congratulatory squeeze!"

"Not quite yet!" Frank warded him off. "The riches still lie both in time's womb and in the unknown future. As cautious people, we must expect that my villa and your farm could disappear into insubstantial vapor. Being a born Saxon and a learned slyboots, I don't doubt at all that my hopes will turn into the most beautiful fulfillment, but for congratulations I'm not quite ready yet. I'm ---"

He was interrupted by the engineer's voice of sudden concern, "Ellen! Where's Ellen? I don't see her!"

After many days, the young girl had seen her first grass here, even some flowers, and had wandered off to pick a bouquet for her father. The pond's moisture enabled vegetation to grow in the defile and continued farther up from there. Ellen had incautiously entered the opening, picking a flower here and there until she came to a bend. Suddenly she remembered that she was not supposed to separate herself that far from the others. Just as she was about to return, three men rounded the bend, three armed Indians. The girl froze in fright, wanting to call for help, but couldn't utter a sound. The Indians, quick-witted by training, acted swiftly and decisively. Barely had the three seen the girl when two of them threw themselves on her. One pressed his hand over her mouth, the other brandished his knife and threatened in broken English, "Quiet, or dead!"

The third Indian scurried forward to find out who the white girl belonged to. It was certain that she wasn't alone. In a couple of minutes, he returned and whispered a few words to his companions that Ellen did not understand. Then she was dragged away, not daring to raise her voice.

Soon the defile came to an end. It terminated in a high slope whose lower portion was overgrown with bushes, its upper reaches changing into forest. Ellen was pulled through the bushes into the trees where a group of Indians was sitting. They had their weapons lying beside them, but grabbed them and jumped up when their fellow braves appeared with the white girl.

Ellen understood not a single spoken word. But the threatening looks she received made her believe she was in imminent danger. All of a sudden she recalled the totem Little Bear had given her on the ship. He had told her it would protect her from any harm. "Its shadow is my shadow, and its blood is my blood; he is my older brother," was its message. She pulled out the string with the totem, took it off, and cautiously held it out to the Indian who she thought was the most dangerous because of his fierce looks.

"Nintropan-homosch," she whispered fearfully, while handing it over, remembering Little Bear's name in his native tongue.

The redskin unfolded the leather piece, studied the markings, voiced an exclamation of surprise and passed it on to the next. It went from hand to hand. The faces became less threatening and the brave who had earlier spoken to Ellen, asked, "Who - give -you?"

"Nintropan-homosch," she replied.

"Young chief?"

"Yes," she nodded.

"Where?"

"On a ship."

"Big fire canoe?"

"Yes."

"On Arkansas River?"

"Yes."

"That true. Nintropan-homosch was on Arkansas. Who men back there?" he asked, pointing towards the defile.

"Winnetou, Old Firehand and Old Shatterhand."

"Uff!" he exclaimed and with more "Uffs!" the others expressed their surprise. The brave was about to continue asking questions when the bushes parted and from three sides the hunters appeared. Winnetou had discovered tracks and immediately initiated pursuit. The Indians made no attempt to defend themselves since they knew they were not about to be attacked. The braves' speaker had recognized Winnetou from a previous encounter.

"Great Chief of the Apaches!" he called out respectfully. "The white girl possesses the totem of Little Bear and is therefore our friend. We took her because we were not sure whether the men she is with would be our friends or foes."

The redskins wore blue and yellow colors on their faces causing Winnetou to ask, "You are Timbabatsche braves?"

"Yes."

"Who is your chief?"

"Tschia-nitsas."

His name translates into Long Ear. The man must be known for his acute hearing.

"Where is he?" Winnetou asked.

"At the lake."

"How many warriors are you?"

"One hundred."

"Are other tribes gathered there?"

"No. But two hundred warriors of the Navajos will arrive soon to fight the Utes. Together with them we will move north to seek the Utes' scalps."

"Beware that the Utes do not take yours. Did you post guards?"

"What for? We do not expect enemies."

"More are coming than you will like. Is Big Bear at the lake?"

"Yes, also Little Bear."

Winnetou and the other two exchanged looks. "Then lead us to them."

At that moment, several rafters exited from the defile leading the horses and the captives. The hunters had of course tracked Ellen on foot. Everyone mounted up, the Timbabatsches ahead as guides. No one was happier than the engineer about the outcome of Ellen's adventure, which had caused him no little worry.

The group continued up the slope beneath the trees. Beyond the ridge the ground gently dropped off again and soon they saw water sparkling.

"It's Silver Lake!" Old Shatterhand breathed, turning to his companions. "We've finally reached our goal."

"But I don't think we'll find peace here," remarked Old Firehand. "We'll probably smell quite a bit of powder yet."

A short while later the entire grand scenery spread out before them.

Towering rock formations, shimmering in all colors like the ones in the canyon, enclosed a valley two hours' ride long and half as wide. Behind the surrounding rock towers mountains rose, one above the other. Unlike the previous terrain, these mountains were not bare. The many canyons cutting through them were overgrown with bushes and trees and the lower the elevation, the denser the forest became, reaching almost all the way to the lake's shore. Only a narrow strip of grass remained between forest and lake, where stood several teepees with a number of canoes moored nearby.

A small green island lay in the middle of the lake, circular in form, its diameter about a hundred paces. In the center stood a curious tiled building, overgrown with vines, a garden behind. It seemed to date from a time when present-day Indians had not yet displaced the aboriginal people.

The forest crowns reflected in the lake's waters and the mountains threw their shadows on the lake, which was neither green nor blue nor dark-hued, but rather shone silver-gray. Not a breeze stirred the waters. If it were possible, one might have thought he was gazing at a mercury-filled basin.

Near the teepees camped all hundred Timbabatsches. The whites' arrival caused a stir among them, but when they recognized their fellow braves ahead of the group they became more at ease.

The group hadn't yet reached the teepees when on the island two men stepped from the tiled building. The Apache cupped his hands and shouted across to them, "Nintropan-hauey! Winnetou has arrived!"

A response was given, then the two Bears, father and son, climbed into one of the canoes on the island to paddle to the shore. Although they were surely surprised to see the well-known faces, they didn't show the least expression. When Big Bear stepped from the canoe, he shook hands with Winnetou and said, "Great chief of the Apaches is everywhere, and wherever he arrives, he brings joy to the heart. I greet also Old Shatterhand, who I know, and Old Firehand, I come to know on ship!"

When he noticed Aunt Droll, a shadow of a smile crossed his face. He remembered the first meeting with the amusing character and said, shaking the hunter's hand, "My white brother is brave man. He killed panther; I bid him welcome."

He went from man to man shaking hands with each. His son was still too young to act on a par with the famous warriors and hunters, but with Butler's daughter he could talk. Once Little Bear left the canoe, he walked up to Ellen who had just climbed down from her chair between the ponies. During his travels, the boy had observed how ladies and gentlemen greeted one another. Now he found it irresistible to demonstrate his knowledge of it. Taking off his hat, he waved it around a bit, bowed slightly, and said in his broken English, "Little Bear had not thought to see white girl again. What is your travel's destination?"

"It's here at Silver Lake," Ellen answered shyly.

A joyous blush crossed his face and he could not help showing his surprise. "Then the miss will stay a while?" he asked.

"For some time even," was her answer.

"Then I ask to be her companion at all times to show the trees, the plants and flowers growing here. We can fish in lake and hunt in forest. Yet I always need be close since there are wild animals and hostile people. Will she permit it?"

"I'd like that. I'll feel much more secure with you then being alone and I'm happy to have found you again."

She offered her hand and, lo and behold, he raised it to his lips and bowed like a true gentleman.

The groups' horses were taken into the forest by the Timbabatches to the same area where they kept their own. Their chief had proudly stayed in his wigwam and only now came forward, rather annoyed that he had not been given any attention before. He was a rather sinister-looking fellow with great long arms and legs, giving him somewhat the appearance of an orangutan. He was no less surprised by the sudden arrival of that many whites, but didn't find it appropriate to his dignity to show any of this. Rather he gave the appearance as if their arrival was of no consequence to him. He kept his distance and peered intently across to the mountains as though he had far more important matters on his mind. But he had miscalculated, for Aunt Droll walked boldly up to him and asked, "Why isn't Long Ear coming closer? Doesn't he want to greet the famous paleface warriors?"

The chief murmured something incomprehensible in his language, but had chosen the wrong man for this in Droll. The hunter tapped him on the shoulder like a fine old acquaintance and said, "Talk English, old boy! I haven't learned your dialect."

The redskin mumbled something else, causing Droll to say, "Don't feign ignorance! I know you speak some decent English."

"No!" the chief denied.

"No? Do you know me?"

"No!"

"You've never seen me?"

"No!"

"Hmm! Try to remember! You must remember me."

"No!"

"We've seen each other at Fort Defiance."

"No!"

"Oh, quit your 'nos'. I can prove it to you. We were three white and eleven red men. We played a bit of cards and drank a little. But you redskins drank a lot more firewater than us whites and finally none of you knew any longer who and where you were. Then you slept all afternoon and through the night. Do you remember now, old one?"

"No!"

"All right! But since you answer my questions, it's proof that you understand me. I'll therefore continue. We whites also bedded down with you Indians in a wooden shack, since there was no better place to go. When we woke up, you folks had disappeared. Do you recall where to?"

"No!"

"Well, along with you redskins my rifle and bullet pouch had also disappeared. I had 'A.D.' for Aunt Droll engraved on my rifle barrel. It's very peculiar that these letters can be seen on the barrel of your rifle. Might you know how they got there?"

"No!"

"And my bullet pouch had been embroidered with beads and also carried the letters 'A.D.' I wore it on my belt, just as you do. And I notice to my heartfelt joy that your bullet pouch also shows those same letters. Do you know how such an amazing coincidence could have happened?"

"No!"

"But I do. I even know how my rifle and bullet pouch got into your hands. A chief carries only those items he has taken as booty; stolen items he disdains. I shall liberate you of them."

In an eyeblink, he tore the rifle from the surprised redskin's hand and the pouch from his belt and strode away. Just as quickly Long Ear followed him, demanding in rather understandable English, "Give back!"

"No!" Now it was Droll's turn to play the 'No!' game. "This is my rifle!"

"No!"

"Also this pouch!"

"No!"

"You are a thief!"

"Give back, or I'll make you!"

"No!"

At this last refusal the redskin pulled his knife. Instantly those who were not familiar with Droll expected a bloody encounter would ensue, but the hunter only broke into hearty laughter and exclaimed, "Am I now to be a scoundrel who steals my own things? Would you think it? You're Long Ear and I know you. Your ears are not the only exceptionally long members of your body. Admit to the truth and I'll let you keep what you took. I've long ago replaced the loss. Truthfully, do you know me?"

"Yes!" Long Ear answered against all expectations.

"We were together at Fort Defiance?"

"Yes!"

"And you were drunk?"

"Yes!"

"And you disappeared with my rifle and bullet pouch?"

"Yes!"

"Then you may keep both. Here, let's shake hands on it and be friends. But you must speak English and no more filching. Understood?"

Droll took the redskin's hand, pumped it up and down and returned the stolen items. Long Ear accepted them without expression, but then said in a far friendlier tone, "My white brother is my friend. He knows what is right and returned the things he found on me. He is a friend of the red man and I like him!"

"Yeah, real friends!" replied the hunter dryly. Then careful to conceal his scorn, he added, "And I like you too. To prove it, let me tell you that if we hadn't come, you would all probably lose your scalps."

"Lose our scalps? Who would take them?"

"The Utes."

"Oh, they not come. They have been beaten by the Navajos. We shall soon follow them to take many Ute scalps."

"In that you're very much mistaken!"

"But you have chiefs and warriors of the Utes as captives. Therefore they must have been defeated."

"We've captured these few Utes on our own account. The Navajos, though, have been beaten ignominiously and have fled this way. The Utes are following them in great numbers and may arrive yet today here at Silver Lake."

"Uff!" exclaimed Long Ear, his mouth gaping in surprise.

His braves too cried out in perplexity.

"Is it possible?" asked Big Bear. "Is this Aunt speaking truth?"

"Yes," answered Winnetou who, being the most familiar with the environs of Silver Lake, had spoken up. "We shall tell you everything in detail but only after we have ascertained that we cannot be surprised by the enemy. We can expect them to appear at any moment. Fifty Timbabatsche braves may ride immediately to the canyon with Humpy-Bill and Gunstick-Uncle accompanying them."

"Me too!" volunteered Hobble-Frank.

"Also me!" added Droll.

"All right," agreed Winnetou, "you go along too. Ride to the spot where the canyon narrows and take up a position behind the rocks. There are enough projections and recesses for your protection. The Utes will push the Navajos so they will probably arrive almost simultaneously at Silver Lake. You two will assist our friends and send a messenger as soon as you see the enemy so we can come to help. Water your horses before, and drink sufficiently yourselves since there is no water down there. Big Bear will give you food to take along."

There was enough meat. It hung drying from thongs between the trees. And there was more than enough water. Several brooks tumbled from the mountains and fed the lake. At one of them the horses had been assembled to drink.

Soon the fifty Indians and four whites were ready to depart. Little Bear asked his father to ride along and was given permission. The boy knew the locale of the lake and the canyon better than the Timbabatsches, which might be of advantage.

The mountain valley of Silver Lake extended from north to south. It was inaccessible from its eastern and western slopes and could be reached from the north only through the canyon the whites had taken. In the south, the lake's waters drained into a gorge, although, with some difficulty, it was still possible to access the valley from that direction.

The enemy was not expected to arrive from the south; only the friendly Navajos were anticipated to come from there so no defensive contingent needed to be posted there. Only the northern approach required attention.

If Silver Lake's northern extent were investigated, one could conclude that in an earlier era, the lake did not drain southward but to the north. Nowadays, however, what looked like a rather wide earthen dam blocked drainage in this direction. The dam had to be artificial, built by human hands, hands which had done this work and had long since turned to dust. On top of the dam grew trees no less than one hundred fifty years old. What had been the purpose of this dam? Was there still a human being alive to answer such a question?

The detachment Winnetou had assigned to guard the narrows rode off into the canyon. At first barely ten feet wide and shallow, it gradually cut deeper and deeper. The deeper it became, the more it increased in width. Vegetation thinned shortly past the dam, then trees and bushes petered out, and soon not even a blade of grass could be seen.

The group barely traveled ten minutes before the canyon walls had risen already to a hundred feet. Another quarter of an hour and they seemed to reach the sky. Here the riders had to traverse rounded pebbles and rocks, a difficult task for the horses. After another quarter hour, the canyon suddenly widened to twice its previous size. Its walls were widely fissured from the bottom up to their highest point. These monumental walls were like rock columns between which one could casually amble but where it was also possible to find perfect concealment.

"Here we stop," said Little Bear, riding in the lead with the whites. "There are many crevices to take cover." The boy was speaking the best English he could manage.

"We better take the horses some distance back," suggested Droll, "so they can't be seen if it comes to a fight."

This was accomplished as the fifty braves sought cover on both sides of the canyon. The whites kept Little Bear with them to benefit from his knowledge of the surroundings. Like an experienced warrior, he seriously and sensibly inquired about the events of the past few days. The boy could hardly believe that the Utes had been overcome by the whites. His appreciation of the whites' accomplishment grew as the story unfolded.

"My white brothers acted as courageous and deliberate men," he said. "Navajos, though, were blind and deaf. They should have won since Utes did not expect them yet. If they entered valley like sly fox to attack the Utes, they could have defeated them. But they screamed and fired their rifles too soon and so had to lose some scalps. Now Utes have superior forces and if the battle draws close to Silver Lake, we ---"

" --- will have a little word to say ourselves," Droll interrupted, finishing Little Bear's sentence for him.

"Yes. My weapons will talk too," added Frank. "I'm eager to try the rifle Lord Castlepool gave me against these fellows for the first time. What's the situation here, Little Bear? Does the canyon have other entries?"

"No. Only one, the one you came through and that one is not known to Utes."

"How about the Navajos?"

"They do know of it, but only the Navajo reinforcements will come from south. The Navajos pursued by the Utes must come from north and ---"

Little Bear stopped to listen. His sharp hearing had caught a noise. The others also heard it now. It sounded like the tired stumbling of a horse across the rubble. A moment later, a single horseman appeared, a Navajo, whose horse was barely able to walk. The brave appeared to be wounded; his shirt was bloodstained. Nevertheless, with both hands and legs he continued to urge his steed on.

Little Bear stepped from his hiding place. As soon as the Navajo spied him, he reined in his horse and exclaimed in relief, "Uff! My young brother! Have the Navajo warriors already arrived?"

"Not yet," replied Little Bear in the Navajo tongue.

"Then we will all be lost!"

"How can a Navajo brave give up so quickly?"

"The Great Spirit has forsaken us and gave his blessings instead to the Ute dogs. We attacked them in the Elk Valley to finish them off, but our chiefs lost their minds and we were defeated. We fled, the Utes pursuing us. They had more warriors than we; nevertheless, we would have prevailed. But this morning a new large group has joined them. Now they are four times our strength and have crowded us mightily."

"Uff! Then you have been wiped out?"

"Almost. A distance of ten rifle shots from here rages a battle. I was sent to the lake to get help since we expected our other braves to be here by now. But now our warriors are lost."

"Not yet. Dismount and rest! Help is already here."

To the brave's surprise, the fifty Timababatsches and the four whites came out of hiding. The four hunters had not been able to follow the Navajo's report since they didn't understand his language. They now had it translated by Little Bear. The report completed, Droll said, "If that's the situation, the Navajos must retreat at once. One of us must ride there quickly to have them come up here. A second messenger must ride to the lake to fetch our companions and the other Timbabatsches."

"How can you think that!" objected Hobble-Frank. "If we follow a plan like that, the Navajos are truly lost."

"How so?" asked Droll surprised. "Do you think I'm such a poor frontiersman?"

"The best frontiersman can have a poor thought at times. The Navajos face such a superior force that they'll be destroyed if they try to flee. The Utes will simply ride them down. They must hold their position until the fight comes to a standstill. For that to occur, we have to act."

"That's so, Frank, you're right!" Humpy-Bill agreed.

And Gunstick-Uncle chimed in, "Oh yes, yes, yes, they must stay there - for us to chase the Utes everywhere!"

"Good!" nodded Hobble, pleased with the approval he received. "We'll dispatch a Navajo brave to ride speedily to the lake to call for help; three others must stay here with the horses so they don't go astray, and the rest of us will scamper as fast as we can to help the Navajos. Let's go!"

The suggestion was executed at once. The four whites with Little Bear in the lead, followed by the Timbabatsches and the wounded Navajo, broke into a run, advancing as quickly as the uneven ground permitted towards the battling Navajos. It did not take long for them to hear a shot being fired, then another. With both friend and foe armed mainly with bows and arrows, no major rifle salvos rang out. But soon afterward they heard the sounds of the struggle as the combatants came into view.

Yes, it stood poorly for the Navajos. More than half of their horses had been killed. The carcasses offered the only cover here, the canyon walls being smooth with no clefts to provide protection. The Navajo fighters seemed to be running short on arrows for they refrained from shooting carelessly and let fly only when they were sure of their target. The most courageous among them ran about collecting the Utes arrows to whizz them back against their foes.

The Utes were so numerous that they stood several rows deep across the canyon's width. They fought on foot, having left their horses behind so they would not become casualties. This was fortunate for the Navajos. Had the Utes been mounted and stormed them, not a single Navajo would have remained alive.

For a moment the battle cries fell silent when both sides saw the reinforcements arrive. The four whites came up behind the Navajos and placed themselves openly in the midst of the canyon where they knew the Utes would be within reach of their bullets. They leveled their rifles and opened fire. The Utes' screeches confirmed there had been hits. Another volley was answered by renewed cries. The Timbabatsches for their part hunkered down and crept forward beyond the whites to get into arrow range.

Humpy-Bill offered the opinion that the four hunters should not fire in unison, since it caused too long a pause for reloading. They agreed that instead two would load and two would shoot.

Quickly it showed what four brave men armed with good rifles could accomplish. Each shot hit its target. Those Utes in possession of rifles now no longer aimed at the Navajos, but at the whites. This gave the Indian defenders some breathing space.

Alongside the frontiersmen, Little Bear had knelt and used his rifle to everyone's admiration. Shot after shot hit home. Enveloped in a cloud of bullets and arrows, the Utes began to withdraw. Only the ones equipped with rifles remained, but their weapons were inferior and their bullets fell short; they dared not come closer. Seeing the retreat, Hobble-Frank called to Little Bear, "We five will stay. The Navajos in front of us should withdraw. Tell them!"

The chief's son followed his instruction. The Navajo redskins leaped up and ran back past the whites to find whatever cover there was. It was a sad sight. Only now was it evident how much these braves had suffered. They counted at most sixty, with fewer than half still having a horse. Fortunately for them, the Timbabatsches held their positions to keep the Utes in check, who should have been ashamed that they had not undertaken a quick, decisive rush onto their enemy. But that would have meant a number of deaths of their own which the Indian generally tries to avoid. He prefers to attack only when he has little to fear.

So it happened that the Navajos fell back, after which the Timbabatsches and the four whites and Little Bear also retreated a bit without being hindered by the Utes who had filtered back and now simply followed them slowly. The Utes conserved their arrows and continued to fire sporadically with their few rifles. In this way, one party retreated for a distance, the other trailing, until the defenders reached the location of their former cover. The whites directed both groups of redskins to quickly conceal themselves in the rock crevices, Little Bear translating, then --- a sudden general scattering, and the hard-pressed defenders disappeared. They had found protection against any kind of shot, while the Utes were forced to remain in the open canyon. If the expected help arrived soon, the besieged Navajos could look forward to renewing hostilities.

* * * * * *

Back at Silver Lake help was under way. Winnetou told Big Bear in a few words what had happened earlier. The Tonkawa frowned and said to Old Shatterhand, "I warn the Navajos and say to wait for all warriors to come. But they thought Utes not yet gathered all braves and wanted to destroy their small groups one by one. Now they suffer same fate they intend for enemies."

"Not yet!" Old Shatterhand said. "The Navajos haven't yet been eliminated."

"You think this? I of different opinion. I know gathering places of Utes. After Navajos flee from Elk Valley, they must pass several such places and Utes can encircle them. And even if Navajos escape to mountains, Ute numbers will increase from place to place. I see maybe one thousand warriors arriving at Silver Lake. Whether Navajos can reach lake under those circumstances very doubtful."

"And how about you? Will the Utes treat you as an enemy?"

"They will."

"Then you're in great danger."

"Big Bear not in danger."

"Because you have the Timbabatsches here and expect more Navajos?"

"No. I not rely on one, nor other, only on Big Bear."

"Then I don't understand you."

"I not fear a thousand Utes."

"Again, I don't understand what you mean."

"I only need raise hand and they will lose. One movement and all die."

"Hmm! All of them?"

"You don't believe? Yes, you cannot comprehend this. Palefaces perhaps smart people but none of you has such a thought."

He said this proudly. Old Shatterhand's looks swept the lake and the mountains, then he answered with a slight smile, "But you're not the only one who had this idea."

"No? Who says this?"

"I do! We whites can conceive -- but not entertain -- such a thought, because we're Christians and shy away from mass murder. But we're wise enough to look into your souls."

"You think you know why I not fearful of a thousand enemies?"

"Yes."

"Speak!"

"Do you really want me to give away your secret, Big Bear?"

"Old Shatterhand not give away since it not possible for you to get right idea. It is secret known today only to two people, Big Bear and Little Bear."

"And to myself!"

"No, paleface. Prove it!"

"All right. You say you can kill a thousand Utes in an eye blink?"

"Is so."

"While they're in the canyon?"

"Yes, in canyon."

"That cannot be done by knives, rifles or other weapons."

"No. So how to do, you cannot know."

"But I can! By a force of nature. By air, that is a storm? No. By fire? That neither. Then by water!"

"White man's thoughts are true and wise, but you not know more!"

"Let's see! Where is there enough water to kill that many people? In Silver Lake. Will these warriors enter the lake? No. Then the lake must go to the people; it must suddenly flood the canyon. How would that be possible; there's a high and strong dam in between! Well then. This dam didn't exist in ancient times. It was built afterwards and when it was done it was equipped with a feature which allows it to be suddenly opened to flood the canyon with a raging torrent. Am I right?"

Despite the calm demeanor an Indian, particularly a chief, must maintain in all walks of life, Big Bear jumped up and exclaimed, "Is Old Shatterhand all-knowing?"

"No, but I have the power to think."

"You found out, truly, you found out! But you also know how I got secret?"

"By inheritance."

"And how is dam opened?" demanded Big Bear.

"If you permit me to check, I'll soon answer your question."

"No, I cannot permit. But can you guess why dam was built?"

"Yes."

"So. What for?"

"For two reasons. The first was for defense. The conquerors of the southern areas all came from the north. This large canyon was a preferred route for these conquerors. The dam was built to close it off and, in the event of an attack, to suddenly release the waters of the lake it created."

"And second reason?"

"The treasure."

"Treasure?" the chief asked aghast, stepping back a pace. "What you know of treasure?"

"Nothing. But I can guess much. I see the lake, its shores, its surroundings and contemplate them. Prior to the dam's construction there was no lake, but a deep valley through which the creeks, like today, flowed through the canyon they had carved over the eons. A rich people lived here who fought the continued advance of new conquerors for a long time. They finally realized that they had to abandon their homes, had to flee, but perhaps only temporarily. They buried their precious belongings, their holy vessels here in the valley and erected the dam to create a large lake whose waters were to be the unconquerable sentinels of this treasure."

"Silent, be silent, or you give away all, everything!" Big Bear exclaimed, suddenly frightened. "We not talk more of treasure, only of dam. Yes, I know how to breach. Big Bear drown a thousand and more Utes while in canyon. Shall I do at moment they come?"

"For God's sake, no! There are other means to subdue them."

"Which? With weapons?"

"Yes. Then there are the hostages lying over there in the grass. They're the most famous chiefs of the Utes. To save their lives the Utes will accede to many of our conditions. For this reason, we seized them and brought them here."

"Then captives must go to safe place."

"Do you have a suitable location?"

"Yes. Give food and drink first; then we bring them there."

The captives' hands were released. They received meat and water to consume after which they were bound again. With the help of some of the Timbabatsches, the hostages were then transported by canoe to the island. Old Firehand, Shatterhand and Winnetou also came along to get to know the interior of the only building on the island.

The structure's ground floor was separated into two rooms by a masonry wall. One of them held a fireplace, the other was used as a living room. It was poorly equipped and contained a hammock and a simple bedstead. That was all.

"Is it here that our captives are to remain?" asked Old Shatterhand.

"No. Here they not secure enough. Big Bear know much better place."

He pushed the bedstead aside, which consisted of a frame of wooden slats covered by rushes and blankets. Where the bedstead had been, a square opening appeared, from which a notched tree trunk, serving as a ladder, led downward. The chief descended; Old Shatterhand followed. The others could lower the captives one by one.

Enough light fell through the opening that Old Shatterhand oriented himself readily in the cellar-like room. It was larger than the upstairs living room, its extension facing toward the garden side. The opposite side was blocked by a wall with neither a door nor any other opening. When the hunter tapped the wall, it sounded thin and hollow. There had to be still another room behind, located underneath the fireplace room. Yet no access from there to this cellar room was apparent.

The Utes were handed down and laid side by side. Looking around, Old Shatterhand worried that the hostages would have insufficient air down here. When he queried Big Bear, the Indian answered, "From ceiling holes go through hollow bricks to outside. Ancient people who build structure know very well what they do."

Without allowing it to appear intentional, Old Shatterhand stamped hard on the floor several times. The cellar's floor also sounded hollow. This led him to believe that the island's center, the building, had been built before the lake's creation, and had been surrounded with a water-impermeable rocky and earthen wall. Could it be possible that the treasure was secreted down below at the bottom of the island?

There was no more time for additional inspections. The last prisoner was in place and the chief had ascended. Old Shatterhand needed to follow.

Below the building's eaves hung large pieces of dried and smoked meats. Some of it was taken to the lake shore for the next meal. Just as the party arrived there, the Navajo messenger who had come from the canyon to seek help galloped in full tilt, his horse foaming. Until they heard his story neither the Timbabatsches nor Big Bear thought the enemy was already so close. Everyone reached for his weapons and rushed to his horse.

Ellen had to remain behind but could not be left without protection. Since no one else was prepared to stay back, it was her father who took on the responsibility. Big Bear advised him to paddle to the island and to remain there for their best possible security. Although probably little danger threatened them, caution was in order. While the others raced off in a cloud of dust, the two boarded a canoe and made their way to the island.

Pushing their horses as hard as they dared, the rescuers covered the distance through the canyon in one-third the time the initial group had needed. When they arrived where the horses had been left and heard shots being fired, they swiftly dismounted and left their own horses there as well. The group split to the left and right of the canyon without being spotted by the Utes and rushed forward to the clefted walls, which were serving their friends as cover.

The defenders were greatly relieved by the arrival of additional reinforcements. Humpy-Bill recounted what had happened so far and Hobble-Frank was gratified by the praise he received for his battle strategy.

The Utes were of the opinion they were still dealing with the small force they had already seen. They had at last come to the conclusion that they could have finished the defenders by a quick rush, and were now prepared to make up for their earlier deficiency. The foremost defenders in the canyon clefts watched the Utes gathering and informed their rear echelon for everyone to prepare for the assault.

Without warning, a wild war cry arose, as cacophonous as an army of wolves. The Utes rushed forward, but into a withering fusillade. After barely two minutes of continuous gunfire and showers of arrows from the defenders, they withdrew leaving behind a great number of dead and wounded. From behind one of the rock shelters Old Shatterhand had fired many shots, but had aimed to incapacitate only, not to kill. Now he saw the Timbabatsches rush out to scalp the fallen, their chief among them.

"Hold it!" he thundered. "Leave these people be."

"Why? Their scalps are ours!" protested Long Ear.

At that, he pulled his knife and bent down to take a Ute's scalp. In a moment, Old Shatterhand stood beside him, revolver to his head, and threatened, "One cut and I kill you!"

While Long Ear had the guts to steal a rifle and a bullet pouch, his courage failed him under threat of a bullet in the brain. He rose and said ingratiatingly, "What have you got against it? The Utes would scalp us."

"If I were with them, they wouldn't do it either. I won't tolerate it; at least not to the living."

"Then the living may keep their scalps, but I shall take them from the dead."

"By what right?"

"I do not understand you," the redskin said, confounded. "A killed enemy must be scalped!"

"Many lie here. Did you kill them all?"

"No. One of them I hit."

"Which one?"

"I do not know."

"Is he dead?"

"That too I do not know. Although he was hit, he was still able to run off."

"Then show me the dead man whose body holds your bullet. You may scalp him then, but not before!"

Grumbling the chief withdrew to his hiding place, his people grudgingly following his example. At this moment, a great shout of incredulity went up from the repelled Utes. When Old Shatterhand was standing in the midst of the Timbabatsches, he had not been recognized. Now that he stood in the open, the cries resounded from the walls of the canyon. "Old Shatterhand! The Magic Rifle, the Magic Rifle!"

That this man could be here was inconceivable to the Utes. His presence was devastating. Demonstrating his courageous spirit, he slowly advanced and once in earshot shouted to them, "Retrieve your dead and wounded! They're our gift to you."

One of their leaders stepped forward and answered, "You will shoot at us!"

"No, we won't."

"Do you speak truth?"

"Old Shatterhand never lies."

At that he turned and went back to his crevice in the rocks.

As perfidious as these redskins were, they did not expect perfidy from this paleface. Worse yet was the shame suffered by Indians who forsake their dead and wounded. For this reason, the Utes now tentatively dispatched two of their braves who approached slowly to pick up one of the wounded and carry him away. They returned to carry back a second one. When there was no sign of hostility, they became more confident and several more joined in the retrieval.

Old Shatterhand stepped forward once again. The Indians grew frightened and started to run back, but he called out to them, "Stay! Nothing's going to happen to you."

They stopped, still suspicious. He approached them and asked, "How many chiefs are with you?"

"Four."

"Who's the most famous?"

"Nanap Varrenton, Old Thunder."

"Tell him I want to speak with him! He may walk half the distance, I the other, for us to meet halfway. We shall leave our weapons behind."

The Utes moved away to deliver the message and shortly returned with the reply, "Nanap Varrenton will come but he will be accompanied by our other three chiefs."

"I'll bring only two companions they may know. As soon as you're done here, the chiefs may come."

Soon the four approached with Old Shatterhand, Firehand and Winnetou coming from the opposite side. They acknowledged each other with curt nods and sat down face to face. Pride prevented the redskins from speaking immediately. Their features were difficult to make out under the heavily-applied facial paint, but their look of wonder was unmistakable as they stared at the other two famous men beside Old Shatterhand.

In this fashion the two parties eyed each other for some time until the eldest redskin, Old Thunder, lost patience and decided to speak. He stood up, assumed his most dignified position and began, "When all the earth still belonged to the sons of Great Manitou and there were no palefaces in our great hunting grounds, there ---"

"That's when you could make long speeches and for as long as you liked," Old Shatterhand interrupted. "But we palefaces prefer to be brief and that we shall be now."

When the redskin begins a palaver he will be hard put to come to an end. Their intended talk could have taken hours had Old Shatterhand not cut off the chief's first words. The redskin gave him a half-reproachful, half-angry glare, sat down again and said, "Old Thunder is a famous chief. He counts many more years than Old Shatterhand and is not accustomed to be interrupted with such disrespect. If the palefaces intended to insult me, there was no use of coming here. Howgh!"

"It wasn't my intention to offend you. A man may count many years, yet may be less experienced than a younger one. You wanted to talk of the times when there were no palefaces here. We, though, intend to speak only about today. And since I'm the one who called for you, I must also be the one to speak first to tell you what I want from you. Howgh!"

This was a sharp reprimand, telling the redskin who it was that would speak and who would make demands. The Indians glowered in silence, so Old Shatterhand continued, "You used my name, which tells me that you know me. Then you also know the two warriors sitting here beside me?"

"Yes. They are Old Firehand and Winnetou, the chief of the Apaches."

"Then you must know that we've always been friends of the red man. No Indian can say that we responded with hostility even when insulted. We often have even waived our right to revenge and forgave where we should have punished. So why do you pursue us?"

"Because you are the friends of our foes."

"That's not true. Big Wolf took us captive without our showing him the least enmity. Several times did he seek our lives; several times did he break his word. To protect our lives, we had to fight the Utes."

"Did you not knock down the old chief at the Forest of Waters and take other chiefs and warriors hostage?"

"Again, only to protect ourselves."

"And now you are with the Navajos and Timbabatsches who are our enemies!"

"Only by coincidence. We were coming to Silver Lake and encountered them here. We heard that a battle would arise between them and you and hurried to make peace."

"We want revenge, not peace, least of all from your hands."

"Whether you accept it or not is up to you, Old Thunder. We think it's our duty to offer it to you."

"We are the victors!"

"Until recently, but no longer. You've been seriously offended; we're aware of this. But it's unjustified to take revenge on innocents. Our lives have been threatened repeatedly by you. Had it been up to you, we would have died at the stake long ago, like the other palefaces in the Elk Valley."

"What do you know of that?"

"Everything. We buried them."

"Then you were there?"

"Yes. We were in your midst. We heard the words of the Utes and saw what they did. We stood below the trees when the Navajos attacked and observed how you repelled them."

"That is impossible. It cannot be true."

"You know I never lie," Old Shatterhand said, looking Old Thunder directly in the eye. "Ask the chiefs of the Utes who were present."

"How are we to ask them? They have disappeared."

"And do you know where?" Old Shatterhand asked innocently.

"Are we supposed to know it?"

"Well, have they been killed by the Navajos?" he continued.

"No. First we thought so, but we did not find their bodies. Then we thought they had been captured. We pursued the Navajos hard but did not see a single captive among them although many fell into our hands. The chiefs of the Utes are not with the Navajos."

"But they cannot have disappeared!" Old Shatterhand was inexorable.

"The Great Spirit may have called them."

"No. The Great Spirit doesn't want such perfidious and treacherous men. He has delivered them into our hands."

"Into your hands?" Shock played across Old Thunder's face.

"Yes. Into the power of the palefaces you want to destroy."

"Your tongue does not speak truth. You speak these words to force peace upon us."

"Yes. I'll force peace upon you but I also tell you the truth. That evening, when we were in the Elk Valley, we captured the three chiefs."

"Right under the eyes of their warriors?"

"No one was there to see or hear us. We knocked them down without their uttering a sound. Am I not called Old Shatterhand?"

"This cannot be so. You would have been seen."

"There's a hiding place in the Elk Valley which we know but you don't. I 'll prove to you that I speak the truth. What is this?"

He pulled from his pocket a leather belt, which was adorned with cylindrical buttons made from the Murex shell or Venus Comb, and held it up to the chief's face.

"Uff!" Old Thunder exclaimed, stunned. "It is the wampum belt of Yellow Sun! I know it very well."

"And this item?"

He pulled out a second belt.

"The wampum belt of chief Four Buffalo! I know it too."

"And this third wampum belt?"

When he showed the third belt, words seemed to stick in the old chief's throat. With a gesture of shock, he stuttered, "No warrior yields his wampum belt, for it is very much valued by him. Who has the wampum belt of another has either killed or captured him. Are the three chiefs still alive?"

"Yes."

"Where are they?"

"In our power, well kept."

"At Silver Lake?"

"You ask too many questions. Consider the others we have also captured, all chiefs and brave warriors who are sure to become chiefs later."

"What do you want with them?"

"Life for life, blood for blood! Make peace with the Navajos and Timbabatsches and we will release the captives!"

"We too have taken captives. Shall we exchange them, man for man?"

"Do you think me a callow boy that I wouldn't know that a chief is worth at least thirty braves? Consider my proposal and think which is better: to achieve freedom for your leaders or to kill another hundred or two hundred enemies."

"You do not take the spoils into account?"

"Booty? Pah! There'll be no loot, for you will have none unless you're victorious. Now we face you, fifty white hunters. We were the captives of the Utes and laughed in their faces. They had to let us go, even deliver their chiefs. This we accomplished when we were tied up. Think what we can do when we're free and unhindered! I tell you, if you don't make peace, few of you will return to your wigwams!"

From his somber look, one could see that this image did not fail to impress Old Thunder. Shatterhand pressed on, increasing the impact of his previous words. "Your chiefs were after our lives. They fell into our hands and we had the right to render them harmless, even the duty to kill them. We didn't do it since we mean well to them and to you. If we now counsel peace, it's meant just as well, for we know that otherwise we'll beat you for sure. Decide before it's too late."

At this, Old Firehand, bored and tired of all the talk,stood up, stretched his giant figure and said, "Pshaw! Why all these words when we have our weapons! Old Thunder should tell us quickly whether he wants war or peace. Then we'll know where we stand and shall give him our answer: life or death!"

The chief's reaction came at once with the answer, "We cannot decide that quickly."

"Why not? Are you men or squaws?" Old Firehand demanded insultingly.

"We are not squaws but warriors. But we must first talk with our people."

"If you're truly chiefs you need not do so," said the hunter contemptuously. "I see you want to gain time to come up with some cunning, as is your custom. But no deception will help you against our rifles."

Deeply offended, Old Thunder spoke in a voice of menace. "Old Firehand ought to speak calmly in the same fashion that we answer him. It does not behoove a man to speak in hot blood. We shall leave and consider what to do."

"Consider then that it'll be night in half an hour!"

"We will tell you by nightfall what we have decided. Whoever wants to talk, you or us, may fire a shot or shout. He will be answered. Howgh!"

He rose, nodded quietly and left, his three fellow chiefs following him.

"Now we know just as little as before!" Old Firehand grumbled.

"My brother spoke in anger," Winnetou said mildly. "He should have let Old Shatterhand continue. Old Thunder had become thoughtful and was on the verge of gaining the proper insight."

Taken aback, Firehand seemed to realize the truth of the reprimand and did not respond. When they returned to their companions, Long Ear received them with the question, "There were four Utes. Why did only you three meet with them?"

"Since we were men enough," Old Firehand responded testily.

"There were other men. I too am a chief. I ought to have been part of the powwow as well as you."

"There was enough useless talk without need for more."

Long Ear remained silent, but had his face not been covered by all his paint, one could have seen how furious he was. He was in a bad mood anyway. He had been ridiculed by Droll without being able to relieve his grudge. Then Old Shatterhand had insulted him in front of his warriors by preventing the scalping. The chief lacked the courage to openly resist, but the anger he didn't show boiled ever more in his innards.

Dusk fell, turning slowly into night. Although a surprise attack by the Utes was unlikely, measures had to be taken to respond to any incursion. Guards were posted. Long Ear volunteered to take on this duty with some of his people, a task which could not be denied him. In order to keep an eye on this unpredictable chief, Old Shatterhand assigned him and his braves precise positions, demanding that they advance no farther.

Five men including the chief were formed into a line stretched across the canyon. Long Ear was given the rightmost position. With his front line established, Old Shatterhand felt safe to crawl forward, hoping to listen to the Utes' conversation. He quickly and completely succeeded, avoiding three posted sentries. He even dared to slip between them and saw that the enemy had positioned themselves side by side across the point where the canyon widened. He returned satisfied.

Long Ear had observed the hunter's reconnoiter and was angered that he had not been given this honor. He, the chief of a noble red tribe, would know how to do it better than any paleface. On and on rage gnawed at him. He longed to show these whites that he was an important person not to be bypassed. What if the Utes were still planning something and he could be the one to overhear it! This thought left him no peace and he finally decided to act on it.

He crept forward, farther and farther. But it was more difficult than he anticipated because the rocky rubble was not packed firmly, but moved under his long limbs. He had little choice but to pay closer attention to what lay underneath him than what lay ahead. Again a pebble rolled. A dark figure rose beside him, another in front. Two powerful hands wrapped themselves like iron clamps around his throat cutting off his breath; two others held his arms to his sides. Long Ear lapsed into unconsciousness.

When he came to again, he found himself between two men who held the points of their knives against his bare chest. His hands and feet were tied, his mouth gagged. He made a slight movement, which was quickly noticed by a third man squatting behind his head. The man spoke in a quiet voice while putting his hand on his captive's head, "We recognize Long Ear. I am Old Thunder. If Long Ear is wise, nothing will happen to him. But if he is foolish, he will taste the knives on his chest. He may acknowledge whether he has understood my words by nodding his head!"

The captive nodded without hesitation. He was between life and death and he found it preferable to choose the former.

"Long Ear must indicate to me also if he will speak softly once I take the gag from his mouth," Old Thunder continued.

Long Ear nodded once more and the gag was removed. Again Old Thunder warned, "Speak a loud word and you die. But if you will ally with me, everything will be forgiven and you shall take part in our loot. Answer me!"

Loot! At this word, a thought, a great, precious thought, occurred to the Timbabatsche. He had previously overheard a conversation between Big Bear and Little Bear, a conversation still resounding in his ears word for word. Loot! Yes, booty there was to be, booty like never before shared after a battle! A great satisfaction overcame him at the thought that he would now be able to take revenge on the proud, conceited whites for the slights and insults he had suffered. From this very moment, he was, body and soul, totally devoted to the Utes' efforts.

"I hate and despise these whites," he answered. "If you help me, we shall destroy them."

"Also the Bears?"

"Yes. But my braves must stay alive!"

"That I promise. But why were you my enemy before?"

"Because I did not know what I know now. The palefaces insulted me so much that I must have their blood."

"Revenge will be yours. I shall see soon enough whether you are truthful or wish to deceive me."

"I will be faithful to you and shall prove it better and more completely than you can foresee now."

"Then tell me first if it is true that the palefaces hold our chiefs captive!"

"It is true. I have seen them."

"Then these dogs are in league with the Evil Spirit; otherwise they would not have succeeded at what is impossible for other people! Where do they keep the chiefs of the Utes?"

"In the house on the island of Silver Lake."

"Who guards them?"

"A single paleface and a girl, his daughter."

"Is it true? A single man and a girl guard that many brave and famous warriors! You are lying!"

"I tell the truth. Remember, the captives are tied up."

"If that is the case, then I can believe it. That is the island; but how many warriors are at the shore?"

"None."

"Long Ear, has your mind been taken by the wind?"

"I said none and I say none! The whites and my Timbabatsches were there, no one else. And all of them rode to the canyon to fight you."

"What folly! And that I am to believe is the truth?"

"It is no folly, because these dogs think you are no danger to them since you cannot get to the lake without their knowing."

"It is possible then?"

"Yes. And by telling you how, I can prove my honesty to you."

"Uff! Then the path up this canyon is not the only one? There is another one?"

"Yes. If you like, I shall guide you."

"Where is this path?"

"At a distance down from here, there is a gap between two outcroppings, through which one gets to a deep rocky basin after crossing a plateau. From there, another canyon leads up to the lake. I have ridden this path with Big Bear."

"And there are truly no warriors at the lake?"

"No, provided the two hundred Navajos have not arrived yet."

"They cannot have arrived yet or they would otherwise have rushed here to fight us. How long does it take by this other route to get to the lake?"

"Three hours."

"That is a long time, very long!"

"But the reward is large. All enemies will fall into your hands. You will free your chiefs and warriors, and ---"

He halted.

"And --- speak on!"

"And in addition you will find booty as you have never seen before."

"Booty? From the Navajos? You mean their horses and weapons? Nothing else can be found with them."

"I do not speak of the Navajos, but of the two Bears and their Silver Lake, on whose bottom lies immense treasure: gold, silver and precious stones in large quantities."

"Who put this foolishness into your head?"

"No one. I heard it from the two Bears themselves. One evening I lay below some trees when the two approached. I remained close by without revealing my presence. That's when they talked about this immense treasure."

"How does it come to be in the lake?"

"A people who lived there long ago, and were subjugated, immersed them."

"Then they must long since have spoiled. And how could one raise them from the bottom of the lake? Are we to ladle it empty?"

"No. What is nowadays a lake was once a dry valley. These ancient people built a tower whose top now forms the island. From this tower, a strong tunnel was built crossing the original valley ending at the mouth of the canyon. Then they built a sturdy, broad dam so that mountain streams could no longer flow north. The valley filled with water and became the lake from which now rises only the top of the tower. Once the lake was full, its waters drained to the south. The tunnel's end was hidden by rocks."

"And all that is supposed to be true?"

"Entirely. I proved it to myself by secretly moving the rocks and finding the tunnel. Where it begins lie torches needed when traversing the tunnel. At the lake's bottom, it leads to the tower in whose lowest chamber the treasure is stored. The tunnel can also serve to drain the lake's waters and to kill any enemies in the canyon. When a blockage in the tunnel is released, water enters and flows out into the canyon drowning everyone in there."

"Uff! That would serve us well, if we could drown the palefaces!"

"That must not be, since my tribesmen would also drown."

"That is correct. But if everything is as you say, the whites will be lost in any case. Your truthfulness will be shown. Are you ready to take us to the lake now?"

"Yes, I will gladly do so. But what part of the treasure will be mine?"

"I shall decide that after I have convinced myself that you speak the truth. I shall have you untied now and give you a horse. Remember, though, that on the first attempt to flee, you will be killed."

The chief quietly issued his orders. Soon all the Utes had mounted up to ride back down the canyon, but with great caution to avoid any noise. They reached the place where the whites had turned off toward the rock basin and followed the same direction.

The ride at night was even more difficult than during daytime, but the redskins had cats' eyes and helped their horses find their way. They crossed the slanted rise and descended into the basin, exactly the same way the whites had done. The final half of the ride was made easier by the crescent moon, which illuminated the shallow canyon.

Three hours had passed according to Long Ear's estimate when the Utes arrived at the point where the trees began. They stopped and sent several scouts ahead to determine if they could safely proceed the final distance. Less than five minutes later a shot sounded, then another. It did not take long for the scouts to return, carrying one of their own. He was dead.

"The palefaces are no longer in the canyon," they reported. "They have positioned themselves at the lake's entrance and shot at us. A bullet hit Eagle Claw. He was careless enough to stand up in the moon's light."

385

This information raised Old Thunder's distrust. He wondered if Long Ear was cheating on him, still remaining in league with the whites and having himself purposely captured so he could deliver the Utes in front of the whites' rifles. But Long Ear succeeded in dispelling Old Thunder's mistrust. He denied that he had ever entertained such an intention and added, "The palefaces did not feel secure in the canyon since they are fewer than you. The have retreated in the darkness to the lake where they believe you cannot surprise them. The entry to the valley is so narrow that they can easily defend it. Now, in the night, it is impossible to force it, but you can outflank them from their rear."

"How will that be possible?"

"Through the tunnel I described. Its entrance is only a few paces from here. We open it by casting aside the rocks, then light the torches and follow the tunnel to the tower. From there, we climb up to the island. A few canoes are always moored there which we can use to get to the lake shore. That puts us in the rear of an enemy we can easily defeat, particularly since my Timbabatsche warriors will join your side once I have given them the command."

"Very well! Half of our braves will stay here, the rest will accompany us through the tunnel. Show it to us!"

The Utes dismounted. Long Ear led them along a diagonal path to the mouth of the canyon. There a rock pile stood against the wall.

"These are the rocks we need to remove," said the Timbabatsche. "Then you will see the opening."

When the blockage was cleared, a dark hole of three by five feet in size became visible. The two chiefs entered and after a short search brought back a supply of torches coated with elk and buffalo tallow. Using punks, they lit several and distributed them, after which they led the column of Utes into the tunnel.

The air inside felt sticky but there was no moisture anywhere. The tunnel must have been solidly constructed and heavily reinforced for it to have resisted the lake's waters for such a long time.

To limit exposure to the stale air, which was not improved by the smoke of the torches, they quickly but cautiously advanced for what seemed to be an interminably long time in the chilly gloom. At last, and with considerable relief, the first twenty exited the tunnel into a large room. Before their eyes, lit by the flickering torches, lay scores of blanket-covered packages against the walls.

"This has to be the lowermost floor of the tower," Long Ear said. "Maybe these packages contain the treasures I spoke of. Shall we look?"

"Yes," answered Old Thunder. "But quickly. Let's not waste much time here. We need to get up to the island. There will be more time later."

When one of the packages was unwrapped, torchlight illuminated a glittering golden idol. This figure alone was worth a fortune. A civilized person would have become drunk from sheer delight; the redskins, though, were unmoved. The idol was covered again and everyone prepared for the ascent.

Small steps had been built into the masonry wall, wide enough to accommodate only one person at a time. The redskins prepared to climb single file.

Long Ear, torch in hand, took the lead. He had not yet reached the uppermost step when he heard a shriek from below, followed by a chorus of panicked shouts. He stopped and peered down. What he saw filled him with horror. From the entire face of the tunnel, which still held scores of Utes, water was gushing! The torches illuminated the dark, gurgling flood, which had already reached half a man's height and was rising with terrible speed. Those still in the tunnel were already drowned and lost. Those still standing on the steps below Long Ear were doomed too. They pushed upward, each and every one trying to save himself, but succeeded only in toppling the others. Some dropped their torches to have both hands free, but none managed to keep a foothold on the steps. The flooding proceeded so swiftly that within a minute from the moment of the first scream, it had reached the necks of the desperate Utes. Some were buoyed, some swam, fighting death and each other --- but in vain.

Only five or six, already high enough, managed to escape, Old Thunder among them. Their only remaining torch was in the hand of Long Ear. A small opening in the ceiling led to the next floor from which more steps ascended.

"Give me the torch and let me go ahead!" demanded Old Thunder as both men climbed the wall.

He reached up but Long Ear refused to hand it over. A brief struggle ensued, long enough for the water to advance and spread across this floor as well. Since the room was very much smaller than the one below, the flooding was greatly speeded up.

Long Ear, younger and stronger than Old Thunder, tore free and with a violent shove tossed the old chief back down onto the flooding floor. But now other Utes scrambled up the steps and attacked Long Ear who had no weapon and only one free hand to defend himself. One of the braves aimed his rifle. "Stop!" Long Ear screamed, "or I drop the torch into the water and you will be lost. If you can no longer see how to climb, the water will overtake you." That helped. The Utes realized that only with light would they be able to save themselves. Already the water had reached their waists.

"Then keep the torch and climb ahead, you dog!" Old Thunder shouted from below. "You shall pay for it soon enough!"

The Timbabatsche hurried on up. Through another small opening, he entered the next level. The old one's threat was serious, Long Ear knew. Only if all the Utes died in the flood would he be able to survive. As soon as he passed through the opening to the next floor he stopped to look back. Behind him appeared Old Thunder's head.

"You call me a dog and want your revenge on me," Long Ear yelled. "You are a dog yourself and shall die like one. Get back into the waters!"

Long Ear's forceful kick into Old Thunder's face caused the Ute to lose his foothold and disappear from the opening. The same happened to the second man, also the third. Suddenly all was quiet. No more heads appeared. Only water now came through the opening. Long Ear was alone, the sole survivor.

He kept on climbing, level after level, with the water following him. Then he noticed the air getting better. The ascending chambers had become so narrow that no further steps had been built. Instead, notched logs leaning against a wall served as a ladder. With his foot already on one of the notches, Long Ear heard a voice from above, "Stop! Stay where you are, or I kill you! The Utes intended to destroy us. Now they suffer their own fate and you shall be the last to die."

The Timbabatsche recognized the voice of Big Bear, speaking in his native tongue.

"I'm not Ute. Don't shoot!" he shouted in terror.

"Who are you then?"

"Your friend, the chief of the Timbabatsche."

"Oh, Long Ear, the traitor! Then you in particular have earned death."

"No, no! You are mistaken!"

"I am not mistaken. You somehow insinuated yourself into my secret and gave it away to the Utes. Now you may drown just as they have."

"I did not tell anything!" protested the terrified redskin, with the waters already reaching his knees.

"Ah, how insidious is your forked tongue!"

"Let me come up! Remember, I have always been your friend!"

"No. You stay down!"

From behind Big Bear another voice made itself heard, that of Old Firehand. "Let him come up! Enough terrible things have happened. He'll admit to his misdeeds."

"Yes, I admit it. I shall tell you everything, everything!" Long Ear assured them, with the waters having risen by now to his waist.

"All right," said Big Bear grudgingly. "I shall give you your life and hope you will be grateful for it."

"My gratitude will be without bounds. Tell me what you want and I shall comply!"

"I will keep you to your word. Now, come up!"

Long Ear dropped his torch in the water to be able to climb using both hands. Once up, he found himself in the room with the fireplace. A fire burned in front of the open door. In its light he saw Big Bear, Old Firehand and Old Shatterhand. Fear and exhaustion caused him to slump to the ground, but he recovered sufficiently to cry out, "Away, away from here, or the rising water will drown us all!"

"Stay!" Big Bear told him. "You need not fear the water any longer. It cannot rise higher inside the tower than the level of the lake. You are safe and shall tell us now how you left your post to show up here."

* * * * * * *

The events leading up to the dreadful fate of the Utes began several hours earlier when Old Shatterhand returned from his daring reconnoiter in the canyon. His companions and the Timbabatsches were lying quietly in their hiding places, alert to any noise should the Utes decide to steal up on them.

Perhaps an hour had passed when Old Shatterhand thought to check the guards once more. He went over to the position nearest the canyon wall where Long Ear had been posted. It was empty. He approached the closest Timbabatsche guard and learned that the chief had crept away.

"Where to?"

"To the Utes. He has not returned yet."

"How long ago did he leave?"

"Almost an hour ago."

"Then something must have happened to him. I'll look."

Crouching low, the hunter moved off in the direction where he earlier had seen the enemy's guards. They were gone. Where the Utes had lain across the entire width of the canyon, not a single one was left. With utmost caution, Old Shatterhand checked farther down the canyon. Finding neither a Ute nor the Timbabatsche chief was cause for serious concern. He returned to his group to fetch Winnetou and Old Firehand to help him reconnoiter. Their collective efforts were in vain. The three men advanced down the canyon for a goodly distance without finding any sign of the enemy and returned to their men certain now that the Utes had slipped away. This would not have been an incomprehensible or terrible event had not Long Ear also disappeared with them.

"They got him," said Big Bear. He dare too much. This be end of him."

"Us too," suggested Old Shatterhand.

"Why us too?"

"There must be a special reason for their leaving. The circumstance of having caught Long Ear cannot by itself be the reason for their unexpected retreat. However, the chief must have been the catalyst for their withdrawal."

"What could be reason?"

"Well, I just don't trust Long Ear. I never did care for him."

"Big Bear not have reason not to trust him. He never show enmity to me."

"That may be. Nevertheless he's not the man I'd want to rely on. Does he know the locale here well?"

"Yes, well."

"Does he know the path leading to the lake via the rocky basin?"

"He must, since he once there with me."

"That tells me enough. We must leave at once for the lake."

"Why?"

"Because he betrayed us by telling the Utes about this path."

"I do not expect this of him."

"But I think he's capable of doing it. I may be mistaken. He may have talked freely or under pressure. It doesn't matter. I'm convinced that the Utes left here an hour ago and will appear at the lake within the next two hours."

"I think so too," agreed Old Firehand.

"Long Ear does not have a good face," offered Winnetou. "My brothers may ride for the lake as swiftly as possible or the Utes will be there first and take Butler and his daughter captive."

With the three men being of the same opinion, Big Bear lost some of his confidence and no longer argued against an immediate departure. Everybody mounted up and rode up the canyon as fast as darkness permitted.

It took perhaps an hour to reach the entry to the lake valley. Rafters were posted as guards since they no longer could trust the Timbabatsches with their chief gone.

Butler and the girl were no longer on the island. Earlier when they were sitting together on the top floor of the building, the hollow sound of the captives' voices had penetrated upstairs from below. It sounded so unearthly that Ellen became frightened. She begged her father to leave the island. He gave in to her request and paddled across to the lake shore. When nighttime came, he lit a fire, but was wise enough not to sit by it; rather the two sat in the shadows overlooking the illuminated area without being seen themselves. The lonely and dangerous place felt sinister to them and they were more than happy when their friends and the Timbabatsches returned.

Since the Utes were not expected to arrive for another hour, it was sufficient to post only half the rafters at the valley's entrance. The hunters and Butlers gathered around the fire. The Timbabatsches started a second one for themselves where they mulled over the disappearance of their chief. They were convinced that he had fallen into the Utes' hands entirely against his will. That the whites suspected him of treachery had been carefully withheld from them.

Since their arrival, Watson, the former work boss from Sheridan, had had no opportunity to speak with Big Bear, who also had paid little attention to the white man. Now that they sat close to each other by the fire, Watson said to the Indian, "My red brother has not talked with me yet. Would he now please look at me, then tell me if he remembers me."

The Bear gave him a searching look, then answered, "My white brother now wears longer beard, but Big Bear recognize him."

"Who am I?"

"You are one of two palefaces who spent long winter up here when Ikhatschi-tatli, our great father, was still alive, but when fell sick was cared for by you until he gave up his spirit."

"Yes, we took care of him, and he was grateful for it. He made us a present, as Big Bear may recall."

"This present I do remember," nodded the Indian, in a way, though, as if he disliked the fact.

"It was a secret he divulged to us, the secret of a treasure hidden away here."

"Yes, but our great father was wrong to speak of secret. He was old and weak and gratefulness made him not remember he swore eternal silence about it. Only to Big and Little Bear, his inheritors, was he permitted to talk about secret. Secret items not Ikhatschi-tatli's property so could not give away. Especially to palefaces he must be silent."

"Then you think I have no right to speak about these things?"

"Big Bear cannot forbid."

"We had a drawing of it."

"It is useless. Follow it, but you not find anything. I have moved all away."

"And the new place is to remain unknown to me?"

"That so!"

"Then you are less grateful than your father!"

"I do my duty, will not forget you were present when Great Spirit called him. You not try to exploit his secret, but every other wish I gladly fulfill you."

"Are you serious?" Old Firehand asked quickly over Watson's shoulder.

"Yes. My words always meant as spoken."

"Then I will present a wish in place of our comrade here."

"Do this! If it in my power I gladly give."

"Whose land is it we're on?" Old Firehand was now pursuing his plan.

"This land belong me. I acquire from the Timbabatsche and one day I pass on to son, Little Bear."

"Do you have title to it?"

"Yes. Among red man word good enough. White men, though, require paper with black letters. I have such paper made up and signed by white chiefs. It has big seal. All land around Silver Lake, all surrounded by mountains, belong to me. I can do with as I want."

"And whose is the rocky basin we passed through today?"

"It belong to the Timbabatsches. White chiefs surveyed whole area and made drawings of it. After that, white father in Washington signed, made it property of Timbabatsche."

"Then the Timbabatsche can sell it, rent it out, or make it a present, just as they wish?"

"That so, and no one can speak against."

"Then let me tell you that I wish to buy the rock basin from them."

"My white brother can do that."

"You're agreed?"

"Big Bear cannot forbid them to sell, not you to buy."

"That's not the question; it's rather whether you like or dislike getting us as neighbors."

"All of you? Not just you? Do all wish to live in basin?"

"We do. I also want to purchase the land up to your border, to the mouth of the canyon."

Big Bear's face assumed a knowing expression as he asked, "Why does paleface want to live in place with no water, where no single blade of grass grows? Whites purchase only land, which brings them great gain. I know what my brother is thinking. It is rock which has value for you."

"That's correct. But it gains value only with the availability of water."

"Take it from lake!"

"That's what I wanted to ask you for."

"My white brother may have much as he needs."

"May I build a conduit?"

"All things that you need."

"You'll sell me the rights for which I will pay you?"

"If purchase necessary, I not say no. You decide price, but I make it present to you. You have made great service to me. Without you we would have fallen into hands of Utes. I now glad to fulfill all your wishes. Other man who earlier talked with me wanted secret treasures of Silver Lake. That I not permit. Instead, I help you exploit basin's treasures. You understand I already guess what is about. Big Bear happy if your hopes are fulfilled."

"That's marvelous," whispered Hobble-Frank to his cousin. "The water we've got now. If the gold will flow just as well, we can soon play Crassussens."

"Don't you mean Croesuses? Wasn't Croesus the king with that immense wealth?"

"Don't you start like Fat Jemmy, who always picks the wrong counterpoint! Crassus is the proper modulation. If you want to remain my friend and cousin, then --- listen!"

A whistle sounded from beyond the dam near the canyon's mouth, the agreed-upon signal from the rafters. The whites leaped up to rush there. The redskins remained where they were. Muffled hoofbeats were coming up the canyon. Quickly, everyone took up positions behind trees ready and waiting for whatever was about to happen.

Ahead stood rows of bushes, the gaps between them illuminated by moonlight. Hobble-Frank and Droll who had scouted ahead lay side by side, keeping a close eye on a wide, open space in front of them.

"Look!" whispered Frank, "Isn't something moving to the left by that tall bush?"

"Yes. I make out three dark shapes. They must be Ute scouts."

"Very well! They're about to feel right now that I'm the proud owner of a fine rifle."

He leveled his weapon just as one of the Indians, clearly outlined in the moon's light, rose to vault across the open space. Frank's shot cracked and the Indian fell, hit in the chest. His companions jumped for him to drag him back. Another shot from a rafter missed. Then the two remaining Utes disappeared with the dead man. Frank and Droll retreated back to the defensive line.

Some time passed. Nothing more was heard or seen. That was peculiar. Puzzled, Winnetou crept forward to search the surrounding area. After a quarter of an hour, he returned to where Old Firehand, Shatterhand and Big Bear were waiting and reported, "The Ute braves have divided. Half of them are remaining with the horses close to the left of the canyon's mouth. The other half went to the right of the canyon entrance. There they opened a hole into which they are disappearing."

"A hole?" Big Bear asked, shocked. "Then they know of tunnel and my secret is lost. Only Long Ear could do. How he learn it? Come with me! I must convince myself that is true."

He hurried off along the crest of the dam with the other three following closely behind. Once hidden among the trees, they could clearly see the canyon's mouth yawning open below them. The rock pile had been moved and by the moonlight they watched the Utes entering the tunnel.

"Yes, they do know secret," Big Bear said bitterly. "They want to get to island to come behind us and they want Silver Lake treasure. But that not happen. I must get quickly to island. Old Firehand and Old Shatterhand may accompany. First I show Winnetou something."

He led the Apache several dozen paces forward to a place on the opposite side of the lake's waters where the dam dropped vertically. Here, a gigantic boulder rested on a support of many small round rocks arranged in the shape of a pyramid. The boulder was placed directly above a spot where the tunnel burrowed under the dam.

Big Bear pointed to one of the supporting rocks and said in the Apache tongue, "As soon as Winnetou sees me start a fire on the island, he must push this little rock away and leap back quickly. The boulder will then roll and drop. My red brother must not be alarmed about the great crashing sound it will make."

"Why does Big Bear want the boulder to be dropped?" Winnetou asked.

"You will see later. No time now for explanations. I must leave quickly."

He ran off, the two hunters keeping a close distance behind him. At one of the fires near the shore, Big Bear snatched up a flaming brand and leaped into one of the canoes. While the Tonkawa fought to keep the flame alive, Old

Firehand and Shatterhand pushed off and paddled for the island. As soon as the canoe's keel scraped the shore, Big Bear quickly jumped out and ran for the building.

He stopped just long enough to hand the burning brand to Shatterhand, then rushed into the room with the fireplace. The entire fireplace structure rested on a swivel base enabling Big Bear to swing it aside effortlessly. An opening appeared where the fireplace stood. The Indian knelt down to listen intently.

Several moments went by, then he jumped up, exclaiming, "They come! Time to light fire!" Seizing a large bundle of dry wood from a stack next to the fireplace, he hurried outside, took the burning faggot from Old Shatterhand and touched the flame to the dry wood. It took almost immediately and moments later a blaze threw light across the water.

"My brothers may listen!" breathed the Indian expectantly, pointing to the place beyond the lake where Winnetou was waiting. At first only silence, then slowly a rolling, grinding noise resounded across the lake, followed by an immense crash of the falling boulder shattered the roof of the tunnel. Tons of rock, soil and debris collapsed into the opening, sealing the tunnel and cutting off any Ute retreat.

"It succeeded!" Big Bear cried exultantly, breathing deeply. "The Utes are lost. Come inside!"

The three men re-entered the building and knelt around the opening to the floors below. Sounds of the warriors' steps as they ascended the tower galvanized Big Bear to action. "They are in tower," he said. "Now water in there quickly!"

He ran outside behind the building. What he did there the two hunters were unable to observe, but when they rejoined him at the water's edge he pointed to a spot on the lake and asked excitedly, "You see water moving there? It makes whirlpool sucking lake down into tunnel where I have opened."

"By God! The Utes will drown miserably!" shouted Old Shatterhand.

"Yes, all! Not a single one is to escape."

"Horrible! Was that not preventable?"

"No. None must escape to tell what has seen there."

"But you've destroyed your own construction!"

"Yes, it is destroyed and can never again be entered. Treasure of Silver Lake lost to mankind. No mortal can find again, for island tower will fill with water to very top. Come inside again!"

A cold shudder gripped the two whites. The rising waters were pushing the stale air up; they could smell it coming from the opening. This meant the death of over a hundred human beings.

"But what about our hostages in the next room below!" demanded Old Shatterhand urgently. "They will also drown!"

"No. Wall will hold for some time. But soon, yes, we get them out. Listen!"

A noise from below was followed by the appearance of an Indian's head protruding from the opening in the floor. It was Long Ear. Big Bear wanted to let him drown too; only Old Firehand's pressing refusal prevented another cruelty. Barely had the Timbabatsche reached safety when the water level inside the tower equaled that of the lake. The whirlpool disappeared.

Long Ear collapsed by the fire, unable to stand any longer. Big Bear sat down opposite him and spoke to the chief in an Indian language they both knew very well, assuring him that he was now safe from the rising waters. Then, pulling a revolver from his belt, Big Bear said in a threatening tone, "Now the chief of the Timbabatsche may tell us how he came to enter the tunnel together with the Utes. If he lies, I shall put a bullet in his head. He knew the island's secret, is that not true?"

"Yes," Long Ear admitted.

"Who told you?"

"You yourself."

"That is not so!"

"It is! I sat over there by the big oak when you came with Little Bear. You remained standing nearby and talked of the island, of its treasure and of the tunnel through which it is possible to drain the water into the canyon. Do you remember?"

"Yes, that is true. We stood there and talked about it. We thought ourselves alone."

"From your words I learned that the tunnel began at the rock pile. The next day when you were both out hunting for elk, I used the time to move part of the rock pile. I crawled into the tunnel and saw the torches. That told me enough and I replaced the rocks."

"And today you went to the Utes to tell them my secret!"

"No, I only wanted to spy on them, but I was discovered. In order to save my life, I told them of the tunnel and the island."

"That was cowardly. Had Old Shatterhand not noticed your absence, your treachery would have succeeded and our souls would be in the Eternal Hunting Grounds tomorrow morning. Did you see what was stored below the island?"

"Yes."

"And did you open the packages?"

"A single one only."

"What was inside?"

"A god made of pure gold."

"No human eye will ever see it again, not even yours. What do you think you have earned for this?"

The Timbabatsche thought any reply inadequate and remained silent.

"Death, a tenfold death! But you were once my friend and comrade and the palefaces do not wish that I kill you. You may live, but only if you do what I demand from you."

"What is it you want?"

"I will demand an oath from you, a most grave oath. An oath that you will never --- and to no one --- reveal anything about the island and its treasure."

"I am willing to swear to it."

"Not now, but later. Then I also require you to accede to Old Firehand's demands. He wants to live in the rock basin and buy it from your tribe. The Timbabatsches will sell him the basin, also the canyon leading into it from Silver Lake."

"We have no need for the basin; it is useless. No horse finds pasture there."

"What do you ask for it?"

"For that I need to talk first with other Timbabatsches."

"They will ask you what to demand and you will have to set a price. I, therefore, will tell you now what price you are allowed to ask. Old Firehand will give you twenty rifles and twenty pounds of powder, ten blankets, fifty knives and thirty pounds of tobacco. That is not too little. Are you agreed?"

"I am agreed and will argue for the others to agree too."

"You will need to go with old Firehand and several witnesses to the nearest chief of the palefaces to validate the purchase. For that you will receive another gift, large or small, much or little, as you earn it or as it pleases Old Firehand. You see that I am looking out for your advantage and I hope you will help me to forget your treachery. Now, call some of your people from the shore to collect the hostages so they will not drown too!"

Long Ear obeyed this directive at once. It was high time to get the captives to safety. When the last of them had been taken outside the building, a cracking, a crash and a rush of water could be heard. The pressure had pushed in the dividing wall and flooded the adjacent room. Had they waited any longer, the Ute chiefs and their braves would have drowned too.

The reprieved men were transported by canoe to the shore and entrusted to the Timbabatsches for safekeeping. Their own chief was not allowed to return to them since he was hardly considered trustworthy. Instead he was compelled to come along to the canyon mouth where the rafters were still at their posts facing the remaining Utes.

These braves were not yet aware of the enormity of their losses. Most of the Utes who had been assigned to attack through the tunnel had already been far along before it collapsed under a mighty mass of the boulder and accompanying earth. Many of the invaders had been crushed in the collapse. The tunnel had been totally closed off so that the lake's waters could not flow into the canyon.

The Utes who had not yet entered the tunnel had withdrawn in fright and returned to their rear guard to tell what had happened. No one knew whether those in the tunnel had been lost, or if some of them had managed to reach the island. If so, then an attack on the whites from behind could be immanent. Waiting minute by minute for something to happen, they finally had to give up hope and assume that all their comrades had become victims of some catastrophe.

Day broke and still the Utes waited with their horses at the assigned place. Finally, Old Shatterhand appeared between the trees, demanding to talk to their leader. Seeing no harm in a powwow, the remaining chief, White Cloud, walked toward the hunter. When they met, Old Shatterhand told him, "You know that we're holding several chiefs and warriors of yours hostage?"

"I know. They are our most famous men," answered the Indian with a dark scowl.

"And you know what happened to your warriors who entered the tunnel?"

"No. What evil have you done them?"

"The tunnel collapsed, water entered and they all drowned. Only Long Ear escaped. The two hundred Navajos we expected have just arrived. We have a far superior force now, but we don't wish for your blood, rather do we still offer peace. The hostages don't believe that so many of your warriors died in the lake. One of you must tell them if we're to convince them. If they are not willing to make peace, they'll die within the hour and we'll chase and hunt the rest of you until you are no more. Be wise and come with me! I'll take you to the chiefs. Talk with them. Then you can return here."

White Cloud stared ahead for a while contemplating his reply, then said, "Old Shatterhand does not know treachery. White Cloud believes you will let me return here. I shall trust the paleface's word and come along."

He informed his people of his intent, laid down his weapons and followed the hunter to the lake. There things had become rather hot, for the Navajos had indeed arrived, eager to avenge their earlier defeat at the hands of the Utes. It had taken more than the usual persuasion to dispose them towards peace-making.

The hostages had been freed of their bonds and were sitting together under heavy guard when Old Shatterhand brought their fellow tribesman. Long Ear and White Cloud were called to describe the course of the catastrophe. No one else entered into the conversation. The Utes had to see for themselves that no further help could be expected.

A dialogue among the Ute chiefs ensued and continued for a long time. Then Long Ear reported that the Utes had yielded and would accept the peace offer. This led to a solemn conclave in which both the prominent whites and redskins took part. It lasted several hours during which many speeches were given until finally the peace pipe made its rounds.

The result was a permanent peace treaty agreed to by all parties. No compensation was to be given by either side. The captives were released and all Utes, Navajos and Timbabatsches committed themselves to maintain peaceful relations with the palefaces who were going to live in the rock basin --- and to assist them wherever possible.

For the whites, most difficult of all now was to treat Big Wolf as a friend. It was he who had offended them most. He alone carried the blame for all that had happened. But even he, eventually, was excused his treachery and made part of the peace process.

Then Long Ear was called aside, and in the presence of Old Shatterhand and Firehand as witnesses, had to swear solemnly to Big Bear never to reveal anything about the treasures he had seen at the base of the now flooded tower.

After all this, a great hunt followed which lasted until evening and produced a rich bounty of game. It was devoured in a feast in which the redskins strove to accomplish the impossible by consuming huge quantities of meat. The festivities lasted well into the morning hours.

During the course of the long night, Old Firehand inquired about the whereabouts of the drawing that the colonel had been carrying. No one knew. It had disappeared. It would have been of no use now anyway. The rising sun saw the heroes of the peace treaty wrap themselves in their blankets to fall into exhausted slumber.

It was to be expected that the entire day was used for sleeping. Departure did not take place until the following morning. The Utes traveled north, the Navajos south. The Timbabatsches, too, returned to their wigwams. Long Ear promised to sit in council concerning the sale of the rock basin and to let the whites know the result quickly. It was only a matter of three days before he returned to report that the council had accepted the price set by Big Bear. It was now simply a procedural matter to confirm the purchase with the authorities.

It remained now only to register the location of the mining operation, then to prepare for the initial dig. This was to be as soon as possible, leading to enthusiastic and hopeful expressions in which only one man took no part --- Lord Castlepool. He had hired Humpy-Bill and Gunstick-Uncle to take him to Frisco, but the two had lost interest in that venture under the new circumstances.

Although they had already accumulated a nice sum in the lord's record book --- which would certainly have grown further by additional adventures on their way to San Francisco --- they could expect much more from the mining operation. They preferred to stay at Silver Lake, and Castlepool was understanding enough not to take it too badly. Besides, since work in the basin could not commence for some time, the lord decided to stay on for a while and roam the mountains with his two friends, seeking a new adventure or two before the mining operation would begin.

With agreement by all parties in hand, Old Firehand rode with Big Bear and Long Ear to Fillmore City, where the purchase was properly registered. This was also the place where Firehand could order his required tools and machinery. Aunt Droll accompanied them to attest at a notary, with the help of witnesses, that the colonel had been killed in the course of his pursuit. Droll now qualified to receive his share of the bounty.

A beautiful sibling-like relationship was evolving between Ellen and Little Bear. Every day the boy spent time with her and those times he needed to be absent she missed him dreadfully.

Finally, after almost a month and a half word came that the machinery and equipment could be picked up. A sizable party of men headed into town, while the lord used the opportunity to look over inhabited areas where he could likely find new guides.

When the party arrived in Fillmore City, it caused a great stir. Everyone had heard of the mining enterprise and wanted to learn more about it. But the miners-to-be maintained total silence, since it was not in their interest to have all kinds of riffraff close by.

When all the equipment had arrived back at the lake, Engineer Butler dived happily into the project. The basin's bottom was first tackled and the water pipeline was laid.

Flour, beans and other provisions were brought in to last for many weeks. Meat was provided by a group of three hunters, changed day by day, while the others worked at mining. Ellen took charge of providing the meals, a great comfort to the roughhewn backwoodsmen.

The hope everyone had placed in the basin came to fruition. The sand was rich in gold flakes and an even richer silver yield could be expected from the hard rock. Gold dust and nuggets accumulated day by day. Each day's yield was weighed and recorded and when the result was as gratifying as usual, Droll would whisper happily to his cousin, "If it continues like this, I can buy my farm pretty soon. Business is excellent."

To which Hobble-Frank responded regularly, "And my villa is mostly completed, at least in my head. It will be a composing building on the beautiful banks of the Elbe, and the name I shall give it will be even more composing. Howgh!"

ABOUT THE AUTHOR

Karl May (1842 - 1912) is today hailed a German literary genius. His unequaled imagination gave birth to a whole collection of characters that lived through exiting and realistic adventure tales that captivated generations of German readers both young and old. Yet his writings were never available to English readers in their unadulterated glory.

Until now …

ABOUT THE TRANSLATOR

Herbert Windolf was born in Wiesbaden, Germany, in 1936. In 1964 he emigrated to Canada with his family to provide his German employer with technical services for North America. In 1970 he was transferred to the United States and eventually became Managing Director of the US affiliate.

Semi-retired, he resides these days in Prescott, Arizona, where he, among other things, teaches courses on scientific subjects at an adult education center. He has translated several literary works from German into English, among which is Karl May's, "The Oil Prince", published by Washington State University Press. His subsequent endeavor has been this translation of one of May's most popular novels, "Der Schatz im Silbersee".